M000218274

Firehurler

Book 1 of the Twinborn Trilogy

By J.S. Morin

Cover Art by Duncan Long
duncanlong.com

ISBN: 1-939233-01-1
ISBN-13: 978-1-939233-01-1

Dedication

To my mother.
For being there for the first words I ever wrote.
Here are the first words I ever published

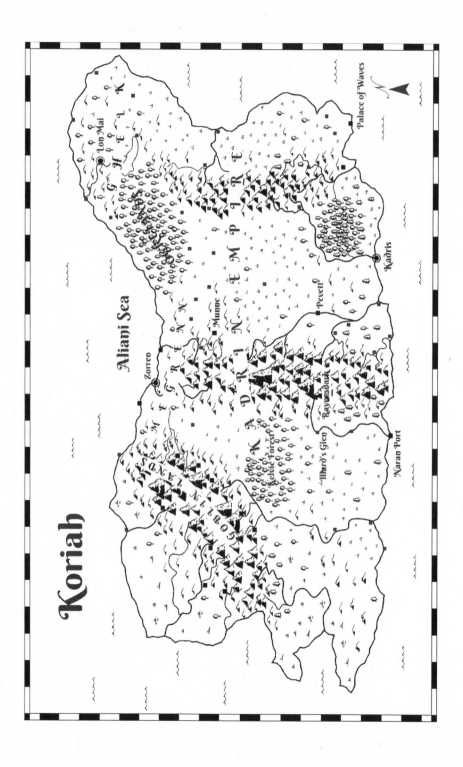

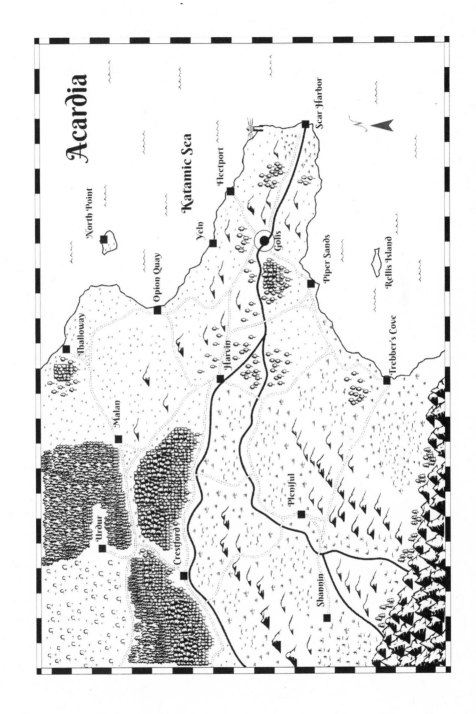

Chapter 1 - The Forest Trap

With his breath coming in ragged gasps, the soldier crashed through the forest. He had ceased to hear any sound of pursuit several minutes ago, but he knew they were still coming. In his heavy chain armor, he also knew that the goblins would be able to keep up with him easily; they could afford to be stealthy. Of course, they had little need for stealth, as there were hundreds of goblins in the forests, spreading out to finish off the stragglers.

The screams of his dying comrades still rang in his ears. They were long, agonized cries, as the goblins ignored the mortally wounded to pursue those soldiers still able to run. He was one of those running. Running from the hopeless battle against a foe that had been expecting them. Running to keep from hearing those gut-wrenching screams coming from his own throat. Running with the hope of finding living allies before the goblins got him. Running from the slaughter that he had just witnessed ...

* * * * * * * *

"Fine day, is it not, Sir Lugren?" Sir Brannis Solaran called out as he approached the older knight.

Brannis Solaran was the youngest of the knights sent into the Kelvie Forest to hunt for goblin scouting parties. He was also in charge of the Imperial Army's Eighth Battalion, with one hundred men at his command. Brannis was tall and lean, traits common in his family, though he carried a great deal of muscle on his frame. There was not a man in camp who could do better than look him in the chin when standing face-to-face with him. His straw-colored hair hung loose down to his shoulders, framing a strong face with prominent cheekbones and a rather longish nose. A pair of bright green eyes peered out, wide and alert, seeming to study rather than just see.

Lugren had seen forty summers and was greying a bit at the temples but showed every sign of being in his physical prime. Broad and muscular, Lugren had served the Kadrin Empire for more than half that lifetime as a knight and before that as a squire. He turned to fix Brannis with dark brown eyes that showed a bit of eagerness in them.

"Fine day for swordplay, do you mean?" Sir Lugren asked in reply.

Lugren had a fondness for all things competitive, and recognized the spring in Brannis's step as a sign that his commander was spoiling for a match. While Lugren was a loyal knight and served Brannis to the best of his abilities, it chafed at him that his commanding officer was little more than half his age. He enjoyed the chances he got to put the upstart in his place.

The youngest son of Maruk Solaran, one of the twelve members of the Inner Circle, Brannis had been expected to grow up to be a sorcerer. With Brannis born on the summer solstice under a confluence of unusual celestial events, High Sorcerer Gravis Archon had foretold that extraordinary powers lay in his future. What turned out to be there instead of sorcerous power was years of frustration and humiliation at the Imperial Academy, trying to learn magic without any real talent for it. When it was finally decided that Brannis would never blossom into the prodigy the high sorcerer had predicted, he was expelled. From there, after much argument with his stubborn father, he had managed to get himself accepted to the School of Arms, the path to the knighthood, and because of a keen mind for strategy, had risen through the ranks quickly.

"I do indeed," Brannis said. "What say you?"

"Any time, sir," Sir Lugren replied.

The older knight retrieved his sword and a special set of leather padding to cover the blade for the bout. While all the knights were given goblin-swords for combat against their foes, none left behind their "real" weapons. It was a matter of honor to carry a true sword at one's hip, since the specialized swords for fighting the goblins looked ridiculously like pointed riding crops. Had the goblins' reputation for quickness and ferocity not been so well known, most knights would have refused to carry them altogether.

Brannis borrowed a sword from Sir Aric and another set of padding for it. Using his own sword was out of the question. Brannis was the only knight in any of the three battalions in Kelvie Forest to have the good fortune of possessing an enchanted blade. Upon receiving his knighthood, his father had given him the sword, named "Massacre," as a gift. It was an heirloom that a family of sorcerers had little need of. It was a misfit weapon, suitable for a misfit son; Brannis's father was happy enough to be rid of both. It had made him uneasy just to wield the blade when he had first gotten it. The sword was wickedly serrated down its entire length, and the hilt was carved to resemble a dragon breathing out the blade. When wielded, the blade glowed green except where the runes were etched into it, and a pale greenish mist hung from the sword and poisoned anything it touched other than the wielder. Even covered in padding, it could be lethal to use in a sparring match. Brannis had since grown accustomed to the sword's brutal appearance, and accepted it as a remarkably effective weapon when used properly.

Sliding the padding over his borrowed sword and tying it securely to the cross guard, Brannis circled his opponent. Lugren likewise circled his young commander, his sword held in front of him in a guard position. Lugren was an excellent swordsman, and he watched for his commander to make the first move, preparing to counter. While Brannis was easily the strongest of the knights in the expedition and had an advantage in reach of several handspans over Sir Lugren, he lacked the long winters of training his opponent possessed and was a rather less-polished fighter.

As word spread throughout the camp that Sir Brannis and Sir Lugren were going to spar, the soldiers not obligated to other duties drifted into an impromptu ring around the combatants. For the knights to practice swordplay was not uncommon in the camp, but their commander's fights always seemed to make for the best shows. There was something about the way Brannis fought that was exciting, a ferocity that rarely entered into the more subdued contests among the older knights.

Lugren's attack came as a series of measured strikes. First a lunge—more controlled than Brannis's had been—aimed at Brannis's chest, followed by a feint to the same spot and a low sweep toward Brannis's legs as his opponent's sword came across to parry the feint. Each strike was planned before the previous maneuver had ended, Brannis knew; Lugren did not expect to end the fight in one blow.

Brannis was working his sword back and forth in front of him, rhythmically beating away Lugren's attacks, which were starting to get predictable. Every third lunge was a feint, which Brannis made certain to at least flinch at so that Lugren would not figure out he was on to the pattern. Brannis was impressed, as always, at the precision of Lugren's moves; every strike, every parry was executed cleanly and with no wasted motion. It was almost pointless to wait for the older knight to make a mistake, since Brannis knew his own technique could be generously described as serviceable. He would slip up long before the more experienced Lugren so much as caught a poor angle on a parry. Brannis needed to make a breakthrough in the fight.

Brannis knew he could never outdo Sir Lugren at his own fighting style, but he needed to lull his opponent back into his routine. Then, with a quick change of footwork, Brannis had his right foot leading well ahead of him and slightly to his opponent's left. He brought his sword around in a wide arc at arm's length, but with the sword's point at an awkward angle aimed straight at his opponent's chest. It was a trick that looked like it was angled to avoid a clean parry but Brannis had learned otherwise long ago. He had tried the move with his first tutor in swordsmanship at the School of Arms and had been neatly and cleanly disarmed. His tutor berated him severely every time he had tried the maneuver, but every youngster had gotten it into his head at some point during his training to try things that would get him killed in a real battle. Brannis had learned that lesson well, and he had not had a relapse in his match with Sir Lugren. However, he had baited a trap.

Sir Lugren had taught swordsmanship at the School of Arms for several summers; Brannis knew that and counted on it. Lugren brought his sword across point down in a parry that would look almost as if he would punch the sword out of Brannis's hand. He caught Brannis's blade gave a fierce push near the crossguard, strong enough to break Brannis's grip on his sword. But Brannis released his grip, and offered no resistance as his sword went spinning off toward the watching soldiers.

There would have been no time for him to recover from the awkward strike had he allowed Lugren to complete his defense properly. Instead, Lugren overbalanced as the resistance he expected from Brannis just was not there. Brannis caught the wrist of Lugren's sword hand as it went by and bowled his opponent to the ground in a clatter of armor. Lugren landed awkwardly on his left shoulder with Brannis atop him. With the fight reduced to a wrestling match, the advantage was Brannis's. Easily forcing his opponent face-first onto the ground, he wrested the sword from Lugren's hand.

"I yield," came a resigned mumble from the dirt, and it was over.

The fight had been a friendly match, so Brannis had merely pinned Lugren rather than roughing him up. The two men helped each other to their feet. Both were dirty and sweaty from the fight, and Brannis started to remove his armor but paused as he noticed Sir Lugren staring at him.

"Who goes there?" came a shout from the sentries that called away all attention from the sparring knights.

* * * * * * *

The errant soldier was insensible when the sentries dragged him into camp. It was obvious from his clothes and boots that he was one of their own; each of the common soldiers had been equipped with the same gear from the army quartermaster just before they set out from Korgen. Other than his clothing, though, he had nothing else with him, neither armor nor weapon, nor even any personal effects. He was exhausted, hungry, and nearly mad with fear. The sentries heard him muttering something about goblins—something that sounded urgent.

Though Brannis wanted very much to give the man some space to collect himself and gather his wits, he could hardly reprimand his men for their curiosity; he shared it in full measure. Nearly every man in camp gathered around the fire where the two sentries brought the poor soldier and sat him down. Someone thought to bring the man a blanket, for he was covered in a cold sweat. One of the cooks brought a fresh bowl of quail stew remaining from the night's meal, and the soldier gratefully accepted it with hands still shaking from the aftereffects of what had to be fear.

As the wayward soldier downed a few mouthfuls of the delicious dinner, the rest of Brannis's men waited in respectful silence, taking a cue from their commander. Brannis sat across the fire from the man and watched his eyes. They seemed to clear as he ate, the delirium of a full day of fearful flight no doubt being replaced by the reality of good food and friendly company. The color started to return to the man's pale face as the warmth of the fire and the food in his belly replenished his depleted strength.

Drawing a deep, shuddering breath, seeming to remind himself of the reality that he was now relatively safe, the man looked around the assembly of faces that had gathered about him.

"Thanks. I ... I need to talk to your commander—whose battalion is this? I've got horrible news."

"I am in command here; these are my men. I am Sir Brannis Solaran. What is your name, soldier, and how did you come to find us here?"

The man turned to meet Brannis's intent gaze and quickly lowered his eyes to the dirt.

"Jodoul Brect, sir, that's my name. They're gone, sir, all of 'em."

There was a collective feeling of shock among the troops gathered around the fire, and a buzz of discussion started to grow and steadily increase in volume with the passing seconds as Jodoul's declaration hung in the air. Brannis waved one hand in a downward motion, urgently gesturing for his men to quiet down. The poor soldier—Jodoul—had obviously been through some ordeal and had not quite recovered mentally. Being in the eye of a storm of speculation and questioning would do him no good. Still, Brannis needed answers, especially if his suspicions about what Jodoul meant proved to be correct.

"What do you mean? Who is gone?" Brannis asked in a measured tone, trying not to upset Jodoul.

"Gone, dead, all of them. All of Sir Ferren's battalion, dead except for me. The goblins came and there was nothing we could do to stop 'em. They was like evil spirits, sneakin' up in the dark of night and swarmin' over our camp. There was fire fallin' from the trees and the air was filled with steel and screamin'." Jodoul gritted his teeth and squeezed shut his eyes. "I can still hears them, even now. I wish I could have done somethin' to help them, I—"

"How did you get away?" Sir Aric interrupted. "How is it that you managed to be the only one, if it is as you say and all the others are dead?"

"I think that is enough for now," Brannis said. "Triple the sentries; all men are to carry arms; everyone into your armor, even for sleeping. I know it is uncomfortable but so is a spear-tip in your gut, you can be sure. We must be ready for them to attack anytime now."

Brannis watched as his men started off to carry out his orders. He then turned to his knights and Jodoul.

"Let us continue this discussion in private, in the planning tent," Brannis said. "Iridan, you should join us as well." Brannis gave a nod to the sorcerer assigned to his battalion.

The planning tent was the only one large enough to accommodate a standing human. It was set up as a meeting place for the knights to lay out their maps and plan strategies without exposing either map or man to the elements. They removed the small table that was normally kept inside the tent, which normally sported a map of their immediate vicinity, and set it outside. They then gathered inside, eight knights—the other two were seeing to the tripling of the watch— along with Jodoul and Iridan, seated themselves on the ground. The tent was originally meant to hold eight men standing around a table so ten men seated, even without the table, was rather cramped. But Jodoul was in no condition to stand for any length of time, and they needed to know everything he had seen, so they accommodated his present weakness.

Over the next several minutes, Brannis and the others came to understand the scope of the enemy they were facing. Jodoul's account was quite thorough in its description of the carnage and the strange happenings resulting from goblin magic. Jodoul, though, left out his own actions around the time of the battle, Brannis noticed. There was something in the way he avoided such mention that made Brannis suspect the man had not acquitted himself well; Sir Aric most likely had the right tack in questioning why he was the one who survived, but Brannis had more immediate concerns than potential cowardice in the face of the enemy.

The goblins were now no doubt aware of their location—that much was easily inferred from Jodoul's account of how they hounded him like a game hare. The only matter remaining unsettled was when they would arrive in force. If the goblins knew they were here, the campfires would only be of aid to the human army, for goblins tended on the whole to see much better in low lighting that their human counterparts. Dousing the fires would not serve to hide them but rather help to hide their small foes from them.

"Iridan, bring up a fog in and around camp," Brannis ordered his friend.

Iridan nodded, then half-closed his eyes and began to chant, *"Zoina emintari koactu fununar,"* at the same time sweeping his hands back and forth in front of him, palms downward, in a close approximation of a swimming motion. He repeated the chant and continued to gesture. A fine wispiness coalesced in the air about his fingers, growing into a light fog and drifting to the ground. Within moments, the fog had spread throughout most of the campsite and was growing both thicker and deeper by the moment. Brannis, who knew the chant at least as well as did Iridan, caught himself silently mouthing the words in time with the chant. He could almost imagine that it was his own powers creating the fog in response to his own chant. As he watched the ever-growing fog, his better sense grabbed hold of his daydreaming and shook it aside.

"Umm, Iridan, stop before you get it chest-high—your chest, not mine— because we still want to be able to see where we are walking. I just want to make it higher than the goblins can see over."

Iridan was nearly a foot shorter than Brannis, so the admonition was not an idle one. Brannis wanted to be sure that his men had every advantage he could manage to find.

* * * * * * *

Iridan finished the spell, satisfied that the human soldiers would still be able to see over the thick bank of fog that now obscured the campsite. It was a simple enough spell and had hardly tasked his strength at all. He glanced around, trying to think of anything else he could do to help prepare for the expected attack. Remembering the wolves, he whistled to summon them to his side. A few seconds later, he felt hot breath on his legs and heard their panting. So effective was the fog cloud that he could not even see the animals, though they were right in front of him.

Hoping that the wolves' sense of smell would serve them well enough to navigate in the blinding fog, Iridan gestured for the wolves to move out into the surrounding woods. It was a command he had taught them so would aid in the search for game. He hoped that the wolves would not make too strong a distinction between deer and goblins as far as acceptable prey was concerned. He was not too worried, though—the creatures seemed to be quite territorial. Had his magic not deluded them into thinking of humans as part of their pack, he was sure the wolves would have attacked the soldiers already.

Iridan wracked his mind thinking what else he might be able to accomplish before the battle started, but could not come up with any more ideas. He looked around, hoping to catch sight of Brannis or one of the other knights to see if one of them might have need of him. He was carefully picking his way across camp toward Brannis's tent when he heard a pained yelp from the woods to the east. Iridan winced at the sounds of a struggle: growling, snarling, a rustling of the underbrush, and finally nothing but a few whimpers that quickly died out.

* * * * * * * *

They had been waiting for hours. After the goblins had killed their wolves, Brannis had expected that they would attack the encampment soon, while they might still gain some surprise. But there sat Brannis and his knights, with Iridan as well, still waiting. Reluctantly Brannis had ordered the men to try to get some rest and there had already been two changes of the sentries. Few could sleep, though, knowing that their enemy was lying in wait, preparing to attack at any moment. Sleeping in chain armor was difficult enough without it also serving as a reminder of the imminent attack.

Brannis finally gave in and decided to try to get what sleep he could while he still possessed a choice in the matter. His eyelids were drifting lower by the minute and it was taking a conscious effort to hold them up. He left Sir Lugren on watch and he would be in command for the first few moments of battle should the enemy attack while Sir Brannis slept.

* * * * * * * *

Iridan watched as his friend pillowed his head on a bundled bedroll and tried to sleep wearing plate armor, right in the middle of the camp with the rest of the knights. Even as he saw Brannis grimace in discomfort as he tried to find a position where his armor did not push at him awkwardly, he envied his friend. For his part, Iridan was planning to stay awake as long as it took, for if his magic was a few seconds too late when battle was joined, he might never join it at all. Goblins were cunning and they would likely make an early target of the humans' only sorcerer. Iridan meditated to try to get at least some rest without fully giving in to his body's demands for slumber. Getting up to renew the fog as the fires slowly burned it away also helped to keep his mind alert. The channeling of aether might drain the body, but there was something about it that invigorated the mind—something not entirely unlike the effect of jumping into a body of cold water. The effect was quite temporary but Iridan needed whatever aid he might find in keeping awake.

The other knights drew lots to determine who slept and who would keep watch. They did it for form's sake mostly, since there was little sleep to be had that night in any event. Every cricket, every toad, every breeze might have concealed the sound of approaching goblins. It was more a matter of who would take watch standing and who would lie awake on the ground. As Iridan mused on the curious arrangement, he heard a slight throaty rasping. A smile tugged at the corner of his mouth as he recognized the sound of snoring. Brannis, at least, had found a way to get to sleep.

Chapter 2 - Dawn of Morning

Dawn's first rays of light peeked through the open window, illuminating the small, sparsely furnished room. Kyrus Hinterdale groaned and rolled over, turning his face from the offending light, knowing it was his own fault for leaving the window open last night. It was late spring, and the same window that had let in such fragrant, refreshing breezes overnight had robbed him of an hour's sleep at the least. It was not that he particularly needed the extra sleep; he was quite well rested. But the sun's unwelcome intrusion had interrupted a most interesting dream, a dream about ...*Drat! Now I cannot even remember!*

Kyrus often remembered bits and pieces of his dreams, not just in the groggy moments immediately after awakening. As a scribe, Kyrus had little enough to add excitement to his days, without forgetting the interesting bits his slumbering mind conjured up for his entertainment each night.

With a resigned sigh, he sat up in bed, rubbed the last remnants of sleep from his bleary eyes, and threw off the bed sheets.Shambling across his small room, Kyrus reached the basin he kept on a table in the corner. He splashed some tepid water over his face and looked at his reflection in the small, polished, silver mirror that his employer, Expert Davin, had given him. Kyrus saw what he had seen each morning since he'd received the gift: a pale, angular face, blue-green eyes, and a mop of sandy-blond hair, adorned with a sickly little beard, so light it was barely noticeable. He would have shaved it off, but he looked young enough that on the rare occasion he indulged in wine, the barkeeps would always ask him whether he had reached the age of accountability, which indeed he had—five years ago.

Once out on the city streets after a quick breakfast, Kyrus stretched and let out a yawn, filling his lungs with the fresh morning air. If there was a better way to start off a day, Kyrus was not aware of it. Kyrus managed a leisurely pace, his full stomach slowing his normally brisk pace somewhat. He used the extra time his early rise bought him to give himself a chance to try to figure out what Expert Davin was planning. Expert Davin had been telling him all week that he had a big surprise planned for him. The old man was normally quite jovial, but this whole business with Kyrus's "surprise," whatever it was, had him nearly giddy of late. Kyrus resolved not to consider the subject of his employer's recent strange behavior and to focus directly on his work for the day. It was a high-minded plan and one that deep down he knew was doomed to failure, but until he actually sat down to start working, Kyrus entertained thoughts of keeping to it.

The problem was that nothing he could think of made much sense. Davin had been promising for some time now that he would get Kryus admitted to the Scriveners Guild as a full member, but that was almost a formality. Kyrus's work was exemplary, even if he did say so himself, and a brief perusal of his work would have been enough to gain him membership, if Expert Davin recommended him. He could not picture Davin getting as worked up about the whole affair if that was it.

His favorite theory, which had Davin playing matchmaker for Kyrus with some mysterious "niece," would at least explain why Davin had been so jovial lately. Davin had expressed concern a number of times to Kyrus that if he did not get out more, he would end up like Davin: an old man with no family of his own. However, Davin had told Kyrus he had only one sibling, a brother some eight years or so his senior. Kyrus snorted in amusement at the very thought. Davin was nearly old enough to be his own grandfather, and any niece Davin might have would have to be at least his mother's age.

And my dear Juliana, I would like to introduce you to your future husband—Oh my, wait. That cannot be any apprentice of mine, looking like some sort of ink-speckled shut-in.

Kyrus grinned to himself, trying to imagine Davin introducing him to some fictional niece he could not possibly have. It was a bit of a stretch of course; Davin was less likely to notice a bit of ink and an unruly mop of hair than he was to suddenly grow his own hair back. Still, he should keep up appearances for the sake of Davin's reputation among his colleagues, who, if he had gathered correctly from Davin's veiled hints over the course of the week, were likely to be in attendance this evening. And besides, who knew when he might run into a woman without Davin having arranged it for him.

With no promising new theories coming to light on that particular walk, Kyrus arrived back at his employer's establishment. The wooden sign above the door hung out toward the street on a wrought-iron bracket, and swung gently in the morning breeze, proclaiming the building to belong to Davin Chartler—Expert Scrivener. The carved wooden letters were bold and plain, and had been painted over in white to make them more visible against the dark-stained background. The letters were the only feature of the sign, which made it quite unique among the establishments of Scar Harbor. Most other businesses would have carved a symbol on their signs, indicating what sort of work went on there, many without even lettering to accompany them. A great many of the folk who lived in the kingdom of Acardia could not read and found the places they needed by picture. A horseshoe indicated a blacksmith, a loaf of bread adorned the bakers' signs, and a needle and thread meant a tailor's shop. Expert Davin had little use for the illiterate professionally, so he forewent the customary quill-and-ink pot that graced the signs of scribes throughout the rest of the kingdom. His stance had likely cost him a bit of business over the years, penning letters and writing up contracts for those who could not write, but his moral stance had gained him respect among the guild membership and freed up more of his time for other work he considered more rewarding.

Shutting the door, Kyrus was once again surrounded by a stuffy feeling in the air, at once both comfortable and a bit stifling. Visitors to the establishment frequently complained that it smelled strongly of equal parts musty old books and cat. The cat was a grey mongrel of indeterminate breeding named Ash, who had free run of the building. Ash was a mouser, and quite a good one. He had worked for Davin longer than Kyrus had by some years, and his skills had given him quite a large girth; he weighed more than some dogs Kyrus had seen.

Ash's eyes followed Kyrus's path as he crossed the main room to his chair, which Ash was currently occupying. The chair was high-backed and solidly built out of oak, and the hard seat gave Kyrus awful aches—or at least it used to. Ever since he had gotten a cushion to pad the seat, Ash had taken to napping on it. Knowing he would not be allowed to remain in his favorite napping spot once Kyrus managed to cross the cluttered room, Ash stretched himself out and, with a sidelong look at Kyrus, hopped to the floor. Kyrus lost sight of the animal as he stepped around a small table with a chessboard on it, careful not to disturb the pieces. As he got over to his chair and sat down to begin his day's work, he caught a glimpse of Ash padding up the stairs. Kyrus could not help but smile. The door to Davin's room did not shut quite right, and if Ash was determined to get in …

A string of curses punctuated Kyrus's thought: "What the…? Pltheah! Get your tail out of my face! How many times do I …"

Davin's voice trailed off, and Kyrus turned to his desk and dipped a quill into his ink pot.

Good morning! Kyrus thought, then chuckled to himself.

* * * * * * * *

It was nearly half an hour later before Davin emerged from upstairs, suitably dressed to meet the day. He was of an age at which a more wealthy man would have considered retiring to the countryside. Over the years, Davin had grown thick around the middle from good eating and little strenuous work, though he could hardly be considered fat. He occasionally joked that his hair behaved like a flock of sparrows: each year it migrated north, but unlike the sparrows, it inconveniently forgot the trip back south. What little was left of his once-black hair had long since gone to grey. His eyes seemed to be those of a much younger man, twinkling from behind a pair of wire-rimmed spectacles and reflecting the joy from a broad smile.

"Fair morning, my boy! How does this fine day find you?"

"It finds me quite well," Kyrus replied, returning his employer's infectious smile. "Has it found you yet?"

Davin took the jest in the spirit in which it was given, and they settled into their morning routine. Kyrus watched Davin write for some time while feigning interest in his own work. His own quill had grown bone dry, and he had been scratching at the same beleaguered piece of parchment for over an hour. Several times, as Davin continued to write, Kyrus tried to peek over the top of his employer's writing desk, raising himself in his chair as much as he could without drawing attention to himself. He did not want to upset Davin by spying on him, especially when tonight was supposed to be the end of his week-long ordeal of curiosity, but he could not help himself. His work had fallen behind, but he silently assured himself that he would be able to catch up starting tomorrow, once he knew what all the mystery lately had been about. Until then, he more or less just gave up and tried to covertly indulge his curiosity, hopeless as it might seem with Davin apparently committed to keeping his secret until the promised time. Davin was an honest man, almost to a fault. But if the king ever had need of a spy, Kyrus doubted he would be able to find one craftier than Davin. Kyrus got the feeling that Davin had been hanging clues in front of him all week, enjoying the opportunity to have a little fun with him. He was sure that whatever Davin was writing had something to do with what he was going to find out that evening.

* * * * * * * *

When evening finally came, Kyrus gratefully put away the parchment that had been tormenting him for the past few hours—a treatise on the enlightened state of the kingdom's justice system commissioned by the local magistrate, Lord Kenrick Lionsvaen. He wiped his ink-stained fingertips on his handkerchief as best he could, though a black tinge of it remained, which never seemed to go away anymore. Hurrying up the stairs, he splashed a little water on his face and ran his more or less clean fingers through his hair to straighten out the tangles a bit. After a glance at his reflection in the mirror, he pronounced himself fit for public viewing. Kyrus generally did not give much thought to his appearance, but tonight was likely to be a bit of a spectacle, if he had judged Davin correctly. He would hate to be an embarrassment to his friend should he arrive looking like he had just lost a fight with his own ink pot.

The streets were quieting down as Kyrus made his way to the Brown Elk Tavern to meet Davin. The sun had just cast its last rays of light over the horizon and was giving way to twilight. Shopkeepers were closing their doors, peddlers packing up their carts and wagons, and fest halls were admitting their clientele for the evening. Kyrus passed a man carrying a large tin jug, reeking of kerosene, who was making his way down Westfall Street, lighting and refilling the lamps that kept the cobblestone street lit through the night. Kyrus nodded a greeting to the man, whose name he had never learned, and received a sidelong glance in return. Kyrus paid little heed to the indifferent response, since he evoked similar reactions from the majority of the people in town. He was not rich, or good-looking, or even particularly sociable, so he figured he had no reason to expect any better.

As he walked, he tried to mentally prepare himself for a letdown, knowing that he had built the whole thing up in his mind all week to the point where anything short of a knighthood or a visit from King Gorden himself would have been a disappointment. Whatever it turned out to be, he would not want Davin to think he was not pleased with it, even if it turned out not to be as grand as he had thought. The old man had been so kind to him over the years of his employment that he could not bear the thought of hurting his feelings. He practiced beaming his best surprised smile until it occurred to him that he must have looked like a simpleton to the few passersby he came across, grinning at nothing in particular as he walked.

He eventually reached the front door of the Brown Elk Tavern, a modest two-story structure with whitewashed walls and brown shutters. Light shone from the yellowed windows, casting a blurry tableaux of shadows onto the street that hinted as to what transpired inside. Raucous laughter and shouted conversation mixed with the tinkling of glass and stoneware to give the tavern a welcoming air. He breathed deep and steeled himself for whatever lay inside, then painted his best expectant look on his face and pushed the door open in front of him.

The Brown Elk was a well-loved establishment among the locals of Scar Harbor. Most nights, the large common room was filled to capacity, and on busy nights, the mezzanine level overlooking that common room would be close to overflowing its railings. That night, however, things were a bit out of sorts. A number of the small square tables that normally stood scattered about the room had been pushed together by one wall to form a makeshift banquet table, with a large tablecloth draped across them all to make the whole arrangement look quite proper. Crowded around the table were a great many people that Kyrus was familiar with, though many were just passing acquaintances. There were several members of the Scriveners Guild from both Scar Harbor and several nearby towns, a few neighbors from the buildings adjacent to Davin's shop, merchants with whom he dealt frequently, and some men he recognized as friends of Davin. At the head of the table sat Expert Davin Chartler himself, laughing at something one of the men next to him had said and hoisting a mug of ale. Next to Davin, and not taking a seat, was a distinguished looking older gentleman, dressed in black and standing straight, as if a board had been tucked down the back of his shirt.

A great cheer greeted Kyrus as his arrival was noted, and a number of tankards and mugs were raised.

"Kyrus!" they shouted in unison, giving the impression they had rehearsed the welcome ahead of time.

"Have a seat, friend," said Greuder, owner of a local pastry shop, who sat near the far end of the table from Davin.

Greuder then stood and pulled out a chair for Kyrus, the seat exactly opposite Davin's, at the other head of the table.

Kyrus's face flushed bright crimson. Twenty or so people were more than he spoke to in a typical day, and he felt out of place at the center of their attention, like an actor thrust into a role at the last moment, never having read the script.

Words failed him utterly. He must have stood there stunned for longer than he thought, because the next thing he knew Greuder had a hand on his shoulder, guiding him to his seat.

"Am … Am I late?" Kyrus managed to stammer out once the initial shock wore off.

"No, no, not at all, my boy!" yelled Davin down the length of the table. "You are here right on time, as usual. It is just that I had arranged for everyone else to be early, you see."

Davin smiled, apparently at his own cleverness. Greuder managed to deliver the guest of honor to his seat and then resumed his own seat just to Kyrus's right. Once everyone had settled down, Davin stood up and produced a small cylindrical case, the same case that had piqued Kyrus's curiosity earlier in the day. He withdrew the contents—several sheets of parchment—and tapped them on the table to straighten them out a bit. Turning his attention to his guests, he cleared his throat.

"Well, let us get down to the reason for this little gathering, shall we?" Davin said. "Friends and colleagues, as you may have already surmised, I have a great announcement to make. This gentleman to my left is Kornelius, steward to His Majesty, King Gorden."

At this, several guests gaped openly, and there was a bit of murmuring.

"He is here at His Majesty's behest to aid me in setting my affairs in order before I leave for Golis. I have been offered, and most gratefully accepted, His Majesty's post as the next royal scribe."

Davin paused here, no doubt fully expecting his friends' reaction. There were several who clapped, some cheered; Kyrus felt faint and could only stare dumbly at his employer.

"I have been given this opportunity because our dear colleague, Mr. Oriedel Conniton, heretofore His Majesty's personal scribe, has fallen ill with an affliction resulting from his advanced years and has resigned the position to spend his remaining years with his family. I have already conveyed my well wishes to Mr. Conniton and his family, and I shall be visiting them on my way to Golis to deliver my respects in person.

"As a member in good standing of the Scriveners Guild, I would like to toast His Majesty for his continued support of our craft, despite the ever-intrusive designs of the typesetters and their infernal presses. To King Gorden, may his wisdom be passed down through all the ages!"

Everyone raised his mug and drank deeply, including Kyrus, who found that someone had pressed a tankard of ale into his hand while he was not paying attention.

"Now, of course, there remains the small matter of what will become of my shop once I have moved out of it," Davin said. "I must admit that over the years I have grown to become quite fond of the place, and I am loath to leave it behind. But, of course, duty calls, and I must answer! Therefore, I have made the decision that I must sell my beloved home, for that is what it is to me, as much as it has been a workplace. And as His Majesty is currently without the services of a royal scribe, the sale must be made in all haste. Since I could not bear to sell it to a stranger, I had thought to ask one of you to buy it from me. We shall auction it right now, with payment due immediately. Let us begin as modestly as possible, at a single eckle."

There was a general bewilderment at this sudden turn of events. That the men gathered at the table were ill prepared for such an undertaking was obvious. Kyrus could not believe what was happening. Davin was auctioning off his home ... *his* home—the both of theirs. While it was perfectly within his right to do so, Kyrus could not believe Davin had not forewarned him.

"Well, anyone ... one eckle?"

There was a general muttering up and down the length of the table, muttered excuses of coin purses left at home and the like. Greuder gave Kyrus an elbow in the side, and Kyrus noticed that nobody at the table would admit to having so much as a single one-eckle coin among them. Fumbling in his vest pocket, Kyrus withdrew the first coin his fingers closed on. He gave a quick glance at the denomination and slapped it down on the table.

"Ten eckles!" Kyrus cried as everyone turned their gazes in his direction.

Silence fell over the gathering as they waited for someone to respond.

"Well, we have a bid of ten eckles. Do I hear any other bids?"

Silence followed Davin's question. After a moment, Davin deemed it suitable to continue, having given everyone enough time to protest should they so choose.

"Ten eckles it is, then."

Davin smiled at Kyrus and beckoned to him with one hand—the hand not holding the speech that had turned Kyrus's world on its head that evening.

"Congratulations, my boy. Let us just get the deed signed over to you, which Kornelius has conveniently brought along."

At a nod from Davin, the old steward retrieved a small strongbox from the floor in the corner of the room, where it had lain unnoticed. Kornelius placed it on the table and withdrew from it some papers, a quill, and ink. Starting to put the pieces together and figure out what precisely was going on, Kyrus cautiously made his way down to Davin's end of the table. The whole thing gave Kyrus the impression of one of the old, trite plays that Davin so enjoyed watching.

Kyrus and Davin both signed the contracts that Kornelius had drawn up to complete the sale, and Kyrus could not help but get the feeling that there was something missing. As if on cue, Davin interrupted his musings.

"Of course, to keep the old place in use, there will have to be a member of the Scriveners Guild there to oversee things. Now, Kyrus, I know you have been painfully aware that I have been remiss in my duties to you as a mentor of late. You are long overdue for your journeymanship, as I have long admitted. Now close your eyes; I have something for you."

Kyrus did as he was told and shut his eyes, grinning broadly. At last, he would get his official membership in the guild. He had waited perhaps a year longer than was considered the norm, but today would make up for all that. He would also be the only journeyman in Eastern Acardia to own his own shop. He could hardly contain his excitement as he first heard Davin step around behind him and then the clatter of a fine metal chain. He felt Davin lower the chain over his head; it had to be his journeyman's medallion, a symbol of his new status as a guild member.

"Now," Davin said, "I know that the guild does not forbid a journeyman from maintaining his own shop, but the general public does not place their trust lightly, and it is difficult for a journeyman to gain that trust, not having been recognized by the guild as an expert in his field. You should not have to worry, though."

Kyrus's eyes shot open. He looked down at his chest and did not see the journeyman's medallion he had first expected. What he saw was the emblem of an Expert Scrivener: a golden "S" curled around a quill. He spun around to face Davin, the question on his mind written upon his face as clearly as his gifted hands could ever have managed.

"At the last meeting of the guild, when I found out about my new station, I remembered to recommend you," Davin said. "I had some of your work along with me for them to review, and I had to somewhat sheepishly confess to my own dereliction in not presenting your case sooner. Needless to say ..." Davin reached over and gave Kyrus's medallion a meaningful flick. "... they were impressed. Oh, to be sure, there were a few who thought that despite your talent, you should progress through the ranks the same way everyone else has to, but these are difficult times. The Typesetters Guild is gaining prominence as they refine those blasted machines that make a mockery of our art. We cannot let a brilliant scribe languish as a journeyman when his works should be heralded as those of a true expert. Now enough of all this seriousness. Let us celebrate!"

Davin picked up his mug of ale, and the other guests did likewise, raising their voices in toasts of congratulation for Davin and Kyrus both. Another mug found its way into Kyrus's hand, and he lifted it along with the others. Few among the guests were hard drinkers, and the night's revelry was fairly brief. Kyrus, who rarely drank anything more potent than wine, was the first to pass out.

Chapter 3 - After the Bloodless Night

By dawn, most of the men were emotionally spent. With the long night finally past, the threat of the goblin attack seemed to diminish. It was almost as if, believing the goblins would attack at night, the threat seemed over with the arrival of the morning sun. Few of them had slept much during the night, between the added watches and chain armor pressing down on their chests like the heavy hand of waiting death.

The cheer of morning seemed to banish such dark thoughts. The singing of morning birds and the rosy cheer of the day's first rays of sunlight seemed at odds with the thought of death lurking out among the trees. There was some talk that perhaps the goblins had thought better of their attack, and silently withdrawn back from wherever they had come. Some believed what they were saying; others just needed to hear some words of confidence to assuage their uncertainty and nervousness. Brannis did not like it.

Let the men say what they would, but Brannis had the nagging feeling that the goblins were scheming something. *They would not have delayed their attack just to cost our men a night's sleep, would they? Perhaps ...*

There had been no hunting the previous night, so the morning meal was to be nothing but cured meat strips and water—hardly an appetizing prospect. Brannis made his way over to claim his dawn feast from the army's stores and ran into Iridan, his eyes sunken and bloodshot, appearing a bit wobbly on his feet.

"Fair morning, what say?" asked Brannis with a smile.

Brannis had managed a restful sleep despite the circumstances and felt refreshed. His dreams had been growing more vivid of late and he seemed to sleep the deeper for it, not awakening throughout the night as so many of the other knights had.

Strange to have such vivid dreams about such mundane drivel. What about copying texts for stodgy old men should be so worth remembering? Am I trying to tell myself I would be best off retiring and taking up a trade? The thought amused Brannis. He had never used to remember what he dreamed at night and wished it was not always the same bland stuff. *Why not fair lasses and glorious battles some night?*

"I would not know; it is still last night for me," Iridan said. "I never thought I would envy anyone a night's sleep in full armor. Guess I was wrong on that count. Hey, when can we call off the goblin watch and let me get some sleep?"

"I will have some patrols search the surrounding area for signs of the goblins.

I do not think they can hide from us in daylight in any threatening numbers. If the patrols do not turn anything up, well, I guess we will see about letting you sleep a bit." Brannis leaned closer and added in a low voice, "I can see now why necromancy is forbidden. I cannot imagine anything dead would look less horrible than you do right now."

Despite his fatigue, Iridan could not help but smile and chuckle a bit. The playful swat that he aimed for the back of the grinning Brannis's head missed badly, and drew an amused snicker at his expense from the few men nearby.

"Sure, Brannis, enjoy this now. I will be getting you back once I have ..." Iridan paused for a yawn. "... gotten a good sleep in me. I will not be forgetting! Maybe the next wolves I bring into camp will be doing their business in *your* tent." They had been friends since childhood, so Iridan was freer than most to joke with the battalion commander.

He looked at Brannis out of the corner of his eye and tried to feign a menacing look. This drew a good-natured laugh from everyone, as Iridan was hardly in any condition to look menacing. Brannis nearly toppled his friend with a hearty clap on the back and helped him to a seat and dawn feast.

* * * * * * * *

"Goblins!" one of the sentries screamed.

While the goblins were as silent in daylight as at night, there was no denying that they had given up some advantage in stealth with their dawn raid. One of the sentries had spotted them.

"To arms! Form a shield wall just inside the camp perimeter," Brannis ordered as he plunked his helmet onto his head and secured the chinstrap. "Keep the shields low and remember that the goblins cannot reach above your shields, only under and between."

The knights were gathering behind the rapidly forming wall of men with shields and spears, each wielding a pair of "goblin swords"—whip-thin rods of steel meant to overcome the goblin advantage of quickness. Only Brannis, carrying Massacre, was differently armed. And, of course, Iridan, who was neither armed nor armored, though he had been given a chain shirt identical to those of the commoner soldiers.

Poor Iridan, thought Brannis, *no sleep for him after all.*

The young sorcerer had shunned the armor he had been given, planning to rely solely on his own magic for his defense. If the goblins were half as smart as everyone claimed, they would pick him out of the crowd easily enough anyway, and he preferred to be free of the awkward armor to better cast his spells.

"Indreithio anamakne ubtaio wanuzar pronedook," intoned Iridan.

Brannis spared a glance over his shoulder to check on the spell Iridan was casting. He was holding his arms skyward, fully extended, with his fingers slowly weaving an intricate pattern in the air. Brannis recognized it as a shielding spell, and from the way Iridan was gesturing, one meant to form a barrier overhead to prevent the goblins' thrown weapons from penetrating, like giving a house a sturdy roof to keep out the rain.

Brannis was just behind the front lines when the first of the goblin missiles sailed in. He shouted for his men to keep down behind their shields and not to raise them up. All but a handful managed to put aside their instinct to bring their shields up to cover their heads.. A second wave of thrown spears and daggers quickly followed the first and with few targets presenting themselves, those few went down quickly amid a storm of hurled blades.

The sound of the goblin sorcerers' spell chants were drowned out by the sudden war cry of their first wave of infantry, a horrible chattering cacophony bringing to mind a flock of startled chickens in an echoing canyon. Yet the spells were cast—heard by the defenders or not—and a blast of lightning shattered the ranks of men to one side, while two bolts of white-hot aether hammered into Iridan's shielding spell, illuminating the transparent barrier for a flickering moment. The shield appeared almost to buckle, but it held and the aether-bolts dispersed.

The goblins pressed their advantage where the lightning had cleared a hole in the Kadrins' shield wall. Two knights rushed in to fill the breach, a burning scent heavy in the air around them. They stood over the bodies of the fallen soldiers and continue serving their duty on the line.

Both sides now had to contend with the effects of the fog.. There was still enough visibility at head height that the humans could clearly make out where their allies were. The goblins, mired in thicker fog whose nature they had somewhat underestimated, were having difficulty finding their footing. Brannis sported a rather wicked, self-satisfied grin when he heard the startled yelps of the goblins that stumbled into one of the vast number of latrines his men had been digging the last several days. He had figured that a waist-deep hole to a man was plenty to take a goblin out of the fighting.

The goblins, however, were nothing if not adaptable. One of their sorcerers quickly cast a spell that created a gale of wind that dispersed the remaining fog in the span of but two breaths. Another created a dimness in the air not entirely dissimilar to the fog, but which acted to dim the light from the morning sun over the battlefield, creating an artificial night.

Iridan acted quickly to counter the latter effect, and nullified the advantage that goblin eyes held in the dark.

"Aleph kalai abdu."

He quickly spoke the few necessary words, and made a quick circling gesture with his right hand, with the tip of his middle finger touching his thumb. It was the simplest of all spells and the first one taught to every student at the Academy. It was a spell simple enough that Brannis nearly had the strength to cast it. Instantly the false night was replaced by an equally false noontime, as a bright ball of light appeared overhead near Iridan's outstretched hand, the harsh white light cutting through the dimming spell the goblins had fashioned.

The spell had worked well, and taken back the advantage that the goblin spell had bought for the few moments prior. But it had also marked Iridan clearly in the eyes of the goblins. The way the spell was worded, it was difficult to make it appear more than a pace or so from the hand from which it originated. In fact, it took some skill and practice even to keep the light from emanating from one's own fingertip. Iridan might as well have painted a sign reading "Sorcerer" and hung it around his neck.

* * * * * * *

Brannis had been calling out orders, orchestrating the Kadrins' defenses, when he heard a high whistle sound above the noise of battle. It came in two quick bursts, a longer whistle, then two more short: goblin signals, he realized. He had not yet become engaged in the combat; his own sword was far too dangerous to have it drawn and swinging about in close quarters with his own men. They were holding up well. They had resisted the urge to break ranks and attempt to press the goblins back into the forest, which was now starting to burn. Iridan's shielding spell had somehow managed to turn a ball of fire from one of the goblins back at their own ranks. Brannis watched to see what came of their enemy's whistle.

From behind the lines, Brannis was the first to notice the goblins' reinforcements charge in from the south and west. They were not as numerous as the main force attacking from the east, but they presented a tactical problem: no defenders were prepared to hold those sides against attack. The shield wall had held so far, and the knights had done well to prevent the goblins from coming around the flanks, but this they were not going to be able to stop in time.

"Pull back and bring the shield wall around to face the south as well!" Brannis shouted.

* * * * * * *

As the knights helped direct the troop movements to carry out their commander's orders, Iridan watched Brannis draw his sword and prepare to defend the interior of the camp. Iridan himself was behind the lines and knew they were unlikely to survive this battle without his magic, so long as the goblin sorcerers still lived. He stayed watching both his friend's position and for places his spells might be needed.

The first attackers among the goblins stopped short. They had been eager to rush in against a lone human knight and an unarmed sorcerer, relishing the glory of cutting off the head of the army. But the sight of an almost ogre-sized human, wielding an enchanted sword that glowed a foreboding green and trailed a strange mist in its wake, gave them pause. As the goblins at the forefront slowed, those lagging behind caught up to the front of the charge, and their renewed numbers swelled their courage once again, and they recommenced the attack en masse.

Iridan saw the goblins heading for Brannis and started another spell.

"Haru bedaessi leoki kwatuan gelora."

Iridan held his arms wide with his fingers spread apart. Then, rapidly, as he finished his chant, he drew his hands together and, just before they met, turned his palms upward and raised both hands overhead. He was only a few paces from the cooking fire and that was what had inspired this particular spell. As the aether flowed through him, he directed it into the various pots, spoons, bowls, and ladles that the Kadrins had brought along with them. These various items rose quickly into the air to hover around waist height and with a commanding gesture from Iridan toward the onrushing goblins, they flew.

In all of Kadrin history, there was perhaps no instance where the contents of a larder had been put to such deadly use on the field of battle. A storm of crockery hurtled through the air with the speed of a diving hawk. The great clanging and splattering sounds that resulted hinted at one of the greatest culinary assaults of all time. Though itsounded quite incongruous in the middle of a battle of spell and steel,the charge from the west was brought near to a halt.

* * * * * * * *

Just a few steps away, Brannis was beset by onrushing goblins, leading with their spears. Three-wide they charged;three at once they were cut down. The goblins were astonished by the speed at which the blade cut through the air ... and spears ... and goblins. That is, all but the first three were astonished, for those at the forefront of the charge never realized what had become of them.

The rest of the goblins charging Brannis drew back and began to try to encircle him, staying just out of his reach. Brannis kept Massacre waving back and forth in front of him, leaving the green mist wafting in the air behind the blade, and forming a hazardous barrier for the goblins to cross.

The goblins were sensitive creatures, naturally better attuned to the aether than were humans. Theycould sense the power in the weapon and thus had some misgivings about letting the mist touch them. One who had gotten a bit too close was already unsteady on his feet and did not look well at all. Several gave up on Brannis altogether and instead tried to get past him to the sorcerer, whom they saw was much distracted by other concerns.

"Brannis, the shield wall!" Iridan called out, drawing Brannis's attention to a gap that had formed.

As Brannis turned that way, he heard Iridan immediately began another spell: *"Kanethio mandraxae."*

Iridan crossed his palms, facing outward, and aimed toward the breach. A blue-white ray of light shone out from him, wide as his shoulders, and he ducked his head to keep the brightness from hurting his eyes. The blast was one of pure aether force, and left a large number of goblins missing entirely when the blinding glare left the spot and everyone could see there again. But the smoking ruin of a gap was once again quickly filled by a few of the remaining goblins.

Iridan winced in pain as the aether blast took more power to cast than his body was accustomed to. Brannis knew that every vein in his thin body must have been like a river of fire. Brannis had studied along with Iridan at the Academy, before being expelled for lack of talent. The pain was really in the mind, and Iridan's body would still function if he had the will to endure through it.

Brannis had taken advantage of the blinding light to cut down most of the goblins facing him. His back had been to the blast and his adversaries had seen it directly, blinding them temporarily and giving Brannis an easy time of dispatching them. With the quick respite in the battle, Brannis took stock of his army and was dismayed. Both sides had been ravaged during the fight. Fewer than half of his troops were still standing and goblin bodies littered the battlefield. Even as he pondered this, a plume of fire erupted from nearby and engulfed several more of his men.

Brannis spotted a goblin sorcerer—one of two that he had figured remained in the battle—at the source of the fire. Distractedly slashing through a goblin that had thought to catch him in an unguarded moment, Brannis charged across the battlefield toward the deadly goblin sorcerer.

The goblin spotted him as well and began another spell. Brannis understood nothing of goblin speech or how they used magic. Not the fleetest of runners, he could only hope he was fast enough to close the distance in time. He saw the goblin cup his hands together as something grew between them. It began as a tiny puff of golden light and expanded as Brannis watched, his eyes intent on nothing else. The energy grew into a globe the size of Brannis's fist. The goblin sorcerer was struggling to hold it in check, squeezing it between its bony hands. He tried to slow himself as he saw the goblin bringing its hands around behind the globe, realizing he was not going to be able to close the distance in time. His momentum was too great to dodge to the side. The goblin let his spell loose straight at Brannis's chest.

Brannis saw the blast coming and did the only thing he could think to do. He brought his sword up in front of him, tip pointing down, into line with the oncoming missile. With his left arm, he tried to shield his face from the blast.

He felt a wrenching pain in his right shoulder, and the sword was torn from his grasp. There was an impact on his breastplate that felt like someone had just slung a sack of flour into his chest but he managed to keep his balance and hardly break stride.

When he brought his other arm away from his face, Brannis caught sight of one particularly astonished goblin who stood gaping at him. The little creature turned to run but Brannis was running full out, and dove onto the sorcerer before he could get more than two steps away. Pinning the goblin was child's play as Brannis easily outweighed the sorcerer five times over. The goblin tried casting one last spell, but two heavy blows from Brannis's gauntleted fist were more than the creature's frail body could endure.

* * * * * * * *

Iridan and the last remaining goblin sorcerer had torn into each other's forces in a fury of magical power while not directly encountering each other. The goblin sorcerer had seen too much of the human's magic to want to test himself against

Iridan directly, but now he had a much better chance. Having snuck around the fallen left flank of the human army, he crouched low by the brook and, quietly as he could, timed a spell for when Iridan was most vulnerable.

Iridan had just cast another aether blast spell, figuring that his own body was a price he was willing to pay to save the rest of the army. He was beginning to feel nauseous with the pain of his last casting, once more having pushed himself too far, when he heard a crackling sound to his left. Turning, he saw a ball of lightning heading toward him and panicked.

Iridan raised his hands out in front of him and reflexively drew in all the aether he could muster. Without a word of arcane or a conscious thought, a translucent barrier formed in the air between his body and the balled lightning, bowl-shaped and facing his enemy. When the two forces collided, Iridan felt the impact in his shoulders, as if his outstretched hands had been supporting the barrier. The barrier flashed but remained intact. The goblin's spell rebounded from the barrier and right back at him. The goblin had no time to react.

Iridan had another problem, however: he had drawn in more aether than he could control. It felt like a wildfire had been ignited behind his eyes. He clutched at the sides of his head and fell to his knees, screaming incoherently. With what little of his mind that was not muddled by pain, he tried to force the aether out of his body and into another vessel. His training would have had him divert the aether into fire and heat the nearest water available to him but he was too blinded by the pain to find the stream, and so he randomly started to release the aether wherever he was able.

The few goblins that had not begun to retreat when they saw their last sorcerer fall tried to take advantage of Iridan's infirmity and finish him off. They did not realize their mistake until they burst into flames as they drew too near the human sorcerer.

The ground around Iridan began to steam and the grass withered to ash within several paces of him. The dozen or so goblins still able to move were now in retreat, and the few Kadrins still standing sought some way to aid their sorcerer's plight.

There was little any of them could do, though, and a moment later, with a convulsive gasp that sounded like a horrible mixture of pain and relief, Iridan collapsed onto the blistered turf.

Chapter 4 - Disturbing Dreams

The city's clock tower struck the hour, the count of chimes lost in the remnants of a lingering dream. Kyrus Hinterdale dragged himself out of bed, stiff and sore, and made his way slowly to the window. The room was dark except for a sliver of sunlight streaming between the closed shutters. When Kyrus drew them open, he had to squeeze his eyes shut against the brightness, only opening them in a squint once he had turned his head. He ran his tongue around the inside of his mouth to clear away the sticky, gummy feeling he had. He took up the pitcher he kept for filling the washbasin and drank a mouthful. The water was warm, as it had been sitting on his dressing table for days but he cared little. It was the second day since Expert Davin's announcement of his new office, and the second morning in a row that had greeted him with a hangover.

Kyrus went to the little mirror that hung from his wall and wiped it clean with a shirtsleeve. The face that looked back bore some passing resemblance to his own. The green eyes were bloodshot, the sandy-blond hair was wilder than was his custom, but it was him. The close examination was more work than his eyes were fit for. He squeezed them shut as a defense.

To keep his mind away from the rioting headache he was experiencing, he tried to put the remnants of yesterday in order in his thoughts …

* * * * * * * *

It was destined to be perhaps the shortest day of Kyrus's life. It began shortly after noon, when he found himself staring at the ceiling of his own room, both wondering how he had managed to get back home, and not wanting to move for fear of his skull splitting in two from sheer pain. His dreams, plagued by nightmares of fire and blood, did no justice to the waking torment that greeted him along with the early afternoon sun.

Davin had brought him a steaming cup of coffee, an extravagance Kyrus rarely had the chance to enjoy, which had cheered him more than relieved his headache. Still, it was enough to coax him out of bed. Davin and the king's steward Kornelius had hired porters to pack up the old scribe's personal effects, so Kyrus's help had not been needed during the morning hours. Davin wanted to spend some time with his young successor, though, before he took his leave. The two of them left the king's man to oversee the packing and went to find a suitable eatery for what they expected would be their last luncheon together for a long time.

Dremmer's Pub was a rich man's dive. It was situated on the outskirts of the wealthy side of Scar Harbor, toward the docks but not near them by any stretch of creative geography. Still, the decor was that of a dockside tavern, with trophy fish hung on the walls and rustic, rough-cut furnishings of unfinished wood. The bottoms of the table were kept scrubbed with seawater to give the place just a hint of the briny smell that reminded sailors of the sea. It was all show, however, for the food was excellent and the prices a bit too high for most to afford easily or regularly. Any real sailor that set foot inside would have had a good laugh at how anyone could mistake the clean, well-tended tavern for a sea-dogs' watering hole. It was a place where the genteel could get a taste of danger without actually experiencing it, making it a common destination for wealthy visitors to the city, as well as a few well-off locals with nautical pretensions.

Kyrus and Davin had taken a seat just under a stuffed swordfish, at a small table in a corner of the common room. Kyrus had never before set foot inside the expensive establishment. He could not help but gawk a bit at the important personages that had stopped by to take their lunch there. He noticed two of the local merchant guild masters, discussing something over bowls of chowder. A lord, whose name did not come readily to his mind, sat by himself, looking through a ledger of some sort. There was Admiral Rand, a pensioner of the Royal Navy and a regular at Dremmer's, sharing old war stories with Lord Harwick's eldest son, Tomas. Kyrus felt out of place among his social superiors.

"The place is all yours now, my boy. I know you will do it proud," Davin said over his plate of shrimp.

Kyrus looked down to the Expert Scrivener's medallion that hung about his neck. It was so new it still smelled of silver polish. It felt like it belonged around someone else's neck.

"You know, all the secrecy the past week when you refused to tell me what you were up to ... I somehow never guessed this," Kyrus said and gave the medallion's chain a tug. "Greuder had me convinced you were setting me up with some long-lost niece of yours."

Davin laughed. "My elder brother's only girl is your mother's age. Tell that baker to stick to his pastries and leave prognostication to more gifted charlatans."

Kyrus gave a little grin and shrugged. "What can I say? He had *me* convinced."

Davin waved away his comments. "Kyrus, you have a good mind between those ears. You just need to get out more. Everything will work out in the end, there is no need to rush things. Besides, now you have a shop of your very own. Respectable member of the Scriveners' Guild and all that."

Davin spent the rest of their meal explaining to Kyrus how to manage the business of the scrivener's shop, and filled him in on the details of the commissions that he had yet to start work on but which Kyrus would be taking over. There was a good deal more to it than Kyrus had realized, and he tried his best to remember everything Davin said. Though it had lessened with the passing hours and continued to abate as he took in some good food and drink, a bright pain still dwelt behind Kyrus's eyes; he was sure it had caused him to miss more than one morsel of advice from his mentor.

What was that about the best prices on colored inks? Ah well, I am sure I shall have a thousand things to learn on my own regardless and one more cannot hurt much. Do not want to spoil the old man's lunch by making him think I am not listening.

The rest of the day had been spent seeing to the last of the packing and to making arrangements for Kyrus's smooth transition to ownership of the business. It was frightfully dull and dry stuff: papers to be filed with the guild and negotiating with merchants to reestablish deals made by Davin in Kyrus's name. Kornelius had been a remarkable help, for his position as a king's man had lent importance to their activities and caught the attention of otherwise slow-acting officials of the merchant guilds.

Interspersed among their bustling, Kyrus and Davin managed to conclude a game of chess that had been set up between their two writing desks. A book entitled *On the Stratagems and Underlying Premises of the Game of Chess, Insights of Lord Arvind Kendelaine III* sat nearby, well worn and well loved. It was the first commission that they had worked on jointly, and the game had been the first thing that Expert Davin found himself to have in common with his apprentice. It was in playing the game regularly that their friendship had developed. As they played more and came to discover that they were well-matched adversaries, Davin came to respect Kyrus's intellect and his ability to analyze. In the years since then, Kyrus had come to be almost a partner to the Expert Scribe, rather than an apprentice in his tutelage. Kyrus almost wished he had lost the game so that Davin could leave victorious.

By day's end, a carriage had been loaded with all that Davin cared to take with him and at the end of the night, he and Kornelius were to depart for Golis. But Davin's other friends had not been idle. The announcement of Davin's appointment as King Gorden's new scribe had been a cause for a celebration of Davin's own making the night before. For the occasion of Davin's departure, however, they had arranged a party of their own to send him off properly.

Having barely recovered from the aftereffects of Davin's surprise revel, Kyrus had made a concerted effort to moderate his celebrating a bit that time. He could not say how well he succeeded at his goal, however, for the night's carousing seemed vague in his memory, though he remembered seeing Davin and Kornelius into their carriage as the driver drew them away from the city. He was fairly certain that he had managed his own way home from the revel as well, but recalled little else.

* * * * * * *

Kyrus decided at that point to swear off drinking entirely. It was unlikely that another occasion would come along soon that would demand a toast, let alone five or more in one night, so for the time being, it should have been no problem to go without. Taking another swallow of water from the pitcher, he poured the rest into the washbasin and splashed some onto his face. He noticed a bit of blood had reddened the water as he washed, and he soon found a cut on the knuckle of the index finger on his right hand. It did not look serious but his careless ignorance of it had reopened the wound, which he had presumably received last night.

I hope I was not in a fight, he thought.

His reflection in the mirror was a wreck, but Kyrus smiled back at himself. For the first time, he truly saw himself as a grown man. *I am a guild member!* The medallion still hung proudly from his neck; he had not removed it since Davin had placed it there two nights before.

Yawning and stretching purposefully, Kyrus was determined to will away his fatigue and headache, and continue about his day. It was overly ambitious of him, but the chipper attitude he forced on himself helped him ignore the pain a bit and focus on more pressing matters. As his mind cleared a little, something struck him momentarily, a fleeting bit of a dream that seemed out of place.

He remembered something about using magic for the first time. He had long dreamed during his childhood of being a great wizard like in the fairy tales, rescuing maidens and battling dragons. But it seemed that even in his own dreams, he was destined never to be able to use magic, no matter how long or hard he tried. He had not recalled dreaming of it for many years, and he remembered his dreams more often than not. Last night, he had dreamt differently, he knew—or thought he knew. The memory was gnawing at the edge of his conscious thoughts, just out of reach. Concentrating, he tried to bring to mind his dreams of last night but the harder he tried, the further they slipped, as was often the way of dreams. The drinking had only made it worse.

Kyrus gave up for the time being, and turned his attention to the more immediate tasks of the day ahead of him. After washing and dressing, he headed downstairs to get to work. As he passed the door of Davin's room, which was slightly ajar, he could not help but wonder anew at the thought that his old friend was really gone. It still seemed strange to Kyrus, something he did not expect to become accustomed to for some time. He wondered what he should do with the room, for he had little enough need of the space his own room provided. Perhaps he could rent the room to a boarder. The thought that he might take on an apprentice of his own had not even entered his mind.

The day's work seemed tedious now, without Davin around. There was still just as much work and now half as many scribes to do it. Surely Davin's work had slowed recently due to his advancing years and aching joints, but he still was able to write a vast number of pages each day. Kyrus missed both his contribution and his wit. He set himself to his task, though, and made it through a greater volume of work than he was normally capable of, since he and Davin often broke off from working for one reason or another during the day, when they felt the need. Kyrus, feeling the pressure of filling his mentor's place as the preeminent scribe in Scar Harbor, pressed straight through the day with naught but a short break at noontime for a small lunch of soup and bread.

At sunset, he put down his quill for the evening. It was nearly summertime, and the days were already long enough in Kyrus's estimation without lengthening them with lamplight. Kyrus flexed the cramps out of his wrist and decided to take a walk to get his idle legs a bit of limbering. As he opened the shop's door to go out, he received a small but not unwelcome surprise.

"Ash, what are you doing here?" Kyrus asked the familiar feline that had been lying patiently on the front stoop.

In answer, the cat stretched languidly and walked past Kyrus into the shop. Apparently he had his own opinion on where he wished to live.

"I see. Well, I shall have to write Davin and see what he wants me to do with you, but you are welcome here for the time being."

Kyrus did not feel the least bit odd talking to the cat, though a woman closing up a vegetable stand for the night looked at him strangely. Kyrus had acquired Davin's habit of talking to Ash as if he were another person, a trait he had developed during the years he lived alone with the cat before taking on Kyrus as his apprentice.

Kyrus shut the door behind the cat and started off down the street with no particular destination in mind. The fresh, mild air felt good as he filled his lungs, and cleared out the musty feeling that had settled there from being cooped up indoors all day. The sky was clear. In the dusk, Kyrus was just able to start picking out stars as the deepening gloom of falling night revealed them one by one. He tried to let all the worries and pressures of his new responsibility drift up and float away into the vast canopy of the heavens. It did not quite work but he felt the better for having tried.

As he walked around Scar Harbor, shops were closing and taverns were filling. Civil servants were about with brands, lighting the oil lamps that kept the main streets safely lit throughout the night. Mothers called their children home from play and sent them off to bed. The city streets grew quieter and more somber. Most folk about were heading somewhere for the night, whether that be home and bed, or a night of revelry. He exchanged greetings with a few people he knew and accepted congratulations from several relative strangers who happened to notice his newly acquired Expert's Medallion, before he self-consciously tucked the chain under his shirt so as not to draw attention to it.

On the other side of the street, walking his way from the other direction, Kyrus spotted Abbiley Tillman. Abbiley was a girl near to Kyrus's own age, one who had caught his eye some time ago, and continued to do so whenever he saw her. He did not know much about her, just that she was an artist and sometimes a singer, and that she supported her younger brother since their parents had died. She seemed shy and he had never gotten up the nerve to talk to her. He was equally shy, especially around pretty girls. She had short, dark hair that she wore loose, the prettiest blue eyes, cheeks that dimpled when she smiled—Kyrus was shocked from his musings when he saw that she had noticed him looking her way.

He quickly turned away, but an inspired bravery struck him at that moment and he gathered up the courage to look back and smile. He was greatly relieved and elated when she actually smiled back. It was a shy little smile but it was clearly directed his way. He raised his hand to wave to her and was about to call out a greeting when a horrified look crossed her face. Kyrus's heart fell immediately, thinking he had pressed his luck too far.

Thunk!

A sharp blow struck him blindside in the head, and he blacked out.

Groaning, Kyrus opened his eyes to be greeted by the faces of a pair of concerned bystanders, framed by a backdrop of the night sky above him. His head stung both just above the right temple and directly in the back, where presumably it had hit the cobblestones.

"Are you all right?" one man asked. "You should watch where you are going. You walked right into a lamppost."

Please do not let Abbiley have been watching, Kyrus thought in despair. Luck was not with him, though, for he heard hard-heeled shoes hurrying across the cobblestones toward him.

"Oh my, are you hurt?" asked a concerned voice.

As the speaker came up next to him and crouched at his side, he easily matched the voice with its owner: the shy—but apparently caring—Abbiley. He had not realized until just then that he had never so much as heard her voice before. All that he had learned of her had been through acquaintances.

Kyrus took a handkerchief from his pocket and dabbed at the side of his head. It came away speckled with blood but not as much as he had feared to see.

"I should live," he announced. "But I would swear that lamppost was a full pace or more farther to the right just a moment ago."

He managed a slight, rueful smile at his own expense. Those gathered around him shared a chuckle and knew he was not badly hurt. Abbiley did not join in the mirth, though, for she seemed genuinely concerned about his injuries. She remained as the rest of the small crowd dispersed.

"I am so sorry. This is all my fault. Please forgive me," she said.

"How do you figure that?" Kyrus asked, rising to a seated position. "Are you the one who decides where to place lampposts on this street?"

She tried to hold back her amusement and not be sidetracked. "It was my fault. I distracted you and you walked into the post. If it had not been for me, it would not have happened."

"Well, if by that you mean if you had not been so captivating that I could not help but look your way, then I accept your apology." Kyrus kept his tone lighthearted but it still made Abbiley blush. "Though ... it was my own fault that my legs kept moving in one direction while my eyes drifted in the other."

It must have been the blow to his head but Kyrus could never remember having such a long conversation with a beautiful young woman before. He normally was stumbling over his words long before this point.

She helped him regain his footing and stand up. "My name is Abbiley," she introduced herself, not realizing that Kyrus had already known that much.

"Nice to meet you. I am Kyrus."

"Oh, you were Mr. Chartler's apprentice, the new Expert Scribe?" she asked, clearly impressed.

"Yes, that would be me," Kyrus admitted.

"Well, I must say, I had expected you to be much older. I guess I just always thought of experts as being old men, like nice old Mr. Chartler. I was sad to hear he was leaving."

"Well, I cannot say much about your expectations but I am working on the 'getting older' part. I still have some work yet to do on it, and walking into too many posts will not do much good toward that end, but I promise to keep trying."

Seemingly relieved that Kyrus was apparently all right, she laughed.

After a pause, he continued: "Davin was a good friend and I am going to miss him, way off in Golis. The shop seems so empty without him around and it has only been one full day."

"Umm ... Well ... maybe I can come by tomorrow, you know ... to see how you are faring?" she stammered out, trying to avoid looking Kyrus in the eye.

He took her hand in his. "Thank you. I would like that," he said.

She looked up at him then and saw him smiling down at her. She licked at her lips and swallowed.

"Oh ... I have got to go. My brother is going to wonder what has become of me." She gently pulled her hand away from Kyrus and turned to hurry away. "So I shall see you tomorrow, then?" she asked over her shoulder.

"Mind the lampposts!" he called out to her, smiling.

She quickly turned her attention back to where she was going, but not before a wide smile spread across her face.

Who was that? Kyrus thought.

He did not mean the girl, either. He vaguely recognized the voice as his own, but where were those words all coming from? It was as if every clever thing he had ever thought to say to a girl—but could not—had suddenly sprung to the tip of his tongue. While he had promised to avoid walking into posts, he seriously considered running his head into a few more to see what other wonders they could induce. He shook his head—until realizing that it hurt to do so—at the strange development.

His walk was taking him generally back toward the shop, though he was barely aware of his surroundings. His thoughts were revolving all around Abbiley and that pretty smile she had shown him. The image was fixed in his mind as if she had painted it there herself. He continued in a daze until something strange caught his attention.

One of the lamps had gone out.

In and of itself, it was not so unusual an occurrence. The lamps ran out of oil despite the light-keepers' best efforts to prevent it and sometimes a strong wind or mischievous children would climb the posts and blow them out. What was unusual was the familiar feeling of standing by an unlit lamppost in the dark.

The dream!
It came back to him suddenly …

* * * * * * *

He was stumbling along in the dark, unsure of quite where he was going. Shadows stretched in front of him from a small light some distance behind. Feeling in front of him with his hands, Kyrus caught hold of the post of an unlit lamp and used it to steady himself. It was an effort to maintain his balance for some reason.

This all seems wrong. I never dream about things from my real life, yet that was clearly Scar Harbor. All my dreams take place in a world that exists only behind the lids of my eyes, and have for as long as I can remember. There are no lampposts or streets like the ones we have in Scar Harbor; the world in my dreams is like something out of the fairy tales I had always loved when I was little. I am a mighty hero there, a knight. I have never dreamed about wandering in the dark, drunk … not that I can remember, at least.

"Sh … Shtoopid lamp."

He tried to shake it, but the post was firm in the ground.

"Can't shhheee where I'm going. Turn back … on."

He tried again to shake it, but gave up when once again nothing happened.

"Oh, shtubborn, huh? I'll show *you*," he threatened the lamp.

"*Alephhhh… kalai… abdu,*" he slurred out, pinching his fingers together and inscribing a circle in the air.

Kyrus felt a chill wind rush through his body. The tip of his finger burst into a soft white light. He brought the glowing finger up in front of his face, so close that his eyes crossed. He blinked and pulled his head back. It did not hurt and it certainly did not look like fire, but he could not tell what was making his finger light up.

That is not right at all! Magic never worked for me before in any of my dreams. I have tried before—many times. It was a recurring nightmare years ago, the same incantation, performed just as the instructor had said, yet nothing happened. Other students snickering, succeeding so easily where I had failed …

Kyrus shook his finger, trying to extinguish the light as if it was a flame, but it clung stubbornly to the tip of the index finger of his right hand. He tried to wipe it off on his shirtsleeve, with no better result. Dumbly, in his drunken state, he thought to light the lamp with it, in the hopes that it would be transferred and leave him. He pushed his finger inside the glass of the lamp and held it there, but the glow would not leave him.

Down the street, another reveler was walking his way, seeking his home after a night's drinking. Panicking, Kyrus tried to hide the offending digit, certain that it would be trouble if anyone else caught sight of it.

He thrust his hand into his pocket, but the glow was bright enough that it shone through the fabric, illuminating his pants from within. He tried covering it with the fist of his other hand, but light seeped out the cracks between his fingers, casting ominous shadows all about; that just made things worse. At last, and in desperation, he stuck his finger in his mouth and was satisfied to see no light pouring forth.

Turning away from the person approaching in the darkness, he hurried away as best he could towards the shop. Fear had lent him some relief from the dizziness of the alcohol in him, and he managed an awkward run, one arm swinging in time with his stride while the other was held up in front of him, keeping the weirdly glowing finger safely hidden in his mouth.

* * * * * * * *

He thought it odd that all of the reverie came back to him just then, but as Kyrus looked around him, the environs in his dream looked much like where he was right then. The similarity was striking, even down to the fact that one of the lamps had blown out. Kyrus assumed that the sight of a street so akin to the one in his dreams must have been the cause of the sudden remembrance of the dream.

It still seems so odd that for the first time for as long as I can remember, my dreams have included elements from the waking world.

His head still bothering him as he walked, Kyrus dabbed again at the wound above his temple. There was only a little blood this time but as he looked down at the handkerchief, he once again noticed the cut on the knuckle of his index finger—the one on his right hand. Kyrus felt dizzy as blood seemed to rush to his head. He held the finger up for a closer look, then, glancing about to see that nobody was watching, put his finger in his mouth, just as he had remembered from his dream. He winced as the cut fell right in line with his teeth. His breath started coming short.

How much of that was a dream? This cannot be real. There is only one way to find out, though.

Kyrus hurried through the streets, the frantic beating of his heart causing his head to throb in the two places where he had hit it earlier. All thoughts of Abbiley and what for a moment had held the promise of being one of the best days of his life, flew from his mind. He reached the shop after just a few minutes and burst through the door, drawing a startled yowl from Ash as he was rudely awakened.

Kyrus tried to calm his breath, for he was near to hyperventilating. He would not be able to tell for sure until he tried it and he needed his voice for the attempt.

Hopefully, he thought, *this will all just turn out to be a weird coincidence of a nightmare and a drunken stupor.*

When he had finally mastered himself to the point where he felt he could speak without his voice trembling, he went up to his room and closed the shutters. After a moment's reflection, he decided that it might be best to use Davin's vacant room instead, just to be on the safe side.

He remembered the whole rigmarole he had learned in his dreams, in that faraway realm in his head where they had finally told him to stop trying to create magic. It was the incantation his dream self had tried for so long with no results, hoping to see just the tiniest bit of an effect for all his hard work. He swallowed hard and then began.

"Aleph kalai abdu," he recited, while carefully touching the tip of his middle finger to the tip of his thumb and carefully tracing a small circle in the air.

The tip of his injured finger burst into a soft white light.

Kyrus stared at it for just a moment … and then passed out.

Chapter 5 - Hard Time

Choonk ... choonk ... choonk ... choonk—CRACK—choonk ...

The heavy hammer swung rhythmically, slamming into the rubble of more rocks than he could count. Denrik Zayne paused a moment to wipe the sweat from his bald head before any more of it dripped into his eyes. He was of average stature and not a solidly built man, but he had a body that had long grown accustomed to hard labor even before coming to this place. His skin had a weathered, leathery look, tanned by sun and rubbed raw by the ocean wind.

Denrik was a sailor by trade, and had spent more years at sea than some of the other prisoners had seen in their whole lives. He had been in the New Hope penal colony on Rellis Island for nearly three years, and he was to see seventeen more before he would ever again be a free man. He regretted nothing more than having been caught, for he was unrepentant of his crimes. Indeed, many at his trial clamored for the reinstatement of public hanging, claiming that if ever there was to be an exception to the king's wish that no prisoner be executed, it would be for Denrik Zayne, Scourge of the Katamic Sea.

Denrik had been one of the most successful—and the most feared—pirates in the region in recent memory. During the height of Denrik's power, few were the merchant ships that left port without an escort from the Acardian navy. He had even been so bold as to engage and sink naval vessels when he could catch them alone. Piracy was a profitable way of life, but one that created a great deal of enmity. In the end, the Acardian navy had caught his ship in a blind inlet, hiding away while being repaired, and he had reluctantly surrendered. He found out during his trial that one of his former crewmen had betrayed the location of one of the sheltered ports he used.

The crack of a whip overhead had Denrik back to his chore quickly. The prisoners spent all day breaking large rocks into smaller rocks, and then sweeping them into sacks to make room for new large rocks to be brought in. Denrik knew it to be a pointless exercise, designed to punish the prisoners and break their spirits by forcing them to perform backbreaking labor all day, every day. He knew the game, though, and played along, biding his time and keeping in as little trouble as his nature allowed him.

They were each stripped to the waist and chained in a long line by the ankles. There were six men together, five others and Denrik, and though the order might change day by day, Denrik was carefully kept from the positions on either end, where a prisoner got to have one leg free at least. As little hope as there was for a prisoner to break free of their chains, Denrik carried a foul reputation, and the guards took any precaution they could think of.

When the prisoners were given their break for lunch, they remained in the work yard. Guards brought out a thin gruel that had been warmed by the blazing noontime sun to the point of making it nearly inedible. The prisoners who were attached to Denrik's chain were not allowed spoons for their gruel, for the warden had strictly forbidden that anything that might be used as a weapon come within Denrik's reach. The order had caused Denrik to be something of a pariah when he first arrived and was assigned to a work crew, just as the warden had intended. He had gotten past that social impediment by agreeing to take the members of his chain-crew into his protection. Once it became known that anyone who gave trouble to someone on his crew would have to answer to Denrik, only one prisoner tested his resolve. The rest of the prisoners on Rellis Island learned an important lesson that day when they discovered that though Acardia no longer executed criminals, Denrik Zayne had no such reservations. When the body was found, Denrik was safely locked away in his cell with the rest of his crew, but nevertheless suspicions ran strong among the more superstitious prisoners that Denrik had done the deed himself.

The guards stood watch over the prisoners while they ate. Each guard was dressed in loose-fitting garments of light linen, all a dusty shade of white. Wide-brimmed straw hats kept them well shaded during the hottest parts of the day, and on that unseasonably hot spring afternoon, the prisoners dearly envied them that shade. In a land with trees and shade and cool water to drink, the day would have seemed beautiful and bright, but not in New Hope. The ground was barren of plants of any sort, the whole of the island being little more than an oversized outcropping of rock jutting from the sea.

"Eat yer grub and be quick about it," ordered one of the guards, a fat surly man by the name of Pierson.

Despite the lightweight uniform and all the other comforts afforded the guards, he was dripping rivers of sweat and in a foul mood. Seeing little response from the prisoners, who in spite of his remonstration were already eagerly slurping up the stomach-turning meal, he cracked his whip over their heads. Several men were startled and fumbled the bowls containing their lunch, and one even spilled the remains of his meal.

Denrik, who had with long practice trained himself not to flinch at the sound of the guards' whips, merely looked up at the guard with dangerously narrowed eyes.

Pierson scowled back at him. "What're you looking at?"

He cracked the whip again, this time within a few inches of Denrik's head. Denrik clenched his jaw and willed himself not to move, but betrayed himself slightly by blinking when the tip of Pierson's whip drew close. Salvaging a bit of authority from the exchange, Pierson let the matter end at that.

Secretly many of the guards were a bit afraid of Denrik Zayne. The name had been synonymous with piracy in Acardia for well over a decade, and even years after his capture, something about the name still commanded fear and respect. He was so unlike the rest of the prisoners on the island; they knew not what to make of him. Most of the men sentenced to hard labor on Rellis Island had been criminals because they knew no honest trade or had taken too easily to the lure of undeserved riches. They were generally an undisciplined, unruly bunch, and prone to much violence when left too long to their own devices. Though little of Denrik Zayne's earlier life was known, it was apparent that somewhere along the line, he had acquired a nobleman's education. Though he spoke little when the guards were about, his accent and vocabulary singled him out clearly among the rest of the rabble incarcerated on this island, and he carried himself calmly and with a strange, offended dignity, as if imprisonment were beneath him. It struck a strange chord in men's minds when they reconciled his demeanor with the reckless brutality for which he had been convicted.

* * * * * * * *

At the end of the day, the prisoners were led back to their cells. The cell block was built from stone native to the island, which had a distinctive reddish-brown color to it, and which Denrik had always thought gave the place a rather cultured look, as far as prisons were concerned. His crew was led into their cell, a stone-floored, square room with no windows and a heavy steel door with a small, closeable door set into it at eye level. There were six bunks, three hanging from each of two opposing walls and with little space between them in any direction. Once the door was locked, the guard handed through the eye-level portal a key ring that would let them unlock their manacles and unchain themselves. Failing to hand both the key and chains back to the guard promptly, through the little door, was always cause for a good punishment, and so the crews each learned to perform the nightly ritual with admirable efficiency.

With their chains removed and the guard having left them locked in and to their own devices, the exhausted men relaxed. Each of them climbed into their bunks, as there was little enough room elsewhere in the cell, and collapsed gratefully onto the not-so-soft wooden planks. The room's stench told of years of sweat and blood soaked into the wood of those bunks and to a lesser degree into the walls and floor, mixed with an entirely different smell from a large bucket shoved back into the far corner of the room. It had become home to them, welcoming only in comparison to the rest of the barren rocky wasteland of New Hope. But in their cell at least, there was no one to whip them for talking and no rocks to break. To the beleaguered prisoners, that was enough.

"Cap'n, how much longer we gots to wait?" asked one of the men.

The men of Denrik's crew had taken to calling him "Captain" as a sign of respect, for they found it seemed to improve his mood.

"Not so much longer, Jimony, not long for this place anyway. Just two more days. I have been counting them, and I do not lose track … unlike some of you."

The last bit was a rare show of humor from their taciturn leader, and it was met with a chorus of chuckles from his crew, except for Tawmund, who was the butt of that particular jibe.

"I can't wait to sees the mainland again," muttered Jimony dreamily.

Their captain had promised that he had a plan to get them off the island and make them all free men again. He had told them few details of it, though, except that it involved them getting as many of their own crew members assigned to help unload the next supply ship as they were able. Bribery was difficult, as the prisoners were allowed few personal effects, but Denrik had managed something along those lines. Getting himself appointed to a loading detail was out of the question, however; for while the guards were careful to keep him away from sharp objects and anything that might conceivably be made into a weapon, the warden had promised to personally hang any guard "who lets Denrik Zayne within sight of any boat."

"Just keep playing their game, by their rules, until their rules do not matter to us anymore," Denrik said.

He realized that he seemed unusually talkative this night and in better spirits than normal. Thus his men took that to be his well-concealed excitement over their impending escape.

"Um, pardon me asking, Cap'n, but when we gettin' to find out the rest o' yer plan? Um, I'm not meaning no dis-ree-spect or nothing, but it's just that we ain't as smart like yerself, see. I mean, what if we's taking some time to learnin' it all?" asked the largest of the group.

"It is alright, Andur; you will do fine. You are all well suited to the parts you will play. The difficult part will be my own, and if I fail, all you need to do is nothing. You will never be suspected should things go awry—um, wrong."

Denrik had to have a care how he spoke among his men. There had been hard feelings and some ticklish situations that had come about from them misinterpreting words they were unfamiliar with. Andur in particular had become nearly frantic when he first heard that Denrik planned to see all of them "emancipated." He had promised to kill any man who tried "emancipating" him.

"Now enough about the plan," Denrik said. "We do not want to risk one of the guards happening to check the cell block while you men are carrying on about how you are looking to break out of here. Now get some sleep."

In truth, the odds were against the guards checking up on the prisoners during the night. They were just concerned with keeping the prisoners from storming their own barracks. Rellis Island was three miles of rough sea from the nearest mainland coastline, the small port town of Trebber's Cove. There was nowhere to hide on the island, either. Though nearly a mile long, the island was only a few hundred yards across, and the terrain was rocky and barren, with very little cover. Any prisoner who broke out of the cell block would either have to make a swim for it against incredible odds or avoid the penal colony's guards until they were eventually captured anyway.

Denrik did not care for his men's questions, though. They were pawns, and he wanted it to remain that way. If he had to explain everything, there would inevitably be suggestions to change things this way or that, or for the men to question if it would work. Things had been arranged too carefully for Denrik to suffer his imbecile henchmen throwing the chaos from their bedraggled minds into his carefully constructed scenario.

The silence lasted not nearly long enough: "Hey, I'm thinkin' of something. Try and guess," called Andur softly into the darkness.

"Is it something on the island here?" another voice whispered.

"Nope."

Despite the pitch darkness in the cell, Denrik found himself squeezing his eyes shut, willing his idiot companions to shut up.

"Well, is it something on the mainland?" asked another voice from the bunk just above Denrik's.

"Nope."

"Hey, wait a minute, it has to be one or the other ..."

Of all the inane activities Denrik's crew engaged in, this was his least favorite. It was an insipid attempt to fill the quiet darkness with something human, Denrik believed. The others were weak-minded and needed the comfort of knowing that there were other people with them in the still dark of night, lest they be overcome by fear.

But let them tell tales or brag of what they will do when they are free, thought Denrik, *or even sing if they have to.*

The game could last hours, so poor were they at it. Despite his best efforts to block it from his mind, Denrik could hardly help occasionally trying to guess, though he kept his questions to himself. If he was going to order them to stop, he would have put an end to the game long ago, but he had chosen not to. He reminded himself that though they deferred to him in almost anything when he made his will known, these were not his ship's crew, nor was he really a captain here. There was a limit to how far he dared push these men and how much resentment he was willing to risk creating. And so he allowed them to continue, though it pained his quick-witted mind to listen to it.

Denrik tried to block the silly banter of questions from his mind as he sought to find the peaceful rest needed to meditate. His muscles were still relaxing from the long day's work, and he was still sweating out the late-evening heat from his body—he was not ready for sleep quite yet. And so he drifted into introspection, fleeing the ennui of his present and wandering rather unwillingly into his unpleasant past. If only his wandering mind was as obedient as his waking one ...

* * * * * * * *

"Ow, watch it with those," he complained, rubbing the sore shoulder where the apple had struck him. He was a small boy again, perhaps eight years old.

"Oops, sorry, Deni," his brother Kennon called down from above, amid his giggling amusement at his little prank.

Denrik hated this memory.

Kennon was four years older than Denrik, and the two were nearly inseparable, despite the fact that Kennon teased him and picked on him all the time. It could hardly be helped, since Father would not let him go anywhere unless he agreed to stay with his older brother. Given a choice between the two of them, Denrik chose his brother's company every time.

Denrik tried to duck the next apple as it sailed down at him, but it clipped him in the shoulder anyway.

"Stop it, Ken!" he whined up to his brother.

Kennon was sitting up in the higher branches of an apple tree and was supposed to be tossing apples to Denrik to put in the sack he carried. They were not supposed to be in the Climmons' orchard, but it was late summer and the leaves on the apple trees were thick enough to conceal them rather well if they drew no other attention to themselves. Kennon's horseplay was causing more noise than Denrik had hoped they would make. Denrik was scared of the beating they would get from Father if Mr. Climmons caught them stealing apples.

He saw a third apple coming right at his face and only had enough time to turn his head before it clobbered him just above the ear. Denrik lost track of the next couple seconds and saw grass just inches from his face when he reoriented himself.

"Yeah, bull's-eye!" came a triumphant cry from above.

Putting fingers to the side of his head, Denrik felt a sticky mix of apple juice and a bit of blood running down toward his face.

"You asked for it!" Denrik yelled, forgetting for the moment his fear of being heard.

Fallen apples around the tree far outnumbered those still in the branches within Kennon's easy reach. Denrik began hurling them back up at his adversary. Dizzy as he was, and with the scrawny arms typical of very young boys, few came near the mark. Ken taunted him from the branches, saying he threw like a little girl and daring him to come up and get him. Then chance, aided perhaps by a bit of anger and wounded pride, helped one apple find its mark. Kennon threw his arms up in front of him as it was coming for his face, and in his panic, he overbalanced.

Arms flailed as Kennon toppled backward off the branch he had been sitting on. He grabbed at the lower branches as he crashed by them, but he could find no hold to stop his fall, and in grabbing just ended up jerking his body wildly in his fall.

Crunch!

Denrik remembered the sound vividly, even nearly forty years later. Kennon had fallen headfirst to the ground a few feet from the base of the tree and lay their motionless. When his brother continued to lie completely still, Denrik stood staring and his breath quickened. He did the only thing he could think to do. He ran to the farmhouse as fast as he could to find Mr. Climmons.

The old apple farmer seemed to gather from Denrik's panicked confession and plea only that someone was hurt in the orchard. He let Denrik take his hand and nearly pull him out the door of his own house and into the orchard.

"You have to help him, he is hurt real bad, see?"

Denrik pointed under the tree where he and his brother had been fighting. Next to the discarded sack, still half full of stolen apples, lay Kennon. The boy's neck was twisted at a grotesque angle.

The older man put his hand around Denrik's shoulder. Denrik could almost feel the rough firmness of it again, setting heavily on his slender frame. It was as if he could feel the old man's grief pressing down on him.

"No, he is not hurt, son. Not anymore. The dead do not feel pain. Now come on, let us get you inside. I will see that someone goes to get your pappy and tell him."

That night, Denrik was beaten worse than he thought possible. When it seemed like the beating had gone on forever, he found himself suddenly alone on the floor of the woodshed behind his father's barn. He could not get up. Everything hurt too much. In the hours it took him to cry himself to sleep, he could not help but remember the farmer's words: "The dead do not feel pain." He repeated them in his head until slumber rescued him.

So long as he could still feel the pain, he was still alive.

* * * * * * *

Denrik wished his thoughts would stop wandering down those dark paths from his youth. The memories still seemed fresh in his mind, even after so many years had passed. But there was no longer the same sense of horror that overcame him when he thought back on how his father nearly killed him that day. Even in the pitch darkness of the cell, Denrik held his arm up in front of him—as best he could with another bunk less than a foot overhead—and imagined he could make out the scars left by his father's belt.

To help banish the fearful remembrances of that night, he forced his thoughts down a more satisfying path. He pictured again his father's bedroom, the blankets drenched in blood, his father's eyes opened in one last split second of shocked horror. He saw in his mind's eye the hand of a fourteen-year-old boy—still bruised from defending himself from a beating the day before at the hands of the same father that seconds later became a corpse—holding a knife meant for butchering chickens.

Those were his last thoughts for the night as sleep finally claimed him. Then he dreamed of freedom—and of vengeance of a different sort.

Chapter 6 - Flight from the Battlefield

What have I done? That was Brannis's first thought as the realization of the battle's end sunk in. All about him lay the unmoving bodies of the men he had shared a meal and tales with over the previous night's dinner, intermingled with the scrawny forms of their goblin adversaries. There were few survivors of the battle on either side. With forces well matched and a fierce determination to prevail, both sides had fought to near annihilation. It was not until the goblins lost the last of their sorcerers, and presumably whoever had led them, that they realized that the remaining humans outmatched them, and they fled. Iridan's pyrotechnics had been the final seal upon their decision to withdraw.

Iridan!

Quickly Brannis turned to regard the spot where his friend had fallen, wincing at the sharp pain the movement caused his right shoulder. The shoulder was not dislocated, he knew, for he still had some use of the arm, but the blast he had deflected with Massacre had wrenched it horribly. Brannis saw the few remaining men of his command congregating near a scorched spot on the ground, the center of which held Iridan's still body. It was as if the sorcerer's loss of control had created an artificial desert of parched and barren land around him, more than the length of two tall men in every direction. None of the soldiers or knights dared cross the "border" where the living grass gave way to the dead, scorched dust. They had all seen what happened before when one approached, for charred skeletons of former goblins lay alongside Iridan.

Brannis lost track of time in a blur, his thoughts churning. He was vaguely aware of running across the battlefield and pushing past his men. Next he knew, he was kneeling beside Iridan's crumpled form, turning him and laying him flat on his back on the baked turf, which was still eerily warm to the touch. Iridan made no movement, and his limp limbs flopped helplessly as Brannis rolled him onto his back. Bending over Iridan's body, Brannis put his ear to his friend's nose. He could hear no breathing, but a rhythmic tickling of air brushed past his ear—Iridan yet lived. Brannis let out an audible sigh of relief.

"He is still alive," he announced to the anxious men surrounding him.

With worries for his friend at least momentarily allayed, he turned his attention to the remains of his battalion.

"Any of you who are injured, see first to your own wounds. Those who are able, we must check to see if there are any who yet live among the fallen. And check the goblins, too, for it would not surprise me if some felt it prudent to impersonate a corpse rather than risk becoming one."

Taking stock of his own health, Brannis found that he had suffered no worse than the shoulder injury, which nagged at him. His armor bore a scorched mark in the center where the goblin blast had struck him after Massacre had turned aside most of its strength. The sword bore no mark of the impact when he found it, lying several paces from where it had flown from his hand. The weeds and grass around where the sword had lain were all dead and withered, but the mist had ceased to fall from the blade. It had depleted its reserve of aether and would feel heavier and slower than it normally did, and the mist would not return until someone replenished the sword's store of aether.

Brannis aided in the search for survivors, though he did his best not to stray far from the spot where Iridan lay. It was a grim task for all, to search among the faces of the fallen and see friends and comrades. The goblins, it seemed, had seen fit even in the heat of battle to spare a spear-thrust for a downed human. Knights were plentiful among the dead as well. The attention that a knight drew on the field of battle outstripped the extra protection his superior armor provided, and the joints between plates sheared spear tips easily when they were thrust between, as the goblins intended. Of all the knights, only Brannis and Lugren now remained. Sir Aric, made of tougher stuff than he would probably have wished, had been found still alive despite a blade broken in his side, and he had suffering greatly. Having neither the means to remove the blade nor carry him without further harming him, it was with a heavy heart that Brannis took it upon himself to carry out the older knight's last request, gasped out between pained, shallow breaths. It was the first time Brannis had ever killed another human.

When it was determined that there were no more survivors among the fallen, Brannis took count of his men. Aside from himself and Sir Lugren, he had only ten soldiers left to his command. Estimates varied from man to man as to how many of the goblins had managed to escape, but all agreed that at least a handful of the little runts had managed to elude the fate of their comrades. There had been no chase, for goblins could outrun men easily enough, given how lightly they traveled.

As Brannis looked into the weary faces of his men, he took note of one whom he did not expect to see among them.

"Jodoul, when did you join the fighting? We gave you neither armor nor spear, and yet here you stand, both armored and bloodied from battle. How came you by that armor?"

Though Brannis felt obliged to ask, he dreaded the likely answer. The grim necessities of war oft require unsavory deeds, but the thought of stripping the dead left a poor taste in his mouth.

"Well, I saw your sorcerer was unarmored as the fighting broke out and made no move to find it afore he started his spells. Well, in my company, our man Kelurian was always grumblin' 'bout having to go about dressed like us grunts in heavy steel and all. I figured yours musta refused to wear his, and so I sneaked to his tent when things started getting hairy and nicked his mail shirt and cap.

"I couldn't just sit on my arse while everyone else was fightin'." He grinned sheepishly. "Sorry, sir."

"But wait, there were no extra spears in camp, or shields," Sir Lugren cut in. "That at least I am sure of. How did you not get torn to bits by goblin spears?"

"Well, sir, I took up one of the bows your folks kept around and made use of it like a club, see? As for the shield bit, well, I never exactly made my way to the shield wall with the other fellows. I sorta snuck 'round the side o' the battle a bit and came up on them from behind, quiet like."

"I see," Brannis replied, intrigued despite his weariness. "Well, we shall talk of it later. Right now, we must get clear of this battlefield. If the survivors among the goblins manage to return with reinforcements, we had best not be here. Gather what supplies you can carry and assemble at the riverbank."

There was an uneasy stirring among the men, and they hesitated before slowly moving to obey their commander. Brannis knew what they were thinking, and he understood their reluctance.

In a quiet voice, he added, "I know, it pains me as well. They are our friends and brothers in arms. To leave them here to be found by wolves and crows does not do these brave men justice, but neither would our deaths, and that is what remaining to burn them would bring. It is too great a task for so few to do in haste. Our duty lies in returning to the Empire with news of these battles and the strength of the goblin presence in Kelvie Forest. Each of us must remember that, for if anyone becomes the last survivor among us, he must carry on this task. Now make haste, for we cannot know when our enemies may return in strength!"

At this pronouncement, his men quickened to their chore, for they heard their own anguish echoing in Sir Brannis's words. They knew that though the leaving of their comrades' bodies was a callous thing to do, they did it for a greater duty that pressed on them.

The gathering of all that was fit to be carried took less time than Brannis would have thought, and for entirely the wrong reasons. Fire and blasts of aether had been hurled about with wanton savagery that it had left little unscathed among the provisions. There was food to be had and skins of water left undamaged, but there still was not enough to fill the packs of the men who were fit to carry them. The cookware had been flung far afield by Iridan's magic, and lay blood splattered and dented in a wide swath of woods just outside of camp. Many tents were burnt and others flattened, and Brannis decided that they would leave them behind anyway as they were cumbersome to pack in haste. The bows and arrows that had been used for hunting were not to be found and were assumed to have been consumed utterly in magical fire, and even the bow that Jodoul had taken as a club had been snapped in twain in the line of duty.

So it was with little more than spears and what foodstuffs they could carry that the men of Brannis's command gathered near the banks of the river.

Brannis's own pack clattered under the heavy burden of eight swords and as many signet rings—heirlooms of the knights that had fallen in battle and which needed to be brought to their kin. From tent poles and canvas, they had made a litter on which to carry the still form of Iridan, for until the gravest peril forced them otherwise, they would carry with them the fallen sorcerer who had saved their lives that day.

The fording of the river was a simple—if unpleasant—task, with only the concern for keeping Iridan from going beneath the water slowing their progress. The river was only some fifty paces from bank to bank and chest-deep at the middle. The current flowed at a leisurely pace that did little to hinder them as they crossed, though the bottom was muddy and tugged at their boots each time they lifted them.

* * * * * * *

They were exhausted and still damp when they stopped at midday to rest and take a meal. Miles lay between them and the river, and they had traveled mainly north, bearing slightly eastward. The woods were lighter than they had been around the campsite, with warm, bright sunshine streaming down between the canopies of tall, thin trees that Brannis could not name. Several men removed their chain armor and the garments beneath to air them in the warm breeze and drive out the wetness that had clung to them since their fording of the river. The rest quickly followed suit, with even Sir Lugren and Brannis taking off their heavy armor and letting it dry in the wind.

"Well, now that we have run blindly north throughout the whole of the morning, it is time we made a plan," Sir Lugren said. "We have put distance between ourselves and the goblins, and bought time enough to let cool heads decide our course."

"I have already figured out our course," Brannis replied easily. "My mind was not idle as we trekked through the woods. Had we turned south immediately after the battle, we could have made for Korgen and reached it in two days, perhaps. But our message needs to reach the high command so they can gather a force large enough to rout these goblins. A messenger from Korgen would either have to cross the Bay of Naran by boat, or turn back north and take the pass through the mountains. No, from here we turn our course eastward and make for the High Pass. We shall cross over there and get horses from the garrison at Tibrik. There we can leave those fatigued or suffering small injuries and send the rest ahead to Kadris to deliver news to the Sir Garibald and the high command."

"I stand corrected then, for our flight was not so blind as I had thought," said Lugren, who obviously had wrestled with concern for his commander's prudence during their retreat northward but had kept his thoughts to himself until just then.

"No, you were right that we went blindly. I kept our course facing northward by the sun alone. We had no map left after the battle that was in fit condition to guide our path, and I do not know precisely where we stand within Kelvie. It mattered little to my thinking, for the Cloud Wall Mountains lie east of here and cannot be missed. Once we break through the tree line and reach the foothills in the shadow of the mountains, we can reconnoiter and set our path aright. The High Pass lies just south of the Cradle Peaks, and I daresay we can judge those by sight."

Brannis thought the plan simple enough. Even with no map, the Cradle Peaks were the two tallest points in the Cloud Wall, and could hardly be mistaken, for they rose up as a great pair among the lesser peaks.

Iridan had shown no sign of improvement since they carried him from the battlefield. His breathing was still shallow, and he had grown pale, even compared to his normally light complexion. They had not tried to rouse him to partake of their lunch, worrying that even if it was possible to revive him, it might do more harm than good. It was yet another dark cloud that hung over the mood of the weary soldiers.

* * * * * * *

Brannis led his men northward through Kelvie Forest. After their meal and rest, he decided to hold their course northward until nightfall, turning eastward in the morning. He was hesitant to give away their eventual destination until he shook the nagging feeling that they were being followed. Of course, Brannis was not the only one among them who had such suspicions. Squirrels, birds, even the rustling of the wind in the leaves of the trees above them: all gave pause to those who feared pursuit by a stealthy adversary. Not every sound that was heard was so easily explained away, either. The hours wore on the nerves of Brannis's troops.

It was near to dusk, and they were beginning to search for a spot to settle for the night, when a call was heard to the west.

"Hail, travelers!" called a human-sounding voice in a high alto, ringing clearly through the evening air.

Every one of them turned to see who spoke, and they saw a small figure approaching them. Through the trees and in back-lit twilight, it was hard to make out much about the man until he approached quite closely to the remains of the army. They took some comfort that his silhouette clearly showed his arms held wide in a show of peace, but still Brannis and the others clutched their weapons with suspicious caution.

When the shadow of one particular tree happened to cast the man's form in less harsh a light, it provided enough relief so that his features could be seen clearly, and their tensions eased away. He was a small man, thin and of a stature similar to Iridan, who was the shortest among them. He was garbed in doeskin, unadorned and of inexpert make. His long hair hung loosely about his shoulders, of a blond so light that in the poor light, it looked nearly white. His face was smooth and pale, with angular features and eyes that were a washed-out blue like a hazy sky. His age was difficult to judge, though he appeared to be rather younger than most of the soldiers he approached.

"Who are you?" called Lugren before the man approached too closely.

"A resident of these parts, given to aiding refugees, it would seem. If you are men of Kadrin, I believe I have someone that belongs to you," replied the stranger, smiling, still keeping his arms spread wide to show his harmlessness.

"What do you mean?" Brannis asked, curious whom the strange man could be referring to.

"Just last night, a man clad in armor such as yours came into my care, claiming to have fled a great slaughter. I did not put much faith in his claim, figuring he was a deserter, but it mattered not to me. Seeing you men in such a state, bloodied and dragging a wounded man along with you, lends some truth to his tale."

"Who is he? Where is he now?"

Brannis was heartened at the thought that perhaps another man had survived the battle that Jodoul had spoken of the previous night. It would have been the best news he had gotten since discovering Iridan had survived his ordeal, and even that was a happiness mixed with concern. He had seen far too much killing that morning, and to find another of his countrymen alive after all the carnage would provide a welcome relief from the dull pain his heart felt.

"I have a small dwelling not far from here. It is my habit to walk about the woods by day, but your man wanted rest, and he declined my invitation to join in my daily stroll. He remains at my home," he replied and, with a slight smile, added, "and if he is of any use at all, he will have managed a fire by now."

"How far is it to your home from here? We are weary and were just now seeking a spot to make our camp for the night."

"I do not pace about the woods counting my footsteps, but perhaps this might help. Do you see yonder those two trees growing so closely that their trunks almost touch?"

He pointed to the north and west. Brannis nodded that he did, for he did indeed see two trees matching the man's description, some ways distant.

"I would call it thrice that distance and half again. If we go now it should be little trouble to reach it before the afterglow of dusk fails us."

Brannis turned his attention from the stranger to take stock of his men. They looked a wreck, like ruined men all dirt-covered and bloody, with eyes weary from fatigue and grief. He hesitated to ask even that much more of his men for that night.

"I can take a look at that fallen man of yours as well, if that is agreeable to you. Lonely living in these reaches forces one to learn such skills if he wishes to survive," the stranger said.

It was this last remark that firmed Brannis's resolve. They all owed Iridan their lives, and they would bear a little more, himself included, to see that he was well tended. Their task could spare them this brief diversion to the west. At Brannis's order, they followed the forest hermit to his home.

* * * * * * * *

"I see no wound of any consequence upon him. What befell?"

The hermit had led them to a small cottage among the trees, not even in a clearing but in a space among the trees. It looked well made but of a simple sort, logs forming the walls and thatch serving as roof. A small pond just behind the cottage was home to a large number of pink water-flowers that had the tended look of a garden about them.

There was no sign of the lost soldier when they arrived, though his armor was piled in a heap by the cottage door. The hermit assumed he had gone for more firewood and said nothing more of him, instead turning his attention to Iridan's condition.

"He is a sorcerer," Brannis said. "His name is Iridan, and he saved our lives this morning using magic that was beyond his power to command." Brannis wanted to be sure the man knew of Iridan's bravery and sacrifice, before revealing his foolishness: "The aether raged out of control and nearly destroyed him. He survived but is as you see him now. Can you do anything for him?"

"It is good that you brought him here to rest, for it is rest he needs most. I do not know how far you dragged him along behind you, but it did no good for his condition," the young hermit said. "I can tend to him to speed his recovery, but he would do best to stay put while he convalesces. There is likely no lasting damage, if he has lived this long after the incident, but he has likely burned his body's fluids dry and needs to recover them. He will awake again with a headache I do not envy, but he should wake again."

"How long until he will be well enough to travel?"

"If you are fleeing from the goblins like my other charge was, be at ease. You may abide here until your sorcerer recovers, which could be by morning or in several days. I have seen goblins while walking about these woods, but they do not approach this place. Patience in matters such as this serves well." He waved a hand vaguely about the area. "There is game to be had here, if you fancy more than herbs and plants for your food."

"No, we cannot stay. Even if it is safe here as you suggest …" Brannis glanced somewhat suspiciously as the hermit. "… we need to get word to the Empire of the presence of such a large force in Kelvie Forest. Do what you can for Iridan, but we must leave in the morning."

"Then at least leave your sorcerer here to recover. I admit that it will not harm him further to travel, so long as someone tends to him, but neither will he recover quickly. Think this over before making your choice."

"All right, but I do not like to think of leaving Iridan behind, especially considering what he has just done for us." Brannis stood to go check on the rest of his men as they made ready to partake of dinner before turning in. "By the way, I am Sir Brannis Solaran, commander of the Eighth Battalion of the Kadrin army." He removed his gauntlet and extended his hand to the hermit.

The hermit accepted the outstretched hand with a wry smile. "Solaran, is it? A name for sorcerers, or so I was given to think. Is your young sorcerer friend descended of the Westel line, then?"

The Westels were an influential noble family with a long history of distinction among the Kadrin military. Brannis raised an eyebrow.

"You have more knowledge of the Empire that I would expect of one who lives out here."

"Tales of children raised by wolves are no more than fanciful stories and folklore. Even those who choose to live in solitude come from somewhere. It is only the most recent portion of my life that has seen me living thus." The hermit turned his attention back to Iridan for a moment, then, looking satisfied with his patient's condition, stood up from where he crouched beside the still form of the sorcerer. "I believe I should find out what has become of our deserter friend. It should not be taking him this long to find his way back."

The hermit calmly turned and walked off in search of the soldier who was lost once and appeared lost again. Without the din of his own men's footsteps all about him, Brannis noticed that the hermit made hardly a whisper of sound when his soft shoes touched the forest floor, though he made no visible effort to quiet his footfalls. It was not until the strange young man was out of sight that Brannis realized that his offer of his name had not been returned in kind. The man's question about Iridan's ancestry and the comment about his own family legacy of sorcery had put him off his guard and distracted him from his first line of thinking.

Who is this peculiar man who lives in Kelvie Forest?

For whatever reason, the comment about Iridan nagged at him. He and Iridan had been close friends ever since they met as students at the Imperial Academy, which was as far back as Brannis's recollections of childhood stretched; he could hardly remember a time in his life before they had known one another. It had always been a sore point with the sorcerer that he came from common stock. His magical talents had developed at a very young age, and he was taken in as a ward of the Academy to hone his skills in service of the Empire. Most of the students at the Academy had sorcerous bloodlines that could be traced back innumerable generations. A few talented peasants and children hailing from the occupied lands were allowed admittance but were widely scorned by the better bred students. Small and frail, as unimposing as a child can be, Iridan's life would have been miserable if a certain gregarious prodigy had not taken him under his wing. Brannis had originally felt a sense of *noblesse oblige* toward protecting Iridan, a strong sense of superiority being a trait learned early as a scion of the Solaran clan. Eventually a genuine friendship had developed and then remained into their adulthood. Iridan was, in fact, the only sorcerer who was willing to join the expedition under Brannis's command without being coerced. It was little wonder of course; Iridan owed him many favors. He still remembered the first ...

* * * * * * * *

"Ouch! Hey, stop it! Help!"

A young boy lay on the grassy courtyard of the Academy grounds, pinned by one his fellow students, who was pummeling him. It was mid-winter, and the chill in the air kept all the students bundled warmly in woolen coats, hats, and mittens at the insistence of their instructors. Despite the fact he could not make out the features of either combatant from where he stood, some dozen paces distant, Brannis recognized the voice of the boy being beaten. It was that quiet boy, Iridan, the one who had taken to following him around for most of the week since he had first arrived. It seemed that he could not leave the kid alone for even a few moments without him getting bullied.

Well, hopefully the mittens help keep the punches from hurting too much.

A quick sprint covered the distance that separated Brannis from the action, and he tackled the boy who had pinned Iridan. He landed heavily atop the aggressor and knocked him clear of where Iridan was lying, pinning the bully in turn, face down in the cold grass.

"Thank you, Master Brannis," young Iridan addressed his savior.

Iridan scrambled to his feet to get out of the way of the fighting. Brannis was the tallest boy in their class, and this was not the first occasion when he had to step in and defend his diminutive friend in the short time they had known each other.

Brannis did not answer back right away, instead struggling to roll his opponent over to pay him back for hitting Iridan. The boy was Brannis's size, which meant he must have been an older student from one of the other classes, and he was putting up a mighty struggle to get out from under Brannis. Still, Brannis was determined and held the advantage of leverage. Eventually he managed to turn the older boy over so he could punch him in the face a few times, just as he had done to Iridan. Just as Brannis had drawn back his fist to land a wicked punch, he stopped short, stunned.

She is a girl!

There were nearly as many girls enrolled at the Imperial Academy as there were boys. Still, the last thing he expected to see when turning over the "boy" who had been beating Iridan was a pair of sparkling green eyes looking back into his own—the eyes of someone who was, quite clearly, a girl. Brannis's moment of surprised inaction was short lived, for along with those eyes came the furrowed brow and clenched jaw of a very angry young girl who happened to be a bully.

After a brief moment of darkness, Brannis's vision cleared, and he saw the sky framing that same face of the girl who had, as far as he could tell, just slugged him in the face. Another blow followed the first, as the girl had pinned Brannis in turn—but he was not Iridan. Heaving the girl off him, he rolled back on top of her, but he could not very well punch a girl. After another brief struggle, Brannis managed to pin the girl face-first on the frozen ground, and this time, instead of trying to hit her, he simply sat down on her back.

"Hey, get off me!" she yelled.

She kicked her feet and tried to punch at Brannis, but she could not put any strength behind her punches. When she tried to struggle to her feet, Brannis just pushed her back down. There may have been little difference in their height, but Brannis was clearly the heavier of the two; the girl was tall, but scrawny.

"Not until you say you are sorry to Iridan, and promise to leave him alone."

"What? No, you cannot make me," came the indignant reply.

"Well, I have nowhere to go until dinnertime, and I am not letting you up."

"I will get you for this! You had best let me up." The girl was starting to sound frantic now.

"Well, I would say that is not a very good reason to get off you. What if I do not want to be 'got,' huh? Maybe you just cannot hear me clearly. Lemme help you with that," Brannis said and plucked the knit woolen hat from her head.

A long cascade of reddish-gold hair fell loosely to the ground about the girl's head, tied with green silk ribbons that would have been quite pretty had they not been crushed up under her hat along with her tangled hair.

"Hey, give that back!"

"No."

She remained silent after that, refusing to give in. Brannis was running short on ideas and was starting to think that maybe he should just let Iridan punch her a couple times and call it even. Then he noticed she was starting to tremble. It was a bitter day, made worse by strong breezes that seemed to cut right through clothing and chill one inside and out. Though the mop of hair that had fallen from her hat obscured her face, he could still see her ears, and they were beginning to redden from the cold. Then there was the sniffling, and that was the deal breaker.

I have gone and made her cry, he thought in dismay.

Trying to maintain his tough attitude despite feeling as low as if he had just kicked a puppy, he pressed the hat roughly back onto the girl's head and got off of her. Still sniffling, though she did not seem to be aware she was doing so, she stood up and glared at Brannis. Hair stuck out every which way from under her hat, which had been pushed down nearly over her eyes, red rimmed and watery. Despite her pitiful state, she looked Brannis squarely in the eye.

"I do not care if you promise or not," Brannis told her, "you are not going to beat up Iridan anymore, got it? He is my friend, and I am not scared of you."

The girl thrust out her chin in defiance but spun about and ran off towards the girls' dormitory before she began to cry in earnest. Brannis then turned around to check on Iridan, who had hidden behind him when the girl got up.

"Umm, Brannis … your nose is bleeding."

* * * * * * * *

Ah, Iridan, how long have I been keeping you out of trouble.

Brannis's thoughts returned to the present. He had always thought of Iridan as sort of a younger brother, though in truth Brannis was the younger by half a season. The girl, he had learned shortly after that incident, was Juliana Archon, the high sorcerer's granddaughter. She was a summer ahead of Brannis and Iridan at the Academy and was now a member of the Imperial Circle.

With so many more pleasant memories of Juliana to choose from, he wondered why his wandering thoughts had chosen that one. After a brief moment of reflection, he supposed it was because he had been thinking about Iridan before he began daydreaming and Iridan had not been present for any of the best ones.

* * * * * * * *

By the time the hermit returned to camp, Brannis's men had set a small fire and begun eating from the meager rations that had been salvaged from their campsite. Having left their broken pots behind, they had taken the liberty of searching the hermit's small home in hope of finding something suited to the task of cooking a meal in. Finding the tiny cottage to be sparse of all but the barest of amenities—less than the barest by some estimations—and with no pots or kettles to be found, they had been forced to spit the meat on sticks and hold it over the fire. Two small bowls were all that the hermit kept to eat from, and they were of little use in cooking meat.

Following the hermit was a brown-haired man carrying an armload of firewood. He was a stranger to Brannis and his men, though Jodoul's mouth gaped dumbly at his first glance of the man.

"Tod! You are alive!" Jodoul cried out in the man's direction.

Forgetting all else, Jodoul let his dinner slip from his hand and fall back into the fire. He rushed over to Tod with almost childish glee. Tod smiled and dropped the firewood in self-defense as Jodoul bowled into him, crushing him in a bear hug.

"Well, for the time being, until you squeeze the last of my breath outta me," Tod said.

Jodoul eventually released him from his grasp and helped him gather up the firewood. During the remainder of the evening, Brannis listened as Tod and Jodoul exchanged tales of their escapes. By Tod's account, he had been lucky to escape with his life. He described the feeling that his flight had been dogged by the goblins, though he could never catch sight of them. From what Tod had been able to gather from the hermit, his course had taken him mostly to the north and east from where Sir Ferren had met his demise. When Tod had come to the river—the same one that Brannis's men had crossed just that morning— he had decided to chance a fording in the hopes that the goblins would not be able to follow. His plan had worked, at least to his mind, for the nagging sense that he was being followed had not returned since he reached the northern bank of the river, and some hours later, he had been found by the hermit.

In his brief time in the hermit's care, Tod had learned little of the man. The odd young man helped clean the small cuts and scrapes that he had incurred while madly scrambling to escape a foe he was sure had followed at his heels. He had then provided Tod with a bit of a meal in the form of some very tasty nuts that were to be found aplenty in the surrounding woods. After that, though, he had mostly let Tod alone to do as he pleased, disappearing into the woods on some unknown and unexplained errand for hours on end. Brannis noticed that in all Tod's account, he never mentioned having learned the hermit's name.

In time, the talk and tales died down as weariness of both body and heart overcame the beleaguered soldiers. The hermit took Iridan inside the cottage to shelter him from the chill breezes that were wont to grace autumn nights, and from any rain that might fall, for clouds had covered the night sky and threatened to storm. The rest of them, the hermit included—for there was no room for two to sleep within the tiny cottage—found what comfort they could on the soft forest floor. There were blankets to be had from the salvage of the battlefield, but not enough for all to sleep upon them. Brannis and Sir Lugren opted to allow the common soldiers what comforts they could find, and went without. The hermit merely sat cross-legged with his back against a tree and rested his chin on his chest, seeming unconcerned by the elements or the loss of the shelter of his cottage for the night.

It had been a long day indeed for those who slept beneath the forest canopy that night, starting at dawn with an ambush by goblins and followed by a long march through the woods carrying whatever they could manage, including an unconscious sorcerer. Within a span of several moments, Brannis heard a chorus of snores and slow, deep breathing and knew that others at least could find slumber. He was keenly aware of his own exhaustion and felt the welcoming call of sleep, felt quite keenly the need to give in and put an end to a day he had wished had never happened, but he could not. Something in him resisted the call; he was sure that the "something" that kept him awake was his conscience, for every time he closed his eyes, he saw Sir Aric's face there, wincing in anticipation of Brannis's killing stroke. Unable to help himself, and sure that his men were asleep, Brannis quietly wept.

A soft touch on his shoulder startled him from his reflection, and he quickly choked back his tears. The young hermit stood over him, though he had not heard him approach.

"Come," the hermit whispered. "This is unseemly, and you would not wish to wake them to see it."

With that, the hermit wove a path among the sleeping men and into the night. Rubbing his eyes to clear them, Brannis rose to follow. The sudden shock had brought his mind back to the present, and his curiosity had been roused. Having some other subject to occupy his thoughts was a welcome development.

The hermit did not look back to see if he was being followed—he seemed to know, though Brannis did his best to tread lightly and make no noise. They walked for a distance Brannis found difficult to judge in the dark, cloudy night, but they had gone well beyond sight of the cottage. That thought made Brannis wish he had carried his sword with him, but he was not in the habit of wearing his sword belt to bed, even on occasions when necessity dictated that he sleep in his armor. Massacre lay safely in its sheath, next to that very armor.

Arriving at last at a large fallen log, the hermit appeared satisfied they had reached a suitable spot, and he sat down upon it. He motioned for Brannis to join him.

"Why would a leader of men cry himself to sleep?" the hermit asked simply.

"What concern is it of yours?" Brannis answered. He had been sure that he was the only one awake, or he would have fought harder against letting his feelings overcome him.

"A fair question. I am one who sees too few people these days, and I make assumptions too readily about those whom I meet. One of my assumptions about you was wrong."

"And just what assumption was that?" Brannis let his annoyance with the hermit's prying push to the forefront of his thoughts to banish his guilt.

"Well, I had assumed you were a typical, cold-blooded, hotheaded knight who dreams of glorious battles and tales sung in his honor. Yet you were grieving for the men you lost today, were you not?"

"Just one, really," Brannis admitted. "He was one of the knights I commanded. He had taken a belly wound and was going to die slowly. It ... was the first time I had ever killed another human."

"Ah, I see." A sardonic smile curled one side of the hermit's mouth. Brannis furrowed his brow in confusion. "It has all been play up until now. The ordering of soldiers about on the field of battle, the salutes, the 'yes, sir' and 'no, sir.' It all seemed like a grand game until things got bloody."

"I have seen battle before, and killed ogres and goblins. I have seen men die, and it grieved me then as well. But this time, I did it myself, with my own sword. Maybe if I had not used my own sword, a cursed thing fit only for striking down foes, not killing for mercy. But there it was next to me, my sword, the one that I used to kill one of my own men."

"Do you feel better now?" the hermit asked. Brannis was taken aback and struck dumb momentarily. "I wager you would never have said that to any of your own men, except perhaps that sorcerer friend of yours for whom you have shown so much concern. So do you feel better having told someone?"

"Maybe ... a little."

The hermit simply smiled.

"And now that I am a bit relieved of that burden, I am reminded of something. You never did give your name when I introduced myself," Brannis said.

"My apologies. My name has often been a source of ill feelings for people and is part of the reason I live here alone in the wilds. By long habit, I do not give it unless someone asks explicitly."

Brannis looked at him, waiting for him to continue.

The hermit smiled back.

"So what is it ... your name?" Brannis finally asked.

"My name is Rashan. I have grown to dislike it but find it a curiously difficult thing to lie about," he replied.

Brannis tried without success not to laugh, despite his mood.

"Well, *that* would explain why you have gone into hiding. What kind of parents could name a child that? No offense, but why not just go by another name?" Brannis asked.

In his time at the Imperial Academy, Brannis had learned of the history of the Kadrin Empire, and the name Rashan was prominent among the annals of the Empire's most bloody era. Rashan Solaran—Brannis was unfortunately a distant relation of the long-dead sorcerer—was the last and most notorious of the Empire's warlocks. A ruthless conqueror in the height of his power, Rashan had been responsible for the destruction of entire armies and had brought many independent realms under the control of the emperor. There was still a phrase in common use, "Rashan's bargain," which was used to describe either a threat disguised as a choice, or a truce used as cover for an ambush. It was used most often by those whose lands had fallen into imperial control during Rashan's time, and it was far from complimentary. It was an accusation of a planned betrayal, worse than negotiating in bad faith.

"I see you know a bit of history then, Brannis. Though since you call yourself 'Solaran,' that would seem only natural that you recognized the name. As for why I chose to keep the name … well, I have considered it from time to time, but I never could get used to any other. To my mind, 'Rashan' and 'me' are one in the same. I cannot think of myself by any other.

"And as far as concerns my parents … think of them what you will. They gave me the name, and I have learned to live with it." The hermit—Rashan— rose from the log and began to walk back toward his cottage. "Now that you have my secret, I trust you not to make a fuss over it in front of your men. I doubt many of them have much of a grasp of history, but that accursed idiom has plagued the name 'Rashan' for all time, it would seem. I do not keep pitchforks or torches lying about, but I am sure the superstitious peasant-folk you command could make do with swords should they decide to rid themselves of an unfortunately named stranger."

"Wait," Brannis called quietly after Rashan, concerned not to let his voice carry as far as where his men lay sleeping. "What do you mean by that? Do you think that my men will kill you just because of some coincidence about your name?"

Brannis got up and followed after the hermit.

Still walking, Rashan replied, "I expect them to think it an ill omen, and yes, perhaps even to try to end my life. I am sure to be blamed for anything that goes amiss. That is how the ignorant get by in life: they blame that which they do not understand for their troubles. I know these woods well and could probably elude any of you for longer than you would care to look, but I do not wish to be driven away. I am concerned for your sorcerer friend, Iridan, and would not leave him untended if I am able."

He shot Brannis a sharp look, and his point was all too clear.

He will take care of Iridan, but I must ensure that the rest of the men do not find out his name. I wonder if I should not have asked him in the first place.

Brannis followed Rashan back to the cottage in silence. His mind was now a blur of varied worries, and the dark thoughts that had haunted his mind and driven away sleep now had company in plenty inside Brannis's head.

What drove this hermit, Rashan, into seclusion? Was he persecuted because of his name, or was there some other reason? That was something to consider, certainly. Brannis sighed, knowing as well that he had gotten caught up as keeper of an unwanted secret. *What if I let slip his name in front of one of the commoner soldiers? Would he really be in danger from them?*

As Brannis lay once more on the soft forest floor, the weight of his fatigue pressed down on him anew. But now without the recurring vision of Sir Aric's face to afflict his thoughts, he was able to surrender, finally, to the urgent calling of his body for rest.

Rashan, who had watched through half-closed eyes until the rhythmic rise and fall of Brannis's chest proclaimed his slumber, quietly arose from the tree against which he rested and went to check on Iridan.

Chapter 7 - Bearers of Bad News

The morning sun was high above the horizon and the dew that had graced the leaves and wild grasses had burned away already. There was a nervous edge to the mood of the goblins as they took their morning meal. Jinzan Fehr was stomped through the camp, his glare clearing a path before him as he the human sorcerer waded among his goblin hosts. He sought out G'thk to find out what had befallen.

"What is this about?" Jinzan demanded of G'thk when he found the goblin general. He was ill-kempt and bleary-eyed from having just awakened, having come directly from his tent, seeking neither grooming nor dawn feast. "I was supposed to be informed as soon as the runners arrived with news of the battle! Here it is, full morning, and yet I was not awakened!"

[They have not returned yet,] G'thk replied simply and calmly. This stopped Jinzan short. [You were not alerted due to this event not happening. Had we received news from the battle, this news would have been yours to know as well.] The two of them each understood the other's language but each spoke his own. Jinzan could hack and cough out bits of the harsh goblin tongue when he had to but prefered to spare his throat the pain it caused him. G'thk would grow winded with all the vowels of the Megrenn dialect of human that Jinzan spoke.

"What do you mean? The runners should have been sent as soon as there was word. The battle should have been over hours ago. Send out a search party immediately to find out what has become of them," Jinzan ordered, not even bothering to beg askance of the goblin general.

G'thk's eyes narrowed. [My commanders are given discretion to choose how best to carry out their orders. I ordered that the humans be eliminated and that none be allowed to escape. I ordered that runners come with news when news is to be had. I gave no order that runners must be back in time for dawn feast so as not to anger human sorcerer and plan battle accordingly. I gave no such foolish orders. You will wait, as I do. Go eat.]

"Has there been any word on the progress of the construction efforts in Tnk'Ch'Nck?" Jinzan asked as the general turned to leave. He stumbled over the awkward goblin city name but had nothing else to call it.

[I have received no news of any new progress. The tinkers are still working with the plans you provided, and their last report was favorable. This device is new to my people, but we are eager to learn more about the wondrous things you have described to us. Do not despair, sorcerer, for your plan seems sound.

56

We will build your device by the time it is needed.] The general patted Jinzan on the arm. [Have faith in our metallurgists and alchemists.]

Jinzan kept his face impassive but nodded an affirmation to the general. Inwardly he groaned.

Of course ... faith, Jinzan thought. *Everything comes down to, that with you goblins, does it not?*

Jinzan had lived among the goblins for a more than a season and had learned a great deal about their culture, including their religion.

The goblins believed that so long as they followed their dragon gods' precepts, everything would work out in the end. It was a philosophy that grated on Jinzan, for he had never believed that anything would go right unless he forced it to do so by his own will. Nevertheless the belief in the rightness of their own actions made the goblins fearsome opponents. The very fact that goblin sorcerers engaged in combat at all—especially given that most human sorcerers considered magical combat one step removed from suicide—showed that this belief system aided his plans. Without goblin sorcerers on the battlefield when the time came, his plan might be revealed too soon.

Surrounded by a small army of goblins, Jinzan had little choice but to obey the general, so he made his way to the mess line. He more poked at the mush that made up dawn feast than ate it, though, as he was preoccupied with the lateness of the army's report. By all accounts, the raiders should have made it to the Kadrins' campsite before midnight, and he could not imagine a scenario that could cause the battle to be so prolonged that it would still be raging come morning.

Jinzan had not half-finished his mush when the goblin sentries raised the alarm thatthe survivors of the battle had been spotted. Initially the sentries believed them to be runners bearing news of battle, and they sent them directly to G'thk. Jinzan discarded the remains of his meal hurriedly, eager to hear what had happened.

Eleven goblins in all had returned, the survivors of the battle with the Kadrins, but they only had five spears among them. All were fatigued from having fled the battlefield at a run. Jinzan suspected he was not the only one to think these looked less like runners than they did deserters.

[Report! How went the battle?] G'thk demanded. There was nervous shifting among the survivors, as none seemed to want to step forward and admit what had taken place. [Well, which of you is the runner? One of you had best answer me.]

A garbled mess of goblin-speech followed as several of the survivors began to speak at once, each relating their version of events, which Jinzan struggled to understand. G'thk quieted them with a raised hand and pointed to one of the goblins who had been speaking.

[We ... We were defeated, General G'thk,] the selected goblin said. [Our sorcerers, three even, could not overcome the humans' sorcerer. One of the human knights wielded a foul sword that seemed enchanted to belch forth fumes, which harmed all that they touched. We fought them well and killed many. The human sorcerer lost control of his aether and began to throw flames wildly. If he is like our firehurlers, he must be dead now, as he fell to the ground and lay still afterward. The human knight with the sword we could not kill, though, and the few of us left could not fight off the last of the humans.]

Jinzan kept outwardly calm but his mind was spinning. *How can this be? The Kadrins should not have been able to withstand the attack. The scouts reported that their numbers were few, and three sorcerers should have been enough.*

The survivor's report held but one bright spot, which was the apparent demise of the Kadrin sorcerer who had defeated three of his own. The Kadrins were not know for employing firehurlers in their battles; the term referred to inept sorcerers with so little control they could manage no better than to ignite aether as a weapon—a crude tactic, wasteful of aether, and dangerous. It was not uncommon for goblin firehurlers to draw in more aether than they could safely handle in the heat of battle. When overcome in such a manner, it was almost always fatal to the goblin that had lost control. The bodies became burned-out husks, charred from the inside. Goblins were not above bringing such dangerous liabilities among their number, but the Kadrin sorcerer had to have been better than that. He had bested three goblins who were far better than the common firehurlers G'thk had originally wanted to bring along before Jinzan objected. If the Kadrin had been overcome by the aether he had drawn in, it was possible he had survived; maybe not likely, but possible.

G'thk turned from the survivors and clasped his hands behind his back. He appeared lost in thought. Jinzan, however, was not so pensive.

"What are you doing back here, cowering like misbehaving children?" Jinzan demanded. "Why did none of you think to stay behind and watch over the army." Jinzan paused, seeming to take note of the blank look on the goblins' faces. They did not understand a word of what he was saying, though they could understand well enough that he was furious with them. Angrily resigning himself to using goblin, he tried again: [Why you soldier goblins not stay and die or stay and see? Now soldier humans leave, you not know where! We blame you! Plan say we not have humans know we come. My plan, and you break it!]

"*Haru bedaessi leoki kwatuan gelora,*" Jinzan quickly growled out under his breath and then made a sweeping gesture with his arms. The goblin who had given his report to G'thk went flying through the air, landing in a bush a score of paces away. The surprised screech the goblin let out at being lifted into the air by magic gave way to a yelp and a dazed moan, as the unfortunate soldier apparently survived his flight.

[No fail plan, or more goblin-birds there will be,] Jinzan warned all the goblins present, survivor or not. He turned and stalked back to his tent to think in peace.

* * * * * * *

It was a disaster in the making. Jinzan sat fuming in his tent, trying to think of a way to prevent word of their army's presence in Kelvie Forest from reaching Kadrin. Surely they must have already been suspicious, thought Jinzan, or they would not have sent an armed force into the woods to investigate. They had obviously underestimated the goblins' presence, for if they had known of the true strength of the expeditionary force, they would have sent far more troops than they had.

Jinzan was also troubled by the presence of a knight armed with a magical sword. Such artifacts were rare indeed, since sorcery was required to create them and sorcerers had little use for them. Most were gifts given to heroes of the Empire in reward of great achievement, and they were passed from generation to generation. That could mean that either the knight was distinguished among his peers for his accomplishments, or was the descendant of such a one. The only other aether-forged swords that Jinzan knew of within the Empire were those that had been wielded in the bygone days of the warlocks. While he considered it unlikely, Jinzan knew that there existed the possibility that this was a warlock's sword, given to the knight for this assignment due to an especial effectiveness in combating goblins. It was not a comforting thought.

Jinzan needed to find answers. He hugged his arms closely to his body, shut his eyes, and lowered his head. He took a deep, steady breath. As he focused on each breath in turn, he gradually extended feelings into the aether, and he began to discern the Source of every plant, every goblin, and every stinking oxen in the area. With his eyes closed, he could see the flows of aether wafting from each Source, stream into river, river into ocean, filling the very air around him.

Every muscle in Jinzan's body tensed as he willed his consciousness into ever-clearer focus. He was not attempting to create magic, but to find it. Two human soldiers had been marked by the assassin Gkt'Lr during the night of the first raid, a bit of tracking magic to help locate them should the hunters lose their quarry. Gkt'Lr was no sorcerer, though, and the magic had been a paltry thing. Jinzan had monitored the fighting, waiting for the marking magic to appear to him and had kept tabs on the two men until the magic on one of them failed. The one that he had been able to watch had been found by G'thk's raiders and had led the way to a second human army camped in Kelvie Forest. The loss of the other man still nagged at Jinzan and he now sought to find either one of them, hoping to pick up some trace of the marking magic.

Jinzan's musing was broken by someone opening the flap of his tent. Turned from his introspection, he was suddenly aware of a clamor of activity outside in the goblins' camp.

[Sorcerer, we are moving out. We are going to occupy the humans' campsite and lead our search from there. If any returns to the battlefield, our sentries will find them,] G'thk called into the tent.

Good, thought Jinzan, *they are not going to sit idle.* Still, Jinzan worried that the humans had a head start in their escape, for surely they would not have remained long after such a battle.

"Send for that assassin. Have him meet us at the Kadrins' camp," Jinzan ordered G'thk.

G'thk glowered at Jinzan, who realized he had overstepped himself. The infraction went unmentioned, but Jinzan knew he had only so much rope before his noose pulled taut.[I will dispatch a runner to fetch him. Do not worry, sorcerer. My people do not leave business unfinished in such a way. We will hunt those humans down and finish them off before they give away your plan.]

G'thk managed to save a little face by that last remark, subtly pointing out that it was Jinzan's plan—and not his own—that was going awry. With three of his sorcerers apparently killed by the Kadrin humans and without even the small protection that the assassin's presence would have afforded him, G'thk was in no position to have a confrontation with the dangerous Jinzan Fehr.

* * * * * * *

The runner had been sent to seek out the elite goblin assassin, Gkt'Lr, and the goblin army had set out toward the battlefield, guided by the survivors of the slaughter. The camp had been broken down in a remarkably short time. Tents were packed up, gear was stowed, oxen were laden, and troops were assembled. Quartermasters had overseen the whole of the operation, and Jinzan could quite honestly say that he had never before seen such an organized group in his life. Each knew where everything belonged and directed soldiers to move each item quickly and accurately onto the proper ox. Jinzan lived in the huge port city of Zorren and had seen many cargo ships loaded and unloaded in his lifetime. Those chaotic productions could hardly be any more at odds with the neatly efficient coordination of the goblins.

Many of the officers had climbed atop the oxen to ride at leisure rather than walk among their men. G'thk smirked down at Jinzan from his perch atop the back of an ox, as if lording his authority over the human sorcerer as he watched Jinzan plod along among the common soldiers. Jinzan had bluntly refused to have anything to do with the beasts of burden and made every effort to keep himself upwind of them as he walked. G'thk had been quite tolerant of his human eccentricities during his stay with the goblins, but Jinzan knew that he had begun to push the limits of their friendship with his presumptions. Jinzan was important among his own people, but the goblins had scant interest in an alliance with the Megrenn. Their current arrangement was one of mutual convenience. At some point, he would have to smooth relations with the goblin general.

Jinzan had never been a great lover of nature, and the beauty of the woodland surroundings and the fresh, clean air were lost on him. The sea he could respect, but the woods were a place where things lurked. There were myriad little scents to it that meant nothing to him, and the sight lines were so short that anything might lie in wait just beyond his vision. It was not his place, and he disliked the strangeness he felt traversing it.

The walk itself bothered him just a little, though he was careful not to let any sign of weakness show. Jinzan's magical powers had slowed his aging greatly, so that he appeared to be in the hale summers of his middle twenties despite twenty additional summers' wisdom to the contrary. His time was spent at activities of mind more often than those of body, however, and his limbs were ill accustomed to long exertion. He grimaced in pain as a cramp worked its way into his calf. Mindful of the watchful eyes of the goblins, he ran his fingers through his thinning hair, a nervous habit he had developed long ago that he used to draw attention away from his facial expressions as he composed himself. A meditative trance or a spell to mask the pain in his aching muscles could have made short work of such simple aches but he did not wish to be seen as frail by the goblins.

How strange, he thought, *that I worry these twig-limbed runts will think* me *frail.*

They paused a short distance from the battlefield and sent scouts to search for signs of any enemies left lying in wait around the area. When the scouts reported the area to be clear of Kadrins, the army proceeded into the area.

Jinzan saw straightaway that the battle had indeed been an incredible slaughter. Camp debris lay scattered and destroyed about the clearing. Many holes had been dug about the perimeter, more than a few containing the broken corpses of goblins who had been so unfortunate as to fall into them with enemies near at hand. Bodies, both human and goblin, littered the area and the surrounding forest. Most of the bodies bore battle wounds from spear or sword, and there were scorched and burned corpses in abundance as well.

Hardened as Jinzan was to Kadrin misfortune, he might have felt some sympathy for the fallen had any of them been lying wounded and suffering. There was something primal and awful about the nearness of death that tugged at his carefully buried compassion. He had never been able to abide the torture of even his most hated enemies, though on more than one occasion, he had held sway over the fate of Kadrin prisoners. But there was nothing on the forlorn battlefield to give him pause—just worthless corpses. The dead were beyond pain, beyond his pity.

As he surveyed the battlefield, two areas caught Jinzan's eye as he tried to piece together what had transpired. First was a cluster of corpses within a few paces of each other that bore strangely garish wounds. They appeared to have been slashed by a sword, but the wounds festered, looking gangrenous and discolored. Even on skin that had no cut upon it, there were blisters and a rash-like reddening. It was the work of that enchanted weapon, Jinzan had no doubt. The other spot of interest was the scorched region in the middle of the camp. The ground had been burned elsewhere in places, but here it had a baked, cracked look to it, as if there had been an incredible heat for some time that had parched the ground and made it look like a desert. A moment of conferring with the survivors marked the area as the spot where the human sorcerer had collapsed.

Jinzan cursed his lack of woodcraft, for he could not tell which way the humans had gone when they fled the battle. Untold days of occupying the site had left footprints and tracks all about, and he could not judge which were the most recent. He sighed in frustration and knew he was going to have to wait for the assassin to track down the Kadrins.

Throughout the afternoon, the goblins went about the unsavory task of clearing the bodies from the battlefield. It was a large job, considering that there were nearly as many dead as there were goblins to bury them, and the human bodies required several goblins to move. It could not be helped, though, if they were to occupy the campsite; the carnage was already beginning to attract scavengers. With their small spades, a score or more of goblins began digging graves just outside camp. Jinzan noted with interest, despite his impatience, that the goblins were preparing the humans for burial as well. He could not tell whether it was a show of respect for the enemy dead, or a mere extension of the pragmatism they showed in laying their own dead to rest where carrion-eaters could not reach them. He knew that his own people likely would have just piled the bodies and set them ablaze. It was quite obvious to Jinzan how little thought the Kadrins had given to the dead.

* * * * * * * *

It was nearly dusk when Gkt'Lr arrived in the newly erected goblin camp. The runner that had been sent to retrieve him had not yet returned, though; the fleet-footed assassin had outpaced the runner and left him behind by more than a league. Gkt'Lr's business often required covering long distances quickly, and he was as fast as any member of the Assassin's Guild. He held the rank of Master of Eternal Night, second only to the Grandmaster of Darkness in the Cult of Knives hierarchy, a position that could not be attained by those lacking in any of the guild's deadly areas of expertise.

Wasting no time, Gkt'Lr approached the goblin general and presented himself. [Your summons was urgent. What task do you have for me? Has your pet human displeased you?] the assassin asked with a touch of dark humor.

Jinzan could not quite keep his nervousness from being reflected in his face, and he found himself running an involuntary hand through his hair yet again.

[There was a battle fought here at dawn,] G'thk responded, letting the jest slip, though a smile betrayed that it privately amused him. [A group of humans escaped. Among them are at least one knight, wielding a deadly magical sword, and possibly a wounded sorcerer.]

[How many are there?]

[We do not have a count.] G'thk gave a sidelong glare toward one of the goblins who had survived the battle. [But it was fewer than a score, by the account the survivors gave.]

[Am I to kill them all, then?] the assassin asked casually, as if it was a task of no consequence.

[That is your task. I will pay whatever price your guild demands for this service.] G'thk hoped to avoid any lengthy haggling over the assassin's fee, for fear that the humans' head start might allow them to reach safety before the assassin caught up to them.

[Very well, then. I will begin my pursuit at once. I trust you will not forget this promise, once the job is complete,] said Gkt'Lr, and it was G'thk's turn to shift uncomfortably at the assassin's remarks.

The assassin made a search of the immediate area and concluded that the humans had crossed Grey Crag Brook. The goblins' earlier search had noticed the number of tracks near the riverbank, but they had assumed that the humans had merely used the brook to wash; it was too deep for a fording, by their estimation. Gkt'Lr scoffed at their foolishness, pointing out that either the Kadrins used magic to cross, or that the water must not have been too deep for the taller humans to wade.

Undaunted by the prospects of crossing the water, Gkt'Lr reached into a small pouch at his belt and pulled out a pair of items that drew strange looks from the onlooking goblins. They were small wooden pieces the shape of an axe head, but much smaller, with strings hanging from them. The end of the axe-head shape was hollowed out, and the assassin slipped his toes into the hollows and secured them by tying the strings behind his ankles. The result looked something like a goblin with duck feet.

Ignoring the whispered wisecracks from among the soldiers looking on, the assassin began to use some sort of magic. Gkt'Lr bowed his head and closed his eyes, muttering something under his breath. Jinzan strained to make out the barely audible whisper of the assassin's voice, or to discern the subtle motions of the goblin's fingertips as he traced tiny patterns in the air in front of him, but to no avail. He felt the aether swirl into the assassin as the magic came to a climax and was completed. The assassin looked up, appearing satisfied. He took a few running steps in place, his legs moving in a blur, then started toward the brook. In three running paces, he hit the water, and to the astonishment of the soldiers watching him, he kept running. Ring-shaped ripples of water echoed from each shallow footprint left in the brook's otherwise tranquil surface as the assassin sped across, lightly running on the water. In less time than it took the goblins to overcome their surprise, the assassin reached the far bank, where he removed the devices from his feet and quickly disappeared into the forest.

* * * * * * * *

Gkt'Lr had little trouble following the trail once he was free of the jumbled mass of footprints that had been left at the campsite, both from the battle and from occupation by human and goblin armies. There was starlight and moonlight in plenty filtering through the treetops, and goblin vision was little impaired by dim light. The heavy feet of the humans marked their path clearly, and there was no evidence that his quarry had made any attempt to obscure it.

The assassin followed the humans' trail all through the night and the next day, pausing only twice for a quick bit of sleep and a small meal consisting of dried strips of meat. The humans seemed to be traveling due north, which made the task much easier. Still, Gkt'Lr was wary of deception. The Kadrin Empire lay to the east, across the Cloud Wall Mountains, and there were smaller outlying colonies and settlements to the south. North of Kelvie Forest was disputed territory, where the humans were more likely to find enemies than allies. He was watchful always for their path to turn or double back. He knew it cost him time to be so careful, but part of his reputation was earned by never failing a job; that meant that he never allowed himself to make foolish mistakes.

In the waning hours of the night, not so long before dawn would brighten the eastern sky, his vigilance paid dividends. The humans had stopped and milled about for a while, then turned west. It was a baffling decision, and Gkt'Lr could only assume that they suspected pursuit and were trying to throw off the trail. After all, travel far enough to the west and they would end up in goblin territory.

He followed the trail west and very soon came upon a small cottage nestled among the trees. It was a curious sight, as Gkt'Lr knew of no inhabitants of this part of the forest. Woodcutters made large camps that were clearly marked by large swaths of felled trees. Perhaps this was a trapper's dwelling. The assassin approached for a closer look and could just make out the sleeping forms of a number of humans. He saw no sentries or anyone awake and on guard at all.

This is too easy, he thought, drawing his dagger from its sheath.

He paused briefly, closing his eyes and trying to feel around the area for Sources of aether that would mark hidden animals or humans that might raise an alarm if startled. He was surprised by the amount of aether in the area but could sense nothing that would indicate that a human or nocturnal creature was creating it. It seemed to be coming from the plants in the area—a particularly aether-strong species to be sure.

He crept toward the sleeping Kadrins, assured now that only a failing of his own stealth lay between those humans and their deaths. His progress was slow and deliberate as he savored the moment before his easy task was over. Only his own self-discipline kept him from crying out then, when suddenly he felt his dagger being plucked from his hand. Quickly he spun about, still silent despite the sudden movement. He caught sight of a flash of white as something disappeared behind a tree some distance off.

He broke into a run to pursue whoever or whatever it was that had pilfered his dagger from his hand, the luxury of stealth lost to him and replaced by the need for quickness afoot. When he got to the tree, he saw nothing there, and as he looked about, he caught sight of the running form of a human cresting a low rise and being lost to his view.

Gkt'Lr ducked low as he approached the top of the small rise, and he crawled the last few feet on his belly. He peered over the top and quickly pulled his head back down as he saw a human looking directly at him. The human was sitting on a fallen log, with an amused expression on his face. The assassin's initial reaction had been a reflex, wrought of long winters in a profession where paranoia was a boon. With a moment to reflect, he decided that the human was neither running nor hunting him but rather waiting. Standing up and trying to sort through the bizarre situation in his head, the assassin approached the strange human and hoped for a parley.

The human sat watching as he approached, and Gkt'Lr noticed that he now held his dagger in the upturned palm of his hand, as if offering its return. The human was a strange one indeed. He was small, not really so much larger than Gkt'Lr, who was considered rather imposing among his people, and his hair looked white in the starlight. His clothing was crude, though—animal skins stitched clumsily together—and did not look like it would provide protection in battle.

"Waaat youuu waaant?" the assassin asked in Kadrin as well as he was able.

[A bit of an explanation about your intentions, if it would not trouble you too much,] the human said, astonishing Gkt'Lr with his fluent goblin-speech. The human smiled at the assassin's obvious surprise—a sight that unnerved the normally cool-headed assassin.

[So you speak my language, human,] Gkt'Lr replied. [But I see no reason to answer to you. You do not look like a soldier, so I do not believe this involves you.]

[Perhaps not to your mind, no. But I did not notice you carrying any other weapon, so if you are thinking about murdering anyone in their sleep, I do not expect you shall have much luck. I do not imagine you could strangle any of them to death without waking everyone up.]

The human casually tossed the dagger into the ground at his own feet, the point sticking into the soft earth.

[So what will you do then, human?] Gkt'Lr asked, inching forward with the thought of making a grab for his dagger.

[Just warn you. I am not going to let you bring harm to the humans who lie sleeping by my house. I merely stole your dagger to bring you away from them, so we would not wake them with our talk. I could just as easily have buried it in your throat, as slowly as you reacted,] the human answered, and Gkt'Lr stopped his approach toward the dagger. [So do you want this back?] The human reached down and picked up the dagger again, grasping it by the hilt.

Gkt'Lr did not know how to answer. Was the human toying with him, or bargaining? Should he make a break for cover and hope to evade the human who had snatched a dagger from his alert grasp? He thought back to his own exploits of the previous night, when he had used a spell to speed his own movements. Biding his time, he focused his thoughts into the aether, and tried to discern if the human was using a similar spell and whether it had worn off yet.

A sudden look of horror crossed the goblin's face, and his thoughts snapped back out of the aether. He stared directly at the human once more, terror evident in his wide eyes.

It cannot be, he thought.

[Something wrong?] the human asked mildly, arching his eyebrows.

The assassin did not stop to answer but turned and fled toward the west, the easiest direction away from the dangerous human. He was not silent and no longer cared, having found something far more urgent than his assignment for the moment. There could always be another attempt on the humans, but he knew he stood no hope of succeeding that night.

A flashing blur sped past Gkt'Lr's face, and he recoiled quickly, hearing a solid *thwack* just inches from his head. His dagger quivered slightly, embedded to the hilt in a tree just to his left.

"You forgot your weapon," the human remarked in his own language, standing just a few feet away.

The assassin looked at the human in continued amazement, wondering how he had appeared so close by without a sound, then looked back to the dagger just for a moment. When his attention turned back to the human, he was gone. Gkt'Lr scanned the area but saw no sign of him. His immediate, reflexive thought was to peer into the aether winds to check for signs of him, but he dismissed the idea out of hand. After all, he knew he could not find the human that way.

He gave a tug at his dagger, but it was stuck fast—not surprising given how deeply it had been sunk into the wood. Calming himself a bit, the assassin used a spell to remove the hopelessly stuck weapon from the tree. Still trembling from the worst fear of his life, Gkt'Lr set off back toward goblin territory. He needed reinforcements.

Chapter 8 - A Magnificent Curse

Kyrus blinked a few times to clear his eyes of bleariness and looked around. It was light outside the shuttered windows of the bare room where Davin had slept just two nights past. Groaning, Kyrus eased himself up to his elbows and attempted to gather his thoughts. The left side of his face felt sore, apparently from having it pressed against the wooden floorboards all night. Sometime after he had passed out, he must have rolled into a position where he was lying with neither of the two lumps on his head resting on the hard surface. He shook his head ruefully at the thought that having his face flattened against the floor was the most comfortable position he was able to find while he slept. It seemed that the part of his mind that watched out for him as he slept was an idiot.

No, that was not right. The part of his mind that watched as he slept had seen many things, and had been quite preoccupied last night. He remembered a harrowing walk through a forest, and a feeling of relief at finding out that a friend of his—figment of his imagination or no—was recovering from a nearly fatal injury. He could still see, if he closed his eyes, the stranger with the long, white hair who had allowed them to take shelter outside his home, and who was tending to his friend—seemingly just a few moments ago, on the other side of his eyelids. It all felt so real, so vivid, that the memories seemed not to fade in the few moments after he awoke, as was common with dreams. He remembered it as well as he could recall the previous night.

Kyrus drew a shuddering, deep breath to calm himself as he thought back to the events that had taken place in that very room the night before. Had it been a strange part of his dream? Had he fallen asleep before that, only to fall asleep once more within his dreams? Kyrus suspected not, but there was only one way to find out. He stood up and closed his eyes, steeling himself against the possibility that he was right.

"*Aleph kalai abdu,*" Kryus calmly spoke, gesturing with his right hand.

A rush like a cool breeze swept through him. Then he felt the brightness, even through the lids of his eyes. Swallowing hard, he looked to confirm what he already knew in his heart. There was a glow in the air before him. It lit the room better than the rays of sunlight that poked in around the edges of the shutters, and Kyrus hoped that the light outdoors was bright enough that it was not noticeable from the street. He did not want to have anyone inquiring as to what was going on before he himself could figure it out. He needed time to sort things through before anyone else found out about this strange phenomenon. That is, if he was ever going to be ready enough to have the world think he was either a lunatic or a freak.

That sobering thought brought Kyrus's attention back to the softly glowing ball of whitish luminescence hanging a handspan in front of his face. He stared at it with a mix of child-like wonderment and an all-too-adult sense of anxiety. He knew that he had created the light, but he was not entirely sure how. It had seemed natural to him, as easily remembered as the catchy tune that children learn to remember their letters or the fluidly sprawling lines of script that flowed from his quill each day: things that had become a part of him through repetition over years and that he could hardly conceive of *not* knowing anymore. Until the previous night, though, as best he could recall, he had never so much as practiced at such arcane nonsense, let alone had anything of the sort actually work.

The light remained aloft and stationary under Kyrus's scrutiny. It became neither brighter nor dimmer. It did not change color or flicker, as would a candle. It did nothing at all and seemed content to remain that way, inexplicably lighting Davin's old room ... somehow. He reached out and passed his hand through it, probing tentatively at first, then waving it about in the midst of the glowing region when he encountered no resistance. Kyrus realized just how impossible the light should have been, burning nothingness, attached to nothing, and hanging adrift and motionless in midair, but he felt strangely unconcerned by how out of place it was. He was far more worried about how he would explain it to someone else, should they happen by, than he was with trying to reconcile it within his own, normally logical, mind.

Kyrus sat down cross-legged on the floor and stared up at the light, trying to decide what to do about it. He rested his chin on his clasped hands, feeling the fine, rough stubble of his unshaven face as he thought. That subtle reminder that he had just slept through the night on the floor, fully clothed, served to galvanize his thoughts; if he did not come up with something soon, someone would likely stop by the shop and find a crazy man with bloodied head wounds, sitting on the floor of an otherwise empty room, staring at a light that should not exist. Remembering the cool, breezy feeling that had spread through him when he had created the light, and how it had momentarily relieved the awful headache he had woken up with, Kyrus decided to see if repeating the magic would reverse the effect.

"*Aleph kalai abdu,*" he spoke quietly as he gestured in the air, mindful that anyone at all might be on the street below his shuttered windows.

Immediately he felt the coolness wash through him again. Being prepared for it to happen, he noticed subtle nuances the second time through that had escaped his notice previously. It was not a breeze that seemed to blow through his veins and cool him from the inside, but dozens, even hundreds of tiny little breezes, permeating every inch of him and swirling into the very center of his being before they coalesced ... into a second ball of light, hanging closer to the floor than the first, just in front of his face as he sat. Fortunately for Kyrus, two of the lights seemed no brighter than one—though that did not make any sense, either—but now he had two of the blasted things to get rid of before someone saw them!

The feeling that accompanied the creation of the light had momentarily alleviated the stabbing pain behind his eyes and dulled it to the point where he could think a bit more clearly. He realized that the spell—and he knew nothing else to call it by—was something remembered from his dreams. That meant that the answer to getting rid of the lights was probably also something hidden away in the back of his mind, where his forgotten dreams lay dormant till he slept again. His immediate problem was that, aside from his dreams that night, he only remembered very broad concepts from his dreams, not minutiae such as how to dispose of unwanted balls of light. Kyrus spent several moments with his eyes closed, trying to conjure up images from his dreams, but all he could remember was a rain-soaked wilderness hike accompanied by a bunch of grim-faced soldiers, a friend of his who seemed to be injured, and a stranger who acted like some sort of enchanter or wizard like in the old children's stories. None of them had banished any lights with magic in his dream, so until he could pay more attention in one of his dreams and inquire of someone as to how such a feat might be accomplished, he was on his own.

Kyrus drummed his fingers against his cheek as he sat there pondering, beginning to grow anxious that he would have to either get rid of the lights or find some way to hide them until he could figure how to manage it. He could not sit here all day without making people suspicious. Someone was bound to stop by the scrivener's shop sooner or later; Davin saw two or three patrons at least, on most days.

Abbiley, he thought suddenly.

Of course someone was going to stop by the shop sooner or later. Abbiley had promised as much the night before when she had spoken to him after his mishap. He could not very well let her see him like this.

Why, yes, my head feels fine. No lasting effects of smacking it on that light pole and the ground last night. When it bothers me a bit, I can always just poof these little balls of light into being out of nothingness, and it feels better for a little while—What? No, I do not need to lie down. Watch and I will show you: "Aleph kalai…"

No, that was not going to go over well at all. He needed to come up with something fast.

He tried concentrating on the feeling that accompanied the spell he used. He tried to imagine the feeling of those tiny little breezes all converging in him, cooling his body and clearing his mind. He closed his eyes, took a few deep breaths, and tried to ignore the throbbing that was starting to grow worse in his head, the sounds of the early morning drifting in from outside, and everything else that might distract him. After a moment or so, he began to feel it, slowly at first and then steadily growing.

Yes, I did it! All right, now what?

Kyrus opened his eyes slowly, still basking in the pleasant chill of whatever it was that he was drawing into himself—whatever it was that he had made the light out of. He was at a loss to describe it, but he could almost "see" the tiny currents of some unfamiliar wind drifting about the room and "see" some of them being pulled toward him. It was nothing that obscured his vision of the room around him; he could still make out the walls, the floor, his clothes, the two weird glowing balls of light … yet there was something deeper, something that he was not accustomed to being able to see, underlying his vision of the world around him.

Kryus's musings about his newfound vision were abruptly cut short when an urgent feeling began to grow inside him. He suddenly felt as if he had drawn a deep breath and needed to exhale, yet he did not know how. The flow of the tiny ethereal rivers as they were drawn into him slowed and came to a halt, and then seemed to try to reverse their course. The feeling that had been cool and pleasant just seconds earlier faded, only to be replaced by one of building pressure and heat, as if something trapped within him was trying to escape. Kyrus began to panic, realizing that he had no idea how to stop what was happening. His vision began to grow hazy, and he felt dizzy. As the pressure within him grew, it became a searing pain, dwarfing the headache he had been suffering already. Kyrus squeezed his eyes shut and grimaced in pain, then collapsed onto the floor.

His mind began to burn, and he knew that somewhere he had seen this before. There had to be an answer somewhere in his memories. There was little time to act, the sensation was growing stronger by the moment.

Memories of my dreams … Think, Kyrus, quickly …

* * * * * * * *

Kyrus remembered standing on a battlefield, littered with the bodies of the fallen. There were men in plenty, and creatures shaped like men yet much smaller, and with a rough, greenish hue to their skin that he somehow knew to call "goblins." He turned his head to look around and saw everything and everyone about him moving far more slowly than they should have been. The thud of spear against shield, the cries of the dying and the victorious, the crackle of the many fires that burned here and there: all seemed to echo from far away, rather than right around him. When he saw a smallish man dressed in soldiers' garb—minus the armor—trading magical bolts of force with one of the goblins, he recognized this as the place he saw in his dreams.

He saw the sorcerer, for he knew that was what his friend was, turn one of the goblin's bolts back at its creator, destroying the creature. Then the sorcerer, whose name came not readily to his mind though he was certain he knew it, collapsed to the ground, clutching at the sides of his head and letting loose an agonized scream. Kyrus tried to race to the sorcerer's aid, yet it felt like he had been yoked to an oxcart and was pulling a load of stone blocks behind him. He watched goblins approach his fallen friend as he struggled to close the distance. He was too far away to save the sorcerer from the spears of the tiny adversaries that were sure to reach him before Kyrus would. Yet as Kyrus looked on helplessly, the goblins' eyes grew wide and they tried to turn and run away, then they caught fire and were consumed in less time than it took Kyrus to gasp his surprise. He saw the ground all about his sorcerer friend begin to steam … the morning dew boiling off of it …

Same problem I am having, but offers no help …

* * * * * * * *

Kyrus's thought bubbled and churned as he dug through them hurriedly. He saw a vision of a familiar barn, weather-stained brown and unpainted but otherwise in a serviceable state. There were fields all about, and a fenced pass leading up to the front of it. The memory felt so real he could smell the fresh manure and the distinctive scent of cows, gathered in large numbers.

Someone rushed past him, carrying a bucket, and then another. He recognized them as two of his older brothers, Melluck and Vohn. A third brother, Kedan, slammed into him as he rushed by as well. The older boy was thrown off his stride, and he spared a quick glance back.

"Sorry, Kyrus," Kedan said, regaining his balance and rushing off with a bucket as well, water sloshing out the sides from his encounter with his younger brother.

No, that is one of my own memories. They were rushing to douse a fire that had started in the barn. I do not think dunking my head in a bucket is going to fix this, but it might be worth a try.

I really need to find something from my dreams. That is where they know how to deal with this.

* * * * * * * *

Kyrus shook his head to clear the last memory, and found himself seated on a small stool in a room with stone walls. There were young children, perhaps half his age, seated to his left and right. There were roughly a score of them, all told, seated in a semicircle around a middle-aged man in very important-looking clothes. All the faces seemed somehow familiar, though he struggled to put names to them. The movements and sounds seemed as strange to Kyrus as they had on the battlefield, but there was something else that felt odd as well.

Kyrus looked around the room, which seemed to have especially high ceilings, then at the children all around him, then *up* at the man who was apparently some sort of tutor or instructor.

How short is this stool? Kyrus found himself thinking, looking down at it.

When he looked at the stool, he also noticed that he was no larger than the children seated to his sides; he was a child just like them. He was one of the students.

The lecture being given was nearly incomprehensible to Kyrus. The teacher spoke at length of something called "aether," which he did not explain well enough that someone who had never heard of it could gather much use from his instructions. But as he spoke of the dangers of the "aether," Kyrus began to grow interested. The teacher told of how harmful it could be to hold onto more than one could handle without releasing it immediately, and then proceeded to demonstrate the proper and safe way to vent excess aether.

The teacher drew the students' attention to a very large basin of water, nearly as wide as a grown man is tall and deep enough to bathe in, which stood in a corner to one side of the room. Kyrus had not thought much of it when he glanced about the room upon discovering himself there, yet it seemed to be central to the teacher's point. The teacher then muttered some nonsensical syllables under his breath and waited. After a moment of tense anticipation experienced by all the children watching, sweat beaded on the older man's brow and he gritted his teeth in apparent exertion. The children were startled to hear the water in the basin suddenly begin to bubble and boil, filling the room with steam and obscuring vision.

When the steam cleared, the teacher stood, at ease and unharmed, with a superior look on his face of someone who has just proven his point beyond argument.

Aha!

* * * * * * *

Kyrus rolled around on the floor, trying to find the release for the so-called aether that he realized he had trapped within himself. His eyes were squeezed down into narrow slits as he fought back the pain, but he could see clearly enough to notice that the floorboards were scorched. He knew what would happen to him if he set the building on fire in the condition he was in.

Scrambling awkwardly to his feet, he stumbled out of Davin's room and across the hallway into his own. There he found what he hoped would be his salvation. The washbasin that he kept on his dressing table was still half full of water. At a loss for any other means of ridding himself of the aether he had drawn in, he focused on the water and imagined it boiling. He thought of the flows of energy he had pulled into himself and tried to push them back out towards the basin. It was difficult and painful, far harder than it had been to pull it into his body, but he saw steam rise from the water and could feel the pressure easing within him. The aether burned all through his body on its way out of him, but it felt ten times better than the ever-growing feeling of a tea-kettle boiling over that it had replaced.

Kyrus breathed a long, ragged sigh of relief as the last of the aether was purged from him. He cautiously peered into the washbasin, which was now steaming gently like a fresh bowl of soup. The water was nearly all gone, and the bowl was too hot to touch when he experimentally put a finger to it. Sucking on his mildly burned fingertip, Kyrus crossed the hallway back toward his original problem: the magical lights he needed to be rid of.

To Kyrus's great relief, there was only one remaining when he entered the room. The first one he had created was gone, most likely having expired of its own accord. Kyrus calmly and prudently waited several minutes until the other light abruptly vanished as well, and then went about setting his morning back on path.

The washbasin had cooled enough to handle again by the time Kyrus got back from the well with fresh water to refill it. He hurriedly washed and combed through his hair—carefully avoiding the painful lumps he had received the night before. He decided against any attempt to trim his beard. His hands still trembled slightly, reminding him of the scare he had just experienced a few moments ago. Kyrus just was not used to being nearly incinerated.

The newest expert of the Scrivener's Guild made little attempt to perform actual work that morning. His hand was not yet steady enough to be trusted with any work on behalf of his patrons. Instead he bustled about the shop, tidying things up that had been put in some disarray when Davin had removed his personal belongings from among the vast mess of the shop. The two of them had come to an understanding when it came to clutter. Both had agreed not to move anything from where the other had left it. Since Kyrus and Davin were both gifted with excellent memories, they were able to find anything they needed, so long as things stayed where they were put. The system worked marvelously, but in the process of vacating the shop, Davin and the king's steward had been forced to dig through piles that contained things both had left there. Kyrus figured that it was as good a time as any to go about finding where everything had ended up.

Working with an efficiency borne of a desire to drown his turbulent thoughts in the reality of his task, Kyrus set about sorting and stacking the innumerable loose pages that covered nearly every available surface. He found more than a few pages that he had long since given up as lost and since rewritten, as well as the remnants of a number of small projects he had rather forgotten having worked on. There was a collection of ruined invitations to the wedding of Lady Clarissa, which Kyrus had doggedly worked through an awful cough several months ago to complete; many of the invitations had splashes of ink or suddenly scratched lines across them. Another whole stack contained manuscripts that were never meant to be finished works, but rather they were pages Kyrus had written as practice during his early apprenticeship and then could not bear to part with, despite the raw script and poor spacing that his first works exhibited. It served to remind him just how much he had learned from his old friend, when he looked back at how undisciplined his calligraphy had looked just a few short years ago. Kyrus smiled to himself and sighed, then carefully set them aside in their own separate stack where he would not lose them again … at least for a few months anyway.

A knock at the door startled Kyrus into dropping several leaves from a history text Davin had written before Kyrus had even been born, sending yellowed pages fluttering to the floor. Normally the door to the shop was kept unlocked during business hours, but Kyrus had been too preoccupied to remember to do so that morning. Quickly gathering the fallen sheets in a pile and putting them back more or less where they had come from, he made his way across the room to see who was calling.

"Sorry, Ash," he said to the cat as he stumbled over Davin's old chair, where the plump feline lay curled in the morning sunlight that washed in through the window. Ash gave him an imperious look, but only briefly, before squeezing his eyes shut again and resuming his repose.

Kyrus slid back the bolt from the door and took a deep breath, trying to compose himself and present a professional demeanor. Smartly, he pulled the door open.

"Good morning. Sorry about the door—" And Kyrus stumbled over his words as he saw that it was Abbiley at the door, come to see him. "Um ..."

"Good morning to you as well, and it is no bother. How is your head?"

"Um ... much better, thanks. Lots better. Um ...you would hardly know it was a pole I had walked into; would not think I had hit it on anything more than a bedpost." He smiled at his own self-deprecation.

"Well, your wits do not seem *too* addled." Abbiley grinned back at him. "Let us get you something to eat, shall we? They say you should not try to mend a wound on an empty stomach."

Kyrus had never heard that before, but he was certainly willing to let the idiom pass unchallenged. He had not been prepared for her visit and was surprised to have made it this far without making a fool of himself. He saw she was carrying a cloth-covered basket in her hands. The basket was fairly large, the kind one might carry a day's shopping in from the market, and had a delicious smell wafting from it, though he could not quite place it.

He held the door aside and allowed her in. She smiled as she walked past him, surveying the room as she entered.

"Oh my," she said, idly stopping to pet the shop's elder resident. "Ash, how did you let this place get in such a state?"—the latter spoken in the tone of voice many people use when addressing animals or small children.

"Oh, I was not aware you two had met."

"You see that painting up on the wall?" Abbiley asked.

Kyrus glanced over at the wall and nodded. There was a painting of Ash, curled up in repose on a window sill.

"I painted that."

"Really? That is remarkable. It is the very image of him. I had always known it was a portrait of Ash—it is too exact a likeness to have been a painting of another cat that Davin had found—but I had not realized you were the artist. Do you paint much?"

"Indeed. It is what keeps a roof over myself and my brother. I had been having some hard times when Mr. Chartler asked if he could commission that portrait of Ash. A kind old man, your Mr. Chartler was. He had been a friend of my pa before he passed, and did me the kindness. Bragged to his friends about it for months after, to boot. Got a lot of work after that ... and have ever since."

"That is wonderful," Kyrus said. "I hope I am not too forward in proclaiming your artistic prowess on another front as well: that basket gives off the most sumptuous aroma."

"Well, I had hoped to make sure you got a good meal in you at midday. Seems like there is not a fit place to set it down in here, though. I know Mr. Chartler had always kept the place in a bit of a state of an old bachelor, but it has seemed to have given up under the care of two of them," she said.

"Hmm, then perhaps we can find a more suitable place for a picnic. Shall we have a walk down to the sea-wall and watch the ships come in?"

Kyrus was not sure where this was all coming from, having never spoken more than a brief exchange of greetings or a professional conversation with a pretty girl. He certainly hoped he could stop dwelling on it long enough, though, that he would not ruin a good thing that he had gotten started on.

Abbiley smiled. "What a wonderful idea. Let us do that … if you are feeling up to it, of course."

Thoughts of work and head injuries stepped gracefully aside, knowing their services would not be required for a while.

"I think I ought to be able to manage."

He extended his arm, and she took it. Kyrus had never felt more pride than he did escorting Abbiley down to the waterfront, grinning like a fool the whole way. The door to the shop was not locked and possibly was not even properly closed all the way. Those thoughts were less graceful and got themselves shoved rudely into a closet, as Kyrus was well and determined to have a singular focus at that moment.

The lunch was delicious. It consisted of sandwiches of a sort, a nice cheese made by someone just outside Golis who was the father of one of her brother's friends, and a nice ale that Kyrus did not recognize as one of the ones he normally drank. It was almost a shame really, the wonderful food, since all Kyrus remembered afterward was the prettiest pair of blue eyes and the sound of her voice.

Chapter 9 - A Walk in the Woods

He felt stiff all over but was more refreshed by far than he had been the previous night. Brannis rolled over onto his stomach and pushed himself up to his hands and knees, stretching out his limbs and working out the tightness that had set in after resting from the long day of fighting and hiking. Climbing to his feet, he looked around the impromptu camp that he and his men had set up the night before. He was the first of the group to awaken—not so uncommon an occurrence, as rising before dawn was far more to his habit than his recent oversleeping—though a few men had begun to stir at the noise Brannis had made in getting up. Brannis made a quick count of his men and found none missing—no small blessing considering the losses they had suffered yesterday. Rubbing the sleep from his eyes, he walked as quietly as he could to the cottage to see how Iridan was faring.

The door to Rashan's cottage opened outward and had a ratty bit of rope for a handle. Grasping the rope, Brannis slowly pulled the door open and peeked inside. Within, he saw Rashan bent over Iridan's resting form, his back to the door; he showed no reaction to Brannis entering. Brannis stepped inside and closed the door behind him, taking care not to shut it too loudly and disturb Iridan. He leaned over the hermit's shoulder to see what he was doing.

"Brannis ... who ... is this?" Iridan's voice called out weakly, little more than a dry-sounding whisper.

Brannis smiled down at his friend, whose eyes were open just a crack, but who was awake and aware enough to have recognized him. Rashan brushed a few strands of Iridan's longish blond hair out of his face, then turned to Brannis. He allowed his patient's friend to introduce him as he saw fit.

"He is a hermit who lives in Kelvie Forest, north of where we were camping. We carried you from the site of the battle after you fell, and happened upon him. He offered to help take care of you, and we accepted, since none of us really knew how to treat aether burn," Brannis told him. "By the by, that was quite the light-and-fire show you put on back there. Please do not do it again."

"I felt like I was floating. I know it was probably just a dream, but I feel like I was just drifting along. It was nice ... My head did not feel like someone was stabbing me in the temple every time I blink." Iridan winced as if even talking was causing his headache to bother him.

"Well, we carried you for the better part of yesterday on a litter we made from one of the tents you did *not* incinerate. That probably explains the floating.

I feel like I have been trampled by a horse, though. I have scant practice at carrying sorcerers around, and my muscles have decided to rebel in protest."

"Probably. Hey, Brannis ..."

"Yes?"

"Remember just before the fighting started, I told you I would get you back for that comment about me looking like a zombie? Consider it payback." Iridan smiled weakly and closed his eyes for a moment. "Can I get a little more water, please?"

"Of course," Rashan answered softly.

Brannis noticed the half-empty bowl next to the hermit. Rashan lifted Iridan's head and brought the bowl up to his lips. The sorcerer seemed to drink very little, for there was nearly as much in the bowl after his drink as before. He licked his lips afterward, as if to moisten them. They were cracked and dry, and looked as if they might split and bleed just from the dehydration. It was understandable, of course; Iridan had baked much of the moisture from his body during the episode yesterday when he had been overcome by drawing in more aether than he could safely control. He was lucky he had not burned away more than just water. It would not have been the first time an overreaching sorcerer was charred to ash by his own power.

Iridan laid his head back down and sighed. As he drifted into sleep or meditation—Brannis could not tell which—Rashan told him that he had forbidden Iridan the use of aether until he recovered fully. Brannis nodded at the wise precaution and left to see about getting his men ready.

"Do you still plan to leave today?" Rashan asked in a low voice, catching Brannis by the arm as he exited the cottage.

"Of course, all the more so now that Iridan has awakened. There should be no doubt now that he will recover. He just needs to build his strength back up. We can still carry him," Brannis replied, sounding optimistic.

Rashan looked back at him, nodding to himself and looking pensive, as if the response had been expected. The hermit followed Brannis outside.

"Very well," Rashan replied, "I will accompany you, then. I do not approve of your decision, but I will come along to see that he is properly tended."

"What? Why? No, we will be fine on our own, though I thank you for taking care of him. Iridan is a dear friend of mine, and I am grateful for all you have done, but we cannot ask you to come along."

"Fine, then it is settled," Rashan replied, smirking, and turned to walk away.

"Huh? What? Did I just miss something?" Brannis asked, confused.

"Oh, I am going to see about finding you something for dawn feast besides those hideous field rations you have brought along," Rashan told Brannis, ignoring the intent of the question.

"That is not what I meant, and you know it," Brannis called after him.

Rashan turned back to look at him, frowning, and brought a finger up to his lips. Brannis had not realized how loudly he had just spoken.

Brannis asked again in a lower voice, "What do you mean, 'it is settled'?"

"Well, you said you could not ask me to come. I had already decided to come before then, and I had not sought your permission, nor had you said I was not welcome, so it sounded like a closed deal. Do not worry, I am very little bother, and I can find my way quite well. I am sure that before you reach the safety of your home, you shall be glad I was along."

With that, he once again turned his back to Brannis and headed off deeper into the woods. Brannis frowned at Rashan's back but did not say anything, watching as the hermit receded from view. There was something that bothered him about Rashan, but he could not quite say what it was. His demeanor was light and casual, and he seemed to ignore anything he found inconvenient—things like not being asked to accompany Brannis's men, but deciding to anyway. Brannis could not help but wonder at the quick mind the hermit had displayed, subtly manipulating him into a situation where he would feel silly objecting to Rashan's offer to stay with Iridan until he had time to recover. Rashan was certainly right about one thing: he was little bother. Since they had arrived at the hermit's cottage, Rashan had probably not said a handful of words to anyone besides Brannis and perhaps Iridan. The hermit did not partake in meals with them, kept out of sight for the most part, and seemed to prefer wandering the woods to their company. He wondered what in the hermit's past might have engendered such an aversion to human companionship.

* * * * * * * *

They broke camp near noontime, which was later than Brannis would have liked, but all of them seemed to have needed the extra time to recover from the aftereffects of their long day of fighting and carrying heavy packs through the woods. Iridan was conscious and able to sit up on his own by then, but his legs wobbled under him when he tried to walk, so it was resolved that they would still have to carry him for the time being. The young sorcerer was feeling well enough to crack a few jokes at his own expense, promising to return the favor and carry each of them in turn once he had recovered. The very idea of Iridan carrying anyone was rather comical. The sorcerer had long been the object of jests regarding women having thicker arms than his, most often at times when he seemed a bit too full of himself or started showing off with his magic. Given Iridan's weakened state, though, the survivors let his boasts pass unchallenged.

Brannis led them east from the hermit's cottage. The trees of Kelvie Forest were sparse enough in that region that no blazed path was needed for them to make good progress. True to his word, Rashan was little trouble to the soldiers. He hung back a ways, staying rather near to the pair of men who carried Iridan at any given time, never letting the sorcerer out of his sight. Still, there were whisperings among the men as the day wore on. Some had begun to take note of the unnatural silence that surrounded the hermit's footsteps despite the din every other pair of feet made among the twigs and small plants that were in abundance on the forest floor. He also had a strange look in his eyes whenever one of the soldiers happened to meet his gaze. All who noticed this seemed to find an unusual intensity there, staring more *into* them than *at* them, though his expression showed no such emotion to match. Brannis, at the head of the group, did not see any of it, though.

The forest was easy terrain for trekking long distances on foot, gently rolling hills graced with trees spaced far enough apart that one could walk a straight line at most times. There was a refreshing breeze that cooled the early afternoon air as they searched for a spot to rest and take a meal. All of them seemed grateful for the pause, when finally they came to a low hilltop shaded by tall oaks and deemed that the time for an afternoon meal had arrived. The soldiers were tired from bearing the weight of their armor and, at turns, carrying the recovering Iridan, and Brannis was carrying the swords of the fallen knights in addition to taking his turn in bearing his injured friend.

From the hilltop, they could hear the murmuring of a stream not far off, and throughout the afternoon, men drank deeply from the few canteens that had remained after the battle against the goblins.

"Denair, Kun, come with me," Brannis ordered, selecting two of the remaining conscripts from his battalion. "Gather up the water skins and let us go find that stream." Brannis loosened Massacre in its sheath in case they encountered any trouble while isolated from the main group. "Sir Lugren, you are in charge in my absence. I hope not to be long about this."

"Mmm," Lugren grunted in reply, nodding brusquely in acknowledgment.

The older knight watched as Brannis and the two soldiers left camp laden with all the water skins they had salvaged from the battlefield. The hermit, who seemed no worse for the day's journey, moved to check on Iridan.

The sorcerer was feeling much improved since he had first awakened earlier that morning. His headache had subsided and his thoughts felt clearer than they had since before his accident. Sitting up, he took one of the pieces of hard tack that the soldiers were eating and nibbled at it, trying both to placate his grumbling stomach and not to upset it by putting too much in after having eaten nothing for over a day.

"Well, it is good to see you feel like eating. Your body is recovering," the hermit commented, crouching down beside Iridan.

"Mmm, I know I must be truly hungry. This awful stuff is actually tasting good," the sorcerer replied between bites.

"Not to destroy your illusions, but you are just imagining—those rocks you call rations do not taste like anything at all. Hmm, maybe it is time we saw whether your mind is recovering as well as your body seems to be."

The hermit grabbed a twig from the ground nearby and broke off all the little forked branches that split from it, making it into a crude implement for writing in the dirt. He drew a square on the ground in front of Iridan, large enough to stand both feet in, and then divided it into smaller squares—a grid eight squares by eight. Iridan watched curiously, his eyes widening in understanding as the hermit began drawing symbols in the two rows of squares closest to each of them.

"Your move," he told Iridan, and handed him the stick. The hermit had drawn a chessboard on the ground. "Let us see what is left in there."

He pointed a finger at Iridan's forehead. The sorcerer smiled, amused.

"Oh my, how does one play this game?" Iridan replied, his too-innocent voice dripping with sarcasm.

"Oh, I think you shall pick up a rough idea within a few moves," the hermit said with a chuckle. "It is common knowledge that they teach young sorcerers to play this game to sharpen their wits. Let us see if this 'crazy woodsman' can best one of the Academy's finest."

Iridan said nothing in reply but scuffed out one of his pawns and then redrew it in another square. He handed the stick back to the hermit with a smug look on his face. Iridan fancied himself a rather expert player of the game, even if Brannis had begun to trounce him regularly in recent summers. It was something of a mark of honor at the Academy to be a good player. There were few opportunities to test magical skills in direct opposition—dueling and anything of that sort was strictly regulated—so the game became a sort of proxy duel that allowed students, and occasionally masters, to engage each other in battles of wits.

The hermit took the stick and casually sketched a new pawn of his own, erasing one with his thumb, mirroring Iridan's play. It was the sort of bland, unimaginative move that Iridan would have expected of a merchant or tradesman—someone not much practiced at the game. He planned to enjoy beating the hermit and tried not to let his smile show, with limited success.

It continued thus for a handful of moves, with the two men passing the stick back and forth in silence. The hermit handled himself much better than Iridan had initially expected, and he had found no clear advantage. He studied the board for several moments before deciding to try distracting his opponent.

"So who are you anyway? All this time, and you have not so much as given your name," he said, making a noncommittal move and passing the stick to the hermit.

"Oh, I have already gone through that whole business with your friend Brannis. I have grown unaccustomed to giving my name. Talk to Brannis later if you are truly curious. I think he would explain things better than I."

"What sort of answer is that? If you have already told Brannis, what harm is there in telling me?" Iridan found that the stick had somehow wandered back into his hand. The hermit had made his move while Iridan had been talking.

"None really, I suppose."

Iridan waited.

"Well?" he asked. "Are you going to tell me, then?"

He made another move—a rather defensive one that closed off what appeared to be an imminent attack by the hermit's rook—just to get the hermit to move while he talked, and passed him the stick.

"No, I think not. I shall let Brannis enlighten you when he decides to," the hermit replied. "Are you sure you have played this game before?"

Iridan's attention was brought back more fully to the game, and he watched as the hermit took a decided advantage—the rook had been a diversion. Iridan saw now that he would lose in just a matter of a few moves.

"All right, let us try that again. I was distracted," Iridan snapped, upset with himself that his trick had backfired.

The hermit smiled and patiently rubbed out the drawn pieces and set the game up once again.

The game resumed anew, this time with the hermit taking a more aggressive approach than he had in the first game. Iridan immediately found himself struggling to defend his pieces.

"From your accent, I take it you are originally from the Empire," Iridan probed, now genuinely curious about the hermit. "What did you do before you left?"

"Oh, a number of things. Odd jobs and the like, for one of the highborn families. I would fix things, deliver messages, that sort of thing. Primarily they had me working as a butcher. Eventually I tired of it—the slaughtering of helpless animals. Mostly I think I grew tired of all the blood. I felt that I just had to get the smell of it out of my nostrils, so I left."

"You just left?" Iridan stopped playing for the moment and made no moves, his attention fixed for the moment on the hermit.

"It was a thankless job. After one particularly long day's work, I decided I'd had enough, and I just left." He snapped his fingers. "Just like that. Not a word to anyone. I came to live out here. That was winters ago."

The hermit nodded back to the game, prompting Iridan to move.

* * * * * * * *

Sometime later, Brannis returned with the two soldiers who had accompanied him to refill the group's canteens. Brannis looked curiously at the two men sitting together—his best friend and the strange hermit that he did not quite trust yet—and went over to see what they were up to. Rashan turned toward Brannis as the knight approached him from behind.

"Well, your friend seems to have suffered no lasting effects of his unfortunate mishap, presuming that he was rather dim-witted before the incident," Rashan commented, smiling lopsidedly.

"Do not listen to him, Brannis, he is really good. I bet he would even give you a tough time of it," Iridan interrupted, defending his maligned wits from the hermit's sarcasm.

"Please," Rashan said. "I have never known a knight who could get out of his own way in a game of chess. They make a few moves and start whining about a draw if there is no obvious advantage right off. No offense."

"None taken," Brannis said. "I actually first learned the game at the Academy, not the School of Arms. I spent several winters there before they gave up on me ever becoming a sorcerer. I know how to play both ways."

It was true that the two institutions had markedly different ways of playing the same game. To those at the Imperial Academy, chess was a game of wits to determine who was the better. They played by what they considered the "pure" rules, with all options available until one player was defeated or the game became stalemated. At the School of Arms, the game was used as a microcosm of a battlefield. Pawns were only considered expendable if there was a clear gain, and more important pieces were defended heavily and rarely were they captured or lost intentionally for any strategic gain. Draws were common, often after only a handful of moves if neither player had gained an advantage. Headmasters presided over the game and judged performances based on territory—or number of squares—that a player controlled, and what kind of "casualties" had been suffered. True victories as the sorcerers saw them rarely happened when squires played. The knighthood had long held that the game gave great insight into the minds of sorcerers, and revealed the most important reasons why they never be given command of troops.

Brannis decided to give the remainder of his men a bit more rest and indulge the hermit in his game. He was curious to discover what he could about their deeply layered companion.

Maybe I can start piecing him together like a puzzle if I can see him from enough angles.

Brannis took Iridan's spot across from the hermit and quickly scribbled his pieces back in their starting locations, then put his opponent's pieces back, even drawing them upside down so they faced the Rashan.

"Not too bad. You seem at least passingly familiar with the game," the hermit admitted. "I shall make the first move."

Brannis played Kanix's Defense, an advanced and complicated opening sequence that looked to unbalance the board and give both players ample opportunity to attack. It was a test, to see if Rashan had learned the game at any advanced level. As the hermit responded, Brannis noted that he took none of the standard attacks but still seemed to be making strong plays and threatening his position at every turn. Not having seen any style of play Brannis was familiar with from either the Imperial Academy or the School of Arms, he carefully worked to a more neutral position. He then decided to play his usual manner: a long-term plan that did not look so much to score wins in pieces or get a particular gambit to work, but rather to gain the most use out of each of his pieces, gaining options and restricting his opponent's.

"Falling back to the knights' way, then?" Rashan commented as he saw Brannis's play grow less aggressive and threatening.

"Not exactly," Brannis replied, exchanging one of his knights for one of the hermit's bishops.

Several moves later, Rashan seemed to finally notice that Brannis had been subtly marginalizing his remaining bishop, to the point where it was nearly useless to him.

"Where did you learn that?" Rashan wondered aloud, shortly before scrubbing out his dirt-drawn king and admitting defeat. "I am not accustomed to losing, and I would like to know: what just happened?"

"You lost. That happened."

Brannis smiled at being able to play the same game the hermit liked to play with words, ignoring half the question to give an unhelpful answer to the rest.

"A rematch, then," Rashan offered, and he began to set the board up again.

"I do not think now is the time for another game. We have to get moving again," Brannis continued.

Looking about the hilltop, he could see that most of the men had already finished eating their lunches and were just sitting or lying about, taking what rest they could.

"They are tired, you know," Rashan said. "You are pushing them too hard. You will not make it back to the Empire like this; you will lose half your men to exhaustion."

"We have no choice. If we do not get word to Kadrin and arrange for reinforcements, those goblins could wipe out Korgen, or maybe Illard's Glen. We shall get horses once we cross into Kadrin territory, then it will be easier on everyone."

"Very well, then." Rashan sighed. "Perhaps I can help you with something."

The hermit turned his attention to the trees above and raised his right hand, palm up. Then he began making melodic twittering noises, reminiscent of the calls of birds they had heard each morning they had been in Kelvie Forest.

A few breaths later, a small sparrow flew down from the trees and landed on Rashan's outstretched hand. Rashan gently closed his hand over the bird, and he began stroking the back of its head with his thumb. Brannis and Iridan looked on in amazement, for the hermit had seemed to work no magic. The bird had merely come to his call. Brannis could tell that Iridan was resisting the urge to stretch his senses into the aether to confirm what he had seen, no doubt because he did not want to risk taxing his mind when he was just beginning to feel like himself again. Several soldiers who had seen the bird fly in now began gathering about, wondering what was going on.

"Brannis," Rashan said quietly, seemingly to avoid disturbing the bird. "Where *exactly* do you want your message delivered? Mind you, somewhere where someone who would not be struck dumb seeing a bird delivering one might be found."

"Umm … The capital … Kadris," Brannis replied skeptically. "I guess at the palace. Someone from the Imperial Circle would likely find it."

"Very well, I know where that is. It should prove little trouble. Now I will need you to speak two messages. The first will be heard by whoever first finds the bird, and will need to tell them to whom the bird need be delivered. The second will be the true message, and you should choose someone who will not discount the word of sparrow." Rashan could not help grinning at that. "Also, it should be someone who will recognize your voice, for sparrows cannot speak with one of their own," Rashan added, as if it were somehow natural that they should speak with a voice that was *not* their own.

Brannis thought for a moment. Who should he send the bird to? Juliana was the first sorcerer who came to mind—as she often did—but she was young and not of high rank in the Imperial Circle. It might raise eyebrows if he sent such an important message to her instead of someone more senior. Brannis's father would certainly be respected enough to bear such news to the rest of the Inner Circle and to the High Command of the knights, but he would sooner kiss a goblin than rely on his father to take his warning to heart. Truly the message would best have been delivered to his immediate superior, Sir Garibald, but he could hardly imagine the stodgy old knight conversing with a sparrow. At last, Brannis decided on his elder sister, Aloisha. She would most likely recognize his voice, though they spoke seldom to one another, and she carried a great deal of respect among her peers. As a bonus, it would seem all well and proper that his sister receive the message, rather than a young sorceress to whom he had once been betrothed.

Brannis nodded to Rashan that he was ready, and the hermit calmly held the sparrow up closer to Brannis face. Feeling silly addressing a bird, Brannis began his first message.

"This bird bears a message for Aloisha Solaran of the Imperial Circle. You are hereby commanded to convey this messenger immediately to the lady's presence, for the matter is most urgent."

Brannis looked expectantly at Rashan, and the hermit nodded in approval, holding up two fingers. It was time for the second message.

"To my sister Aloisha, I give greetings. This bird bears a message from Brannis Solaran, with news of the search in Kelvie Forest. The goblin presence is greater than we feared. We have confirmed the loss of Sir Ferren's battalion with but two survivors, and my own command has suffered heavy casualties. There has been no word from Sir Dennever's battalion, and I fear it has been lost as well. The goblins are gathering in numbers, likely for an invasion of the western empire. I return to Kadris in all haste."

Brannis nodded to Rashan once more, and the hermit raised his hand quickly, releasing the sparrow, which flew away immediately, heading east.

"How did you do that? I did not see you use magic," Brannis asked, confused.

"I thought you could not see magic at all, so I do not find that surprising," the hermit replied sarcastically. He seemed to enjoy picking at Brannis's words.

"You know what I mean: you did not cast a spell. The bird just came when you called it."

"Small children have been doing bird calls since long before I was born. I doubt they relied on magic to do it."

"And the message? I suppose that was a child's trick as well," Brannis pressed, meaning to get answers from the mysterious hermit.

Rashan seemed always to be acting helpful and speaking in circles. It was beginning to grate on his nerves, for he knew not whether the hermit was being playful or deceitful.

"Well, now you get to the meat of the question, so to speak. Yes, I have learned a few tricks over the winters. Any crazy old coot can talk to animals, but it takes some skill to get the animals to talk back." Rashan looked around to all the soldiers who were gathering their belongings, and then he began to walk eastward. "Come on. We can afford a more leisurely pace now, but since you have no intention of indulging me in a second game, I suppose we should be on our way."

Iridan was feeling much improved after having eaten, well enough to walk on his own, much to the relief of all those who had been taking turns bearing the litter that had carried him for a day and a half. The sorcerer chose to walk with Rashan, and the two conversed through the long hours of the journey that afternoon. It seemed to Brannis that the hermit had taken an unusual interest in Iridan, which gave further credence to his growing suspicion that Rashan had at least some minor training in sorcery, whether he would admit it or not. He also could not help but notice how similar the two were. Iridan was only the taller of the two by a little, and heavier only by grace of a healthy diet and little strenuous exercise. Both were thin-limbed and fair of complexion, though the hermit was far paler than appeared healthy. Rashan most likely saw Iridan as a kindred spirit, Brannis decided, one who made his way in life by wit and magic, just as the hermit seemed to.

The day turned foul some hours after the break for replenishing the group's water supply. The trees that had thoughtfully allowed the warm sunshine through their leaves to cheer them all day had now permitted the dark clouds that gathered above to soak them with a cold rain—more typical of the late autumn, but far less welcome. The storm had come on them suddenly, sneaking up from the west at their backs, unnoticed until they were caught up in its midst. The winds that brought the storm also blew the rain hard at their backs, the only blessings being that it gave them a tailwind and kept the rain from their faces. To the knights and soldiers wearing heavy armor with thick padding beneath, the rain soaked them and was absorbed in great quantities by their undergarments, chilling them and weighing them down even further under the weight of their packs. Iridan seemed to have the worst time of it, just recently having recovered the strength to walk on his own, worrying Brannis. The hermit Rashan seemed entirely unconcerned and unbothered by the weather.

As they traveled along the rolling forest terrain, they came to a shallow valley between hills where the rainwater had pooled and made mud of all the ground. Men grumbled as the ground sucked at their boots while water splashed into them, drenching their feet. Then a few of the men stopped, whispering to one another. Curiosity and gossip quickly brought the whole group to a standstill, with the first few who had stopped all staring in the direction of the hermit. Soon all eyes turned to Rashan, who stood with raised eyebrows, seeming to wait quietly for someone to mention why they were staring at him. One of the men pointed to the ground behind him, and the hermit turned and looked down. So did everyone else.

There were no tracks.

There was an uncomfortable silence as all eyes turned once more to the hermit. The commoner soldiers seemed to be extremely wary, unconsciously leaning away from the hermit, but not taking so much as a step away. Iridan seemed more surprised than wary, thinking that this was something he ought to have noticed, or at least felt, if magic was about.

Brannis was the one to break the silence: "Well, care to explain this?" he asked, trying not to sound too accusatory.

The hermit cocked his head to the side. "Explain what? You really ought to try being more specific. You give me more credit than is my due if you think all is known to me."

"The footprints … Why are there none? Is that specific enough for you?" Brannis said.

The foul weather had worn his patience thin.

"Ahh, there we go, a proper question. Well, it seemed rather bothersome to trudge about in the mud, so I chose not to."

"Well, stop it. You are making us all uneasy, working strange magics without letting on that you are doing so … and now that I look closer, you are not even wet!"

Rashan rolled his eyes and blew a long, weary sigh. "Very well, I shall muck about in the mud with the rest of you, but I will not get rained on just for your peace of mind. I hate going about in wet clothes for no good reason." And with no warning, the hermit sank a finger's-breadth with a soft splash and a squish of mud. He crossed his arms over his chest and asked, "Better?"

"All right, but let me know before you use magic again," Brannis said, a little bothered by how easily the hermit performed such minor feats of magic.

He had heard of woodland sorcerers before—those who called themselves druids—but he had been taught that they lacked any real talent with aether. Supposedly they only drew on the aether in living plants, and very rarely the aether of animals. Such limitations combined with no organized training reputedly made them an insignificant force compared to the sorcerers that the Academy trained. If Rashan was a druid, then druids were more adept than the masters at the Academy had let on.

"All life is magic, Brannis. Shall I inform you each time I breathe?" the hermit asked.

It was a simple enough question, and the logic flowed right from Brannis's remembered lessons from the Academy: Life is magic. Aether flows from life.

"Never mind. Just do not hide things from us anymore. You have proven yourself to be a friend by your help in tending to Iridan's affliction. You need not worry that we are ungrateful, or frightened of small bits of sorcery worked about us. Now enough of this gawking; we are not getting any closer to Kadris this way."

Brannis turned away from the sideshow at the back of the group and resumed his march. The men about him were less trusting of the hermit now, though, and were slow to turn their backs on him, but eventually had to return to their duty to keep up with their commander.

* * * * * * *

Iridan and Rashan were the last to resume their march, hanging back from the rest of the company. Rashan took hold of Iridan's upper arm and held him gently at bay. With feigned innocence and a mischievous little grin on his face, Rashan seemed to rise up a finger's breadth, and there was a slight sucking noise from the mud beneath his feet. A heartbeat later, Iridan felt his own body lighten suddenly and his feet pulled free of the mud in which they had been mired.

"Since they already know about this little trick," Rashan whispered just loudly enough to be heard over the noise of the storm, "it is hardly a secret anymore. Let us take the day's walking in leisure and leave the mud to them."

He cast Iridan a conspiratorial look. There was a twinkle in the hermit's icy blue eyes that told Iridan that he was not taking the matter nearly as seriously as Brannis had made it out to be.

Iridan considered for a moment and decided that the hermit was right. He had just regained the strength to walk, and he had begun to tire some time ago. Complaining did not seem likely to buy overmuch sympathy from the men who had been carrying him in shifts in addition to their own gear, so he had not mentioned anything to Brannis. With the help of the hermit's magic, he would be able to keep up with the soldiers' pace as they slogged through the mud. A grin slowly spread across Iridan's face as he returned the hermit's gaze. Suspicion remained in the dark recesses of his thoughts, but Iridan found himself liking his strange new companion. The two men hurried their steps, splashing along the surface of the shallow, muddy pools of water, and tried not to attract too much attention as they caught up to everyone else.

Chapter 10 - The Time to Act

He was all alone in the dark cell, sitting on the edge of his bunk. He rested his elbows on his knees, and his hands were clasped tightly together; his heart was racing in eager anticipation.

The day is finally here.

Denrik's men had been taken from the cell shortly before dawn as part of a work detail that would unload the supply ship that was to make its monthly visit to Rellis Island that morning. All told, a dozen men would take part in the job of carrying the food and other goods ashore and stocking them in the small warehouse that held the penal colony's supplies. The guards picked the fortunate prisoners based on behavior, bribery, and often on a whim. The rest—a group that unfailingly included Denrik—were locked in their cells until the ship had once again departed. The fact that all five members of Denrik's crew happened to have been selected this once caused no concern among the guards, for of all the prisoners on the island, only Denrik was deemed to warrant extraordinary precautions.

The waiting was necessary but growing tiresome on Denrik's nerves. He needed to time his maneuvers properly, even if he had built considerable leeway into his plan. Inside the cell block, there was no light from the sun, and judging the passage of time was tricky—in fact impossible with any degree of precision. Since he had never been on one of the supply details, he had to make countless inquiries of the other prisoners who had. Not all the prisoners were friendly with the former pirate, and some had taken to taunting him with tales of their little treks aboard the supply ships, knowing that it bothered him that he was not allowed to accompany them. Bitter though the stories were, Denrik milked them for all the information he could gather about how the operation was run—and that was quite a lot.

* * * * * * * *

Jimony glanced all about as he walked, fearing that the guards knew what he was preparing to do. To his mind, guilt was written clearly upon his features, and he was a doomed man. The guards were not so perceptive that they made anything of it, and merely thought the prisoner to be fearful of the bared weapons that they carried. Normally the guards on duty carried just whips and clubs, lest the prisoners rise up in numbers and overpower them should they get hold of anything truly dangerous. When a ship was docked, that changed. All the guards were on duty, outnumbering the prisoners unloading the ship twofold, and they carried swords. In the hold, the ship's crewmen were similarly armed, ensuring that the workers caused no mischief to the ship or the cargo.

They had already made one trip, carrying barrels of freshwater and sacks of flour into the storehouse. This next trip into the hold was the one. Captain Denrik had told them all what to do, the five of them that were loyal to him. If the other seven prisoners went along with the plan once it was revealed, everything would be fine. If not ... Well, things might get bloody. Jimony glanced around to assure himself that his comrades were all present. He fervently wished that the captain had not put him in charge of this part of his plan.

The prisoners marched barefoot up the gangplank and then down into the hold of the ship via a short flight of rickety stairs. The ceiling of the hold was low, giving rise to fears of hitting one's head while merely walking upright. Sailors stood to either side of the door, and others among the cargo, watching the prisoners' movements with drawn swords.

Jimony cleared his throat. "Beggin' yer pardon, mister, but I'm not for thinkin' we're gonna get off this ship," he told the nearest sailor, trying not to sound scared.

"Huh?" one of the prisoners who had not been in Denrik's "crew" uttered dumbly.

"Of course, and you need not get off," the sailor said. "We surrender."

The sailor's words were matter-of-fact, and he laid his sword carefully on the floor. The other sailors did likewise. Jimony could hardly believe how easy it had been.

* * * * * * * *

Denrik had waited long enough. Time or not, he was unable to sit idle any longer. He would have rather tested his luck being too early than see all his planning wasted were he to be too late.

He moved to the steel door that had caged him in for so long, and smiled. Irrationally, he felt it was time that the door received its due punishment for the all the years that it had held him captive. He felt along the rough, metal surface to locate the lock. Satisfied that he had found just the right spot, he took a half step back and crouched low, bringing the lock to his eye level.

"Kohtho ilextiumane veeru," he spoke softly and then held the tips of his index fingers just a hairsbreadth apart—no mean feat considering the darkness.

He felt the cool rush of aether into his body, a welcome feeling that he was too seldom able to indulge in among the superstitious fools with whom he dwelt. Being a pirate was a serious enough offense—one that had nearly been enough for the Acardians to reinstate public execution—without compounding it by being caught practicing witchcraft.

There was no visible change to the lock at first, but slowly a red glow began to illuminate the gloom of the darkened cell. The heat created enough light for Denrik to see what he was doing, as the area around the lock grew ever hotter.

The smell of burning filth wafted from the door as the grime that pervaded the cell block caught fire inside the lock. Sweat beaded on Denrik's bald head, but from exertion and not the heat of the melting metal. His skills with magic were considerable, but he lacked the power to make much use of them. The spell he was using to heat the lock was fairly simple, yet he felt as if he was straining to hold a cannonball over his head, so quickly it sapped his strength.

With a gasp and a few heavy breaths, Denrik ended the spell, and the red glow from the door began immediately to fade. He ran a hand over his head to wipe away the sweat, a gesture that still felt odd to him with no hair. He supposed that once he was free of the lice-infested prison colony, he could grow it out again.

Foolish guards, he mused, *they have not let me so much as see a razor. Did they ever wonder how I managed to keep clean-shaven?*

Denrik had been using magic to keep the stubble both on his face and scalp at bay, not wanting to suffer the misery that so many other prisoners went through with the biting parasites that infested the place. He shook his head in derision at the thought that in the three years of his captivity, no one had questioned how he managed it.

Regaining his strength after a moment, Denrik stood and pushed gently on the door. It swung open just a crack, the locking mechanism no longer in any shape to continue performing its duties. He peeked out into the hallway, squinting against the sunlight that streamed in from a barred window above the guard post. It was unmanned, of course, since all the guards were out ensuring that the supply ship was protected.

How amusing: if there was someone on duty here, that ship would be a whole lot safer.

Denrik made his way down the hall, his bare feet slapping against the stone floor. He did not care if anyone heard him or not. The prisoners were of no concern; none of them would raise an alarm, even if they did believe something to be amiss. There was no love lost among the various inmates of the New Hope colony, but they all stood united against their common enemy—the guards.

The door out of the cell block had no lock and really never needed one before. The island was thought to be secure from escape, and the locked cells were mostly to protect the guards. Denrik walked right out of the cell block unopposed, leaving the door to his own cell wide open. He relished the thought of the guards' expressions when they eventually came back and saw that their prized prisoner was gone.

The morning sun was high in the sky, and a few fluffy white clouds were the only ornament to grace the clear blue above. Denrik never cared much for landscapes or trees, or any of the beauty that poets ascribed to them, but there was something about a clear sky that he could appreciate as a man of the sea. It was a fine day to set sail!

He headed straight toward the water, away from where the ship was docked. He kept low and used the naturally rocky and uneven terrain of the island for cover. The guards were likely preoccupied with the prisoners unloading the supply ship, but he was too close to his goal to take any unneeded risks. The chilly water of the Katamic Sea lapped at his feet at he reached the shore, apparently without being spotted. Not hesitating in the least, he plunged into the water. The sudden cold shock of the dunking felt invigorating—he supposed in no small part due to the fact that he knew he was nearly a free man. He slowly began to make a circuit of the small island, swimming around to where his salvation was docked.

It was the riskiest part of his plan. Denrik was a strong swimmer, but he could only make so large a concession to stealth. To completely avoid detection, he might have swum out to sea a ways and doubled back on the ship from the far side. But there was limited time, and he needed to make sure he was on board the ship before it weighed anchor. He was going to need a bit of luck to avoid being seen by the guards as he came within a hundred yards of the shore and then approached the ship.

* * * * * * * *

The guards were growing impatient. The lazy good-for-nothing prisoners had been in the ship's hold for too long. What was the delay? There was a protocol to the business of the supply ships; the sailors took great pride in their job and were touchy about the guards coming on board to boss them around. It gave little comfort to the colony's guards, however, as they waited on the short pier for their prisoners to emerge with the last of the supplies.

They heard no sign of a struggle from the ship's hold, and had heard no calls for help from the crew. There was nothing to be done but wait for the prisoners to come back out, at least not without causing trouble with the ship's crew. There was going to be a debt to pay after the ship was unloaded, though.

* * * * * * * *

Denrik was almost disgusted at how easily he reached the ship, named the *Bringer of Hope* as a reminder that the prisoners had little of it themselves.. If the guards were so oblivious, he wondered why he had not just stowed aboard one of the ships years ago. Of course, Denrik knew better than to seriously think he could have succeeded. The crew would almost certainly have discovered him and fed him to the sharks, even if he had managed to get free from his cell without having his cellmates all out of the way on work detail. He grabbed the rope that anchored the ship in the water and pulled himself hand over hand up to the deck. It was just one more thing that was going according to his plan; the anchor was not attached by a chain.

He crawled across the deck to the stair leading below into the hold and slipped down into the belly of the supply ship. It was all going as planned. There were his men, as well as the other prisoners, and the crew of the ship all tied and seated against the wall.

"Cap'n, you made it!" Jimony exclaimed, his eyes widening in disbelief. He somehow had not expected the plan to work.

"Yes, good work, men," Denrik said to his crew. "Have they been cooperating?"

"Uh-huh. They gived up them swords and let us tie 'em up, real easy like," Jimony replied.

"We have done as we were instructed, Captain Zayne," one of the ship's crewmen said to Denrik. "Your man made everything perfectly clear."

"Huh? We didn't tells ya nothin' but we wasn't gettin' back off 'n this here ship," Jimony said.

"Do not worry," Denrik assured his men. "You were not the one he was referring to. Some of my former associates have been quite helpful in arranging this little jailbreak for us. The crew is being paid well to go along with this little charade of a commandeering."

"Huh?" Andur asked, the simple-minded one of the group speaking the thoughts of several of Denrik's men.

"This was all planned ahead of time," Denrik boasted. "My old first mate bribed these men to let us take over their ship. They say we overpowered them, and pocket a king's—or should I say pirate's—ransom for it. Now we have to make good our escape."

After confiscating one of the cutlasses his men had taken from the crewmen, Denrik headed back up to the deck. He motioned for his men to follow, noting that four of the five at least had held his ground and not followed the other prisoners back off the ship; it was better than he had expected. Hopefully the rest remembered their role in the final part of the plan.

Denrik slunk over to where the line for the anchor was tied. The knot was too heavy and too tightly pulled for him to have any hope of untying it, but there was little need. He used his new cutlass and began to saw at the rope. Watching from the top of the stairs to the hold, Jimony waited for Denrik to signal him. When the rope snapped free and slithered over the side rail and into the water, Denrik turned and gave a quick nod to his men.

All pretense of stealth was abandoned as the men of Denrik's—or more appropriately Captain Zayne's—crew rushed out onto the deck, weapons drawn. The guards were stunned momentarily but recovered quickly and burst into action, making their way to the gangplank to board the ship. But the prisoners were prepared. They made immediately for the only way onto the ship, loosing the gangplank from the deck and dropping it into the water. They then set off quickly for the remaining rope lines that tethered the ship to the dock, hacking away at them to free the vessel. Denrik was a one-man crew as he rushed about preparing the ship to sail. He only needed to do enough to get away from the dock before he could painstakingly instruct his landlubber crew in the operation of a ship. The guards, with their drawn swords and no apparent means to board the ship, looked lost and confused.

Denrik felt the ship lurch and knew that the vessel was floating freely, cut free of the dock at last. The rest was simple. In no time, the ship was making its way slowly out onto the open sea. He could not resist running over to the railing to call out to the guards.

"Thank you all! This ship is not quite to my preference, but it will have to do for now. Remember that I know each of your names. If I hear that word of my escape reaches the mainland within a fortnight, your families will pay dearly. Farewell," he cried.

The guards did not respond. They did not know how to respond. They had been given one clear mission that took precedence over all their other duties: keep Denrik Zayne from ever sailing again. They had failed.

* * * * * * * *

Captain Zayne had taken the uniform and boots from the sailor closest to his own size, and had ripped off the naval rank insignia that the uniform bore. He had no hat, as he had customarily worn in the days when he had a real crew and a real ship of his own, but his bald head was deeply tanned from the long days spent breaking rocks, so he could survive without one for a few days. The jacket and pants fit well enough, though he felt foolish dressed as a midshipman in the Acardian Navy, but it was far preferable to going about clad in the rags of a prisoner. He let the vestments of his captive life drop overboard and swore that he would never be forced into such a wretched state again. His pride had been wounded during his time on Rellis Island, but he was not going to forget the indignities he suffered, or let them go unpunished.

The crew was pathetically inadequate in all things nautical. He had made an attempt to teach them enough to maintain the basic functions of the ship, but even that had apparently been beyond their comprehension. He had finally set everything in order himself, handed the ship's wheel to Andur, and ordered that he hold it still. Two others he charged with alerting him should anything change at all, putting them on watch over the rigging and sails. Shaking his head at his hopeless crew, he went below deck to see to his prisoners, bringing Jimony in tow.

The prisoners were lined up along a wall of the hold, ten men in all, and aside from the one whose uniform Denrik had stolen, all looked in relatively good spirits.

"So were all the arrangements to your liking?" he asked, knowing that the men were in no position to object at that moment.

"Yes, sir, Captain Zayne. We did everything just as your mate instructed," replied the apparent leader, a lieutenant in the Acardian Navy.

"And you told no one of our arrangement? It would not do for anyone to find out, you know," Denrik said.

"No, sir, everything was kept quiet. We shall be rescued once you run the ship aground, and we will tell everyone that the great Captain Zayne was too much for us." The man winked at Denrik.

"Excellent," Denrik said with a grin that was not the least bit reassuring to the sailors. He turned to Jimony. "Cut their throats and throw them to the sharks. It is better than they deserve."

Denrik turned to head back up top.

"Wait! What about our deal? I swear we told no one!" the prisoners pleaded, eyes wide with fear.

Denrik spun about, a hard, ruthless look in his eyes. "The next one who talks gets thrown in with a belly wound ... to be eaten alive!"

He stomped up the stairs, leaving an uncomfortable Jimony to finish the gruesome chore.

Jimony looked from the blade in his hand to the helpless prisoners who cowered before him. He was beginning to understand why Captain Zayne was known as the Scourge of the Katamic.

Chapter 11 - Old Habits

By mid-morning the next day, Brannis's troops met up with the main road that led down from the Cloud Wall Mountains and forked south into the forest toward the Kadrin town of Illard's Glen and north toward Megrenn. It was a well-cleared path of dirt, wide enough for two wagons to pass each other comfortably. In days gone by, it was a busy thoroughfare, as it was the primary land route between the heartland of the Empire and the far-flung settlements west of the mountain range. That was before the seas had been well-secured by the Kadrin fleet and shipping lanes had been plagued by privateers, making them a risky venture; wagons were thought to be the surest way for merchants to see a return on their investments. Though still in use, the road was now quiet much of the time, and so it was when Brannis led his men onto it, grateful to a man for a straight trail to follow, after days of tripping over roots and crashing through underbrush. The mild upward grade the whole way was the only downside for the weary bunch.

With his route clear before him, Brannis's thoughts moved onward to what lay ahead of them. The road would lead them up into the mountains along an old pass, cleared by magic hundreds of winters before. Lingering constructs of aether were supposedly still protecting the pass, their silent and invisible presence reassuring them of safety from avalanches and collapsing rock faces.

Of course, Brannis thought, *I would never notice if it was not here until we were buried beneath a pile of rubble.*

He briefly considered asking Iridan to feel his way into the aether to see whether they were still protected, but decided against it. After Iridan's last attempt to draw aether, Brannis hesitated to give his friend another chance to re-injure himself.

The thought of asking Rashan to do the same thing lingered a trifle longer before he finally decided against that as well. There was something he did not trust about the odd little hermit, and despite every indication to the contrary, he could not shake the feeling that Rashan was a potential threat. He had taken care of Iridan when he collapsed from self-induced aether burn. He had allowed Brannis and his men the meager comforts of his forest home. He had—or at least claimed to have—sent a message to Kadrin for them. He had accompanied them quietly, helpfully, and unobtrusively for days, and seemed to be getting on companionably with Iridan, whose health he was still careful of. But the sums just did not add up in Brannis's mind.

Should a forester, living off the land and being out of doors constantly, not be more … forester-like? Should his body not be hard and tough? Rashan looked as if a rowdy chipmunk could topple him. Should his face not be unshaven, weathered, tanned? Rashan was as fair as a sheltered noble lass of eight winters age, and no hairier, it seemed. Should his clothes not be dirty and worn? His homemade garments were certainly not fashionable but they looked newly made and undamaged; even Brannis's own clothes seemed worse for wear after just a few days travel through Kelvie Forest. Should a man cut off for winters not be awkward among strangers? Brannis had instructors at both the Imperial Academy and School of Arms who were less eloquent, less sure of themselves. No, Brannis decided to forge onward into the mountains, trusting that either ancient magic, or luck, would see them safely to their destination.

The destination that Brannis had most immediately in mind was a small fortress, kept up by the Kadrin military, which guarded the crossing of Two-Drake Chasm. The pass had gotten its name in the early days of the imperial expansion, when a group of mountaineers was sent to survey a route for a path to be carved through the Cloud Wall Mountains. During the expedition, two brothers, Carlen and Mortimer Drake, fell to their deaths in a chasm that split the eventual main route through the mountains. Finding no better route along safer ground, the fortress was built to guard a drawbridge that allowed the Kadrins to control access through the pass. During the height of the pass's use, the fortress became a strategic bottleneck for the defense of the heartland, giving the Kadrin merchants quick access to the west, and providing the Kadrin Empire a good income from taxing foreign merchants for its use. However, just like the pass itself, the fortress had fallen from prominence, though not entirely from use. A small garrison of Kadrin soldiers manned it and guarded the drawbridge, and it was these soldiers Brannis was counting on for support.

"Brannis," called the hermit quietly from just behind, "might I have a word with you?"

Brannis had not heard Rashan come up behind him, and was a little startled, as it was rare for him to leave his place beside Iridan, taking up the rear of the march.

"Sure, what is it?"

"Iridan seems to be much improved. By tomorrow, I expect he will be free to call aether again without harming himself."

"Well, that is good to hear." Brannis sighed with relief.

"Yes, and I think that means I have about played out my time with you. You should not need me any longer, and I should be heading back to tend my gardens. I shall take my leave of you once you are safely on your own side of the fortress."

"Who said anything about a fortress?" Brannis asked, giving the hermit a sidelong glance.

For, indeed, he hadn't mentioned it to his men nor had he overheard anyone mentioning it to Rashan.

"I did not grow up in the forest here, Brannis, you know that. I told you I was born in the Empire. I passed through that fortress autumns ago. It is an open road still, you know," Rashan replied a bit impatiently, as if he expected Brannis to have known better.

"There you are!" came a call from behind them. Iridan was hastening up to join Brannis and Rashan as they walked side by side at the lead of the line. "I turn my attention away for moment and it is like you have disappeared."

"I just had to speak with your commander for a bit," replied the hermit, smiling and looking a bit amused.

"Oh," said Iridan, sounding just a touch hurt at being left out. "Anything I might be interested in?"

"Just that I will be parting ways with you all when we reach the fortress that guards the pass."

Iridan stopped in his tracks. The rest of the Kadrin contingent kept right on walking, and the young sorcerer was left gaping for a moment as he was slowly left behind.

"What?" Iridan said.

Brannis turned back to see Iridan jogging to catch up to Rashan, who was facing straight ahead and grinning to himself as he kept pace with Brannis. Iridan got ahead of both of them and stopped in the road, blocking the hermit's path.

"What do you mean you are leaving? You cannot just leave us, just like that." Iridan snapped his fingers in the air.

"I have a flower garden that will die without my care. It may already be dying, as I have neglected it these past days. It is a delicate species and requires a great deal of attention. Besides, you should be safe once you have reached more of your own men. That, and by tomorrow, you should be able to gather and hold aether without it hurting. You will not be needing me."

"Flowers? You cannot be serious!" Iridan shouted. "You have been away a long time; come back to the Empire with us. I can hear it in your voice every time you mention it, that you miss it there."

Rashan's eyebrows rose slightly as this.

"And how can you know I will not need you, that tomorrow I shall be able to use aether without any problem?" Iridan asked. "You are not even the same sort of sorcerer as we have in the Empire, you said so yourself."

Brannis was a little surprised at hearing this, but the effect on the hermit was more pronounced.

"No, I am not," Rashan returned evenly, his expression stern and his nearly colorless blue eyes flashing in anger. "But I do know what I am talking about. You would think you could show more respect for my knowledge, seeing as it saved your life the other night. Yes, I quite think you would have died had I as little understanding as you are now attributing to me. But anyway," and with an abrupt change, the hermit's mild tone had returned, "we ought not pass the day just standing here. Onward, eh?"

The entire group had halted when Iridan had blocked Rashan's path and forced him to stop, and all had been watching the whole scene unfold. No one seemed to know quite what to make of it, though, and everyone, including Iridan and Brannis, seemed a bit ill at ease. There were certainly none among the soldiers who would shed a tear at the strange hermit's parting.

The rest of the trip up the mountain passed in uneasy silence. Rashan seemed to be unaware of the discomfort he was causing to those around him. Brannis and the soldiers had found his sudden small burst of anger troubling, especially now that he had apparently admitted he was a sorcerer of some sort—though they were all quite suspicious already after the bird-messenger incident, despite never having seen him perform anything that looked like spellcasting. Iridan, on the other hand, seemed to be nursing a case of hurt feelings. It seemed that he had grown rather fond of the hermit and had been quite grateful for the care he had received from his injury. But, no doubt, he could not help but feel rejected and neglected when Rashan had snuck off and told Brannis of his coming departure, and not told him first.

The mountain road was in exceedingly good condition with a low grade and smooth surface. Brannis hoped it was evidence of a healthy aether construct at work—wards buried under the dirt, down in the bedrock, and in the side of the cliff faces themselves—keeping things in order and preventing the hundreds of tons of rock overhanging the pass from falling on them. With the lack of voices in the air, the only sounds to be heard were the creak of leather boots as they trudged along the rock, the clatter of the soldiers' gear, and the sound of the wind moaning between the mountains.

The view nearly made up for the miserable company his fellows were being, Brannis thought. As they ascended, he could see the treetops of Kelvie Forest, green and lush, with no sign of the turmoil of battle and marching armies. Brannis had looked back often, wary of signs of pursuit, or of the movements of the main goblin force, but the goblins were far too clever to give themselves away by, for instance, creating great smoking bonfires at their encampments.

The men were in reasonably good spirits as they approached the safety of the garrison at Two-Drake Chasm. It promised a rest from pursuit and a good meal, and possibly horses for making the final leg of their journey back to the Empire proper in good time. And thus it came as quite a shock when they finally came within view of Tibrik, the fortress that Kadrin kept garrisoned to defend High Pass.

The garrison itself presented a drab, grey wall of fitted stone to those who approached from the western half of the pass, weather stained and ancient looking. The top of the wall was crenelated, and arrow slits broke up the monotony of the otherwise unadorned facade. A drawbridge of iron-bound timbers blocked the gate, and its absence precluded any attempt at crossing the chasm on foot. What was out of sorts was that the fortress *should* have been adorned. Thin iron rods jutted out along the top of the wall, meant to be hung with the red and gold of the Kadrin flag. There were six of them in all, and all were bare.

It was not a comforting sign.

In its heyday, the garrison housed upward of fifty soldiers and could still accommodate stopovers by merchants and other travelers. The whole fortress had bustled with activity as a miniature trading town along a lucrative road. Even in modern times, it should still have been at least manned to the point of having a lookout to have hailed them by now. That the Imperial Colors were not flying was an even worse sign. Brannis hoped that nothing horrible was about to happen.

"Hello there," Brannis called across the chasm as they reached the point where the drawbridge should have ended, were it to be lowered.

"... there ... ere," his voice echoed back to him.

"I am Sir Brannis Solaran, Knight of the Empire. I say, is there anyone on duty?"

"duty ... uty."

He waited, but there was no reply from inside.

"I guess we will have to work out some other way of getting across. Iridan, do you think you are up to doing a little heavy lifting?" Brannis asked, turning to the sorcerer, who had been conferring with the hermit in hushed tones off to the side a ways.

Brannis was not sure he cared for how close the two of them were becoming. It was not jealousy as such but more of the caution of an older brother, worried that his younger sibling was getting involved with unsavory associates. Best friends though they may have been, Brannis had always been sort of watching out for Iridan as long as he had known him. Brannis's musings were cut short, though, as a reply was finally forthcoming from the fortress, though not the type that Brannis had really hoped for.

"Fire!" someone from inside shouted.

"Fire ... Fire ... ire."

The air erupted in arrows, and bows thrummed a deadly tune as the garrison sprang from its slumber and attacked. The chasm was not particularly wide, and there was no cover worth mentioning. It was quite an efficient and forthright defensive position; it was constructed in a time when builders were advised by generals rather than merchants and noblemen. The archers who were manning it now were also no fools. They had waited and watched, and knew who the leaders of Brannis's group were. Incidentally, Brannis's proclamation of his own rank may have helped confirm who was in charge.

Of all the arrows fired in the initial volley, there were only three men picked out and targeted: Brannis, Iridan, and Rashan. Brannis felt the arrows pound the breastplate of his armor and deflect off, thankful for the excellent, runed armor his family was able to afford. He wished he had made Iridan wear the conscript's armor he had been issued. The sorcerer stood out enough already without drawing more attention to himself, and was a sitting duck.

Instinct took over as Brannis and the soldiers scrambled back down the pass as quickly and as low to the ground as they could. Brannis had the presence of mind, as well as the foolhardiness, to hang back and cover his men's retreat, trusting that his armor would turn aside any arrows that struck the enchanted metal. Trying not to think of all the areas his armor did not fully cover and what an arrow in them might feel like, he nevertheless spared a glance back toward Iridan, ready to go back if he showed any sign of having survived the barrage. What he saw made his blood go suddenly cold.

Standing slightly in front of Iridan was the hermit, Rashan. His arms were outstretched to one side, as if he had reacted to block the arrows aimed at the sorcerer. In fact, arrows had pierced Rashan's hands and one arm, apparently leaving Iridan unharmed. Both men still stood. As Iridan came to his senses and headed for safety down the pass, Rashan simply stood there, bringing his hands in front of him. As he turned a bit, Brannis saw several arrows sticking out of his chest and stomach. It seemed as if what had just happened somehow failed to register in his head and had not told him to fall dead.

Instead he clenched both fists and swatted an arm across his front, shattering arrow shafts. A somewhat confused and less organized volley of arrows followed from the fortress, as the archers slowly started to realize that something was very wrong. Six or eight arrows ought to have been enough to fell a slightly built young man, the brighter ones surely reasoned. The more slow-witted of the archers rapidly caught up with those forward thinkers when their second volley of arrows hung briefly in midair, then dropped harmlessly into the chasm.

Not everyone in the fortress that day had been assigned to the wall with a bow and arrows, so not everyone had been privy to the sight of the unkillable hermit and his arrow-stopping magic. So those uninformed individuals were unaware as to what was befalling their captured fortress until the screaming started.

Brannis and his men stood there mutely, unsure whether to be confused, relieved, or horrified; most of them went with all three. Someone may at some point have uttered something to the effect of "What in the name of all that is holy is going on in there?" but it went unanswered.

After shrugging off several mortal-looking arrow wounds and halting a second volley mid-flight, the hermit had leapt across the chasm and landed on top of the wall, then disappeared from view into the fortress. It looked so simple, but Brannis had not heard any magic being used, and there was no hand-waving or finger-waggling that he would have recognized as proper spellcasting. Rashan simply shot across the gap as if fired from a ballista.

Shortly after Rashan crossed, sounds could be heard from inside the keep. It began with confused shouting and yelling, and progressed through clatters of metal on stone, wet crunching noises, and roaring flames. Throughout most of it, there was a lot of screaming—not battle cries or screams of fear, though some of those may have been drowned out in the din—but the screams of men dying less than quick deaths. The horrible fascination and surrealism of it made it seem like an eternity, but in quite short order, the sounds of battle ended, replaced by the rhythmic clanking of the hoisting mechanism for the drawbridge being released.

There was no one standing on the far side to greet them when it finished opening.

No one moved. No one spoke. The silence coming from the open drawbridge was distinctly asking "Well, are you coming or not?" but no one seemed to want to be the first to cross.

Finally Brannis decided to assert his command and announced, "Well then, we cannot very well stand here all day," and then stepped onto the drawbridge.

As he got halfway across, Iridan got up his courage and ventured onto it himself. One by one, the rest of the troops followed suit.

On the far side, Brannis began to take stock and realize what must have gone on during the hermit's vicious assault. Bodies were flung against the walls like rag dolls, with limbs torn off and blood everywhere. One soot-stained stairway seemed to contain three or four bodies, but no one seemed to be of a mind to pick through the greasy mess of charred remains to get a good count. Swords and shields lay scattered about, the former being rather incongruously clean compared to most of the devastation around them. From the looks of the uniforms and what he could make out from the bodies, the men appeared to be from Megrenn.

Megrenn was a former part of the Kadrin Empire, conquered over a century ago, and which had regained its independence when Brannis was still just a small boy. There were a handful of regions like it, conquered during periods of particularly fierce expansion of the Empire, left to drift back to their old governments when a more peaceful emperor or more frugal high commander let control slip back to the hands of the locals. The Megrenn were a seafaring people from the northlands, and for a time, the bounty of their whaling fleets was much prized by the nobles of Kadrin. As shrewd Megrenn merchants took advantage of fads in kerosene lamps and scrimshaw knickknacks, petulant nobles began to consider cheaper alternatives. The cheapest they decided on was to annex the country. Of course, fads never lasted forever, and kerosene lamps fell out of popularity in favor of good old-fashioned aether, and scrimshaw gewgaws came to be viewed as cheap and tawdry, and Kadrin natives never quite developed a taste for whale meat. So when the Megrenn decided to revolt and oust the Kadrin garrison, they had little trouble about it. The garrison had already been cut to a skeleton crew, and the remaining forces were overwhelmed … and butchered.

The Megrenn were not amused by their time under Imperial rule. They had not been content merely with liberation; they sought reparations, and knowing that the Kadrins were not the type to go in for that sort of nonsense, they went about taking by force what they felt they deserved. Of course, their winters of subjugation had left them bereft of any real military might, but they made a nuisance of themselves, sending sanctioned bands of brigands on horseback, whom they referred to amongst themselves as the "light cavalry," to harry and obstruct Kadrin traders traveling abroad and in the remote reaches of the Empire itself.

By all appearances, they had done quite well for themselves in taking over the fortress guarding Two-Drake Chasm. There were no signs of Kadrin remains among the fallen, so presumably they had been in control of the garrison for at least a little while and had set themselves up comfortably enough, with provisions and everything, as if it were actually under Megrenn command. Brannis had not counted the bodies but guessed that there were roughly two dozen men, all now dead, who had been stationed there. Certainly they should have been able to slaughter a small, weary, under-equipped command group, even one with a junior member of the Imperial Circle to aid them. But they had not counted on some strange, secretive hermit leaping the chasm and butchering them.

"Butchering … them …" Brannis murmured under his breath.

He could feel his pulse pounding in his ears, and his stomach went a bit queasy. He turned from his musings and set off down the eastern side of the pass before his better judgment could dissuade him.

Brannis did not have far to go. The hermit was sitting a short ways ahead, in the middle of the road. His knees were pulled up to his chest as he stared into the distance, his back to Brannis as he approached. The late-morning light streamed through the gap in the mountains, and Brannis realized that he had never really gotten a look at Rashan in full daylight. The forest canopy, the rain, the shadows of the mountains … but now brilliant, warm light cast a clearer picture as the hermit turned, sensing Brannis's approach. His hair was not merely a platinum blond, it was snowy white, and the pale face seemed like smooth-polished ivory.

"I have missed it, you know."

"You are really him." Brannis tried not to sound accusing. "You are *the* Rashan. Warlock Rashan Solaran, who died a hundred summers ago."

"Brannis …" There was a long pause. "If you could be a sorcerer, would you go back and try the Academy again? Iridan told me that you were popular there as a child, that you were the best student, until they tried you at real magic."

"What are you talking about?" Brannis was caught off guard by the abrupt change from accusation to interrogation.

"Would you give up all you have now to go back and take the life you thought you were going to have? Could you face all the people who you left behind and act like nothing ever happened? If it turned out you could do it, would you *want* to be accepted back in?"

"I am not sure, I guess. I do not see what this is getting at, though. You are evading the question again."

"Not really, this time. Yes, I am Rashan Solaran. I am probably some great uncle of yours a handful of generations removed. I thought the day would never come when I would return to the Empire. I am not even sure what is left there for me anymore. I do not know whether I am a deserter, an expatriate, a traitor, or merely returned from an unusually long sabbatical. One hundred and two winters is a very long time."

"But you were not a young man when they say you died," Brannis said as diplomatically as he could think of. "And you are still alive. You must be nearly 250 by now."

"Who is the oldest sorcerer ever known to have lived?" Rashan asked.

"Umm …" Brannis searched back in his mind to academy history lessons. "Gelverick Archon, was it not—212?" he ventured.

"Not bad, but it was 218." Rashan seemed rather pleased. "The text in third-rank history is off on the dates but a good reference overall. They have it right in Colverge's *Introductory Longevity*, which I imagine you were not still around for in seventh-rank Practical Magic."

Brannis's mind was working in circles now. This was not the conversation he had been expecting at all when he came to confront the "hermit."

"Come now," Rashan said. "I taught for twenty winters and more at the Academy and attended it too of course, when I was a boy. But then, that was a *very* long time ago."

Rashan fixed Brannis with a meaningful stare.

"All right, I will take your bait. What is the trick? Is there some magic potion to take winters off a body, or a place where the aether runs time backward, or are you just some sort of prodigy in life-prolonging, using all your powers on keeping young?"

"Almost spot on with the last one, excepting of course that it is hardly a drain on my Source to keep me vital. No, I am merely immortal. My Source is closed; I do not bleed aether like mortal creatures do. My own aether sustains me now."

"But that is not possible," Brannis said. "That is basic magic. They teach it the first day at the Academy. It is the first thing you teach small children about where magic comes from. The definition of a living thing is that it gives off aether; anything else moving around that does not is some sort of undead abomination or a—"

"—demon," Rashan finished for him, nodding. "Yes, as you understand it, I would be classified as a demon. The others find it casts them in too harsh a light and prefer being referred to as immortals, but I do not mind the term, really. It has a certain ancient authority about it, referenced in mythology and legend, fearsome creatures of magic and rage, eternal and mighty."

"Others?" Brannis asked.

"Brannis, this is going to get long and complicated. The Megrenn had plenty of horses for your men. I left them all alive, so we can ride the rest of the way. It is only three days if we push ourselves a bit early and late in the days." Rashan sighed. "I cannot return now, so instead I will go back. I shall answer what questions you might have as we ride."

"Do you think you could stop talking in riddles? What do you mean 'cannot return … have to go back'?"

Brannis found himself talking to the warlock's back, as the little man—little demon?—strode past to where the horses were stabled.

"Probably not, but if you start listening in riddles, you might find your answers quicker."

* * * * * * *

"Well, you see, when something is immortal, the population of them tends not to shrink much."

Rashan rode along, his horse even with Brannis's at the front of the group. They were making good time, but without being able to change horses, they carefully managed the beasts' stamina.

"Even if there were only one to emerge every hundred summers, you would still see the number of them grow. Mind you, demons can be killed, but it is not so easy. All demons are comfortable with magic, our bodies are sustained by aether, not reliant on flesh and blood to maintain life. Most also take the time to reshape and refine their bodies, making them stronger, or tougher, or more intimidating—whatever they wish. A smaller body is weaker physically, but takes less aether to maintain."

"So what you are saying is that you reshaped yourself into the form you have now. You are physically weak but do not require much aether to keep yourself alive?" Brannis asked, intrigued by this more than he expected, and less horrified, though he realized he probably should be.

"Yes and no. This form is essentially my body from my younger days. By the time I was able to harness immortality, I was well along in summers, and despite my excellent age control, I was feeling the age of a non-sorcerer nearing fifty summers. I look, as best as I could recall, as I did just as I entered Imperial service. And as to the other half of your question, I could break your neck with hardly an effort. Strength is relative. If I had crafted a body the size of an ogre, I ought to be able to crush boulders in my fists and stave in castle walls. Why bother with that, though, when through aether I can accomplish all that and more, without the nuisance of looking like a monster."

Brannis sat back in his saddle. He noticed he had been leaning in, rapt attention on every word Rashan had spoken, but he needed to digest this information. He had only seen the aftermath at the fortress, a result of angering this diminutive demon who had apparently once subdued half the continent through force of arms, but it was difficult to reconcile with the pale, frail, wispy young woodsman who sat atop the horse next to his.

Chapter 12 - Masterless Apprentice

Kyrus stared into the bluish glow lighting the lantern on his desk. It was a gentle, pleasing light, soothing and comforting, despite its other-worldliness. He had been practicing at length—hours a night—and had made progress in modifying the light to suit his desire. A bit of a change of inflection and he could adjust the brightness or the hue. Subtle changes to the way he moved his fingers could make it last longer or shorter, how close to him it formed, and whether it would stay fixed in space or follow an object as if attached to it. He was feeling rather proficient at it; everything seemed familiar once he tried it, and it came almost naturally to him.

Regarding his latest experiment, he scribbled some notes about how he had managed to light the lantern just so. He had already managed to get it in shades of white, yellow, and orange. Blue was the first one he had tried that had made it a color that he had never seen in a fireplace. As he finished his notations, he let his senses drift into that other place, where the aether was visible, and mentally tugged at the light. It went dark, as if a candle had been blown out.

He had been quite relieved to discover that trick, since as he performed the ritual more and more precisely, it tended to last much longer of its own accord. The previous night, he had left one aglow to see how long it might last and had fallen asleep before it so much as dimmed. It had been unchanged in the morning, and he had felt better snuffing it out lest anyone discover it, preferring caution over curiosity. Still, one day, he ought to figure out the limits of this magic, and to do so would require someplace more discreet than a scrivener's shop on a city street.

By the light of a normal lamp, Kyrus gathered up his night's notes in a neat pile and set them in a drawer, along with notes from his previous few nights' work. Sooner or later, he thought, he would have to get them bound up, lest they become disorderly. A whole new world was opening up to him, he could feel, and he did not want to miss any part of it.

Kyrus went to bed determined to peer into that other world he saw so often but remembered so little from. Things had been getting easier to recall, though, the more he practiced with the lights. Something familiar to that world was making the connections to the rest that much easier. There were things there he wanted to see, to learn, to understand. There was more to magic than simple tricks of light; *that* he was certain of. It would be akin to learning a language by watching children play: haphazard, unfocused, and never certain of a correct example, but until he discovered a better way, he would watch and study.

If he were to dream instead of Abbiley, that would not be so bad, either. Alas, he saw naught but the same magical world, same as ever.

* * * * * * * *

The morning's work seemed interminable. Kyrus scribbled his way through one page after another of the new bylaws passed by the Shipping Guild. He had finished two copies already and was midway through a third. Eight had been commissioned by Expert Harone, enough copies to allow each of his shipping masters to keep a copy. While he appreciated that Expert Harone had gone the traditional route, rather than bring such a repetitive tasks to the typesetters who specialized in such jobs, he was growing weary of it. The saving grace was that the shippers were not going to be as picky about the niceties of penmanship as some of Kyrus's other clients; they just wanted accurate, legible copies of the document distributed among their membership.

And Kyrus was in a rush. He had woken up with a fresh memory of another bit of magic to try. He had seen and heard it quite clearly, across from a campfire: an incantation to lift and move small objects about.

"Haru bedaessi leoki kwatuan gelora."

That was how it went, and the one who spoke those nonsensical words had also gestured at the same time. He had started with his hands out at his sides, then brought them together as if to clasp them, but at the last moment turned and lifted them instead, and the subject of his spell lifted off the ground a foot or so. After that, he had seemed to be able to control the movement of the objects—in this particular case the remnants of the campfire-cooked dinner—but Kyrus could not see how he had managed that. He could not wait to try, and to figure it out.

As Kyrus's hand flew across the pages of the shippers' bylaws, he could not help but notice that there were things written within it that he likely should not know. There were all the usual mundane procedural rules and whatnot, but couched within the otherwise trite old standbys were a number of rules they had set up, whereby they regulated the trade of the city and much of the kingdom. There were rates set within it that could not be undercut by any of the members, though they were free to charge more should they be able to get more money from a customer, keeping the prices higher than if they were at each other's throats for business. There were lists of contraband items that could not be transported, but there were also notable listed exceptions for those with certain paperwork, signed by the proper officials, and who those officials were. There were lists of nations and their various tariffs, and brief lists of what they considered contraband in their own lands. It listed what nations were lax about enforcing these restrictions, and which were not. There was a notation about two nations, the Empire of Sak Qual and the island kingdom of Silk Waves, which only allowed their people to travel under certain restriction and with official permission. All told, it was not just the rules of the tradesmen, but an insight—

albeit a commercial and nautical one—into the wider world beyond Acardia.

As the day wore on, Kyrus scribbled away relentlessly to get through the shippers' commission. He was making more mistakes than usual, he knew, and was probably making it take longer than if he slowed down and did a more careful job, but he was unable to contain his excitement. He crumpled yet another sheet, walked across the room to the stove, and tossed it into the fire.

* * * * * * * *

When finally he penned the last line of the last letter of the last sheet of the last copy of the shippers' bylaws, Kyrus let out a deep sigh. He would take them to the binder in the morning—a simple, inelegant job, just enough to hold the sheets together—but for now he was done. He set aside the eight stacks of paper and opened the drawer that contained his latest notes from his dreams.

He gathered them up and took a quick stop in the kitchen. He opened a drawer containing various culinary implements and selected a single spoon. Satisfied, he headed up to his bedroom, notes and spoon in hand. Ash, not usually the curious type, nevertheless followed him up the stairs, padding along silently behind.

Kyrus laid his notes out on the little desk by the bedside and sat down in the small, worn wooden chair. Scratched out hastily in the foggy aftereffects of slumber, the notes were something of a puzzle in and of themselves. The first part of Kyrus's experimentation would be deciphering his own notes. Normally, if he had jotted something down in haste, he would have taken clues from the context to help him unravel the meaning of the words and identify wayward and misbegotten letters. These notes were different, though; they included a lot of nonsense, and intentionally so. The words Kyrus needed to remember were words that were not spoken in Acardia, or any part of Tellurak that he was aware of, and he suspected they might not be spoken in any land he had ever heard of.

Kyrus eventually decided that he would have to rewrite his notes as he went along. After some time and a trip back downstairs to retrieve a quill, ink, and more paper, he set about trying to figure out the mysteries of the universe. He took a deep breath to calm himself, then went over and closed and shuttered the windows. He was left with only the light of a single candle on the desk. He sat down and blew the candle out, and the room was suddenly pitch dark.

"Aleph kalai abdu."

A warm yellow glow lighted the room, as if a cheery fire shone in a hearth, except this light did not flicker as would a fire, cheery or otherwise. It lit the room fully and effectively, banishing shadows from all but the farthest reaches under the bed, and certainly removing from the ambiance any hint of the creepy, macabre, or occult—or so Kyrus hoped. There was still some part of him that rebelled against the possibility that this was actually happening, that he was not actually tapping into forces of unknown origin and moral character. A brightly lit room to work in made it seem more scientific, like being a chemist, or an astronomer—*No, wait, that does not work at all; they work nearly exclusively in darkness.*

No matter. Kyrus had felt the rush of cool aether invigorating his mind as a reminder that he knew this power and had already plumbed its shallowest waters. It was time to test somewhat deeper waters.

"Baru bedoessi leokl kwatuan gelana."

Kyrus remembered the accompanying gesture much more clearly than the gibberish the magician in his dreams had spouted and thus swept his hands inward and then upward.

Nothing happened. Kyrus had some small hope within him that it would have worked on the first try, but he was not so fortunate. He squinted back down at his notes and tried to figure out where he had guessed wrong at his own writing. He tried also to remember from his dream how everything had sounded, felt, looked, as the spell came together.

"Baru bedaessi leokl kwatuan gelana."

Still nothing. Perhaps that first "b" was supposed to have been an "n"?

"Naru bedaessi leokl kwatuan gelana."

Again, there was no result. But Kyrus was not easily deterred. He pored over the letters and phrases, trying to see how his half-sleeping self had been forming letters by comparing them to words he could figure out.

Several more attempts later, and …

"Haru bedaessi leoki kwatuan gelora."

Success! The spoon on the desk lifted to chin height and hung there, suspended by aether. In his dream, it appeared that there was nothing holding up the plates and pans his unwitting mentor had levitated, but here in the waking world, Kyrus could feel and "see" the aether as it supported the spoon, with wisp-like tendrils of the magic stuff tethering it to him. Kyrus stared at it in wonder.

After the initial mesmerizing effects of his newfound magic passed, Kyrus reached out and gently touched the spoon. It drifted away from his finger as if it were a toy boat on a still pond. The magic seemed to be holding it somewhat level in the air at a constant height but did not prevent it from floating about. Kyrus gave it a bit harder push and could not help giggling as it bounced off the wall and ricocheted awkwardly back in his general direction.

Kyrus caught the spoon as it returned, and steadied it in the air, leaving his hand beneath it. He reached his mind back into the aether and sucked in what was wrapped around the spoon. Just as it did with his lights, removing the aether ended the magical effect. The spoon dropped smartly into the palm of his hand. He clenched it in a fist.

"Ha! I am getting good at this."

Kyrus beamed. Ash, unnoticed on the bed behind him, could not disagree. Kyrus turned the spoon over in his hand and examined it. It seemed unharmed. The wispy tendrils of aether had left no trace on the spoon, neither of physical nor an aetherial nature—as best as his knowledge of aether allowed.

Kyrus set the spoon back down gently on the desk and repeated the incantation. It lifted off the desk, same as before. Kyrus reached for his quill and a fresh sheet of paper and began writing out the spell properly. He noted the inflection of each syllable he had used, and began to write out a detailed description of the gesture but stopped short; he intended to experiment with the subtleties of the spoken component of the incantation as well as the motions, and a lengthy longhand accounting was going to be cumbersome. He needed some quicker symbology for his work.

Kyrus paused a moment to think of what he should start out with. He held no illusion of coming up with a perfect solution straightaway. He expected that he would refine his methodology, and that it would improve along with his newfound mystical talents.

He began to draw a pair of hands, held apart, just as they would be when the spellcasting began. However, he noticed a problem almost immediately. Despite his extensive expertise at writing, he was no artist. The blotchy little squiggles that appeared on the paper more resembled a glove—discarded and trodden into ill-repair in the gutter of a thoroughfare—than of a human hand. His sense of perspective was awful, and the fingers were uneven, differing in length and thickness, with no anatomical analog to where they seemed to bend. Despite several attempts, he saw no way that an uninformed observer would ever decipher what motions he was trying to portray.

Slightly discouraged, Kyrus decided to have a little fun.

"Haru bedaessi leoki kwatuan gelora."

He levitated the pages that held his poor attempts at documentation, lifting them as easily as he had the spoon. They began to drift slightly, as even his breath was enough to set them adrift, but he reached out and steadied them a bit. Then, reaching into the aether, he drew some of the magic essence into himself. Not using it for any spell, he just refocused it on the paper. Remembering the heat such an action produced, he was unsurprised when, before long, the paper smoldered then caught fire. He watched the aether around the paper lose its grip as paper turned to ash, and ash sprinkled to the ground, cut loose from the bit still unburnt. Eventually there was nothing left unburnt, and the aether no longer held anything at all.

Brushing aside the need to figure out how best to document his research, Kyrus figured on spending the rest of the evening playing and practicing. There would be time to be a scientist and wizard later. He might well wake up the next morning and find that his powers had disappeared as swiftly as they had been discovered, or so he told himself; he ought to enjoy it a bit at least.

Kyrus tossed the spoon in the air, quickly repeating the incantation: *"Haru bedaessi leoki kwatuan gelora."*

He lifted his palms and finished the spell just before the spoon touched the floor. With the spoon hovering a handspan above the floorboards, he slowly continued to raise his hands, trying to get the spoon to rise higher. The spoon did a fair impression of his own movement, moving up as fast as he moved his hands, just as he had hoped. Kyrus extended his arms fully above his head, then got up on his toes; the spoon was nearly waist high.

Kyrus lowered his hands again and was able to set the spoon down on the floor. He repeated this game a few more times, finding that he could move it not only up and down, but to the side as well. He kept at it for longer than he had meant to and was interrupted by his light abruptly winking out of existence.

"Aleph kalai abdu" and a quick circle with his fingers, hardly given any thought, turned the room to near daylight again.

"Hmm," muttered Kyrus, "maybe that one would be better to start with."

With that, he sat down at the desk again and attempted to write out the spell. Startled by the sudden disappearance and reappearance of the light, Ash sneaked across the room and up into Kryus's lap, seeking comfort.

"Well hello there, old boy. Did not like that little eclipse, did you?"

Kyrus reached down absentmindedly to pet Ash and noticed something unusual. While he was aware that his own body gave off aether, he was just noticing how much Ash emitted. It was considerably more than Kyrus had seen other people produce, even more so if one were to consider the size of his much smaller body. Kyrus had surreptitiously watched passersby to see what they and so many other things looked like in the aether. A lack of perspective prevented him from getting a good sense of his own Source's output of the stuff. He could not help but wonder if the fairy tales—with their talk of witches' familiars and keeping cats—did not hold some element of truth behind them. He could easily see how keeping such a strong source of aether around could be useful. It would be like a farmer working the most arable land available, or brigands lying in wait on the most lucrative trade routes.

Still pondering this new revelation, Kyrus began jotting down his trusty light spell on the paper in front of him. As Kyrus tore his gaze from the lazy miasma of aether wafting out of the cat in his lap, he decided to have another stab at notating spell gestures. He blinked at the paper in front of him though, not immediately recognizing what he had just written. There were strange, otherworldly symbols on the page that he did not quite recall meaning to write. They were in no language he had ever written, and yet he knew quite well what they said. *Aleph kalai abdu*, with unique symbols that conveyed not only the sounds, but pitch, inflection, and relative quickness of each syllable. Intermixed were other symbols that had no pronunciation: these were the notations that described, in quite adequate detail, the motions that were required for the spell. Kyrus's hand had done it nearly of its own accord, as if it were so rote an activity as writing his own signature.

Kyrus was a scribe, and long years of practice had long since dissociated the thought of writing from the act of writing. A word existed in his mind, and when he willed it to paper, his hand knew what to do. He did not concern himself over what strokes of the quill went into making a Q or an F; he had progressed past the stage of having to consciously worry about those minor details long ago. If he was copying something, he almost did not need to think at all. His eyes would see the words, and his hand would repeat them. This, though, was new. Not only had he not really thought specifically about what he was writing, he wrote something he had never seen before. That was puzzling. Even more puzzling was that it was so easy for him to understand its meaning.

Slowly and deliberately, Kyrus lifted his quill. Staring suspiciously at the strange text he had written, he attempted to duplicate it just below where he had penned the original. His hand effortlessly went through a series of sweeps and scratches, neatly and professionally. While there were several lines to each symbol he wrote, there was a certain order that just made sense, a flow to the quill strokes that seemed well thought out.

Kyrus was certain he had done this before. There was no way this was the first time he had used this script, written these symbols, practiced writing out that spell. Somewhere in his memory, memories of dreams long since consciously forgotten, he had done this before, and by the ease with which it came to him, he had done it a lot. The action was rote, unthinking, and easy. Much the way he could knot the laces of his own shoes, his hands knew better what to do than did his mind.

Initially the thought of a repository of knowledge, contents unknown and cached away deep in the hidden nooks of his own brain, disturbed Kyrus. But as he pondered it further, he realized that he was not entirely guessing at this whole business. Some part of him, at some level, knew what it was doing, what *he* was doing. Somewhere, sometime, whether his dreams were real or a prophetic delusion come true, he knew what he was doing. Kyrus had long enjoyed the diversion his dreams offered, but it was the first time he had realized he may have been getting an education all his life as he slept.

The hour had drawn late and Kyrus experimented and pondered, and he was beginning to notice that his eyes had started to ache and burn with fatigue. He slumped back in his chair and blinked hard a few times and tried to rub the fatigue out of them with his fingers. He did not want to sleep. There was too much new and exciting to discover.

Pushing back his chair, he disturbed an anxious but comfortable Ash, who had been quite content to curl up in Kyrus's lap as he worked. Jumping to the floor as the lap he had occupied disappeared from beneath him, the cat followed Kyrus as he headed downstairs to put on a kettle of tea. Kyrus's steps were a bit heavy and clumsy as he fought back the urge to curl up in his nice soft bed and give up on wizardry for the night. Ash kept back a bit out of prudence, lest he be stepped on.

Outside the bedroom, night had claimed the rest of the residence. Kyrus had been up and down these stairs thousands of times, though, and was not concerned, darkness and fatigue hardly registering. Nevertheless he would need light to make tea by.

"*Aleph kalai abdu,*" and most of the ground floor was lit.

The tiny rush of aether was refreshing, and Kyrus paused just long enough to consider whether keeping up those little rushes of exhilaration would be enough to keep him awake. He continued down the stair, shaking his head.

No, I need a good strong tea; at least I know how that works.

111

Kyrus poured a kettle of water and dropped in the tea leaves, a mix of exotic herbs that Abbiley had introduced him to at a little shop across town. It was a bitter drink, but it had a really invigorating quality to it. It was imported from faraway Krang, where tea brewing was supposedly elevated to an art form, with most respectable citizens having their own personal blend of leaves and spices.

The stove was cold, and Kyrus had little patience to start a fire. He held the kettle at arm's length by its wooden handle and began diverting aether into it. Slowly at first, and ever quicker as he got a feel for it, Kyrus brought the kettle to a whistling boil in mere moments. Kyrus set it atop the stove for a few minutes to let the tea steep, then poured himself a cup.

The aroma of plants that Kyrus would probably never see in his lifetime filled the room. The sharp, bitter flavor of the first sip he took quickly began clearing his head, first with the hot, steamy vapors, then with a burst of something contained within the mysterious mixture. Kyrus had never met a Krangan, but he was sure the one who had concocted his tea was a genius. Kyrus felt focused and alert by the time he finished the cup, though there was a strange, almost disembodied ache throughout him—fatigue he was now able to set aside and ignore for a while.

Kyrus walked over to the stove to pour himself another cup to bring upstairs with him as he continued his work, when he caught sight of his work desk. On the corner, stacked neatly, were his pages for the shippers' bylaws. The original was set next to them separately. Kyrus had been almost interested enough to make himself a ninth copy earlier in the day. Perhaps he had another diversion to keep his spell practice interesting. He took his second cup of the Krangan tea, walked over to his desk, and sat down. Picking up the eight commissioned copies, he set them aside, away from the ink pot and where he intended to try his next experiment; it was far too likely for some small thing to go wrong and he did not want to have to redo an entire day's work—or research how to remove ink from paper magically.

Kyrus set up a fresh sheet of paper in front of him alongside the original copy. The original was little more than a set of notes, not needed beyond Kyrus's use of them, and if something were to happen to them, it could be explained away, at least. Kyrus selected a quill and uncovered his ink well.

"Haru bedaessi leoki kwatuan gelora."

The quill lifted gently off the desk. Kyrus moved his hand slightly, willing the quill to follow his motion, and ponderously guided it through the air and dipped the tip into the ink. He pulled it out again, even managing to gently wipe the excess ink from the tip. He brought it over to the page and began painstakingly crafting letters on the blank whiteness of the paper.

Kyrus held his hand crooked as if it actually held the quill, rather than it being a handsbreadth away and suspended in midair by an aether that only he, as far as he knew, was able to see. He took his hand through the same motions he would normally use to write, though much more slowly, still unsure of how well the quill and the magic would be able to keep up with him. Letter by letter, though, word by word, page by page, Kyrus sped his hand, and the quill kept pace.

Kyrus had not paid so close attention to the actual mechanics of his profession in a long time. He was exaggerating his movements, going through them as technically soundly as he knew in his head they should be. He was aware that his hand had long practice and its own ideas how letters ought to be written, but he was more keenly aware of the quill this time than he was of his hand's daily activity, and as a result, he was working his hand in ways it was unused to. Halfway through finishing his personal copy of the bylaws, his hand cramped up suddenly.

The quill kept going. Forgetting the pain in his cramped hand, Kyrus watched in fascination as the quill ignored the movements of his hand—now clenched nearly shut in a spasm—and finished the word he had been in the middle of.

Kyrus grinned, working his left hand against the knotted muscle in his right to ease the cramp, and concentrated not on the movements of his hand, but on the movements the quill should take. It was awkward at first, and the writing not so crisp and clear as when he had used his own writing as a mental model for the quill to mimic, but he picked right back up where he left off. Faster and faster, Kyrus pushed the quill to see how quickly it could follow his thoughts, and indeed it was quick. Words flew down onto the paper. Trips to the ink pot and back left tiny trails of ink flecks, and Kyrus cared little. Letters were formed haphazardly as the quill was often at a poor angle to write, but Kyrus chalked it up to something he would get better at with more practice.

Within a short time of realizing his hand was not needed to guide the quill, Kyrus had finished the extra copy of the shippers' bylaws. Kyrus's very own copy of the world-wise men's view of life beyond Acardia—and how to exploit it for profit—was now set out in front of him.

Kyrus was giddy. He poured another cup of his new favorite tea and thought about what he should try next. He noticed his hands were trembling with fatigue as he poured, though. He noticed also that his head was feeling heavy and a bit fuzzy. While he might possess magic, the tea was merely an extraordinary concoction of the mundane, and he had discovered its limits. Finally giving in to practicality and the needs of the clumsy vessel that carried around his brain, Kyrus set aside his cup of tea unfinished and headed up the stairs.

Ash, who'd had enough of magical shenanigans with the lights, chose to remain below and curl up atop the stove with the still-warm kettle. As Kyrus ended the light spell illuminating the work area, Ash yawned and quickly went to sleep.

Kyrus collapsed into his bed fully clothed. He ached throughout his body and mind, but it was the exhausted ache of a victorious gladiator. His battle had been fought and won, and he now needed rest before he would be ready to begin anew. He had turned lights on and off, made tea, and written a set of guild rules rather poorly, but he had done it with magic.

He felt like one of the mighty wizards of the fairy tales.

Chapter 13 - Returning Home

"How's that now?" Jodoul asked. "What do you mean that we can't go back to bein' soldiers?"

He rode atop one of the pilfered horses from the garrison and was now embroiled in a conversation about what they would do once they got back to the Empire proper.

"You have seen too much, been too close to me, witnessed the way I was living out there. I cannot have you mixing back in with the common soldiers like it never happened," Rashan replied.

They were all riding close together and talking loudly enough for all to hear. Rashan had slowed their progress back to Kadris, assuring everyone that the message about the goblin raiders had arrived. Rashan's change of heart after the massacre had quickly resolved itself into a determination to resume his place atop the pecking order of the Kadrin sorcerous hierarchy.

"This is no free pension to live out your days in luxury, but you are not going back to front-line duty or digging latrines. I shall find places for you all, once everything has fallen back into place."

"You are assuming you will be welcomed back so easily? Surely High Sorcerer Gravis is not going to step aside and cede you the position," Iridan chimed in. He rode right next to Rashan on one of the smaller horses, a white mare that had a grey streak down her chest.

"Of course not. I do not plan on making it a choice, though. By all rights, I outrank him, even now. The position of high sorcerer is still a lesser one than warlock, and I never officially resigned. Traditionally the role of high sorcerer is assumed by a warlock as well, but I may allow him to keep his title and role as second in command should he be cooperative during the transition."

Iridan looked visibly concerned. "'Cooperative?' High Sorcerer Gravis is not known to be one for compromise, let alone ceding rule of the Inner Circle to someone who has not set foot in the Empire for a century. Suppose he is not cooperative? What then?"

"Do not worry. Leadership of the Inner Circle has always been a small part politics and a large part aetherial might. Despite not being current with the doings at court and the petty backstabbing amongst the Imperial Circle, I shall have no problem demonstrating that I am the rightful leader of the Empire's sorcerers ... and the knighthood. I suspect we will find far less resistance on that front, however."

"Why is that?" Brannis asked. "I have been through both the Academy and the School of Arms, and if anything, the knighthood is more hidebound and traditional than even the sorcerers." Flanking Rashan on the other side from Iridan, Brannis had been the counterpoint to Rashan's arguments since he began making hints to his post-return plans for the Empire. "They will not just step aside and allow you to take charge of the order."

"Well, I think they value tradition more than you even know. Those old war-mules have always looked back on the 'better times,' every generation of them. And let me tell you this much: those better times nearly always coincided with the ascension of a warlock to lead the Empire in battle. There is no glory in parades remembering someone else's wars. Plunder, conquest, the expansion of the Empire, and throwing down the broken corpses of old foes: those make for the tales that the old men tell. Most warriors, when they reach the age where creaking bones and failing sight limit them to hearth sides or their beds, want nothing more than to relive the glory of their youth and see wonder and admiration in the eyes of their young kinfolk. Pity the ones who have no tales to tell ... or who cannot lie.

"No, the old guard will put up enough of a resistance to show they care, and they will make sure I have convinced them thoroughly that my claim is authentic, which I have no worry of accomplishing. Then they will salute and step aside."

Brannis noted that Rashan now sounded confident. His demeanor had changed markedly. He was no longer quiet and unassuming, content to let Brannis lead them and keep out of sight, back with Iridan. Now when he asked questions, he sought only information, or to make one think of something in a new way. He no longer asked permission or even hinted that it might be necessary. He seemed to just have naturally taken over command. If his claims were all true, it seemed he was even within his rights to do so.

"What if they charge you with abandoning your responsibility to the Empire?" Brannis asked. "A Kadrin officer could never get away with a long unexplained absence without charges being brought. What will you tell them of the time you spent outside the Empire's borders, with no word."

"Perhaps they shall try that, though I think the circumstances are certainly unusual enough and the justification legitimate enough, that I will weather questioning well enough," Rashan said, somewhat more quietly.

"If'n you do not mind me askin', just what was the circumstances?" a soldier named Tulok asked from the back of the group.

"Do you know the history of the Necromancer Wars?" Rashan asked.

There was general muttering at the question.

"I do," Brannis said.

Iridan nodded.

"What of the Battle of Farren's Plain?" Rashan continued.

"No, I cannot say that I know that one," Brannis responded. He had been a good student and had an excellent memory, especially battles. The Kadrin Empire had a rich history of wars, and Brannis knew them all quite well. He looked skeptically at Rashan, possibly having caught hold of a thread that could unravel his story.

"Well then, what do you know of the last great battle of the Third Necromancer War?"

"Well, that would be the Battle of the Dead Earth. That is when Warlock Rashan—err, you, I suppose—unleashed a magic of unfathomable power that consumed both armies. There were no survivors, and the land itself was cracked and broken, with every plant, animal, and man not just dead but reduced to skeletal remains. Nothing grew there for winters." Brannis recounted the story as best he remembered it being taught to him as a boy.

"So they ended up calling it the Battle of the Dead Earth, did they?" Rashan mused. "Would you like to hear the rest of the tale?"

Rashan didn't wait for a reply: "It had begun to rain as the final blows rang out from the forge. It was an open-air smithy that adjoined the royal stables. The work had taken much longer than I had expected. I am no blacksmith, nor was I then, but I felt it was something I had to do myself. My handiwork was good enough to pass the muster of many a smith in the Empire, though candidly I must admit I used aether to guide my hammer. And I did not just guide the blows of the hammer to shape the metal of the blade, but I forged aether right into the alloy, and not without structure, either. The blade had a purpose, and just as that purpose was finished being crafted into it, one of my apprentices, a promising young man named Sarthon, spoke up.

"'Your work does not pass unnoticed,' he told me. I always valued thinkers who spoke their mind over the obsequious bootlicks the others in the Inner Circle seemed to prefer, so I asked him what he meant by that.

"'The heavens themselves cry at what you have wrought here,' he said, gesturing up to the rain-soaked sky. I had paid little attention to the weather, but it was indeed a foul day he was attributing to my handiwork. I took no offense, for indeed I had created something terrible. It seemed Sarthon was a bit of a poet, and I liked the image he had conjured in my mind.

"'Well then,' I replied, 'I shall call the sword "Heavens Cry."'" It seemed somehow appropriate. The task I had set out for was an unpleasant one, and I was equal to it. I had spent winters fighting back the legions of dead that Loramar and his underlings kept creating and expanding. Several of the Empire's protectorates had been freed from our reign in the aftermath of the previous wars, and this time, Loramar seemed intent at striking at the heart of the Empire. He had been bypassing the larger cities in favor of sacking villages and moving quickly, carving a path that one could see led straight to Kadris.

"Here was our dilemma, though. You probably recall their name, Brannis—as might you, Iridan—but for the rest of you, should you not remember your history, my men were called the Red Riders. I stole them from the Imperial Academy and trained them as knights. Their magical training I diverted toward a single purpose: maintaining their hold on their own Source. You see, such was the evil of the necromancers that even approaching them was fatal. They drew aether not just from the world around them, but straight from living Sources. They could, and did, kill men outright, just by draining them dry inside. A man killed like that was easier for them to re-animate, and sounder of body, than one who had been rent apart by blades or magic. Armies of foot soldiers would march into battle under one banner and end up fighting for their enemy.

"My Red Riders could wade into the middle of the fray, hacking down the dead. Our steeds were fashioned from nothing but aether, constructs I had made myself that were difficult and time-consuming to unravel, and sturdy enough to bear the rigors of battle. We brought nothing and no one with us that could be turned against us. I stole half a generation of sorcerers from Kadrin, but it was needed.

"I had known that blades alone would not be enough. They were too many and we were too few. My own power I used mostly to defend us from the other tricks the necromancers knew, though even at that I had to be wary of all the dead aether that followed the walking corpses everywhere they went. That was why I created Heavens Cry: to destroy an army.

"The fateful day we met Loramar's army in Farren's Plain, we faced the entire might of the Great Necromancer and all his apprentices. It was his final march toward Kadris itself, and he was preparing to do battle with all the forces we could muster. I had left scouts a day's ride behind us, so that if we failed to stop them, word would reach Kadris for everyone to evacuate before the battle for the city. All who lived there were weapons waiting to be wielded against the Inner Circle should the dead army get that far.

"Farren's Plain was farmland in those days. The wheat fields were knee high—not quite tall enough for a good ambush, had our hundred or so had any need for stealth. Stealth was not an option for what I intended.

"Each time we had fought Loramar, we would attack and withdraw. We would break his dead soldiers and ruin them so they could hold aether no longer, then ride off without letting him have any more corpses to replace them. It was wearying work, but we had been able to eventually wear down his armies and win two wars. But in the third war, Loramar had done better. He kept his armies far from the territories the Red Riders kept safe and amassed a huge force, one that our strike-and-flee tactics could not combat quickly enough to protect the heart of the Empire.

"That day at Farren's Plain, we charged into the vast legion with no thought of escape. The necromancers had grown used to our attacks and weathered them, rather than putting serious effort to destroying us. I had thwarted them each time they had tried, and they had grown weary of wasting aether against my defenses. But that day, they saw blasts of aether and pieces of the dead flung like leaves on the wind. They realized I was no longer on the defensive, providing cover for the Riders. No, I was carving a swath straight for them, safe at the center of a sea of dead bodyguards. They panicked, and they attacked.

"My Riders had been trained to protect their Source, but I had done better. My men could be overwhelmed by the sheer force of the necromancers' combined powers, but my Source I had turned into a fortress. You see, I had already by this point gone beyond my mortal limits. The quest to find a way to defeat Loramar had led me to the perfection of my defenses against him. Unfazed by their impotent assaults directly on my Source, they tried conventional magics on me, but those were pitiful, atrophied powers, forgotten lessons that could not be relearned in the midst of battle.

"I cut my way to the heart of their army, within sight of Loramar, the only one who posed a threat to me personally. As my men died around me by the dozens, I unleashed the power I had crafted into Heavens Cry. I drove the blade into the earth at my feet with all my might, nearly to the hilt, and I drew all the aether I could. I drew from anything and everything I could grasp hold of, and I fed it into the sword. The ground cracked and split beneath my feet, in an ever-widening area. From the cracks a caustic fog arose and clawed at the flesh of the living and the dead alike. Nothing could bear its touch for long. Loramar withstood it best, but even then, it seemed unsatisfying how quickly he succumbed to its power.

"But I became the center of a maelstrom. I had made sure the sword could finish its task. Whether I survived the day or not, I wanted to ensure that none of the necromancers made it out of that field alive. The sword continued to draw all the aether in the area. The field of wheat, Red Riders, Loramar, his apprentices, and the animate dead, all were drained to the last wisp of aether as the sinister fog grew and spread. Cloth and leather, skin and sinew, the fog devoured it all, save my own flesh; I was its creator, and in its crafting, I was able to ensure at least that one small self-protection. My Source was safe from it as well, though I could not teach it to let that be. I was immortal already, a demon as you would call me, and my Source had no weakness through which aether might be pulled.

"Minutes passed, and I stared at nothing but the ground where the blade had entered. When I looked up, there was almost nothing left. Where I had moments earlier ridden into battle beside a hundred men and faced an army of uncountable thousands, there was nothing left that moved. The fog dissipated soon after the last of the aether had been burned off, and I could see to the horizon in all directions, and there was little left but cracked earth, fallen weapons, and a few bits of camp debris to tell there had been living men there at all. Bits of skeletons lay here and there, not fully consumed before the fog had gone, enough to hint at the vast scope of the carnage.

"I felt dizzy and sick. My life was war and carnage, and such a clean battlefield was nothing to my sensibilities, having seen the guts of friend and foe alike spilled an arm's length from me more times than I cared to count. No, it was being a conduit for all that aether, and not just aether, but dead aether. Imagine if you had gorged yourself at a feast, only to find that half the food was rotten with maggots.

"I felt infested, unclean. It was a nearly indescribable sensation. I stumbled away from the battlefield, confused. I am not one who is used to uncertainty, but I did not know how to cleanse myself of the aether that had gotten into me, that had merged with my own Source. I did not want to bring that back to Kadris with me, nor to anyone I wished to remain safe, so I set off alone to find seclusion and hoped that I could cleanse myself of the taint I had acquired.

"The rest is a tale longer than the trip we have remaining before us. Perhaps I shall tell bits of it, but understand that I left the Empire after ending its greatest threat in centuries, and then stayed away for its own good. If I stayed longer than perhaps necessity dictated, I would say that I earned it."

And with that, Rashan left them to consider his tale … and the missing bits of history that he had just revealed.

Brannis knew well that the historical account said no one had lived through the Battle of the Dead Earth.

* * * * * * * *

The rest of the day passed more quietly. After finishing his tale, Rashan became somewhat subdued, as if he had perhaps given them a bit too much insight into his past. When Brannis, Iridan, and all the rest had eagerly tried to find out what had happened thereafter, Rashan told them that they would have to wait for another time when he was feeling loquacious.

The open farmland they had been passing through gave way to a small town called Pevett. It sprawled on either side of the Thadagar River, a few hundred houses, mostly with thatched roofs, a marketplace, and some mills. More importantly to Kadrin, it was a shipping port for transferring goods up and down the Thadagar as well as dispersing the riverboats' cargoes to the smaller surrounding villages. Most importantly, within its borders was the West Way Bridge, one of the main crossings of the slow, deep Thadagar River, and where Brannis and his remaining command were intending to cross.

The town was surrounded by a wall of rough-cut stone and mortar, with sentry towers at infrequent intervals. Pevett was far enough from the borderlands that the wall defined the town more than it defended it. It was kept in good repair, as Pevett was a prosperous town and the local lord who ruled it, Lord Fenrigar Whitestag, was a responsible, prudent man. Pevett was a hub of commerce, and Fenrigar believed that if war ever came, it would be a valuable target for disrupting the western half of the Empire proper.

Brannis took the lead as they approached the gates. Heavily armed though they were, they bore imperial garb and insignia, the golden fist upon a red triangular background. Brannis did not expect difficulty. The gate stood wide and there was no move to bar or defend it as they drew near.

"Hail, Gatekeeper!" Brannis called out.

"Gatekeeper" was perhaps overly formal, given that the lone man preventing their entry was a bored-looking young man from the local militia, wearing Lord Fenrigar's green-and-black livery, with a sword still sheathed at his hip. He also carried a slate and chalk.

"Peace, Sir Knight. Identify yourself and state your business here in Pevett. We were not expecting any envoy from the knights."

The sentry's voice was thin and reedy, and he did not pause once in his greeting, rushing it all out in one long breath. He looked over the group, nodding to himself at each, and made a series of marks on his slate.

"I am Sir Brannis Solaran, commander of the Eighth Battalion, and this is what remains of my command. We are en route to Kadris to report and receive new orders. And this is Iridan Korian, of the Imperial Circle. He was assigned to accompany my command and lend the Circle's support to our efforts," Brannis replied. Then he added in a lower voice, "And we are rather road weary and seek soft beds for the night before we travel onward."

"Very well, I shall send word ahead to Lord Fenrigar. If you would be so good as to follow the main thoroughfare to the town center and bear left, you will find a warm welcome at the keep. Lord Fenrigar has always been a friend of the knighthood." A deep breath and then, "My name is Snead, and if you require anything, please allow me to assist you."

Brannis wondered if there was some sort of condition that the man suffered from that made him gasp out his speech thus.

"Thank you," Brannis said, "but we do not require—"

"Actually, Snead," Iridan interrupted, " if you could be so good as to point my way to the Circle's meeting place here in Pevett, I would much like to confer with my colleagues." And aside to Brannis, he confided, "I would like to confirm that our warning was received, and send word ahead of our impending arrival. Pevett has a speaking stone unless I am mistaken."

"Very well," Brannis said, "show my friend the way to the Circle's home in Pevett, and the rest of us will find ourselves accommodations for the night. We are no dignitaries, merely soldiers who must report back to Kadris with all practical haste. It would be unseemly to be feted by your most gracious Lord Fenrigar when we have such pressing business. Please pass our regards along to his lordship, and should he still require our presence, we will of course oblige."

Brannis had always been a natural at sidestepping social occasions he did not care to become entangled in.

"Very well, sir. If you insist." Snead seemed nonplussed by their declining Lord Fenrigar's hospitality. "If you head for the dockside, you can find—"

"We shall manage fine on our own," Rashan said. "I am familiar with the town."

It was the first Rashan had spoken since they arrived at the gates. He had agreed to let Brannis, uniformed officer and knight of the Kadrin Empire, smooth the introductions, but he clearly still viewed himself as the one in charge. He urged his horse forward and past the rest of the group. Brannis and the others fell in behind, and Iridan split off to go seek out the local sorcerers. Brannis nodded a brief acknowledgment to Snead as they passed.

When they were well out of earshot of Snead, Rashan spoke: "I have not been here in a long time, but while I suspect it may be under new ownership, the Rockshore Inn and Tavern, or its successor, ought to still be just a short walk from the dockside.

"I am curious, Brannis. If he had asked the rest of our names, what would you have told him? The truth, and count on a general ignorance of history to make it just slip by unnoticed? Would you have lied, or better yet, would you have proudly announced you were bringing the great Warlock Rashan back home with you?" Rashan chuckled, clearly enjoying pondering what Brannis might have done.

"I suppose I could have let Snead decide. I cannot be held accountable for a man's education, nor for his lack of one. I think you underestimate yourself, though, if you think your name forgotten. 'Rashan's Bargain,' remember? Perhaps he would not know the origin of the phrase, but the name would have likely stuck in his ear, possibly enough to bother him into inquiring further, if he did not know the tale already," Brannis said.

For whatever reason, the way Rashan asked questions worked its way past any thought of whether he should answer or not. He seemed to take an interest in dissecting his own thought process aloud.

"Ahh, what an unfortunate association," Rashan said. "I know, I have heard the phrase enough times, even before leaving the Empire. You have not seen a face go quite as red so quickly as when someone realizes they have been overheard by the warlock whose name they have just used so disparagingly. Believe what you will about me—and I know my reputation is as bloody as it is well-earned—but I have never taken retribution for such casual disrespect. I save my vitriol for my enemies, and I have no enemies among my own people. I am their champion, their defender, their weapon. I am the bloody right hand of their emperor, loyally cutting down whatever His Highness directs me against. All I have done has been to carry out the emperor's will, for good or ill."

Brannis noted that Rashan grew increasingly impassioned as he spoke, clearly proud of his service in the emperor's name. The streets were busy, and among the noise of the crowd, no one was paying them enough attention to bother eavesdropping, though anyone who had would have been fascinated.

"So all the wars, all the conquests, it was all the emperor's idea?" Brannis asked.

"Emperors, plural. Mind you, Brannis, that I was far from young at the Battle of Farren's Plain. I served four emperors, each with their own way of keeping the Empire. I first took the mantle of warlock during the reign of Escelon the Fourth. He was old and knew his health was failing. He told me that he wanted his empire secured before his son took the throne. He had me drive back the goblins—likely ancestors of the ones you recently encountered—from the northwest of the Empire and back up into the Granite Talons Mountain Range. I took ships and sank the fleets of Gar-Danel that had preyed on our merchants. I was preparing to launch a full-scale war against Megrenn when Escelon died one night in his sleep.

"Tameron the First was his heir and did not see things as his father did. He had me stop my planned invasion and focus my efforts on building the strength of the Empire from within. He wanted me to train others to be warlocks and to teach our sorcerers how to do battle—and I assure you there is a difference." Brannis nodded. "Under his long rule, Kadrin waged no war of aggression, but twice fought off smaller foes who sought to steal small stretches of land while we seemed passive. I also killed three of my own sons trying to make warlocks out of them." Rashan paused for a moment and sighed, seeming to drift away mentally from the conversation for just a moment. "It cannot be done so easily, you know. The talent is either there or it is not. It was a hard thing to learn.

"After Tameron was Liead. Liead the Only, for he forbade his ancestors from reusing his name. He and I were friends. I had educated him as a boy, and he grew up as more like a son to me than to the emperor. He shared my views and saw the Kadrin Empire for what it could be, and not what it was. It was he who gave me wide latitude to expand the Empire wherever I could. It was under his reign that my Megrenn invasion took place, whence my appellation was earned, and when we added Tuermon, Ghelk, and Safschan to the Empire. Loramar was Ghelkan, and his rise was a consequence of our conquest. The First and Second Necromancer Wars were both fought during Liead's time as emperor.

"When Merenon the Second took the throne, I was well entrenched as his main adviser, having been his father's most trusted friend for over sixty summers. He was a brilliant strategist; I made sure of that. It was his idea to form the Red Riders," Rashan said, sighing yet again, "and doom so many of our young sorcerers to a life of battle against the dead. But his idea was what saved us from Loramar. Well, saved Kadrin anyway; I suppose I would have survived in any event."

* * * * * * * *

"So what you are saying is, you would almost have preferred that I reveal you as the great and powerful Rashan, long-lost warlock of the Empire and returning hero," Brannis suggested. "Trying to stir the stew a bit before our arrival in Kadrin, letting rumor be your herald?"

Rashan slit his eyes at Brannis. The boy was no fool. Rashan had always preferred for his words to have two meanings when possible; it was just more efficient. Most who heard him would only listen to the obvious, the blustering of an old war-mule of a sorcerer, claiming to be Warlock Rashan. He liked to discover who actually paid attention to why he spoke, and not just the plain meaning of the words. Those who did were the ones who were useful beyond carrying out orders; they were the thinkers who could act on their own and succeed. The young knight's motives were simple enough to read, so he had no doubt of Brannis's loyalty to the Empire, and being kin made it even simpler. Yes, he would put Brannis to use.

"No, merely amusing myself at the possible scene it might have caused. You are right, though: that man Snead may well have figured it out, even if he would not have believed it," Rashan said. "Besides, we are not going to be sneaking up on anyone. They will know rather quickly when we are to be arriving, and who you are supposedly bringing with you."

* * * * * * * *

The Imperial Circle's home in Pevett was a hexagonal granite tower of modest size, rising to a copper dome three stories up. The tower was surrounded by a wrought-iron fence of ornate design, artfully distracting from the spikes at its top. The gate stood open, allowing convenient access to the cobbled path to the main door. There was no hitching post out front, so Iridan tied his horse's reigns to the fence.

Iridan took the path at a slow walk, taking in the carefully manicured grass and small flowers that made up the courtyard that surrounded the tower. Though admittedly he had not seen the lord's keep on the other side of the town, it was the only landscaped part of Pevett he had seen. Stone benches and tables were interspersed across the grounds but were unoccupied. The hour was growing late, and if anyone had partaken of the pleasant autumn weather, they had already sought shelter from the chill that dusk was already beginning to bring.

The door at the end of the path stood atop three wide stone steps and was a massive thing of carved panels, stained a deep reddish-black with brass adornments at the edges where time and use might have otherwise worn it. Iridan imagined that it was probably oak, but he was no good with trees and what their wood looked like. There was no guard posted outside, since no one with any sense would trespass on the Imperial Circle's land. Carved in the stone above the door was the motto "Herein Lies Power," written in the syllables of arcane text. He took hold of the ogre-headed knocker and rapped thrice on the door—*thock, thock, thock.*

A moment passed and Iridan waited before the door finally opened, revealing a middle-aged servant dressed in a tidy brown tunic and trousers, bearing a small emblem denoting service to the Circle: a small lightning bolt within a flame, stitched in yellow thread, meant to look gold at a casual glance. The servant's hair was grey and only ringed the periphery of his head. He wore a tiny pair of spectacles and appeared rather scholarly.

"Greetings, young man. What business brings you here?" the servant asked.

He glanced up and down at Iridan, which reminded Iridan that he was dressed most intentionally *not* to look like a sorcerer, given the hazards of his recent assignment.

"My name is Iridan Korian, Fourth Circle. I am returning from an assignment with an army regiment scouting beyond the Cloud Wall Mountains in Kelvie Forest. This is the first town we have come to that has a speaking stone, and I would be obliged if I could make use of it."

Iridian knew his rank of Fourth Circle was enough to at least garner a modicum of respect from someone who would realize that it was rather an advanced position for someone of his apparent age, though with sorcerers, trying to determine age by sight could be misleading.

"Oh, and I might ask if I could trouble your hospitality for a change of uniform. I was deployed to be inconspicuous among the soldiers I accompanied."

"Well, enter then, Iridan Korian. I will announce you to the master of Pevett Tower, Haridiar Stellarus of the Second Circle. You may make your requests of him. In the meantime, avail yourself of a late repast in the dining hall."

The servant clapped his hands, and a younger man, no larger than Iridan, came from around a corner so quickly he must have been awaiting his summons.

"Geofard," the servant said, "take our guest to the dining hall and see if the cook has kept something warm for him to sup on."

With that, the servant bowed quickly and turned to depart, leaving Iridan to Geofard's care. The young man led Iridan to a small but elegant room with a polished wood table, lit by magic, as would be the case all throughout the tower, he knew. Sorcerers left few opportunities unexploited when it came to using their magic to make their homes more comfortable. Lighting that would react to a mere gesture or word was too dear a luxury for many to consider lighting with candles.

The boy mumbled a few pleasantries and trundled off to presumably get him some dinner. Iridan had not come with the thought of a free meal in mind but found he was hungry enough not to argue, and expected that the sorcerers of Pevett were unlikely to deny themselves a fine kitchen staff.

Iridan's conjecture bore out, and he was halfway through a fine venison stew when the master of the tower arrived. The man was taller than Iridan by a head and built like a merchant. That is to say, he was rotund and looked unfamiliar with the concepts of fresh air and manual labor.

"So, back from the borderlands, I hear." Haridiar stalked across the room to clasp hands with Iridan as the latter quickly set down his spoon and stood to meet his superior. "Good lad. Way to make a name for yourself, hold one over the heads of all those pompous fools who think they will learn all about magic sniffing at the same aether from dawn to dusk. Haridiar Stellarus, Master of Pevett Tower."

"Iridan Korian, Fourth Circle, sir. Thank you for your hospitality," Iridan responded. He was about to continue, but Haridiar was quicker.

"So my man Delft says you have a favor to ask, want to use our speaking stone, is that so?" he asked.

"Well, we had sent a report back via an enspelled bird, you see, but we have no means of ensuring our message was received and understood. I would be much reassured if I was to know our warning had been heeded."

"'Warning,' you say? What sort of warning? Things not all flowers and tea cakes in the borderlands?" Haridiar's already considerable interest in Iridan seemed to suddenly grew.

"No, sir, not at all. I accompanied one hundred men, ten of them knights, into Kelvie Forest. Two other commands of similar size went as well and spread out to investigate reports of goblin activity. Fifteen remain now, including myself, and of the other two commands, we believe all are lost save two we rescued in the wood; they are included among the fifteen.

"We also picked up a traveler, a woodland hermit who gave us shelter and aided in healing a bad case of aether burn I suffered in battle. We head on to Kadris come morning, and I had hoped to convey all this to someone in the Inner Circle before we depart."

"Well, that's quite disturbing." Haridiar's face grew pale. "Nearly three hundred lost. I presume the other groups had a sorcerer assigned them as well? Do you know their names—the ones the Circle may have lost?"

"One was Kelurian Donarte, Fifth Circle, I believe. The other was Randul of Sarcen, Fourth Circle. I do not believe any others were assigned to the expedition. We have no physical evidence of their demise, but we strongly suspect it."

Iridan was glad that Haridiar was more concerned about his fellow sorcerers than about finding out details about their newest acquaintance. He was not sure how to truthfully give the tale without making himself out to be a fool or half crazed. Had he thought Rashan was lying, he could give a faithful account without casting his own credibility into doubt, but he was fairly convinced that Rashan was who he claimed to be. Let Brannis be the skeptic; Iridan *wanted* to believe.

"Terrible tragedy. Terrible tragedy." The master of Pevett Tower shook his head sadly. "By all means, take your leisure with the speaking stone. I shall leave orders that you are not to be disturbed. Until you are given leave by the Inner Circle, I will ask no further details of you. You have sated my curiosity enough that I can in good conscience allow you access to our stone. I shall press for no details that you may not be at liberty to divulge." Haridiar gave Iridan a wink. "Come right this way. Follow me."

And with that, he headed for the stairs. Iridan followed close behind. Down they went, two levels underground, the stone walls smooth and well cared for at either side of them as they descended. A fine rug hugged the middle of each stairway, thick reddish-purple fabric deadening their footfalls and reducing the echo of the stone stairwell. The sorcerers in Pevett clearly took excellent care of their home.

Haridiar stopped before a door marked "Room of Words" in arcane text. *"Geknu feroll benah,"* he intoned and then made a series of twisting motions with his fingers and wrists.

Iridan watched in the aether as the wards protecting the door unraveled. It was a common enough spell, but to unlock a particular ward required either knowing the correct gestures to pull it apart, or long hours of guesswork figuring them out. Iridan was not sure he had seen what Haridiar had done well enough to copy it, should he have the need.

"Do not worry. I shall leave it unwarded behind you. My sorcerers and servants alike are trustworthy and will leave you in peace."

With that, Haridiar left Iridan to enter the Room of Words.

The room itself was sparse. A stone table stood in the center of the octagonal room, an O-shaped rug encircling it. Four comfortable-looking high-backed chairs surrounded the table, with padded seats, backs, and arms. Set into the surface of the table was a geodesic sphere of glass. While the glass itself was of ordinary, though excellent craftsmanship, it was enchanted to communicate across vast distances with others like it.

Iridan would be trying to contact Kadris, where the Imperial Circle had their own speaking stone. He had no idea who might be attending to one at such an hour, but someone would be. He walked over to one of the chairs and sat down. He took a deep breath to calm his thoughts and reached out with both hands, laying them on the stone.

Woooom!

The stone pulsed with aether, causing a moment of dizziness to Iridan as he accustomed himself to the link. Tendrils drifted far off into the vastness of the aether, and as Iridan envisioned Kadris and the tower of the palace that the Inner Circle called home, the tendrils veered off in the direction of the Empire's capital.

Iridan lost some sense of perspective as he could simultaneously perceive his backside cushioned on the seat of a chair in Pevett while his mind felt like it was suspended in the aether halfway to Kadris. After what seemed to be just a moment or two, he heard a voice echo in the aether.

"Who is this?" the brusque voice came clearly enough, though the echo would make it hard to identify someone by voice. It was clearly male, though. *"That had best not be you again, Haridiar. I shall make my move when I make it. I will not let you harangue me into making a mistake."*

"Um, no, this is Iridan Korian, Fourth Circle. To whom am I speaking, if I might ask?" Iridan spoke aloud, knowing that his voice was carrying across the aether as well.

"I am Caladris Solaran, boy. You were sent to Kelvie Forest with my nephew," the voice responded.

Caladris had no need to identify himself by Circle; he was Inner Circle. All sorcerers in the Empire knew who the twelve members of the Inner Circle were. It would have been almost pompous of Caladris to dangle his rank about when he knew Iridan was well aware of it … which is why it surprised Iridan slightly that he had not done so. Brannis's kin were not known for their humility.

"Why are you using the Pevett Tower speaking stone?" Caladris asked. *"Have you news? We received a messenger bird, but it told little."*

"Well, that relieves me greatly. The first thing I had wanted to do was confirm that the Circle had received our warning. We were nearly wiped out. Goblins overran our camp. We believe they followed the survivors of Sir Ferren Jessair's command; his was wiped out as well, and there were but two survivors, sentries who had been cut off from the fighting. Of Sir Dennever Taldeen's force, we had heard nothing and suspect the worst."

Iridan was sweating. It was not so much the exertion of the speaking stone link—that was rather undemanding—but rather the fact that he was having this conversation with Caladris Solaran of the Inner Circle …

... and eventually he would have to mention the one member of their entourage that was going to be uncomfortable to explain.

"Tragic. Kelurian and Randul were their sorcerers, at least for the expedition. I suppose neither of them survived." There was a long sigh from Caladris, who seemed genuinely mournful. *"How did you manage to escape their fate? Was it by trick or fortune that you survived when so many others did not?"*

"We were victorious, after a fashion. We had deduced after one of the fugitive sentries arrived that he would have been followed, if not directly, then at least tracked to us. Sir Brannis had us dig in and ambush them as best we could. The losses on both sides were staggering, but I do not think more than a handful of their assault force survived to flee," Iridan said.

He felt a small swell of pride for the first time since the battle, considering how his actions had helped ensure their survival. He had not really given much thought to how the other two Kadrin forces had been destroyed utterly, and how they had actually prevailed, albeit at a terrible price.

"And what did you do in this great battle? You were sent in support of Sir Brannis's command, but if it was as wiggly a spot as you describe, I suppose you must have intervened. How did you represent yourself? Did you give a good and professional accounting, a credit to the Circle? We will have reports from the others, and your stories will be checked against one another ..." Caladris trailed off ominously.

Iridan swallowed, not entirely sure he was not going to be called to task very shortly. "I prepared the battlefield ahead of time. I had tamed wolves to patrol our perimeter, and they were the first to give warning of the assault. I gathered fog to obscure the vision, though only high enough to hinder the goblins; it was also to conceal pit traps that Sir Brannis had instructed his men to dig. When the battle joined in earnest, I used shielding spells to ward off the attacks of the goblins' firehurlers. When they gained an advantage on us, I used telekinesis to hurl debris from the campsite into their midst, killing several."

"So you are blood-drunk now, are you? Got a taste of killing?" Caladris asked. *"Have a care, boy. I know the thrill of battle can be exhilarating, but it is a path that leads to self-destruction—"*

"I was nearly overmatched by a sudden blast," Iridan interrupted, surprising even himself, but he could not let himself be lectured about self-destruction after what he had recently been through, "but was able to catch it in time by instinct, bringing up a barrier. I was too hasty, though, and blacked out. I suffered a near-fatal case of aether burn. I know no further details of the battle, as I was carried senseless from the field by the soldiers."

"A hard way to learn a lesson, but one you shall not forget." The voice had softened some, as if it had heard what it needed to hear from its interrogation, and became sympathetic. *"So, Iridan Korian, you have indeed survived. One moment."* There was a pause where Iridan felt contact with the Kadrin speaking stone break off. *"All right now. Name for me the others who survive and are returning to Kadrin with you. I shall be making a report, and I expect others will be wanting to know about their loved ones."*

"Well, apart from myself are Sir Brannis, who seemed to have suffered no lasting harm in the battle; Sir Lugren, who I believe injured his sword arm in the battle, and who has seemed unusually subdued ever since. I daresay I cannot recall more than a few words he has spoken since I recovered. Among the conscripts were Maeron, Jorafir, Braegor—"

"Do you know their family names?" Caladris interjected.

Iridan froze. He was not a part of the regiment, officially; he was merely attached temporarily for this endeavor. He had never seen the men's names, nor sought to learn them.

"Um, no, I cannot say that I do. I feel dreadful now that you mention it, but I never had reason to learn them." Iridan was not sure how well his heartfelt contrition sounded across the aether link. "Could you possibly consult someone from the army who might have a roster of names?"

"Hmm, I suppose. Carry on."

Iridan breathed an audible sigh of relief, then immediately froze up. Had Caladris heard that?

"Yes, well, there's also, um, Tulok, Fardro, Liopan, Denair, Kundragar, Huane, and Urnar." Iridan mentally ticked off the names in his head as he visualized the faces of the men he had been traveling with the past fortnight, proud that he had remembered Kun's full name. "Then there are the two survivors from Sir Ferren's force: Jodoul Brect and Tod Hellet. We questioned them upon their arrival, so I had cause to learn their surnames."

"Very well. The hour is late, and I would much like to retire for the evening. We shall be expecting you in, say, four days' time? You shall be expected at the Tower." Caladris referred, of course, to the Tower of Contemplation, the northernmost tower of the Imperial Palace and the seat of the Imperial Circle's power.

Iridan took a deep, steadying breath. "There is one other with us. We found him living in Kelvie Forest. He was knowledgeable in treating aether burn, and so they let him help nurse me back to health where I might otherwise have died. He says he lived in the Empire, was even born there, but had not been back in some time. Our encounter seemed to have given him either an excuse or at least a motivation to return to the Empire."

"Fine. What's his name? I shall write it down, but then I am off for a warm spiced wine and an even warmer bed. You lose track of time using this dratted thing, and I have come to understand that it is well past midnight; one of the attendants just alerted me."

"He gave his name as Rashan." Iridan paused to listen briefly but heard nothing but cold, eerie silence from the connection. "And gave his family name as Solaran."

"Preposterous! You have found a madman, or someone who has taken on a most unfortunate pseudonym. Have you noticed any odd behaviors about him? Does he talk to himself, or have a look in his eye of one whose wits do not quite all line up in a row? Is he dangerous?" Caladris's voice sounded nervous and worried. *"Keep a close watch on him. I know you say he helped heal you, and you should be grateful to him for that, but have a care who you take into your trust. He is obviously unstable in some way. Bring him to Kadris if you feel you must, either out of gratitude or prudence. If you feel some remuneration has been*

deserved for his assistance, by all means we can accommodate, but do not leave him unguarded among you. I will not lose a third sorcerer in this endeavor to something like carelessness in the handling of a madman."

Iridan let Caladris ramble as he thought how to put his next words into an order that indicted neither himself nor Rashan as crazed. It was going to be tough to convince Caladris when he still had doubts himself, but too many coincidences had piled up, too many details fit too cleanly into place. Iridan believed in conspiracy, in elaborate plans and deals forged in dark hallways and hidden rooms. He knew that Kadrin and its enemies all engaged in subterfuge and espionage, a game of goblins and ogres to see if a small amount of force could be used to topple a large foe. But for the life of him, he could not conceive of why anyone would want to impersonate a long-dead warlock. If Rashan's claim was false and he was a charlatan, he would be found out and destroyed the first time anyone tested his powers. If his claim was false, yet he was truly powerful, why adopt a guise so implausible as to not help but arouse all suspicion? Far easier to insinuate his way into the Imperial Circle through less conspicuous means. Unless there was a far deeper game afoot than Iridan could imagine—which he was willing to accept was a possibility—then the remaining choice was to believe.

"I have seen no odd mannerisms; in fact, he seems to be the most rational and thoughtful man I have met. His wits are quite intact, I can assure you, for I have seen him work magic, and he has done so as a warlock might: no verbal or gestural aids in his magic. I realize, of course, that plenty of sorcerers can perform the same feat any time they wish, if they are undisturbed. But he is also dangerous; I will not dispute that one. I had left out the detail of the ambush at Tibrik. The garrison had been overtaken by rebel Megrenn. Almost by reflex, he leaped the fortress wall and slaughtered every man within.

"He claims he is a demon. He claims he survived the Battle of the Dead Earth and gave an accounting of how it was won. He says that he was wounded by the necromancer's putrid aether, tainting his Source, and that he kept away to prevent himself from bringing that taint home with him."

Iridan took a quick breath, then, "And I believe him."

"I must know more."

Neither Iridan nor Caladris Solaran of the Inner Circle slept much at all that night.

Chapter 14 - The Smell of Freedom

The waves broke against the rocky shore, sending up a salty spray that scented the air with a briny musk. The sea breeze was refreshing and invigorating, a chill wind that wore away at years of oppression and the rhythmic crashing of wave upon wave eased the mind with the lull of constancy. That same tide had been washing in and out since the beginning of time, but it felt different that day.

Denrik Zayne breathed deeply of the sea air, filling his lungs. He felt free. It had been a week since he had made landfall, along with his makeshift crew. They were stashed away in a rocky inlet, a few miles south of Scar Harbor. The short cliffs that lay to the north and south of them protected them from the view of mainlanders, and there were enough crevices into them that they could easily conceal themselves when ships were spotted entering and leaving the port to their north.

Denrik watched the horizon, not for any pressing need, but rather out of habit—and a feeling of old familiarity. He could almost feel the deck of his old ship, *The Honest Merchant*, beneath his feet again as he stood at the water's edge, letting the ocean fill his vision and ignoring the shoreline. He watched the water for hours at a time, keeping a vigil, not a watch. He knew when ships would pass their camp, when he would direct his crew to cover until the threat of discovery had passed.

"Cap'n! Yer man's here!" Andur called out, breaking Denrik from his reverie.

He turned and made his way back to the cave they had taken as their temporary home. The cave was only just large enough to sleep them all, and they had salvaged little enough from the *Bringer of Hope* before Denrik had lashed the ship's wheel and set it off to sea unmanned, hopefully to run aground somewhere, conveniently misleading those who would seek their recapture. They had gone north from Rellis Island rather than head west to the nearest landfall at Trebber's Cove; if the ship managed to get anywhere near the cove, their eventual pursuers might never surmise them to have landed near Scar Harbor.

When Denrik got there, his men parted to allow him by, and he saw his guest. Robbono Stalyart was a tall, broad-shouldered man, with grease-slicked hair and a beard that he waxed to a sharp point below his chin. His dark eyes shone with genuine warmth, and his easy grin showed pearl-white teeth, giving him an air of a man completely at ease despite the hardened criminals he was visiting. He was dressed in a loose, grey tunic and dark leather vest, left open to reveal a large swath of his hairy, darkly tanned chest. The sash at his waist sported an inconspicuous bulge where Denrik deduced a knife was sheathed.

"Mr. Stalyart, what news?" Denrik asked, feeling more like Captain Zayne each time he spoke with his former first mate.

Robbono Stalyart had escaped during the surrender of *The Honest Merchant* and gotten away free and clear of the charges that had been brought against the other pirates. A phenomenal swimmer and diver, he had eluded the Acardian Navy long enough that they had given him up for drowned. It was he who had spent three years working to arrange the escape of Denrik Zayne from his imprisonment, learning the workings of the penal colony and finding its weaknesses, sending covert messages in amid supplies, and finally bribing the crew of the *Bringer of Hope*. Stalyart had met them at the inlet upon their arrival, having arranged it in advance as their meeting place for after the escape. He had broken into one of the hidden caches that Captain Zayne had stocked away for emergencies, and for Denrik Zayne, imprisonment was certainly justification enough for digging up some of the gold he had plundered.

What Denrik considered truly remarkable was that, given the chance, Stalyart had chosen to risk his own freedom on the plan to spring his former captain from exile. He could have lived well enough on one cache of loot that he would never have needed to sail again, yet here he was, in a small shoreline cave not far from Acardia's largest seaport, plotting a return to the rolling seas with the most fearsome pirate of his day. Denrik could not help but be touched at the loyalty that showed, even if there was as much for him to gain by renewing their plundering reign on the Katamic.

"Captain," Stalyart said, "it is what we have waited for. The *Harbinger* is due in port next week."

Stalyart then handed his captain a folded sheet of paper, which Denrik opened and glanced over quickly. It was a copy of the harbormaster's list of planned arrivals and departures, the second such document Stalyart had brought, beginning with their first meeting. Denrik had used it to ensure that they were all out of sight of the water when they knew a ship would be passing within spyglass range of their hideout.

"It is a frigate, and had a good reputation as a worthy ship," Stalyart said. "They are due for a rotation of crew, with several men having completed their tours, and taking on as many new men. They will also be re-provisioning and taking on a small number of the new long guns that the cannoneers have invented. Since I am known now as a well-traveled merchant, it was not suspicious when I inquired about purchasing the guns for my own ship. I was told they may only be sold to the navy." Stalyart smiled. "It will make it all the more glorious to take them for ourselves."

"What is her complement? How many men will guard her?" Denrik's mind was already formulating a plan of attack. He had long plotted how he would get back to sea with a ship of his own, so rough frameworks of various plots were already lying about in his head half finished. A frigate: it was a grand prize indeed, but a difficult prospect unless they had some sort of edge. "Do you have anyone on the inside? One of the new crew members, perhaps?"

"My Captain!" Stalyart gave a sweeping bow, doffing an imaginary cap he was not wearing. "You ruin my surprises by outguessing me. I have one better than you think, though. My half-brother serves as gunnery mate aboard *Harbinger*. He is not one that is staying behind. He will serve his turn on the berth watch, but I will visit with him when he takes his shore leave. I have no doubt he would rather make his fortune with his brother and Captain Zayne than toil for a gunner's pension in the navy."

"You sure?"

"My Captain, I will throw my brother's life and my own at your feet in this. I know that if there is any betrayal, my life is forfeit as well as my brother's. I know him."

"Err, Cap'n, this mean we're takin' a boat from the navy?" Andur asked. "I mean, ya know, we had us a boat afore, an' we shooed it off to sea empty-like. Why didn't we just keep it?"

Puzzling Andur was one of the least difficult tasks Denrik had ever performed. Even now that they were off Rellis Island, it was a task he still performed almost daily.

"Andur, have you ever *seen* a frigate?" Denrik asked, and Andur shook his head; at least he was being honest. "Well, a frigate is to that worthless little wreck of a supply ship as a sword is to a spoon."

With that, Denrik swept his cutlass, taken from the now dead guards aboard that same supply ship, from its scabbard. *Shhhhinnng!*

"Find yourself a spoon now, Andur, and defend yourself."

Denrik waved the blade in front of Andur, who nevertheless looked suddenly very nervous.

"Um. Uh. That-That," Andur stammered, "don't seem all fair to me. I-I-I don't know how to fight with a spoon!"

There was a general burst of laughter from all present.

"He don't mean for real, ya stinker! Cap'n's usin' one o' them word tricks to make a point," Jimony said with a guffaw.

Even Denrik, who felt better than he had in years, broke out in a smile at Andur's discomfiture. He sheathed his blade before he scared the poor fool senseless.

"With a ship like that, we would stand a chance against nearly any ship in the sea," Denrik said. "I have no intention of shipping wheat or spices when I sail again. I do not plan to offer my services to travelers. I intend to take up my mantle as the most feared pirate in the Katamic!" Then Denrik lowered his voice somewhat: "And I will not get there captaining a creaky wooden barrel with a sail that poor bastard calls a ship.

"So, Mr. Stalyart," Denrik said, purposely changing his demeanor to set a lighter tone, "what do you have for your captain to eat, and to drink?"

* * * * * * *

Denrik's work crew whiled away the hours and days. There was little enough to do, since they could not risk being spotted. That meant no swimming or fishing, no fires, and trying not to be too loud. That meant boring. Stalyart had brought them cards and dice to amuse themselves, but they had no money to gamble with and generally lost interest. None of them were great thinkers, but Captain had given them something that required a great deal of thought.

Denrik Zayne needed a crew. Stalyart had a few men picked out that had sailed with him on his little trading ship, *Nyurissa*, and was counting on his brother's help, but he was still quite short on men. Grudgingly, he had given his Rellis Island companions the option: they could either join his crew and learn the trade as they went, or Denrik would drop them at the nearest port of questionable character, where they might lose themselves among the locals and start anew in a land where their criminal pasts were not known.

Conscripted crews were a great tradition among both pirates and the navy of old. It showed that if properly motivated—by the lash if necessary—any dullard could be made into a serviceable sailor. But the navy had abandoned the practice decades ago with good cause. Not only were they trying to cast themselves in a better light among the reformist government's elites, but they had found that "any dullard" made an awful sailor, and a discontented and potentially mutinous one. None of Denrik's charges was a thinker, and as best he could gather, only two had useful skills he might avail himself of.

First was Grosh—Grosh Mantlegard—who was a tailor by trade. He had been rather newly anointed into the Tailors Guild when he had gotten into a heated, drunken dispute with his employer and stabbed him to death with a pair of scissors. Denrik figured that sail repair ought to be something he could manage with little trouble. As a bonus, he was also a killer, and an unrepentant one, maintaining that his boss had it coming. Such men took better than most to a life of piracy.

Then there was Tawmund Reggelend. Tawmund was the quietest of Denrik's fellow inmates, a kindness he was inclined to repay, but that was not the reason Denrik wanted him in his crew. Tawmund was built like the statue of Ptaw, the old Garnevian god of blacksmiths, that stood in Temple Square of Golis. Thick as an oak tree, and with no discernible neck, Tawmund was frighteningly strong. Years of hard labor had made him leaner, but his bulk was still considerable. He would be a natural for boarding actions and subduing captured vessels. He was also already a pirate of sorts; he was sent to Rellis Island for his part in a gang that ran a number of criminal rackets in Stollen—they were pirates on land.

Jimony was another story, however. He was a thief and a killer of the "knife you from behind" and "slit your throat in your sleep" variety. Denrik did not trust him. Sure, they were all on Rellis Island for good cause, but Denrik was a shrewd judge of character and was an expert on scoundrels in particular. There were criminals whom you could trust to do a job, take orders, and pull their weight because they knew you were good for a payoff in the end. They were the backbone of the pirate trade. Others could be hammered into that mold with the threat of violence hanging over their heads; a bosun with a scourge in hand had made many a poor sailor into an able one. This Jimony, though, was a viper if Denrik had ever seen one. He was not the sort to start a mutiny but rather the sort to try to make off with as much as he could carry after a big haul, probably leaving a few knives stuck in the poor souls stuck on watch the night he did it.

Trapped on Rellis Island, Jimony had thrown in with Denrik out of necessity. All the others in the cell had let him act as their leader, and Denrik's own vile reputation offered a good reason to pause before acting against him. Now that there was a whole world to disappear into, Denrik would not trust the man with his back turned. Sooner or later, he would be rid of him; if he took the deal to be dropped off at some distant port, so be it. If he accepted Denrik's offer to join his crew at sea, well, there would either be some convenient accident, or Denrik would have to find a good excuse to run him through. If it came to it, it might not be such a bad idea to let his new crew know who they were dealing with—and the price for crossing him.

Denrik sighed deeply and contemplated his hardest decision: Andur. Poor Andur was simpleminded, but in an earnest way that Denrik could not help taking a liking to. There was no artifice with Andur: he would say what he meant, whether it was a good idea or not, whether he grasped the situation or not. He took no offense from all the ridicule he bore; for of all the faults he had mentally, he was at least aware of the deficiency. He naturally gravitated to those who told him what to do and how to do it. He had practically been Denrik's puppy on the island. He was not exactly certain of the crime Andur had been imprisoned for, but he gathered it was rape. From years observing the man, Denrik was fairly certain he had been a dupe for someone else's crime, a brawny laborer who worked for a noble family and was too stupid to defend himself from the charge. Worse, he was the sort who could be convinced to confess without realizing the consequences.

He had no second thoughts to the man's character. If nothing else, Andur practically worshiped him and obeyed him unquestioningly. The problem was what to do with him aboard ship. He was too gullible for a bodyguard, too easily confused to be a combatant. Best he could think of was cabin boy, a position usually held by a boy of ten or twelve years. Perhaps he could be taught knots?

Denrik turned his from his musing and surveyed them from where he sat, perched on a rock with the farthest trickles of the waves lapping around it. They were all a bit nervous about being away from the cliffs, where they were better hidden, but Denrik liked being by the water. He knew when the ships would be passing; another trade ship would be hauling anchor in an hour or so, then at dusk, the fishing vessels would make port with their day's catch.

The rest amused themselves as they were able, safe in the shadows of the cliff face. Andur and Tawmund played at checkers, a painful sight to watch as the two men agonized over each move for minutes on end before making a completely pointless move. Grosh napped in the sand, with a sack for a pillow. Jimony whittled at a piece of driftwood with a knife Stalyart had left them along with a number of other basic supplies. Denrik narrowed his eyes. Particularly after his recent musings, the sight of Jimony with a knife in his hand sat ill with him.

Turning back to look out to sea, Denrik listened to the waves and sighed again. Men he might have, and few as they were, but he was even shorter on brains. Stalyart was as good a man as he had sailed with, and he had some hopes for the man's half-brother; ties of blood and a history of naval service were good signs. The handpicked men from Stalyart's merchant crew worried him only slightly. Normally he would be concerned that their loyalties to their former captain might be the ideal catalyst for a mutiny, but Stalyart would have none of that. A man who had gone to such lengths would not throw all his work away just to kill him and take his ship. Would he? Denrik shook his head. He was too far gone now to do this without Stalyart. If he played some deeper game and intended treachery, Denrik would deal with it when the time came—and in both worlds.

Denrik sat there until the time came to withdraw from sight of the shipping lanes, then got up and waded through the incoming tide to where the rest of them were sheltered. He said nothing to them and got nothing but a couple glances of mild interest from them in return. They were growing weary of each other's company in the cramped beach hideaway. They were all so close to freedom, but for the time being, they felt more trapped and cornered than they had on Rellis Island. At least there they had the certainty of a long prison sentence and no thoughts of a new life right around the bend to tease them with its closeness.

Denrik went to his things and took up a pack that Stalyart had brought earlier in the day. Unbuckling the flap, he began removing the contents. There was a well-worn set of tunic and breeches in a drab greyish-brown, a pair of soft-soled boots, a long, heavy black coat with a high collar, and a knit woolen cap dyed dark grey. There was also a small purse. Denrik took a quick look inside and estimated it contained about two hundred eckles, enough for a quick bribe or a couple good meals; it was contingency money for unplanned expenses. The last item in the pack was a small empty sheath, with a strap for buckling it around a wrist or ankle.

Denrik strode across the campsite to where Jimony sat whittling.

"Give me that," Denrik ordered as he snatched the knife from Jimony's hand.

Jimony did not resist, just shrugged and gave a sheepish grin. Denrik shoved the knife in its sheath and secured it around his left wrist.

In front of everyone, for they had long gotten over embarrassment of such things in each other's company, he changed into the clothing Stalyart had provided, save for the coat and hat.

"What's all that for?" Grosh asked, obviously not as sound asleep as he appeared to be, and he sat up. One side of him was covered in sand that had stuck to him as he lay on the beach.

"I do not fancy sailing with men I have never met, let alone stealing a ship with them and risking our lives with them. I am heading in to Scar Harbor to meet with Stalyart's men and his brother. I will take my measure of them and make sure they can be trusted."

Denrik had no reason to keep this information from them. They were not going to meet anyone whom they could betray the plan to, even accidentally.

"Don't that seem a bit dangerous?" Andur asked. "I mean, we's hiding here, so them don't find us. Won't they find you if'n ya go right to 'em?"

"I will be disguised, and I am going after nightfall. Besides, people know me by name and reputation; few have seen me face-to-face. While I am gone, I am leaving Grosh in charge. Grosh, just … do not do anything, alright? Keep everyone tucked away here until I return."

* * * * * * * *

Denrik left the camp shortly after dusk. The tide was low and he took the opportunity to skirt the shoreline rather than scrambling up the cliff wall. There were handholds aplenty, but Denrik was not as young as he once was and preferred the easier route. If the meeting lasted long enough, he might miss his chance to take the same route back before the tide came in, but he would sail that strait when he came to it.

He was dressed in the outfit left by Stalyart. Even in the late spring, nightfall by the water's edge brought a chill, especially so far north. He would not look out of place dressed as warmly as he was, and the hat and coat did much to obscure him when the coat's collar was turned up. The idea was for him to look like an old dock hand. He supposed from his long years of labor and sunburn, he probably looked the part better than if he had tried dressing up as a pirate captain. His cheekbones stood out against a more gaunt face than they had when he was living like a king out on the seas, and his stubble was half gone to grey, making him at once look both older and unkempt. He still had a hard, alert look about him, a slight forward lean, and a gaze that swept frequently out to the sides, which gave the impression of a predator. Old man or not, he was unlikely to be trifled with as he approached the roughest part of one of the tamest cities in the kingdom.

The shoreline was alternately rocky and sandy, with plenty of room to maneuver at low tide. Keeping his hands tucked into the pockets of his jacket, Denrik made good time along the water's edge as he approached Scar Harbor's docks from the south end. Scar Harbor was not naturally a deep-draft port, but a ways out, the shelf dropped off drastically. The piers, therefore, had been built unusually long, and much of the dockside was actually built up on stilts, below the high-tide mark, so as to be closer to where the boats docked.

As Denrik grew nearer to the city itself, he could see plenty of activity. The fishing vessels had come in and were busily unloading their catch—plain fish that would be rendered into oil, made into stews, and sold in poor to fair restaurants. The finer establishments got their fish from some smaller ships that hauled earlier in the day, bringing fresh catches just in time to be prepared for midday and evening meals. The boats that were unloading now were the workhorses of the Katamic, filling the fishmongers' stalls for the common folk to buy from.

Denrik approached the building nearest to the sand, a warehouse right on the edge of town. There was a short ladder up to dock level from the beach. It was good and solid, built from a pair of thick timbers running vertically, with thinner rungs poked through both and lashed into place with rope. The rungs looked newer than the rest of the ladder and the rest of the docks in general, which sported a weathered, grey look. It seemed that the rungs saw much use and spent high tide below the waterline, and so were made to be replaced as needed, and had been changed rather recently. The smell of fresh pitch wafted from the rungs as Denrik scampered up them and to the warehouse.

Men were all about, hefting large baskets of fish from the boats at anchor and hauling them to the front of the warehouse, where they would be picked up in the morning to be taken to market. They were a mix of locals and foreigners, with various accents heard as they shouted to one another while the foreman directed the flow of men and baskets within the warehouse and just outside it. There was a stink like a fishery about, but like many smells the past few days, Denrik found it nostalgic and welcome. He picked his way through the bustle, keeping out of the way as best he could as he made his way through, and then out onto the docks.

"Eh, watchyer!" one exclaimed as Denrik jostled him.

A quick glare was all he received in return, but the man—a pale, haggard, and stout man of middle years, a lower-class Hurlan by his accent—made eye contact with Denrik, and the one look was enough to shut the man up. One did not make a living on the outskirts of respectability by failing to identify truly dangerous men. There was a manner and look about them that weak men heeded instinctively as a warning sign, and that Denrik had from keel to crow's nest.

Denrik made his way down the docks and glanced at the ships as he passed. Most were unremarkable—merchants, traders, fishermen, a pleasure yacht or two belonging to a nobleman—but there was one he had to see. He knew where it was berthed and could see its masts from farther down the dock, but he had to get a good look. There it was, *Harbinger*, the ship he would make his own. It had docked just that morning, and there were men all about it even at the late hour. Some made repairs to the rigging and to the sails that had been taken down and lay upon the deck. Crew came and went, mostly departing for shore leave to take advantage of the brothels and taverns in the vicinity of the waterfront. He walked down the pier to have a better look, trying to look like he belonged among the workers.

It was a fine ship. The navy had taste and style, he would grant them that much. It was a long, sleek vessel with high masts sure to catch any wind it could find. The double gun decks particularly drew Denrik's eye, since its firepower was one of the chief reasons he was so eager to have it. The new long guns would almost certainly not have been delivered yet; he would have to be certain of that delivery before he made his move. It would be a pity to capture the vessel before its latest armaments became available.

"You there, move along," a voice called down from the deck. "This is an Acardian Navy vessel, not a statue."

Denrik glanced up to see a figure in lieutenant's regalia staring down at him from over the rail.

"Shur fine ship, sir." Denrik faked a generic "foreign" accent. "Din't mean nuttin' by it."

With that, he lifted his hand to his cap as if to tip it—though knitted caps were notoriously difficult to tip—and turned to walk away. Under his breath, he added, "Be back to collect her soon enough. You just finish patching her up."

Denrik made his way to The Drunken Squid, a rough, rowdy watering hole favored among seafaring visitors to Acardia. Some locals favored it as well, but mostly due to the motley assortment of characters they met there. It was a place where friends were made over pints of ale barely a step above piss, and business was conducted by men who wanted lots of people around as witnesses, lest they catch a knife in the gut when negotiations went sour. The Squid had a fanciful carved sign hung out front, depicting a whimsically rendered squid hoisting several foaming tankards and sporting a look that could best be described as "lecherous." There was no mistaking it for a high-class establishment, and neither the owner nor the patrons would have wanted it otherwise.

Denrik entered through the wide-open door, which despite the chill outside, was left ajar to vent the heat and smell of many men crowded into tight quarters inside. The din inside was typical of any place where many congregated to socialize, though perhaps a bit louder. The decor was nautical, with unfinished wood weathered to a grey-brown and cargo netting hung up in the rafters, and fish mounted along the walls on plaques. The tables and chairs were of an extremely simple and sturdy design, meant to survive the occasional brawl or at least be easily replaced afterward.

Among the tables of men waded a handful of battle-hardened barmaids. No fairy-tale princesses among them, the women who served drinks in the Squid were sturdy, no-nonsense sorts. Though they dressed with skirts and low-cut bodices, they were as ready to deliver a tankard upside the head as they were to serve it, should the need arise. Men starved for feminine attention tipped well, even when they were not wealthy, but those seeking such tips earned them many times over with the mischief they had to put up with to get them.

Denrik picked his way among the tables to a back corner where he saw Stalyart seated with a number of men he had never met. There was an empty chair—no small feat itself on a busy night—and it was the one directly in the corner of the taproom where its occupant could not be approached from behind. Denrik squeezed his way around the wall and to the seat that had been saved for him.

"Mr. Stalyart," Denrik said with a simple nod of acknowledgment.

"Captain," Stalyart leaned across and whispered, "I believe for tonight, we should be careful with names." Then, adopting a normal volume, "It is good for you to join us tonight, friend. It had been so, so long." Stalyart smiled and held his hands wide.

Stalyart reached into his vest and drew out a small wooden box, slightly larger than the palm of his hand. It was stained a deep brown that had worn away at the edges and had copper hinges. Stalyart undid the simple clasp that held it shut. It contained a deck of cards. Stalyart gave the deck a few perfunctory shuffles as everyone at the table watched, and then set the deck on the table. He reached then for his purse and pulled out a fistful of coins, depositing them in front of him in a pile. As everyone else did quick math to estimate the worth of the pile, Denrik knew almost immediately: it was the same amount he had been left in his own purse. "Contingency funds," indeed.

"Tonight we play Crackle, and drink," Stalyart said.

But Denrik was already ahead of him, pulling out his own purse and dumping its contents in front of him on the table. The others did similarly, scrounging on their own persons for loose cash and forming a ring of seven piles of eckles around a deck of Talis cards at roughly the center of the table.

"Since I know for fact you all are fully aware the rules, I dispense with repeating them," Stalyart said, picking up the deck again.

He began swiftly dealing out the cards, three to each player. Talis was a gentleman's game, played mostly by stuffy old men, their idle wives, and whip-smart young men aiming to impress their way to a better career in the employ of stuffy old men. It was a game of subtlety, guile, and planning, to make the best of good hands and cut your losses on the bad, with an intricate scoring system that would leave one player the winner after an evening's amusement.

Crackle used the same cards as Talis but was seldom played by gentlemen. It was a game children played with their parents' Talis cards—and that grown men played for money. Crackle was not a simplified version of Talis so much as it was a version gone feral. It was a game of opportunity and ruthlessness, seized chances and steel-eyed nerves. It was scored each hand, and the score was paid up in cash. Fortunes swung wildly during a night of Crackle as luck, and often drink, took hold of the players. Most men who played regularly were the poorer for it, but there were savvy players who made tidy profits at the game.

The finest of players had to watch their backs, for even a drunkard could usually tell which way all his money had gone, and a properly presented knife later in an alley could quickly undo hours of properly presented cards on the table. Many of the truly good players were hard, cold men, used to the prospect of violence directed at their persons. Stalyart was one of those. He had taught Denrik the game years ago, when he had first joined the crew of *The Honest Merchant*. Denrik had gotten quite proficient at the game but had never approached Stalyart's mastery of it.

Denrik took a quick look at his cards once they were all dealt, but turned his attention quickly to his fellow players. A Crackle game was more often won by mistakes than gambits, and watching your opponents' reactions to see if they let any hint slip about their cards was half the game. But his opponents this night were inscrutable for the most part. Crackle was not so much a game for thinkers as it was for those with nerve and resolve. Your wits kept you from making truly glaring mistakes, but it did not take a sharp mind to play. These men seated with him might have had the minds of astronomers or stable muckers, but they had the nerve of gamblers.

The game began with a few terse hands as everyone settled into the game. Little was said except what was needful to keep the game apace. But the barmaids came with rounds of ale, paid for by Stalyart, and the tongues at the table loosened gradually. And though Stalyart had warned against using names, he was mostly sensitive to anyone giving Captain Zayne away, and quietly Denrik was able to learn the identities of his would-be crew.

First to his left was Nimrul Scradd, a wiry, thin man with dark hair and a prominent Adam's apple. His eyes flicked about like houseflies trapped in jars, never lighting long in one place. He was apparently a quartermaster aboard Stalyart's trading ship. He had been one of the first that Stalyart had taken on when he began his run of playing at captain.

Next to Scradd sat Jon Marshfield. Marshfield was Golish, a broad, thick fellow with a big round face and a tousle of blond hair above bright green eyes. His easy smile and guileless manner suggested a farm-boy's upbringing, but his shrewd play with the cards told another story.

Next to Marshfield was Mr. Stalyart's half-brother, Rogur Crispin. While he had his Acardian mother's name, Crispin was in all other ways his father's son. He and Stalyart might have passed for twins if Stalyart was not nearly a decade his senior and darker of complexion. They had the same dark hair, the same build, even their noses sported a similar hooked downturn. Crispin was dressed in a navy sailor's work clothes: a simple sweat-stained white tunic, loose grey slacks, and deck shoes. He had thankfully left behind the silly little white hat the navy's noncommissioned officers wore on duty. He was not half the player his elder brother was, but he held his own and, in conversation over the table, gave tidbits of information about the ship and crew they were planning to confront.

Across from Denrik sat their host, and the mastermind of Denrik's escape, Robbono Stalyart. Denrik's admiration for the man had only grown since his escape plan's success. Stalyart had flourished out on his own, free from Denrik's service. Yet here he was, willingly throwing back the yoke onto his own back to haul his captain back up to his rightful place on the seas. Denrik Zayne had not made his mark in piracy by naïveté, but it was clearly touching how much Stalyart looked up to him. Denrik had come to realize during their planning of his escape that his former mate wanted his place in the history books as Denrik's indispensable right hand, rather than as a captain in some thick tome entitled *Katamic Sea Pirates of the Zayne Era: An Alphabetical Listing*. It was Denrik's sincere hope that the man was not becoming too competent and charismatic to be left alive.

After Stalyart sat Dorin Kelgart, a stout older man with a grey beard streaked through with bits of the original dark brown. He was Stalyart's carpenter—and the worst player of Crackle at the table. His short, stubby fingers held the cards awkwardly, as if the game was possibly somewhat newer to him than to his compatriots. His play was steady and safe, and too conservative to win against experienced opponents. His face, though, was a mask of granite. His expression barely changed through the night, and even when he spoke, his mouth moved little and was further obscured behind his beard. He may have also been the only one not having fun with the encounter. Denrik took an immediate liking to him—all business and almost certainly not a troublemaker.

Past Kelgart was Stevin. Stevin gave no family name; he was an orphan who had never adopted one. His skin was pale with an orange-yellow tinge to it, suggesting he had been born in Khesh, or perhaps Feru Maru. Denrik judged he might be as old as twenty, but he would not have been surprised to learn he was younger. He was just a sailor in Stalyart's service, but he was conditioned to survive and scavenge, having been on his own for most of his life. Stalyart vouched for him as a hard worker, and he seemed eager and amiable.

Lastly, just to Denrik's right, was Marfin Holyoake. Denrik was ashamed to admit he had not recognized the man at first, though that was plainly to Holyoake's advantage. Anonymity had its privileges. Holyoake was one of Denrik's crew on *The Honest Merchant*, and his inclusion in the hijacking was a great comfort to Denrik. He had been worried about all the men involved who were loyal first and foremost to Stalyart, and who may eventually prefer him as captain over Denrik. But Holyoake had gotten out of prison not long after being convicted of piracy, in a tale he swore he would give in full and glorious detail once they were at sea. Holyoake was Captain Zayne's boatswain and as reliable as a pirate could be. Older even than Denrik, he was showing his years physically. He had thinned since Denrik last saw him, and his hair was nearly all gone, but he was feisty as ever. He took his pipe from his mouth only long enough to drink, and resumed smoking before his tankard even hit the table.

The game and the drinking lasted for hours. Money changed hands, but mostly came out even, though Stalyart's pile seemed to have grown a bit. Denrik had gleaned useful information about the minutiae of the *Harbinger* and had a rough outline of the life stories of the men he was taking on as a crew, but he needed to start battening down a plan.

"So you take night watches, do you?" Denrik asked Crispin, who nodded by way of reply. "When will you be on deck?"

"Tomorrow night, midnight to predawn. Then four days hence, dusk to midnight," Crispin answered, speaking low so that no one at the other tables might hear him. He was a navy officer and seemed concerned that someone from his ship might overhear him giving away information that was of use only for nefarious purposes.

"Tomorrow night is too soon," Denrik said. "The new long guns will not be aboard yet, and we won't have much time to make arrangements. We will move four nights from now, on the first night watch."

He looked slowly around the table and met the gaze of each man. This was the one thing he had to know for sure: whether he had their full attention. Each gaze was met, and every man passed one other test: Denrik could see the fire in their eyes. These men were not nervous; they seemed determined and hungry.

He turned his attention back solely to Crispin. "How many will be aboard, and where will they be?"

"A few men will end up waking in the brothels in the morning, and two have family in Acardia that they will stay with. Most will spend the night drinking ashore, though, or taking their pleasures and returning later to the ship. If we move before ten bells, most of the crew will be ashore. The ones still on board will be the ones who take their bed early, or prefer to drink and gamble belowdecks. Perhaps twenty men."

"Hmm," Denrik said, pondering. "And is it a single watch while in port, or do you keep double?"

"Double most nights."

"All right. The plan is simple enough," Denrik said even as he thought it through. "Stalyart, get your own ship loaded with whatever valuables you have. The night we attack, have it set out to sea and anchor a few miles out. Make sure you have at least one loyal man aboard to make sure they surrender when we board. They will be our first mark once we are back in business.

"Crispin, you will be in charge of keeping things quiet until we are aboard. If it is a two-man watch, your job will be to make sure the other sentry does not take note of us. Upon your signal, we will rush the gangplank and make our way aboard. I do not care how you dispose of the other man on watch —get him dead drunk, wait until he is in the head, knife in the gut—just make sure that when you signal us, we can make it to the deck before anyone is the wiser."

Crispin nodded once in reply, his expression mirroring the seriousness of the task he was just set.

"Stalyart, you are going to need to get a hold of any weapons you are able. I have two cutlasses stolen from the *Bringer of Hope*, but that is it. We will need more blades at the least, and as many pistols as you are able to gather in four days. Mind you, I will have four more of my own men along, so have something for them as well. Oh, and an axe or two ought to get us free from the moorings quickly. If we raise a general alarm in the port, we will need to be off quickly."

Stalyart nodded. "Of course. I have six pistols already, and I shall see if I can manage more in time."

He seemed like he was about to expound, but Denrik started right up again: "If Crispin does his part, we shall be on deck unnoticed. I need two men to start getting the ship ready to sail. That will mean cutting the ropes mooring us, then seeing to the anchor and sails. If things go badly, I will give the order to cut the anchor and start immediately on the sails.

"The rest will go below deck and run through anyone who does not surrender quick enough. We shall take prisoners, and maybe Crispin can pick out a few that we might make use of."

"What of the captain?" Stalyart asked. "Surely he must be aboard. Old man, eh? Not so young to be taking drink with sailors."

Crispin pondered briefly. "Well, Captain Rannison has dinner with various councilors and lords when he's in port. He's from an old family and has got connections. Still, I'd plan for him being in his cabin. You know, just in case."

"I shall deal with the captain myself, if he is aboard," Denrik said. "If there are no objections, this is our plan. If there are changes to be made, I shall send word with Stalyart."

With that, Denrik rose from the table, scooping his winnings into his purse. With a minimum of fuss, he made his way through the crowded taproom and out into the night.

* * * * * * * *

Elsewhere in Scar Harbor that night ...

"Just wait! It has been like this three nights running now," whispered a timid-looking man crouched by the corner of an unassuming building. The building bore an indecipherable sign with no picture to indicate whose shop it was or what they sold.

"Mister Lierson, you are trying me. What is this all about anyway?" The figure next to the timid-looking man was less timid by far, going perhaps as far from timid as "stern," "annoyed," or "put upon and about to give someone an impolite haranguing." That type of expression came naturally to constables, and they were quick to put it on when they felt their time was being wasted.

"Sorry, Constable, but you won't believe me telling you. Just wait, it can't be long now, I promise," Lierson said.

Constable Darren let out an impatient sigh but said nothing.

They waited nearly twenty minutes, and the good constable was very nearly ready to dress down Lierson for wasting his valuable time, but there was a stirring inside. A light came on, bright enough that it peeked through the shutters of the storefront.

"Haru bedaessi leoki kwatuan gelora," came a muffled voice from within.

Constable Darren turned to Lierson, who widened his eyes and gestured with his head back toward the window in an unmistakable "Yes, this is what I was talking about" manner. Constable Darren then moved closer to the window to try and see in. The shutters did not fit quite perfectly, and he was able to catch an edge with a fingernail and pull them outward until the latch caught and stopped them. It was enough.

The room inside was lit with an unnatural glow, tinged slightly blue, and seemed to fill the room with no shadowed corners the way a lamp would. Hovering in the air were a number of quills, no hand touching them, that the constable saw dip themselves in an ink pot one at a time and move out of the narrow view the shutters afforded. He heard scribbling, though, as if the quills had begun to work on their own.

"Haru bedaessi leoki kwatuan gelora." The voice was somewhat clearer this time.

Then Constable Darren saw a teacup float past his view. A moment later, a youngish man walked into view, sipping tea and looking down, presumably overseeing the quills at their work.

Constable Darren ducked down and crept as quietly as he could back to where Lierson crouched. He took Lierson by the arm and led him to the building next door, a building sporting a shoe and boot for a sign. It was Lierson's shop, Mr. Lierson being a cobbler and the neighbor of one Kyrus Hinterdale: scrivener and, it would seen, amateur wizard. Lierson's bedroom was also above his shop and happened to be directly across from Kyrus's bedroom.

"For three nights now, Constable. He makes these awful chants, and things glow and float and whatnot. I do not consider myself a superstitious man, sir, but *that* is witchcraft!" Lierson said. "I do not feel safe living next door to someone using black magic."

"Well, I did not think I was superstitious, either, until now. What I saw, though, just is not natural, and I cannot abide that sort of thing going on unchecked. If he's at it again tomorrow night, we shall catch him in the act, and I'll have more men with me to apprehend him."

"Thank you, Constable Darren. I shall put in a very good word with your superiors after this mess is sorted out. My name may not carry much weight, but I am a law-abiding citizen and concerned for the safety of the city.

"I believe the penalty for witchcraft is burning, is it not?" Lierson added.

"Well, um, no, sir. Before they stopped executing criminals, I believe it was hanging," Constable Darren replied. "Never saw a real case of it before, though."

"Oh, I'm sure they'll make an exception this time. We won't be safe so long as that Mr. Hinterdale lives."

Chapter 15 - Rook Takes Pawn

Jinzan awoke refreshed. He felt better than he had in a long time. His plan was finally about to start paying back all the work he had put into it.

As he pushed back the flap and exited his tent, he found quite a different attitude among his goblin hosts. The autumn air had grown frosty, and the frail, scrawny creatures had little love for the cold. The camp was filled with bored goblins huddling around sorcerer-warmed stones, bundled up in raccoon furs and trying to keep busy until the remainder of their forces arrived.

They had been camped on the forested hills just outside of Illard's Glen for two days. The small farming and trade community sat across the Neverthaw River. The Neverthaw was a deep, wide river that would bar any reasonable attempt by the goblins to cross, short of building ships. Illard's Glen had a wide bridge that would allow the army to cross.

Despite their proximity to the town, they were reasonably secure in their ability to remain undetected. Illard's Glen was woefully understaffed with sorcerers. The goblins' own magic-users had been keeping up a constant veil of illusory trees to keep them out of view of the town itself, making the nearby woodlands seem denser to conceal G'thk's encampment. The few Kadrins who had ventured near enough to notice something amiss had been enspelled to believe they had seen nothing. One of the goblins had even hunted a deer and stuck one of the humans' arrows in it before sending them on their way with their prize.

Jinzan breathed in the cold morning air and found it invigorating. He wandered over to the cooking area and grabbed two bowls of the goblins' mush dawn-feast rations. The soggy mixture steamed lightly, the cauldron of it having been warmed over a few stones the sorcerers had heated to a reddish glow. The goblins were not fond of winter, and even the autumn mornings were more than enough to sour them on the weather. Jinzan had spend much of his youth in colder climates, and found the morning unworthy of a heavy cloak. The smaller, thinner bodies of the goblins just did not hold heat well. They typically dwelt underground in the winter, with their communities half above and half below ground in more temperate weather.

[Good morning, sorcerer,] came a voice from behind Jinzan as he searched for a place to sit with his food.

"Good morning yourself, General," Jinzan replied, recognizing G'thk's voice. He turned to look at the goblin, not wishing to be any more disrespectful than usual.

[How you are not cold continues amazing me. You humans are either crazy or half bear. Join me over here while you take morning meal.] G'thk gestured to the seat beside him on a cut log.

It always amused the sorcerer that the goblins made furniture for their general whenever they stopped for more than a day or so. They were industrious little creatures even if they were weaklings individually, and he took full advantage. When Jinzan's secret weapons arrived, he was eager to see just how clever they had been.

"Any word of the assassin?" Jinzan had almost added "that you sent" to the end of his question but did not want to be diverted over an argument of who was to blame for his disappearance.

[It has been too long,] G'thk conceded. He had been insisting for days that the assassin would be back any time. It was the first time he admitted something might be wrong. [We have no choice but to pray he was successful, and continue with the plan. We will not turn back.]

Jinzan had been pressing for details every night since the assassin was sent to dispatch the Kadrin survivors. He knew little about Gkt'Lr's skills, but G'thk seemed to have every confidence that he would be able to finish off the half-score or so of humans that had been left after the battle at the river.

"Do you think he might have had troubles with that magical sword?" Jinzan suggested. "We expected the ambush to destroy them as well; perhaps we have underestimated them a second time."

G'thk's eyes narrowed as he glared at Jinzan. [I dislike you sometimes, sorcerer. You are right too many times when we disagree. I think this time you are only half right, though. For my guess, I say that the sorcerer the humans had was stronger than we reasoned. The scorched spot where there was an aether burn; there was no human body in that spot. Maybe the sorcerer of theirs survived. If he was strong enough to battle three of our own sorcerers, perhaps he was able to thwart Gkt'Lr. A human sword-knight should not have seen Gkt'Lr coming, but maybe a sorcerer did.]

"It is possible, I suppose. I wonder how much use anyone who caused that aether burn would be, though, so soon after. He must have overextended himself severely to do that sort of damage just with excess aether. I would rather think that they just kept his body. The Kadrins think much more of sorcerers than they do of their dead soldiers. But if the assassin was defeated, I could see a sorcerer's part in that. I know I do not fear him," Jinzan boasted, not entirely idly. While the assassin might well kill him in his sleep, he was not so easy a mark to sneak up on as most.

Jinzan was adept enough that he could perceive the aether even while using his normal sight. It was a half measure of attention to be sure, like a sort of peripheral vision, but the assassin's Source was stronger than most, and Jinzan was generally aware of all Sources within a few paces of himself at all times. Most sorcerers, at least among humans, really only saw aether when they blocked out their normal sight. It was yet another reason sorcerers kept out of pitched battles as a rule. Jinzan was not so sure how goblins perceived aether and reality at the same time, though. He suspected that the ability to watch aether and reality at once might be somewhat less rare among their sorcerers, and might possibly be why they were more willing to fight with magic.

[Either way, if the assassin was not able to stop the humans reaching help, we may have to deal with reinforcements. I doubt the humans will be able to rally enough forces to stop us, though, especially if your weapons work as well as you claim.]

"They will. Your artisans are skilled. I think they will be able to follow the plans I gave them. If they build them right, we will have no troubles. Illard's Glen will be a test. We could take the town with just normal forces, but we want to be certain that the new weapons are working as intended."

[I am eager to see them in action. You are very certain of their effectiveness for something that has never been made before.]

Jinzan simply smiled.

* * * * * * * *

It was that same afternoon that the rest of the goblins forces arrived. Their presence would be nearly impossible to hide with the number of troops swelling to over one hundred thousand, filling nearly every available part of the forest within a mile of the tree line.

As waves of goblins and entire herds of oxen ambled into the general area of the original campsite, Jinzan searched out the quartermasters of the goblin army. Fortunately, for Jinzan, the goblins were a nimble people generally, and Jinzan saw the path before him clear as he moved. To the goblins, he might as well have been an ogre. There was much chattering as he passed, with many of the newcomers never having seen a human before. Jinzan had a hard enough time picking up conversational goblin-speech in small groups, but to his ears, the multitudes might well have been crickets chirping or hens clucking for all the sense he could make of it.

As he passed, he would pick out officers by their uniform and ask a single question in his rudimentary goblin: [Where new weapon?]

[Back, at end,] he kept hearing.

He waded onward, careful lest he step on one of his allies and possibly provoke violence. At the distance of a spear throw, he would take his chances against half an army's worth of the little runts, but all about him and armed, he wanted to take extra care to avoid any misunderstandings.

After half an hour that seemed like a day, Jinzan made it to the back of the procession. There he found an unusual group. Oxen were the common beast of burden among the goblins, but this was an animal he had never seen before. There were several eight-legged lizards, nearly Jinzan's height at the shoulder and even broader across, their bellies slung nearly to the ground. They were massive, powerful creatures who plodded along hauling carts, each bearing a cargo lashed down with tarps.

Jinzan waved his hands over his head as he approached, carefully keeping to the side of the gargantuan lizards' path.

[Hold!] he shouted, or at least tried. He nearly choked trying to yell in goblin.

The rider of the lead lizard stopped, and the rest followed suit. Had he not been so eager to inspect their cargo, Jinzan would have been fascinated by the lizards and their riders. The riders sat not on the lizards backs, but saddled to their heads. Due to their multitude of legs working in alternating stride, the backs of the lizards weaved side to side as they walked, but the heads held very steady. And despite the cold-blooded nature of lizards and the chill in the air, the lizards seemed plenty warm. In fact, Jinzan could feel the heat radiating off them as he approached; it seemed to come from a harness of tubes crisscrossing the beasts, attached to a large bladder on their backs.

[What, human? What you want?] crackled a wizened old goblin from the head of the lead lizard. [You the one who drew these devices?]

The goblin was wrinkled and his skin had a more greyish color to it rather than the typical green hues the younger goblins showed. From what Jinzan knew of goblins, unless this one knew age-slowing magic like humans used, he was probably well past thirty. The old goblin wore thick spectacles and a wide, flattened conical hat that tied under his chin. He was bundled in raccoon furs like most of the other goblins, but Jinzan noticed a pack on his back that looked similar to the one on the lizard; presumably the tubes went underneath his furs.

[Yes. Me one who make—] but the old goblin waved a hand and cut him off.

[You hurt my old ears. I can understand human speech just fine. Speak your own tongue and leave ours in peace. By the great dragon Ni'Hash'Tk, you shriek like an old lady,] the goblin said, then chuckled.

"Fine, then. Yes, I am the one who drew the plans for these weapons. I wish to see them. Show me," he demanded.

[Just like a human. No patience,] the old goblin said, cackling in amusement. He yelled to some of the nearby soldiers to unbind the tarps and remove them. [My name is K'k'rt. I am the one who oversaw the making of your weapons. Let me tell you, we are *two days late* because you make,] and there was a word Jinzan did not know, [like a little child. We had to remake them right and fix a lot of mistakes.]

Jinzan was a little worried now, as the goblins rushed over and climbed onto the cart, scrambling up the sides by the very straps they were about to remove. He was aware that the goblins would have their own way of doing things, but he thought his specifications were unambiguous. He had hoped that they had not made them different enough that they did not work now.

Soon enough, he had his answer. As the last of the goblins got down from the cart, a pair of them pulled off the tarp. K'k'rt swung the lizard's head around to get a better view, and the creature contorted its body so that it was nearly bent in two. The reins of the lizard's bridle gave the rider control not only over the lizard's walking, but over which way it faced its head.

Jinzan's breath caught in his throat, and he gasped in wonder at the sight before him. He approached and reached out to touch the goblins' creation: a long cylinder of polished bronze with silvery bands of a metal he did not recognize reinforcing it toward the open end, for indeed one end of the device had a hole that extended down inside.

It was a cannon. Jinzan had never actually seen or felt one before, though it was familiar to him as his own robes were. He had seen them nightly in his dreams for a long time. The craftsmanship was exquisite, the surface gleamed, and the bore was straight as a plumb line. It was better than he had hoped; the goblins had outdone themselves.

[Ha-ha, you like it human?] K'k'rt asked, smiling. [Once we fixed your mistakes, it worked much better].

Jinzan's head snapped around, and he looked K'k'rt with surprise. "You have tried it?"

[Ha-ha, of course. Silly human, we do not make things and bring them to a battle with no testing. Ha-ha, we had a wonderful time playing with them before we worked out the models you see here. Your burning rope triggering for it was the first thing we got rid of.]

Jinzan looked at the breech end of the cannon. There was no fuse, nor any place he could see to put one. Instead he found a box-like contraption welded onto the outside with a metal handle dangling from a chain. The chain seemed not so much to be attached to the box as attached to somewhere inside the box.

"What is this?" Jinzan asked. "What have you done with the fuse?"

[Bah, your silly rope. Your exploding powder needs fire. You put a burning rope in it? Ha-ha, what a bad way to get fire inside. Too hard to get the timing. We made a mechanism for lighting the blasting powder that is quicker and more reliable. Just pull the chain and it makes sparks inside.] The goblin chuckled as he spoke, clearly enjoying the feeling of superiority over the cannon's "inventor."

Jinzan grasped hold of the chain and looked askance of K'k'rt.

[Go ahead and pull. Quick tug. Not too hard, it was made for my kind to use. Do not break it,] K'k'rt instructed, miming a tugging action.

Jinzan pulled the chain and heard a scraping, metal-on-metal *snick* from within the box. When he let go, the chain pulled itself back to its original length. Jinzan did not perceive any aether at work and was not sure how they had managed that unless they had developed some sort of spring-return mechanism on their own. Jinzan carefully avoided turning to look at K'k'rt, but he was starting to wonder if perhaps he should have taken a slower approach and taught his own people how to make the cannons. It might have been a decade before they got it right, but he was starting to question the wisdom of giving these clever creatures a head start on technology.

"Excellent work," he said quietly.

Then Jinzan walked over to the other carts. There were twelve cannon in all, and several more carts bearing cannon shot and black powder. He kept a careful distance from the latter, as even in the dream world, the storage and handling of black powder was a twitchy thing. These goblins were new to the stuff and were much more tolerant of risk-taking than most humans were. If they had not had a safer design for the cannon figured out in time, they would have certainly just made do with the initial design. Abandoning the project out of concern for the newly appointed goblin cannoneers would not have occurred to them.

* * * * * * * *

By the following morning, the cannons were in place on the hilltop. The trees that were in the line of fire were half cut, ready to be brought down by the sorcerers when the signal was made to begin the battle.

When G'thk gave that signal, the sorcerers gave a great blast of wind, toppling the trees away from the direction of the camp. In a riot of reds and oranges and yellows, the fall colors of the canopy rushed to the ground in front of them. The powerful aether-driven winds stripped the leaves from the fallen trees as well and sent them swirling off in the direction of Illard's Glen.

With the view of the city now exposed, Jinzan and the commanders of the army could see the massive goblin force closing on the city. Armed only with spears, the goblin infantry rushed forward toward the walls of the town. It would be several minutes before they covered the prairie between the hilltop and the wall, and they carried no easy means of surmounting the wall. That task would be left to the cannon, and if that failed, the sorcerers—particularly Jinzan—would have to clear up the mess.

The Kadrin forces that defended Illard's Glen had been oblivious to the goblin presence in the forested hills around their town, but the goblin sorcerers had given up wasting aether on illusions, and the crack of dozens of falling trees could be heard even from town. Within seconds of the toppling of their tree cover, Jinzan and the goblins heard the watch bells ringing frantically from Illard's Glen, and they saw the north facing gate being closed.

Jinzan moved in directly behind the cannon. All twelve were trained on the city walls, their crews awaiting the order to fire. They were dressed as the common soldiers were, with one exception. Each was fitted with a leather helmet, thickly padded inside where it covered their ears, and a pair of goggles. It had not taken the goblin artisans long to realize the noise and smoke their new creations caused, and to devise methods of protecting their crews.

As their hearing was muffled, the signal G'thk gave was simply to point to the cannoneers, then to the wall. The crews turned from their leader to the chains of the cannon, and in remarkable unison, pulled the chains.

Kthooom! Kthooom! Kthooom! Kthooom!

The concussion was thunderous. All the goblins not wearing protective helmets grabbed for their ears, even those well away from the cannon. The ground hammered on their feet from the shock wave, sending a few stumbling. The cannoneers scrambled as the recoil from their siege engines sent them backward into their midst.

Jinzan just smiled. His ears rang from the blast, but he had stood his ground and barely flinched. The cannon's report was like music to him. He felt like a young boy, always barred from the tavern on nights when bards were playing, listening to muted notes that the wall allowed through. Now, finally, he was allowed to hear the music in all its glory.

Seconds later, the cannon balls hit. Two plumes of rocky dust exploded from the wall. The rest either overshot or undershot their mark. The disoriented crews had seen the two plumes as well and realized that ten of the cannon had missed their marks. They gestured frantically amongst themselves as they struggled to push the cannon back into position and reload. There was clearly a disagreement over which had been aimed properly.

Jinzan was paying closer attention, though. He strode over to the cannoneers and pointed emphatically to one, then to another, then motioned for the nearest goblin to remove his helmet. The goblin complied hastily.

[That two hit. This one, up three tick.] Jinzan pointed to a third cannon. [That one, up two tick.]

Jinzan ran through the rest of the cannon as best he could estimate how much they were off and giving instruction as to how to adjust the ratcheted mechanism the goblins had added to the cannons to adjust and hold their aim. The aiming device was an excellent idea, but he was unfamiliar with just how much each "tick" actually represented. Since Jinzan had only seen where a few of the shot had impacted, aside from the two that hit the wall, he was largely guessing at the adjustments anyway.

[You see this time. I no see all time for you.] Jinzan's voice was already growing hoarse from speaking goblin.

The one he had instructed quickly relayed his commands to the rest, and they began trying to heft the cannon back into position. They had wheels, but in the soft dirt, the blast had driven them into the ground a little, meaning they were pushing uphill, if only slightly.

"Haru bedaessi leoki kwatuan gelora."

Jinzan set the cannon back roughly where they had started as the startled goblins—who could not hear his spell—scrambled to get back to work loading.

The loading process was amusing to watch. What would have taken a couple humans just muscle power, the goblins had developed a whole process for. There were stepladders, small carts, and a two-goblin cradle for carrying the shot. Jinzan was not any sort of physical specimen, but he could still lift one of the cannonballs in one hand, with some difficulty.

The second volley was less chaotic than the first. The commanders and sorcerers who remained on the hill knew to plug their ears as the command was given to fire. The crews kept out of the way from the recoil. Goblin sorcerers were ready to lift the cannon back into position as soon as they fired. And nine of the twelve hit the wall, and the ones who had not made adjustments of their own.

A third volley was much the same, and the town wall was breached in several spots. A cheer went up from the goblins on the hilltop, as the first of the infantry reached the wall and found passage through. Arrows and grapeshot rained down among the swarming masses of the goblin invaders, but so great were their numbers that they hardly slowed.

The cannoneers began to stow their equipment and prepared to move down to the town. It would be in goblin hands long before they arrived.

* * * * * * * *

Small footfalls echoed in the vast cavern. Gkt'Lr could have moved more quietly, but it would have been irreverent to attempt stealth, given the circumstances. The only other sounds were the faint crackling of the torches along the walls and a steady sound like a bellows.

Gkt'Lr approached the center of the cavern, where there was a promontory overlooking the shadowy depths of the lower portion of the great chamber. The torches had been placed such that their light did not reach down below. As he reached the edge, he glanced down. Seeing nothing, he let his vision delve into the aetherial realm. He saw a wash of aether flowing from a single, vast Source.

[Great Ni'Hash'Tk, I bring important news.]

Gkt'Lr carefully pronounced the difficult name so as not to cause offense. He swallowed hard, nervous as he had been only once before in the last several winters, which happened to be the reason for his audience. He waited for a response.

There was a great stirring below. A great creaking of leather and sinew gave way to a scratching of massive claws on stone, and the Source closed the distance to Gkt'Lr. As it grew very near, he brought his vision back to reality and saw the face of his goddess.

The enormous reptilian head of the dragon was covered in steel-hard greenish-brown scales, framing a pair of glowing yellowed eyes with slits like a cat's and a parted jaw filled with teeth longer than Gkt'Lr was tall. A tongue darted out quickly, tasting the air near the assassin.

[Your name is known to me. You are Master of Eternal Night; you have the esteem of my attendants. I do not think you are one who would dare waste my time on a petty matter. Speak,] Ni'Hash'Tk ordered, her deep voice rumbling throughout the cavern.

Gkt'Lr could smell the carrion on her breath. The assassin was no expert on meats, but he knew it was probably caribou meat he was smelling, from the herds raised just to satiate the dragon's appetite for her favorite meal.

[The plan to secure your whelp's lair is in jeopardy. The humans have allied themselves with a demon.] Gkt'Lr did not want to waste the dragon's time by dancing around the real reason for his urgency.

The dragon's eyes narrowed. [Explain.]

[Your Holiness, the scouting parties ran into an unusually strong resistance from a small force of humans. One strike force was lost almost entirely, and the humans were nearly wiped out as well. The few survivors fled, and I was sent to make sure they were not able to reach help and raise an alarm against us. I found them easily but was ambushed by the demon, who claimed the humans were under his protection. The demon toyed with me and let me flee. I came here to warn you.] Gkt'Lr hoped that would be sufficient but suspected not.

[So you have failed?] the dragon asked.

That was the topic he had sincerely hoped the dragon would overlook.

[Yes, Your Holiness.] Gkt'Lr bowed his head in contrition. [If I had persisted despite the demon's warning, I still would have failed, and none would have known of the demon's presence with the humans. I wished to relay a warning.]

[How are you sure that it is a demon? What did it look like?] Ni'Hash'Tk asked.

Gkt'Lr was not sure if the dragon believed him, and offered a silent prayer to Ni'Hash'Tk that he be spared. It was a brief moment, but Gkt'Lr almost laughed when he realized his logical error.

[It looks human, though small for one of their kind, with white hair. It looks young, but not child-like. I knew it was a demon because of my aether-sight. The demon sheds no aether,] the assassin explained.

[Perhaps it is a fault in your aether-vision, then?]

[Your pardon, Holiness, but I do not believe so. In my aether-vision, you are a vast shining beacon of life, and all lesser creatures are smaller lights. I use my aether-sight to help track my prey, and I assure you, this demon was the farthest opposite of you. In the aether-sight, he is a ghost. I can see his body with my eyes, but there is no Source to be seen. He is not alive, but he is powerful. Is that not the definition of a demon?]

[In my lifetime, I have not seen a demon, but all you say of this one strikes true to the tales of them. There are sorcerers among the army gone to claim my Ruuk'Pt'Kaan his lair, but none that I would trust to stand against a demon.

[I will go, and I will see that this demon does not spoil the conquest of the human settlement that Ruuk'Pt'Kaan will take for his new home,] Ni'Hash'Tk said. [Attendants!] the mighty dragon bellowed, shaking the walls and causing the torches to flicker.

A maelstrom of activity ensued, with scores of goblins in brown robes flocking to their goddess's call. They swarmed the promontory and filled the area behind Gkt'Lr, barring his path out, though that consideration was far from their thoughts.

[Prepare me for battle. I will go to war,] Ni'Hash'Tk growled. [And lore-keeper, let it show that Gkt'Lr has performed admirably. There will be no mark of failure upon his record.]

The dragon-priests in attendance sprang into action, for there was much to be done before the vainglorious dragon-goddess would deem herself fit to fight. There were oils to be rubbed into her leathery wings. Teeth and claws to be filed and sharpened. Scales would be checked for cracks and chips, and cleaned of debris. The headdress of gold and silks that Ni'Hash'Tk wore when venturing out from her lair would be cleaned and refitted to the dragon's ever-growing head—she had not worn it in ages. Then there was an entourage to assemble; no infantry to slow Ni'Hash'Tk's passage, but swift-mounted riders from among her loyal attendants. Ni'Hash'Tk would not fly to battle, but walk among her retainers—a swift pace to be sure, but it would not do for her to outdistance her servants by taking to the air.

There was much to be done but little work for Ni'Hash'Tk herself. She settled down to enjoy the pampering of her priests. She had planning to do, though, and hoped that it would all sort itself out before she arrived. If they had a demon among them, she would prefer it show its powers against her worshipers first, before she had to deal with it.

Chapter 16 - Some Explaining to Do

Towers rose in the distance, seen above the rooftops of the small building that had been built outside the city walls. Kadris had outgrown its wall long ago, and the Empire was secure enough that the populace felt safe just being within sight of it. The buildings outside were a diverse assortment of small shops, inns, and dwellings. As the city expanded as a trading hub, the need for more places to put the vast number of visitors outstripped the ability of the old city to provide.

Brannis could make out the Imperial Academy, various noble houses, the largest among the watchtowers, and the Tower of Contemplation, attached to the Imperial Palace. Iridan had told them they needed to report there first, the morning after returning to the inn where the rest of their small band had actually gotten a night's sleep. Brannis was a little worried about what he had been up all night discussing with the sorcerers back home but trusted that Iridan had not cast him in too bad a light.

On horseback, they had little trouble making their way down the main thoroughfare of the outer city, as folks generally had the good sense to clear a path for a dozen horses to pass. Had they been on foot, the crowds would have made it difficult for them all to remain together. Men and women of various kingdoms were in abundance, though still outnumbered tenfold by local Kadrins. While much of the Empire was segregated by choice to either native-born Kadrins or conquered peoples—with a fair number of loyal Kadrin soldiers garrisoned among them—in a given city, the capital itself was quite metropolitan by comparison. The architecture of the outer city was especially worldly, with much of the more modern expansion coming via the developing trade with lands across the seas—folk who had little historical reason to distrust Kadrin, unlike many of their continental neighbors, most of whom either warred with Kadrin or had been conquered by them sometime in the past few hundred winters.

Brannis rode at the head of the group, followed by Iridan and Sir Lugren. Rashan rode in the middle of the conscripts, not wanting to draw undue attention to himself quite yet. The city gates stood wide open and, as a sign of Kadrin power, were never closed, so certain was the city of its defenses. There was, however, a token force of guards at the gate and, on this particular occasion, a herald.

"Hold and be recognized!" came the herald's shout as they approached.

Brannis drew up just short of the guards and their brandished halberds. *This is apparently going to be a formal affair*, Brannis mused. The herald was dressed in white finery, with a pinched face and sporting long blond hair and tiny spectacles, giving the impression of a white mouse that had learned to read. He carried a scroll, held open before him.

"I am Sir Brannis Solaran, commander of the Eighth Battalion, returning from investigating Kelvie Forest," Brannis replied.

"I am Sir Lugren Malchea, serving under Sir Brannis." Lugren's reply was the most he had spoken in a week.

"I am Iridan Korian, Fourth Circle," Iridan said.

"I am Tod Hellet—" Tod began, but the herald cut him off with a dismissive wave of his hand.

"Sir Brannis, Sorcerer Iridan, you are hereby ordered to accompany me to the Tower of Contemplation and answer the questions of the Inner Circle. Sir Lugren, and the rest of you, please dismount and accompany these guards to Imperial Army command," the herald said matter-of-factly and then closed the scroll.

"No."

"What was that?" the herald demanded. He carried orders directly from the Inner Circle and no doubt was aghast at having been contradicted.

"I am Rashan Solaran," a voice from the middle of the pack said evenly, and a horse rode to the front, "Warlock of the Empire, High Sorcerer, and the blood-stained right hand of the emperor. I will see the Inner Circle, and I will take orders from none but the emperor himself."

Rashan stopped his horse just short of the herald. The tidy, fussy man who had initially been outraged was now petrified with fear. Unarmed and dressed in poorly made clothes, Rashan's presence was still unnerving.

"Do you understand?"

"Yes," came the meek reply.

Brannis wondered whether some magic was at work to so cow the man, or if he was just familiar enough with the busts decorating the Academy and the Tower of Contemplation that he was familiar with the face of the warlock.

Am I the only one who is not convinced? Brannis wondered.

* * * * * * *

Rashan had left orders, and made the herald confirm them with the Circle's borrowed authority, that the soldiers and Sir Lugren be taken instead to The Harp and Lute, a rather pricey inn that had been in business since his own time. The herald had a horse tied nearby, and the four of them—Rashan, Brannis, Iridan, and the herald himself—rode across the city in silence; three of them seemed worried.

The streets were crowded, but the path before them always seemed open. Slightly suspicious, Iridan focused on the aether for a moment and saw why: Rashan was using magic to gently push aside anyone who came near to getting in their way.

"Kemu nantalo chanisi quega," Iridan muttered, and touched the index finger of

each hand to the palm of the other.

"*What are you doing?*" Iridan spoke telepathically to Rashan.

"*Making this into a procession,*" came the reply.

"*You are going to start trouble. Please stop.*"

"*I am drawing attention, but there will be no trouble. I want people to know I have returned. When the rumors begin, I want plenty to have borne witness,*" and with that, the communication was cut short. Iridan was not sure how Rashan had managed that, but if he wanted to contact the old demon again, he would have to work the spell a second time.

When they arrived at the Tower, the herald led them around to the side entrance. There were two main entries to the Tower of Contemplation, one through the palace itself and the other was the way they were taking. The Tower was a masterpiece of magical architecture. Like the rest of the palace, it was built of Ghelkan marble, mostly black with highlights of green streaked through it. The whole of the palace was also accented with filigree and statuary, and silver-capped towers of smaller height. The Tower of Contemplation was carved with runes of old protective spells, shielding the sorcerers of the Imperial Circle from enemies of magical power both near and far; the runes could turn aside mighty spells and prevent spying.

As they dismounted and allowed stable boys to take the reins of their horses, Brannis could not help but wonder anew at its beauty. He was born and raised in Kadris, but he spent much time away. It was easy to forget how wondrous the capital could appear. Iridan also could not help but take in the sight of his order's seat of power, having only been up close a few times and only inside even fewer. The Circle's herald barely gave the Tower a second glance, having just come from it earlier in the day, and having been in and out of it a dozen times a week for many long summers. Rashan, however, stopped entirely. He looked up, and his gaze swept each balcony, each carved gargoyle, every rune, and all the greenish swirls of the exotic marble. Brannis thought he might be harboring second thoughts about bullying his way in to see the Inner Circle, but Iridan thought he seemed more wistful.

When they finally did enter, the guards did not budge to challenge them. Brannis suspected, though he had no way to look into the aether to tell, that their overly stiff posture was due to Rashan holding them at their posts by magical means. A sweeping set of stairs circled almost endlessly upward around the circumference of the main chamber of the Tower, the ceiling of which was obscured in shadow over a hundred feet above them. Rashan took the lead, marching straight for the middle of the room. Brannis and Iridan followed. The herald remained behind as the three of them began to rise on a platform that formed itself beneath them out of nothing but aether. While Rashan had been the one to activate it, it was not his magic that was at work. It was an accommodation for the many elders among the Circle, for whom the number of stairs was daunting if not entirely impossible. The levitation platforms let the older sorcerers attend Circle meetings without needing their own magic to ascend the stairs. It was in very poor taste for young, able-bodied sorcerers of the Third Circle and below to use them.

As they gently ascended, Iridan leaned close to Rashan. "Do you think you might have changed clothes? You ... You do not quite look the part at the moment," he whispered to the purported warlock.

"I am just hoping he does not decide to kill them all," Brannis muttered under his breath.

He panicked, though, as Rashan chuckled; he had not actually intended to speak that aloud. Rashan did not answer either of them, however, and kept to himself as they rose.

As the platform made its way up toward the topmost levels of the tower, they drew curious stares from those on the landings and on the stairs who were going about their daily business in service to the Circle. Clerks and scribes, messengers and sorcerers, all bustled about, entering and leaving the various chambers and corridors that branched off from the landings at each level. The sight of the three travelers was extraordinary enough that much work was interrupted to gossip about the unusual visitors.

Brannis had not really stopped to think about it at first, but Rashan's shabby attire was probably low among their interests. Here Brannis was, still dusty from the road, armored and bearing a magical weapon. It was the last that he regretted. Had the herald not been so disconcerted by Rashan's bullying, he likely would have disarmed Brannis, or at least required him to leave the sword below. Brannis fingered the dragon-sculpted hilt of Massacre and wondered if he might be able to leave it with the guards who would be stationed outside the Inner Circle's Sanctum.

Brannis's musings did not have long to fester and gnaw at him with worry. If the Inner Circle was going to feel threatened by his sword, so be it, because as soon as they reached the top of the inner chamber of the tower, Rashan strode off. There was naught else at the landing but a short corridor leading to the stairs up into the Sanctum. A pair of imperial guards flanked the bottom of the stairs. Each wielded a weapon like a trident, with the center tine greatly shorter than the outer two. Neither of them so much as flinched as the three approached, and even Brannis had caught on as to why.

I suppose they would not do much good taking custody of it anyway, Brannis reflected, consciously removing his hand from the hilt of Massacre and assuming a normal gait.

The stairs led up into the Sanctum proper. They emerged at the lower circle, a great, ornate chamber with a floor inlaid with runes of protection, both from physical harm and from more subtle invasions against the privacy of the proceedings. Around the walls of the chamber were portraits and busts showing past high sorcerers, set into shallow alcoves in the stone. Iridan could feel the faint hum of harnessed aether, both from the room's wards as well as from the members of the Inner Circle and the various protections they carried.

The Sanctum had a mezzanine level all around. A complete circle was formed of twelve seats behind a chest-high wall, with stone desks hidden from view below. Those seats held the twelve members of the Inner Circle itself. Each had a commanding and imposing view of those stranded below in the lower circle, who by their lack of a seat above were already deemed to be lower in rank to the Inner Circle—only the emperor could command them, and the emperor did not petition at the Sanctum but would hold audience in the palace itself.

There were faint noises of surprise as Rashan entered ahead of Iridan, with Brannis following in lastly. The assembled sorcerers had not been prepared for their guests to have arrived already.

"Markham, what is this? You had not leave to bring them in yet! Markham?" called Gravis Archon, High Sorcerer of the Kadrin Empire, seated directly opposite the entrance, looking down at them.

Even seated, it was clear he was a tall man, gaunt, with intense green eyes. His hair was streaked through with grey, but his narrow face was only slightly wrinkled. He appeared to be a man in his late fifties, though really he was more than double that age. Like all the rest of the Inner Circle, he wore black robes trimmed with red and gold; neither insignia nor regalia marked him as the leader.

When there was no response, and after a somewhat uncomfortable pause, Iridan spoke up: "High Sorcerer, the herald remained below. He gave no reason but did not follow on the lifting disc," his voice quiet and meek.

"I shall deal with that later," Gravis harrumphed. "So, Iridan Korian, you have returned to us safely and reported on troubling goblin activity in the vicinity of Kelvie Forest. Caladris has passed along the information you have shared with him already." Gravis nodded in acknowledgment of Caladris Solaran, seated three seats to his left. "We will, of course, be interested in further details, especially on two subjects. Firstly, we would like to hear Sir Brannis's account of the events you described. By your own admission, you were incapacitated in battle and did not recover for some days thereafter.

"Secondly, the matter of this vagrant you have brought back with you. Caladris told me of his claim, though there seemed not to be much evidence to support it," Gravis said.

Iridan carefully kept his attention on the high sorcerer, but something was amiss. He had gone to great lengths detailing the things he had seen Rashan do in their short time traveling with him, and relayed at least the gist of the stories he'd told. Clearly either Caladris was withholding information from the high sorcerer, or Gravis Archon was disdainful of the evidence Iridan had given.

"I would not have been troubled had you taken it upon yourself to slay him for his temerity, young Iridan."

Rashan smiled. "That certainly would have been entertaining."

"Silence!" shouted Gravis. "In this chamber, you will speak only when answering a question posed by one of the Circle."

"What is your name, then?" Rashan asked innocently. "I am sorry, but I did not even think to inquire as to who was high sorcerer these days."

The high sorcerer's face flushed. "How dare you! I am Gravis Archon, and I just—"

"Little Gravis? You grew up to be high sorcerer. I can scarcely believe it." Rashan laughed a little.

Had the wards in the Sanctum not prevented nearly any form of magical violence, likely Gravis would have struck him down where he stood.

"Guards! Remove this vagabond! Place him in one of the warded cells." Gravis was nearly apoplectic. "If he wants to pretend he is a warlock, let us see him figure a way out of there."

"Pretending to be a warlock? Hmm," Rashan mused.

The ill-fitted leathers he wore began to melt and flow. Before the guards could make it up the stairs, Rashan wore a black tunic and loose pants, trimmed in red and gold not unlike the Inner Circle's garb. However, he'd added a cape as well, with plate-armored epaulettes of gold. It was a warlock's traditional uniform.

Rashan smiled and cocked his head to the side. "Is that better?"

At that point, the guards made their way in, and the reason for the unique weapons they carried became clear. They dropped the trident heads to either side of Rashan's neck, and the long side tines of the weapons curled around like collars, leaving the short points nearly impaling him. Several of the Inner Circle seemed lost in concentration. Iridan supposed that Rashan's little trick had given them cause to look into the aether. He wondered if in the aether-rich chamber, they would be able to notice his lack of a mortal Source. Seeing that Rashan's emitted no aether might be too much to ask with so much else to see.

"I would like to speak with the Emperor Dharus," Rashan stated, unfazed by the weapons that had captured him.

"Remove him," Gravis ordered the guards, pointedly ignoring Rashan's request.

While Gravis's attention was elsewhere, Iridan caught Caladris's gaze. The older sorcerer—Brannis's uncle, who was a stout man, not nearly so tall as most of the Solarans—gave a subtle half wink, acknowledgment enough for Iridan to know that Gravis was not acting in full knowledge of what he was dealing with.

Brannis watched everything transpire and hoped that he would be overlooked. This had gone nearly as badly as he could have imagined without resorting to open warfare, though it remained a possibility. He had seen the aftermath at Tibrik. Whether or not Rashan was truly the ancient warlock returned, as he claimed to be, he was dangerous.

Surprising both Brannis, and to a lesser extent Iridan, Rashan allowed himself to be led from the chamber by the guards. As he was walked down the stairway, his garments faded back to their original shape. Without turning back, he called out, "Third Law of Aether, recite!"

"A sorcerer must always—" Gravis caught himself mid-sentence.

His flush of anger had begun to fade only to be replaced by an even deeper flush of embarrassment. He remained silent until the prisoner was removed entirely from within earshot. None of the Inner Circle knew about his difficulties as a young student at the Academy. They did not know how many times he had been kept after class, memorizing the Laws of Aether and reciting them back to the instructors. They had kept him at it for hours on occasion, the talented but unfocused son of one of the Inner Circle members of those days. They did not allow him to fail and hammered every lesson into his head before they would let him go to his supper. They were times he would have preferred to bury somewhere where they would stay buried.

As the chamber fell back into a semblance of order, Gravis swept his gaze across the room, surveying the faces of his fellows. To his chagrin, he noted that several were rather amused and took little care to hide it. Two of the members of the Inner Circle, though, seemed concerned. The outburst had worried them.

"Now that *that* is resolved, let us—" Gravis began, but was cut short.

"No, I do not think that was resolved," interjected Dolvaen Lurien, one of the ones who had appeared concerned at both Rashan's actions and Gravis's reaction. A powerful sorcerer despite coming from an undistinguished bloodline, Dolvaen was the likely successor to Gravis Archon. Hard faced and hard eyed, he seemed always to have his brow furrowed in concentration and had a direct, almost rude manner that put him often at odds with the rest of the Circle. "I know what I saw just then. Who else bothered to look? That was a demon."

"How would you even tell in here? There is aether upon aether in the Sanctum. Can you pick one fish from a school and say it is not moving? Pick out one bird in a flock that is not flying quite right? In here, he could easily have been faking," claimed Maruk Solaran, Brannis's father.

The old man is ever the ornery skeptic, but this is the first time I can remember agreeing with him, Brannis thought. He kept his thoughts to himself this time but could not help feeling an unfamiliar swell of pride in his father.

"Faking? You cannot be serious," Dolvaen said.

"Did you not play at being demons when you were a boy at the Academy?" Caladris asked, drawing a scowl from Gravis Archon, who would have preferred to be off the topic of the Academy entirely. "Draw just as much as you give off, or as close as you can. You look a bit like a demon in aether-sight. Children cannot keep it up long, but I would wager any of us could have managed for as long as that fellow was in here."

"Hmm, interesting observation, Caladris," Gravis said. "And I was certainly unimpressed with his transmutation of his clothing. Surely most of us could manage a mentally cast spell in an aether-rich spot such as this, with no distractions about."

"What of his parting barb? A lucky guess? I would surmise not," suggested Stalia Gardarus, her light, high-pitched soprano a stark contrast to the deeper, more hard-edged voices from the male members of the Inner Circle. She was the second most junior of the twelve, with all the look of youth about her, belying her nearly three-score springtimes.

"A fine point. Would that have worked had I said it, Gravis?" Caladris jested, though his comment was meant also to support Stalia. "I cannot say I have ever had you sputtering Academy drivel before—"

"Can demons read minds?" Brannis dared to ask, and all eyes momentarily turned downward to where he and Iridan stood, half forgotten. Brannis's natural curiosity had just bested him, and it was too late to suggest "best two out of three." Curiosity had drawn blood and already been awarded the point.

"It is certainly possible in the general sense, but not here. The wards would not allow such a thing," Dolvaen responded, and to Brannis's relief had taken the question seriously. "But I just realized we are overlooking an obvious source of information. Sir Brannis, Iridan, what can you tell us about that person?"

Brannis noted that none used Rashan's name. He was hopeful that the skeptical Inner Circle might yet relieve him of the sinking feeling that Iridan was right about the "hermit."

"We found him in Kelvie Forest, growing lotus flowers," Brannis said. "Or should I say, he found us. As we retreated from our battle with the goblins, we wandered near his dwelling, and he took us in and tended to Iridan. None of us knew how to treat aether-burn, and he did. He traveled with us while Iridan recovered, and afterward for reasons he did not share. When we were ambushed at Tibrik, he destroyed the Megrenn soldiers who had occupied it. He went in alone, so we only saw the aftermath, but he was unharmed and they were ..." Brannis searched for an appropriate and tactful way to describe the horrific sight. "... thoroughly dead.

"I have seen him work magic, but never cast a spell. He also told us a version of the Battle of the Dead Earth that does not quite match the histories. In his version, Rashan Solaran walks away from the battle as the only survivor, leaving behind a sword he had named Heavens Cry." The Inner Circle looked a little uncomfortably at each other. Brannis was not sure what part had caused the disquiet, or whether it was just the whole thing in general. "I must say, though, that I am skeptical of his claims but have been able to find no definitive proof either way."

"Iridan, what have you to add?" asked Gravis, resuming his place as questioner among the Inner Circle and thankful to be on to a different topic. The high sorcerer relaxed back in his chair a bit.

"Well, I am certain that he is indeed a demon. I have observed him enough in the wilds where the aether is easier to read. He neither sleeps nor eats, though he briefly kept up a charade before he revealed his nature to us. His magic comes easily to him. As Brannis said, we never saw him use his magic in any manner but silently. I have no recollection of him using any spell of particular power, just a great number of lesser magics.

"He also very clearly wiped out the occupiers in Tibrik, but he rushed ahead of us, crossing the chasm before the bridge was down. I saw nothing of how he managed the feat, nor whether it was an exception to his subtle spellcasting," Iridan said, shifting his weight from one foot to the other. The eyes of the Empire's greatest sorcerers pierced him on all sides, and he could not get that thought out of his head as he recounted. "His tale of the Battle of the Dead

Earth—which he referred to as the Battle of Ferren's Plain—differed from what I was taught but seemed internally consistent."

"Well, that's one strike against his claims for certain. There were no survivors of that battle. The investigators that found the battlefield searched thoroughly; no survivors, no one fled. It was a complete annihilation of both sides, the only such incident in recorded history," Stalia said. "I might add that it is unlikely that Rashan Solaran would have left behind such a weapon as Heavens Cry. That dreadful thing was too valuable for him to leave, and too dangerous. He would not have risked who might have taken custody of it."

"Hmm, agreed. That is true," Maruk said then nodded in agreement, and much of the Inner Circle followed suit. "For his faults, he was a responsible protector of the Empire. He gave his life to save us all from Loramar. Let us not forget that, when we complain about the troubles with the enemies he forged for Kadrin."

Brannis expected as much; his father was always willing to push the family legacy when he had the chance.

"I believe him," Iridan said softly. In the echoing Sanctum, though, few voices went unheard, and he might as easily have shouted his statement. "I cannot say quite why, aside from all the evidence I have given. I just felt a connection with him. He seems unlike what I would have thought a demon would be like."

"Someday you will learn wisdom, young Iridan. You show much promise," Gravis said. "But be wary of the easy answer: it may lead you past the harder questions."

"Indeed, he shows much promise," Dolvaen said. "I hear that he is among the strongest of the Fourth Circle, and with his performance on this assignment, I shall sponsor his petition to advance to the Third." Dolvaen was often a champion for the advancement of sorcerers who were not a part of the selectively bred sorcerous bloodlines. He felt it served the Empire well to foster new blood where talent was to be found.

"That is neither urgent nor germane, Dolvaen. Let us consider the options before us," Gravis said. "This creature is either a demon or not. He is either Rashan Solaran or he is not. He claims he is both. What does he gain from each, were he to be lying?"

There was a general agreement among the Inner Circle. Among other traits, Gravis was a scholar and no fool. His leadership of the Inner Circle was more than just a feat of magical power.

"Well, it would seem reasonable to assume he is a demon. I mean, what advantage is there in that lie?" asked Fenris Destrier, who had been silent until that point. He spoke little at council, until the more talkative sorcerers had cut to the heart of an argument. "If he means to pass as one, surely he would be found out eventually."

"Perhaps his plans for the ruse are short term, and he feels he could maintain the deception long enough to pull it off. He was certainly convincing enough in front of the twelve of us, and we are no peasant farmers to be fooled by cheap tricks," Maruk reasoned.

"But to what advantage? If nothing else, we are more suspicious of him now. If he meant to sneak among us, he has failed already," Fenris said.

"If he wants everyone to believe he is Rashan Solaran, he needs to explain how he is still alive. Being immortal certainly covers that." Brannis could not help but point out what he considered to be the obvious answer, rather than wait for the Circle to shake it out via debate. He hoped he was not overstepping his bounds.

"Aha! Now that would seem sensible," Gravis said. "If we acknowledged him as Rashan Solaran, and thus as warlock, he would outrank us all. Certainly there must be inherent value in that. Whatever other scheme he may be working, access to everything in the Tower and palace, command of the Circle and the army.

"He must have studied up on the warlock, perhaps having infiltrated the Academy, or even House Solaran for details that he could use to make himself convincing. I am practically the only one in the Empire old enough to remember him firsthand, and I was a mere boy. My recollections are poor at best."

"It seems you have a rather compelling narrative, Gravis," Stalia said. "I feel inclined to agree. This charlatan, whether he is a demon or not, seems intent on gaining power over us. Whether the details of your conjecture bear out, I believe that you have caught this one by the tail."

Pouring a glass from a decanter under his desk, Caladris added, "Or we are all witnessing a return of the meanest, cruelest warlock the Empire ever knew. One or the other."

There was a long pause where no one spoke, and Caladris drained his wineglass. More than a handful of his fellows wished they kept spirits hidden away in the Sanctum as well, at that thought.

"Well, enough for now. We all have much to consider. The prisoner will remain sealed in a warded cell until we determine a course of action," Gravis stated, trying to reclaim the mood of order and efficiency in the Sanctum that he preferred. "Sir Brannis, I regret having detained you so long. You surely have a report to give to your commander. You and Iridan are dismissed," and he waved them away.

There was little ceremony among the sorcerers, so Brannis and Iridan merely turned and left the way they came in, unescorted.

* * * * * * * *

As the two guards hauled him down the height of the tower and toward the palace dungeons, Rashan fought to control himself. There was one tenet that had kept him alive for over two centuries, and he had to convince himself that he was not violating it now, despite the fact that it certainly felt like he was. That tenet was: *"Suffer no enemy to live once they have offered violence."*

The trident points poised at his neck were no real threat to him, but the guards did not realize that. They were just loyal men of the Empire, following orders that were just and proper. It was he who was playing at games, Rashan reminded himself. He was risking their lives against his own lack of control.

As they walked down the corridors that ran beneath the palace, Rashan could envision the walls painted red with their blood, and their bones and flesh in a sloppy pile below. He could easily destroy them with his bare hands, or with a quick blast of lightning, or—

Stop it! he interrupted his own train of thought. *This is why I was exiled. Killing is too easy—my solution to too many problems.*

He let himself be led the rest of the way to a special section of the dungeons. The guards alerted a Third Circle sorcerer, whose job it was to help with such matters, that they needed a cell opened in the warded area.

There was no proper door where the sorcerer laid his hand, fingers tracing runes in a purposeful order from among the hundreds that adorned the wall. When he finished, a section of the wall opened, and the sorcerer stepped back quickly. The guards shoved Rashan inside, none too gently, and quickly released the grasp they had around Rashan's neck. A touch to the wall outside of the cell closed it quickly.

The room was utterly dark. Neither window, nor lamp, nor construct of aether was left to the unfortunate prisoner in the warded cell. Rashan was untroubled by the lack of light. He was so accustomed to aether-sight that he preferred it anyway, and his aether-sight could see plenty well.

The walls and ceiling were of basalt, covered in runes that were inlaid with silver. The center of the room was the only spot left bare. It was where the prisoner belonged. The runes were a nasty framework for an aether construct that drew aether out of the room. There was a constant pull even against the prisoner's Source, stronger the closer he got to the walls. The only relatively safe spot was the very center of the room, on the floor, for the ceiling bore such runes as well. Tiny holes disguised among the runes allowed in enough air to keep the prisoner alive, but little else. The cell was meant to feel like a water-filled chamber with just a small pocket of air to breath. It was a cell for keeping sorcerers helpless. Drawing aether against the runes' pull was nearly pointless; they were too strong and would just draw it back anyway if it was not used immediately. There was no stray aether floating about, so any spells cast would have to draw from the prisoner's own Source, a dangerous endeavor.

It was devious and possibly a little extreme, but Rashan was proud of it. The Empire had used them for ages, but he had made the most recent modifications. He could still see his own handiwork in the crafting. It was not his best work, he admitted, but it had been such a long time ago. The aether construct upon it had been rebuilt since he had left the Empire, but that was no surprise; such things wore down over time, how quickly depending on how well they were formed in the first place.

But Rashan's Source was sealed against such mild influence as the draw of the runes, and his small demon body used only a fraction of the aether his Source produced. He was constantly working small magics just to burn off the excess. He waited an hour or so for things outside to have quieted down and then proceeded to let himself out of the cell.

Rashan's aether snaked through the wall to the same runes the Third Circle sorcerer had used to open it the first time. The cell tried to draw the aether apart and pull it away from him, but Rashan's control was too finely honed. There was no fraying edge of a spell for the wall's magic to grasp hold of and unravel it by.

He smirked as the door opened. The cell would hold just about anyone, from an Academy novice to a high sorcerer, or even a warlock, but a demon—especially one who had created it—was too much for it.

As he stepped out of the cell, casually touching the wall to close it behind him, he looked up and down the corridor. The dungeon was cheerier than he had remembered it. Whoever had last renewed the lights had not much of a flair for the macabre. Dungeons were not intended to be pleasant places; half their function was to demoralize prisoners. Rashan reached out and dimmed the lights just a little and reddened them a bit, making it more like torchlight.

He felt as if he had arrived home after a long holiday to find out the caretakers of his estate had redecorated in his absence. It was all so familiar, but the trappings had changed. Rashan allowed the tiniest bit of doubt to steal into his heart.

Can I have everything back, as if I had never left?

He picked a direction and strode down the corridor, heading out of the dungeons. He had a lot to do.

* * * * * * * *

As they rode through the city streets, the soldiers' mood lightened. Per Rashan's orders, they were being treated as important guests of the Empire. The guards who had originally expected to be dragging them before their superiors to answer a lot of uncomfortable questions were instead escorting them to one of the oldest and most respected inns in the city. Along the way, they were headed to the market. Jodoul had the idea shortly after leaving the city gates that they were on free horses, which had become theirs fair and square through being at the right place at the right time when Rashan killed their previous owners. Thus they were going to sell them.

As they entered the marketplace, even those who had never been to Kadrin found it unusually crowded. The tailors, clothiers, and food stands of all kinds were doing the heaviest business. It did not take them long to realize that they had arrived back to Kadrin just in time for the Bygones Festival. It was the traditional day to dress up as someone you spent most of the cycle of seasons at odds with and get drunk together.

The Bygones Festival was held just after the harvest ended. Harvest time mattered little to the urban residents of the capital, but the festival dated back centuries. Back then—and even in modern times in the farmlands—it was a time just after the hardest work of the season had been finished, when tempers were just cooling after a lot of people with differing agendas and needs all just finished their wrangling over prices, transporting goods to market, and other business dealings. It gave everyone a chance to literally see themselves as others saw them and to diffuse feuds with humor and drink before everyone was stuck indoors all winter together.

Sir Lugren had taken his leave of them once he was free to do so, parting just after the gates. The rest of them made their way to the market, sold their mounts, and, for the first time in their lives, were considering a proper Bygones Festival celebration. None of the conscripts had a valuable trade or any family wealth—otherwise they would not have been conscripted—so it was a new experience shopping for costumes. They had horse money filling their pockets!

The stalls and carts that clogged the marketplace offered choices aplenty. There were merchants from Safschan selling black silk that could be made into a fine likeness of the Imperial Circle robes, a popular costume among the army. Traders from Gar-Danel sold polished wooden swords that many a sorcerer would wear sheathed on his hip come nightfall. Many professions had traditional rivals, whether through daily conflict throughout the season or through a history of excellent salesmanship levering a rivalry into place where none seemed quite to fit—the shepherds and fishermen were something of a stretch, for example. For the Bygones Festival, the merchants made sure they had something to sell to practically everyone.

"Figure this fella! Thinks I'm gonna give him two lions for this here little rag of a robe," Jodoul complained to the marketplace in general, turning his back to a man who had tried to sell him a sorcerer costume.

"It's silk, what'd you expect?" Tod retorted, seemingly less interested in shopping than in getting to their fancy accommodations and having a good long rest. "Just pick out something simple and be done with it."

"My wife made mine out of wool, dyed black. Sewed it all herself. Fits me like my own shadow," commented one of the guards escorting them. Being ordered to treat someone like an "honored guest" gave them considerable latitude in catering to their requests. An hour or two poking about in the markets with their charges was a better way to spend the afternoon than at their post, so the guards were in no rush to get to the inn.

"Well, I never had a proper costume before, so I wanted something, you know, maybe a bit nice," Jodoul replied. "I ain't had this sort of money before. Are you gonna get something a little stylish, Tod?"

"Prob'ly not, my horse had got bad teeth they said. Only gave me three lions, five hawks for the beast. I don't want to dunk it all on a Bygones costume. I did not get seven lions, like you did. Hey now! That reminds me, you still owe me from our dice game," Tod said.

"Wow. In all the confusion out there, it had escaped my head entirely. I can't say I even remember how we'd left off." Jodoul chuckled. He glanced sidelong at Tod to see if he was going to get any leeway with this tactic.

"Four lions, three hawks," Tod answered dryly, raising an eyebrow to glare back.

* * * * * * * *

Brannis and Iridan went their separate ways leaving the Tower of Contemplation. Brannis headed for his family's estate on the outskirts of the city, and Iridan to his own rooms, in a boarders' house near the city's western gate. Brannis wanted to change and wash before reporting to his superiors; Iridan just wanted some rest. While Iridan had been attached to Brannis's command for the excursion, he was not part of the army's chain of command and had only to answer to the Circle. If the generals wanted answers from Iridan, they would have to ask Gravis Archon.

The roads around the palace were usually busy, but with the upcoming Bygones Night party the palace held each autumn about to begin a few hours hence, there was a heavy flow of people and foodstuffs heading toward the palace as he tried to leave. As Brannis eased his horse through the wagonloads of wine barrels, carts of fresh fruits, and various other conveyances filled with delicacies, he was glad of the direction he was headed. In a few short hours, the palace would be filled with revelry and merriment of a sort Brannis wanted no part.

As a knight from a respected family, he would have been welcomed at the palace celebration. For most holidays, Brannis was more than happy to accept an invitation to the royal celebrations, but the Bygones Festival was his least favorite time of the cycle of seasons. He loved the colorful displays of magic that lighted the night skies on Founding Day, the elaborate banquets that were served at the Summer Equinox, and the drunken revels of Promise Day, but the costumed puffery of the Bygones Festival he wanted no part in. Tradition would have him dress as a sorcerer for the night, just as all the sorcerers at the palace would be dressed as knights. Brannis had spent nearly his whole youth pretending he was a sorcerer, and it was a time in his life he was glad to put behind him.

As he made his way clear of the worst of the crush of bodies trying to get to the palace, he urged his horse to a trot and made good time through the side streets. Kadrin was a large city and the seat of government, with guards and knights and sorcerers in abundance, but still had dangerous areas that decent folk avoided, especially after dark. Brannis did not need to worry about being accosted as he took the shortest route home through areas where a drunken merchant had a coin flip's chance to make it through with his purse. It was hours yet until sundown, and Brannis was hardly the sort to invite trouble at any hour. Mounted and armored, carrying an ornate sword and wearing the adornments of both the army and House Solaran, no sane criminal would risk impeding him.

The ride home was not a long one, less than half the time it would have been had he followed the main roads. He rode onto the grounds of Solaran Estate and took a short gallop over to the stables. Situated on the southern bank of Dragon Lake—so named for the small island that nearly cut it in half running north-south, giving it the look of a reptilian iris—the home of one of the most respected families in the Empire was extravagant. The main building covered acres and was of construction as fine as the palace—understandable, since it was constructed around the same time period by many of the same sorcerers. Towers and parapets rose to heights carefully kept just shorter than those the emperor's home boasted. The grounds were manicured green grasses, with gardens, topiaries, and orchards of exotic fruit trees imported from all over the world. The estate also included stables, a number of outbuildings to house the servants, a boathouse, docks, and fountains. There was also an area of flat black marble that was inscribed with numerous runed circles, glyphs, and other magical devices of general purpose for aiding in certain spells.

Brannis ignored the commonplace wonders of his familial home. He had been seeing them all his life, and while he was aware of how spectacular the sights were, he was jaded to them. His current goal was a simple one: get cleaned up and report to General Sir Hurald Chadreisson on the Kelvie mission.

He left his horse at the stables and jogged up to the entrance and opened the door. The wards on the door knew him as a member of the Solaran family, so he did not need someone else to allow him entry. It was good enough security that no servant manned the door unless guests were expected. That served Brannis's needs just fine, as he was in a rush and preferred not to get the whole "Welcome home, how was your little adventure?" treatment from some servant who had known him since childhood—and at Brannis's still-tender age of twenty-two, there were a fair number who had.

For once, Bygones Night was kind to Brannis, as much of the household staff was let off work early to prepare for their own celebrations. The family was nearly all invited to the palace for the evening, so the servants were not needed around the house that night. Brannis made his way up to his room without incident.

The room had been kept immaculate in his absence, in a way that it could never be when he was regularly at home. The bed linens were all cleaned and tucked tightly and there were no clothes or weapons or armor left about. The wardrobe was closed—Brannis never bothered closing it—which meant it was likely filled with his cleaned clothes.

Brannis closed the door behind him and began stripping off his road-worn, battle-stained uniform. He struggled some getting out of his armor without help, but with some trouble was able to manage, leaving the discarded plates at the foot of the bed. He tossed Massacre on the bed in its sheath. While it was perfectly acceptable to visit army headquarters armed, even when speaking to a general, most in the army and the knighthood were uncomfortable around that sword. While Brannis was far from the only knight with an enchanted blade, his was a particularly nasty piece of work, and those who knew its powers were leery of being too close to it. He studied the workmanship of the hilt and wondered again why something so fierce was adorned so whimsically. The sculpted dragon made it uncomfortable to wield in his bare hand; the maker obviously had been less concerned about utility than aesthetics when it he forged it.

Brannis pulled on fresh pants from the wardrobe and made his way bare-chested over to the wash basin. The servants had kept it filled, but the water was tepid. Any other adult in the family would have heated it with aether without a second thought, but with no servant handy to get him hot water for it, Brannis was forced to wash up with cold water.

After toweling off, he put on a clean uniform, emblazoned with the Solaran family crest. It had taken some research for Brannis to discover the crest when he had been knighted. Traditionally sorcerers wore no family coat of arms, so despite their prominence in the Empire, none of the family had known what their centuries-old crest had looked like. Brannis had eventually found a rendering in an old book on the families of the Kadrin Empire and had a seamstress embroider one from the picture to have on his tabard.

Suitably attired for polite company, Brannis headed back down to the stables to retrieve a fresh horse and to answer for the loss of his unit. He just hoped Sir Hurald was not already dressed for Bygones Night. Being dressed down by a man in sorcerer's robes was the last thing he needed.

Chapter 17 - For Lost Time

Rashan walked casually through the halls of the palace, not even pausing as he enspelled the guards to ignore him. He had come up from the dungeons and proceeded directly to the residential portions of the palace. The building was ancient, and there had been no significant remodeling done in the hundred winters he had been gone. The decor had changed somewhat, a combination of evolving fashions and the personal taste of the current emperor, Dharus, of whom Rashan knew little.

Emperor Dharus was a recluse by all accounts, preferring solitude and holding court infrequently, letting his advisers run the day-to-day dealings of the Empire. He would appear at his balcony to make proclamations and speeches, then retreat to his quarters, or more frequently his country estates. Rashan was guessing that he would make at least a token appearance at the Bygones Night festivities, however.

Rashan had been focused when he arrived in Kadris, but not so much so that he had overlooked the obvious celebratory preparations going on in the city. Times changed, but Bygones Festival was still one of the favorite holidays in the Empire. Tradition held that the emperor had no rival, no adversary to placate once an autumn, thus he attended any function of Bygones Festival in his normal royal garb. In some ways, it isolated a man in an already lonely position at the highest level of power in the Empire, to not truly take part in the revels that his subjects enjoyed so much. However, it was too much to pass up the sight of so many of the important personages of the Empire making asses of themselves impersonating one another.

Rashan had every intention of crashing the party that was to be held in the palace that evening. The building thrummed with excited energy as the main ballroom was decorated for the occasion. Food and drink from the finest merchants in Kadrin were brought in and set out in buffets. Coming up through the dungeons was easy enough, but in the upper levels of the palace, the bustle of so many people made staying unnoticed difficult. He had to quickly hide the shabby clothes he wore before he drew attention. He transformed them into a messenger's outfit much the same way he had made them look like a warlock's ensemble earlier at the Tower of Contemplation. A messenger who walked purposefully and looked like he knew where he was going was seldom interrupted.

Rashan did have a purpose and most certainly knew where he was going. It was a matter of what he would find when he got there.

He found his destination at the end of a hall that was seldom visited. The floors were kept clean, but there was little other reason to come down this way. The door in front of him was outlined in runes, both on the door and on the stone frame it was set in. The two lines of runes matched up, with identical symbols on each, directly across from one another. A faint, subtle pull of aether fed the magic of the door's locking spell. Unlike the crude cell down in the dungeons, this work was a masterpiece. While it was not designed to harm anyone, it was a bit of self-regenerating magic, an aether construct that would repair and renew itself, rather than slowly give way to the passage of time, weakening until it ultimately failed.

Rashan wove a complicated web of aether, touching just the right places at the right times. It was so ingrained in him that he did it with hardly a conscious thought. This was his room.

It was much as he remembered leaving it the day he departed with the Red Riders for Farren's Plain. There were the discarded clothes he had worn the day before, ready to fall apart with age. The wardrobe stood open. Upon the shelves was a collection of books, a few of which he had written himself.

Blast! he thought. *Someone got in here.*

There was a book missing, and after a moment's thought, Rashan knew which it was. *The Warlock Prophecies* was gone from its spot. The immortal warlock sighed deeply. He hoped that the book had not caused any trouble.

Rashan had always possessed a dark sense of humor. In his younger days, when he was feeling annoyed with someone he could not justify killing, he would often retire to his room and write prophecy. Rashan had no gift of foresight, but it was cathartic to write of doom and woe in the most cryptic and vague ways he thought someone might someday believe. As he wrote them, he took his petty vengeance on the generations yet unborn who believed in prophecy and would get what they deserved for reading his. He had always hated prophecies and the passive, helpless thinking they engendered. Rashan carved his own history with steel and aether, and the thought that fate or some unknown agent of the universe controlled his actions was anathema to him.

In those younger days, he had taken a sinister glee in the thought that weak-minded fools one day would follow his prophecies as some sort of grand revelation that could save them from the dooms they predicted if only they deciphered them. Now he just hoped that whoever had broken into his room and stolen it had not taken it seriously. He could not recall everything he had written, but some of it likely applied to the current era.

The entry into his room had been no small feat. Whoever had managed it must have studied the locking aether construct extensively. There were a number of steps required to disarm the layers upon layers of aether guarding the construct. It would have been simpler to have confronted the wards guarding the physical structure of the door and just blasted it off its hinges. The latter would have required considerable power in its own right, but was far less complicated and painstaking. However, Rashan had not built any means of inflicting harm into the door's protections; it was in the middle of the palace, after all, and he had no reason to harm overly curious palace staff or mischievous young sorcerers. It was simply a matter of ensuring the sanctity of his own privacy—and if forced to admit it, to show off how well he could craft it.

Whoever had broken in had certainly earned himself a modicum of respect from the warlock. To take on the tedious task of figuring out the lock rather than the idiot's method of caving in the door bespoke someone who also wished to show off their cleverness. However, to have taken—near as he could tell—only the prophetic writings, damped that respect markedly.

Rashan double-checked the rest of the room. His recollections were a century old, and while he possessed a good memory, time played tricks with even an immortal's past. Still worried he might have overlooked something missing, he concluded that it was probably just the book.

What Rashan had really come to his old room for was easily found. On a special rack made just to hold it, hung his formal garb. Identical to the robes and cloak he had imitated before the Inner Circle, these were the genuine article. The tunic was of a rare spider silk that was naturally black and shimmered iridescent in certain lighting. The gold trim was actually gold-infused thread, and the red trim got its color from ruby dust. The cloak was dragon hide, with meteoric iron pauldrons that were trimmed in plated gold. The pauldrons were joined together in the front and back as a single piece, and Rashan pulled them over his head as he finished changing.

Rashan reached under the back of his collar and pulled his long hair free where it had been caught under the cloak, shaking it loose and letting it fall back into place. He stepped over to the mirror and casually swept away the century's worth of dust that had accumulated, using a small wind called up from the aether. He looked himself over critically. He looked younger than the last time he had seen himself in that mirror, the wrinkles at the corners of his eyes gone along with the dark circles that often hung below them. His hair was pure white now as opposed to blond and grey, and covered all the areas it had formerly retreated from. Age had been kind to the exceptional materials his warlock's gear was crafted from, but not nearly so generous as the gifts immortality had granted him. Still, two items were missing.

The boots Rashan had preferred were lost at the Battle of Farren's Plain. *Fine, "Battle of the Dead Earth" if that is what they insist on calling it.* They were a practical pair, suitable to the dirty work of fighting necromancers, unlike the finery he had just donned. He had no other pair like them. Walking barefoot over to the bed, he reached under and found a nice pair of house slippers that looked enough like soft shoes to avoid embarrassment, and slipped them on.

The last piece he was missing was hovering in the air over its sheath, which hung from a pair of hooks in the wall just below it. *Ahh, Avalanche, how long has it been? Too long, I think.* Grasping the hilt, he pulled the sword from its perch atop nothingness. The blade had a bluish tint to its steel, but the blade and crosspiece were otherwise not unusual for a broadsword. He gave it a couple effortless sweeps through the air, holding it in one hand; though in battle, he had always used two. He was much stronger now than he had been as a mortal; the changes he had wrought in his body were more than cosmetic. He was careful to avoid hitting anything with the blade. Avalanche was a weapon that was difficult to impede. He could put it through the wall if he was not careful with it.

He let the blade go for a moment, and it resumed hovering exactly where it was left. To test its enchantment, Rashan leaned heavily against the flat of the blade and could not feel the slightest give to it. Satisfied, he retrieved the sheath from the wall and buckled it onto his belt. Taking control of the sword once more, he slid it into its sheath with a satisfying *snick*. Only in its sheath, or when wielded, could Avalanche be moved.

Walking back to the mirror, he rechecked his appearance. The shoes were not very noticeable, he was relieved to find. The sword seemed lacking, though. While the workmanship was fine, and he had carried it habitually through much of his tenure as warlock, he knew that it was unimpressive to look at. The sword and hilt were finely crafted, but certainly no more so than most knight's blades. Whoever had crafted it, ages ago, had been primarily concerned with utility. Rashan had always appreciated that aspect of the sword since he had used it often and found it served its purpose admirably. For now, though, he wanted something showier, something that would cause a bit more of a stir.

He wanted to retrieve Heavens Cry.

Making sure the door was secured behind him, its wards back to their silent sentry duty, he turned and set off to get it.

* * * * * * * *

Well, that could have gone worse, I suppose, Brannis thought, feeling drained.

He had just returned from army headquarters and his meeting with General Sir Hurald and Sir Garibald, the commander of Kadrin forces and his own commander, respectively. The older knight had thankfully been in his army uniform still, despite being expected at the palace shortly thereafter in foppish sorcerer's garb. They had listened to Brannis's accounting of the mission, the battle, and the return trip home in silence, not asking any questions until he had finished.

That was when Sir Hurald revealed that Sir Lugren had already reported in, and had a different take on Brannis's story. Lugren had told Sir Hurald that the army had been unprepared for the goblins' arrival despite vain efforts to make them so. He reported that Iridan was unable to effectively counter the goblins' own sorcerers, and that many of their casualties were a direct result. He had complained about the efforts of carrying the stricken Iridan with them when no effort was made to bring any of the fallen soldiers along, and of the time they had wasted with the delusional hermit that eventually claimed to be Warlock Rashan.

Brannis's own account had agreed on all the wide-sweeping facts, but on the minor details and interpretations, Lugren had disagreed entirely. While Sir Lugren spoke well of Brannis's combat acumen, he had convinced the general that Brannis was unfit for command. Even though Brannis held a higher rank on the mission than Lugren, Hurald chose to take the older, more veteran knight's word on the matter, especially since Brannis seemed to at least entertain the idea that the hermit they met might really be the former Kadrin warlock.

As he walked though the house and up to his room, Brannis could think of little aside from finding his bed and sleeping through the rest of Bygones Night. The growling of his stomach asserted itself, though, and he corrected his thought. He could think of little else but sneaking some food from the kitchen, heading up to his room to eat, and sleeping away the remainder of the evening.

When he reached his room, carrying a battered turkey leg and a tankard of ale, he received a shock. Upon opening the door, he had seen that someone had stolen in. His heart raced as he realized that the sword on his bed was not Massacre.

He rushed over to the bed, hastily setting his meal down on a side table, and looked to see what was there. Under some fragments that appeared to have once been the dragon-sculpted handle of Massacre, there was a note, written in a brusque, scratchy script:

I wanted my sword back. Take this one. I think you shall like it better anyway. Its name is Avalanche. Be careful with it until you have learned its tricks. It does not move unless sheathed or in hand. —Uncle Rashan

Brannis felt dizzy.
What does he mean by "my sword"?
Brannis picked up the broken pieces of the little dragon that used to perch at his hip. He tried fitting them back together and noticed that they were actually *not* the hilt of his sword, but had actually covered it. There was a hollowed out area inside the sculpture that was the shape of a much thinner handle, one that would have been uncomfortably small for his large hands. It would seem to have been ideally suited to someone Rashan's size, though.

He knew that trying to chase down the demon was pointless. He would not know what to do if he caught him. By the note, he bore Brannis no ill will, but confronting him would likely irritate him at the least. Brannis tried thinking back to when he had first met Rashan. Had he taken any particular interest in the sword? How soon had he recognized the weapon?
Have I really been carrying Heavens Cry around all this time?
Ever curious, Brannis could not help but wonder about the new blade he had been given. He pulled Avalanche from its sheath on the bed and gave it a few experimental swings to test its weight. It felt like almost nothing in his hand.
Probably a lightened weapon for a smaller swordsman, someone Rashan's size, Brannis mused.

He swung it around hard a few times, making a *hwoom, hwoom* sound as it displaced the air. Brannis looked around the room for something to test it on, but his own armor, piled in a heap at the foot of his bed, was the best he could find. Not wanting to ding his armor, he gently tapped at the breastplate with Avalanche.

Crunch!

The sword smashed the breastplate against the floor and took a fist-sized chunk out of the stone. Startled, he dropped the sword and leaped back from it. The sword did not fall, but stayed point down, angled to the floor just as he had left it. More cautious this time, he grabbed the hilt and picked it up again, then let it go in midair. Again it stayed.

Accepting the fact that he could do little about the demon's desire for Heavens Cry, Brannis brightened his mood by playing with Avalanche, seeing what it was capable of.

* * * * * * *

As darkness fell over the city of Kadrin, the lights of the palace shone brightly. From the open and welcoming doors, magical illumination spilled out onto the marble-paved road that ran past the entrance, where carriages deposited their various personages of royal invitation. To be welcomed at the palace that night, one had to be either a noble, a head of one of the trade guilds, a knight, or a member of the Imperial Circle. There was a line of carriages out front, as guests awaited their turn to disembark. Those among the guests who lived closer sometimes walked and thus avoided the long wait for the carriages to unload. In all, there were likely to be over five hundred in attendance before guests stopped filling the palace ballroom.

Rashan watched the procession from the shadows near the entrance gate, far from the doors of the palace but close to where the carriages passed as they entered the grounds. He kept an idle count of the conveyances as they passed, but was mostly looking to see what sort of folk were running the Empire nowadays. There was only so much one could gather from the partygoers at a revel, but at least Rashan saw that the Empire appeared to be prospering; the guests were bedecked in expensive-looking finery, almost without exception. The only ones who seemed to be dressed in less than extravagant luxury were some of the younger members of the Circle, and a few knights and nobles from less well-off families.

There were two in particular Rashan watched for, and he was disappointed on one count. He saw Iridan later on toward the end of the guests' arrivals, on foot. He supposed the lad must have had to scramble to prepare, given that they had arrived only earlier in the day. Rashan smiled when he saw Iridan's costume. While most of the sorcerers of the Circle were dressing as knights, Iridan was in squire's garb. Rashan applauded him for having the humility to poke fun at his own inexperience. He saw too that Iridan was alone. While it was certainly not unheard of to attend a ball unescorted, Rashan had rather hoped Iridan would have had time to find someone to take.

I shall have to do something about that. He ought to have been arranged to someone by now. Can they not see how exceptional he is?

As the last of the carriages finally left, Rashan made his way to the entrance. He strode confidently across the lawns of the palace, taking the shortest distance rather than following the curve of the road. With his cloak flowing out behind him and Heavens Cry bouncing at his hip, nearly dragging on the ground, he was like an apparition from the past. Ever mindful of the Empire's best interests even in small matters, he kept his feet from touching the grass as he walked.

The entrance was guarded, but ceremonially so. With everyone in costume, a pair of armored simpletons could hardly tell that one petite warlock did not belong at the party. The guards would have prevented drunken peasants from wandering in, but Rashan needed no magic to slip by them without raising their suspicions. The herald, however, was another story. The wizened old man whose voice called out the names of those who entered made a career of knowing who belonged in the palace, with emphasis on knowing who belonged at the various revels.

"Sir, I do not know you," the herald told Rashan, stepping into the warlock's path. "Might you enlighten me, such that you may be properly introduced?"

While his words were formal and said in the most polite tone, there was a clear implication that Rashan was in the wrong.

"What is your name, Herald? I would properly address you before I give mine."

Rashan wanted to know this man, whom he expected he would deal with much more once he slipped back into palace life on the emperor's staff. He could easily have befuddled him with magic but chose not to. Some were a bit more sensitive to it than others, and even if he did not recall being enspelled, the herald would deduce it later when talk of a gatecrasher spread throughout the city.

"I am Lonford, sir, Royal Herald." He nodded graciously—and expectantly.

"If you have had cause to visit the Sanctum in the Tower of Contemplation, you may recognize my face. I am Rashan Solaran, Warlock of the Empire, High Sorcerer, and the blood-stained right hand of the emperor. I have been away a long time, and it is a tale I have no time to tell now. I am home now and intend to resume my service to the emperor and to the Empire."

Rashan drew his sword as slowly and nonthreateningly as he could manage, pulling it with his off hand and grip reversed, cradling it along his right arm as he pulled the blade free of its sheath. He used his magic to levitate the blade in front of Lonford for inspection.

"This is Heavens Cry, no crude copy, but the real blade itself, forged by my hand. Tonight is my first night back in Kadris, and since it happens to be Bygones Night, I plan to make the Inner Circle a peace offering, for the best interest of the Empire. I will, however, leave it to your discretion whether you would like to announce me—with the title as I gave it to you—or just allow me to enter unannounced."

"What game do you play at, sir? I will not be made a fool of." Lonford sounded indignant, but maintained his temper.

"No game, Lonford. I am back. My magic has kept me alive longer than any of my predecessors, and I have been away for too long, but I am here, and I am indeed Rashan Solaran," Rashan told him in a calm tone. He thought he might be able to convince the old herald, or he would not have bothered talking to him at all.

"I do know your face. I am a student of Kadrin history, of course. You know that if you are using magic to look like him, scores of sorcerers inside—including all the Inner Circle—will see right through you," Lonford said.

Rashan merely nodded slightly in reply.

"And you are not worried?"

Rashan shook his head, just barely.

Lonford swallowed visibly. "Very well."

Rashan followed Lonford down the short hall to the ballroom. The sounds of flutes and drums and lutes wafted in as they approached, as well as the general din of a hundred conversations taking place. At the entrance of the room, Lonford paused, turned, and looked askance of Rashan. The warlock nodded in reply.

"I present Rashan Solaran, Warlock of the Empire, High Sorcerer, and the blood-stained right hand of the emperor." Lonford winced as he added the last part, though he no doubt knew that it was nearly as good as an official part of the title.

The music played on, but the conversations halted as if they had tripped. Rashan looked out into the sea of the men and women who represented the elite class of the Empire. The sorcerers were decked out in parchment-thin armor of silver or gold, with fanciful and mirthful crests emblazoned on their tabards. Most of the would-be knights carried thin, dull swords made of cheap steel, and a few had on fake mustaches to poke fun at the knightly pretense of neatly groomed facial hair in which so many indulged.

The knights, for the most part, were dressed in what appeared to be ill-fitted bed linens, with necklaces of dangling baubles and pointed hats that had fallen out of fashion before even Rashan's time—with everyone except those who wished to lampoon sorcerous pomp.

The nobles and merchants Rashan could hardly tell apart, for they tended to focus on more specific impersonations, and by his accounting, there was little difference between the two groups. The nobles were greedy, manipulative snakes who felt they were superior by birthright. The merchants were greedy, manipulative snakes who felt they were superior because they were good at being greedy, manipulative snakes.

The ladies present were mostly not costumed, as such. It was unbefitting a lady of standing to admit to having rivals, and if they were to, they would've had to have been forced to dress much the same regardless. The exception to this were the ladies of the Imperial Circle, who were dressed as knights much like

178

their male colleagues. The women sorcerers of the Empire had even better cause to satirize the knighthood, as there were no women among their ranks. Everyone enjoyed the sight of the ladies' armor and the very large—often magically lightened—swords they carried.

All these various people stopped and stared up at the entrance where Rashan stood smiling, giving the impression of being happily returned to them after a long time away. Most of those doing the staring were surprised and confused; the name was familiar to everyone, though some of the poorer students of history might not quite have recalled from where. The sorcerers of the Inner Circle were aghast. While they knew that Rashan, or at least someone claiming to be him, had returned to the Empire, they all believed that person to be safely stowed away in the most secure cell they had. One person, and only one person, was not surprised at all that he had escaped imprisonment; Iridan merely sighed and hoped he was not going to kill anyone.

While the entrance was up several steps from the ballroom floor, Rashan's lack of height meant that only those nearest the entrance saw that he was armed. None of those close enough recognized the weapon for anything but a prop, as least as far as they let on. As he descended down into the crowd, a few conversations started back up, and some took on a whole new tenor as the guests speculated as to what was transpiring. Rashan smiled and nodded, acknowledging any who made eye contact with him. He picked his way through the crowd until someone approached him.

"What are you playing at?" growled Gravis Archon under his breath from just inches away from Rashan. He was wearing plate armor and a green tabard with a crest that depicted a fat, sleeping bear, and wore a rapier on his belt that was twisted like a corkscrew and flopped a bit as he walked.

"That is the second time someone has suggested that this is a game. While I will admit to enjoying myself thus far on my return home, this is no game. If you wish to hear the long and sordid tale of my time outside the Empire, I shall tell it sometime, but for now just know this: I am back, and I intend to stay."

"So you think you can just walk back from a century of neglecting the Empire and be welcomed as a returning hero? If you really are Rashan, you have become a fool," Gravis replied.

Rashan just looked up and down at Gravis's outfit and smiled, cocking his head as if to say: Which of us looks the fool?

Gravis frowned. "You make light of this? Is this all a farce to you? You cannot expect me to be convinced you are our long-dead warlock by acting the jester."

"You were just a boy. You never knew me, but I was always the jester. You can only surround your heart with so much death without it consuming you. However, if you would like a more serious topic, who has been in my room?" Rashan asked.

For the first time, it seemed he had hit his mark. Gravis's face went ashen.

"What do you mean, 'Who has been in your room?'"

"I mean, I went up there to retrieve some of my old things, and I found something missing. Someone besides me has been in there."

"You got into Rashan's chambers?" Gravis asked in a hushed tone. "That lock has thwarted all attempts at entry since he died."

"*My* chambers ... and of course I got in. I hardly have to think about it to disarm the wards. But someone has gotten in. You do not know who that might have been, by any chance? Oh, and while we are being incredulous, I worked on the wards in the dungeon. Getting out of there was simple as well." Rashan felt he had Gravis convinced now.

"As I said, no one has gotten in to the best of my knowledge. We have tried here and there, but it is a puzzle. There is a standing offer of immediate graduation for any student of the Academy who can get in there. Can you prove you actually got in?" Gravis asked.

Iridan had quietly made his way within earshot of the conversation, and he was very curious to hear the answer to that one as well.

"First of all, this costume is actually the genuine article. Look at the aether, and you will see it." He paused briefly as Gravis Archon concentrated. "And while you are noticing that the garments are unaltered, please note that I am immortal," he added casually.

Gravis frowned slightly, and his eyes unfocused. "You *are* a demon!" Gravis gasped, taking a quick half step backward. His coiled sword bounced comically in response.

"How else would I still be alive? I am two hundred and forty-seven summers old, unless I lost track somewhere along the way. You are less than half my age and showing your winters," Rashan said. Despite the vast difference in age, Rashan indeed looked barely past adolescence, and Gravis appeared at least thrice his age.

"Oh, I might add that I figured out where you had hidden this." He patted Heavens Cry at his hip.

Gravis's eyes widened as he realized what weapon the demon was carrying.

"You really should not have given it to poor Brannis to drag around. With no aether to control it, it must have been as dangerous to his men as it was to his enemies."

"You have broken Heavens Cry loose of its bindings? Why?"

Gravis seemed perplexed. Several of the Inner Circle were hovering nearby now, listening in and ready to intervene if necessary. Iridan noticed them and kept back just a little farther than the subtle circle they had formed a short way from the two senior sorcerers.

"First of all, because it is mine. Secondly, because I think it helps bolster my case for my identity. Thirdly, because there is the small chance that some fool one of you is going to try to attack me and embolden others to do likewise," Rashan answered simply. "While I think I would be able to defend myself even without it, I prefer to have more weaponry than I need rather than less."

"So you expect us to take you back? Just like that? You make a strong case.

You certainly know things that Rashan Solaran should know, but you still may have come by this knowledge by other means, demon."

Gravis tried to hold his ground in an argument he was clearly losing. Whispered conversations were taking place behind him among the Inner Circle and many of the other guests who had been drawn away from the music, food, and dancing by the high sorcerer's meeting with one of the Empire's ghosts.

"A draw, then," Rashan said. "I challenge you here and now, for leadership of the Circle. By rights, I should not even have to, but I shall prove my point. There should be water enough in the fountains out front to soak up your spent aether at the end." Rashan smiled, baiting the high sorcerer.

* * * * * * * *

Iridan's eyes widened and a smile grew on his face, unbidden. Now *that* would be a sight to remember: a draw between Rashan and Gravis Archon.

Cut that pompous old fool's ego to shreds, Rashan, Iridan wished.

Iridan had always loved a good draw, even as a young student at the Academy ...

It had been late morning on that day not so many autumns ago, and the fog had just lifted on Dragon Lake and the surrounding countryside. The Academy lay just on the north side of the lake. That day, on the grounds overlooking the water, the faculty and student body of the Academy were gathered, along with many curious onlookers from the palace and the army.

It was Ranking Day. Students below the age of fourteen were ranked solely on their academic success, but thereafter, each springtime the students would compete in a draw to see who would be first among them, and second, third, and so forth down to the bottom of the class. They would compete both against students their own age, and against the whole student body. It had long been considered essential to bringing out the best in the top students, to force them to compete against one another.

It was to be the last day Brannis spent at the Imperial Academy, as it was the first time he had been eligible for Ranking Day and took part in his first and only draw. It was the day he had had to make the painful admission before everyone that he was not only incapable of competing, but of even properly witnessing the event. He was no better than the knights and courtiers who came just for the excitement and to see who were the up-and-comers among the young sorcerers. After a single bout, he accepted a disqualification and the bottom rank in the Academy, rather than be trotted out to be defeated repeatedly by the weakest students in the class until it was certain he was worst. That same evening, High Sorcerer Gravis Archon would take Brannis aside to test him for any sign at all of hope for his magical abilities, and finally give up on him.

For Iridan, however, it was a day of glory. He had been a modest student, competent but unexceptional, solidly lodged in the middle of his class. He was a nobody, from a family with no history of magical aptitude, and despite showing promise, he had never been taken terribly seriously. He was the sort of student that Ranking Day was created for.

The draw was a civilized sorcerer's alternative to dueling. Two sorcerers stood a short distance apart in an area of sufficient and reasonably balanced aether. A number of other sorcerers stood in attendance, and either one sorcerer or a small group of them would stand in judgment. At the command to begin, each combatant would draw as much aether as he, or she, could. As the two drew aether in, the judges would watch for a current to form in the aether, showing who had the more powerful draw. If one was clearly the stronger, the flow of aether would be noticeably stronger toward that sorcerer. If the two were closely matched, small interferences from outside the competition would make it too close to determine a winner by flow alone. If such was the case, as the aether in the immediate area began to be used up, one judge would declare a "hold." At that point, each sorcerer stopped gathering in aether and tried to contain what they had drawn for as long as possible. The first one to need to release aether, either during the hold or anytime before, was declared the loser. Large quantities of water were always on hand in case the sorcerers were unable to use the aether productively in a spell.

As for Iridan, he had spent the morning embarrassing his classmates and had carved a swath through the older students as well. The ability to draw aether could be improved over time with practice and techniques, but much of it was raw natural ability, which, as it turned out, Iridan possessed by the wagonload.

The first matches had been uncompetitive, with the judges quickly awarding victories from a clear dominance of the flow of aether shortly after the matches had begun. The students his age fell by the wayside, with only a couple putting up much resistance. He was glad that one of the other students had eliminated Brannis, because that was a match he had not relished having to win.

Once he got paired with the older students, he found the going a little more difficult, but not difficult enough to actually cause him to lose. Iridan was still drawing aether faster than any of them, and he had yet to have a hold called. There was a satisfaction that few could understand, when a boy of no family worth noting defeated an Archon, or a Gardarus, or a Solaran, or any boy or girl who had grown up with every advantage granted by a sorcerous bloodline. It felt *good* putting a few of them in their place.

Iridan's last opponent now stood across from him. It was Garrelos Gardarus, a lad of seventeen whom Iridan hardly knew. Three summers older, Garrelos was hardly one to socialize with a young boy with no social connections. He was a bookish sort, solidly built but not what one would ever confuse with muscular, with intense brown eyes and a round face. He had been having just as easy a time of it as Iridan, except he'd had fewer age groups to advance through, starting as he was in the eldest rank of the Academy.

"Begin," High Sorcerer Gravis had announced.

Both boys drew aether as fast as they were able. Iridan noticed immediately that he was being outdrawn, and he redoubled his efforts. The older boy probably held a small advantage over him, but the judges were always careful not to call a bout too early if it was close. The hold was a much more reliable method of determining a winner. When Iridan got the sense that a hold was coming, he eased off just a little, hoping to have to contain less aether than his opponent. It was a sound strategy, and more often used by the one winning, but Iridan found that as he backed off, so did Garrelos.

"Hold," came the call, as both had expected.

Iridan quickly stopped drawing aether. It was more than he had ever held. He knew it was more than was safe to hold. He trusted that all the senior members of the Imperial Circle were there and would rush to the aid of either participant if there was an accident, but he did not want to lose like that. He calmed himself and tried to hold in the aether that rushed around within his Source, a throbbing, pulsating, burning sensation; it felt like taking a mouthful of stew that was too hot and only grew hotter.

Iridan tried to focus on just his own predicament, but he could not help but keep an eye on his opponent. Garrelos was clearly straining, and Iridan watched to see when he would fail. Built up with confidence from a dozen and more bouts already, it did not occur to Iridan that he might go down first.

Suddenly Garrelos lurched forward. Plumes of steam jetted up from the large basins that stood behind him. Iridan was declared victorious, and a cheer rang up from the audience. The Academy's top-ranked student had been determined.

But Iridan was not done yet. He had been practicing something special all on his own. The students of his rank had been taught the basic concepts of silent casting, but no more. Iridan had taken that lesson well to heart, however, and practiced a few spells until he was rather good with them silently. Ever since he began winning earlier in the morning, he had started planning what he would do if he won.

Iridan calmed himself as best he could and bled a little aether out into the basins where Garrelos had just dumped all the aether he had held. It was just enough to regain control from the edge of feeling like he was about to explode, and he had used Garrelos's basins instead of his own, just to keep up appearances a bit.

Kanethio mandraxae, he thought, but did not say aloud.

He felt his palms crossed in front of him but did not move them. He felt the spell about to take hold and thrust his fist into the air.

The crowd gasped as an impressive aether bolt sundered the sky, leaving a hole in the clouds above and letting in a small ray of sunshine on the overcast morning. The cheering erupted anew, and his best friend Brannis rushed out to crush him in a hug, then lifted him up on his shoulder. People crowded in to congratulate him.

It had been the best day of his life.

* * * * * * * *

Iridan found himself very much hoping the high sorcerer would accept Rashan's challenge. Iridan loved the spectacle of a draw and even went back to the Academy each Ranking Day to watch. He often made some spare coin betting on the contests. A contest between Rashan and Gravis was one he would pay a month's wage for the privilege of watching.

"I think not," Gravis replied, and more than just Iridan were within earshot and disappointed by the news. "We can discuss the matter further tomorrow in the Sanctum. If you can offer further evidence to back your claim, we will hear it then."

"Would you not rather settle the matter right now and be done with it?" Rashan said.

There was a hungry look in Rashan's eyes that betrayed how much he wanted to confront the high sorcerer.

I wonder how many men have died with their last sight being that look on his face, Iridan mused.

"No, and since you seem to prefer such responses, I shall list why. Firstly, I have nothing to gain in victory; I would only achieve a stalemate. Secondly, I am aware of the history of how you came to be warlock, and will not repeat that mistake," to which Rashan averted his gaze and looked sincerely chastened. "And thirdly, it is Bygones Night, which is anathema to the draw. Now, if you will pardon me, my wife would much enjoy my company for the rest of the evening."

With that, Gravis turned away from Rashan. Iridan was impressed, despite hoping for the confrontation that apparently was not forthcoming. He had yet to see anyone best Rashan at wordplay, despite he and Brannis being around each other so much, and Brannis being pretty good at twisting people around in a conversation.

"Have you seen the emperor?" Rashan called after him. "I had hoped to present myself to him tonight."

Gravis spoke over his shoulder as he walked away: "Emperor Dharus does not like these affairs. He keeps to himself mostly."

Frowning, Rashan set off to make the acquaintance of the important personages of the modern empire. Iridan followed after and caught up with him.

"I had really hoped to see you draw against the high sorcerer," he said. "I bet you would have beaten him."

"Of course I would have. You yourself could offer him a challenge. I was just offering a quick answer to the mystery he does not want solved, and I would have offered it up with a fistful of humiliation. However, I was not planning to kill him," Rashan said.

"Why would you kill him?" Iridan asked, puzzled.

"I knew you overheard the second reason he gave. I assumed you knew the story. I skipped my final two ranks at the Academy to become warlock and enter the emperor's service. On Ranking Day, after brushing aside all the students, I called out the high sorcerer, my grandfather, and challenged him to a draw.

"Well, he cursed me and insulted me, but he could not rightly refuse. He did take the time to remind me of the only previous time a student had challenged a member of the Circle—in that case one of the faculty of the Academy. That draw had resulted in the faculty member winning, and he used his stored aether to kill the student where he stood for his 'impudence.'

"Well, I took that poorly, and when I bested High Sorcerer Kormar Solaran, I blasted him to ash. Then I went over to the emperor and offered him my services as warlock. Escelon the Fourth liked the thought of having a warlock and had never gotten on well with Kormar, so that was that. I made many enemies that day, but I made the only ally that mattered.

"Gravis obviously suspected he was to play the part of Kormar tonight. Sadly I just wanted to prove a point. I have no grudge with him, despite the whole incident with the dungeon earlier. I practically goaded him into it."

"So what will you do now?" Iridan asked.

"The hour is late. If he is not attending the revel, I will not disturb the emperor tonight. I shall see him in the morning," Rashan said, shrugging nonchalantly. "I think—"

"Oh, I do not think the emperor is in Kadris," Iridan interrupted. "He is likely at his seaside palace this time of autumn."

Rashan frowned. "Hmm. If I set out tonight, I could make it there on foot by morning."

Iridan gave him a skeptical look.

"I would prefer to skip dealing with Gravis and just have the emperor reinstate me," Rashan said. "Even peace-loving Tameron would not have refused the services of a warlock, wanted more like me even, to defend the Empire. This Emperor Dharus will surely prove reasonable.

"If you will excuse me." Rashan nodded to Iridan and started for the door. "Oh, and Iridan, try to find some company. This is a revel."

Rashan smiled back at him as he made his exit.

Chapter 18 - Usurpers Usurped

Rashan could have used magic to cross the distance to the Palace of Waves in but a few heartbeats, but with all night to spare, he wanted to see his homeland as he traveled. Using magic to speed his stride, he jogged across the countryside quick as a startled hare.

He crossed rolling hills of pastureland and plots of furrowed rows of corn and wheat and barley that had been harvested earlier in the season. Under the night sky, the colors were muted, but forcing his vision to the world of color and light, he could make out enough to experience the simple beauty of the Kadrin landscape.

Where the moonlight caught the trees, he could make out yellows and oranges and reds among the foliage, and fallen leaves crunched lightly under his step. Towns and villages dotted the land, their lamps and candles showing pricks of light against the slumbering darkness of the mortal world. Rashan could name all of them in this millennia-old corner of the Empire; there were so many things in the heart of the Empire that changed slowly enough that even an immortal could recall them from his youth.

On and on he ran, leaping over small streams and dancing lightly across the Darfall River, its smooth flowing water shimmering under the moon's glow. He cut through Reislor, a small township where they made the wine he had always preferred, darting through the streets and giving the nocturnal residents a moment's pause before they dismissed his passing as a trick of the eye. He noticed the faint change of light and knew that the predawn was approaching, and so altered his course and headed for the seacoast.

He raced down the rocky beach and veered straight into the water. The shoreline was on the Fallreach Inlet, and he meant to cross the short way, avoiding an hours-long detour by land. Leaping atop one of the larger rocks, he vaulted up above the waves, continuing his run on the water as he landed, as if he were in meadow of undulating earth.

On the far shore, he could see his destination, the Palace of Waves, set on a rocky cliff overlooking the sea. The palace was a coastal fortress, as functional as it was luxurious. Many an emperor had made it his adopted home, with the natural beauty of the sea to the south and east, and pastoral countryside and the villages of Brekt and Puhr just inland to the west and north, respectively. The quiet available away from court in Kadris was also a compelling reason to spend much time at Waves.

He had timed his journey well enough. He would be there shortly after dawn. He hoped Emperor Dharus was an early riser.

* * * * * * * *

Rashan made a quick check of his garb, cleansing it of dust and sea spray he had accumulated on his trek, then levitated up the side of the cliff, to the level of the palace. Built of piled and fitted granite blocks fifteen centuries ago, it was not half the work of art the Imperial Palace in Kadris was, but it possessed a gravitas that accompanies extreme old age in a structure. The palace and surrounding lands had been a part of the Empire so long that most folk had forgotten it was conquered land. Folk had long stopped thinking that Brekt and Puhr were odd words in the Kadrin tongue, and merely added their own dialect atop the names to make them sound right. The palace had once been the seat of power of a kingdom known as Strachlann, and which once ruled nearly half the continent, in the days when they boasted twin brothers who were both warlocks.

But now the palace was an escape for the Kadrin emperor from the duties of rulership. He could retreat to the Palace of Waves and leave the running of the Empire in his advisers' hands. For many an emperor, it was best that they rule little and delegate much. From the lack of concern of the emperor's absence, Rashan suspected that this emperor was one of those. It mattered little once he was taken back in. He would serve the emperor via explicit orders, or by vague ideas and a license to carry them out at his discretion, whichever his highness preferred.

Rashan walked around to the front gate and announced himself to the sentries on duty. The unfamiliar garb of a warlock confused them, but it bore enough resemblance to the vestments of the Inner Circle that they hurriedly sent someone to fetch one of Emperor Dharus's councilors. Despite the guards' protestations, Rashan did not wait outside but walked right past them and to the audience chamber.

After but a few moments, a tall, broad-shouldered woman with black hair to match her black robes entered the chamber as well.

"Who are you really?" she demanded, crossing her arms and attempting to look stern.

Rashan had seen such bravado too many times, though, and saw through the front put forth and realized the fear it hid.

"I am who I said I am: Rashan Solaran. I have returned, and I would give my fealty to Emperor Dharus, whom I have regrettably not yet met," he replied, with a slight bow at the waist.

"Emperor Dharus does not wish to be disturbed. He has a standing order that none but his personal attendants enter his presence. I apologize if you have come all this way, but you will not see him," the sorceress explained.

"I think it is time he consider an exception to that order. Go to him and tell him that I am here. I doubt his tutors would have left me out of his history lessons. He will change his mind," Rashan said.

His patience was waning by the moment. He was unaccustomed to having to deal with lesser advisers of the emperor obstructing his access to his liege.

"Sir, if you are a loyal servant of the emperor, you will honor his wishes and—"

"What rank are you? Fourth Circle?" Rashan snapped, interrupting her practiced dismissal. "What is your name, child?"

"Um, Shaeila Archon ... and I am Third Circle," she added indignantly.

Before she could resume her attempt to send him away, Rashan continued: "Well, Shaeila Archon, Third Circle, I am Warlock in this Empire, and if you do not head straight to His Majesty and present my petition for audience, I am going to rip the Source clear out of you," Rashan spat. "Now, GO!" And he pointed back toward where, he knew from many previous visits, the emperor's private suites were located.

Without even replying, Shaeila Archon took a few quick steps back away from Rashan, then turned and fled from the room. Rashan missed the days when he could issue orders and they got obeyed with little to no fuss. He sensed a clear lack of strong leadership and discipline among the upper echelons of the Empire these days.

Rashan paced the audience chamber and waited for the Archon girl to return. He looked at the throne and could picture Liead sitting there, with his empress seated on the arm and little Merenon in his lap. He wondered what kind of emperor this Dharus would turn out to be, though he knew in his heart he would not find another like Liead again.

"He will not see you," Shaeila called from the doorway where she was peeking out. "Please, return to Kadris and serve the emperor by serving High Sorcerer Gravis."

She pulled away from the doorway and scurried down the hall. Rashan, though, would have none of it.

He may tell me whatever he likes, but I will speak with Dharus.

He started down the hall she had taken. He could hear her footsteps racing away ahead of him, growing distant. If she thought to elude him, she need not have bothered. He knew very well where he was heading and cared little for whomever else he might find along the way. He was finished taking their excuses and diversions, and had no intention of waiting any longer. Rashan headed right for the emperor's suites.

The double doors to the sitting area of the suite were locked with a ward, but he tore the ward to shreds and pushed the doors open anyway. The sitting area was empty, but he heard voices out in the gardens. He made his way through the velvet-covered furnishings and out into the garden.

Despite the brisk chill in the air, the outdoor garden was kept verdant through magic. Species of flowers and other plants from throughout the empire and from lands beyond bloomed in a mosaic of colors all about the garden. Rashan had taken to growing lotus flowers of his own, but mostly for the aether they produced in abundance, not for any love of botany. The splendors of the garden were lost on him in his foul mood.

On the far side of the garden, he saw two sorceresses: Shaeila and an older blonde woman. Both were conferring with a lounging figure, in white silks, that ought to have been the emperor.

"Rashan Solaran, I presume. Be gone, I say. Back to Kadris with you. You would serve me? So be it, but do not disturb me," the emperor called across the garden in a lilting tenor that gave every indication of idleness and indolence. He sounded as if he could not be bothered to meet Rashan.

Rashan, however, paid the voice little attention. Something that the two sorceresses clearly had not counted on was that Rashan preferred aether-sight almost exclusively. He saw clearly in the aether that there was no emperor in the garden. What was being shown to him, what was speaking to him, was an elaborate puppet constructed of aether. Rashan's eyes narrowed dangerously as he strode toward the two presumptive puppeteers.

"Stop! I command you, as your emperor, stop!" the puppet called out.

Rashan reached into the aether and grabbed at the tiny loose edges available to be found on the excellently crafted spell. With a mighty mental effort, he began unraveling it as he approached, and the "emperor" wavered and flowed and then dissipated entirely.

"Where. Is. The. Emperor?" Rashan spoke slowly and clearly, lest there be the slightest misunderstanding.

He pulled Heavens Cry from its sheath. Neither of the sorceresses had likely ever been threatened with a blade before, and both were clearly unnerved by both Heavens Cry—a wicked-looking implement to be certain—and its wielder, who was either a madman or a warlock, and very possibly both.

"W-W-Warlock Rashan," the elder sorceress stammered. "That was all the emperor there was."

She fell to her knees and hung her head, expecting to die. Her hair fell in front of her face, and there was a sniffling whimper as she began to cry. Shaeila leaned away, as if hoping to pass unnoticed as Rashan's attention was fixed on her companion.

The crying sorceress began to lift into the air, until her head was up even with Rashan's, or just slightly above, so he could see her face.

"First, you will tell me your name and circle. Then you have possibly ten breaths to explain what you just said. Speak truthfully and I might not kill you."

Much more than ten breaths later, after a lengthy conversation with the older sorceress, Rashan himself rose into the air, and a great shimmering sphere of aether enveloped him. The air shook with power, and aether from every direction rushed in a torrent into it. When it suddenly vanished, Rashan was gone as well.

And neither of the two sorceresses had been killed.

* * * * * * * *

In the courtyard before the Tower of Contemplation in Kadrin, a shimmering sphere of aether appeared briefly. When it suddenly vanished, a very angry warlock dropped lightly to the ground. Had anyone been close by when this happened, they would have noted the somewhat incongruous scent of a dozen or more species of flower before it dissipated in the fresh morning air.

Rashan stalked right toward the tower, drawing in aether as he went. He tore open the door, nearly wrenching it from its hinges. The startled attendants just within scrambled to clear a path for the warlock as he made for the stairs. Rashan moved purposefully as he ascended, but did not rush; he was still drawing in aether.

By the time he reached the top, many of the lower floors of the tower were cleared of staff. Rumors of Rashan's return had spread, and the furious demon marched up the tower stairs as he sucked in more aether than any of them would have believed in a tale; that was reason enough for most sensible folk to find elsewhere to be.

As he walked into the Sanctum, those of the Inner Circle who kept one eye to the aether were forced to blink back to normal vision, lest they be blinded in their aether-sight; Rashan was nearly as bright in the aether as the sun was in the sky.

"Warlock Rashan," Gravis Archon said, "this council has other business to attend to. If you will kindly return after highsu—"

A hand clasped around Gravis's throat. The high sorcerer gasped as he was slammed against the back wall of the Sanctum, where a leaping Rashan Solaran had just pinned him, Heavens Cry held poised to strike in his other hand.

"For nearly forty winters, there has been no emperor?" Rashan screamed the question in Gravis's ear.

The rest of the Inner Circle, those who had already been in attendance in the Sanctum at least, looked on in horror. Those who had been busy in their offices below came up to their desks cautiously to see what was befalling.

"We did what we could when Tameron the Second died suddenly, leaving only a boy for an heir. When Dharus died not long after, we had no other choice," Gravis gasped.

Rashan noticed the high sorcerer trying to draw aether and slammed him against the wall to break his concentration. The sorcerers watching from within the chamber winced collectively, but none dared intervene; Rashan was nearly glowing in the visible light range by that point.

"No other choice? What of cousins, uncles? There must have been a legitimate heir somewhere," Rashan insisted.

"We were better suited. The Circle has always been the guiding hand of—"

"TRAITOR!"

* * * * * * *

On the streets of Kadrin that morning, the ground shook and a noise was heard unlike any before, a great thunderous crash. Those who had a clear sight line to the Tower of Contemplation could see a cloud of dust and smoke rising from a hole near the very top.

And those with very good vision could make out the black-clad figure standing in that hole, one foot set upon the blasted rock that was once part of the rune-carved wall, surveying the empire that he had, quite possibly, just conquered.

Chapter 19 - That Witch I Fear

A harsh knocking awakened Kyrus, coming from downstairs. He squeezed his eyes tightly shut to gather the strength to open them properly, and blinked several times to clear the blur he saw at first. The knocking repeated as he rolled out of his bed and found his shoes. He had fallen asleep fully clothed, which left him one way-marker of etiquette closer to being able to answer the door to polite company. He stumbled down the stairs as he tried to bring his mind around from its torpor.

"One moment," he called down ahead of him, hopefully forestalling any further knocking. He paused briefly to run his fingers through his matted and tangled hair quickly before opening the door.

"Expert Kyrus, I do not take kindly to being kept waiting," the client at the door said.

He was a rotund man with a beard that ran down both sides of his face and up through a mustache, but skipped the chin. Speaking to his apparent years, the facial hair and what remained atop his head had gone well and truly grey. He was dressed expensively, and a carriage waited behind him on the street, its door ajar with a footman beside.

"Lord Derrel, my apologies. I know your daughter's wedding invitations were a rush job. I stayed up the night finishing them. I will fetch them directly."

Kyrus disappeared back inside briefly. He returned shortly with a carefully tied bundle, which he handed to Lord Derrel, along with a rolled parchment.

"There you are, Your Lordship, eight hundred-odd invitations and the copy of the guest list you provided. I beg your pardon for my appearance and lateness in arising this morning."

"Well, Expert Kyrus, you made good your promise. Expert Juren could do no better than a week, so I was leery of your boast of two days, but I needed those invitations quickly. When you did not answer my knock, I suspected you had failed your commission. Thank you." Lord Derrel inclined his head in acknowledgment and reached into his vest pocket. "Your payment, and perhaps a bit extra." He winked at Kyrus.

"Would you like to untie the bundle and have a look, to make sure you are satisfied?" Kyrus asked.

"No, no. No time for that now," Lord Derrel said as he turned back toward his carriage. "I must arrange for these to be delivered. With just over a month to the wedding, far-flung guests will have barely enough time to make arrangements to attend. If I find they are not in proper order, you shall hear of it, though," he said, then chuckled.

Kyrus locked the door as soon as Lord Derrel had departed. That one job had earned him thirty-five hundred eckles, plus whatever tip his lordship had alluded to. He could afford to close up shop for a week and not notice the loss, so he planned to enjoy the day, especially since the morning had not gotten off to a promising start, what with waking to an impatient client nearly staving in his door, but there was time enough to rehabilitate it.

Continuing to try to rub the sleep from his eyes, Kyrus headed back upstairs. He washed up properly and changed into fresh clothes. He levitated a comb through his hair a few times, but shaved in the more conventional manner, as he was still not confident enough of his new power to trust it with a blade near his throat. He would have skipped the shaving entirely, but Abbiley had expressed a preference for his appearance without the beard.

He regarded his reflection in the mirror and saw his clean-shaven face staring back at him with red-rimmed eyes. The late nights were taking something of a toll on him. With clients calling at what most folk would consider reasonable hours, he could ill afford to be lying abed until noon or later each day. Sooner or later, he would have to either choose to alter the way he ran Davin's old scrivener's shop or to find a more secluded place to practice his magic—maybe move to a new building that had a cellar, or maybe somewhere in the caves along the beach south of town. However, the former would require saving up enough coin to purchase a new building and the latter seemed rather inconvenient. He sighed and resolved to think more on it later. For the time being, he would save his hobbies for after dark.

Though he looked a bit bedraggled, he felt much better after having gotten himself sorted out and more a suitable sight to be out in public. He hefted the large purse that Lord Derrel had given him, which he had set down on the bedside table. It felt heavy and substantial in his hand, more money than he had ever made from a single job. Even copying an entire book usually pocketed him less, but Lord Derrel had been desperate to have his daughter's wedding arrangements settled quickly. Kyrus was no fool and realized when Derrel had approached him that his daughter must have been expecting a child. Kyrus had priced the job accordingly and trusted in his magic to help him do the job speedily enough.

The arrangement worked out to the satisfaction of both, even if Kyrus might seem to have taken advantage of the desperate nobleman. But Lord Derrel had coin to spare and needed to protect his reputation. Kyrus, on the other hand, had reputation to spare and needed the money. Kyrus could not help but wonder how much better a businessman he could become once he knew a wider array of magics to help him deliver otherwise impossible results.

That thought prompted Kyrus to wonder when he would learn any new spells. His counterpart in the other world had spent much time on the road of late, and his two magical companions had seemingly been less interested in showing off their magic than they had in just getting to their capital city. Kyrus hoped that now that Brannis was back in a city of magic, he would have ample opportunity to see new spells. Perhaps he could find a way to more explicitly convey his desire to Brannis.

"Hello? Sir Knight? Brannis? If you can hear me, go find a magic show to watch, or a good book of spells to read or something," Kyrus spoke aloud.

He was not sure if Brannis was aware of him the way he was aware of Brannis, but he supposed it could not hurt to ask.

Kyrus made his way back downstairs in slightly less haste than on his previous trip. He looked around the work room and saw the quills lying about, along with half-emptied ink pots.

I ought to get that put away, in case anyone stops by. They should wonder what kind of establishment I run if I have a dozen quills and ink pots everywhere.

He started to walk over to tidy up—"tidy" being a relative term, given all the other books and papers lying about—but stopped himself short.

No one will be coming today, and if they do, they shall find the shop closed.

Resolving to worry about the mess later—and after all, he would just be back at work and needing them again later on—he turned for the door. Locking the shop behind him, he headed off to see Abbiley, whistling a happy, off-key melody as he went.

As he passed the cobbler's shop, he acquired an admirer. This admirer had been waiting all morning for him to leave his shop, watching the door and biding his time. As the admirer fell into step several paces back, Kyrus walked on, in ignorance.

* * * * * * * *

Kyrus sauntered down the streets of Acardia, in no particular rush. He knew that Abbiley would have work to do and that he would be interrupting her, so he decided to take his time in getting to her studio. She had stopped by his shop often enough during the middle of the day, though, that he was nearly certain she could afford at least a part of the afternoon in leisure.

As he passed near Greuder's, he caught a whiff of the midday pastries and veered off on a new course. He realized that he had not eaten yet, and his stomach took over navigation and steered him toward spiced crescents. The noontime rush had dissipated along with noontime, and there was no line waiting to get in. Kyrus slipped inside and took a table.

"Good morning, Greuder," he called out, smiling.

The dining area was not quite empty, but most of the patrons seemed closer to finishing their meals than beginning them. Kyrus recognized most, but there was no one that he knew well enough that he felt obliged to strike up a conversation.

"Well, well, Expert Kyrus. You seldom come here for luncheon, and you would be late even if you were of the habit. Clock tower's bell not loud enough for you?" Greuder said, raising his voice to be heard across the room from behind the counter where he was beginning to clean up after the day's baking.

"Oh, I had a late night of it, working on a rush job. Took the early hours off and decide to push 'morning' back until after midday. Seemed sensible, since I would much prefer a few spiced crescents over a bowl of stew," Kyrus said.

"Well, then, I fear you have made a grave error. I have only five of them little morsels left, and I had promised them to the alley cats. The little dears have been waiting quietly out there all morning, and I could not bear to disappoint them. Now if you had come in at a respectable hour ..."

"Oh, Greuder, if you have five left, I shall purchase them and *promise* to share them with the cats. I might go so far as to pitch in a little extra so you might find them a saucer of milk to wash it down with." Kyrus winked.

Greuder, of course, had made no such promise for the last of the spiced crescents, feline or otherwise, and Kyrus was soon slaking his hunger on the finest breakfast to be had at two hours past noon. Despite being in no rush, he gulped down the sweet pastries as if he had not eaten all day—which he had not.

"So, Mr. Expert." Greuder sat down across from him as the last of the other patrons departed. "You have yet to stop smiling since you arrived. I know how wonderful my spiced crescents are. I actually know *precisely* how wonderful they are, but they are not *that* wonderful. Out with it, Kyrus. Have you found yourself a girl, or have they just gone ahead and made you High Overlord of All Scriveners this time?"

"Is it that plain to see?" Kyrus asked, trying his best to look sheepish but falling short of the mark.

"Aye, it is. Do tell."

"Well, it seems that I have a rather unique and remarkable gift, and my fellows in the Scrivener's Guild—"

Greuder cut him short with a cleaning towel to the head, which got them both laughing.

"No, really, boy. Who is she? You intend to keep it secret?"

"Not hardly." Kyrus grinned. "I doubt I could had I wanted to, given how transparent I apparently am. Do you know Abbiley Tillman?"

"You mean old Geremy's girl, the painter?" Greuder asked.

"I suppose so. I had never known her father, but she is a painter," Kyrus replied.

He knew that Abbiley was orphaned and that she had a younger brother she helped to raise, but he knew little of her parents. He could think of no delicate way of asking about them, and he was unsure whether she would want to be asked. Kyrus saw his own family infrequently enough, but he felt reassured in the knowledge that they were safely at home on their farm, just a half-day's ride to the west.

Kyrus had always been the odd piece in the family puzzle. His parents loved him and raised him the same as his brothers and sisters, but farm life had never caught hold of him. His mother taught them all to read and do simple ciphering—the sorts of things they would find useful in buying supplies and selling goods at market one day when they were in charge of running the farm. With Kyrus, however, he wanted more of the "book learning" and less of animal husbandry and crop rotation. He took care of his chores—at least as much as any young boy would—but never was interested in his older brothers' rough sports, which even his sisters found more interesting than did he.

When Kyrus had been shipped off to Expert Davin to become a scribe, he and his family knew it was right for him. They were never going to make a proper farmer of him, so they let him find his fortune in city life. He visited on occasion and took comfort in knowing he was always welcome. He had not severed ties with them so much as taken a different direction.

With Abbiley, she had lost her parents some years ago, though Kyrus did not quite know how. He briefly considered asking Greuder about them, but he somehow did not feel right about it. He would hear about them from Abbiley when he felt comfortable enough asking her.

"Well, she always seemed like a nice girl. You be good to her, Kyrus, you hear me? Else there will be no more seat for you in my bakery." Greuder winked at Kyrus, possibly only half-joking.

"I will. I promise," Kyrus replied, and he meant it.

* * * * * * * *

"It is beautiful," Kyrus remarked, looking at the first painting Abbiley showed him.

After Greuder's, he could not help but head right over to Abbiley's studio, where she worked mostly on commission, painting portraits. The rest of her works were done in her ample free time, portraits being a service of infrequent and unpredictable demand. The one she was showing him was a painting of the Katamic Sea during a storm.

"How did you manage to paint this without getting the canvas ruined in the storm?"

"I painted it from memory. I see the Katamic often enough that I know its look, and then I just painted it the way I saw the storm change it. I actually ran in as soon as the heavy rains blew in." She laughed. "That whole painting would have been naught but a blur if I had kept it out in that downpour."

The painting was mostly greys and dark blues, showing the Katamic at its angriest. Waves broke against the rocky point north of the city, where the lighthouse sat, overlooking the harbor. Kyrus remembered the storm, some two years earlier, and had spent much of the night with Ash curled up in his lap, terrified. Halfway through the storm, the wind had blown in the shutters on one of the windows, and he and Davin had scrambled to find a way to secure it again. They had lost a lot of the papers they had been working on to the windblown rain that came in, and they did not see Ash until the following morning, when they found him hidden in the back of one of the pantry cupboards.

"It is amazing. You would swear this was a window, overlooking the storm," Kyrus commented.

He could make out the brush strokes when he looked closely enough, but from a step or two back, it looked so real he would have expected to get his hand wet touching it. He certainly would not have wished to trade places with the lighthouse keeper than night.

Abbiley set the painting back down against the wall, next to the rest of her works. She had no gallery to show them off, so simply kept them propped against the walls when they were finished. She had nearly a dozen of them. On occasion, someone would purchase one, supplying Abbiley and her brother with a bit of extra income, but these were the ones that still awaited a buyer—if they were ever to have one.

Kyrus walked over to another and knelt by it. "Who is this?" he asked.

"That is Neelan, my brother. I painted it years ago. It does not look so much like him as it used to."

The painting showed a lad of perhaps eight years, perched on a stool with his hands folded in his lap. He looked stiff and sullen, his posture too straight to appear relaxed, and no smile on his serious little face.

"It looks as if he was an unwilling subject." Kyrus smiled.

"You know not the half of it. I was still practicing at portraits, hoping to be skilled enough at it to feed us. It was all I could do to keep the rascal in one spot. At one point, I threatened to bring the cooper over from next door and nail him to that stool." Abbiley laughed. "I have yet to get him back onto that stool, though nowadays I would say I do not need the practice as I once did."

"So where is your brother? I would much like to meet him."

"Oh, someday you will, to be sure. He may have grown since that portrait, but only in size. I cannot keep him under one roof. When he was little, I could make him behave, but now he is bigger than I am, and less afeared of a whipping if he causes trouble," Abbiley said.

"So what does he do all day while you work?" Kyrus asked, genuinely curious.

"'Odd jobs,' he says. Helping haul crates and unload fishing boats down at the piers, helping foreign merchants set up carts and stalls in the market, making deliveries, that sort of thing. He brings in coins, but I wonder where they really come from. I doubt he does half what he claims."

"Have you any worry of him getting mixed up with lawless sorts?"

"Oh, plenty of worries, but he is not a bad boy. I think he just feels like he ought to help put food on our table rather than just eating it."

"Have you thought of finding him an apprenticeship? I think a lot of boys just need someone to keep them on a narrow path, and a good tradesman should be able to manage that."

Kyrus hoped he was not overstepping his bounds. Abbiley had been raising the boy for years, and he had never even met him.

"Oh, to be certain, but he is a willful one. I expect they will make a merchant out of him one of these days, though I am not sure what type he would be," she said with a wink.

Kyrus let the matter drop and wandered among the rest of the paintings. There was a vase of flowers depicted in one—the sort of things one would expect any younger painter to try a hand at. There were more landscapes, which seemed to be Abbiley's specialty—a shame since it did not pay as well as portrait painting.

"Is this one a self-portrait?" Kyrus asked, pointing to the last painting, near the far corner of the studio.

It was a remarkable likeness of Abbiley: the eyes were the same deep blue, the cheeks had the pretty little dimples as she smiled, the hair the right color, but styled somewhat differently, though Kyrus knew little enough of women's fashion that he could not put a name to the difference. Her hair was shorter than in the painting; that much he could say with certainty. The style of the painting itself was somewhat crude in comparison to the rest. The brush strokes were a bit more noticeable and the colors perhaps a bit more vibrant and less realistic.

"No, though you are not the first to have thought so. That there is my mum. It is the first one I painted that was worth keeping. She was the one who taught me to paint, and she sat for a portrait for me. I was about eleven when I painted that," Abbiley said.

"Your mother was quite beautiful. The resemblance is remarkable," Kyrus said, still looking at the painting.

He thus did not notice the blush that flushed Abbiley's cheeks a bright red.

* * * * * * * *

Abbiley closed up the studio early that day, and she and Kyrus wandered down to the marketplace. Folks were gathering in larger numbers than usual, as a large merchant-explorer vessel had returned from an expedition to the faraway ports to the south and east, bringing exotic wares back with them. Few had the spare coin to spend on the luxuries they brought, but just seeing the new and different goods they had in their rented shops and carts was enough to draw crowds.

Kyrus and Abbiley held hands as they negotiated the flow of citizens and carts, lest they get separated. Kyrus was not normally one to go down to the marketplace in the middle of the day, but even he could tell that there were more people on the streets than was usual.

"Oh, look at that," Abbiley said. "Those patterns are stunning."

Her attention was fixed on a wagon load of silk cloth. They were all dyed in various colors and designs, with red-gold, blue-green, purple-black, and a few with colors that seemed to change as you looked at them—a trick of the way the light caught them.

"Where are these from?" she asked the lean, dark-skinned gentleman attending the merchandise.

He had a thin face and a long slender nose above a curled mustache and scraggly chin beard. The expression he wore was serene and friendly. He wore a long coat in typical Acardian style, but his headdress was a long piece of purple silk that wrapped several times around and dangled down to wrap around his neck.

"They from Khesh, my lady," he said in awkward but perfectly serviceable Acardian. "You like it, yes? Feel how nice."

He held the end of one of the bolts out to her and pressed it into her hands. Kyrus also ran his fingers over it. The fabric was indeed ... well, silky. Abbiley had no doubt never owned anything so luxurious and could not help but betray her admiration of it.

"Yes, yes, you see now. So soft. Maybe he buy for you?" the merchant said, looking at Kyrus.

"Um, well. I mean ... How much is it?" Kyrus said.

He had never been comfortable haggling in the marketplace. The world-worn traders that set up shop there seemed to be playing a game whose rules he did not understand. He could hardly help but feel he was being played the fool—and he was likely correct.

"For your fine lady, two hundred eckle each arm," he told them, and Abbiley gasped slightly, which Kyrus took to mean that was a lot for fabric. "Good deal. I like see pretty lady wear my silk. It good for business."

Kyrus was unsure how the dressmaking profession worked, but he imagined that it would take two or three arms' lengths of fabric to make a dress out of.

"My lady, pick which silk you like. He buy for you."

As Kyrus struggled for the proper response, Abbiley took him by the arm. "Oh, Kyrus, no. Those are pretty but I could not wear anything fancy like that. I would ruin it with paint inside a day. Come on," she said, then led him away from the wagon and its presumptuous owner.

"You change mind, I still be here," he called after them as they pushed into the crowd and left him behind.

"I just want to look, Kyrus. I do not mean to buy anything. Everything is so interesting, I just want to feel it and smell it and hear it all."

She kept hold of his arm and took over leading them around amongst all the wonders of the foreign traders. They stopped at a small rented storefront that was stocked with distilled liquors from Takalia. They made the strong drinks from local fruits and berries that had no names in Acardian. The merchant who sold them was a well-traveled Golishman who knew the markets well and had given them names like "Moon Berry," "Star Fruit," and "River Dream." He passed out samples poured into thimbles to anyone who looked both interested and with coin enough to purchase. He kept a careful guard against the drunkard beggars who might otherwise drink him penniless.

Kyrus and Abbiley both tried samples. Kyrus picked one called "Honeyfruit" that was sweet and smooth, though stronger than he was used to. He was thankful for the tiny vessel it was provided in, lest he pass out right there in the marketplace. Abbiley sampled "Forgetful Breeze" and blinked several times as the sharp, cool beverage seemed to go straight to her head.

"You shall not find better distillers than the Takalish. They make of it an art form," the proprietor told them. His puffed and ruddy complexion bespoke a certain expertise on the subject that Kyrus felt no inclination to argue with.

"Have you got anything a bit milder?" Kyrus asked him.

While Kyrus was certainly not above enjoying a good strong drink from time to time, he preferred remembering the occasion.

"Well, drinks from Takalia are made to be strong, but I have other wares as well. I cannot afford to give samples, but I have this wine from Feru Maru that they make from mushrooms. I assure you it is worth the price at five hundred eckles," the merchant said.

"Five hundred for one bottle?" Kyrus asked.

He knew that wine was often expensive, but that was what he might make in a typical month. Lord Derrel's commission had fattened his purse but not dulled his judgment.

"Good sir, I make my way to Acardia every other year at the least and have yet to depart with a single bottle remaining. I will keep this shopfront open until I sell what I have purchased abroad and then settle in for the season to enjoy a fine Acardian summer. I shall ship out again with the autumn trade winds and do it all over again, and I shall expect my customers to be eagerly awaiting my return with more. My name is Droon Harwick, and you may ask anyone you like, should you doubt my reputation."

"Well, Mr. Harwick," Kyrus said, "suppose I were to offer you four hundred and the prospect of another loyal customer awaiting you each autumn?"

Kyrus much preferred wine to liquor and thought that perhaps an indulgence while he had the coin in hand would not be entirely unjustified. Besides, it occurred to him that if his plans worked out for using magic to speed his work, he would hardly be short on coin again.

"Kyrus, are you certain?" Abbiley asked.

"No, not entirely. But have you ever had mushroom wine?" he asked her.

"Well, no, but—"

"Neither have I. Why not have a go at it? I just finished a rather large rush job and have extra coin in hand. We should enjoy good fortune when it presents itself," Kyrus said.

"Well reasoned, my good man. Make that four hundred thirty and you shall have your mushroom wine," Droon Harwick said.

Kyrus lacked the wherewithal to bargain further and simply accepted the merchant's price. It was awkward enough having offered so much less than the asking price in the first place. He felt the man had done him a favor in asking back so little.

The wine came in a glass jug with a small chain running through the cork and attaching to a small loop of glass near the top. It required no corkscrew to open. The glass itself had a greenish tint to it but was otherwise clear. The liquid inside had a yellowish hue to it, but Kyrus could not tell how much the color was distorted by the green of the glass.

Toting his purchase at his side, Kyrus took Abbiley by the hand again, and they continued their adventure in the market. They stopped and saw a juggler in an outlandish outfit covered in ribbons and bells, tossing knifes as if he had not a care for the danger. After the performance, he passed around a bowl and accepted coins from the onlookers, many of whom were happy to oblige for the masterful performance they had just witnessed. Kyrus tossed in a few eckles in the hope that such entertainers would continue coming to the city.

They stopped at another cart, this one sporting a series of wooden rods down the length, from which numerous necklaces, medallions, and charms were hung. They ranged from the exquisite to the quirky and the whole spectrum between. The finest appeared to be carved from ivory and jade, and some bore stones that looked real enough. Others were simple carved wood, either painted in bright colors or left to the natural wood.

There was an older man, wrinkled and bent and with deeply tanned skin attending to the necklaces. Like many of the foreigners in the market, he was bundled tightly against the northern cold, though it was only a mild spring day by the locals' standards. He wore a knit hat pulled low to just above his eyes, his grey, wispy eyebrows just poking out beneath it. He kept his hand inside the opposite sleeves of his jacket, which was a collarless, large-buttoned style with voluminous sleeves common farther south.

"You do not want these," the necklace peddler said, his voice gravelly and slightly wheezy with age.

"Pardon me?" Kyrus replied, expecting that he had misheard the old man. The accent was one he was not familiar with, though Kyrus's experience was rather limited in that regard.

"Go away, I said," the old peddler said. "You look, you touch, you no buy. I know you kind. Waste my time."

"Well, we *might* buy something, but we have yet to look," Abbiley said, examining the necklaces nearest her. She seemed especially fond of the jade, which was an uncommon sight in Acardia.

"Hmph," the old man snorted. "Fine. Look. I not stop you."

The old man looked perturbed, and Kyrus began to suspect that yet another crafts trader had just sunk his claws into them. Abbiley picked one of the necklaces from its pole and unlatched it. It was jade shaped to form a tiny dragon, curled up in a roughly oval shape. She dangled it in front of her throat and showed it off to Kyrus.

"What do you think?" she asked him, smiling.

"I think it gives a bit of green to those blue eyes of yours. I think it suits you," he answered.

"Amulet have old magic. Priest bless. Protect who wear it," the peddler said.

Kyrus was immediately suspicious and cast his sight into the aether. He could not help showing a bit of surprise when he realized that it indeed *was* magical. He had heard of swindlers selling "magic" tokens, but until recently, it would not have occurred to him to check their claims. He wondered how many opportunities he might have missed out on to get real magical protection at peddler-in-a-dark-alley prices.

"How much?" Kyrus asked, though the peddler had been speaking to Abbiley and not him.

The old man turned to Kyrus with a critical eye.

"For you, eight hundred," the peddler said and then fixed Kyrus with a stern eye and jutted jaw, in challenge.

Abbiley quickly put the necklace back on the cart, afraid to touch it once she knew the price.

"Two hundred," Kyrus countered. "That spell is old and not so strong. My lady just likes the look of it."

The old peddled seemed to be caught a bit off guard by Kyrus's reasoning, but the last gambit he recognized and understood.

"Six. Amulet still make of jade," the peddler said.

"Two hundred fifty." Kyrus dug in, starting to get a feel for the process. "I know that jade is common in Khesh and Feru Maru. This did not cost you much at all. I shall pay for the trouble you took in bringing it here but will not be fooled to thinking it a rare stone."

"Five hundred. Lot trouble bring amulet here. You get fair deal," the peddler said.

Kyrus was sensing that he almost had the hang of this haggling thing; the peddler was backtracking quickly on his price.

"Come on, Abbiley. We shall find you another at one of the other traders," he called to Abbiley and held out his hand to take hers.

As they turned to leave, the old peddler grabbed Kyrus's sleeve.

"You win. You win. Three hundred," the peddler said. "You take advantage old man."

"Deal," Kyrus agreed, smiling, before Abbiley could object.

He counted out the three hundred and took the jade dragon amulet from the peddler's cart. Handing the wine jug to Abbiley, he came around behind her and looped the chain around her neck, securing the tiny clasp. He took her by the shoulders and led her to the tiny, grubby mirror that sat on the cart for customers to see themselves in. She bent down and inspected her reflection.

She turned and looked up at Kyrus. "So beautiful," she said. "But you really did not have to. Thank you."

"Worth every eckle." Kyrus smiled down at her.

While he meant it in the way Abbiley took it, he also wondered at the magical properties of the amulet. If it truly did offer protection of some sort, he very much wanted to strengthen the enchantment so that it would last and function properly should she need it.

Their wanderings in the market had taken longer than either had realized, and the sun was growing lower in the sky. It was late afternoon, and the shallow warmth of midday was already beginning to wane. More importantly, both were growing hungry.

* * * * * * * *

Kyrus had taken them to a cozy little tavern that straddled the unofficial line between the wealthy portion of town and where the craftsmen plied their trade. The sign above showed a bowl of stew and a ham hock, but its proper name was The Fattened Sow. Davin had told Kyrus about it as a place where the Scriveners would occasionally have their meetings, and he had always described the food in the fondest terms. Kyrus had never been there, but his knowledge of nicer dining establishments was rather limited.

They were also fortunate in that there was a visiting troubadour who had arrived on the trade ship and was performing at the Sow that night. He was a Kheshi native, with pale yellow skin and light blond hair, and eyes that were so deep a brown as to appear black. He wore his hair in a mop of braids that were woven with beads that clacked as he moved his head. His long, thin beard was likewise braided, but tied with ribbons rather than beaded. Kyrus suspected that was because beads would have been a distraction as he sang.

And sing he did. The troubadour, whose Kheshi name Kyrus and Abbiley could not quite understand coming from the butchering the proprietor made of it in introducing him, possessed a haunting voice. While none in attendance could understand a word the chap spoke, the emotion came through clearly. As he sang, he played some sort of twangy-sounding instrument whose strings he struck with a pair of tiny hammers.

The troubadour apparently spoke none of the Acardian language, and a second Kheshi who accompanied him stood between each song and explained it a bit in halting Acardian. They were local folk songs and children's stories that were common in their homeland. Neither Kyrus nor Abbiley had heard anything of the like before.

The two supped on game pheasant and honey-glazed sweet potatoes, some of the finest fare Kyrus could remember, and certainly the most elegant meal Abbiley had ever had. They talked little during the meal, enraptured by the evening's entertainment. They sat together on the same side of a small table, just watching the master troubadour as he mesmerized the room.

From there, they had gone down to the shore, to watch the ships coming in from the harbor as the sun set behind them. They sat huddled together as the chill of the evening deepened. They had gone down at low tide and scampered down to the rocks that dominated the north shore of Acardia and found a seat upon a low flat rock, worn smooth by centuries of waves.

"Khesh is off that way." Kyrus pointed to the southeast. "Our friendly troubadour tonight came a long way to play for us."

He passed the jug of wine to Abbiley, who took a swig. They had stopped to find a blanket at one of the less exotic stalls, but not to find proper glasses to drink the mushroom wine, and Abbiley had been curious to try the drink. They had already passed it several times between them. It was perhaps not the proper way to partake of an expensive wine, but Abbiley was unfamiliar with the etiquette of fine society and Kyrus could not be bothered with it if Abbiley cared not.

Abbiley looked across the sea in the direction he pointed. "A long way to come just to sing to us, do you not think?" she joked. "It was awfully nice of him."

She rested her head against Kyrus's shoulder. They were warm beneath the blanket, but the sea breeze brought a chill that kept them from dozing as they relaxed together. They just sat for a time and looked out into the sea, watching the reds and oranges of the sunset reflect off the waves, and the pink of the clouds as they hung above.

As the last of the fishing ships pulled into port, Abbiley asked, without lifting her head from Kyrus's shoulder, "Have you ever dreamed of sailing the world, of seeing all of Tellurak? You know, exotic places and strange languages, and where music like we heard tonight is common."

"Actually, no. Ever since I can remember, I have dreamed of being a knight, like the ones in fairy tales. Not the stodgy old men that the king knights from time to time in Golis, but a true knight with a sword and armor, who fights battles for glory and honor," Kyrus said.

"The kind who rescues princesses and wins their hearts?" Abbiley asked dreamily, looking up at him.

"I am not quite sure I ever dreamed that far," Kyrus said, smiling. "I think maybe I was not dreaming of being the kind of knight that went about looking for a princess that way."

As the sunset gave way to dusk, the air grew even more chill, and uncomfortably so. Kyrus and Abbiley gathered up the shoes they had taken off to walk on the beach. They scampered quickly through the ankle-deep waves that seemed far colder than it had when they had arrived.

"What a magical night," Abbiley commented, as they brushed as much sand as they could manage from their feet and replaced their shoes.

Kyrus just smiled in reply.

Oh, but what magic I could show you, he thought. *I do not think you are ready to see it, though. I will not spoil a wonderful night by risking it. Soon, though, I promise.*

Kyrus walked Abbiley home, as a good gentleman should, and returned to his shop.

Also returning was a gentleman in nondescript garb, who had been watching him from a distance all evening.

* * * * * * *

Kyrus threw the bolt on the door and sighed as he escaped to his sanctuary of quills and spells. His evening with Abbiley had lifted his spirits and left him feeling a little dizzy in the head—possibly aided by the mushroom wine. It was a wonderful sensation, but Kyrus knew he had work to catch up on. Money aside, he had promises to keep to several clients. He set the half-empty wine jug aside on the table nearest the door.

"Aleph kalai abdu."

Kyrus lit the workroom and began going through papers with instructions on a playbill for the Acardian Theater. It was quite a coup to win the job over the typesetters, since this was precisely the sort of thing they claimed to be best at. He had told the theater's proprietor that he would have a dozen completed by tomorrow evening, and he had split the day between sleeping and enjoying Abbiley's company rather than work on it.

That's all right, Kyrus mused, *I shall just work through the night again. I get much more done with no risk of interruption.*

He walked over to the stove and set on a pot of tea. He was far from drunk, but a bit of wine and the late hour had him less alert than he would have cared for.

Making a circuit of the room, he laid out an array of blank pages, using any available flat surface he could find, and setting a quill and ink pot down next to each. By the time he had cleared enough space to work on all the playbills at once, his tea was done steeping. He poured himself a cup and went over to stand by his writing desk, where he had one of the sets of quill, ink, and paper, as well as the instructions on how to compose the advertisement.

Setting the cup down, he spoke, *"Haru bedaessi leoki kwatuan gelora,"* sweeping his arms together and up, and the quills rose in unison along with them.

Just at that moment, there was a great crash. The door burst open and three men rushed in, one in the plain coveralls of a laborer, the other two dressed in the uniforms of the constabulary.

"Surrender, by decree of the king's justice!" one of the uniformed constables shouted.

Kyrus stood agape, frozen in sudden fear as he looked alternately from the intruders to the floating writing implements and back again. The men carried clubs, and both uniformed constables had shackles hanging from their belts.

The constables looked shocked as well, seemingly unsure how to proceed through the cluttered maze of tables and papers without having to *touch* one of the bewitched quills. The constables' resolve mustered itself first, however, and they charged across heedless of the tiny floating obstructions.

"Whoa, wait!" Kyrus said, but quickly changed tactics as his startled exclamation failed to halt the oncoming lawmen. *"Haru bedaessi leoki kwatuan gelora,"* he said as quickly as he could, casting the levitation spell again.

They were by far the heaviest objects he had lifted, but in his panic, he drew in aether to spare. Up rose the tables from the floor, and Kyrus sent them tumbling at the constables.

Papers flew and ink spilled, the constables cursed, and Kyrus ran. He knocked over his tea as he made for the kitchen. There was a back door that led to the alleyway behind the shop where old stews got dumped and chamberpots were emptied. Overturning cookware in his wake, he crossed the kitchen in two strides and pulled the door open. He grabbed the door frame as he ran through to make the turn down the alley quicker, but slammed into something solid.

Another two constables had been waiting around the back entrance of the shop, and he had just plowed into one of them. The constable grabbed Kyrus as they collided and, with a shift of his weight, brought both himself and Kyrus to the ground as they overbalanced.

Kyrus hit the cobblestones with the back of his head leading the way. Had he been conscious by then, he would have heard the second constable tell him that he was being arrested for the crime of witchcraft, and that he ought not to resist.

The second, at least, was no issue, but Kyrus would have to wait until the morning to learn of the charge against him. Brannis Solaran, however, would have to wait until the following night to find out, as he was startled awake from a terrible dream before finding out how it ended.

Chapter 20 - I Am Indeed Me

Brannis awoke suddenly, gasping in shock. He felt the throbbing beat of his heart in his chest, and his breath came raggedly. He threw off the bedclothes as he sat up and looked around the room.

It was his bedroom, but moments ago, it had not been. He had just been in an alley, behind a scrivener's shop. He was being chased by constables—city guardsmen—and was about to be apprehended.

It was such a nice dream up until the end. He remembered everything, from the meeting with the nobleman client to the shared jug of wine by the seashore. He had even gotten another indulgence of his secret desire to work magic. He closed his eyes as he recalled the clean, fresh feeling of aether cascading through him and into those quills.

Just the very last bit was fuzzy. It seemed safe enough to presume he had lost consciousness in the dream. He hoped that was all that it was. It ended so suddenly, so unexpectedly, that he wondered if the man he was in his dreams had just been killed. The thought chilled him.

He had been experiencing his dreams so vividly of late that it seemed much like a second life that he resumed upon falling asleep. He could recite the names of dozens of people in a city he had never visited. He knew stupid little details of complete stranger's lives, from the guests at a nobleman's "headsman's wedding" to the going rate for spiced crescents made by a local baker. He had seen so much of this other life that he had grown attached to it, as if it were his own.

Brannis was worried.

* * * * * * * *

Brannis dressed and made his way down to the dining hall for dawn feast, worries about this Kyrus fellow gnawing at him. The worst part was that it was such an *odd* thing to be worried about, he did not know to whom he could look for counsel.

Father, there is a neophyte sorcerer in my dreams who has gotten himself in trouble. I do not know what has become of him and would like to lend him aid. What would you advise?

Well, that certainly would not pass muster.

Brannis reached the main dining hall as much of the family had already finished their meal. For all his abruptness in waking, Brannis had overslept, and by some hours, it seemed. The productive members of the family had all departed for their daily business, leaving only his cousin Danil—short for

Danilaesis—and his grandfather, once High Sorcerer of Kadrin, but now too infirm to use his magic for anything but life extension.

"Uncle Brannis," Danil screamed when he saw Brannis enter the hall.

Danil was of an age when he was looking for a guiding male presence in his life closer to his own age than his father, and Brannis had been anointed. The small bundle of excess energy leapt from his chair at the dining table and sprinted headlong across the room to crush Brannis in a hug around the waist.

"Good morning, Danil," Brannis greeted him as he absorbed the impact. "Have you been good while I was away?"

"Yeah," the boy replied, though Brannis suspected otherwise.

Danil was seven autumns old and a whirlwind of mischief. He was the youngest son of Brannis's uncle Caladris and his aunt Felia, who were both rather too busy and important to look after him. Danil was left mostly to tutors and servants, and occasionally overseen by his grandfather—the latter being the likely cause of his free-spiritedness. While the tutors lacked the authority to truly punish the boy—seen as a potentially great sorcerer one day—his grandfather was both doting and growing in senility; what behaviors his grandfather did not outright allow, were often permitted through neglect or obliviousness.

"Brannis, my boy?" his grandfather said to him from across the room. "If that is you, then come here and let me have a look at you. Each day passing I expect to be my last, and you have been away too long."

The ancient and infirm sorcerer's eyesight had deteriorated to the point where he rarely bothered with it anymore, preferring the indistinct view of the world through aether-sight over the blurry view that normal vision offered. Aether-sight used the eyes differently, though, and through it, Axterion Solaran was able to manage despite his normal vision having been nearly lost to cataracts.

Brannis obliged the old man, walking the length of the fine polished oak table that took up most of the room. He knew that his grandfather's view of him in the aether was poor due to his own rather closed Source. Axterion would have to make do with seeing his grandson in the light if he wished to see him at all.

"How have you been, Grandfather? Has Danil been causing trouble?" he inquired.

Axterion had always been kind to Brannis, even in his disgrace of failing out of the Academy. Axterion was unable to work magic anymore, lest his failing health give out on him, so he could at least somewhat understand Brannis's plight, though he was coming at it from the other end, after a long and distinguished career of magic.

"Hmph, that boy can cause no trouble. He can scarcely draw aether properly. His parents worry too much about him. He is a small boy, and in my experience, he is doing precisely what they are supposed to do." The old man chuckled at his own observation. "But, Brannis, I hear there is true trouble come to call. Your father and uncle both say that you brought back a demon with you, who claims to be Rashan."

"You hear truly. I met him in Kelvie Forest, on an assignment. We were fleeing from a battle and came across him living in the woods as a hermit," Brannis replied.

"None of that sounds like the Rashan I knew. You found him in the direction opposite a battle? Living in squalor, with no one around to command? No, not like him at all," Axterion mused, seemingly almost to himself.

"But, Grandpa, what about that big boom, when the floor shook?" Danil piped in. "I could see smoke from my window, coming from the palace."

The boy might have been young and a rascal, but he was no fool.

"Indigestion, nothing more," Axterion replied, apparently not entirely grasping what the young boy had said.

"What 'boom,' Danil?" Brannis asked.

"Just before you came down to dawn feast, you must have heard it," Danil insisted. "The whole floor shook, too!"

"Sorry, but I was soundly asleep, I fear," Brannis told him. "No one has said what it was?"

"It is probably an invasion! With dragons and warlocks and ogres and forest spirits and wyverns and—"

"Enough, boy!" Axterion snapped. He muttered something under his breath to the effect of "not raising a blathering idiot," then continued: "If that is a demon you brought back with you Brannis, Rashan or no, I suspect that to be the cause."

Brannis's heart sank again. If Rashan—or whomever he turned out to be— was an enemy of Kadrin, Brannis might bear responsibility for whatever had just befallen at the palace. He was now unsure whether he was worse off in real life or in his dream life.

"I should go, then, and find out," Brannis said, then turned to leave.

But his grandfather caught him by the arm. The old man's grip was feeble, but Brannis was too respectful—and careful of his grandfather's health—to pull free.

"Sit. Eat. You may command soldiers, boy, but you are just a pawn here. The Inner Circle knows of your involvement, and if they wish to consult you on the matter, they will send for you.

"Cook," Axterion called out. "Bring out more mutton and eggs. We have one more left for dawn feast."

Reluctantly Brannis sat down. Axterion was still head of the family, though he exerted his privilege infrequently. Brannis had a lot of leeway to disobey, given that his advancement in the knighthood had little relation to the Circle's politics, but he also knew that his grandfather was in the right. While he might offer some assistance to the Inner Circle, he would have to wait for them to call for it.

Brannis tried to enjoy the mutton and eggs the cook brought out, but was too preoccupied to appreciate them properly. On top of it, he had developed a headache. It felt as if something had hit him on the back of the head.

* * * * * * * *

The expected summons came an hour or so later. Brannis had gone back to his room and dressed properly for a formal visit to the Tower of Contemplation, and buckled on Avalanche at his hip. To bide his time until the messenger arrived, he had been playing with Danil, something that few in the household had patience for.

The messenger arrived on horseback and had gotten the grooms of the Solaran stable to saddle one of their horses and ready it for Brannis. The message itself was curt to the point of rudeness: "Your presence is required in the Sanctum. Be quick about it." The messenger was clearly uneasy, though Brannis could get no details. When he pressed for answers along the way to the Tower, the best answer he got was: "They shall explain when you arrive."

There were a number of guards at the gate when they arrived, far more than the token presence the Tower of Contemplation usually warranted. Upon entering the building, there were sorcerers milling about everywhere; it appeared that most of the Circle who lived within Kadrin were waiting in the entry hall of the tower.

The messenger took the stairs, and Brannis followed, wondering if there was any particular reason they were taking the slower way up. All eyes turned to follow him as he walked up, keeping pace with the briskly ascending messenger.

The messenger was short of breath by the time they gained the top landing. Brannis had gotten used to traveling in armor, however, and without it, he felt a bit lighter of foot and not quite so quick to tire. Both men took a moment to gather themselves before approaching the Sanctum. Brannis then followed the messenger up the short steps to the chamber itself.

"Sir Brannis Solaran," the messenger announced him, then quickly withdrew. He brushed past Brannis on his way down the stairs, his eagerness to be elsewhere clearly apparent.

Brannis walked up into the Sanctum with some apprehension, which only heightened as he observed the daylight streaming in. His worry changed to confusion when he noticed that it was Rashan Solaran, and not Gravis Archon, seated in the high sorcerer's seat directly opposite the entrance. Brannis entered the chamber and found Iridan there as well, along with his sister Aloisha, and a young sorcerer he did not know by name.

"Good morning, Brannis," Rashan said. "As you can see, there have been changes made this morning. Now that all of you are here, I shall explain this just once.

"Gravis Archon is dead, by my hand, on the charge of treason against the Empire."

As Rashan spoke, Brannis took quick stock of the Inner Circle. There were two empty chairs, not including the one that Rashan now occupied.

"Yes, Brannis, I see you checking. Your father Maruk Solaran was complicit as well, as was Stalia Gardarus. Both are dead, also by my hand."

Brannis stared at Rashan in shock. He hated his father, but in a way that many boys do. He resented and quarreled with him, and sought his approval for so long that he had given up trying to achieve it—though always secretly hoping he would find it regardless. He had not wanted his father dead—perhaps chastened, but never dead.

"What had they done?" Aloisha asked, ever the practical one. She was tall and slender, as were most of the Solarans, and resembled Brannis enough that no one would doubt their relation.

"There is no emperor," Rashan stated simply and then paused, letting the reality of that brief sentence settle in. "Some forty winters ago, Tameron the Second died of a sudden illness. His successor, Dharus, was a young and sickly boy, and he died not long after. Rather than seek out the next closest in line for the throne, those dead today conspired to replace the imperial line with puppets of naught but aether, controlled by the sorcerers handpicked by the high sorcerer.

"While I know that others were most certainly aware of this arrangement ..." Rashan glared around the room at the remaining members of the Inner Circle. "... I will not further weaken the Empire by seeking out and executing everyone who knew about the plot. For those still breathing, there is a second chance. I am forgiving this transgression, but I shall not forget it entirely."

"So what now?" Iridan asked quietly.

Brannis noted that Iridan did not seem fearful of Rashan but still seemed disturbed by the events that had taken place.

"We will do what the Inner Circle should have done in the first place," Rashan said. "We will search through the royal bloodlines and find the rightful heir and have a coronation. It will be a new dynasty, but it shall be a legitimate one. In the meantime, I will act as regent." Rashan let that last part hang, awaiting a challenge, should anyone offer one.

"By what right would you rule, if you just struck down Gravis for the same offense?" asked Dolvaen, perhaps foolishly. He was ever the righteous one among the council, claiming that he was not beholden to a bloodline family and was thus more free to speak and act by his conscience.

The others in the room collectively held their breaths, wondering if there soon would be a third empty seat in the Sanctum. Rashan glanced about the room at the reaction, frowning slightly.

"Three today were killed for treason, and I have already said that those remaining were to be given a second chance. Whatever my reputation has become over the past century, I do not slay sorcerers of the Empire for asking questions.

"I have no more right to the position than Gravis Archon. That much I will grant. His treason, however, was not that he stood in regency over the Empire, but that he was complicit in supplanting the dynasty in the first place. Had the imperial royal family died during his tenure as high sorcerer, it would have been fine for him to seek regency until the succession could be resolved," Rashan said.

"And how do we fit in?" Brannis asked, spreading his arms wide to indicate himself and the three sorcerers with him in the middle of the chamber.

"Well, Jurl is just here to act as herald. Many things will need to be explained and announced, and I was made to understand that Jurl has a rather excellent memory," Rashan told them. "As for the rest of you, there are changes to be made. The Empire is in need of a bit of upheaval.

"I find that the warning we had given regarding the goblins in Kelvie Forest has gone largely unheeded. While the threat was acknowledged, the generals of the army seem to have decided that there are sufficient troops in the region, and any potential reinforcements would not make it so far in time to matter. They are leaving the western reaches of the Empire to their own resources.

"We have apparently been making a habit, these past few decades, of relinquishing lands we conquered, as we are driven out of them. Megrenn is free and sacking our outposts, and we have done nothing substantive about it.

"Brannis, I am putting you in charge of the Imperial Army. You have the mind for it, and I know you can be trusted. The latter cannot be underestimated, given that I may face challenges from within, should my largess regarding amnesty be taken advantage of. This current crop of knights feels weak to me, as well. I have heard little so far, but what little I hear is enough to turn my stomach. We have bred a generation of tower guards and called them knights. You fight to win. When we are finished here, Jurl will accompany you to army headquarters, where you will relieve whoever is in charge these days."

"That would be Sir Hurald Chadreisson, Warlock," Caladris added sullenly. His normally jovial demeanor was, quite reasonably, dampened by the recent death of his brother.

"Well, he will not be in charge much longer," Rashan said. "Your first assignment, Brannis, will be to find where the goblins intend to invade and to drive them back. We will discuss this later and in greater detail. I have not fought a war in far too long, and I will not sit idly by for this one.

"As for you two …" Rashan gestured to Iridan and Aloisha, still standing roughly in the middle of the chamber. "… we have two seats to fill here. Aloisha, you will take the seat that Stalia Gardarus once occupied. We will have someone from House Gardarus come to fetch her things later today, and you may have her offices as well."

Aloisha looked stunned. She had long expected to one day ascend to the Inner Circle, but she had always thought it would be many long summers away.

"But I am not next in line," she said. "There are others with seniority who—"

"And they will continue to wait," Rashan said. "Seniority is something of an issue for me. It bespeaks laziness and entitlement. Power was always supposed to matter, and competence as well. Sitting comfortably in these throne-like seats in a tower as the Empire shrinks around you, *that* is what leadership by seniority accomplishes. Aloisha, I hear nothing but good things about you, from what little time I have had to decide on a replacement. You are also kin, and I am not ashamed to admit to favoring House Solaran when there is little else to go by."

"Yes, Warlock. I accept the honor you are bestowing on me," Aloisha spoke, still seeming numb and dizzy with the heady realization that she had just been given one of the most powerful positions in the Empire.

"Lastly you, Iridan. I must confess I have done wrong by you." Rashan paused and swallowed, as if unsure how to continue. "You have struggled and fought against a system that favors the purest of the bloodlines. Brannis told me that you finished top ranked your final four summers of the Academy and still garnered only token respect for it. You entered the Imperial Circle as a nobody, albeit a talented one. You were not arranged a wife, since a lone sorcerer in a peasant bloodline is just a fluke, not to be trusted until generations of sorcerers had proceeded from your line. How do you feel you have been treated by the Circle? Speak plainly now," Rashan commanded.

"Held back," Iridan answered, seemingly uncomfortable with saying so in front of so many that had been in charge of the system that had favored weaker sorcerers from better families over his. "Like I would never be good enough because my parents are peasants."

"Do you think that traditional wisdom is wrong? That the blood does not tell? That talent may turn up unexpectedly, even in the most unlikely of places?" Rashan asked one question after another, giving Iridan no time to answer in between.

"Yes, I think I do," Iridan answered proudly, lifting his head.

Rashan was about to elevate him to the Inner Circle, Brannis realized, and Iridan seemed to want to end the talk that his pedigree was not good enough.

"You are *wrong*!" Rashan shouted.

Iridan's eyes widened in shock. It was surely not the response he was building up in his head.

"Iridan, you have the purest blood in this room," Rashan said. "You are no more a fluke than I am. When you were born, I was not ready to return to Kadrin, but I wanted you to be raised in the Empire, without revealing that I was still alive. You are *my* son, not the son of those kindly farm folk we left you with."

"What?" Iridan whispered. "I ... Son?"

"Yes," Rashan said, "I did not choose to follow your band of refugees from Kelvie Forest because of my distant relation to Brannis, or the fact that he carried Heavens Cry and did not know it—though I admit that intrigued me as well. I followed you because I heard about your battle with the goblins and how you acquitted yourself," Rashan rambled, getting caught up in finally revealing his relation to Iridan.

"But I ... I nearly killed myself," Iridan said.

"But you did not," Rashan countered. "You took an instinctive step on the path to becoming a warlock. You used silent spellcasting in the furor of battle successfully. You have a natural talent; the rest is merely training."

"Wait, what? Warlock? Me?" Iridan sputtered.

Brannis could understand that Iridan felt overwhelmed—on two fronts, no less: first, hearing that he was going to be elevated from Fourth Circle directly to the Inner Circle, then being told that Rashan Solaran was his father. Now he was to be trained as a warlock as well?

I suppose I should have seen the resemblance, Brannis mused, feeling curiously detached from the proceedings.

It was all too impossible to be real. His dreams actually felt more plausible than his own life, where he had just been the beneficiary of some sort of well-meaning reverse coup, where the usurpers had just been overthrown, and which had resulted in him being given an army.

There is a hole in the side of the Tower of Contemplation. Three members of the Inner Circle are dead, including my father. Rashan is Iridan's father? I am supposed to orchestrate the attack to drive back the goblin army. Oh, and apparently there has been no emperor in my lifetime.

I would much like to wake up from this dream, too.

* * * * * * * *

Brannis did not get to wake up from the strange world he was now being dragged into. Instead he found himself at the center of a small parade, headed for the army headquarters. At the head of the procession was Jurl, who had transcribed Rashan's proclamation into a set of written orders, which the warlock had signed. Two sorcerers walked next to him, his cousin Hernus Gardarus, and Iridan—*Solaran?* Brannis mused. Surrounding the lot of them to the sides and rear were a dozen of the Tower's honor guards.

The inclusion of Iridan—at his own request no less—made Brannis a bit more comfortable. He was unsure of the reaction he was about to receive. Just the previous evening, he had been in Sir Hurald Chadreisson's office, taking the reprimand he knew he had coming for the loss of so many of his men. Now he was on his way to deliver orders requiring Sir Hurald to cede command to him. The general would be furious, to say the least.

If Rashan had known the general, he might have sent more guards along.

The trek across Kadris to army headquarters on foot was long enough that word spread ahead of them. The streets were lining themselves with Kadrin citizens, eager to begin putting the puzzle together of what had occurred that morning. Gossip was clearly raging already, and people shouted questions at them as they passed, occasionally calling out to the members of the procession by name if they recognized someone they knew. The guards were able to keep the curious at bay—a trick that being armed and accompanied by sorcerers made easier—but the press of onlookers blocking their path slowed them considerably, as the numbers in the streets swelled.

They slowed to nearly a halt as the mob grew too large to get out of its own way, the ones nearest the procession being pushed forward by those far back trying to move closer.

"People of Kadrin," Jurl called out, "stand aside, in the name of Warlock Rashan."

This caused a buzz to go through the crowd as ale-room historians and quilting circle politicians circulated fresh gossip based on this newest revelation.

Not one in four truly knew who Rashan was the night before, other than perhaps knowing the name from "somewhere." By midday, all would have heard news of his return, and his history.

The crowd was curious but had not been especially spurred to react in any sort of path-clearing manner. The foremost rows directly in Brannis's path tried to edge sideways, but the constant press from behind would only allow for so much movement.

From beside him, he heard Iridan chant, *"Glaenu chukchaawe sevaani mafalu anahio."*

Brannis turned to see what he was gesturing, but Iridan was quick; he finished before Brannis had a chance to see what he had just done.

A clear, shimmering liquid spread beneath the feet of Brannis, Iridan, the other two sorcerers, and the guards. It formed a small pond under them all, and once it had everyone supported, it began to rise up from the cobblestones. The feeling was disconcerting initially, but the gooey liquid seemed sturdy enough—akin to standing in very wet mud.

"Nicely done," Brannis congratulated Iridan.

But his friend was paying him scant attention. Iridan's eyes were unfocused, likely lost in aether-sight, Brannis guessed. Once they had risen above the heads of those in the crowd, the liquidy mass began to move. Unfortunately it did not pull everyone along with it; Iridan began to walk, and the rest followed his example. The surface tugged at their feet slightly as they lifted them, and there was an echoing ripple of sound, similar to a drop of water falling into a full bucket, with each step. The sound of sixteen pairs of feet made for an odd symphony as they walked. Fortunately the honor guard had been assigned to the Tower of Contemplation for long enough that unannounced bits of magic were merely unusual, rather than shocking.

Iridan had not lifted their conveyance much more than head height, and hands reached up from the crowd to touch the magical walking-water as it passed above. Magic was quite far from unknown in the Kadrin Empire, but most often it was done out of sight of the common folk. It was a rare treat to see such a display, and diverted much of the crowd's immediate attention from gossip to wonderment. In the meantime, Brannis, Iridan, and the rest of Brannis's escort made haste for Kalak Square, where they would find the headquarters of the Imperial Army.

A few paces into their midair journey, Iridan shook his head, clearing his sight back to normal vision and reorienting himself as he walked.

"Thank you, I quite like this one," Iridan said, belatedly accepting Brannis's compliment.

"So, um, Iridan," Brannis began, "I guess this means we are ... cousins."

"I will need to see a family tree at some point, I suppose, but I think we are four generations or so apart from being cousins. I cannot rightly say what we are. For all I know, I could be your thrice-great uncle, despite being just a month older," Iridan replied.

It seemed to Brannis that he had already given the topic some thought.

"Welcome to the family, in any event. I imagine that you can move to the family estate if you would like. It seems rather clear that Rashan favors you," Brannis observed dryly. "You might ask for any room you like."

As soon as Brannis mentioned rooms at Solaran Estate, he thought of his own room. Then he thought of the dream. His stomach twisted inside him as the anxiety returned, worrying what was going on in that world he saw at night.

"Are you all right, Brannis?" Iridan asked. "You just got this look on your face like someone just told you that the beef stew you just ate was not actually made from beef." Iridan walked a pace ahead of Brannis and turned to look him in the face head on. "Really, are you well?"

"Lot on my mind, is all. The world changed a lot on us today, I feel. More so for you and me than for most, perhaps, but it changed for everyone. I think I know what it feels like now, when a pawn advances to the back rank. I am not sure what piece I have become, but I am fairly certain I am a pawn no longer," Brannis said.

"Rook, I would say. You have a rookish quality to you," Iridan joked, and got Brannis to chuckle. "Always go in a straight line, once you get set on something."

The gnawing worry was still within Brannis, but Iridan helped keep his mind off what he knew he could not control, at least until nightfall. Brannis was not sure who was in control in his dreams, whether he was just an observer or whether he was the one deciding what to do. A lot of what this Kyrus fellow did seemed rather naïve, but it was an endearing sort of naïve that Brannis envied a little. Maybe in that world, he was just a more innocent version of himself.

He hoped that the innocent self of his dreams was ready to face whatever was to come. That innocence would ill serve him, if Brannis's *second*-worst fears were realized. If Kyrus had just died last night, all was moot anyway, and it seemed there would be no repercussion to Brannis. However, if Kyrus had been captured, Brannis still did not know how their fates were twined, and the worst might still be yet to come.

Brannis's thoughts, it seemed, could wander off without him, despite Iridan's best efforts.

* * * * * * * *

"What is all this?" Sir Hurald Chadreisson demanded as Jurl opened up his message in the main entry hall and began to read it aloud to Sir Hurald and everyone else within earshot.

As Brannis's entourage entered the army headquarters, soldiers, functionaries, and officers had begun to congregate. As with much of the rest of Kadris, they were privy to an unusual sight ... and curiosity was the surest lure of men.

"'This morning, the seventy-third day of Autumn, six thousand two hundred seventy-nine summers since the Founding, three members of the Imperial Inner Circle were executed for the crime of treason regarding the circumstances of the death of Emperor Dharus Kadrin. These included High Sorcerer Gravis Archon,

Maruk Solaran, and Stalia Gardarus. Those who may have been aware of their treasonous conspiracy are granted conditional clemency, insomuch as there will be no formal inquiry beyond what justice has already been meted out.

"'These circumstances have necessitated changes in leadership at the highest levels of the empire. While there is no specific charge leveled against anyone in the Imperial Army and no officer thereof shall be singled out for dishonor, at this time I must place loyalty and competence above seniority and the standard chain of promotion.

"'Thus I hereby bestow upon Sir Brannis Solaran the title of Grand Marshal of the Kadrin Imperial Army, with full and complete authority over all men and materials of the army, and discretion to use them as he sees fit, subject solely to my direction and oversight.

"'Furthermore, all senior officers in the Imperial Army are ordered to appear in the Great Hall of the Imperial Palace at sunset tonight, to receive further details. All questions regarding the change of command may be held until that time.

"'Under no circumstances will anyone interfere with the transition of command to Grand Marshal Sir Brannis Solaran or disobey his orders. Anyone who does so will answer directly to me.'

"Signed, Warlock Rashan Solaran, High Sorcerer and Regent of the Kadrin Empire," Jurl finished, and walked calmly over to Sir Hurald and handed him the decree.

There was a stunned silence in the hall. Many of the onlookers shifted uncomfortably, awaiting a reaction from Sir Hurald, who had listened less than stoically to Jurl's recitation of the decree. His pale, pasty skin had flushed a bright red where it was not covered by beard, and he was breathing heavily. It seemed all he could do as he listened not to cross the few paces between himself and Jurl and run the sorcerer through.

"Preposterous!" Sir Hurald thundered. "This is a coup. Take this lot prisoner immediately," he ordered to no one in particular, gesturing to Brannis and his entourage. "These are traitors to the Empire!"

Hurald's hand went to the enchanted sword at his side, but instantly the honor guards' halberds leveled in his direction. Several officers moved to General Sir Hurald's side, though they were careful not to draw their own blades. While the honor guard was little tested in battle, they had a reputation for efficiency and obedience that left none to question whether they would die carrying out their order to defend the "usurper," regardless of what Sir Hurald might wish.

Others had watched from the entrance hall or the walkways above that overlooked it, but there was no great haste to take sides. On the one hand, they were suspicious of these orders, having just heard about the deaths of three of the most influential members of the Inner Circle at the hands of the one who gave them. On the other, the military was quite fond of history and educated its officers well on the subject, especially Kadrin's rich and bloody history of conquest. Unlike the peasant-folk outside, these men knew who Rashan Solaran was and wanted no part of defying him. Rumors had already spread that the old warlock was truly returned.

"What are you waiting for, men?" Sir Hurald looked around the hall and up at those watching and waiting. "Draw steel and subdue these intruders. Are you cowards?"

There was some element of truth to Sir Hurald's accusation. The honor guard was the least of the troubles they saw. Three sorcerers of the Imperial Circle were among the entourage, and many had heard second- or third-hand accounts of Iridan entering combat in the Battle of Kelvie Forest. Sorcerers were always risky to fight, since when faced with death, they had no reason *not* to try to fight with aether, to the winds with consequences. Foremost, though, was that Brannis was known to carry Massacre. None in the hall had noticed—or knew enough to even tell the difference—that he was carrying Avalanche instead.

"There has indeed been a coup," Brannis replied. "It is over now, the usurpers killed. Rashan Solaran is Regent of the Empire now. This is a fact. The Imperial Circle already recognizes him as such. He meets with the nobles even now to inform them. Your summons for this evening is your time to see for yourself. I have seen him already."

"You shall not take the army without a fight!" Sir Hurald proclaimed. "I have served at the emperor's command for nearly my entire life, and I will not allow some reckless pup to steer us into catastrophe. If none of you will draw steel to defend the fate of the army, then I will."

And Hurald drew his blade, a fine piece of both sword-smithing and aether-smithing. The blade shone like silver or seemed black as night depending on the angle of the light. It was scribed down the length with runes, keeping it razor sharp and easily balanced in Hurald's hand. He presented it in the classic fencing salute.

"I challenge you, Brannis Solaran, to a duel," he spoke formally, but intentionally left off the "Sir" and any mention of rank.

"Hold," Brannis spoke softly, raising his hand to forestall the impending halberd charge he felt was coming from the honor guards.

He drew Avalanche from its sheath, slowly, and with a reversed grip. He took two steps closer to Sir Hurald as the honor guard parted slightly to allow a clear path between the two men. Still moving slowly, he raised his sword, blade still facing downward, until his arm was fully extended.

With a sudden, explosive thrust, Brannis drove the sword halfway to the hilt into the solid granite floor of the entry hall. Those nearby turned, threw up their hands, or covered their faces to protect themselves from the stone debris that flew up every which way from the sundered floor. To his credit, Sir Hurald only flinched, never lowering his sword from guard position.

"I could cut you in half," Brannis spoke, loudly enough for everyone in the now quiet hall to hear him clearly, despite being only a few paces from the old general he was addressing. "But that will not make me any more right. If you were to dodge my strike and run your sword through my heart, you would not prove your point, either.

"Rashan Solaran is back. Yes, he is the very same warlock who destroyed Loramar and ended the Necromancer Wars, and who survived the Battle of the Dead Earth, contrary to what we once thought. He had been gone just over a century, and he has much to explain about his whereabouts in the interim, and why he has not returned before now. That I will grant.

"This is no raw lust for power; he has all that he could want and more already. I know little of his tale, but I know this much: Warlock Rashan was able to survive the final battle with Loramar because he had become an immortal, a demon. However powerful and dangerous history's record says he is, he is more so now. Though I was not present to witness it, I have reliable accounts, confirmed by the Inner Circle, that Gravis Archon confessed his crimes and tried to rationalize his way around them. When Warlock Rashan chose to summarily destroy him, the former high sorcerer was helpless to defend himself.

"Though you will doubtless hear much the same from him tonight, Warlock Rashan does not intend or wish to remain regent, or to style himself as the new emperor. Having traveled back from Kelvie Forest with him, I feel I know him at least a small bit. I believe he was homesick and wished to return to the emperor's service, as he once served so long ago. Upon his homecoming, he instead found a grand conspiracy that had been perpetrated in his absence.

"He is upset. He is angry. He does not yet know whom to trust among the circles of power in Kadrin. Thus he has instated me, his kin and someone whom he has shared travels with, as custodian of the army, at least for the time being. I know not if this promotion will last a week, a month, or become permanent.

"You, Sir Hurald, have not been demoted as such. The position of Grand Marshal may be above yours but has not been awarded in many summers. I expect you will continue to serve the Imperial Army and obey the orders given by me or by the regent. If you have issue with this arrangement, and frankly you have made it sufficiently clear that you do, take it up with Warlock Rashan tonight when you meet him. Contrary to what you might think, he will not kill you for challenging his decision; he may even appreciate it. He finds our knights soft and passive, and you might do well to show otherwise.

"I will let you think on this. I have no intention of issuing sweeping orders to change the army wholesale. My one order for today is that you find me an office, which I will take residency in starting tomorrow." Brannis paused as if to consider something, then continued: "And please bear in mind that the warlock may visit this new office of mine. While I consider myself to be good humored and reasonable, I find Warlock Rashan to be somewhat less so, and he might find it *inappropriate* if he has to meet with me in some converted pantry or one of the stables."

Brannis pulled his sword from the ground as easily as if it had been stuck in snow, and returned Avalanche to its sheath, locking his gaze on Sir Hurald as he did so.

"I may still ask to face you in combat over this, Brannis," Sir Hurald said, more calmly than he had spoken earlier. Warily, he slid his own blade back into its sheath as well.

"I will see you this evening, then. I shall be in attendance as well, as I am now a senior officer of the army," Brannis replied.

Brannis turned and began to walk back toward the main doors, and the honor guard fell in behind him.

As they exited army headquarters and the view of those inside, Iridan leaned in to Brannis and whispered, "Well played, indeed. I thought for a moment you really were going to cut him in half in front of everyone."

Without turning, Brannis muttered back, "So did I. I am still surprised the arrogant mule put his sword away."

Iridan suppressed a chuckle.

* * * * * * *

Brannis parted ways with the honor guard and the two sorcerers at the gate to Solaran Estate. He needed some time away from the chaos that was quickly overtaking him, at least long enough to regroup and adjust to the sudden change in rank and importance. Iridan remained behind when the rest left.

"Would you like me to show you around the place? I know my father did not like having you around, but that would seem not to be an issue anymore," Brannis said.

Despite their longstanding friendship, Maruk Solaran had never approved of Brannis associating so closely with a "peasant" sorcerer. Though his stance had softened somewhat as Iridan showed himself more and more capable as he advanced through the Academy, Brannis's father had never allowed Iridan to feel at ease at the estate.

"I would like to see the place a bit. From the couple times you sneaked me in when we were younger, it seemed nearly as nice as the palace," Iridan replied. "Not today, though. I think everyone should get some time to get used to me being Warlock Rashan's son, not the least of them being me. I woke up this morning as Iridan Korian. I think I shall try falling asleep as him tonight as well.

"By the by, you could use a good night's rest yourself. I know you have had as interesting a day as have I, but you look the worse for it," Iridan said in that bluntly insulting manner that only close friends are wont to get away with on a regular basis.

"I slept poorly last night. I had a particularly vivid nightmare, and it has gnawed at me all day, despite the numerous distractions that you might think would take my mind off it entirely," Brannis confided. There was no one else around now, and he felt confident that Iridan knew him well enough not to read too much into it.

"Must have been quite the nightmare. Were you falling perhaps, or trapped by some monster or another? I have never found the end of one of those falling ones; I think the mind does not quite know what the end is supposed to feel like, so you just wake up," Iridan said.

"No, I always see the same place in my dreams, the same people. I am always the same person in my dreams, not Brannis the knight, but some lowly scribe. Last night, I was accosted by city guards after they caught me doing magic, which I think was illegal, possibly. Anyway, I got caught and knocked out. I do not know what happened from then on," Brannis said. He was not sure Iridan would understand, but at least he felt he could unburden himself somewhat in Iridan's presence.

"Oh, Brannis. It still pains you even though the Academy was winters ago? You get to play at magic in your dreams and get persecuted for it? That is just awful. Quite a clear recollection of it as well. It must have made quite the impression on you."

Iridan sounded empathetic, but Brannis knew he could not understand the frustration that those winters of failure and ultimately ridicule had caused him. Still, as thoughtful as Iridan's kind words were, they missed the mark.

"Well, yes, but that is not the half of it. I remember it all, the whole thing, morning to night, and I do every night. I did not use to remember my dreams much at all, but I think possibly because they bored me so. Things have been going better of late in the dream world, what with learning a little magic and meeting this girl—"

"Aha," Iridan interrupted him. "This whole dream thing is about the parts of your life you would like to change. You are still pining for Juliana, too, I would wager. You claimed you were past that, but you still carry on hoping because technically no one called off your betrothal. It was just a given that once you left the Academy that it was over. How many lasses have you bedded to convince yourself you did not still want her? You are a general now—"

"Grand marshal," Brannis corrected him quietly, barely slowing Iridan's narrative momentum.

"Err, yes, a grand marshal now, and have the support of the new high sorcerer. Surely you could just, uh, follow through? How could she refuse you?" Iridan asked.

Brannis could not help but admire how his friend was trying to help him out, ill-conceived though the attempt might have been.

"It is not so much that; I just worry what has happened in my dream. I do not want to lose everything I have there," Brannis said.

"Brannis, it is just a dream. Dreams are all in your head. If you lose what you have there, maybe you can take my advice and seek it while you are awake." Iridan smiled mischievously. "Is she pretty?"

Brannis frowned in reply. "Do you have an appointment with a tailor you ought to be seeing to this afternoon?" Brannis said, diverting the conversation because Iridan was just having fun with him now.

"See you tomorrow, Brannis." Iridan turned and waved as he departed. "And get some real sleep tonight. The Empire will need you, after all."

* * * * * * * *

Brannis attended the officers' summons to the palace that night. Rashan held audience in the throne room but stood beside the empty throne the whole time. All officers stationed in Kadris were in attendance, since the order had left off mention of what ranks were considered "senior" enough to attend. Rashan made no comment on the size of the crowd.

Brannis kept himself distracted by the audience, as he had heard the details of the conspiracy already, and knew more of the travels from Kelvie already than Rashan revealed to the rest of the officers. He could not stop his worries about Kyrus and his fate, now that he had time enough to let them run wild.

He was half-listening to Rashan and was aware enough of the crowd's reaction to realize that the warlock was an inspiring speaker. It dawned on Brannis that *these* were Rashan's people, much more so than the flabby old sorcerers that sat in ornate chairs in a tower and spent their days debating and delegating. These were men who would bear arms into battle and emerge bloody and victorious, or at least might have in their younger days, in some cases.

The warlock appealed to their sense of imperial pride and talked of the glories of the Empire that were dying in the fields like overripe vegetables. He actually compared them to those vegetables: soft, worthless, and rotting inside. He offered them a new path back to what the Empire used to be, when he was last its warlock.

The rousing speech noticeably lifted the morale of those present, though obviously some remained unconvinced. The one phrase that stood out to Brannis as an omen of the Empire's future was thus: "I will reunite the Empire through diplomacy, and I am a diplomat of fire and steel." There was actually a book in the library at the School of Arms entitled *The Diplomacy of Fire and Steel*, which had been written after Rashan's apparent death, describing his use of diplomacy and deception in the cause of war.

It was said that the emperor wielded the army in his left hand and the Circle in his right, the two tools by which he controlled the Empire. Brannis wondered if he was about to become the blood-stained left hand of the regent.

Sir Hurald did not seek Warlock Rashan's permission to challenge Brannis to a duel that night. Brannis did not expect to sleep the better for it.

Chapter 21 - On My Own Behalf

What happened? Kyrus wondered in a daze.

He had a headache that only a man bound for the chopping block would envy. He was lying down on some hard surface that felt like wood. Opening his eyes to try to get his bearings, the light sent shooting pains through his head, and he closed them again quickly.

There was some sort of commotion that sounded like it was in the next room, but he could not tell with any certainty. There were raised and angry voices, but too many of them, and the overall effect was too loud; it was making his headache worse.

His whole side hurt from whatever wooden surface he was lying on. He felt as if he must have been insensible for a long time, for his muscles had grown stiff due to lack of movement. He stretched out a bit and heard a clanking of chains; his ankles were shackled together.

What he had first dismissed as a bad case of dry mouth was actually some sort of gag. He reached up to pull it loose but found his wrists shackled together as well, and bound to a chain around his waist.

Oh, this definitely is not a good sign.

Opening his eyes just a slit, Kyrus managed to survey his surroundings. He was, unsurprisingly given the shackles, in a cell. Kyrus had never been to Scar Harbor's jail—a failing of his cultural upbringing no doubt—but was clever enough to puzzle out that it was his present location. He was surrounded on three sides and above by stone bricks, with a wall of bars completing the room. The floor was dirt covered, but Kyrus suspected that it, too, was stone or bedrock not far down. He was lying on a wooden cot, with the only other furnishing in the room being a chamber pot. With a supreme effort, Kyrus rolled enough that he could look at the wall he was lying nearest, and saw that there was a small, wide, barred window above him near the ceiling of the cell. The window allowed in fresh air, a little—unwelcome at the moment—light, and the noises from the street that he had been hearing.

Kyrus knew only one, modestly effective, cure for headaches. He relaxed as best he could and drew in a bit of aether. The cool rush cleared his head a bit. It did not eliminate the pain, but it helped markedly in clearing the foggy haze that the pain left in his head. He was able to sit up without the world spinning and decided that it was worth an attempt to do so.

Though he had drawn in little aether, after a few moments he became irritatingly aware of the fact that he was holding it. As it began to burn, and it occurred to Kyrus that he had not the ability to cast any spells, bound up as he was. He looked about for a likely place to dump the excess discretely and found that they had left him no water. He was almost glad he had not yet used the chamber pot, sparing himself that unsavory odor, should he have boiled it off. He decided on the bars of the cell door as his likeliest option and diverted the aether there. He saw no visible effect from it, but knew that the bars would be, at the least, rather uncomfortably warm to the touch.

* * * * * * *

The bars of the cell had surely cooled by the time the bailiffs arrived to drag Kyrus from his cell. They were two stocky men, cut from the "just obeying orders" cloth. Both were dressed in official uniforms of a drab brown with minimal adornment, and carrying clubs slung from their belts. One carried a ring of keys and unlocked the cell door. The grating metal-on-metal sound of the key in the rusted lock pierced Kyrus's still-sensitive ears and drove tiny daggers of pain into his brain.

The door opened with the creak one might expect of an un-oiled iron cage, and the bailiffs strode in. Without so much as a word, they hoisted Kyrus up under each arm and carried him bodily from the cell, shackled feet dragging along. Kyrus could not have kept up with their pace had he wanted to, hobbled as he was, and doubted he would much care for where they were taking him. They carried him down the row of cells beneath the jailhouse, and to the stairs heading up.

Well, at least this bodes well for seeing the light of day again, Kyrus mused darkly.

He had worried that he might be taken somewhere worse, and usually that sort of thing would suggest down rather than up, if the storybooks he had read were any indication. As they took the stairs, Kyrus contorted to dodge his head below one of the low rafters, causing his headache to renew its efforts. His feet bumped along at each step as they hung limply; Kyrus was too tired to make the effort to pull them up or back and out of the way.

When they reached the top, they made their way past a short row of waiting constables, who fell in beside them as they proceeded. The jail was cleaner and more orderly up on the ground floor, with desks and storage rooms and hallways connected by barred doors. Kyrus tried to make a map of it in his head, in case he were to attempt some sort of daring escape. To date, his most daring endeavor had been courting Abbiley, so he expected that there might be a bit of a learning curve in regards to jailbreaks. Still, what other options was he going to have?

Well, I can always try denying everything. Only a few officers of the constabulary saw anything, and it was late at night. They could have been overwrought and misinterpreted what they saw. Or maybe I can insist I was practicing parlor tricks, and it was all an act. Surely not enough people in Acardia are superstitious enough to believe in magic. Certainly not a magistrate.

Kyrus had managed to make himself feel rather better about his prospects by the time they got him to the door. He would make his appeal to the magistrate—which is where he supposed they were bringing him—and convince everyone that the whole notion of magic was preposterous. Acardia was a rational, enlightened kingdom: too sensible to be overcome by fears of witchcraft.

Of course, once Kyrus passed clear of the door, the crowd, which had gone relatively quiet in the hours of waiting to see the "witch," was re-energized. Thoughts of appealing to the better nature of a learned man of law and justice were quickly replaced with a sudden fear that he was going to be burned at the stake!

"Begone, fiend!"

"We do not want your kind!"

"Get rid of him!"

"Hang him!"

"Leave us alone, witch!"

"Burn the witch!"

The latter was shouted more than once and was eventually taken up by the mob at large as a chant. Kyrus suspected that he was being carried because any sane man would have likely tried to bolt if he was walking on his own. The two bailiffs carried him to a waiting wagon and hefted him into it, then climbed in with him. The constables kept the crowd back and away from the horses as the wagon drover got them moving. Kyrus tried to slouch down below the level of the sides of the wagon to get out of sight of the crowd, but one of the bailiffs grabbed him and hauled him back up.

"Aww, no hidin', Mister Witch," the bailiff told him in his gutter accent. He seemed the sort who chose a life of thuggery in the service of law as a career option favorable to a life of thuggery outside it—and only because the pay was steady. "They wants to see ya, so they gets to see ya."

Kyrus hung his head and tried to block out the jeers and calls for his immolation, but there was only so little room inside one's own head in which to hide, and Kyrus was beset on all sides. The ride to the courthouse was a short one, as it was located convenient to the jail, but it seemed an eternity to Kyrus, whose confidence in the rationality of Acardians was severely shaken. He could not understand how the citizens could be convinced so quickly when he had only been arrested hours earlier, and no charges had yet been lodged against him officially.

* * * * * * *

Across town, at a certain shop whose sign bore no picture, another crowd had gathered. This one was less angry and more curious, but still very excited. Constables had formed a loose ring around it and were keeping folks back from it. Inside, some of the more senior members of the sheriff's staff were rummaging through papers and books, gathering evidence. They had already found Kyrus's notes, both those written in plain language and those that were written in an indecipherable and otherworldly script.

The crowd was uninterested in the investigation of the shop. They had all gathered to catch a glimpse of the otherworldly light that shone out the door that had been left ajar. A light that had no visible origin, yet just kept glowing …

* * * * * * * *

"Expert Kyrus Hinterdale, how do you answer these charges?" Lord Kenrick Lionsvaen asked.

Kyrus had formally been charged with the practice of witchcraft and attacking officers of the peace. Two men with crossbows aimed at his back stood just behind him as he sat in the dock, where he had just finished listening to the preliminaries of the case presented against him. He had been given to understand that if they heard anything that sounded like it might be magical in nature, he would be shot, but at least they had removed the gag from his mouth.

"I have done nothing wrong, Your Lordship," was all Kyrus could manage.

He was terrified and disoriented. The shouting of the crowd had done little good for his still-aching head, and he had never had much interest in court cases, so he was unfamiliar with how things were to be handled.

"Sheriff Marsemal, please present the evidence," the judge intoned.

The judge was an elderly man with a regal bearing. He wore the traditional black robes of a jurist, which hung loosely off his gaunt frame, and skull cap to match. His wrinkled face was pale and ashen as someone who had worked a lifetime indoors. His hooked nose supported a pair of gold-rimmed spectacles that caught the light strangely and obscured his eyes, making it seem as if he was not seeing what took place around him and giving him a detached air.

"Your Lordship." The sheriff of Scar Harbor bowed slightly to the magistrate as he arose. "I have five men who were witnesses to the sights in Mr. Hinterdale's shop last evening, three of whom can attest to having seen actual witchcraft performed in front of their very eyes; seen it, heard it, and had detritus from about the shop flung at them by means of it.

"Also, Your Lordship, we have the accused's own notes, describing the methods and means of his dark art, written plainly in Acardian. We also have a number of pages containing notes in an unknown language. I took the liberty of awakening the esteemed Professor Wittingham of the university's department of language and foreign studies, who could not so much as identify the characters or symbols being used.

"If these were not enough, Your Lordship, there is still, as of the last of my hearing, a light of inexplicable and unknowable origin shining from within the main work area of Mr. Hinterdale's shop.

"Your Lordship, I am not a superstitious man, and a week ago, I would have thought it impossible. Today I stand before you and ask how this can be anything else but witchcraft," the sheriff concluded.

Kyrus could not help but be impressed at the man's oratory ability, despite his predicament. Sheriff Marsemal could have been a thespian, or perhaps a city councilor, but instead stayed on year after year as the sheriff in Scar Harbor. Kyrus wondered if he kept the job because he had grown to like having everyone hang on his words as he made such speeches in court.

"Again, Expert Hinterdale, I would ask you to respond to this evidence," Lord Lionsvaen instructed Kyrus.

Kyrus's mouth was dry, but somehow managed to get even drier. "I ... hurt no one," he croaked. He cleared his throat, fearing that the nervous crossbowmen would fire quarrels into his back, but needing to make a case for himself. "It is all harmless. Parlor tricks and such. This is all being taken much too far."

There was a general murmuring of dozens of conversations that began in the gallery at the first hearing of Kyrus's defense. Many who had never met him just heard this "witch" speak for the first time, and he was hardly a threatening specimen. Kyrus had barely been aware of the spectators within the courtroom until they started making noise. After the crowd outside and their calls for his gruesome demise, the relatively civil citizens in attendance had barely registered themselves in his consciousness—his consciousness being somewhat tenuous at the moment itself; he was feeling faint.

"Quiet now!" Lord Lionsvaen shouted, and the audience composed themselves once more. "Mr. Hinterdale," he continued in a more professional tone, "you admit to these acts?"

"Yes, but—"

"And I have seen for myself, as Sheriff Marsemal took me by your shop this morning, that there is indeed an unhallowed sort of light that comes from nothingness."

"Well, you see—"

"Stop interrupting me, child, or it shall go badly for you," Lord Lionsvaen said. "And the lawmen you assaulted are rather upstanding and honest men, whose accounts I believe in spite of the fantastical nature of its description."

"Your Lordship, I think that this is an instance where we might justifiably request an exemption from the prohibition on executions," Sheriff Marsemal said.

At that mention of execution, Kyrus heart began to race even quicker. He felt his breath coming shallow and rapidly.

"I am not a fearful man," the sheriff said, "but the existence of one such as this disturbs me to the core. I think ..."

And that was the last that Kyrus heard before he lost consciousness, having passed out.

* * * * * * *

Brannis woke with a start. It was the middle of the night, but there was no denying how he felt. His head hurt for no reason he could rationalize—other than that Kyrus's head hurt, and that he had just been there in it, watching. He was not so debilitated by it as Kyrus had been, but he could feel the spot where

Kyrus had hit his head on the cobblestones of the streets of Scar Harbor behind his shop.

Have I gone mad?

The question hung in Brannis's mind as he lay in bed, staring up at a ceiling that was too dark to see. The shock of his dream was enough to bring him fully awake, though he was still slightly disoriented. Acardia felt too real for Kadrin to have fully sunk in just yet.

That is the real question, is it not? If I have lost my faculties, then this is all really just a dream, and I can ignore it—perhaps even find a way to rid myself of the dreams entirely. Surely there are potions, or magic to cure me, or even just taking to strong drink at night to sleep in oblivion.

Brannis thought more about it for a few seconds.

I could hide it, I think, never speaking of it to anyone. If I am strong enough, they will never catch on. I would have to be careful never to let slip anything I know that does not belong to the waking world. If I am lucky, I could take the secret to my grave never having breathed a word of it. I have just been given the chance of a lifetime; I cannot risk losing it. Can I?

Brannis thought of all the wonderful things he had seen and felt in his dreams. Kyrus was not well-traveled, but had experienced friends and a budding romance, and even felt the rush of the aether. It was the latter that tugged particularly at Brannis's conscience. He knew that he had never imagined how it could feel to actually draw aether. He doubted his mind could have conjured such a euphoric feeling. Had it given the same joy as lovemaking, he could have accused his dreams of plagiarism, but the drawing of aether was entirely different. It was like standing in a hurricane untouched, as the wind blew through you, cleaning out the mind and body and leaving it feeling pure.

It has to be real. If it is real, Kyrus needs me. If I am to help, all I can give is knowledge. The only knowledge that might save him is magic.

Brannis threw off the bedclothes and stumbled in darkness over to the window. He drew open the heavy, velvet curtains that had so effectively cloaked the bedchamber in darkness. Pale moonlight wafted into the room, giving everything a ghostly quality, nearly devoid of color.

Brannis's eyes adjusted to the light, and he could make out the clothing he had worn the previous day. Though they smelled of stale sweat, they would serve his purposes, and Brannis quickly dressed. As he finished pulling on his boots, he walked swiftly for the door, then hesitated. He considered for a moment whether he ought to bring his sword but then dismissed the idea. He was not going far— not even leaving the estate.

Brannis walked down the heavy-carpeted halls of Solaran Estate in thankful silence. Had his family been less indentured to comfort and luxury, he might have had to walk down a hall of bare stone, and would have needed to pad his steps if he wished to avoid causing commotion. The thick, red Safschan carpets, hundreds of summers old and preserved by magic, cushioned even his booted steps and muffled them to a whisper. A soft glow lit every hallway of the building at night, lest anyone seeking a late-evening snack—or just arriving late to bed—need to carry illumination of their own.

He made his way to the family library, which his father had, until quite recently of course, taken custody of as his personal study. Doors within the estate were never locked, and Brannis opened the rightmost of the double doors and quietly entered. The heavy, ornately carved wooden door made not the slightest sound as it swung. Unlike the halls, the library was dark. Brannis felt his way across the dark room by only the scant light that came in from the hall. When he reached the window, he drew it open the curtains to cast enough light, hopefully, to read by.

It was difficult to find a light source anywhere in the estate. Even his cousin Danil was enough of a sorcerer to light up anyplace he chose. Brannis was so rarely at home that he did not keep a lamp or magical light device about for his own use. It was fortunate that the moon was high and mostly full that night, and that the clouds were too thin and wispy to block much light, else Brannis would have been unable to find anything at all. As it was, he could only read the titles of volumes whose spines faced the window.

Brannis scanned the ones he could see: *Trontor's Alchemy. Native Species of Tuermon. The Hurac Dynasty: A Sorcerer's Perspective. The Warlock Prophecies. The Life of Fexil Solaran. Artifacts of the Early Imperial Era.* Then a title written in a language Brannis could not read. Then, *Geography and the Flow of Aether.* And then, *My Journal: Telemuron Solaran.*

Brannis thought the last sounded promising and pulled it from its shelf. Brannis scanned the first few pages. They were yellowed with age but bore the distinctively smooth feel of magical preservation.

Talking about his early life … Goes on a sea voyage … Meets foreigners and shows them magic … More sea voyage … Drat, he was naught but an explorer. Nothing about how *to do any magic.*

Brannis shoved the volume back into place with somewhat less care and respect normally due a four-hundred-odd summer-old book. He picked up where he left off.

Predatory Avians. Geology as Pertains to Underground Structures. Collected Maps of the Ocean Currents. Coins. Sighing in annoyance with himself, Brannis could not help but wonder from the scant title what that one contained. He quickly pulled it off the shelf and looked inside. There was page after page of coins from various kingdoms and eras, sketched in fine detail by someone with ample free time. He angrily slammed it back into place and looked at the last two volumes on that shelf. *Corporo Kannis: Merchant King. Ways of the Old Gods.*

Brannis moved to the next shelf down and continued: *Dark Tales for the Fireside. Adventures of Boppy the Rabbit. Seram's Children's Stories.* Brannis quickly browsed the rest of the shelf—nothing but children's books. Maruk may have taken the library for his study, but it was still the family's library.

He continued scanning title after title. There were scholarly works, biographies, and storybooks, but he had yet to find anything that he could use. He needed instructions, notes, something substantive that Kyrus would be able to remember and make use of. He started taking books from the darkened shelves on the other side of the room and bringing them over to the window to read the titles.

He discovered more of the same, perhaps with a few more personal journals of his ancestors. He was finding it difficult to believe that in a household of perhaps the most influential bloodline of sorcerers in the Empire, that there were no books on how to perform magic. Brannis admittedly had not looked at every book in the library, but he was getting the sense that if there were books in there of the type he was after, he ought to have found at least one so far.

Brannis moved to his father's desk and gave it a quick check as well. It did not take long to decide that it was devoid of helpful writings as well. His father had either kept it very tidy, or some ambitious relatives had already absconded with anything of value.

He must have kept everything in his offices in the Tower of Contemplation, Brannis decided.

That presented problems of its own, but not insurmountable ones. Brannis had already committed himself this far; he was prepared to do whatever it took now and deal with the consequences later.

Brannis hurriedly drew the curtains closed again and made his way in the semi-darkness back out of the library. He considered his options. He could simply awaken someone and beg their assistance. Any number of sorcerers in the house could find him spells to escape from Kyrus's situation; there was a reason the palace had warded cells for magic-capable prisoners. He could also ask either Iridan or Rashan for assistance. However, Iridan had already dismissed the dreams as nothing to worry about, and Rashan … Well, Rashan was not someone he was hoping to seek help from just then.

He could sneak back into the Academy, but there were so many ways that could be misinterpreted that he shuddered to think how it would be seen if he were to be caught. He bore little love for the instructors and the feeling was mutual. Rummaging through their libraries might even be portrayed as some form of vengeful vandalism.

The Tower of Contemplation seemed most promising. His father's office had been there, and if it had not yet been cleared of his personal effects, then his notes and reference materials ought still to be there. Plus, if he was unable to find anything useful in his father's office, there were other libraries in the Tower as well.

Kyrus headed down the hall toward the main stairs but then paused a moment. Backtracking, he jogged down to his room and retrieved Avalanche. Poking around his family's home was one thing. Snooping around in the headquarters of the Imperial Circle was a different matter. If questioned, he had plausible enough excuses to offer for being there so late, but it felt better to prepare for the worst.

* * * * * * *

Brannis had decided to go on foot, rather than alert the stable hands on both ends of his journey. Taking the same route he had taken just the previous night coming back from the Bygones Day preparations, he set off for the palace at a jog.

He found the usual rather lax security at the Tower of Contemplation and let himself in. He wondered idly if he ought to mention increasing the guard contingent of the Tower to someone. No thief in his right mind would break into the Tower, but that did not prevent the insane thieves from becoming wealthy if they dared to try it and got lucky. Brannis counted himself among the latter for the night, and though it was not wealth he sought, he was certainly hoping for a bit of luck.

* * * * * * *

He found the door to his father's office warded, and having no means to open it short of using Avalanche to stave it in, he had slumped against it as he considered his next plan of action. Sighing, he banged his head lightly against the door, wincing at the expected pain that did not actually materialize.

At least I seem to have gotten past that headache. I hope that means Kyrus is doing better.

He needed to think of something quickly, before it was too late to help. He tried to remember all the special assignments that Rashan had given out to the rest of his surviving men from the Kelvie expedition. The warlock had wanted to keep them close by to prevent silly rumors from spreading about the time before he arrived back in Kadrin. He had neither seen nor heard from Sir Lugren since they had arrived, and the common soldiers had been given various assignments in and around the palace and Tower.

That works! Brannis realized. *Tod and Jodoul are guards for one of the Tower libraries. If I cannot get in past those two scholars, I am hopeless.*

Brannis pulled himself to his feet and headed back downstairs three floors to where he was fairly sure the North Library was located. It was, unsurprisingly, on the north side of the Tower, if only he had managed to get the floor correct.

Brannis wended his way through the corridors until he saw them and confirmed that he had chosen correctly. There were Tod and Jodoul, fancied up in their pristine new red-and-white Circle Guard uniforms. They were leaning on their halberds and carrying on a conversation as he neared them.

"Well, I know first thing I plan to get is a place of me own," Tod commented, not even looking down the hall where Brannis approached from.

"A woman for me, I thinks," Jodoul replied, matter-of-factly.

"Aww, not wastin' it all on whores, are ya?" Tod sounded disappointed in his friend.

"Naw, think I got the coin now to court a girl proper. You know, get me a wife, like?" Jodoul said just before noticing Brannis coming right down the hall at them.

Both men scrambled to arrange themselves in proper guard pose—upright and holding a weapon usually covered it.

"Easy, fellows," Brannis said as he got close enough that he would not have to yell to talk to them. "Just here for the library, not any sort of official inspection."

"Aww, sir, you ought to know we cannot let you in," Tod said.

"Orders and all," Jodoul agreed, "right from Warlock Rashan. This is our first night at it, and we cannot botch it up right off."

Brannis could not help noticing that they largely dropped the gutter slang when addressing him.

"You stand relieved. Go get some sleep," Brannis ordered.

Neither man budged.

"Warlock Rashan's orders, sir," Tod told him.

"He does not want folks poking about at night until it settles down a bit," Jodoul said. "Come morning, I am sure you can get him to let you have a look."

Brannis felt himself growing exasperated. "Listen, boys, I have no time to explain properly, but I need to get into that library. I do not have time to wait until morning. Go have yourselves a good night's rest. I will make sure no one *else* gets in."

Brannis tried to sound calm and reasonable, but his sword hand was across his body, resting on the hilt of Avalanche. The point was not missed by either of the two guards. For all their other shortcomings, Tod and Jodoul were survivors. They had heard of the incident at army headquarters, where Brannis had driven that same sword an arm's length deep into the stone floor.

"Yes, sir," they said in unison.

Neither of them saluted as they stepped aside and let Brannis pass. As Brannis opened the—thankfully not warded—door, they made their retreat down the corridor. Brannis shut the door behind him. The room was well lit, with light just sufficient for comfortable reading anywhere in the room, and no more.

Brannis picked a row of shelves at random and started browsing titles: *Aether Theory for Plants. A Decomposition of Fire Magics. The Sorcerer's Travel Companion. Ward Maintenance. Care and Nurturing of Familiars for Increased Aether Generation. Maximizing Spell Effects with Minimal Aether. Guide to Silent Casting: A Novel Approach. Magics of Stone and Earth.*

Brannis nodded to himself. *All right, that one sounds promising. Kyrus is in a cell of stone blocks.*

He pulled the volume off the shelf and examined it. It did not look especially old, but he suspected that extraordinary measures were likely used to keep old books intact over the course of centuries. He flipped through it and found that it was written in rune language, which he was fully capable of reading, and it was even illustrated with diagrams showing what various forms of spell could do. Brannis took it over to one of the many small tables scattered about the library and sat down to study it.

There was a spell to crush rock and another to form rock dust into larger pieces. He found a spell that was a more effective way of levitation that was suited specifically to rock and earth. He found one that could burrow and one that could make solid stone turn to a runny sort of mud.

Brannis knew he was probably going to have to leave Kyrus to his own devices to get the gag out of his mouth enough to speak, but the problem he kept seeing was that all of the gestures for the spells involved motions that could not be done while he was shackled. He kept reading, hoping to find one that was a one-handed gesture, or something just done with the fingers. He scanned quickly through the rest of the book to see if any were simpler spells but found that it was not the case.

Leaving that book open on the table to the page with the burrowing spell, Brannis went back to the shelves. He wanted to see if there were any books that might help with getting Kyrus unshackled. He looked for titles that dealt with metals, skipping over the rest for now.

Manipulating Metals turned out to be about changing alloys to improve sword performance. *Cold Steel* was actually a book describing how warlocks combined sword and spell in battle.

Melting Metal was actually a scholarly work describing the ways that metals were smelted, but it was written for the hobbyist sorcerer who practiced metallurgy in his free time. In between passages explaining the necessary temperatures to get various metals to melt and the most advantageous mineral additives to strengthen them, there were helpful variant spells that worked well for achieving those temperatures. Unfortunately it was poorly organized and each section referenced other works where further information could be found. If Brannis were to get any use out of it, he would have to search through to find the basic spells the author kept referencing, and then work out how they would need to be modified to heat a particular metal most economically. The economy of aether was good to note, since Brannis had no basis for comparison as to how well Kyrus drew aether.

Brannis was taking *Melting Metal* over to the table to read when he heard the library door open. His hand immediately went for his blade, but he did not draw it. Staying behind the shelves for cover, he stood quietly and waited.

For what seemed like hours there was no sound at all, and Brannis was getting ready to dismiss the sound of the door as paranoia. Then, down the end of the row, he saw a head poke around the corner.

"Aha, there you are," Rashan said, chuckling. "Your two friends are better soldiers than you gave them credit for. They came straight to me after you got rid of them."

"So it would seem," Brannis commented flatly, trying to see where the warlock was going with this.

"So what brings you down to the libraries at this hour? Have you been trying to study up to graduate the Academy? What was so important that you had to threaten your way past the guards?"

Brannis struggled to find some excuse for being there. His excuse for nearly anyone else would have been that he was working on orders from Rashan, but that was unlikely to work in his current scenario.

"Oh, stop trying to think up a lie and just tell me. Unless you are a spy for Megrenn or a goblin sympathizer, it is not as if I would kill you for whatever reason you have," Rashan said.

Brannis cursed silently in his head. The warlock was too clever to be stalled.

"Well, I suppose that ought to reassure me. I do not think it absolves me of being thought a madman, though. I admit this is all quite suspicious," Brannis admitted.

He could feel his heart starting to quicken in his chest. He did not want to have Rashan think that he could not handle his new position and take it away from him this soon.

"Brannis, I have been thought dead for a century, and less than a day after returning, I find I have to kill a quarter of the Inner Circle for treason. You shall hardly have a monopoly on being thought a madman, regardless of your tale. Besides, now you have piqued my curiosity, and I shall not be denied whatever story you have. Be warned: I have been lied to by many of the best liars in Kadrin—the nobles—and can generally sniff out a false tale."

Brannis swallowed hard. *At this point, if I admit it, maybe I can get him to help. I do not know if I will get a good enough plan together in time at the rate things are going now.*

"Well, this might take a bit of explaining," Brannis said. "We should sit."

Brannis went over to the table where *Magics of Stone and Earth* sat open, and settled into one of the chairs. Rashan dropped lightly into one of the chairs opposite him, twisting his head around to make out the title of the book Brannis had been reading.

"Studying fortifications and how to destroy them with magic? Commendable, but not 'emergency in the night' fare, I think. Out with it now; what sordid tale do you have for me?"

Brannis took a deep breath to steady his nerves. "Well, this is about my dreams. I have … I do not know quite what to call them—visions?—of another place. I see things through someone else's eyes," Brannis began, wondering if he could get Rashan to jump in and offer insights.

"Fascinating," Rashan commented, his tone light and his eyes fixed on Brannis's, as if he were hearing the opening to a fireside storyteller's yarn.

"Well, in this other place, this other person has gotten himself into some trouble. I know he can learn things that I have seen, so I was looking for a spell to get him out of his predicament." Brannis phrased that about as mildly as he could think of without straying from the truth.

"So what sort of predicament? Surrounded by goblins? Backed against a cliff and facing doom at the hands of angry ogres? Just caught in the bedchamber of a princess? Brannis, you are a lousy storyteller. Details, please," Rashan said.

"He has been locked up for being a 'witch,' and he is likely trapped in a cell awaiting execution. He is shackled hand and foot, and gagged. I am looking for a spell that could get him out of a stone dungeon cell, or out of a set of iron shackles, preferably both," Brannis said.

Rashan looked pensive for a moment. Then he did something Brannis had yet to see from the warlock. He cast a spell.

"Denek iliaru estatta pogulu benna tetga fenex refleragna," he said and pressed his hands together, rubbing them quickly in tiny circles.

Rashan's form became hazy and indistinct, then fully transparent. Brannis watched the warlock pass his hand through the table. After a moment, he solidified again.

"It allows one to pass through solid objects and requires minimal hand movement," Rashan explained.

"Any suggestions on how to get the gag out of his mouth?" Brannis asked, hoping perhaps the warlock would give him all the answers he would need. He had not honestly considered that Rashan would be nonplussed by the whole affair and decide to help him.

"Well, if your alter ego can use aether at all, just burn it through. If he is about to be executed otherwise, I would think a few burns would be worth the cost. Oh, and if he fails to escape, at least have the historical sense to go out with something noteworthy ... like a plume of flame engulfing everyone in sight. Sorcerers are not meant to be rounded up and beheaded like thieves. Do not start a precedent." Rashan winked and stood to leave.

"Thank you, Rashan. Now I just need to get back to sleep so he can use this information," Brannis said. "Would anyone mind if I slept here until morning?" It was certainly an unusual request, but Brannis thought it by far the least insane thing he had done that night.

"By all means. Here, let me help," and Rashan appeared to concentrate on Brannis, and he started to feel just a bit dizzy. "Brannis, you are far too resistant to magic for your own good. If that Source of yours were shut any tighter, you would be a demon, like me. I might be able to tear you in half with lightning or cremate you where you stand with a firestorm, but I cannot affect you directly with a simple sleep enchantment," Rashan said. "Let me try from a bit closer."

Rashan got right up next to Brannis and held his hands out just to either side of his head. As soon as Brannis closed his eyes to try and help out by relaxing, Rashan balled his right fist and slugged him, hard, right in the temple. The warlock was quick to react, catching the much larger knight as he slumped out of his chair and laying him sprawled out on the floor.

"Good luck," Rashan wished him and retired from the library.

Chapter 22 - Good Help Is Hard to Find

"I'd never before thought of a life at sea, but you make your point, Cap'n," Grosh replied when asked if he would join Denrik as part of his crew. "I have no trade without acting outside my guild, and who has heard of a rogue tailor? At least with you, sir, I know where I stand."

Denrik nodded in acknowledgment. *That makes one of the ones I wanted, at the least.* He stood with his men arranged about him in a semicircle, and was going about finding out once and for all who was staying on with him. It was to be their last night camped among the low cliffs to Scar Harbor's south. By morning, they would either be sailing as free men, or be dead. None among them wished to be recaptured.

"And you, Jimony?" Denrik asked.

"Good coin, ya say? I got you on that one, right? We get loot and get rich?" Jimony asked, his priorities transparent. The wiry viper's eyes gleamed as he imagined piles of treasure akin to the stories in *Neiron the Kingthief* and pictured them for himself.

"Better than knifing old men coming home from the tavern, certainly," Denrik replied dryly. "Learn a trade aboard ship, and you shall earn a full share of the loot. Same goes for all of you lads. Work as a pirate, get paid as one."

"Aye, Cap'n. Count me in," Jimony replied enthusiastically.

Denrik was chagrined but little surprised. It was the easiest money a lowlife like Jimony could imagine, preying on merchants and traders who quickly became much more interested in saving their own skins than in protecting their investments, and far from the reach of any sort of law. On the open waters, it was the Law of Guns: whoever possessed the most cannons was in charge.

"Oh, me too!" exclaimed Andur. "Loot for everyone!"

Everyone laughed, and Denrik supposed he was stuck with Andur for the foreseeable future.

Denrik did not ask again but simply turned to Tawmund and looked questioningly at him. As a man of few words himself, Tawmund understood the implied query.

"Yeah, sure," was all Tawmund said, but from Denrik's perspective, that was all he needed to hear.

Whether they would change their minds later once they found out that life aboard ship was not for everyone, and certainly was not day after day of plunder interrupted only by port calls for drinking and whoring … Well, he would just wait and see how they took to it.

* * * * * * * *

Stalyart arrived for one final visit early in the afternoon. He seemed in good spirits as well—and why not? For, his plan to take to the seas with his old captain was about to come to fruition. He was dressed more plainly than the other times he had come to them, in the plain drab-brown coveralls and boots of a dock worker. He was lugging a large sack along with him.

"Mr. Stalyart, good news I hope," Denrik said as Tawmund and Grosh moved to help him unburden his load.

"The best, as always, Captain," the grinning Stalyart replied. "I have brought everything we will need and perhaps a bit more. I like games of chance, but this is no game, so I take no chances." He chuckled at his own joke. "Dark clothing for everyone. I guessed sizes, so make the best if they do not fit as you would prefer. There are long knifes for each—better than cutlasses, easy to hide. Two more pistols also. My men are ready as well. We will meet at the docks an hour after sunset and wait for my brother's signal."

Denrik always admired his first mate's efficiency. With five more like him, it would little matter what dullards the rest of the crew were. Fortune being what it was, there was only one of Stalyart. He was still going to be woefully short on good men who knew their trades. His most pressing reason for bringing his Rellis Island crew was simple manpower. Under normal circumstances, he would have been able to afford the luxury of picking an experienced crew, but he had need of every willing and able body he could muster.

"What news from the city? Are the cannons aboard? What of the captain?" Denrik peppered him with questions, his own eagerness showing through.

"The captain, I am afraid, will likely be on board. No great harm, though. We can take care of him. The new cannons are *so* beautiful; I see them for myself when they load them. The news from the city, though? Ahh, this shames my other little newses. The sheriff has caught a witch! He even admitted it in his trial this morning. In the witch's house, there is a light that does not come from anywhere. I went for myself to see it."

"So you believe them?" Denrik asked.

This was truly news worth hearing. Denrik's own powers were so limited.

A real sorcerer in Acardia? Now that might be useful.

"Yes. He was not sentenced today. They want to get permission to execute him, but need to have to ask the lords in Golis. He is not dead yet, but he borrows his days," Stalyart replied.

"What do you think, Stalyart?" Denrik asked him.

Stalyart was among those on his crew who were aware of Denrik's mystical leanings, so Denrik knew that Stalyart had something more in mind when he brought him this news, otherwise its inclusion with the day's plans would have been nothing more than a distraction.

"I think the winds are not so strong tonight. I think we take less chance by bringing this witch with us than we do trying to outrun pursuit on a calm night," Stalyart replied.

"If this witch has real magic, how is it that he is kept captive?" Denrik asked, drawing nods of agreement from Jimony and Grosh, who otherwise had the sense to keep out of the conversation.

"He is kept shackled and gagged. They keep him so he can work not magic," Stalyart explained. "I hear that even to eat, they hold a crossbow on him."

So he is unskilled, or at least unschooled. I can work with that. A fully trained sorcerer could easily escape such mundane imprisonment, which is why no one with sense takes one prisoner. Jinzan could have broken out the minute they left him alone.

"How did they capture him?" Denrik asked, trying to get a feel for how much of a sorcerer he was dealing with.

"They broke in his door in the middle of the night and took him by surprise."

Denrik sat down and thought for several minutes. No one interrupted him. The look on his face was of such an obvious calculating nature that they just waited for him to speak and then decide.

* * * * * * * *

Kyrus came back to the land of the conscious and found he had been returned to his cell. It was a small comfort, knowing that he was likely just awaiting the hangman's noose, or possibly a post, some rope, and a pile of firewood.

His headache had improved to the point where he was thinking rationally. Importantly, he remembered everything he had dreamed, including a rather clear recollection of Rashan's spell. He just had to pick the right time to use it.

He worked at the gag in his mouth, trying to dislodge it. Were he to manage that trick, the correct time would be "now," and he would worry about other consequences as they came up. As it stood, the gag stubbornly refused his efforts, and he could not get his shackled hands close enough to hook his thumbs in and pull at it. He would have to settle for a blast of raw aether and hope that he did not immolate himself as the gag caught fire.

That little trick was something he would save until all was quiet. Outside the cell, he could still hear people on the streets, and the constables trying to keep them away from his cell window. There were a lot of angry people out there, he knew, and in this case at least, the constables were on his side; no escape plan would be worth its weight in feathers if he got dragged out by that mob and killed first.

He was roused from his musings by footsteps approaching from down the cell block. Kyrus was no expert on the subject, but it was more than one person, and fewer than a dozen. He got a cold feeling in the pit of his stomach; nothing good had come down that corridor of late.

He was pleasantly surprised to see that it was the jailor and two men armed with crossbows. Well, he was not pleased to see *them* so much as the lovely young lady they had brought to see him.

"Oh, Kyrus," Abbiley gushed after she saw him, disheveled, unshaven, and trussed up in his cell. She was carrying a bowl of something steaming. He also noticed that she was still wearing the jade dragon they had bought only yesterday.

"One word out of you and you will find two quarrels in your throat," the jailor threatened as he unlocked the cell door. Kyrus's eyes were drawn to the ring of keys he carried. "I do not care if it is Acardian or witch gibberish, I shall take no chances. You will get fed, and that is it."

One of the armed men loosened his gag, and then both took up positions on either side of him, weapons leveled, as promised, generally at his throat. Abbiley hurried over and knelt down next to him, then started spooning stew into him. It felt wonderful in his mouth—too hot perhaps, but the first food he had tasted in nearly a day—and knowing that Abbiley would still come see him felt even better. The look in her eyes was haunted and worried, but she was scared for him, not of him.

"Kyrus, are all those awful things they said about you true," she asked.

Kyrus shook his head between mouthfuls.

"You are a witch, though," she stated rather than asked.

Kyrus bobbed his head a bit from side to side, to try to indicate that it was not so clear a distinction. Kyrus was quite mindful of the "no talking" edict and fully intended to carry on a whole conversation via head gestures if he had to.

"So you did magic, but you are not a witch?" she asked, trying to piece together a story from the vague hints he could give.

Kyrus smiled and nodded. This seemed to be working.

He was hungry and devoured whatever she spooned to him, but too late, he realized that his conversation was likely to last the duration of the stew. As the final spoonful made its way into his mouth, the jailor intervened: "That is enough, we are done here."

Kyrus quickly concocted a new plan. Firehurling was supposedly quite dangerous, and he had never tried it, but it was supposedly about the simplest form of magic. He could take out the two armed guards first, then the jailor. Then he could either use Rashan's spell, or get Abbiley to retrieve the keys from the jailor's body. After that, he would blast a path out of the jail and out of the city, and he and Abbiley could live as outlaws until Brannis read up on enough magic for him to set them up in a comfortable lifestyle out in the wilderness. After a time and a better understanding of magic, maybe he could insinuate himself back into society, not in Scar Harbor, but perhaps in Harvin or Udur—someplace where they were still under the rule of Acardia but not so close to home. He could use magic to rise in the social ranks and do well in business—whatever business he chose—and raise a family in wealth and privilege. He could teach his children magic, and they could become the secret ruling class in the kingdom, using magic to take over and institute laws against punishing people for witchcraft.

Abruptly, Kyrus's planning was cut short by the gag being stuffed roughly back in his mouth and Abbiley being led from the cell. As the door was locked behind him, Abbiley turned to look at him one last time.

"Do not worry, Kyrus. I am sure this will all work out somehow. Oh, and do not worry about Ash. I took him home with me until this all gets figured out."

* * * * * * *

Kyrus bided his time the rest of the daylight hours. The fervor of the crowd outside had waned when it became apparent after several hours that the constables were not about to allow them to storm the cell and drag Kyrus out. It was not the type of crowd that would storm a prison without the tacit approval of the constables. They were the sort who liked to make a lot of noise and hope that someone else would do the whole "taking the law into their own hands" bit, lest they end up in a cell of their own.

As near as Kyrus could tell, by nightfall, all that were left outside were a pair of fresh constables who had replaced the ones from earlier. They carried on a bit of idle conversation but otherwise proved to be uninteresting; no news of the rest of the trial or his sentence, no dropped hints of lackadaisical jailors or loose bricks that Kyrus could use. He was beginning to think all the storybooks he had read were going to prove useless.

He steeled himself for what might prove to be the riskiest thing he had tried in his life, and began to draw in aether. Then he started to let it out right into the leather cord of the gag. Slowly at first, then in increasing amounts, he warmed, then heated, then practically boiled the leather.

Hot. Hot. Hot. It is not burning. I am!

Kyrus twisted and squirmed and could smell his own singed hair, and quickly stopped the flow of aether, instead unloading it into the door again. Tears streamed from his eyes as the burning hot cord pressed into the back of his neck, where he had tried to focus the heat. Eventually the heat died down and became tolerable, and Kyrus breathed a sigh of relief.

Well, that was one of the worst ideas I have ever had.

He was still locked up and gagged, and now his neck hurt where the leather rubbed against burned flesh.

Time to see how picky magic is about pronunciation.

"Hmnk wrru uhdhdh poguruh bnnuh dhdhguh vnk rvrurugnuh," he mumbled, mimicking Rashan's gesture of pressing his hands together and making little circles as he rubbed them together.

At first, he thought he felt something weird happening to him, but soon he realized that it was the aether building inside him with no release. He heated the doors some more to let the pressure of the aether escape him.

Kyrus knew that the magic did not care one whit about the words themselves or how he spoke them. It was more a matter of the shapes they made in his mind. But Kyrus was new at this, and the words and gestures were meant to create the right thoughts. He did not know the spell well enough to skip to the end results and just cast it knowing how it was supposed to go.

Kyrus tried the spell again, this time focusing on trying to hear the words correctly in his head, even if his mouth was getting them wrong—due to entirely forgivable circumstances.

Having nothing but time on his hands, Kyrus kept trying over and over as each attempt failed. He began wondering if he would be better off just trying his plan of "blast everything next time someone unlocks the door."

After what, by his count, was his thirty-fifth try, he was distracted by noises outside. In the clear night air, he could more clearly hear the two constables guarding him and the scant few noises of the streets.

"Mind if we have a word with your prisoner?"

The male voice came from outside, not far from Kyrus's window.

"No visitors. Please step ba—"

The constable's voice was cut short.

"Hwp—" a muffled voice began, but got no further.

Kyrus heard two bodies slump to the ground.

"Get to the corner and keep a watch. We do not have much time," Kyrus heard the voice again, same as the first one.

He was not sure what had transpired outside his cell, but he was leery of it. Too many people had called for his death earlier in the day for him to trust that a random stranger was less a threat to him than the men guarding his cell.

"You in there," the voice called.

Kyrus looked up to see a face peering down at him through the bars.

"Are you really a sorcerer?"

The owner of the voice had a darkly tanned face covered in salt-and-pepper stubble, and he wore a black knit cap pulled low.

Kyrus heard the word "sorcerer" instead of "witch," and festival bells rang in his brain. That was the Kadrin term for a witch! Kyrus decided to take his chances with the user of the term less associated with public burning. He nodded enthusiastically.

"Get the back of your head as close to these bars as you can," the stranger instructed.

Kyrus struggled up onto the plank bed and stood straight, turning his back to the window.

"*Kohtho ilextiumane veeru,*" Kyrus heard from behind him.

Suddenly the gag was loose in his mouth. He quickly spit it out, trailing a wad of saliva with it, and worked his stiff jaw to loosen the muscles. He turned to see his benefactor just inches from his face.

"Thank you," Kyrus said. "Are you planning on getting me out of here?"

Kyrus did not ask what had befallen the constables. At that moment, he did not want to know.

"Burning through that gag was about the most I can manage," the man said. "If you are really a sorcerer, now is the time to prove it. Same words I just used, and hold your fingers as close together as you can without them touching."

The stranger then demonstrated the gesture. Kyrus was relieved to find that someone had discovered a spell for casting while shackled.

"Focus on these bars, and once they melt through, we can pull you out."

"Kohtho ilextiumane veeru," Kyrus repeated as he put his fingers close together.

He drew aether and felt it flow like an arrow straight to the point in the bar he directed it. It glowed orange, but Kyrus accidentally touched his fingers together and the spell faltered.

"You must keep your fingers apart or it will never work," his would-be rescuer told him. "You get more power from having them closer, but touching ruins it. Find a way to get it done without ending the spell so soon."

Kyrus tried again, this time with his fingers far enough apart that he could have put his nose between them, had the shackles allowed him that much freedom.

"Kohtho ilextiumane veeru," Kyrus repeated.

The aether flowed again. The bar turned a reddish-orange, but did not seem to be melting.

"They need to be closer than that," the man said. "I am surprised you can heat it at all like that."

Kyrus looked down and brought his fingers much closer. He was no longer watching where he was aiming, but he kept the aether going the same place it had been, so he was hopeful it would still be heating the bar.

He heard a hissing sound and looked up, trying not to move his fingers. He saw the reddish-orange bar turn a bright orange, then white, then become a puddle. Then the puddle started to boil off.

"Great Melethaw, Lord of Seas! What did you just do?" the man said.

Kyrus was not well versed in nautical expletives, but he recalled that Melethaw was one of the ancient Garnevian gods. It did not tell him much about his rescuer, but at least he was classically educated. *Or possibly a cultist,* Kyrus thought, keeping himself honest. There was no use overlooking unpleasant possibilities.

"I did as you asked," Kyrus answered. "I kept my fingers closer together."

"Well, hurry up and do the same to the other three. I had thought we would be at this for some time, but it seems I underestimated you."

The stranger left for a moment as Kyrus repeated the spell thrice more.

His rescuer soon returned with his companion. Kyrus could make out little in the darkness outside, but the second of his rescuers seemed rather a large man. He also noted for the first time that there appeared to be a light rain falling outside. It hissed and steamed as it hit the spots where the iron bars of the cell had once been.

"Get close and we will haul you out," the first rescuer instructed him, stepping aside so his stone-faced companion could appear at the window to grab him.

"One moment," Kyrus requested, and began another spell.

"Denek iliaru estatta pogulu benna tetga fenex refleragna," he chanted quickly, finding it much easier without a gag in his mouth.

As he completed the hand-rubbing gesture, he felt a strange tingling throughout his body. Without warning, he fell through the plank bed he had been standing on. He stopped when he hit the dirt floor, not understanding why it felt solid while all else passed right through him. As planned, the shackles fell right through him as well, crashing onto the plank, which was now at thigh level—and actually within Kyrus's incorporeal thigh. As an unexpected bonus, his clothing fell through him as well.

Quickly dismissing the magic once he had a chance to step clear of the cluttered mess he had just made, Kyrus hastily dressed himself, and climbed back onto the bed. He reached up with his arms and carefully out the first hand's length of the window, avoiding the still-scalding ends of the vaporized bars.

The larger of his two rescuers grabbed his hands. Kyrus braced a foot against a wall and tried his best to angle his head so it would go through without touching. With a sudden heave, Kyrus was pulled through the window, scrambling up the wall with his feet as best he could to avoid banging his hips and knees as he went through.

Despite taking a slight battering and scorching both his shirt and pants, Kyrus was little worse for the wear on the other side. The falling rain felt good, even cleansing. He saw his two accomplices in the jailbreak. The leader was a lean, hard-looking man of middle years and much obvious hardship. He had the gleam in his eye of the type of person Kyrus avoided sharing the same side of the street with, even in daylight. The one who had pulled him through the window resembled nothing so much as a wall of person. Tall, wide, and solid, he seemed to be the epitome of what an ambitious wall aspires to.

"Thank you," Kyrus said.

He was unsure what else to say. His two rescuers were dressed all in black and had just murdered two men who were, even now, spreading pools of blood beneath them. It was not exactly in the "knights in shining armor" mold of rescue, but he supposed he made for a poor maiden. While he regretted that the two constables had to die for him to be free, he was feeling a rather large surge in whatever organ regulates self-preservation, and was willing to overlook it, considering they seemed rather likely to be preparing him for a similar fate.

"What now?" Kyrus asked. It felt like a safe, noncommittal question.

"We have somewhere to get, come on," the leader said, beckoning with one hand. The other he kept against his side, likely concealing whatever blade had been used on the dead constables.

"Where are we heading?" Kyrus asked.

"The docks," the leader said. "We are going to get on a ship and get far away from Acardia. You seem like you could use a new place to live. I have a place for you."

Kyrus's mind skipped a beat. He had never been more than a week's travel by carriage from Scar Harbor. Golis was a long trek by his mind, and a fast rider could make it in less than a day.

"Can I stop at home and pack a few things?"

"We have the time for it, but no. Your house turned into something of a gawking curiosity, since you left a light on. We saw the glow on our way over here. Even at this hour, folks are likely to notice us if we got near the place. You get a fresh start, lad. Not everyone gets so lucky," the leader told him. "Now move. Of all the places to discuss this, there are few worse than right here."

The leader took him firmly by the arm as they slipped away down a side street, taking a long, winding route through the city's worst neighborhoods to avoid notice. Kyrus supposed his new companions were like mountain guides, those curious folk who could walk up nearly sheer surfaces and who were essential companions for explorers seeking the safe ways through the Skelton Peaks. In this case, they were guiding him along the safe passes through the city. He supposed it was a bit of an unfair comparison, since in many ways, the safest path was a knife's reach to either side of them, and moved with them.

Not needing his eyes to guide him, Kyrus slipped into aether-sight to check for pursuers and ambushes along their path. He mostly kept watch behind them, more worried about pursuit once his escape and associated murders were discovered than the prospect of being accosted in an alley while being escorted by two murderers, one of whom was apparently a minor sorcerer.

"There are a half dozen men around the next corner on the right, headed this way," Kyrus said.

The leader did not question how he knew but quickly backtracked them to a side street. They made a circle of the block in the opposite direction and kept moving. They could hear a number of voices; apparently some sort of young ne'er-do-wells were gadding about and causing trouble. Kyrus supposed that on this occasion, he ought not be one to judge.

Twice more on their route to the docks, Kyrus altered their course to avoid bystanders. The leader seemed to take it in stride, but Kyrus got the sense that his larger companion was a bit skeptical of how he was getting his insights. He hoped that the leader was in firm control, lest he end up with another witch hunt to flee from.

Their immediate destination was a vacant warehouse near the northern side of the dock ward, close to the piers. Kyrus warned again of a number of men on their path, but this time, his warning was brushed aside.

"They are with us," the leader informed him. "Everyone," he announced quietly, once they were close enough that everyone could hear his low tone. "This is Mr. Kyrus Hinterdale. He is coming with us."

"Aye, you got him out, eh?" one man said, then chuckled. "Not bad if I says so meself."

"Excellent. Most excellent. Welcome, Mr. Hinterdale," said one man who appeared to also be some kind of leader. "Today you died in Acardia as a witch. Tonight you are born again on the sea as a free man."

Kyrus took in the ragged, hard-eyed men that made up the group and wondered just what they were up to.

"We had no time for proper introductions on the way here, given the circumstances. I am Denrik Zayne, soon to be captain of that vessel just over yonder." He pointed out to a navy ship docked in the harbor. "I know you for what you are, and I accept you as such. Now you know me for who I am, and I am giving you a chance to start a new life. Whatever you had here, they took it from you. Come with me and you shall become rich and powerful. You are a fugitive, as am I. Yesterday you might have thought that you and I had little in common, but today I think you will find that we can use each other. I will take you in, and you can use your magic to aid and protect me and my crew. Are you in?"

Kyrus was amid a dozen or so men—pirates, he supposed—and was nominally being offered a choice.

"What would happen if I said 'no'? Would you slit my throat and dump me in the harbor?"

"We would hardly have to. Just leaving you behind is a death sentence," Denrik said.

"It seems I have little choice but to accept," Kyrus said.

"Well now, you do have choices, and many more than you think. You could turn yourself in, betray us, and plead for leniency for helping recapture someone far more dangerous than yourself. You could sneak off, stow away on a trade ship, and hope to hide out until you get to Feru Maru to start a new life as a fisherman. You could disappear into the city, try and remake yourself as one of the shadow merchants hereabouts. You could even try using that magic of yours to burn the city down; you are raw, but you have a lot of power in you.

"No, what I offer you is not your only choice, but your only good solid choice," Denrik said. "The Acardian Navy took my ship and sank it, since none of theirs would sully themselves at the wheel of it. The Acardian magistrates took three years of my life and kept me from all the wealth I had accumulated in my years at sea. Think about what they are taking from you: your home, your possessions, your livelihood. I am doing something about it; I am taking back what I can. I give you the opportunity to do the same, to take a new life to replace what you have lost. It will not be the same, but it is yours to make of it what you will.

"The same goes for the rest of you. Most of you have never tried a hand at piracy. Some have sailed ships, and some have killed and robbed for money, but all of you have the chance, tonight, to start anew."

"I ... suppose I can give it a try," Kyrus said, not making eye contact with Denrik.

Piracy was not exactly what he had planned as an alternative to the gallows or the stake. Then again, what careers were available to someone deemed a witch and seen as a threat to the natural order of society merely for living?

"Mr. Hinterdale, I see you think yourself a good man. I saw the way you looked at those dead guards at the jailhouse, like you had never seen a dead body. You need to harden this in here," Denrik poked Kyrus in the chest, "or the world is going to chew you up and swallow you. The world comprises sharks and chum. We here are sharks."

"I have seen death before. I have killed more than you might guess. I just never reveled in a man's death, or blocked it from my heart," Kyrus said just above a whisper. More loudly, he continued: "But I suppose that will change in joining with you. Killing is easy enough, but I still hope never to get used to it."

Kyrus was bluffing a bit, but he had all of Brannis's memories in him, and if he could draw on those experiences to give himself a measure of credibility among these shark-like men, he would do so.

* * * * * * * *

Denrik was taken aback a bit. He had always been a shrewd judge of men and could tell a liar better than most. The lad seemed to have as little guile as Andur, yet his claims seemed outrageous. Perhaps the good folk of Scar Harbor had reason enough to wish death on this "witch" after all, without even realizing it.

* * * * * * * *

Grosh had been keeping watch, but as the hour approached, everyone moved near the half-open warehouse door and watched for the signal. Kyrus was at the back of the group, along with Denrik. Neither of them felt the particular need to watch, Denrik because it was exactly the sort of thing that one had crews for, and Kyrus because he just was not that eager to go. They had explained the general thrust of the plan, and really that seemed to be about all there was to it.

They were to wait for Mr. Stalyart's brother, one of the night watchmen on the ship, to give them a signal that meant he had eliminated the other man on watch duty with him. Then they would race onto the ship and overpower however many men were left on board while the rest were drinking, gambling, and whoring the night away. Then they would sail off with the ship. It seemed far too simple to work, but when Kyrus considered the sort of men that were a party to this heist, he wondered how complex a plan they might carry out properly.

Mr. Crispin gave a wave in their direction, the signal that all was prepared. Stalyart signaled back to Denrik, and Captain Zayne gave the order: "Keep quiet and move, quickly. No running, but keep it moving."

The would-be pirates poured out of the warehouse, disorderly but with a single purpose among them. Their shoes clomped along on the wooden boards of the pier as they made their way to the gangplank, playing a percussive symphony. Kyrus was swept along in their wake, with only Denrik behind him, taking up the rear guard position.

Despite living in a port city for several years, Kyrus had never found reason to set foot on board a ship before. The gangplank was intimidating—a long, narrow board with no handrails or ropes to hold onto. It was perhaps as wide as he was tall, but felt all the narrower for having nothing to catch himself on if he were to slip on the steep slope. There were wooden ribs at regular intervals, but Kyrus found them to be less than comforting as a safety measure.

Once he made it onto the deck, the small group had congregated around

Stalyart's brother, Mr. Crispin. He was on watch duty, wearing his navy sailor's cap and heavy coat to keep out the chill. Tight to his body he held a long knife, similar to the ones that the rest of the pirates were drawing all around him. It was an unnerving sight, even if logically Kyrus knew that the last thing they planned was to drag him up here just to kill him.

"The captain is asleep in his quarters," Crispin whispered as Denrik, Stalyart, and a few others leaned in to listen. "The other watchman is in the head, dead."

"Crispin, lead the rest belowdecks. Forestall any alarm by acting as if you just came back from shore and have your own men with you. Let surprise do most of the work for you," Denrik said and then set them off to take care of the crew.

Kyrus watched with a sense of dread and detachment as Tawmund, Marshfield, and a few others whose names he had not gathered yet all headed down to murder the crew.

"Mr. Holyoake, Mr. Stalyart, get the ship free of her moorings, then raise the sails. Mr. Hinterdale, when the sails are up, can you raise the anchor?" Denrik asked, honestly questioning his abilities rather than making the order optional just for him.

"Um, of course. You ... I mean, you do want me to do it with magic, right? Otherwise I shall revise my answer," Kyrus replied.

"Very well, then, do it, soon as I give the command, or Stalyart does," Denrik said.

"Uhh, where is the anchor?" Kyrus asked. He was entirely new to this, and while he knew what an anchor was, he did not know where on the ship it tied up ... or bolted ... or coiled, or whatever one did with them when they were not anchoring the ship.

"Starboard bow," Denrik called back as he headed for the rear of the ship where the captain's cabin lay.

Kyrus looked on as Holyoake and Stalyart went around with small axes and hacked away at the moorings. He wondered if he ought to ask them if he was correct in thinking that starboard with the right side of the ship; he knew that the bow was the front. Kyrus heard someone down below on the docks notice that something was amiss, and all thought of asking for clarification fled his mind.

"Hey, what you doin' up there?" he heard.

Kyrus rushed to the side of the ship to see what was happening. A man in navy sailor's garb was sprinting down the pier back toward the taverns and brothels where presumably he would find his fellows and rally them against the intruders.

Kyrus grew worried. He was now caught between the Acardian Navy and Captain Zayne—*the* Captain Zayne—and things seemed headed for a collision. The thought flickered in his mind to possibly sell out the pirates and try his luck with the magistrates again, but it never took hold.

No, whether I like it or not, they have made me their enemy. I will find no comfort with them. These may be wicked men—no, these are wicked men I find myself with, but only for now. I will ride out this storm and see where I come out of it. If Captain Zayne has magic, I will learn it, and I will get myself the skills I will need to rid myself of his company. I will swallow this bitter elixir and hope that it will cure me rather than kill me.

Kyrus moved quickly to Stalyart's side. "We have been found out. Hurry, and I will do what I can to delay them."

"Very good, Mr. Hinterdale. You earn a place here," Stalyart said.

Stalyart moved to the rigging after cutting the last of the moorings. Along with Holyoake, they were making good time in getting the ship prepared for a hasty departure.

Suddenly there was a shout from the end of the pier. Kyrus crouched low and looked over the bulwark, doing his best to avoid being seen. There looked to be about two dozen men—navy from the uniforms most wore—making all haste for the gangplank. Kyrus had promised to do what he could to hold them off, and he knew he had little time to act.

"Haru bedaessi leoki kwatuan gelora," and Kyrus swept his hands up. He had managed to lift furniture in his shop when the constables arrived to arrest him. Captain Zayne had been impressed with how strong his iron-melting spell had been. It was time for Kyrus to see just how much he could squeeze out of his powers.

As the first of the sailors was about to set foot on the gangplank, it was yanked from beneath him. With a yelp and a splash, one fewer assailant was trying to board. Kyrus lifted the plank and twisted it in the air, orienting it crossways to the pier and up on its side. He held it at thigh height to keep it above the piles and began moving it down the length of the pier, sweeping men out of its path. Kyrus angled it slightly so that it scraped the mob of sailors' off the far side of the pier and into the water. A few of the more nimble ones managed to duck under it as it passed, and several more retreated back down the pier, but many were dumped unceremoniously into the harbor.

Kyrus, despite his fears, could not help but enjoy using his magic openly and to such great effect. He swept the gangplank back down the pier in the other direction, spinning it as it went, knocking even the more nimble of the sailors into the water.

A shot rang out, and the wood of the bulwark just to Kyrus's right splintered.

Well, fun time seems to be over.

He ducked back down behind cover. "Is that gangplank ours, Mr. Stalyart?" Kyrus shouted across the deck.

"Anything is ours if we wish to take it," Stalyart shouted back.

It was a poetic bit of optimism but unhelpful. Kyrus supposed that if gangplanks were supposed to remain with the pier then they could just throw it overboard later. He recalled it and set it down on the deck a few feet from himself.

"Captain, we are under sail," Stalyart shouted.

All pretense of stealth was gone now. The ship had lurched and begun to slowly inch away from its berth. Stalyart and Holyoake were working frantically to raise more sails, having just one to catch wind thus far. No one was yet at the helm, and they appeared to be banking a very mild turn as they got under way.

Captain Zayne came sprinting from the rear castle of the ship. "Mr. Hinterdale, get that anchor up, *now!*" he shouted.

Oops, anchor. Right.

Kyrus rushed over to the bow and found the chain that headed out the side of the ship and into the harbor. While no nautical expert was he, Kyrus nonetheless knew what an anchor was. He grabbed for the chain, the only way he knew how.

"Haru bedaessi leoki kwatuan gelora," and up it came.

He had to cast the spell twice more to get a "grip" farther down and bring the anchor safely to rest. There was a great thunderous crash as he let the chains drop to the deck.

"Mr. Hinterdale, get up here," Captain Zayne shouted again. He had taken the wheel and was guiding the freed ship out of its berth at roughly a walking pace. "Look over there. The navy crew are commandeering that merchant ship in the next berth. They mean to take up pursuit. That ship is armed, and we do not have enough men to put up a fight yet. I will show you this once. Then you use it on the sails.

"Eehu dolkavi esfenetor gelex ajihru," and Captain Zayne thrust one hand forward, palm facing out, with his fingers spread and making a claw-like gesture.

Kyrus watched and thought maybe he felt a little breeze. Based on the captain's comment about using it on the sails, he could only assume it was to make wind.

So this is how it will be? You need something done and you will show me a spell for it. How much are you going to hold back?

Kyrus nodded to affirm that he had gotten it, and Captain Zayne took the wheel again in both hands. He looked over and saw that there was a riot of activity on the vessel on their left—port—side, and the ship certainly looked formidable. Kyrus could see the little trapdoors where the cannons hid in the sides, and the sails looked very large and suited for wind-catching. Their own new ship was a navy vessel, though, and ought to be just as formidable. It might not be running with a full crew, but Kyrus supposed that was why they seemed so glad to have him along.

I will show them, Kyrus thought, starting to feel a bit of self-confidence. *I will show them that they would not be able to manage without me.*

"Eehu dolkavi esfenetor gelex ajihru," chanted Kyrus loudly, mimicking Captain Zayne's thrusting claw hand action. Kyrus made sure to pull hard on the aether as he finished the spell, funneling as much power into it as he could manage.

From nowhere, a gale sprang, catching the sail—which had been slack in the light breeze—and snapping it taught. There was a great and ominous creak of wood straining, and the bow of the ship lifted up as the ship accelerated unnaturally. Kyrus lost his footing and stumbled against the pillar that supported the wheel.

Kyrus was not finished, though. He was tired, and scared, and was suddenly finding an outlet for all the frustration and hopelessness he had found since his capture. He hurried to the port side of the ship and tried something he had been curious about. For all the dangers it was supposed to carry, he figured that there was plenty of water handy to absorb any mistakes. Kyrus leaned out over the railing and extended both hands out toward the merchant vessel that they were starting to pull away from. He did not know if the gesture helped any, but it felt right.

Kyrus just drew in any and all aether he could manage. The normal cool rush of it burned instead as it tore through him, but it did oh so much more once he released it. A massive gout of flame poured across the expanse separating the two ships and rolled up and into the rigging and sails. He stopped short of raking the decks with flame; angry as he was, he was still not a killer at heart, despite the company he had accepted.

"Mr. Hinterdale, if you do not mind me asking ... why did we need to rescue you?" Captain Zayne asked, clearly taken aback by a display of sorcery that was unheard of in his experience.

"That was my backup plan. I was not about to go to the gallows without a fight," Kyrus bragged. He sincerely hoped that in light of the conflagration he had just unleashed, no one would notice the fact that he was shaking.

Over the next few minutes, men emerged from belowdecks, and several helped get the sails set and rigged properly. Stalyart took over the wheel as Captain Zayne took reports on the execution of their plan.

On the whole, they had suffered only minor injuries. There had been a slaughter below, as Mr. Crispin's ruse had gotten them to within striking distance, with knives out, before the crew had even realized something was amiss. Eight men had been taken prisoner and the rest were all dead. Before he took over the wheel, Captain Zayne had gone into the captain's quarters and knocked out Captain Rannison; they went back in after to tie him up. There was no evidence of sabotage or damage to the ship, and there were plenty of supplies stored aboard; the ship had been preparing to leave port in just two more days.

＊ ＊ ＊ ＊ ＊ ＊ ＊

Dawn broke and found Captain Zayne a free and contented man. He stood on the deck of his own ship, so new that he had not yet decided on a name for it. He had considered just naming it *The Honest Merchant* and carrying on as if he had never lost the original, but he knew the name would always ring hollow to him if he did.

Taking a deep breath of the sea air on a clear morning, he turned to survey his prisoners. There were nine in all—eight common sailors and one captain—standing in a row by the starboard bulwark. Captain Rannison was stripped to his underclothes as Denrik had appropriated his wardrobe and given it to Grosh to make alterations. The former captain was also the only one bound, with his hands tied behind his back.

The whole crew was on deck, except for Holyoake at the wheel and Kyrus.

The hero of their escape had taken to his new quarters on the pretense of exhaustion and had shut himself in. He had commandeered one of the senior officers' cabins, making it only himself, Mr. Stalyart, and the captain who had deluxe accommodations. The minor officers' quarters were generally twos and fours, and there were enough of those to go around that none of the crew had to bunk where the navy's common sailors had slept.

"Good morning, gentlemen. I imagine that after last night's events, you are all surprised and perhaps grateful to be alive," Captain Zayne said, speaking loudly enough that all could hear him. "Well, today I am in a magnanimous mood. I have a new ship, and a fresh crew, and the rolling sea beneath my feet again. As you may notice, we are shorthanded. I may go so far as to offer you gentlemen jobs.

"But first, I would like to deal with the issue of your Captain Rannison. I imagine that if you spend long enough aboard a ship, you may come to resent your captain, perhaps even bear him a grudge. It may even be the case that despite your own tenuous situation, that you are enjoying seeing him squirm," Denrik said, though in truth he believed that the old captain's stoicism was very dignified and rather admirable. "So I offer my pistol, loaded, to the man who would take his captain's life. I shall not question your motive; your reason you may keep to yourself."

He offered the pistol, handle foremost, to each of the eight men in turn. None of the men moved.

"I see, so none of you has a grudge you would like to settle today, to end this man's life by your own hand?" Denrik asked. "Very well, then."

Denrik then grabbed Captain Rannison by the shoulder, pushed him against the railing, and shot the man himself. He leaned on the stricken Rannison and heaved him over the railing. No one but Captain Zayne saw him hit the water, but all heard the splash. It was like a punctuation mark at the end of their hijacking.

In the end, each of the eight men was dumped in the water. Denrik had asked Mr. Crispin about each of them, and he was unwilling to vouch for any. Disappointed, but certainly grateful that Crispin was a hard enough man to let them all die rather than take a chance, Captain Zayne set his crew and headed for the meeting spot to transfer men and supplies from Stalyart's merchant ship. It would still be a small crew, but they would work that out in due time.

* * * * * * * *

In an elegantly appointed office in the heart of Golis, Lord Harwick opened the message he had just received. It had been delivered by horse just moments before by a messenger from Scar Harbor who had claimed it was of utmost urgency. The man had ridden well into the night to reach Golis but had been stopped cold by Lord Harwick's own assistants, who would not be persuaded to rouse the aging magistrate in the night for anyone short of the king or the high councilor.

Lord Harwick adjusted his spectacles and read through it. The secretary who had brought the message in watched Lord Harwick's eyebrow raise at first, then saw his brow furrow. After a moment, he saw the lord's face redden.

"Clarsey, do you know what this is?" Lord Harwick demanded.

Clarsey knew enough that his lordship was angry, but not with him.

"No, your lordship. What is it?" Clarsey played along. Lord Harwick was a good man and a keen jurist, so he could be forgiven his occasional theatrics.

"Those superstitious bumpkins in Scar Harbor have found someone guilty of witchcraft. They want me to convince the king to make an exception to the moratorium on executions. And of all people, Kyrus Hinterdale, an expert in the Scrivener's Guild. Same lad who put Lord Kendelaine's treatise on chess into publication; I have a copy of it myself. If that lad is a threat to the society, then I am one of his majesty's hunting hounds!

"Put an order together, Clarsey. I want Expert Hinterdale brought up here and given a new trial. And I want Lord Lionsvaen up here as well, to explain himself. Oh, and draft up something for the council, recommending we strike that silly witchcraft law from the books. It is a farce that we still have that on record.

"That poor boy. I shall see to it that he is cleared of this ridiculous charge."

Once his assistant had left the room, Harwick took up his pipe and clamped it firmly in his mouth. He leaned back in his armchair and laced his fingers behind his head. With no one else observing him, a tiny flame sparked unbidden, lighting his pipe.

Chapter 23 - Dragon Time

Jinzan watched out the window as one of the reins of the great, winged beasts the goblins called a ch'pt'rk was tied to one of the wrought-iron fences in the flower garden of Lord Festrius Feldrake. Jinzan knew that it was a sign of poor leadership and an ill-controlled temper to kill messengers who bore unwelcome news, but he had been sorely tempted to incinerate the pompous skyrider who had delivered Ni'Hash'Tk's decree.

A tenday? Really, dragon, you could not make any more haste than that?

The delay seemed excessive to the impatient sorcerer, who saw no preparations to leave, but rather a settling in among the goblins of G'thk's army.

The citizens of Illard's Glen had fled in great haste as the goblin army overran the town. Many of the defenders had remained behind long enough that most of the refugees had been able to escape. Knights had stood their ground against impossible odds to buy the civilians extra moments to make it to the eastern and southern gates, where they might flee to Raynesdark and Korgen, respectively. G'thk had ordered a token pursuit of the refugees, and his forces had engaged those who had gone along armed to protect the peasants, tradesmen, and others who were ill-equipped to defend themselves. The goblin general cared little for the fleeing Kadrins, however, and quickly recalled his forces before they became too far separated from the main body of the army.

The goblins had swept the city and rounded up all those humans who had remained. The able-bodied men were all killed as a precaution, with the exception of two knights that were taken alive with the hope of ransoming them later. The children and the infirm were taken hostage and reasonably well cared for. The goblins fed them and allowed them proper shelter; they did not mistreat or intentionally frighten them, and left them to be overseen by some of the older girl children. The women were pressed into service as attendants to the goblins, especially the officers. With the knowledge that the safety and well-being of their young ones were at stake, they were docile enough as household servants.

Jinzan tried to remain detached from the goblins' treatment of their human prisoners. His own people had been conquered by these same Kadrins ages ago, and it held a warped and distorted mirror before his face to see the way the goblins casually disposed of and used them. It would have felt more like a proper vengeance if Megrenn soldiers had been the ones to kill the human prisoners, rather than having them burned by the dozen by goblin firehurlers.

More than a week I shall wait in this worthless Kadrin town. And for what, an escort from that great overgrown lizard?

Jinzan had been allowed to meet Ni'Hash'Tk when he had first proposed his plan. While the dragon-goddess was certainly impressive in size and certainly seemed capable of inflicting great harm, he found her to be insufferably vain and naïve. He had known beforehand that Ni'Hash'Tk was looked down upon by the other goblin tribes as a fool, and his plan had relied on it. Convincing the dragon to send her armies to conquer a lair for her dullard offspring worked brilliantly for getting him into the upper mines of Raynesdark.

[Quit looking out the window and come play,] a crackling voice called him from his musings.

Jinzan turned and saw three goblins seated around a small square table. Like many of the human furnishings in Lord Feldrake's manor home, the legs had been cut short by the goblins since they had moved in. What had once likely been a table where the lord and his guests might play at cards was now little more than a platform at shin height. A set of velvet upholstered chairs had likewise been shortened to goblin size, and contained the personages of K'k'rt, G'thk, and N'ft'k, who was the commander of the reinforcement divisions that had recently joined up with G'thk's troops.

"Do we not have more pressing tasks?' Jinzan asked.

He knew the game well enough but suspected strongly that the goblins would conspire against him. Jinzan looked down at the pile of square ivory tiles that were strewn face down on the table. K'k'rt mashed his hands in among them and mixed them vigorously, but with such a practiced hand that they did not flip over in the process.

[Sorcerer, you worry too much. We will have Ni'Hash'Tk's blessing for the final battle. That is all we could wish for. Your toys are most effective and impressive, certainly, but with Ni'Hash'Tk's aid, we cannot lose. Your plan will work now. Enjoy yourself,] G'thk said.

The general had been satisfied with the army's rapid conquest of Illard's Glen, but had been somewhat less optimistic about their assault on Raynesdark, which boasted much sterner defenses. News of their dragon-goddess joining them, though, had erased all his doubts. While Jinzan agreed that the dragon's aid would certainly weigh heavily in their favor, one small detail in the message nagged at him.

"And what of the demon Ni'Hash'Tk mentioned?" Jinzan asked, grateful that at least the dragon's name was pronounceable with Megrenn sounds.

The sorcerer pulled up a large silk pillow to the table and used it for a seat, folding his legs under him. The chairs were cut down so low that his knees would have been up by his chin had he tried to sit in one, and even if he had found one still left at human height, the table would have been too low to reach. The pillow was comfortable, if somewhat undignified.

[That is why she comes. Ni'Hash'Tk will deal with the demon, if it is brave enough to show itself in battle despite her presence,] G'thk said.

The goblin general lazed in his chair and reached to select five of the tiles for himself. K'k'rt and N'ft'k did likewise, taking their starting allotment for the game. Jinzan still felt uneasy playing the game in the first place, but took his five tiles as well.

It was a simple enough game on the surface. The tiles were blank on one side. On the other face, each edge of the square tiles had a symbol. On his turn, a player would play a tile and draw a tile from the middle to replace it. After the first tile was placed, any other tile placed had to lie adjacent to another with a matching symbol. Each player was attempting to make a ring of tiles that enclosed the largest area possible. Once one player completed a circuit, the round would end and bets would be paid out, using a complicated system that related to how large an area was fenced off in tiles, and certain modifiers for combinations of symbols facing inward. Players predominantly played on their own tiles but were free to spend a turn adding tiles to their opponents' rings as well, to hinder them. If a player either had no eligible plays or simply wished to pass, he could drop a tile faceup in the middle and select another as his turn.

Those last two parts were what always concerned Jinzan about playing with the goblins. There were no rules preventing two or more of his opponents from ganging up on him to let one of the others win, and discarding tiles faceup meant that cunning opponents could pass tiles to each other. Jinzan had learned a different variant of the game where the discarded tiles went facedown, but G'thk considered his way to be the "proper" way to play. The goblin's name for the game had no proper exact translation in Megrenn, but G'thk had explained that it came out to roughly "swineherd making fences." Jinzan's people had learned the game ages ago from trade with the goblins and had named it "Avarice." Many a game was lost when someone held out too long for a large payoff and someone finished a smaller ring before their masterpiece was completed.

Jinzan looked at his tiles. He was a rank novice at the game, in addition to his suspicion that the goblins would cheat him out of his money. He had already counted his coins as lost. The tiles he held were as good as any others; he had no grand plan for winning. He merely humored his goblin allies in playing, and wanted to be in on their conversation, especially if he could steer it toward making useful plans rather than counting on their reptilian liege to take care of their affairs for them.

Jinzan picked one of his tiles at random and plunked it down on the table as his first move. They had not yet decided the order of play, but Jinzan skipped over that formality and took the initiative. If this was to be a test of wits and wills—one likely stacked against him from the outset—he would rather be bold.

The goblins exchanged glances, but none spoke against their human ally. Play proceeded as if nothing untoward had occurred. Jinzan began to wonder if anything had. These goblins had their own way of thinking of such things; perhaps he had just stumbled into something they considered socially accepted, taking the lead in starting the game. More likely, though, he had just marked himself as a troublemaker to be dealt with within the game.

[You worry too much, sorcerer,] G'thk said, placing a tile in front of him. [I can tell you would rather we gather up all our troops and charge straight to the humans' mines. Rush in, blast with magic and your new weapons, take what we want.] G'thk picked up a tile, and play proceeded past him as he talked. [Surely I would much enjoy finishing our campaign with a great and crushing success. Sometimes prudence weighs more, though. You think I take the warning of a demon lightly? I do not. I take the assurance of Ni'Hash'Tk's protection very seriously, though. To rush in now, and perhaps face a demon, maybe we lose half our forces. Demons can be all manner of shapes and sizes, and we know almost nothing of this one. With Ni'Hash'Tk leading us, no demon will stand against us.

[So I say we are in no hurry. My kind have a fable we tell, of a fox and a monkey who both wish to get to an island in the center of a deep pond. They have heard that there is a great treasure there and are each eager to claim it. The monkey—]

"Yes, my people have that story as well, or a version of it. The monkey is impatient and gets eaten by monsters that live in the pond when he tries to swim it; the fox waits until winter and walks across once the water freezes," Jinzan said. He absently played a tile and drew another from the center.

[Spoken just like a monkey, too,] K'k'rt said, laughing at Jinzan's expense. [I may hate the cold, but I would like to walk on the frozen water rather than swim with the lake monsters. You would think that humans live so long that they would show more patience. I would wager you are ten summers older than I am, but you sit still as well as a child.]

"I do not care for your tone, tinker," Jinzan warned.

He realized that his temper was growing short. The room had begun to feel uncomfortably warm, and he suspected that it was not the room that was growing heated. He had decided going in to the game that G'thk and K'k'rt were too valuable as allies, but should the lesser-ranked N'ft'k cross him, he was prepared to slay the goblin right at the gaming table. With the performance of the cannons during the brief assault on the defenses of Illard's Glen, he felt he had reaffirmed his value and was prepared to trade some of the leeway that accompanied that for a bit more respect—and fear.

[Have ease, sorcerer,] G'thk said. [We are having a game tonight. Perhaps K'k'rt has had too much of the human lord's wine and has freed his tongue, but perhaps you have drunk too little. Your brain is tied in knots with worry. Wash them loose with wine. I know you tell me the Kd'rn wine is like urine, but it comes from the stores of your enemy. Drink it and think it is their tears and blood.]

"I am not certain tears or blood would taste any better," Jinzan said dryly, drawing chuckles from his opponents. "But if I am to lose all my coin tonight, I may as well enjoy it." Switching over to the Kadrin tongue, he yelled out, "Girl! Bring me wine, the best Lord Feldrake kept in his cellar." Jinzan spoke fluent Kadrin, with a smooth Megrenn accent unmistakable atop it.

The sorcerer let out a long sigh and ran his fingers through his hair. Speaking Kadrin for the first time in years, surrounded by people who viewed him as a curiosity and who likely spoke daggers of him behind his back, it brought back old times for Jinzan...

* * * * * * *

"Today, we continue the lesson on the expansionist wars of Warlock Rashan. As we covered yesterday, the Empire was not always so large as it is today, and we have Warlock Rashan to thank for many of the varied peoples who now pay fealty to Emperor Dharus," their teacher had droned in that uniquely didactic tone that seemed to develop in all classroom instructors if you stood them before students for enough summers. "While these territories have now been assimilated into the Empire proper, Warlock Rashan made many enemies in the process. Who can tell me one of the many epithets his enemies used to describe him?"

"Rashan the Bloodthirsty," volunteered one student, a fresh-faced lad named Krough who was always eager to get himself noticed.

"Good try, but that was how he came to be known here in Kadrin, by those who grew weary of his constant warring," said the instructor, Dolvaen Lurien.

Dolvaen Lurien was a respected member of the faculty at the Imperial Academy, a Third Circle sorcerer who was marked for high places despite his low birth. Jinzan liked him better than the pompous sorcerers from the well-heeled bloodlines. Jinzan had always thought the Imperial Circle's control of the breeding of the major sorcerous bloodlines of Kadrin made them like warhorses or dogs, creatures bred for servitude and only allowed to rut when and where their masters wished. Dolvaen treated the lowborn and non-Kadrin students in his class equally, and Jinzan vowed he would not forget that fact.

"Rashan the Merciless," offered another student, Chessa Destrier.

She was fair and grey-eyed, and had taken the lead among her peers on the path to womanhood. With curves where the other girls were only beginning to hint at them, she drew the attention of all the boys in the class. Jinzan was no exception, but he realized that she was out of his reach. As the pride of the Destrier family, and the granddaughter of Inner Circle member Fenris Destrier, Jinzan would be lucky to escape with his life if he were to ever bed her, and would be lucky to escape with a shred of his dignity if he even hinted to her of the possibility. She was all smiles and curtseys when the teachers were around but was a young tyrant among the students when they were left unsupervised. Fifteen summers of being told she was better than her peers had sunk in well.

"That one hits the mark! Very good, who else?"

"Rashan the Murderer. That was what Loramar called him in the formal declaration of the First Necromancer War," said Jurl.

The most bookish of the students in Jinzan's class, Jurl was a very serious young lad. His ancestry was unknown, or at least partly. He had been born to a whore in Dellanter, and there was plenty of speculation of his father likely being a member of the Imperial Circle. He had always studied hard and was once the top student in the class, but that ended once they were old enough for the

Ranking.

Jinzan was the top-ranked student now. They had teased him for winters, for his darker skin—though their own grew nearly as dark in the summer months—for his accent, for the fact that he was from a lesser bloodline. The latter bothered him the most, since among the Megrenn, he would have been considered exceptionally well-bred. His parents were both sorcerers, though secretly, as it was only recently that Kadrin had granted Megrenn citizens the privilege of taking sorcerous training.

Jinzan had taken Ranking Day as a small sampling of the vendetta he was harboring. He had thrashed his classmates and easily claimed the top ranking, not even bothering to toy with them. He had even beaten the top student of the class ahead of him, before finally succumbing to one of the older and more polished duelists in the Academy.

"Rashan the Deceiver," Jinzan added, unable to keep the contempt from his voice. His accent had been a bit stronger in those days, and he heard a few snickers at the slightly misspoken word.

"True enough. There is no need for bitterness, though. Megrenn is part of the Empire now, and those old grudges have been set aside. Your being here is proof enough of that," Dolvaen said. "But that leads to an interesting topic. Does anyone—besides Jinzan—know how he got that name?"

"Was that when Warlock Rashan negotiated a peace deal and used the signing of the treaty as a cover for a surprise attack?" Jurl said. "That was Rashan's Bargain, right? He offered them a good deal just to get them to agree to the terms, and at the signing ceremony, he killed all their top generals and their king, not to mention a dozen sorcerers."

"I see someone has been reading *The Diplomacy of Fire and Steel*. All the knights read it as a matter of course, but I highly recommend it to anyone who wishes a deeper understanding of Warlock Rashan, or even just warfare in general.

"Does anyone else have other names he was known by?" Dolvaen asked, pausing to give the students an opportunity to respond but hearing nothing.

Jinzan could have gone on at some length of all the things he had heard Rashan called. His people were quite creative when it came to the subject, having been made a laughingstock by the long-dead tyrant. The warlock was eighty winters dead, and still the Megrenn were known for being naïve and trusting, all from that one incident. It had destroyed their identity as a free-thinking land of philosophers and warrior-poets in the minds of the world, and replaced it with the image of a farmer who invited a wolf to make peace with his chickens.

"Very well, then we move on to the war with Megrenn itself. At the time, Megrenn was believed to have been strong enough to withstand an extensive campaign, with allies from across the sea and with the goblins to the west and southwest, as well as favorable relations with the ogre tribes. As we now know, much of Megrenn's strength was exaggerated, both by bards' tales and careful use of spies to spread false rumors of treaties …"

Jinzan could feel the eyes of his classmates drifting to him as the talk centered around his homeland, its deficiencies, and their weaknesses as a people. Jinzan knew that Dolvaen was oblivious to the embarrassment he was causing, but the young sorcerer just hoped his skin—for the half shade darker it was than his pure-blooded Kadrin classmates—was dark enough to hide his blush.

* * * * * * * *

The serving girl who brought the wine was not one of the lord's household staff—those had likely managed to flee with the rest of the lord's household. She struggled with the wine cork, seemingly never having used a corkscrew before. The goblins had rather haphazardly organized their captives according to what they felt needed to be done, with no real attempt to find out who was qualified to what tasks. Presumably, Jinzan thought, they figured that the mundane tasks that would be required of them could be done by anyone.

The three goblins at the table with him shared a laugh at the girl's ineptitude. Jinzan was tempted to just use a little magic to pull the cork out and be done with it, but he found himself distracted by the girl herself. She had jaw-length dark hair, and blue eyes, rimmed red from crying. She looked haggard—understandable given that her town had just been sacked by the very people she was trying to serve wine—but not very old. Jinzan suspected that she probably had a very young child somewhere nearby, being watched over by goblin guards and some barely pubescent girl. Still, despite not looking her best, she was comely enough, and Jinzan had not been among other humans for many long weeks.

[Your turn, sorcerer, make a play,] said N'ft'k, seated to Jinzan's right. [Have the serving girl later.]

The goblins laughed at the comment. Despite not understanding a word of goblin-speech, the girl was savvy enough to get the gist of the comment, and she blushed as she continued to stab at the top of the wine bottle with the corkscrew.

Jinzan turned and looked sidelong down at his tiles, absently playing one. He had given up on trying to win and was just playing for the sake of playing now. His gaze fell on the lesser-ranked General N'ft'k, and his eyes narrowed. The goblin's laughter petered out awkwardly under Jinzan's glare. He turned his attention back to the serving girl, looking her in the eye as he took the bottle and corkscrew from her hand.

"Here, allow me," he told her in Kadrin.

With a few expert twists, he had the corkscrew in and easily pulled the cork out without needing any magic. She set out four goblets and took the bottle back from Jinzan to begin to pour their drinks. After she had poured the first two, he held out a hand for her to stop.

"Just a moment," he told her, still using her own language.

"*Haru bedaessi leoki kwatuan gelora,*" and N'ft'k rose suddenly from his chair. The ceilings of Lord Feldrake's manor home were thrice the height of a man, nearly six times the height of a goblin. Jinzan left the unfortunate goblin pinned heavily to the ceiling, as if leaving a sack of grain atop him. He then took up the two empty goblets and stood.

"I believe I will take my leave of you gentlemen for tonight. Please thank General N'ft'k for his suggestion when he returns," Jinzan reverted to Megrenn, which he assumed the serving girl did not understand, but he knew that G'thk did not speak Kadrin. He cared not a whit whether the tinker could, but he would not have put it past the wily old goblin.

As the sorcerer stalked off toward the room he had borrowed in Feldrake Manor, he gestured imperiously behind him.

"Come along," he ordered in Kadrin.

A swish of skirts and the scuffling of soft shoes on the lord's rugs told him that he had been heeded.

* * * * * * * *

Jinzan let out a long sigh. He felt more relaxed than he had in a long time. He had been so caught up in his plans for the assault on Raynesdark that he had not taken the time to properly celebrate Denrik's return to the seas. Certainly, though, the wine and the exertions of the unclad serving girl curled asleep on his chest had helped some as well.

He did not feel that he had mistreated the girl. He had offered her no violence, and she had not protested, which for Jinzan's conscience was enough, given the circumstances. He could not entirely fool himself into thinking she had gone to his bed willingly, since the implied threat of violence was present, whether he would have carried through with it or not. He told himself that he was better than the Kadrins who had sacked Megrenn in his grandfather's time. The girl, whose name he had not even asked, had been frightened and trembling when he took her away from the goblins. Now she lay sleeping peacefully.

He had come near to killing N'ft'k just a short while ago. It might have been the final hole that would sink his ship, had he gone through with it. G'thk was growing weary of him, he could tell. Perhaps it would be best to keep out of the way of the goblin general for a few days. He had to keep in mind that without the goblins, he lacked the means to take Raynesdark and get into the mines.

The Staff of Gehlen would give him the power to make the Kadrins *truly* pay. The aether-void around its tomb had been impenetrable for thousands of summers, the draw against all aether within a few paces of it was ferocious. The wards that protected it rebuilt themselves and repaired chips that were knocked loose from spears, sling-stones, and arrows. Even catapults seemed unable to harm it enough to break through before it undid the damage the siege engine could inflict. Cannons would be different.

He just needed patience.

He wrapped an arm around the sleeping serving girl, who stirred slightly at his touch. He felt the warmth and smoothness of her skin. He had not been with a woman in far too long. Jinzan laid his head back and closed his eyes, snuffing out the magical light that had kept away the darkness as midnight approached.

It was time to see what Captain Zayne was up to.

Chapter 24 - How to Start a War

Brannis closed the door to the library behind him as he exited, thankful that no other guards had been posted in the meantime. Rashan had allowed him to sleep in the unguarded library for the rest of the night. Brannis head hurt where the warlock had slugged him, but apparently Rashan knew what he was doing, and there had been no blood, and any bruise would likely be covered by the fall of his hair. The latter was just a guess, as the library had no mirror, and Brannis had yet to find anywhere to freshen up. His face was scratchy with stubble, and his clothes had been slept in; he expected that he looked much less the Grand Marshal than perhaps he should.

That demon can explain to everyone why I look like I have just stumbled home from the taverns, if anyone asks.

Brannis eschewed his quest for a wash basin and mirror, or even a morning meal, and headed for the offices of the various Inner Circle members, whose entrances were the floor below the Sanctum. The Tower of Contemplation was ornately appointed and well lit with aetherial lights, but sorely lacked for windows. Brannis was unsure how late the hour had grown, but the activity level in the Tower suggested that it was at least a respectable hour of the morning. There was a general bustle of sorcerers and servants about the main central stairways that Brannis took to be business as usual; he had little basis for comparison, however, since he had only been there previously under extenuating circumstances.

As he reached the door to the high sorcerer's office (now occupied by a warlock), he overheard voices within. It struck Brannis as odd that the Inner Circle would be so careless—or arrogant—as to leave their doors unwarded against eavesdroppers.

Maybe they are so paranoid that the wards produce false conversations to be overheard? Brannis mused. That seemed more in keeping with the sorcerers he knew.

Trying to avoid the impression that he was loitering in the hopes of overhearing them, he knocked smartly on the door. The conversation abruptly halted, and a breath later, the door opened. Brannis stepped quickly aside as a middle-aged sorcerer brushed past him.

"Congratulations, Marshal," Shador Archon greeted him in passing.

Brannis was familiar enough with Shador, a tall, broad-shouldered gentleman nearly his own size. Shador's hair was grey at the temples, but it was his only concession to aging. He was Second Circle and likely one of the sorcerers who had been overlooked for the vacancies Rashan had created among the Inner Circle, though Brannis had never kept such close accounting of the Circle's hierarchy. Shador was also Juliana Archon's father.

"Thank you, Sorcerer Shador," Brannis replied, caught somewhat off guard.

He was not quick enough of wit so soon after waking to formulate a follow-up question. Pleasantries dispensed with, the older sorcerer took his leave, and Brannis could only watch after him as the Questions Ministry within his mind slowly began catching up on its workload.

Brannis, still looking over his shoulder, entered Rashan's office. He turned his attention back to the warlock as Shador passed out of sight down the stairs. He was seated in an overly large armchair, clearly better suited to the late Gravis Archon's stature than his own. The office was bereft of most of its contents, the personal effects of the previous high sorcerer having already been reclaimed by his kin. Heavens Cry rested in its sheath on an otherwise empty bookshelf, and a few notes and books were scattered about the desk, clearly what Rashan had been working on in his brief time back at the head of the Imperial Circle.

"Good morning, Brannis. Close the door behind you, if you would," Rashan said. Once Brannis had complied, he continued: "All is well in your dreams?"

"After a fashion, yes."

"The spell I showed you proved adequate?" Rashan asked.

"It was not entirely how I expected it to go, but generally, yes," Brannis answered, still puzzled by the warlock's interest—and the fact that he had taken Brannis's bizarre quest the previous night so seriously. There was a long pause, and Brannis felt the need to elaborate to fill the uncomfortable silence: "Is there a way to have it bring your clothes along?"

Rashan smiled. "Practice, mostly."

That seemed to be enough to satisfy the demon that he had actually put his advice into practice. Brannis wondered if Rashan was trying to verify whether he really had been able to perform the magic in his dream.

"Come, let us get to work this morning," Rashan said. "There are goblins at work on our western border, and we need to determine their plan. I received a message via the speaking stone in Naran Port that Illard's Glen was sacked three days ago. Refugees have escaped to Raynesdark and Korgen, with messengers reaching Naran Port late last night," Rashan said.

He pushed aside the documents and books that covered the desk and drew a map from one of the desk drawers. It showed the Kadrin Empire as it stood presently. By Brannis's estimation, the map could be no more than twenty summers old, given that it showed an independent Megrenn and what was once Tuermon still a part of the Empire. In Rashan's wars, Megrenn had fallen before Tuermon.

"How many survivors? What of Lord Feldrake?" Brannis was going to have to get used to Rashan's blunt style of delivering even shocking news. Most of the generals that Brannis knew were prone to much more preamble prior to getting to the heart of a matter.

"Wrong question. Think to win first, then worry about the cost," Rashan said.

"How large a force? Was there any indication whether they were settling in to occupy, or just using the city as a way to resupply and cross the Neverthaw?" Brannis tried again.

"Much better. The survivors estimated that there were at least sixty thousand troops," Rashan said, and Brannis's blood chilled. That was no tactical force to strike and flee with. That was a full-scale invasion. "They also had at least a few sorcerers among them, which is not unusual for a goblin army, especially one that size. There were reports of some new siege engine, similar to a catapult, which the goblins have invented. It tore huge holes in the town wall, allowing Illard's Glen to be overrun by goblin infantry. There was an unconfirmed report that there was a human traveling among the goblins, as well."

Rashan stared at Brannis for a moment, then asked, "What do you make of it?"

"Illard's Glen is too small a town for goblins to have sent such a large force. Goblins prefer to attack with a clear advantage, but they could have sacked Illard's Glen with a third that force."

"I agree." Rashan nodded.

"If the report is true that there was a human consorting with the goblins, I would wager heavily that he is Megrenn. Megrenn raiders had taken control of High Pass with none of us the wiser, so it stands to reason that this activity by the goblins is in support of that effort. I think it is safe to assume that there is some degree of coordination between the goblins and the Megrenn to take at least some portion of the western part of the Empire. I would assume if that is the case, then the human is a liaison."

"That seems reasonable. As to your other question, the survivors could make no clear determination of the goblins' intent. They had made no concerted attempts to hunt down the refugees, and were flooding the city with troops, but they could just be consolidating their forces and resupplying. They had not burned the town, so I think it safe to conclude that they are staying long enough to want roofs above their heads at night."

"Illard's Glen is no great prize—no offense meant to those farmers and other loyal Kadrins who live there—so we must assume they will have further plans. East of Illard's Glen is Raynesdark." Brannis pointed at the map, mostly for reference and to help him think aloud. He had no reason to suspect that Rashan knew any less about Kadrin geography than he did. "South along the Neverthaw is Korgen." Brannis pointed again. "And at the mouth of the Neverthaw is Naran Port. Now Naran Port would be quite a prize. They would take over all our western shipping and seriously curtail any ability of ours to land reinforcements west of the Cloud Wall Mountains.

"But that would not explain why they would strike Illard's Glen. Korgen is more directly on the path from Kelvie Forest, and even Korgen could be bypassed by overland routes if they were willing to march openly without tree cover.

"No, Raynesdark is their next target. The mines are still prosperous enough to make it an attractive target. There has not been gold in the Raynesdark mines for ages, but the deeper mines still yield diamonds, and the whole area is rich in iron ore."

"The goblins worship their dragon gods," Rashan said. "If some dragon remembers Raynesdark as rich in gold from ages long past, I could consider that they might have designs to take it for their own. So you think this is a mining expedition?"

"No, not really. It seems too straightforward. The goblins use enough strange minerals in their metallurgy that I doubt iron is a priority for them, and they could likely buy the diamonds from us for less than what this campaign is going to cost them. If I had to make a guess, there is something they want those mines for that they either cannot get by trade, or that they do not wish us to know about."

"What if this is a feint? Maybe they intend to take a flotilla down the Neverthaw, taking Korgen along the way to conquering Naran Port," Rashan said. His tone was flat, suggesting that he was not actually advocating the possibility, merely being thorough.

"It would certainly be a surprising tactic. Given the number of troops the reports indicate, they would need a lot of ships, though. I would think that any ships that were able to get under sail or oar would have departed Illard's Glen at the first sighting of a hostile force. That would mean the goblins would have to build their flotilla in Illard's Glen, and that would negate any advantage of surprise they might think to take—building enough ships would take the best part of a season.

"Besides, if we prepare Raynesdark for an attack, and they make for Korgen instead, we can take a force and pursue them. We would need to be careful, but if we time it correctly, we could arrive in time to pin them between ourselves and the defenders in Korgen."

"Very well, you can detail your plans on the way there. Be prepared to depart early tomorrow morning. I will have sorcerers to support you, and I shall scavenge about the palace for any useful magics that have been squirreled away in the name of the nonexistent emperor. Any questions?"

"Yes. What were you and Shador Archon discussing?" Brannis asked. He was beginning to understand how Rashan thought and figured he would need to be direct to get any useful answer out of him.

"Wrong question. You have a lot of—"

"No, this time I have the question I want. I may have more later, but this is the one I would like answered first," Brannis said.

Rashan looked perturbed, a slight frown creasing his delicate features. After a moment's pause, a smile curled one side of his mouth.

"I am going to enjoy having you leading my armies, Brannis. I spent much of yesterday bullying sorcerers thrice your age and then some, men who had for long summers ruled unquestioned. None of them dared interrupt me, much less contradict me. A few hold back because they distrust me and wish to wait for the ideal time to strike, but for the most part, it is simple fear that stays their tongues. Always remember, Brannis, it is your mind that I value—your insight, your inquisitiveness, even your conscience. If I wanted a swinging sword and an empty helmet, I have a whole army filled with those already to choose from."

"And you still have not answered," Brannis said, folding his arms in front of him.

"Very well. I was speaking to Sorcerer Shador about his daughter. I saw the matchmakers records, so I know she was once promised to you, but I believe it was understood that the marriage was contingent on you turning out to be a sorcerer," Rashan said.

Brannis could not help but flush in a combination of embarrassment and shame. It had been winters since he had put the Academy behind him, but the sting could still be brought fresh to the surface by thoughts of Juliana.

"She is too bright a flower to be unwed at her age," Rashan said. "I thought that she would be an ideal match for Iridan."

"What!" Brannis exclaimed.

He had held some vague illusion that perhaps Rashan had been leading up to explain that a grand marshal would still be a fine and honorable husband for a sorceress of the Archon line.

"Well, Iridan would have been considered for a prime match long ago had the Circle known of his lineage. He cannot just linger around and marry some daughter of a lesser nobleman, or a simple commoner." Rashan sighed. "And he is just the sort, too. I could easily see him falling for some nobody, a sweet little thing from a worthless family, pleasant enough but no fit match to be sure."

"Who is his mother, anyway?" Brannis asked.

"You are the first to ask that," Rashan replied, chuckling. "Is it any wonder that this Empire is slipping away as my conquests come undone? Even Iridan has yet to overcome his shock enough to get to that one. His mother is immortal—a demon, if you will—like me. Unlike me, she was born that way. Among the small community of immortals where I met her, they call it being 'pureborn.' I had hoped being half pureborn would give Iridan a better chance of being born pureborn himself, but alas …"

"I shall want to know more about these other immortals at some point, but there are more pressing concerns at hand," Brannis responded.

It seemed that Rashan had an unlimited capacity to overwhelm his thoughts. There were a hundred things he needed to know, to arrange, to investigate, and to plan.

"Agreed," Rashan said, "so let us—"

"So what did he say?" Brannis broke in, deftly setting aside one hundred things at once. Men had their weaknesses, and for all his troubles with magic, Brannis's greatest weakness was one particular sorceress, as it had been ever since that one summer …

* * * * * * * *

"So what did he say?" Brannis had asked Juliana Archon on that day, trying to control himself from snatching the parchment from her hand and reading it for himself.

He had pulled her aside after her early afternoon lesson in interpreting runes. The messenger had arrived mid morning, and she had opened it as soon as their alchemy lesson had ended. Brannis had tried to talk to her as soon as he had gotten word, but she had played coy and managed to avoid him thus far.

"Oh, are you referring to *this?*" Juliana replied, offering the parchment to Brannis and snatching it away when he made a grab for it. "I could not begin to imagine."

She grinned mischievously and Brannis melted just a little. He had grown completely incapable of getting mad at Juliana and was hopelessly enchanted with her. She was still a bully and a troublemaker, but she had left Iridan alone since the day Brannis had humbled her winters ago. And while she was still tall for her age and best described as rail-thin, she had acquired the curves of a woman and had taken them as her preferred weapon over her fists. It was a good thing, too, for while at eight summers old, Brannis was a hand taller and a gallon or two heavier, now he was nearly a head taller and half again her weight.

Brannis made another attempt at the parchment, and Juliana turned, holding it at arm's length with her body blocking the path to it. When Brannis grabbed her arm, she shifted it to her other hand, giggling as Brannis pulled her around by the wrong side. She twisted away, but relented when Brannis caught hold of her other arm, relaxing back up against him and holding the parchment angled so that he could read it over her shoulder.

Brannis realized he had been tricked when he found himself with his arms wrapped around a willing Juliana, her back pressed against his chest and the scent of the honeysuckle perfume in her golden-red hair filling his nostrils. Brannis had always been the tallest of the boys his age at the Academy and mature for his age, but he had also reached adolescence first. With a deepening voice and a jawline that was, if not bearded, at the very least clearly unshaven, he seemed much older than the other boys. As the girls of his class gained a more adult awareness of the boys, Brannis was the first target of their youthful daydreams. Tall, handsome, and athletic, he was everything most girls could hope for, and Juliana was no exception.

"So this is it?" Brannis asked, after scanning the document. "Everything is settled now?"

"Yes," Juliana replied simply. "I get to keep you."

She grinned and spun free of Brannis's loosened grasp, then leaped up into his arms and crushed him in a fierce embrace, the parchment still clutched in one hand. She squealed in delight, unable to contain her excitement.

Brannis was nearly bowled over but stumbled and managed to keep his footing. A shoulder under his chin was nearly choking him, but he managed to wrap his arms around her and support her weight, easing her to the ground once she had calmed down enough to relax her grip and let him go.

"Oh, Brannis, it will be wonderful. I can stop worrying now that some other girl will get you for a husband. I cannot wait for us to finish up and graduate. These next five winters will be an eternity!" Juliana gushed, staring up at Brannis with eyes that were seeing him as perhaps a bit more than he actually was. While she would graduate in four summers, Brannis was a year younger, so they would have to wait until both finished their studies.

"It is only four winters and two hundred nineteen days actually," Brannis said, grinning.

While he was less outwardly overcome with elation, he was still both relieved and overjoyed that Juliana was going to be his wife one day. Both of them had known from a young age that their marriages would be determined for them by the Imperial Circle's blood-readers, who oversaw the couplings of all the scions of the major bloodlines. The blood-readers had ensured the purity of Kadrin Empire's sorcerous houses for centuries, keeping the most promising blood intermixed. Despite his painfully slow development magically, the high sorcerer's prophecy kept Brannis's name high among the potential mates for young sorceresses. As granddaughter of the high sorcerer, Juliana Archon had been deemed a suitable match.

Houses Solaran and Archon had been crossed so many times that the rivalries that appeared on the surface never ran too deeply. While both were competitive and proud, the familial links were too numerous to allow for things to grow too contentious, and violence had thus been kept largely in check among the Imperial Circle for generations, as the two strongest houses allied themselves in all but name. Had either of them the patience to research their family histories, Brannis and Juliana could have figured that they were cousins some three generations removed.

"Well, anyway, these are going to be the longest four winters and however many days you just said of my life," Juliana replied, punctuated by an overly dramatic sigh.

She twirled away from Brannis's embrace, causing the green silk skirts of her dress to billow out in a spiral to keep up with her. While the Academy provided room, board, and clothing to all students, many of the wealthier ones still saw to their own wardrobes, especially among the girls. Juliana always preferred to adorn herself in the latest fashions, shunning the plain grey and black of the Academy's official wardrobe.

"Nothing wrong with that, you know. We have all the days we could ever hope for. Who says we should not enjoy them now?" Brannis said, smiling cockeyed at Juliana, challenging her feigned martyrdom.

Unlike his newly betrothed, Brannis wore nothing but the plain garments the Academy provided. He stood out in every other way, for better or worse, and did not wish to further separate himself by flaunting the Solarans' immense wealth. He was the best student in class in every subject that did not actually involve performing magic, and even at that, he was technically flawless, just lacking completely in native talent. He was also the largest boy his age, at least in height, and was always favored in the yard when the boys gathered to sport. More than one slight about his ineptitude with the aether had been repaid in bruises or a bloodied nose by "accident" in the Academy's courtyards.

"Why, Brannis ... are you suggesting you intend to court me?" Juliana asked in mock surprise.

In truth, she had been trying to get him to court her for quite some time and found his stubborn naiveté incongruous with his otherwise quick wit. It did not help matters that half the girls in their class made eyes at him and smiled whenever he looked their way, but unlike the rest of them, Juliana was not only serious but had reasonable grounds to believe she was entitled to him. Rumors had been circulating for at least two summers that she was aware of, regarding the two of them being matched. It made sense to her, what with them each being the youngest of one of the major bloodlines—her being the granddaughter of the high sorcerer and Brannis's father being in the Inner Circle.

"If you would rather I did not, we could always just wait until our wedding. No one would—"

"No, I never said that," Juliana interrupted, just a little too quickly to maintain her facade of aloofness.

Brannis's smile widened just a hair. "Very well, then, yes. I shall court you properly, starting tonight. Meet me at the stables after dinner," Brannis told her.

He had been fending Juliana off halfheartedly for what seemed like ages, waiting to find out whether she was going to be the one. He found it awkward talking to other girls, but Juliana was different. He had wanted to court her since his baser urges had started suggesting that such interests ought to be among his priorities, but he did not know how he would have handled it if he had been promised to another. Dinarah Gardarus seemed as likely a match for the blood-readers to make, and Brannis did not want to end up caught between her and Juliana if it came down to that. While Brannis had befriended nearly every boy his own age, he was not sure Juliana had any true friends. Instead she kept company with a small coven of rivals, each constantly vying to outdo the others. They were the highborn girls, all either from the major bloodlines or the wealthier lesser lines. Brannis preferred to keep well clear of them when they were all together, and wanted nothing to do with them fighting over him.

Brannis also suspected that long before dinner, Dinarah Gardarus would find herself someplace quiet and private to have a long, loud cry. For all that she did to his brain when she was there in front of him, Brannis was still aware of Juliana's faults. She could be downright cruel when she chose to be.

That night, Brannis and Juliana had ridden down to the pier at Solaran Estate. Brannis had been surprised how well she rode, since she seemed to spend much of her time at more idle pursuits. She had changed out of the green dress she wore earlier and had donned riding leathers, along with a white silk blouse covered by a black vest, along with a hooded traveling cloak. As ever, her reddish-gold hair was unbound, and it trailed behind her as they rode, occasionally getting in her face as the winds gusted; she seemed not to notice, or at least did not pay it any heed.

They took the long way to get there, skirting the pastures and grasslands of Solaran Estate's off-city side rather than taking the streets. They gave their borrowed horses rein to run and raced once they were safely away from the Academy and could afford to be less than stealthy.

They tied the horses near the pier, and Brannis took them out on one of the small rowboats his family kept for enjoying the peace of the lake, either for fishing or just enjoying the lake for its own sake. It was small and sturdy, ringed around the edge with tiny runes that would keep it from tipping far enough to be dangerous. And while many of Brannis's kin would have propelled it with magic, it was nonetheless kept equipped with a functioning set of oars, which Brannis put to their proper use.

As he rowed them out to Dragon's Eye Island, the little forested oasis at the center of Dragon Lake, he bid Juliana look in the satchel he had brought. Inside was a bottle of ice wine he had pilfered from the Academy's wine cellar, and a rolled-up woolen blanket that was wrapped around a pair of the fancy goblets that were kept aside for when the Academy was expecting important guests. Juliana looked up from inspecting the satchel's contents and smiled her approval. It was so quiet and peaceful out on the lake that they had hardly spoken a word since Brannis began to row. The rhythmic slosh of the oars as they entered and exited the water was the only sound.

The late-spring air was still warm, even as dusk set in and the stars came out as they made their way across the lake. The breeze carried only the faintest of chills that made Juliana huddle beneath the cloak she had worn. She might have worn something prettier than the riding gear she had chosen, but Brannis had told her to meet him by the stables. She had gathered that he was going to have them ride somewhere. It might not have been a masterwork of deduction, but it had still made him feel like she shared his thoughts.

As for his plans for the evening, he left her guessing at the details. He had read enough storybook romances to know that anticipation and mystery were all but essential. Little had he realized at the time, but Juliana had plans of her own, far more adventurous than his.

The maids that kept up Archon Estate were incorrigible gossips. Juliana's ladies' maids and the girl who cleaned the floor where her room was had taken a rather keen interest in her education while she was home from the Academy one winter. After comforting her through the confusion and worry following her first moonflow, they had taken her into their confidence as if she had just passed an initiation rite. No longer guarding their tongues in the presence of "young ears," Juliana had gained a courtesan's education by the time she arrived back at the Academy that springtime.

Brannis could see Juliana's breath come quick by the time they neared the island. With no oars to busy her hands, she fidgeted in her seat, some thought clearly occupying her brain. That night, she told Brannis that he was the kindest, bravest, all-around best boy—no, strike that, he was a man—she had ever met. The Inner Circle had seen fit to let her have him, but she would be flogged before she would wait nearly five winters to claim him.

* * * * * * * *

"What would you expect? Of course he agreed," Rashan answered. "It would only be prudent, in the aftermath of his father's death, to try to solidify his standing in the Circle. What could he possibly hope to gain by antagonizing me by refusing an offer of marriage to my son. The merits of the arrangement itself aside, he would be a fool not to leap at the opportunity to get in my good graces."

"But why Juliana Archon, of all the unwed girls in the Empire?" Brannis demanded.

He suspected that Rashan might be intentionally goading him. Somewhere in the recesses of his mind, Brannis knew he had slipped just past the line where rational arguments resided, and was now practicing a somewhat suspect alchemy of optimism and paranoia: *Maybe he just wants to see if I was still intending to follow through on our betrothal; maybe he was actually talking to Shador on my behalf and wanted to dangle Iridan's name in the way to tease me; maybe ... maybe ...*

"You overestimate the number of candidates, I think," Rashan replied, picking up a hefty volume from his desk and waving it in front of Brannis. "This book has records of all the eligible sorceresses in Kadrin—as well as many who have since been married off. There were perhaps three or four who might have been suitable, perhaps as many as six if I were willing to wait on girls who are still at the Academy. Juliana Archon has the best pedigree of any of them, though. You should be flattered Brannis; it was why you were matched with her yourself."

"How is that flattering, considering how it has turned out?" Brannis shot back. "If my 'pedigree' is so good, why should I not marry her? It was all approved, and I have never actually seen anything that says otherwise. Everyone just seems to have assumed it was all nullified when I left the Academy."

"Would you like me to make a proclamation, Brannis? Shall I gather the Inner Circle and make sure everyone sees that we have followed protocol? By the winds, Brannis! They did it to spare your dignity, and your family's. I have yet to unravel all the political nonsense the Inner Circle has engaged in, but I strongly suspect your father would have held up any new betrothal for Juliana Archon due to the embarrassment of having to admit you were deemed unsuitable.

"Now get hold of yourself, Brannis. Whatever this girl meant to you, it was nine winters ago and you need to put it past you. From everything Iridan has told me, you have no trouble finding women to share your bed, and why not? You have everything in your favor. Heroic young knight, just given command of the Imperial Army, good family, have the ear of the warlock. Take your pick of any woman in Kadrin and she would be yours. What nobleman would refuse you his daughter's hand? What commoner would not be swept off her feet? Find some foreign princess to wed, and secure allies for the Empire. Choose a sorceress from an emergent bloodline if you wish; I assure you her family would be ecstatic to mix with Solaran blood, hoping your talent merely skipped a generation. But the ones in this book ..." Rashan shook the genealogist's tome for emphasis. "... are not for you.

"Kadrin has kept itself strong for thousands of summers by maintaining the strength of the Imperial Circle. I cannot allow the best of our young blood to be diluted. Strength begets strength. If I looked back through enough of these books, I could trace my own lineage back past the Founding."

"I could do the same," Brannis said. "A few generations back, it is even the same ancestors."

"Brannis, there are a thousand others you can have, and a paltry handful denied to you. Why must you insist on being difficult? Do you wish to know why?" Rashan set down the book he had been holding and took another like it from the desk. He flipped through it to the last portion that had been filled in— leaving numerous blank pages in the yet unfinished volume—and flipped back a few pages. "Here. This is your reason."

The entry stood out immediately: *"Brannis Solaran. (F) Maruk Solaran, (M) Lyphaela Solaran (Sharniss),"* the whole of which had been crossed out with a double line, accompanied by a notation in a different handwriting— *"UNSUITABLE."* Brannis felt a chill in his gut and suddenly felt not quite well. He had known his status among the Circle had changed completely when he left the Academy, but somehow he had never fully accepted that he was forever cut out of their plans for the continuation of the bloodlines. The finality of those two thin lines passing through his name was like an iron door slamming shut and blocking off that part of his past.

Neither Brannis nor Rashan spoke for what seemed like hours, as Brannis stared numbly at the birthing records. He saw the names that shared the page with his; he recognized them all. They were his classmates, his friends, the girls he had once flirted with and the boys he had wrestled in the Academy's courtyards. In the eyes of the Circle, they were valuable to the Empire, and he no longer was. What he had turned out to be, they had no use for and wanted no more of.

Rashan finally reached over and closed the book. "Now go prepare for your departure. Expect to leave in the morning. I have many preparations to make, not the least of which is selecting sorcerers to accompany you. Be at the palace at sunset for a late dinner, and I will gather everyone involved to discuss our plans. I would suggest you find a room at the palace for the night as well, so that you might leave as early as possible. The steward will be expecting you and ought to be able to manage something for you as for accommodations."

"Why send sorcerers? Raynesdark will have a few of their own that can handle reinforcing wards and preparing fortifications. I would expect that in battle, any other sorcerers would be as much a hindrance to you as they would be an asset."

"Because I do not intend to accompany you. If I meant to lead every battle for the Empire, I would have little need of you, Brannis. Because I have you, I feel I can trust that the battle will be well conducted without requiring my presence. In the meantime, I have much to do in getting the Empire back under control. I doubt what is said to my face bears much similarity to what they say behind warded doors. I will spend my time unraveling the knotted tangle of lies that obscures Kadrin politics these days.

"In truth, I think I would much enjoy the slaughter I am sending you off to commit in my place. If there were another who could run the Empire without causing further chaos, I would not hesitate to go. What I have done is bad enough, though, without handing the reins of the Circle and the regency over to yet another usurper."

"Very well, then. I shall be at the army headquarters much of the day, learning what I can of Raynesdark's defenses before departing," Brannis said.

* * * * * * * *

As it turned out, Brannis's offices at the army headquarters were neither in the stables nor the wine cellar. They had in fact given him a spacious suite with its own sitting room and a view overlooking Kalak Square. It was large enough to meet with half the senior officers stationed in Kadris at once, with a large oaken table upon which maps could be laid out, surrounded by high-backed chairs. There was a wide, polished oak desk over one hundred summers old that allowed its occupant to sit with his back to the panoramic view of not only the square but much of the city as well. Being on the uppermost floor of the building, it was high enough to see the palace over the surrounding buildings.

Brannis had taken advantage of the planning table to gather all the maps he could find regarding Raynesdark—or rather, that he could have underlings find and bring to him. Brannis was still growing used to the idea that he could give orders to literally anyone in the Imperial Army. He suspected that it would be some time before anyone quite respected him in his new position, but for the time being, the backing of the warlock was all the authority he needed. No one was yet certain just how Rashan intended to oversee the affairs of the army, or how much involvement he would have. Giving command over to a young knight of his own blood was—in their view at least—merely the first of many changes to come. The reputation of Rashan the Conqueror had never been connected with long periods of peace.

Rashan's maps were several winters old, but Brannis worried little that the place had changed. Raynesdark had been built in the Empire's younger days, when gold had been found in the Cloud Wall Mountains. Once the mines opened, the wealth it produced for the Empire allowed—and demanded—the construction of impressive fortifications. To the north side of the city, there had been a quarry since ages long past, providing massive stone blocks that constituted the city's streets, walls, and fortresses. Smaller stones blocks were also produced, which were used in the construction of most of the city's buildings.

As Raynesdark had once been a key to the Empire's prosperity, the army had extensive diagrams of its defenses. Every tower, the keep, and the entirety of the fortress was mapped out in admirable detail. Brannis was torn as to whether he should have someone make copies for him but decided that there was just not enough time for someone to do a thorough job of it. He satisfied himself with going over them all himself and committing them to his formidable memory. Unless they had fallen into disarray in Raynesdark, he could reference their own records once he arrived, should he need to check any details.

Brannis had been going over the layout of the upper mines—once the lifeblood of the empire's gold—when a junior officer interrupted him with a knock at the door and entered quietly.

"Sir Brannis. You had mentioned a dinner engagement at the palace tonight," the officer said.

Brannis looked out the window of his new office and saw that the sun was sinking low in the sky. The light had waned on him so gradually that he had not noticed.

"Thank you, Lieutenant. Dismissed," Brannis replied.

He left the diagrams and maps scattered about the table for his new underlings to deal with and made haste for the palace.

* * * * * * * *

Brannis arrived late for the dinner that Rashan had arranged. As the steward escorted him into the grand dining hall of the palace, he could see the other guests that Warlock Rashan had invited. Brannis had expected to see Iridan there and was not disappointed. He was impressed with the new uniform that had been fashioned on such short notice; it was nearly a copy of Rashan's own, though Brannis suspected that the materials were far less exotic, and the epaulettes attached to his cloak were of shining steel, rather than gold. It was clear that Rashan intended to follow through with his stated goal of making Iridan into a warlock as well.

Iridan sat just to the right of Rashan, who was seated just to the right of the vacant head of the table. The emperor's place setting was empty, likely to show that Rashan was merely regent and had no designs on the crown. The rest of the guests consisted of the remaining members of the Inner Circle, a small number of sorcerers he had not met: Lord Gellard Hallimere and his lady wife Chandelle, old Duke Benklear, and Shador Archon and his daughter, Juliana.

Brannis was fortunate that the palace's formal dining hall could seat hundreds for a feast, and that the single long table set out seemed lost in the large room. It therefore took long enough for a porter to escort Brannis to the table that he was able to compose himself after the surprise of seeing Juliana. Had he been of a mind to try predicting the guest list, he might have seen the logic behind most of the guests seated around the table, but he had been rather preoccupied with military planning on his journey from the army's headquarters to the palace.

The seat to the left of the vacant setting for the emperor was empty as well, and that was the seat to which the young porter brought Brannis. He was to be seated just two seats from Juliana, with only her father between them. As Brannis approached the table, conversations halted.

"And here he is, our new grand marshal. Brannis, I was just explaining to Duke Benklear why you will be taking over command of the army," Rashan called out loudly enough for the whole table to hear as Brannis was being seated.

"I am not in favor of it, young sir," Duke Benklear informed Brannis from halfway down the table.

Duke Benklear would tell anyone who cared to listen that he had seen over seventy-four autumns and that anyone who did not wish to hear his opinions could just wait until he died, at which point he promised to hold his tongue. The Benklears owned much of the land surrounding Kadris, and a fair amount of the city itself. Other than the palace itself, very little of the Empire belonged solely to the crown.

"Sir Hurald has done just fine, I think," Benklear said. "Comes from as good a family as you will find among the commoners."

"Your Grace," Rashan said, "you will find that Sir Brannis has one of the finest military minds. Sir Hurald may be a fine administrator, but I do not think he will do as well by our troops in the field as Brannis would."

"I must admit, it seemed a bit rash to me, as well," Dolvaen said.

Brannis thought that it was a good sign that at least someone in the Inner Circle was willing to voice a dissenting view—even if it was in argument against his new position.

"Agreed," added Lord Hallimere. "He has little experience. A few summers fighting on the northeast borders to keep back the ogre incursions, then a small scouting command that could not be called entirely successful."

Lord Hallimere was technically Lord of Kadris. All functions of governing the city—those that the emperor did not wish to deal with personally—fell within his purview. While his personal holdings in the city were still considerable, House Benklear had a greater share of the city than the Hallimeres. Neither, however, held title to as much of the city as the Solarans. Between the Solarans, Archons, Gardaruses, Benklears, and Hallimeres, nearly all the land in the city was accounted for, and all others were their tenants.

"I have an eye for such things," Rashan said. "I see more than you do, looking at the same events. I watch him think and plan, I have matched wits with him and lost. I have conquered kingdoms and advised emperors, and I have more blood on my hands than any of you have seen in a lifetime. I am an expert on the subject of war, and I tell you that I prefer Sir Brannis to lead my armies."

Brannis could see the effect his words had all along the table. Except for Iridan, these people had not ridden with Rashan, not talked with him at any length. To them, he was history come to life—an ancient, mad demigod of war. He sounded so sure when he spoke, brooking no argument and citing experience at war that he knew none could call into question. Certainly the wisdom of his conquests could be rightly debated—and had been for a hundred winters—but the fact of them was indisputable.

"So then, tell us of this new threat from goblins to the west," Shador said, seeming to be not entirely concerned with the affairs of the army.

"The expedition to Kelvie uncovered the incursion of goblin forces to our western territories," Rashan said. "Word was sent to the Circle, but went unheeded, and now we have word that Illard's Glen has fallen. We believe that they intend to press onward to Raynesdark with the intent to conquer and hold it. Should they succeed, they will be difficult to dislodge, as Raynesdark is built quite well for defense."

"Would that not mean that the goblins will have difficulty attacking it in the first place?" Lord Hallimere asked, and there was a general muttering of agreement with his logic. "Certainly we ought to know how to defend it better than they would."

"That might be the case, but we know that the goblins are no fools," Brannis said. "They know better than to throw their forces at defenses that they cannot penetrate. We have reports that they have created new siege engines and tested them on the walls of Illard's Glen, a town they could easily have taken anyway. Instead they crushed the wall into gravel just to see if they could. Raynesdark will face the same threat soon enough." Brannis hoped he sounded as smart as Rashan made him out to be.

"What makes you certain that they are intent on Raynesdark?" asked Duke Benklear. The scrawny, bald old nobleman sat back and awaited an answer with folded arms.

"We have examined all the possible motives for the goblin campaign against us and concluded that they are intent on the Raynesdark mines," Rashan answered. "I will not bore you with the details of our deliberations, but suffice it that we find no logical reason for them to take Illard's Glen and nothing more, and had they intended to strike us farther south, the delay to take Illard's Glen would have been pointless."

"So what then? You mentioned having a plan," Shador asked. "I am not normally privy to war council. Tell me why we are here tonight."

"Well, firstly, I had wished to congratulate you and formally announce the betrothal of my son to your daughter." There were looks of surprise around the table, but no one spoke out. "Iridan." Rashan motioned for him to stand, and the new member of the Inner Circle got up from his chair, resplendent in his black warlock's robes. "Juliana." He motioned to the young sorceress and she complied. She was wearing the plainer black robes befitting her position in the Sixth Circle, cinched tightly around her slender waist.

She looked much the same as Brannis remembered her, though he had avoided seeing her the past few summers. She still had the same long reddish-gold hair, and her figure seemed to have never fully finished filling out. The fire he was used to seeing in her eyes seemed muted, and she looked a bit self-conscious with the attention of the rest of the attendees on her. She looked around a bit as she stood there, and when she turned to look his way, Brannis quickly averted his gaze to avoid making eye contact with her. In doing so, he happened to notice that Iridan looked a bit nervous with the attention as well.

"We are in no rush," Rashan said. "There will be time for festivities come springtime, with better omens for a marriage. We shall toast a renewed alliance between House Solaran and House Archon."

And with that, everyone at the table stood and raised their wine goblets. There was a general chorus of agreement with the sentiment, though Brannis thought he could make out some sarcastic comment from Lord Hallimere about how little support House Solaran seemed to need these days.

After the toast, they all resumed their seats, with the soon-to-be couple looking relieved to rejoin the rest of the diners.

"And now to the more pressing business," Rashan said. "I feel that we need to dispatch aid to Raynesdark in advance of the expected invasion. I have heard two sentiments tonight that I have agreed with. The first is that Raynesdark ought to be able to hold out, as the city's defenses are indeed formidable. The second is that goblins are clever little vermin and know better than to attack with no plan to overcome those defenses.

"Since the city ought to be able to defend itself, and the goblins clearly have thought of some clever way to change that, I am sending Grand Marshal Brannis over there to match wits with them and counter whatever gambit they intend."

"You really think that sending this boy over there is going to change the course of a battle?" asked Duke Benklear. "If so, I think you are daft. I know Duke Pellaton, and if some unscarred little knight shows up at his castle gates demanding to take over command of his army, he shall have him in chains. I would do the same if I had a goblin army camped in my back garden and some fool came around trying to give me orders."

"In that case, I expect you will approve of my decision to send along a few of the Circle to lend him aid. There will be no confusion over who is in command. Iridan will be going as well. He has experience in battle, and I have given him some advice that ought to help him as well." Rashan paused, as if awaiting objections, then continued when there were none: "I am also sending Ruuglor Megaren, Second Circle, and Faolen Sarmon, Fourth Circle. They have both proven themselves to be competent and have accepted this assignment voluntarily."

Two of the sorcerers Brannis had never met nodded in acknowledgment, making it apparent that they were Ruuglor and Faolen, though he could not gather which was which.

"Lastly, Juliana Archon will be going as well."

The last comment provoked a reaction from Shador Archon, who immediately bolted up to his feet.

"You cannot just send a girl into a war! She is only Sixth Circle and you just arranged her to your own son. You may have aspirations of turning Iridan into a warlock, but Juliana is no warrior," Shador said. "What game are you playing at? Are you trying to get her killed?"

"Relax yourself, Shador. I have no thought as to how long the siege of Raynesdark may last. I had just thought that it would be good for Iridan and Juliana to spend time together, and Iridan will certainly not be staying behind. When the fighting starts, I would expect her to keep out of the fray, along with Sorcerers Ruuglor and Faolen, I might add. Only Iridan would I expect to actually engage the enemy," Rashan said. "And besides, I believe that a man fighting to protect his lady love will always fight to the best of his ability."

The conversation went on for a while longer, but that was the last of it that really sank into Brannis's mind. The lords and sorcerers may have missed his intent, but Brannis had heard it as clearly as if he had spoken it aloud. It was not Iridan that Rashan was looking to goad into excellence, but Brannis himself.

* * * * * * * *

After the dinner was over, one of the palace porters brought Brannis to a room they had made ready for him. The palace was replete with guest rooms, prepared to entertain personages from all over the world, from kings to emperors, lords to merchant princes, and occasionally even Kadrin nobility when they came from outside the city.

Brannis stopped in the room just long enough to allow the dinner guests to go their various ways. Once he felt it was relatively safe to go about without answering a lot of questions, he headed across the palace and to the Tower of Contemplation.

The guards on duty that night were not Tod and Jodoul, but they let Brannis into the library anyway. After all, short of Rashan himself, Brannis seemed to be in charge of everyone, as far as most folk could tell.

An hour later, when Brannis left with a pack that was suspiciously much fuller than when he arrived, the guards said nothing. There were rules about taking books from the library—namely, that no one was to take books from the library—but Brannis was willing to ignore rules until such time as he heard from Rashan that they applied to him. Anyone else was going to have to take it up with the warlock if they did not agree with what he did.

Inside the pack were three volumes: *Basic Wards*, which seemed to have a good overview of the simpler warding spells; *Hellfire's Song*, a whimsically entitled book that nonetheless contained details on a number of battle magics that Brannis thought might be good to know; and *The Way of the Wind*, which discussed at length weather and wind patterns, both from an academic as well as magical view.

Brannis had nearly taken *Magic at Sea: The Tides of Aether and Water*, but had no idea how to justify having it if someone found it. He promised himself to look into it later, upon his return. Kyrus would just have to get by without nautical magic for a while.

Chapter 25 - Sorcerer Ahoy

Kyrus was relieved to find the chair still in place upon his awakening. He had jammed it against the door before going to bed, worried that some superstitious man among the crew might decide he felt safer with no "witch" aboard ship. The gentle swaying of the cabin reminded Kyrus that they were at sea—still in the Katamic, unless he had slept for days. The cabin had no window, and the only light came from the soft blue glow that Kyrus had left there the previous night.

He was surprised how well rested he felt. He had feared that he would not sleep at all, given the motion of the ship and the worry about his safety. After bracing the door, he had curled up on the cabin's lone bunk, which he knew to be a luxury aboard ship, and let his vision drift into the aether. He had never tried it before, but he found that he could watch Sources even through the wooden planks of the ship. It was fascinating—and a bit eerie—being able to see through walls, if only in a limited fashion, but it let him keep track of where the other men on the ship were, and reassure him that they were not gathering outside his door.

However, fascination and falling asleep rarely could cohabitate in the same mind. While Kyrus intended to watch the door for signs of attack, he fell in to watching the habits of his new shipmates. He heard voices and connected them to the distinct look of each Source, and tried to catch names and add those to his collection as well. He was also disconcerted when he noted that he could even see through the floor below him and grew irrationally nervous when he saw men milling about belowdecks under his cabin. He was not yet familiar with the layout of the ship, but he supposed that he was above one of the holds. The men had not congregated below him, just poked around a bit, and he saw a larger group of them lying farther down the lower deck, which he gathered was the crew's quarters.

Shortly after confirming that his impromptu door lock was secure, Kyrus let his vision back into the aether to check the environs outside his quarters. He could hear them at work out on deck, and his aether-vision confirmed that nearly the whole crew was above deck, with a few going to and from the hold. There were in fact a great many more men than he had remembered from the previous night. He resolved to look into it once he had a chance to look around the cabin more thoroughly.

He had been preoccupied with his safety at first and later with the goings-on aboard ship, and had not taken inventory of his new abode. For better or worse, for the time being, he was a pirate, and he had lost all his Acardian possessions save the clothes he wore and the Expert's Medallion that still hung around his neck—thankfully they had not seen fit to relieve him of it at the Scar Harbor jail. Whatever he had in his cabin would become his, temporarily at least. Blinking back into normal light vision, he reconnoitered the room.

The whole of the cabin was done in dark-stained wood, polished to a shine where it had not worn. The single bunk was of a simple design, with little ornament aside from round knobs at the footer. It had heavy blankets, feather pillows, and was quite comfortable for shipboard accommodations. There was a small writing desk, permanently attached to the wall, whose chair Kyrus had used to bar the door. A lantern hung from the ceiling in the middle of the room and was low enough that Kyrus would have to watch his head lest he injure himself on it. He considered removing it, as he would be quite content to use magic to light his room, but he would have time to redecorate later.

The most interesting furnishing in the cabin though was the footlocker. Made of oak and reinforced with iron bands and hardware, it had a formidable look to it. Unlike the rest of the cabin, it showed its age in the smooth-worn areas where a hand would reach to open or close it, and bore scratches and nicks in keeping with a chest that had traveled with its owner for years before coming aboard the *Harbinger*. Kyrus tried to open the lid and found it locked. He took some time to search the room—under the bed, in all the desk drawers, looking for compartments in the lantern—but could find no key. Likely it had been left in Acardia with its owner.

Kyrus studied the lock. He knew very little about locks but was not above learning. He picked up a letter opener he found in the desk and jammed it into the keyhole and wiggled it around a bit, managing nothing aside from marring the edge of the opener. A few minutes of frustration later, he simply repeated the spell that had sprung him from his jail cell:

"Kohtho ilextiumane veeru," he chanted softly and made sure to keep his fingers safely apart.

At first, he merely warmed the lock, but slowly he brought his fingers closer together, and watched as the metal began to glow. Then with a quick burst of aether, he pressed his fingers together, creating a white-hot flash just before his fingers touched. Quickly he reached out and pulled the lid open, keeping his fingers well away from the lock. A whiff of smoke rose from the ruined lock, causing Kyrus to cough and turn his head away. He had managed to keep the wood from catching fire, though, and that was all he had hoped for.

Inside the chest, he found clothing and personal effects. There were Acardian Navy uniforms, a heavy jacket, a pair of worn shoes, a sterling silver tankard, a shaving kit, a dagger with a carved ivory handle, a coffer that was heavy with coins, and a collection of exotic jewelry. Kyrus was careful not to confuse "exotic" with "valuable," as the jewelry consisted of stuff Kyrus would not have given a second look in the markets. There was a shark-tooth necklace, with the teeth polished and dulled enough to not endanger the wearer; a bracelet of carved wood, made to look like it was woven; a belt buckle of hammered tin that showed the insignia of some Takalish distillery; and a ring set with amber that contained a tiny spider.

Kyrus opened the coffer and counted over twelve hundred eckles. It was a tidy sum, hardly enough to retire on but certainly enough for a contingency in case he needed it. Kyrus put the coffer away and took up the shaving kit. There was a small cup and brush, some soap, a razor, a leather strap, and a small mirror with a loop at one end. He looked about and found a hook on one wall, and hung the mirror.

Kyrus had looked better. He was bruised and battered. He had not shaved in days, and he needed to comb his hair. He quickly rechecked the footlocker for a comb, but found nothing. He decided that in all likelihood the former occupant had been bald, or at least kept his head clean shaven. Kyrus angled the mirror a bit to look himself over. His clothes were torn and filthy, and he decided that he would need to find clothes somewhere on the ship that would fit him. His Expert's Medallion was intact and still around his neck, which he was oddly thankful for. There were to be few enough ties to his life in Acardia, and that was one he had at least managed to keep with him.

He took the medallion and examined it, looking over all the curves and lines, remembering the night he had gotten it. It had not been so long ago, less than a month even. Back then, Davin had been around, and Kyrus had little to worry about beyond finishing his day's work. He had little in the way of responsibilities and had spent his free time reading and playing chess with Davin. All the excitement he could crave, he lived out in his dream world, which seemed at the time to be a sensible alternative to risking his own life with a sword and armor.

Since he had received the medallion, Davin had left for Golis to work for the king, and he had taken over the business. He had first discovered that the magic he saw in his dreams really worked, and realized that the knight he saw in his dreams saw Kyrus in his own. And most importantly, he had met Abbiley, a girl he had admired from afar for years yet never worked up the courage to approach. His time with Abbiley had been the best of his life, and he regretted not having approached her sooner. He had not realized back then that he would have so little time with her before the strange turn his life had just taken would separate them. He had seen her just yesterday, yet he was heading the opposite direction with no clear plan to get back to her. He was missing her badly already.

Kyrus was all ready to wash up and make himself presentable when he realized he had no water. He sat down on the edge of the bed to consider that peculiar conundrum. The ship was surrounded by water, but Kyrus had lived by the sea long enough to know better than to expect to drink or wash with seawater. Having to store any freshwater they would use probably meant that the pirates were not likely to use much of it for washing. Kyrus was going to be in the same boat with them, both literally and figuratively.

He went through the clothes in the footlocker and laid them out on the bed. He tried on various articles and found that at the very least, the loose-fitting tunics that the navy wore for working on deck were forgiving of size differences. The previous owner was shorter and stouter than Kyrus, but the billowing garment covered him well enough. While the sleeves were not long enough, the top covered his torso—though would not tuck in as a good navy officer would wear it—and with the sleeves rolled up to his elbows, it did not look so ridiculous as it hung loosely from his shoulders.

Kyrus checked the mirror again. He looked like a lost little boy who had been dressed in someone else's clothing. Slipping back to aether-vision, he saw the dozens of men outside, each one a killer, and wondered how long a lost little boy might last among them. Shifting back to seeing in the light, Kyrus had an idea.

He dug out the strange jewelry from the locker and put on the necklace, the bracelet, and the ring. He looked in the mirror and decided that the bracelet looked silly on him, and removed it. The shark-tooth necklace and spider ring looked just primitive enough that it might give second thoughts about his mystical powers.

Kyrus also snuffed out the blue light in the room. It was easy on his eyes as he worked, but it was too calming and serene for the effect he wanted. Quickly casting the light spell again, he set the color to a deep, ominous red, the kind of light you saw looking through the grating of a wood stove, or in a blacksmith's forge.

While the pretense he was creating stood to give pause to those who might take advantage of the scrawny scrivener aboard, Kyrus had one real protection to add. He took the quill and ink that came with the desk and began drawing on the inside of the door. Brannis had done more in his time in the library than just select books to take along; he had read up on the proper runes for creating a warded door. Kyrus had never created a ward before but had practiced a bit with the rune language, and his hand was steady for the kind of work that was required.

When he finished drawing on the door, he inspected his work, and it looked just as he remembered it from his dream. Knowing that it would not last even the day as ink, Kyrus began tracing over the ink with the letter opener, carving the runes into the wood of the door. It took hours of work, but when he was finished, he energized the runes with aether and threw his weight against the door. By physical means, he could not budge the door at all.

Releasing the ward, Kyrus finally allowed himself out on deck.

* * * * * * * *

Despite his initial apprehensions, Kyrus found himself enjoying his time out on deck. He was still unused to the swaying of the ship at sea but had not actually fallen down yet trying to walk.

The noise and extra Sources he saw were from the ship they had tethered themselves to. After asking around, he found that it was the *Nyurissa*, Stalyart's former trade ship. They were taking on additional supplies and had picked up a handful of additional crewmen. They were transferring aboard all the things

Stalyart had prepared and trading in many of the belongings and supplies from the navy's crew.

Kyrus had made many friends among the men when he had seen them struggling to load crates of rum with the ship's primitive crane. He had sent men scrambling in every direction when he had grabbed the load with telekinesis and easily completed the task for them. Once they had departed and raised the sails, Kyrus had filled them with a strong wind to get them under way.

"Stand by us, Mr. Hinterdale, and you will always have a welcome on this ship," Captain Zayne had told him.

The old pirate had seemed ecstatic to have the services of a true sorcerer aboard, even if he was a bit green—both in the lack of experience and his slight discomfort with sea travel.

Kyrus had spent much of the day making the acquaintance of the rest of the crew. They seemed unscrupulous to a man, and while many seemed eager to endear themselves to the one who could lift their loads and fill their sails, Kyrus was sure that several were uncomfortable having a sorcerer on the ship. There was something in their eyes when he spoke to them; the pirates seemed bold enough by and large, but the ones who could not meet his gaze unnerved him. He supposed that it was partly the bizarre accoutrements he had outfitted himself with, but mostly that he was outside of their realm of knowledge. Of all the crew, the only ones who seemed comfortable around him were Captain Zayne and First Mate Stalyart.

The men themselves had a motley feel to them. They were of all nations and kingdoms, mostly lowborn, but a few had been well bred but disgraced. He lumped both Denrik and Stalyart into the latter category, though he knew not the history of either man. The captain was clearly a well-educated man by his diction, and Stalyart seemed too keen to have gotten all his learning from the docks and alleys.

"Now, what many of you have waited long for," Stalyart called out in the early evening hours, drawing men from all over the ship to the area of the main mast. "This is our first haul. While we did not take the *Nyurissa* in battle, we nevertheless had much gold to bring aboard. This was gold once won by Captain Zayne, and is now his reward to all of you for bringing him a new ship."

As men gathered about, they could see that he had his foot on a strongbox and held a black-bound ledger in his one hand and a quill in the other. One of the men Kyrus had not met opened the strongbox, and those gathered nearest gasped and immediately began to press forward.

"Stay back, you dogs!" shouted Captain Zayne from the quarterdeck, where he was overseeing the disbursal of funds. "You shall each get your share, and no more. See these railings?" He pointed around the perimeter of the ship. "This is the border of our little kingdom here, and within this kingdom there is no stealing. Out there ..." He gestured vaguely beyond the ship to the world at large. "... all is for the taking, but here we are brothers. If any of you smart fellows thinks that your brothers back on land might steal from you, let me just assure you that I do not take kindly to bad blood aboard my ship. When we fight, when we plunder, we need to know that there is no knife at our back. When one prospers, we all do. When one fights, we all do. Theft from one of us is theft from all. Gods willing, there will be loot enough for us all to retire like kings.

"Now, all of you, hang back and wait for Mr. Stalyart to call your name, then collect your share. There is a share for each of you, a share and a half for Mr. Stalyart, Mr. Crispin, and Mr. Holyoake, and two full shares for Mr. Hinterdale and for myself," Captain Zayne said.

With that, the crowd gathered themselves into something just shy of a mob, and waited their turn like hungry jackals, rather than rabid ones. Kyrus hung well back and waited for the crush to die down before bothering to approach Stalyart. He leaned against the forecastle and watched as men slunk off to the crew quarters with handfuls of trade bars of gold. Each roughly the size of a man's finger and square cut, trade bars were used for buying ships and land, or for negotiating ransoms. Few of the crew had ever held one, and most did not know their exact worth, just that it was a lot more than the same weight in eckle coins. Kyrus had a better guess than most, but not by a lot. He figured that each was roughly three thousand eckles, and that most of the crew had just gotten more than a year's wages worth of legitimate work.

When Kyrus's name was finally called, at the end, he received a share of sixteen bars from the nearly empty strongbox. He had been mildly surprised that Captain Zayne had seen fit to give Kyrus a share equal to his own, but he supposed it made sense. If Kyrus used his skill at magic to good effect, he was worth any ten men of the crew. It was a bargain price for what he gave in return. Kyrus was just grateful that it clearly showed the captain's support in front of the entire crew. Few enough men would be brave enough to risk crossing Kyrus the Sorcerer, but hopefully none were foolish enough to anger Captain Zayne, Scourge of the Katamic Sea.

That evening, Kyrus was invited to the captain's quarters, along with the ship's newly appointed officers. Kyrus arrived promptly when informed by one of the crew, a young man named Stevin, that there was to be a dinner in celebration of their ship's "liberation" from the Acardians. He was struck immediately by how much larger and more luxurious the captain's cabin was. Despite their equal share of the loot, there was no mistaking that the real power was centered here.

The cabin was appointed in dark-stained and polished wood, much like the one Kyrus had claimed, but there was a large window at the rear looking out the stern of the ship, and two smaller, round windows in each of the port and starboard sides. The captain had a bed easily twice the size of Kyrus's own, set to the starboard side of the room, and to the port side, situated between the windows, a locked liquor cabinet. The center of the room was dominated by a large table and chairs with a wrought-iron chandelier suspended above it by sturdy iron chains. The periphery of the room had bookshelves, a smaller table with a map and charts, and there was a globe, something that Kyrus had never seen except in the anteroom of the Society of Learned Men. Whereas his own cabin had been plain yet sturdy, this cabin was decorated with scrollwork and carvings befitting a nobleman's parlor.

Captain Zayne was already seated and waiting, and Kyrus was the first to arrive.

"Welcome," he bid Kyrus, "come in and make yourself comfortable. I am in excellent spirits today. The finest wine I was able to dig up aboard this ship is yours to enjoy tonight, along with the rest of the officers, once they arrive. Of course," he added, "the rest will be along a bit later. I asked Stevin to fetch you first, as I wished to speak to you privately, without everyone else around."

"About what, sir?" Kyrus asked.

He remembered to add the "sir" at the end, which was going to take some getting used to. Kyrus had some idea of what the captain wanted to discuss, but he was willing to play dumb long enough to find out what Captain Zayne already knew.

"I think you know, so I will be blunt. Who are you, Mr. Hinterdale?" Denrik asked.

Leaning forward in his chair and resting his chin on his clasped hands, he looked Kyrus square in the eye, and Kyrus could not help but avert his gaze under the scrutiny.

"Until recently, just a scrivener like any other. Perhaps I was unusually talented, if I do say so, but—"

"No, that is not what I meant, and I believe you know that. Mr. Hinterdale, I am neither a fool nor a man to be trifled with. I find it impossible to believe that you learned the rudiments in a book somewhere. From what I have heard of your trial, there was no such volume found despite a rather extensive search of your shop. So allow me to rephrase this question: who *else* are you?" Denrik added, and Kyrus knew what he meant.

Kyrus was not prepared to trust Captain Zayne with the truth. He feared that anything he let on may find its way to the wrong ears in Brannis's world, so he thought fast and tried to come up with an alternate identity.

"In Veydrus," Kyrus said, "I am a highwayman. I work by way of the north road out of Pevett, in the Kadrin Empire, and have a hideaway not a half-day's ride from the road. I work with a crew of five others, and the most recent to join us was a sorcerer who had fallen out of favor with Lord Whitestag and left his employ—I did not ask the cause of his disfavor or the terms of his departure. I have been studying his spells and watching him use them. My learning has thus been rather haphazard."

"Kadrin, are you? Filthy bastards, the lot of them." Denrik sneered. "I had rather hoped you were not one of them, but you have the look, now that I consider it."

"I could not agree more, Captain. I make my living robbing trade caravans, and I see that lot at their worst. I spare most of them—bad business leaving a lot of bodies—but I do not regret when they choose valor over poverty and end up on the end of my blade," Kyrus said.

"A swordsman, eh? Show me," Denrik said.

Still seated, he drew the cutlass sheathed at his hip and handed it across the table to Kyrus.

"Forgive me not being in practice in this world. These muscles will probably not do my skills justice," Kyrus said and then took a few practice swipes around the cabin.

He briefly considered how easy it would be to run the captain through and wondered why he let himself sit at such a disadvantage. The blade felt heavy and awkward in his hands, far more so that Brannis's sword usually felt, but he was fairly certain he could defeat an unarmed pirate of middling years.

The answer struck him of course: *I could try to run him through, of course, but that would hardly be the easiest way to kill him. I could light Denrik Zayne ablaze with hardly an effort from this range, and he knows it.* The pirate captain was brave enough just to be in the room alone with Kyrus, weapon or no weapon.

"You seem a bit scrawny in the arm to be waving that thing around, but I can see that you know how to use it, even if you could not outduel a single man on this ship," Denrik said. "Hand it back here before you break something."

Kyrus dutifully returned the weapon to its owner, and the captain sheathed it once again.

"So you are a highwayman, you say ..." Denrik left the question unfinished, and Kyrus was unsure what answer he was looking for.

"Yes, and what are you, or should I ask ... who?" Kyrus countered.

"In Veydrus, I am a sorcerer, and a powerful one. Here, I can barely draw enough to light a candle, but in Megrenn, I am respected and powerful. I know plenty of magic and was properly schooled, even though I can hardly get much use out of it here, despite the bounty of aether that abounds. I could teach you. My price is service aboard my ship, and that you do not go around acting like a Kadrin," Denrik said.

"Acting like a Kadrin? What do you mean by that?" Kyrus asked, genuinely confused.

He had already started doing the figuring in his head: *Megrenn claimed its independence from Kadrin roughly twenty-one winters—years—ago, and the war ended twenty ago. Denrik must be at least in his middle forties now. He was probably educated at the Academy and very likely fought for Megrenn in the war.*

Kyrus wondered for the first time if he might be able to return the favor Brannis had done him in teaching him magic. Maybe he could find a way to act as a spy for Kadrin. Megrenn outriders had taken High Pass, and it was likely that they were somehow involved in the current goblin problem. Megrenn had always been one for making odd alliances.

"For starters," Denrik said, "resist the urge to conquer anyplace we dock. It may be hard, since it runs deep in the blood, but I insist. I extend this to my ship as well; I will not have you fighting me for command. Also, there must be no talking of Veydrus— or anything at all from the other world for that matter—when any besides myself or Mr. Stalyart are present. He and I are the only ones who know of the other world, and like as not, we are the only two who are not afraid of you just for practicing magic."

"Stalyart? The first mate knows, too?" Kyrus asked.

"Aye, met him during the Freedom War on the other side. He is a trader and scoundrel in both worlds. You would swear you had met the same man if you saw him there. He cannot work a lick of magic in either world, near as I can tell, though he is enough of a Crackle player that I could not say for certain. He used to supply Megrenn with stripe-cats and monohorns for our cavalry, after the Kadrin occupation had left us with so little to defend ourselves. You Kadrins were never much as sailors, and he ran your patrol lines with ease. Tellurak is more developed nautically, and I suspect he used tricks he picked up around here to help him smuggle," Denrik said.

"Are there any others. I mean, not just on the ship? I suspected when you called me a sorcerer that you knew something, but that was the first I had heard of anyone with knowledge of the other world. And I assume that you *know* it is another world, correct? Is it possible that it is just another part of this one?" Kyrus asked.

"No, I think not. Tellurak is a vast place, but between myself and Stalyart, we have seen the mammoth's share of it, with nothing hinting that it overlaps Veydrus at all. Stalyart and I have made quite a career of sharing information between worlds. When you pay close attention, you will find things that you can exploit, one world to the other," Denrik said.

"Such as?" Kyrus pressed, taking a mouthful of the excellent wine Captain Zayne had provided.

"Well, cannons for one," Denrik said, and Kyrus nearly choked on his wine. "And even though I do not have the draw you do, I use magic to my advantage on occasion myself."

"Are you telling me that Megrenn has cannons?"

Kyrus was incredulous. Immediately he thought of the new "siege engine" the goblins were reported to have used at Illard's Glen. Some sort of improved catapult, they said. Would not a cannon be seen as such, especially if they had only seen it from the receiving end.

"You will see them in Kadrin, soon enough. Pevett, you said? Give us a season and you will see them for yourself." Denrik smiled. "There will be a reckoning, and Kadrin will find out what it is like to be occupied."

"Why would you tell me this, after I admitted to being Kadrin? Surely you must suspect I would try to do something to stop you."

"Why would I?" Denrik countered. "I know from long experience that you cannot just bring information from one world to the next with no explanation. No one in Veydrus would believe you, and I doubt you could get through their primitive heads what a cannon was before they saw one used against them in battle. Kadrins know magic, I give them that much, but if you can match their magic on the battlefield, or even close the gap, they lack the military strength Megrenn has.

"You would do well to consider helping the Megrenn cause, Mr. Hinterdale," Denrik offered. "It sounds as if you do not have much love for your countrymen, and I do not imagine that the life of a brigand pays nearly so well as life as a spy. You could never be caught, since you could pass information in this world without ever giving cause to suspect you. Just worm your way into some position of value and feed information through me."

"You have given me much to think on, Captain. I trust I do not need to decide right away," Kyrus said, taking another sip of his wine.

"No, there is no rush. But I think it is high time we let everyone else in and celebrated," Denrik said. "Stevin!" he called out, and the young man opened the door promptly. "Bring the officers in."

"Aye, Captain," the lad replied.

* * * * * * *

The game had been going on for hours. Kyrus had played Crackle a few times, but mostly as a child with his brothers. He had never had much money and certainly had not frequented places where Crackle players could be found. There were no games quite like it in Kadrin, so Brannis had no experience to draw from, either. The trade bars they had been given by Stalyart earlier in the day represented sums too large to be used for a game, but most of the crew had money of their own, of various currencies. Stalyart had a list he chalked onto a slate board that gave the exchange rates, which made it easier for Kyrus to keep track of how much money was actually being passed around the table.

Kyrus had suspected cheating going into the game. The reputation of pirates was legendary, and none of it included fair play. He did not expect to catch any of them at it, since he was so new to the game and they all seemed to be much more comfortable with it—or at least they all made it seem that way. There was a good chance that he would be going to bed a poor man, despite his share of the loot that he had received only hours earlier. He had traded a few of his trade bars for an impressive-looking stack of zimbals, the coinage of Feru Maru. The small, octagonal zimbal coins had a square hole in the center, which Kyrus thought made them look exotic, certainly more interesting than the plain round eckle coins he had grown up with.

Early into the game, Kyrus had been losing regularly and steadily. He apologized for his many miscues in the etiquette of the game, which were easy to forgive when it was someone who was losing large sums. There had been jokes at his expense, and he seemed to be losing some of the mystique he had hoped to create in his persona. He was the land-dweller, the scrivener, the kid.

Kyrus decided to try his own hand at cheating. *Well, if I am to be a pirate, I might as well try their way of playing. Let them just try to catch me at my way.*

Kyrus—or rather, Brannis—had long been able to tell when a sorcerer was lost in aether-vision; he had seen the dreamy, vacant look often enough at the

Academy and in his own family home. He had no reason to believe that Captain Zayne, or possibly even Mr. Stalyart, would miss the telltale sign of someone oblivious to the world of light. As the game went on, Kyrus tried slipping his sight just partly into the aether and, after an hour or so of practice, was comfortable enough with it that he could put his plan into effect.

As the cards came to him, he marked them with tiny wisps of aether, each uniquely identifying the card for him. After several rounds, he had touched every card and could begin taking advantage. Knowing who held which cards made Crackle—a child's game—seem like child's play. Kyrus was careful not to be too blatant about his change in luck, but began to allow his pile of coins to steadily increase. To his zimbals and a pair of gold trade bars in front of him, he now had eckles, darshis, clay-bones, and fonns, collected from stashes that the various players at the table had brought with them from their homelands or acquired elsewhere in their travels throughout Tellurak.

"You are not so bad at this game, Mr. Hinterdale," Stalyart complimented him after Kyrus had taken a rather large pot from the first mate.

The man's expression was inscrutable during a hand, but he became quite amiable when he was not involved, and he seemed to take his losses in stride, which was gracious of him since his pile had grown steadily through the night.

"Aye, Mr. Hinterdale seems to have caught the gist of our little game," Holyoake commented, chomping on the end of his pipe.

Holyoake, though, seemed less charitable than Stalyart, and had been involved in the same hand until dropping out halfway through when he decided that either Kyrus or Stalyart had him beaten.

"Well, I had not played since I was a boy," Kyrus said. "You cannot expect me to jump right in and play with the likes you fellows. Now that I have got my legs under me, I expect you will find me less of an easy mark."

Kyrus tried not to sound smug. He was enjoying winning, and was actually learning quite a lot about his fellow crewmates in the process. Being able to tell what cards they held, he knew when they were bluffing, and when they were trying to trick their opponents by feigning weakness when they were strong. Stalyart for one, seemed to almost be able to tell what the other players held as well as Kyrus could.

I wonder if he has some trick like mine, Kyrus mused.

"It seems our ship's wizard is a quick study. I wonder if he could learn to read nautical charts as quickly," Captain Zayne said. "We have put to sea with no proper navigator aboard. A few of us can manage well enough to get us where we want to go, but it would be good to have someone take over, and frankly, Mr. Hinterdale, you could do with an occupation while at sea."

"I suppose I could learn it easily enough. I know how to read a map, certainly, and the rest ought to sort itself out from there. How hard could it be?" Kyrus said.

He had certainly seen nautical charts before. Davin had a handful of them, which he had taken with him to Golis when he had left. Kyrus had never paid them overmuch attention, but he was at least familiar with the basics of what was included: tides, water depths, hazards, and the like.

"This is serious business, Mr. Hinterdale. You have proven your worth with that magic of yours, but a mistake in navigation could run us aground. I shall have you apprentice to Mr. Stalyart until he says you are fit to plot our course unassisted. I trust you will take his tutelage to heart," Denrik said.

"Cap'n, wouldn't it be a bit, err, safer havin' someone with experience doin' the navigatin'?" Scradd objected.

The thin quartermaster seemed to be in his cups a bit, but there were nods of agreement around the table.

"I am not letting him navigate until Mr. Stalyart had trained him to his satisfaction. I have every confidence that Mr. Hinterdale will be quick as a lightning bolt taking up the trade. If he learns it as quick as he picked up Crackle, he shall be guiding the ship better than any of us within the fortnight," Denrik replied.

Kyrus was a bit dubious at the confidence the captain showed in him but was more surprised that he had not reprimanded the quartermaster for questioning him. Kyrus was no scholar of naval comportment, but he was fairly certain the Acardian navy took a dim view of underlings questioning their superiors' decisions. He had assumed that among pirates, the tolerance for such brazenness would have been nearly nil.

In fact, Kyrus was beginning to question just how much danger he was truly in aboard the Denrik Zayne's ship. Despite most of them carrying blades, he had yet to see anyone draw one in anger against another crewman. With all the drinking during their night of Crackle, there had been no brawl or serious threats, just a general joviality. With the captain and first mate in on the secret he carried, there was even a certain sense of protection from above.

For the rest of the evening, Kyrus kept his winnings moderate.

Let them think I had a run of luck, and nothing more, Kyrus thought.

He even strategically lost a few hands to Holyoake and Scradd, who had seemed the least cordial toward him. He figured that it would be easier to like someone when you can take their money at cards.

* * * * * * *

By the time the game broke up and each of them had retired to their quarters, Kyrus had added a hefty sum to the share of loot he had been awarded. He figured upon it being roughly a haul of sixty thousand eckles, once he converted the various currencies using Stalyart's exchange rates. It was more than he had made in his lifetime up to that point. It was hardly a sum to retire on as a country gentleman, but it was certainly a strong start toward such a fortune.

If Kyrus was ever were to make his way back to Acardia to reunite with Abbiley, it certainly would not hurt to be wealthy by then. He doubted his reputation would allow him to ever settle within the city again, but with enough gold, he could start a new life and take Abbiley along with him. Certainly there was gold enough to be had among these pirates that such a goal was not unrealistic.

Kyrus sighed, thinking about the last night he and Abbiley had spent together, and wishing that he had not left her to go back to his shop and work.

Brannis would have known better, he thought, punching his feather pillow in frustration. *I was a fool to assume I had forever to court her.*

Kyrus walked the few steps to his now warded door and angrily poured aether into it, yanking a bit back at the last moment when he sensed it was about to burst.

Let the ship crash against the rocks; that door still is not going anywhere.

He could still see everyone in his vicinity aboard the ship, their Sources overlaying his vision of the world of light; Kyrus was really appreciating his newfound trick of keeping his sight balanced between the worlds of aether and light. He wondered briefly if the world of aether was truly another world like the one that Brannis lived in, or whether the aether world was common to both. It was a bit too philosophical for the late hour, and Kyrus's moderate drinking had nevertheless taken a small toll on his wakefulness. He resolved to ponder the question another day.

Read a bit more from Basic Wards *tonight, Brannis, if you do not mind*, Kyrus thought before drifting off to sleep, feeling much more secure than he had the previous night.

It was an odd feeling, knowing there was someone in another world watching over you, conspiring with you, sharing your thoughts and memories. Now that Kyrus knew the secret of his connection with Brannis, though, he found it comforting. It was like finding out a childhood imaginary friend had been real all along.

Chapter 26 - For Old Times

Brannis and one of the palace porters clattered down the halls of the palace, intent on the stables. Their arms were filled with the provisions Brannis had expected they might need on the journey to Raynesdark. While Brannis carried the pack with the books he had taken from the Tower library, a number of maps of the countryside, and a few changes of clothing, the porter was carrying much of Brannis's armor, whence came much of the considerable noise they were making.

Brannis wore a traveling cloak over mail armor and a steel breastplate, as well as his Solaran tabard. Mail covered the leather of his leggings down to just above the knee, but his lower legs and boots were unarmored. It was a compromise—armor that would lend some protection if they ran into trouble on their journey, but not so heavy that a journey of a tenday would wear him down physically. He expected to ride hard, at least so much as his sorcerer companions could handle.

Brannis was under little illusion about his companions. Sorcerers among the Kadrin Imperial Circle were not known for partaking of an active lifestyle. Iridan's adventure in Kelvie Forest with Brannis had been by far the exception, and even after the whole expedition, he was hardly in the shape of a common conscript. Juliana—for all else he admired about her form—was built better for the ballroom than the road, with thin arms and slender legs and shallow, graceful
...

Never mind that now.

The other two he knew not, but neither looked the least bit rugged. Ruuglor likely weighed twice his own twenty-five gallons—well, probably not, but it certainly seemed like it. And Faolen must have spent as much time on his appearance as a courtesan, and appeared more dainty than even Juliana, who could at least act the part of the fierce warrior when the mood struck her.

And yet, should we be ambushed on the road, it will be them protecting me, not the other way around, Brannis thought ruefully.

He knew he was being sent to Raynesdark for his leadership rather than his sword arm, but it was still a bit off-putting to know that any of the four of them could almost literally tie him into knots if it came right down to it. Kadrin sorcerers were a far cry from the novices the goblins in Kelvie had thrown at them.

When Brannis and his assistant made it to the stables, they found Rashan waiting for them. Unlike the previous night's dinner, they had arrived in advance of the rest of the attendees. The warlock was dressed in his usual black robes and cloak, but he was carrying an ornate breastplate.

"Fair morning, Brannis," Rashan greeted him. "I ought to have sent word to leave your armor behind, but I have had so many other tasks to attend to that I fear I overlooked that detail. Now, before everyone else arrives, get that stuff off and get changed."

"What do you mean? I have no time for fitting a new set of armor at this point. If you need my measurements to have it fitted while I am away, I use Goloway as my smith. He is the best in Kadrin these days and has all my measurements, unless I have lost girth with how busy I have kept myself this last season or so. Um ... you did not already have Goloway alter that armor for me, did you? I cannot imagine that was made anew in the two days since you have returned."

"No, Brannis, do not concern yourself. It will fit you plenty well enough without alteration. Quit arguing and just put it on. You shall see," Rashan said, proffering the breastplate at arm's length.

Brannis looked about and saw what appeared to be the rest of the matching plates hanging from pegs that normally would have held riding tack, had five horses not already been outfitted that morning.

"Very well," Brannis agreed, reluctantly.

He hoped that the warlock was at least a good enough judge of his size that the armor would not be too uncomfortable. Given the choice of looking like a grand marshal and actually wearing comfortable, fitted armor, he would choose the latter every time. For someone unaccustomed to needing armor, Rashan just would not understand the vast difference between "close" and "just right" when it came to the fit of a suit of armor. Goloway made a princely living for a commoner by being a master at understanding that difference.

He enlisted the porter's help in getting out of his own armor, a task he could manage on his own if time was not at issue. When he went to put on the long-sleeved mail shirt that went on under the plates of the new armor, he found it to be laughably oversized for him. Brannis found that unusual, as he was among the tallest knights in the Empire, and his hands would not even exit the ends of the sleeves until he bunched the mail up at his wrists.

As soon as Brannis had fully donned the mail shirt, it began to shrink until it fit snugly against the padded woolen under-layer he wore. His eyes immediately sought out the warlock and found Rashan watching him with amusement.

"I told you it would fit," the warlock said, smiling.

"Where did you get this? I doubt even five knights in the Empire own aether-forged armor. I daresay none would give theirs up while they yet lived," Brannis replied.

Brannis's own armor was runed but not aether-forged. It held protections that a sorcerer could renew with aether, but aether-forged armor was not only stronger, but also capable of remarkable feats like the resizing trick Rashan's proffered armor has just performed.

"Please tell me that you did not murder some poor knight to get this."

"No, I merely made a search of the emperor's private armory. It was hanging on a display rack, apparently unused since Liead wore it into battle with me," Rashan said, sounding sad.

"So you made this armor?" Brannis asked, impressed.

As he looked over the rest of the plates, he could not help admiring the exquisite detail—etched patterns and writings that were hidden among the raised relief artwork, gracefully flowing lines, and, on the inside, runes.

"No, no. Sadly I cannot take credit for that. It was hundreds of summers old when I first laid eyes on it. I never took the time to research its history, but many an emperor, those that were of a mind at least, wore it when going to battle or when fighting in tournaments. Once long ago, our emperors were not craven canaries, kept in gilded cages to be put on display for the commoners at holidays."

"If this is from the emperor's armory, I should not be wearing it. This should only be worn by the emperor." Brannis began removing the mail shirt.

"Stop that. Be sensible. You talk as if there were an emperor to offend. My all-wise Inner Circle saw to it that the canary in the cage was replaced with the mere reflection of a bird. It did all it needed to on high balconies on feasting days, but I think it lacked the ability to take offense. While I am regent, I will not allow such useful magic to go wasting away in a dusty room while I can put it to use in battle," Rashan said.

"Well, then ..." Brannis trailed off, and he started putting the armor on.

The porter loitered around to help, but the armor went on with ease as each piece was comfortably oversized as it went on and then fitted itself like a second skin as soon as it was in place.

When he had finished, Rashan conjured up a shimmering force in midair that reflected like a mirror. "Well, see how you look. More befitting the Grand Marshal of the Imperial Army, would you say?"

"I must admit, I look the part now, at least," Brannis said.

He was dressed head to foot in gold and quicksilver, materials that would never be used in more functional, mundane armor—quicksilver could not even have held a shape without magic—but as mere vessels for the magic they bore, they were impressive and far more functional than any armor Brannis had ever worn.

"Here is the best part," Rashan told Brannis.

Without warning, the warlock drew Heavens Cry and lunged for him. Brannis could barely begin to lift an arm to ward off the unexpected attack before the blade struck him squarely in the chest. Brannis rocked back slightly under the blow, but instinctively he had expected the blade to pass right through him. More rationally, he had figured that the aether construct worked into the armor would have held firm and he would have just been driven back by the force of the blow, but that had not happened, either. He looked down at the breastplate and noticed a small dent that was already growing smaller as the quicksilver flowed back into a mirror-smooth, perfectly unblemished surface.

"I admit it, that was impressive." Brannis smiled and went back to looking over his reflection.

There were dragon-claw clasps at the collarbone for attaching a cloak, and the ridged blades rode down each arm from elbow to wrist. Similar blades worked their way from knee to ankle. The boots were made with a thick sole to them, making Brannis seem a half hand taller even, on top of his already impressive stature. The gauntlets were serrated on the backs of the knuckles, but the palm side was just leather, which gave them a comfortable feel on the hilt of his blade—and there was a hook on his belt to hang them from when he was attending to less bloody work. The helm was a masterpiece: shaped into the countenance of a demon—the storybook sort, not like Rashan at all—with twisting horns and jutting edges and angles around the open face that seemed to cast the wearer's face in ominous shadows unless lit from directly in front.

Rashan handed Brannis a new cloak as well, bloodred to match the trim of the Inner Circle's robes, as well at the emperor's personal colors.

"There is nothing special about the cloak," Rashan said. "It is just well made and matches the armor better than the plain one you wore back from Kelvie."

As Brannis was fastening it on, the rest of the group arrived, apparently all having just come from the dining hall's morning feast. Brannis, being of a more martial and practical bent, had expected them to break their fast on the road with trail rations, but it appeared as if he had been overruled by the majority.

"Excuse me ... Warlock? What have you done with Brannis? And who is this scary-looking fellow in the sharpened armor?" Iridan asked upon seeing Brannis in Emperor Liead's armor.

Iridan was dressed like Rashan again, in his black tunic and leggings, and steel-epauletted cloak. Brannis supposed it would serve well enough as traveling attire, if Iridan had some magic in mind to deal with the cold.

The other three were dressed more reasonably for the late-autumn trek to the mountains. The robes of the Imperial Circle had been replaced with riding leathers and heavy jackets and cloaks. Brannis had to make a point of not letting his gaze linger overlong on Juliana, as he reminisced about the last time he had seen her dressed for riding.

"I hear he is the new grand marshal," Juliana said. "He must be trying to look the part. I would have suggested a few grey hairs and some wrinkles, myself."

She looked Brannis over with much less discretion than he had used, making him a bit uncomfortable with everyone else there watching.

"Now that we are all here," Rashan began, ignoring the jests, "I will reveal the surprises I have in store for you."

"I hope he does not have one of those outfits for me," Iridan muttered to Ruuglor, whom he seemed to already know.

"I have five horses here, all fitted with runed shoes."

The five would-be travelers looked at each other, puzzled. None of them had been expecting horses with runed shoes.

"They have been fully drained for now, but when charged with aether, these horses will run easily twice their normal speed, and their hooves will not quite touch the ground. That will allow you to cross rough, muddy terrain, as well as bodies of water. Take care not to stop on the water, as the effect does not persist once they stop moving."

"That could save six or seven days off our journey," Brannis said, impressed.

He could not predict how long the goblins would spend consolidating their hold on Illard's Glen before advancing to Raynesdark, if they had not already done so. Six days would markedly increase their chances of reaching the city ahead of the anticipated siege.

"No, it will save three days, four if you press," Rashan said. "Besides allowing you to move faster, the shoes will let you take uncut paths through the mountains. You will not have to take High Pass and follow the Cloud Wall south along the western side. You can head straight west and come at the city from across the mountains directly."

"How will we know where to cross the Cloud Wall if there is no road?" Ruuglor asked.

"You are smart little boys and girls, and Brannis is carrying maps. I am sure you will figure out how to find Raynesdark from the east side," Rashan replied. "Now mount up, and be gone. You have already wasted enough of the morning. Head north along the road for an hour, then activate the horseshoes and begin heading west from there. That should confuse any spies who might take note of your departure. So long as you have privacy when you veer west, you will not be seen again by any who might try to follow you.

"Oh, and I trust that the four of you will support Brannis's claim that he has truly been appointed grand marshal. I want no trouble from Duke Pellaton if he is indeed as cantankerous as Duke Benklear inferred. Brannis is to take charge of all Kadrin forces present, including Duke Pellaton's own troops. And that includes the lot of you and any sorcerers in the city already," Rashan said.

"But, Warlock, the chains of command are entirely separate. I would have to support the senior—in this case—only member of the Inner Circle present, were there to be a conflict," Faolen said, possibly mistaking Brannis's and Iridan's informality with the warlock for permission to act so himself.

"Let me make this clear, Sorcerer Faolen. Marshal Brannis is in charge on this journey, and he is in charge when you all reach Raynesdark. *I* say so, and I am High Sorcerer, as well as Regent of the Empire. I am explicitly ordering you to follow Marshal Brannis's command. Is that clear?" Rashan asked, glaring at Faolen.

They all selected mounts and stowed their gear in the saddlebags. Brannis's load was much lighter now that he was not bringing separate armor for travel and battle; the magical armor was more comfortable even than his own expertly fitted armor—and lighter as well.

"Iridan," Rashan spoke softly, pulling his son aside as the others were busying themselves with the horses. "Take this," and he pressed a plum-sized spherical stone into Iridan's hand. It was carved with hastily scratched runes and had a hole in the middle, through which a leather thong was run. "It is a crude speaking stone I crafted last night. It will only send to me and may not work for long, but should anything go badly, contact me. I can use a transference spell to come to your aid. I have much to attend to here in Kadris, so do not bother me for trivialities."

"How bad should I allow things to get before seeking aid?" Iridan asked.

"Ahh, now that is my son talking. Assume the worst when making your plans, and nothing can take you unawares. Well, I would expect the goblins to have some nasty surprise for you. If it looks as if you cannot counter what that turns out to be, I would think that qualifies," Rashan said.

"Any ideas what that surprise might be?" Iridan asked.

"No. That is Brannis's job. He is the mind of the army now. If I did not think he was up to puzzling it out, I would have to go myself and risk whatever chaos I might find upon returning to Kadris. Ruling an empire is a game more complex than chess, and you do not see all the pieces I have to keep track of."

"I have known Brannis most of my life. If anyone can figure it out, he can. I cannot imagine where he thinks of some of the gambits he tries, but it always seems he is one step ahead," Iridan said. He had always been proud to call Brannis a friend. Even when it became clear that Iridan would become the more powerful sorcerer, he leaned on Brannis to get him through the harder classes at the Academy.

Rashan just nodded and moved to pull Brannis aside before they left.

"I am putting a great deal of trust in you, Brannis. You heard me stake quite a claim against my reputation last night supporting your takeover of the army. Make good use of it. Get those goblins out of my empire, by whatever means you must use.

"Just be warned: those green-skinned devils are smarter than most men. Whatever they have planned, you must counter it, for they must be counting on the advantage they gain from it to succeed."

"The reports said that the goblins have some new siege weapon that obliterated the walls of Illard's Glen," Brannis said.

"Yes? And?" Rashan sensed Brannis was on to something.

"I am rather certain that they now have ... cannons," Brannis said.

He waited for a reaction from Rashan. It was a gambit that he was not sure of, but if it went poorly, he would just muddle his way out of it somehow.

Rashan's face remained a mask. The normally talkative warlock said nothing for a moment, but studied Brannis.

"I see," was all he could say to Brannis's statement.

And from the way he said it, Brannis was not at all certain just what he meant that he saw.

* * * * * * *

The first leg of their journey, still following the North Road out of Kadris, was somber and brisk. A light snowfall had begun overnight, and a thin dusting blanketed the countryside. As far south as the capital of the Empire was, it was unusual to receive the season's first snow so late into autumn; the solstice would be in just fourteen days. As they were to be heading north and west, they could expect to see less of the wintry weather until they crossed the mountains. The Cloud Wall would shield the eastern slopes from most precipitation, but the western side, at higher elevations, would likely have already seen heavy snows.

Brannis called them to a halt when they found a respite from the curious eyes sharing the road with them. They had just crested a hill in a lightly forested area on the outskirts of Podawei Wood, which the road veered northwesterly to avoid entering. Podawei Wood was on House Archon land, and the road had been blazed in ages long past, during a time when the emperor and the head of the Archon clan were not seeing things with the same temper. The wood was a prime hunting ground for elk and caribou, as well as the much rarer mammoth foxes. It was vast and deep and dark, and even experienced hunters only ventured so far within its grasp before turning back. The forest spirits had been driven out of it during the wars that resulted in the Empire's founding, but it was commonly believed that some remained hidden away deep within and were responsible for the disappearances of many a brave huntsman.

Brannis used the tree cover to obscure them from those to their north, while the bulk of the hill they had crested shielded them from view to the south.

"I think we have found our opportunity to throw off any curious pursuers. Time for us to take our leave of the road," Brannis called out to his companions.

As Juliana and Ruuglor, who had been leftmost in the formation, brought their mounts about, Brannis held up a warding hand.

"Wait. We need to have those horseshoes filled with aether. Rashan said that the horses' hooves would not be touching the ground once they gained speed, and if we are careful, we may leave no clue as to where we left the road."

"Ruuglor, Faolen, see to it," Iridan commanded, sitting back in his saddle with a little smile.

He cast a sidelong glance at Juliana to see if she showed any sign of appreciating not having been assigned to work on the horses' shoes.

The two appointed sorcerers exchanged a knowing look as they dismounted their horses. The beasts were well trained and somewhat accustomed to the eccentricities of being handled by sorcerers. This included, among other indignities, grown men crawling around underfoot, fiddling with their horseshoes and making them tingle. Each shoe had to be touched individually and aether drawn and deposited within. It was not difficult work, and most children from homes where magic was common learned to draw aether for their favorite toys from a young age. But in the case of horseshoes, it was dirty and unpleasant work, at least for those who preferred feasts and courtly sitting rooms to stables and the road.

Faolen was nimbler afoot—and crawling around as well—than his portly associate. He took care of his own mount, then attended to "Warlock" Iridan's and Juliana's horses, all before Ruuglor could finish his own and Brannis's.

Ruuglor grunted eloquently as he drew himself up to his feet after completing his job on Brannis's mount. "I would bed the lad myself if it got me out of such work," Ruuglor muttered beneath his breath, just loud enough for Brannis to be the only one to hear him.

Brannis managed to keep his chuckle inaudible as he smiled in response. His back was to the others, and the exchange went unnoticed.

Once they were all in saddle again, Brannis urged his horse at a trot along the road. He immediately noticed the effect of the shoes, as his horse's strides seemed longer and the scenery began to move past at a gallop. After the first few steps, the noise of hoof on dirt vanished, and they rose a handspan above the road. Content that he was no longer leaving a trail of hoofprints, he veered left and headed off the road.

"Follow as soon as you clear the ground," Brannis called back.

The others took off after him, following down the road until their own mounts managed to get ever so slightly airborne, then heading westerly after the grand marshal.

The journey quickened once they were all together and aloft. Their passage was eerily quiet, with the sensation of riding normally being accompanied by the crash of hoofbeats and theirs marked by little more than the rush of air as they passed. Brannis had it the worst, with the flutes and openings in his armor catching the wind and creating all manner of moans and whistles, while the wool and fur that covered the sorcerers allowed them to ride largely in peace.

The monolithic pale grey of the snow clouds hid the sun entirely and looked like it would persist long enough to obscure moon and stars alike come nightfall. Brannis knew the area well enough for the time being, but he feared that they might get turned off course if they did not find better weather by the morrow. At the rate the horses were tearing across the Kadrin landscape, they would be into the heart of farm country by midday the next day. It was unfamiliar land to Brannis, too far within the Empire's borders for the army to bother with garrisons and too bland to be considered worthy of visiting for recreation or study; neither the Academy nor the knighthood had ever shown interest in sending him there.

They kept the pace until shortly after what they imagined to be high-sun, when Brannis bid them stop for lunch. He watched as the sorcerers dismounted to see how the morning's ride had treated them.

Iridan looked stiff and walked awkwardly for his first few steps after regaining his footing on solid ground. His feet were shoulder length apart and appeared content to remain so until such time as his muscles uncramped.

Ruuglor had fared somewhat better. Though he had trouble mounting and dismounting the horse as a matter of course due to his girth, he seemed as if he had made use of one before, and after a brief stretch to work out the kinks in a back ill-treated by the jarring of his ride, appeared to be none the worse for their morning's exercise.

Faolen was in a worse state than Iridan even. He needed assistance to get down and was hardly able to walk without leaning on Ruuglor's stout shoulder.

Juliana appeared fine. She dismounted casually and showed no ill effects from the first leg of their trek. Brannis had once before underestimated her ability with horses, so he kept a tight rein on his surprise and settled instead for being rather impressed. The Archon family had large holdings in the countryside surrounding Kadris, with ample room for horseback riding where no one would bother you, but it was still a pastime more common among the less gifted members of the family, and those high-ranking servants who could afford the luxury in both time and expense to indulge in equestrian hobbies. Though he had intentionally not kept abreast of her activities, he had always gotten the impression that Juliana was more at home at court and in the city than out in the country, riding.

"Let us have our midday meal on the ground, rather than in the saddle. I know you fellows are unaccustomed to riding, so we will have an easy day of it today," Brannis said, rummaging in his saddlebags for what was essentially going to be a picnic.

"I can ride from the palace to the Academy and back just fine. This overland travel is a bit much. I prefer a quieter pace for long times in the saddle," Iridan said as he began boiling away fresh-fallen snow to clear a spot for their meal.

"Bah, better to make it quick, I say," Ruuglor said. "Certainly there is unpleasantness to go along with any long journey, but if it must be done, get it over with rather than prolong it. Warlock Rashan said we could take another whole day off our trip if we press hard."

"Oh yes, you all look so refreshed after our morning's ride that we ought to consider challenging ourselves a bit more," Juliana deadpanned, drawing a chuckle from Brannis.

"We still might reclaim that day, if I think we can manage it," Brannis said. "But we must be careful of the horses. If we tire them out, we shall not only be searching out fresh ones, but they will be unaccustomed to meddling by sorcerers, and we would have to have them reshod as well. A good smith can make quick work of a reshoeing, but ten horses? That would be much of a day's work, even if the new horses do not panic when the runed shoes begin their work."

"Just five horses, you mean. We would not have to wait for these five to be reshod, certainly. We could just leave them with the stable and instructions to have them returned to the palace stables," Faolen said, easing himself down to the now parched spot on the ground that Iridan had just baked.

"Where do you think they will get those shoes? We may not need to wait for these to be reshod, but the smith would at least have to make the time to remove the runed shoes from our horses first," Brannis said.

Brannis laid out a small spread of various salted meats and cheeses for their meal, and everyone partook, though Juliana and Faolen seemed skeptical, and Ruuglor seemed to be expecting there to be a bit more. Iridan had grown accustomed to the meager field rations they had been eating in Kelvie, and he and Brannis knew that the trail food the palace had stocked in their saddlebags was a world better quality than the hardtack and stale bread they had made do with in the forest.

"So what is our plan once we get to Raynesdark, Brannis?" Juliana asked once they had settled in for their meal. She tore into a strip of jerky as she awaited his reply.

"The true plan is to get there quickly," Brannis said. "I have no doubt the goblins are already a step ahead of us in planning the siege. I will need to figure out as quickly as possible what they are planning to surprise us with and then find a way to counter it."

"Well, that is just what Rashan said at dinner last night. What is the real plan?" Juliana countered. "Surely there was more to it than that."

"Not as such, no."

"You mean that we are trekking across half the Empire and crossing the Cloud Wall at whatever spot we find ourselves at, just to figure it out when you get there?" Juliana seemed baffled.

"You have a better plan?" Brannis asked. "If you know what the goblins have planned and a strategy to counter it, I am your attentive servant."

Brannis looked at her expectantly, with a carefully crafted expression of naïve hopefulness painted on his face. He winced in his head as he recalled having used this same annoying ploy on her countless times when he was courting her—when he was just a boy, really. It had become an almost reflexive response to her judgmental outbursts. If he had realized how much more ridiculous that expression looked when wearing gold-and-quicksilver armor with a demon-horned helm, he would have flushed with embarrassment.

"No, but if it had been my duty to put one together, I would have come up with something better that 'I shall figure it out later,'" Juliana imitated Brannis in a fair approximation of his voice.

Faolen snickered.

"Truly, if any of you have a plan, I *am* willing to listen," Brannis said. "I cannot promise I will follow any set course of action until we arrive at Raynesdark and I can assess the situation, but I will give fair hearing to any thoughts you might have. It is a long road yet, and I expect you will have plenty of time alone with your thoughts as the wind carries our words off as we ride."

"Um, actually, Brannis, it is just you," Iridan said. "The rest of us realized that it was that silly armor of yours making all the noise, and that once we hung back a few paces, we could carry on conversation rather easily. In fact, I won a hundred fifty lions for having best guessed when you would finally let us stop for a rest."

Brannis stowed his helm for the remainder of the day's ride and was able to partake in the general conversation as their horses blazed a trail over the snow at a blurring pace, despite pushing the pace hardly at all. As there were only so many practicalities to discuss and hours aplenty to fill, they spoke of many other topics. Brannis felt better about taking men into a war with him if they were less than strangers to one another.

They rode five abreast, with Brannis at the center. They spoke of their backgrounds and families—though Brannis's, and now Iridan's, family was already the subject of much gossip in the Empire—and of what they thought of the future of the Empire now that the ruse of the false emperor had been revealed. It was then that Brannis found out why Ruuglor and Faolen had been chosen to "volunteer" for this assignment.

"Indeed, he gave us a choice, but it was Rashan's Bargain come to life," Ruuglor said, laughing despite not finding it particularly funny himself. "You know it is a trap from the outset, yet you are desperate enough that you have to take the chance that it is not. It was suggested that Faolen and I might begin to help make amends for our part in perpetuating the ruse, if we were to go along and help defend Raynesdark."

"So you both knew?" Brannis asked.

"Of course," Ruuglor replied. "I helped to craft and maintain the aether construct of the body. It truly is a masterwork. I cannot claim credit for much of it; I was one of several involved in the crafting. I would also occasionally repair bits where the construct started to fray."

"What of you, Faolen? What was your role?" Brannis asked.

"I was an occasional puppeteer. I also consulted on matters of fashion and details of the face and jewelry," Faolen said.

"Aye, and he had quite the eye for it," Ruuglor said. "Illusion is his specialty, and not many of them are to be had among the Circle. Our Faolen is an artist of aether."

"So you are telling me that you two are being sent along as punishment?" Brannis asked.

"Not as such," Ruuglor parroted Brannis's own equivocation back at him. "It was just strongly implied that it might forestall some potential future repercussions that might befall us."

"So he threatened you," Brannis stated. It was not a question.

"It was a privilege to watch a master at work!" Ruuglor announced, employing grace about the situation when bitterness might have been forgivable.

"And what threat hangs over your head, Juliana? How did the old warlock convince you to come along?" Brannis asked.

"He asked. If you must attach a threat to it, then the threat of never seeing my future husband again, should the battle go badly," she replied, as if there were no more to it than that.

Brannis had suspicions otherwise but kept them to himself.

"And you, Iridan? I do not suppose you required much to get you to come along," Brannis suggested.

"Of course not. Rashan thinks I have it in me to become a warlock. He gave me some insights into how I should conduct myself on the battlefield, and I mean to put them into practice. If there is a chance I could be the Empire's next warlock, I *have* to try. High sorcerers get portraits painted and busts carved and names written into the history books. Warlocks *make* the history," Iridan said.

Apparently he had overcome the initial shock of Rashan's suggestion that he might become a warlock, and had embraced the idea. Brannis could not help but wonder if he was paying attention when Rashan explained what had become of the other sons he had tried training as warlocks.

By evening, they found themselves too far from any inhabited land to find proper beds for the night. The roads in the western half of the Empire, between the capital and the Cloud Wall, were a tangle of mule paths, old trade routes, and north-south routes that funneled goods to and from the southern ports. Too few roads ran cleanly east-west for Brannis's company to make good use as a guide, and they got themselves stuck somewhere in between Farfield and Marmet, smaller communities to be sure, but plenty large enough to find five beds at the command of the Inner Circle and the commander of the Imperial Army.

Instead they found themselves saddled with sleepy horses who bore increasingly sleepy riders, with no roof to be had close enough at hand to be of use. Brannis found them shelter near the Stoneflow River, where the steep bank was set back away from the low waters with enough room for a proper campsite. The bank was high enough that it shielded even the horses from the worst of the frosty night winds.

Brannis saw to the horses after the others had all dismounted in various states of physical distress. He found a root from a tree along the bank where it had grown out through the surface, and used it to tether the horses. He set about unpacking the small, individual-sized tents that each horse carried, and turned to suggest someone start looking for firewood.

He realized his folly immediately when he saw the sorcerers he traveled with. They had already levitated dozens of medium-sized stones from the riverbed to form a circle around the campfire, which they had already lit. The fire was large enough to warm a feasting hall, and crackled merrily away burning absolutely nothing.

I spent too much of the day remembering that I traveled with a bunch of soft, complaining, useless fops, and forgot that I was traveling with sorcerers. *I may as well have asked a town crier, "What news?" as asked sorcerers for fire.*

The tent-setting went similarly. While Brannis had initially resolved himself that he was not going to put up Juliana's tent for her—let Iridan be chivalrous if she needed the help—the four sorcerers each managed their own in no time at all, using telekinesis to arrange the little poles and ropes and jam the stakes into the cold hard ground. As Brannis went about setting his own up the more traditional way, he felt it pulled from his grasp.

"Sorry, Sir Brannis. I just could not watch that any longer," Ruuglor said, avoiding Brannis's gaze as he set it up for the grand marshal in one-tenth the time it would have taken Brannis by manual labor.

They took their evening meal hot. It was little different from the midday meal, except they were able to add bread and melt the cheese onto it, making the two hard foodstuffs each more palatable. There was also wine to be had—

Brannis truly wondered if the palace stewards had any idea how to properly pack for the road—and there was a small, somber celebration of the fact they made it through their first day on the road.

Upon retiring to their respective tents for the evening, Brannis could not help but notice that Juliana, at some point, had managed to set hers up right next to his own. He was too tired to do anything about it that night but resolved that he would choose his tent site last at the next place they stopped for the night. It was just one further thing he wished he did not have to worry about, but he was hardly eager to get between Iridan and Juliana.

Chapter 27 - Foreign Markets

Kyrus stood at the railing, seeing a foreign cityscape for the first time. The day was warm and bright with sunshine, and the light fog that had hung over the harbor on their approach in the early morning had burned off, leaving a blue sky filled with a scattering of grey-white clouds and the cries of thousands of seagulls.

The weather had warmed in the four days since they had set their course south from Acardia. While the chill of late autumn was icing the air above Kyrus's homeland, it seemed much like a fine spring day in the waters of Ganaad Bay, the gateway to the free city of Marker's Point.

Marker's Point was a small series of islands in the shape of a crescent moon, with the open side facing to the east. The separation of the islands varied with the tides, with interconnections between many of them appearing at low tide only to disappear upon the tide's return. Aside from the main passage in from the east, there was no draft deep enough for seagoing vessels between any of the islands. The whole of the landmass was populated aside from the short, craggy volcanic mountains that predominated the outer side of the crescent. Much had been built out into the shallow waters of Ganaad Bay itself as well, with buildings supported on stilts to keep the floors above the high tide.

In the early days of seafaring exploration, the once-barren island formation had served as a waypoint for voyages across the great expanses between continents. Initially used as a navigation aid—a landmark in an otherwise sparse area of the Katamic—ships would occasionally take shelter in the calm waters of the bay to anchor for repairs or to wait out storms. Eventually the explorers of the early seafaring age gave way to the second wave: merchants. It became apparent to anyone of a mercantile bent that the island chain made an ideal trading post for the various nautically inclined peoples whose shores touched the Katamic. It was not long before it was settled by various shipping and trading concerns. Many were more than willing to cut half the time off their journey to get paid for their wares at Marker's Point instead of their final destination, even if it meant taking a smaller cut; more voyages in more familiar waters made profits quicker and safer than longer voyages across open sea.

Thus the city of Marker's Point had grown up to be inhabited by moneychangers and warehouse owners, shippers and fishermen, fugitives and itinerant sailors, tavern-keepers, pirates, and whores. Few were born in the city—at least outside the brothels—and few spent their whole lives in it. Those hardy few formed the backbone of the island's society, though: the Lord Pon-Aeric Halahari and his family, the Tide's Watchmen who patrolled the waters and kept order, and the Hwann family, whose bank financed most of the major deals in the city.

Kyrus had never seen such a place before, and had only heard it referred to in storybooks and tavern tales as a place of mystery and intrigue, where deals were made in shady dockside saloons and pirates walked the piers.

I suppose the latter is true at least, or will be once they let us dock.

They had been under surveillance by one of the three massive lighthouses that surrounded the islands ever since the fog had cleared. Shortly thereafter, a small single-sailed harbor vessel had intercepted them, and one of the Tide's Watchmen had come aboard. Kyrus had been expecting trouble, considering that they were, after all, pirates. However, the watchman cleared them once he was satisfied that the ship was no longer a part of the Acardian Navy. There were few rules that the Pointers enforced, but "no naval vessels" was one they clung to dearly. It was an unpopular rule among the kingdoms whose subjects might flee to the city, but they felt it was essential to keep trade flowing freely—and they had enough cannons to enforce their decree.

Once the watchman had Captain Zayne's word on their lack of affiliation with Acardia, they issued a reminder that open gun ports in the bay were forbidden. After that, the small harbor ship merely escorted them toward the docks.

Kyrus watched the shore as they neared the berth they had been assigned. The city was vast, sprawling, built entirely around the periphery of the bay and filling any surface that could conceivably support a structure. It would only take a few minutes to walk from the inside beach to the outside beach in most parts of Marker's Point, yet to walk one end to the other might require overnight accommodations. Ferries ran crisscross between various docks along the inside face of the city at all hours of the day and night. Kyrus's eyes were drawn up as well, as many of the buildings were tall, spindly affairs, made from imported stone and winding their way up into the sky to make the most of the scant land available.

Kyrus could only begin to guess how many people lived in the city. Golis was the largest city in Acardia and held over fifty thousand. He might have supposed Marker's Point was thrice that at the least. Kyrus could recall the sights and sounds of Kadris from his dreams—a city the size of Marker's Point and Ganaad Bay combined—but the visceral feel of approaching it was like nothing his dreams could prepare him for. They had not even reached the dock when the clamor of the throngs on the dock reached them. Ships were being loaded and unloaded, with longshoremen shouting at one another in a dozen languages. Trading ships came and went in the harbor, with smaller boats darting in and around them, containing fishermen, city officials, peddlers who rowed from ship to ship pressing their wares on newcomers before they even reached port, and countless others whose occupations Kyrus could not gather upon cursory examination.

The men of Captain Zayne's crew were nearly all on deck, waiting for their chance at shore leave. Not all would be granted the privilege, as men were needed to guard the ship—Kyrus could not *imagine* why—but most would be making for the city proper with all haste. Scar Harbor was a large enough city by most standards, but the stuffy, parochial attitudes of the locals kept much of interest from happening beyond the dock ward.

Kyrus expected that he would be allowed to leave and take in the sights. Captain Zayne had granted him two full shares of loot, so he was obviously not quite subject to the same rules as the rest of the crew.

After all, he knows my secret, and he saw what I did on the docks at Acardia. It is not as if I would disappear into the city and hide away.

Under Captain Zayne's expert hand, the former *Harbinger*—which had yet to be renamed—slid smoothly into its assigned berth. There was a flurry of activity as sails were furled and lines pulled. Men down on the pier shouted up and requested mooring lines be thrown down. Kyrus could hardly contain the wide, childlike grin that was spreading itself over his face. He had never been much of anywhere in his life, and now here he was in Marker's Point.

* * * * * * *

Denrik steered the ship into port easily. Even with years between him and the last time he had piloted a ship, and with the unfamiliar feel of his new vessel, the mild waters of Ganaad Bay made for easy practice.

"Welcome to freedom, lads!" Denrik called out to the crew, to a general cheer.

Stalyart took over the details, directing the flow of the frenzied work on the deck as experienced sailors made ship ready to moor. The green ones had the sense at least to stay out of the way, even Andur, and the work went quickly even with the short crew.

Eager to be ashore, Denrik thought. *I suppose I can understand why. Were it up to me, I would never set foot on dry land again. I did my time in the dirt on that forsaken rock of Rellis Island. We need crew, though, and this is the place to find them.*

Denrik made his way down to where his men were laying the gangplank. Before any of his men made it down, though, first there was someone who insisted upon coming up.

"Who is the captain here?" the man asked.

He was a man of perhaps thirty years by his lack of grey hairs, but a hard thirty. He bore a pair of scars down the right side of his face, yet had been spared the loss of that eye. He walked with a cane, which thumped hollowly on the deck of the ship as he approached Denrik on a hunch. The man was clad in the blue-and-green livery of the Tide's Watch, but the heavy gold medallion hanging from his neck marked him as a harbormaster.

"I am Captain Denrik Zayne. This is my ship," Denrik informed the harbormaster proudly. There were times to conceal one's identity as a pirate and other times to wear one's name as a badge of honor. This counted as the latter.

"Well, the rumors are true, I see. I had heard the scuttlebutt that you had been among a group of escapees from the New Hope colony. This is quite a fine vessel you have acquired. I must admit, we were skeptical when we saw the *Harbinger* approach. Our records show that the *Harbinger* is registered to the Acardian Navy. When you did not fly your Acardian colors, however, we suspected something amiss. I trust that this vessel and the Acardian Navy are no longer associated ..." the harbormaster left the implied question hanging, waiting for Denrik to explain himself.

"That it says *'Harbinger'* on the side is clearly an error. I intend to see it corrected before we shove off," Denrik said, crossing his arms in front of him.

"It is now my duty to ask you: how long will that be?" the harbormaster asked.

"Two days. Maybe four. Maybe a week. I am in need of crew, and it will take how long it takes gathering a good one," Denrik replied.

He would rather have gotten in and out of Marker's Point in a day or two, but he knew better than to take just any man who volunteered. He would interview men and find out what ships they had served on, who their captain had been, and what other skills they possessed. Sailing with the Pirate King ought to carry some prestige, and he hoped to attract the best crew he could lay hands on.

"Well, we will require an advance of a week's berthing fees. If you depart beforehand, one of the harbormasters will be sure to reimburse you for the unused days remaining. The seven days will cost you fifty-six thousand zimbals," the harbormaster said.

Men nearby gasped in shock at the expense, but that was mostly because they did not understand just how worthless a zimbal was. Those who had been to Marker's Point before, or who had traveled to Feru Maru where zimbals were the legal tender, expected to pay as many as a hundred zimbals for a pint of watery ale.

Denrik paid the man in trade bars equivalent to the barrel of zimbals he had requested. He was not at all certain he had gotten a good exchange rate on them, but this was port and he was a pirate. There was a certain cachet attached to being able ignore the minor details in financial transactions such as this. He was out to find himself a crew, and being found to count zimbals was not going to help his reputation any. A captain hard on his luck was not a man would-be pirates wanted to sail with.

When the harbormaster had been satisfied, the gangway was clear and the men started pouring off the ship, jostling and shoving to get down first. He noted with a lack of surprise that Mr. Hinterdale was off to the side, waiting out the press of bodies.

"Mr. Stevin," Denrik pulled the young man aside as he brushed by his captain on the way to the gang plank.

"Aye, Captain?" the boy said, looking confused. He had been just paces shy of total freedom before getting waylaid by Captain Zayne.

"I want you to stick by Mr. Hinterdale today and see that he stays out of trouble," Denrik ordered.

Stevin cocked his head and gave him a puzzled expression. "Aye, sir. O' course. Ya don't mind me ask, but what trouble? I hear he take half da crew off da old ship and burn another," Stevin said.

Rumors had passed to every man on the ship about Kyrus's exploits on the night of the liberation of the *Harbinger*. Accounts varied—as they always did—in the retelling, but all accounts gave the very clear impression that Mr. Hinterdale was rather capable of looking after himself.

"Oh, our wizard may be all that, but he is an easy mark here nonetheless. You speak all the languages around here, true?" Denrik asked, and Stevin nodded in the affirmative. "Well, that lad there speaks Acardian and probably nothing else. He is going to lose all his money and very likely cross someone with a short temper, a sharp blade, and poor social skills today. This place is thick with them. By the waves, it is why we are here! I need those sorts to make pirates of.

"Now you just stay close to him and be his guide for today," Denrik said, looking into Stevin's eyes to make sure the boy knew he was serious.

"What if he don't want me with him?" Stevin asked. "I gotta sneek 'n' watch him?" The boy raised an eyebrow skeptically.

"I would not worry overmuch about that. The lad has never been away from home before. I doubt very much he relishes being on his own anyway," Denrik said.

* * * * * * * *

Kyrus had watched as Captain Zayne had negotiated some sort of payment with the harbor officials, but could not understand a word of it. The harbormaster was speaking something that he could only guess was the language of Feru Maru. After that, the men stampeded for the gangplank, an activity Kyrus saw no reason to put his life at risk for, with only the gain of a minute or so to be had for it.

As the crowd thinned, leaving only the handful who would stay behind on guard duty, Kyrus made his way down himself. He held his arms out to the side to balance himself as the gangplank swayed slightly under his footsteps. When he reached the pier, he turned back to look at the ship. He had yet to get a good look at it, since they had boarded it at night and he had been on it ever since. It was an elegant vessel in Kyrus's eyes, well cared for and lovingly detailed, obviously built by shipwrights with a sense of pride.

A hand on his shoulder caused Kyrus to twist around suddenly. He found that the hand belonged to the exotic young sailor, Stevin.

"Oh, that was just you," Kyrus, feeling relieved.

"Cap'n said I go with you. You don't speak the tongues here," Stevin told him, nodding.

Stevin then pressed a sword belt into his hands, which he had been carrying in the hand that was not on Kyrus's shoulder.

"And you *do* speak all the languages they speak here?" Kyrus asked, skeptical.

"You think I speak Acardian first?" Stevin asked, smiling lopsidedly. "But no. I not speak every tongue here. They speak everything here, but I speak a lot, see?"

"Well, thank you, I suppose. Are you sure you do not mind acting as my interpreter?" Kyrus asked.

"Don't matter. Cap'n says, Cap'n says." Stevin shrugged. "Cap'n says clean deck, I clean deck. Cap'n says haul anchor, I haul anchor. Today, Cap'n says follow Mr. Hinterdale."

"I ... suppose. What is this for then?"

Kyrus held up the sword belt. It was one of the ones they had brought with them on the initial raid on the *Harbinger*, a saber, Kyrus believed.

"Less trouble with you carrin' a sword, hmm? Lotta rough guys around this place. See an easy mark, they get ya," Stevin said.

Kyrus left it at that and buckled on the belt. The weight of the sword felt oddly reassuring at his side, though it was awkward bouncing against his leg, and he could feel the offset weight of the belt already starting to cause it to chafe against his side after the first few paces. Kyrus tried resting his hand on the hilt to steady the blade and lessen the discomfort.

Preoccupied as he was with figuring out how to wear the sword, he momentarily forgot about Stevin, as the younger man had fallen into step behind him as they left the pier where the *Harbinger* was moored.

SLAP!

Kyrus withdrew the stinging hand from the sword hilt and snapped his head around to see what had just happened.

"Stop that. You look like you never use sword before," Stevin chided him, giving him a stern look.

Kyrus looked the lad up and down. He was wiry of build with exotic yellow-orange skin and a mop of blond hair that he kept shaved at the sides. His arms, exposed now that the weather was warm enough for rolled sleeves, were covered in tattoos of dragons, serpents, knives, and the like. Around his neck was a pendant that Kyrus thought he recognized as a Kheshi totem for invoking bad luck on one's enemies. It seemed that Stevin knew his tricks when it came to not looking like an easy mark.

The tattoos in particular were something that Kyrus had been wondering about. Ever since the warm turn of weather as they sailed southward, the crew had more and more taken to rolling up sleeves or working bare chested up on the main deck. As a result, Kyrus had seen a collage of human-based artwork; nearly every man aboard seemed to bear some sort of marking. Some had fearsome collections of beasts and omens inscribed on their bodies to make themselves appear more dangerous—or, as Kyrus occasionally considered, properly identify themselves as dangerous. Names and mottoes were commonplace as well, with men paying tribute to lovers or parents, lost brothers and devoted friends, or expressing the values they lived by—nothing says a man loves gold, rum, and whores like a tattoo that says *"Gold & Rum & Whores."* A few others had patterns that seemed to be strictly decorative, with no deeper meaning.

It finally occurred to Kyrus that he had never seen a tattoo in his dreams of Veydrus. Brannis and his contemporaries were unfamiliar with them. The ogre tribes often painted their bodies for war and rituals, but nothing like the permanent, subcutaneous markings that were so common in Tellurak.

"Stevin, where can I find a place to get a tattoo, like yours?" Kyrus asked.

"Ah, now you thinkin'. No hand on sword, get tattoo. You be scary guy soon, huh?" Stevin smiled at him.

"Something like that," Kyrus replied. He had something different in mind, though.

* * * * * * *

The tattoo den was nestled in a corner of an open-air market, one of the fixed structures that surrounded a plaza filled with carts and booths. Kyrus had been following Stevin around what felt like half the island chain.

The interior was dimly lit by a pair of braziers that were burning some sort of incense. It gave a reddish glow to everything in the parlor. The walls were covered in exotic artwork: masks, little carved wooden reliefs, scrolls with strange symbols similar to runes but which Kyrus thought might be Kheshi script, and tassels with bells on them. There was a low couch to one side of the room with a chair next to it, surrounded by tables with various implements whose purpose Kyrus could surmise, with some trepidation.

Seated in the chair was a wrinkled old man whose bald head, and most of his body, was a mass of intermingled tattoos. The man had a pinched face and puckered mouth, an impression heightened by a long, thin pipe he was puffing at, jetting out little purple-grey wisps of smoke. A pair of tiny round spectacles perched on his nose, and he stared through them at a thin book—a soft-covered piece of trash that was likely made by typesetters, Kyrus thought disdainfully—whose front cover he had curled around the back to allow it to stay open when held with one hand.

Bells had clattered and jingled from the top of the door as Kyrus and Stevin had entered, yet the old man had not stirred from his book. The whole of the parlor smelled of the combined smokes of the braziers and the old man's pipe, a cloying, sickly sweet scent that stung the eyes until they became accustomed to it.

Stevin called something out in a language Kyrus did not understand. Based on his guess about the symbols on the walls, he supposed that the lad was using Kheshi. Stevin seemed to be very polite in addressing the older man, which he gathered meant Stevin respected him more than Kyrus.

I suppose either he was just raised to respect his elders, or he figures that Captain Zayne set him as my nanny for the day, so how much respect should I deserve?

"What are you saying to him?" Kyrus asked, after the two appeared to be holding a conversation rather than making the pleasantries of a greeting as a prelude to a business transaction.

"Oh, I know him long time," Stevin said. "I grow up Marker's Point. He a good guy. You can trust him."

"Does he speak Acardian?" Kyrus asked.

What he had in mind would be a lot easier if he could communicate with the old man directly.

"No. Speak Kheshi," Stevin said, confirming Kyrus's conjecture about the language at least, unhelpful though the information was.

Stevin then launched into Kheshi speech at length with the old man, then took Kyrus by the hands and arranged them such that Kyrus's hands were palm up, spread in front of him.

"Tell him name now," he prompted Kyrus.

"Kyrus Hinterdale," Kyrus said dutifully, presumably a part of a formal introduction.

"(Something Kheshi) Shao," the old man replied, finally setting down the book and mirroring Kyrus's spread palms gesture.

"Grandfather Shao take good care you." Stevin nodded at Kyrus.

"Ask him if he can copy from a design I draw," Kyrus said.

Stevin relayed the message. Grandfather Shao carried on at length before stopping to let Stevin translate back.

"He says ya, just draw it and he put anywhere you want," Stevin said.

"That sounded like a lot more than what you translated," Kyrus said.

"He is proud old man. He say a lot you don't care about; I tell you da good stuff," Stevin assured him.

"Find out how much it will cost," Kyrus ordered.

Again, Stevin launched into a conversation that sounded like it included a lot more than his initial request.

"Six thousan' zimbals. I get you good deal," Stevin said, and Kyrus agreed.

Unlike much of the crew, the math behind just how little each zimbal was worth was not so difficult for him. It would have been about the price of a meal at a nicer tavern.

"Umm, he think you not draw too much. You draw all day, he make you pay more, ya?"

"Well, I can deal with that when the time comes," Kyrus said. "Can you ask him for something to draw on?"

A few minutes later, Kyrus was working on the design for the tattoo he wanted. Stevin seemed like he was not the type for waiting and started getting restless after not terribly long. Grandfather Shao had initially showed some slight interest in what Kyrus was starting to draw, but seeing that he did not recognize the design, he went back to his book.

"Stevin, I think I will be fine here, if you wish to enjoy the markets. I do not think I will get into any trouble here," Kyrus assured the lad.

"You not have tell me twice." Stevin winked and ducked out of the parlor in a clamor of bells before Kyrus could say another word.

Kyrus worked for a few minutes, double- and then triple-checking his work. His final check was less obvious, but the design seemed to hold up to all scrutiny—it held the tiny bit of aether he released into it. He got Grandfather Shao's attention and showed him the design, a vertical series of runes, nearly identical to the ones he had carved into the door of his cabin.

The old man examined it critically, nodding slightly, then looked at Kyrus and raised an eyebrow eloquently, glancing over Kyrus. Kyrus took the hint and worked his way out of his tunic. He described an area of his upper left arm by pointing and outlining with his finger. Grandfather Shao nodded again, seeming satisfied. He gestured Kyrus to recline on the couch and then dragged his chair around to where Kyrus's shoulder was. He took the paper from Kyrus and turned it this way and that, until Kyrus took hold of it and lined it up on his shoulder right where he wanted it. Then Shao took his thumb and forefinger and held them together, then widened them, then narrowed them, and cocked his head and raised an eyebrow.

"Just like it is there." Kyrus pointed emphatically at the drawn version he had done. He had already accounted for the proper size.

Grandfather Shao nodded sagely.

The old man went to a cupboard in the back of the shop and gathered some glasses and jars contained therein. He poured a glass of something that smelled strongly of alcohol, but had naught but a bit of yellow in it to keep it from being completely clear. The old man daubed a cloth in it and wiped the area clean where he was about to work. Then he poured a second glass of another liquid and handed it to Kyrus. Shao made a quick motion with his wrist, which Kyrus mimicked with the hand *not* holding the glass, trying to confirm whether he was meant to drink it.

"If you say so," Kyrus muttered, and downed the contents.

It burned all the way down and back up when he exhaled afterward. While he was certain he had actually swallowed it, the fumes cleared his nose and made his eyes water.

"You could warn a fellow," Kyrus protested.

The old man chuckled.

"You ... do not speak Acardian ... do you?" Kyrus asked.

Grandfather Shao held out one hand and wobbled it side to side, and shrugged. "Mebbe li'l," he admitted, and the two of them shared a chuckle.

Kyrus winced as the first needle pierced his skin, and several times throughout the ordeal Grandfather Shao had stopped his work to cuff him on the side of the head and lay into him in a string of invectives in Kheshi that, despite the language barrier, clearly called into question his manhood.

It seemed like a day, and in truth had taken hours, but at the end—like so many things—it was done.

The whole of his left shoulder felt bee-stung, but Kyrus looked at the result and compared it to the paper copy he had made. If Kyrus had been an Expert Scrivener, then Grandfather Shao had every right to be called an Expert

Tattooist. The markings matched identically, with not a line out of place or a proportion amiss.

The true test was in practice, and Kyrus drew aether. Watching in his now habitual split aether-vision, he directed it into the ward that Grandfather Shao had carved into his arm. It glowed in the aether, just like his cabin door had, and a grin spread widely across his face. Grandfather Shao assumed that he was just especially pleased with the work, and he smiled in return.

"Can you keep a secret?" Kyrus asked, but Shao just looked at him quizzically. "Well, let me show you something anyway."

Kyrus slowly and carefully drew the cutlass from its scabbard, turning away from Shao, lest he feel threatened. With equal care, he pressed the blade against his forearm, gently at first, and when he saw no sign of duress from the ward, pressed firmly. When that showed no sign of affecting the ward either, he pulled back the blade and swung it lightly into his arm. Again the ward held.

Grandfather Shao's eyes were wide; he rambled something in Kheshi that Kyrus could not understand, but seemed rather shocked. Kyrus just slid the blade back into its scabbard and pointed to the markings on his arm, which Shao had just tattooed there. Shao just pointed to himself in confusion, incredulous that he was being credited with the result he had just seen.

Kyrus caught the old man's eye straying to the drawing on the table, where he had left it after confirming it was an accurate copy. Kyrus could see gold reflected in those eyes, which he could understand, even if Shao could not understand that without the knowledge of how to activate it, the ward would be nothing but decoration.

To save Shao some trouble in his future, Kyrus reached over and picked up the drawing. He raised his own eyebrows in imitation of Shao's own gesture, and smiled. Then he incinerated the drawing with a quick jolt of aether, sending it to the floor and ceiling, half smoke, half ash, letting go of it just in time to avoid burning himself badly.

"Sorry," Kyrus said. " I hope this will make up for it."

He pulled a trade bar from his pocket and handed it to the old man. It was worth twenty times the price he had been asked.

"Thank you," Kryus told Grandfather Shao as he stood to leave, gathering his tunic and pulling it over his head.

"Tanks you," Grandfather Shao replied, wide-eyed.

* * * * * * *

Kyrus had a swagger in his step as he wandered the marketplace. He had just put Kadrin wards and Acardian—or, in this case, Marker's Point—tattooing together in a way that he felt was sure to protect him from anything that he was likely to get stuck, slashed, or run through with in the marketplace. He was feeling rightly proud of himself as he casually browsed the wares offered from all across the Tellurak.

It actually reminded him a lot of the day that the trading ships' merchants had set up shop in Acardia. He wished Abbiley could have been there to see all the bizarre sights of Marker's Point's much larger version. It somehow seemed more authentic here, without the backdrop of Kyrus's hometown making everything seem safe and compartmentalized. Here, there was no scrivener's shop to go home to, just a pirate ship.

He wondered what Expert Davin would think of him, signing on with Captain Zayne. *I hope he would be able to see the extenuating circumstances. I mean, I was going to be executed, and Captain Zayne and that big fellow, Tawmund, came and helped me break out of jail.*

While every marketplace had food, drink, and various cloth and baubles, Marker's Point seemed to go well beyond those hawkers' staples. One stall was set up with displays of wicker baskets, each containing a deadly venomous snake. Blades were widely sold, mainly the small, easily concealed type. Though all were considered contraband in Acardia, here there was mindroot, red-leafed clover, ru-spider venom, kokoi grass, firebat fur, dami juice, and lichberries, all sold openly. Kyrus could not even remember which among them were deadly poisons and which were recreational hallucinogens.

Kyrus kept one eye to seeing if he could spot Stevin again, but generally he just enjoyed browsing among the various transient merchants who had set up shop for a week, a season, or longer, depending how quickly they ran out of the wares they had brought from their homelands. He stopped at the more permanent structures as well, mostly run by trading houses and longstanding traders who had goods shipped to Marker's Point just to resell them. It was slow going for a while, until Kyrus learned that with enough persistence, he could usually find someone who spoke enough Acardian to help make a deal.

By the time the sun had gone down, Kyrus had cleared quite a lot of space in his pockets. He had purchased an entire new set of clothing that fit him properly. He wore a new set of low-cut boots that the shopkeeper who he bought them from insisted would help him keep his footing on the deck of a ship. He also found a shop that had a comb made from a seashell, a material that Kyrus was rather indifferent to, just wanting to get a comb of any sort, and purchased that as well. Somewhere along the way, he also bought a rucksack, as his awkward bundle was beginning to worry him. At what he best thought was dinnertime by the ache in his stomach, Kyrus tried eel-on-a-stick for the first time—though possibly for the only time, as it was not terribly tasty. An impulse purchase of salt, pepper, and something nice-smelling called "raosh" rounded out his shopping trip.

As Kyrus wended his way back toward where the *Harbinger* was moored, he found a place with an unbroken view to the west to watch the colors in the sky change. He had never seen the sunset over the water before; Scar Harbor only saw sunrises. The pinks and reds were supposed to mean something about the weather the next day, but Kyrus did not care about that. He just stopped to enjoy the colors over the water, again wishing that he had Abbiley to watch it with.

Night had fully fallen well before Kyrus got halfway back to the ship. He continued along in a circular fashion, keeping the bay to his right hand as best he could manage. There was nothing quite resembling a main thoroughfare in the whole of the city, just an endless web of interwoven streets and alleys. The roads were often lit by lanterns, but many could only be followed by starlight. Even as late as it was, there were the noises of taverns and brothels keeping the night from seeming either peaceful or eerie, merely seedy.

Kyrus had learned a few tricks of getting bearings by the night sky during Stalyart's first few lessons on navigation, and he used them when he was unsure whether he was still proceeding in the right direction. At one desolate intersection, when he stopped to look up, he heard a voice that he could only surmise was addressing him.

"You lost, kid?" he heard from the shadows of a nearby building. The voice spoke Acardian like a native, but did not sound friendly toward its countryman.

Kyrus thought better of answering and just made a hasty decision about a direction and got moving.

"Hey now, no reason to be runnin' off like that," another voice joined in from an alley he was passing by.

"This is our territory here, and at night, there's a fee for passin' through it," the first voice came again, and this time Kyrus could make out a figure approaching him.

Correction, several figures, Kyrus realized as the friends of the first voice came out of hiding.

Kyrus realized he had let his aether-vision slip during his time admiring the offerings in the marketplace, and he fixed his vision back into its hybrid view. Instantly the night came alive in Kyrus's sight. While the roads and alleys were as much of a mystery as before, his antagonists came into clear focus. There were eleven of them, which was a larger number than Kyrus had hoped for, and it seemed that they had all the routes of escape manned.

"I shall pay no fee. I will just be on my way," Kyrus said to no one in particular.

"I thinks ya will," replied a new, third voice. "What's ya got in that sack? We be takin' that fer starters."

"I think not, now stand back."

Kyrus pulled his cutlass from its scabbard. He gave a quick glance at his shoulder and could see the runes clearly even through his tunic, glowing with aether. Kyrus drew in a bit more aether and funneled it into the ward, making sure it would have all that it could need in what was clearly looking like it was going to become a fight.

"O, ho! This one has some fight in him," the first voice called out, now clearly visible even in the scant light. He was a smallish man, his bald head reflecting the starlight, and he was dressed in dark work clothes. He looked like a longshoremen.

Kyrus heard blades being drawn all around him. He spun about to see that the ring of men around him was drawing closed.

"Now why not set that sword down and hand over the sack and whatever else you got on ya," the first man said, clearly not asking despite the phrasing of his statement.

"No man has crossed blades with me and lived," Kyrus bluffed, trying to manage his best impression of Rashan Solaran. He could not help but think that if the demon warlock had been present, these ruffians would have already been washing the cobblestones with their lifeblood.

"Sure. I heard that one before," the first man said, obviously the leader of the group. "Bag him. We can sell him off to that Hurlan merchant ship that's short on oarsmen."

The ring of ruffians responded at once, approaching from all sides.

Kyrus was holding the weapon correctly, as Brannis had learned to wield a sword, but again his brawnier counterpart's training failed him. The first time one of the ruffians tried to hack at him, he blocked the blow full on, and his sword was smashed back into him. The second strike, from behind him, he had no time to even attempt a parry and the ward absorbed the blow. By the third strike, a third man had also closed to arm's reach and joined in as well. Kyrus managed to parry one blow to the side before the other nicked him in the arm— stopped thankfully by his ward—and managed to recover in time to slash back and catch one of his attackers across the chest.

All pretense of proper sword-fighting technique blew away like a fog before a gale, and Kyrus lashed out at any exposed limb or body he could find, trusting in the ward to deflect any blows and his aether-vision to keep an eye behind him.

"What the...?"

"I thought I got him!"

"Hey, what gives?"

His opponents began to catch on that there was something not right. Each blow they landed seemed ineffective. It was understandable when a single cut did not fell a foe, especially one who might have leathers on beneath his comically oversized tunic, but too many hits were being landed for their prey to have shown no effect. Finally one enterprising thug took a new tactic and, with a great swipe, smashed the cutlass from Kyrus's hand after parrying one of his less graceful thrusts.

Uh-oh! Kyrus thought as the sword fight became a wrestling match.

Men who were intent to take him captive and sell him off as slave labor aboard a ship no longer needed swords to defend themselves, and dropped them. Arms grabbed at Kyrus, some pulling away the rucksack that he had carried over his shoulder the whole fight and others latching on to hold him. Someone threw a sack over his head, and all but the aether went dark. With the press of bodies all around him and none of them identifiable by their Source, Kyrus was not sure who was the one who pressed a big, meaty hand over his mouth and nose, but it instantly made it impossible to breath. As Kyrus was already beginning to breathe hard from the fight, the effect was immediately dire.

Kyrus panicked and drew all the aether he could.

A moment later, Kyrus was coughing and choking, gasping in the smoke-filled air to try in vain to catch his breath. He hastily grabbed the scorched rucksack and stumbled away, picking no direction in particular. All around him, buildings burned, and the ring of buildings closest to him had been reduced to fiery rubble. There were screams and panicked shouting filling the night air as people raced to escape the flames, but not from any of Kyrus's attackers, who were now nothing but ash on the night breeze.

* * * * * * * *

Kyrus sat in his cabin, protected behind two wards now, the door's and his own. The smell of smoke was unmistakable about him, even though the scorched rucksack had been thrown into the bay once he had unpacked its contents; the smell had gotten into his hair and clothing as he had escaped the scene of destruction he had created.

He wondered what Davin would say if he had seen him destroy a moderately sized chunk of a city. He wondered what Abbiley would think of him if she knew that he had just killed not only eleven men who had threatened his life—which she might easily forgive—but uncounted others who had just happened to be too close by when it happened. Magic was so alien to their view of the world that the fact of his magic use alone might easily cloud their opinion of him. He then wondered what Iridan would think, or Rashan. He could not help but wonder, despite his own and even Brannis's better judgment, what Juliana would think of him.

I worry that Abbiley and Davin would fear me. Iridan and Rashan would probably applaud me. Juliana ... she would make fun of my aim.

Kyrus was pulled from his musings by someone stopping outside his door. He had not lapsed back into single vision again since the incident with the thugs, so he could see the figure on the other side of his door by its Source. There was a pause for a moment, then Kyrus heard a knocking coming from the wall just next to the door.

Ward works. Kyrus could not help a small smile at that.

"Captain wants to see you," came the voice of Tawmund, who seemed to be settling into a role as Captain Zayne's bodyguard and personal servant.

"Very well. I will be along directly," Kyrus replied.

Kyrus began to sort himself out, taking off the sword belt and tugging at the folds of his clothing to try to air the smell of smoke out of them as best he could.

"Now!" came the impatient reply from outside his cabin door.

Kyrus was sorely tempted to just let the man stew outside while he readied himself, but thought better of it when considering that the captain might be upset with him already if he suspected that Kyrus was involved in the fire.

Kyrus opened the door to find Tawmund just outside. He glared up at the huge thug without saying anything, until Tawmund backed away. Kyrus strode past him and across the deck to the captain's cabin. Kyrus did not think to knock as he opened the door. He found Captain Zayne inside, along with Stalyart. They were looking over papers at the captain's desk. Denrik looked up at his entrance and gazed testily at him.

"Close the door, Mr. Reggelend, and see they we are not disturbed," he called out to Tawmund, who had followed Kyrus to the captain's cabin. When the door had been closed, he turned to Kyrus. "Is this how it is going to be? First night in port and you bring down hellfire in the middle of the streets? If they connect this back to us, we will be lucky to escape with our lives."

"I was attacked in the streets. I tried to fight them off with a saber, but ... well ... I am not much good with one. They disarmed me and grabbed me—the rest was just a reflex," Kyrus explained.

"Reaction? You cast a hellfire spell and call it a reaction? You cannot—"

"No, I just hurled fire. I do not know any real sort of war spells. I mean ... I want to someday, mind you ... but ... it may not be easy to just stumble across someone I can watch to learn them from. I tend to stay away from battlefields," Kyrus said.

"No. Just ... no. I refuse to believe you did that just firehurling," Denrik protested. "Firstly, you would have charred yourself to a husk from the inside channeling that much aether through you raw like that. Secondly, you could not have caused that much destruction. By the waves, boy, we felt that here by the waterfront. I was in the Man-Eating Shark buying ale for every worthless wretch I could find, hoping to find a few pearls among the oysters, and everyone took note of it. The building shook."

"It was very loud, Mr. Hinterdale, and we see smoke block out the stars in that direction," Stalyart added.

"I was ... scared," Kyrus protested weakly.

"Well, one way or another, just think not of leaving the ship until we shove off. Remember that 'Kadrin behavior' we spoke of? Consider this sort of thing added to that list. I shall not have you burning down half of every port city we stop at," Denrik said.

"Well, then, teach me something easier to defend myself with. You said you would teach me magics as I needed them. If this is not evidence enough that I need some spells to defend myself with, I do not know what would be," Kyrus answered back, growing a little bolder. Something was beginning to dawn on him. "If it was not for the ward protecting me, I likely would have died tonight."

"They are called shields, not wards. Wards are for protecting objects," Denrik corrected him.

"Are they?" Kyrus asked.

Denrik looked at him suspiciously. Kyrus watched for the telltale sign of a sorcerer losing himself into the aether and saw it, followed shortly by a look of surprise on Denrik's face.

"What is it, Captain?" Stalyart asked.

"This fool had a ward tattooed into his arm," Denrik told him. "Mr. Hinterdale, you *do* know that thing is going to eat into your own Source, do you not?"

"What?" Kyrus was shocked.

He had not considered that there may be side effects to the protective ward on his arm. It was the same one he had used to protect the door against physical damage, and the door has seemed none the worse for it

"Wards are hungry things. They weaken over time, but rarely fail completely unless they are damaged. That is because they take aether from nearby, bits at a time only, but enough to sustain themselves. By the same manner, if they are too close to a Source, they will drain from that Source to keep themselves going. That is why many sorcerers shun warded garments, and if they do wear them, keep the wards away from their skin. You have just attached a leech to your Source," Denrik said, clearly exasperated with Kyrus's rash decision.

"I do not feel it doing anything to me," Kyrus protested. He had not noticed the ward doing anything to his Source, and if it was, the effect must have been miniscule.

"I admit, your Source is strong, but be warned … that thing will eat away at you until you rue the day you got it," Denrik said. "I am starting to truly question whether you are worth keeping around, if this is the sort of decision you are making."

"Well, then, just remember this. If Captain Zayne is going to be the most feared pirate in the Katamic again," Kyrus said, remembering that on a few occasions he had noted that the captain seemed proud of that particular ignominy, "you are going to have to overcome the fact that the navy captured you, and everyone knows it. Stealing a navy ship might help a little, but having a fearsome sorcerer as part of your crew will help not only your reputation but also your capability. Do you think you would even have been captured in the first place, had I been a part of your crew then? If you are rid of me, I think you might not last long."

Denrik just raised an eyebrow, not having expected Kyrus to talk back as he had. The old pirate seemed like he knew Kyrus had a point, though. If Denrik could keep him reined him in, Kyrus would be an irreplaceable asset to the ship.

When neither Denrik nor Stalyart responded immediately, Kyrus asked, "Will that be all, Captain?"

"Yes," Denrik replied slowly. "Yes, I think that will do, Mr. Hinterdale."

With that, Kyrus turned and left. He passed the stoic Tawmund on the other side of the door without saying a word. He knew without having to ask that the giant had heard every word he had spoken to the captain. He doubted that the brute had understood half the things they had discussed, but there was enough that was unmistakable that it would certainly give the man pause to consider before laying a hand on him. When Kyrus reached the solitude of his own cabin, he renewed the ward on the door and collapsed down onto the bed, his heart racing.

Did I just threaten the legendary Captain Zayne? Kyrus wondered. *I think I just did. And I think it just might have worked.*

* * * * * * * *

"What do you make of him, Stalyart?" Denrik asked his first mate.

The clutter of papers on the desk went disregarded. His earlier discussion of the merits of various men vying for places on the crew—names jotted down on those same papers—was set aside.

"I like him," Stalyart stated. "He does not know what he is doing, but he does it anyway ... boldly! He could have begged from you forgiveness, made promises, but no. Instead he tells you that you need him and threatens you if you toss him off the ship."

"You heard his story about his life in Veydrus. I am beginning to question parts of it. He seems to know more spells than he is letting on. I still do not believe that he was just firehurling when he obliterated that district," Denrik said, looking to Stalyart for confirmation.

"I believe him, and I do not believe him. Think about you. Here you are a pirate, feared and respected, but not by everyone. In Veydrus, in Megrenn, you are the hero; you fought to free your people from Kadrin; you're loved and honored, and respected by all. Are you not the same man as him? If your places were switched, would you live as a saint, using magic to protect everyone in Harvin from harm? Would Denrik Zayne be a pirate in Megrenn waters? I think your own people would hate pirates more than even the ones in this world," Stalyart said. "In the other world, Mr. Hinterdale says he is a robber of merchants, who kills when he has to but not all the time, so he does not attract too much attention. Well, what if this robber was not so strong, and lived where he did not need to rob to make money—maybe he works as a scribe. Maybe that robber takes the easy path of food on the table every day, and no risk of being caught. Then what if that same weak man becomes strong and learns magic. Maybe that weak man learns there is more than meals and safety to be had. Maybe the wolf pup who was raised by sheep grew up and realized it was a wolf all along, that its fangs were not meant for eating grass."

"Interesting theory. You believe him, then?"

"No, Captain. That Mr. Hinterdale is a liar. He is changing things in his story. Some of it is true. Some is not true. I think all things you could try to catch him at, he probably tells you the truth. He is Kadrin, because you could ask him to speak it, and he could not fake knowing it fluently. He knows how to use a sword there—we know because you tested him—and he obviously did not learn fencing as a scribe. Maybe some of the rest is true too, but I suspect all of it for now."

"What makes you so sure he is a liar?" Denrik asked. He trusted his friend's judgment but was curious what made the man so sure.

"He cheated us all at cards."

Denrik's brow drew together and cocked his head to the side, eying Stalyart curiously.

Chapter 28 - Out in the Cold

[What news of G'thk and his troops?] the deep sonorous voice thrummed through the forest, the harsh consonants of the goblin-speech she used among her followers snapped and cracked like the felling of a tree.

The dragon's footsteps did not shake the ground or rattle the trees the way her voice did. The dragon's gait was graceful and balanced, despite the awesome bulk of her body. The long claws dug trenches into the ground as she gained traction with each step, and shallow depressions formed beneath each foot in spite of the cold hard soil of the forest floor.

[The report is that they are eager to conquer but remain respectfully, awaiting your arrival before advancing. The human sorcerer is becoming an annoyance, pressing the general to move sooner,] the priest reported.

[I begin to agree with the human. Order G'thk to move his troops. We will speed our pace and catch up to him as he reaches the mines,] the dragon ordered testily.

Ni'Hash'Tk was miserable in the cold, though she tried her best to hide the worst of her discomfort from the goblins outside of her priesthood. The priests were aware and accepting of both her divinity and her few flaws. They played up the former and helped to cover up the latter when dealing with those outside the dragon's most loyal minions. Ni'Hash'Tk was covered in a blanket of sorts, made from scores of ice-bear pelts, custom fitted to her reptilian form, complete with cutouts to allow her wings a full range of motion; the wings had their own ice-bear furs keeping them warm. She had not ventured out of her lair in winter—and Ni'Hash'Tk cared little that the astronomers insisted it was still only autumn—in centuries and was constantly reminded of why. The world was miserable and cold outside her lair, with snows and winds and ground that might have been ice for all she cared to distinguish.

[I will send word at once, Mighty One,] the priest replied.

[Be sure to send a skyrider. I wish them to make all haste. Let them leave no more than a token garrison. If the humans retake their city, so be it,] Ni'Hash'Tk added.

The human mines were in a mountain that was once a volcano. If she was not mistaken, there should be warmth aplenty within its depths. It would be tempting to winter there and wait until the warmer weather before venturing back to her own lair.

[As you wish, Mighty One,] the priest acknowledged.

* * * * * * * *

Jinzan was standing on the balcony of Lord Feldrake's manor, looking to the north. He could see the Cloud Wall as if they were at the base of it. The mountains were so high that on the two-day trek to Raynesdark, it would barely shift in their view as the army approached it. He was being denied his prize by that arrogant lizard, and it galled him. He knew his plan so well he could have executed it in his sleep. No amount of tinkering or fiddling with it was likely to improve upon it; he had but to be given the opportunity to put it into play.

With the time he had on his hands, he had taken to trying to solve Denrik's problems instead. *That Acardian sorcerer is such an enigma. He had seemed such an innocent, bookish lad at first, overwhelmed by the enormity of the world outside his master's shop. Then he nearly single-handedly holds off a navy crew and burns down a ship with nothing but hurled fire. After that, two days of tutoring and he navigated us into Marker's Point, as if he had been years at the trade. I send him into the city with a guide as good as any native, and he manages to not only lose his guide, but to get accosted as well, and nearly killed. But no, he was not killed; he managed to slaughter everyone threatening him and bring every building in the area down around his ears as well.*

Who is he? Jinzan wondered. *After what Stalyart figured out, I no longer believe the innocent façade. If he can cheat the likes of the men around that table at Crackle, I think wordplay would be but a lark.*

Stalyart—tides bless the man—had picked up on it. The lad was lost in the game at first; he knew the rules but was no match for the type of opponents he faced. He stared at his own cards and the common cards, typical of a beginner. A master such as Stalyart, or even reasonably skilled players such as Denrik, watched their opponents, since no amount of staring at one's own cards will tell you anything new about them. Stalyart had noticed that Kyrus started to turn his "luck" around when he started staring at his opponents' cards and the ones about to be dealt. He lost some small pots but never became entangled for much money unless he was sure to win.

Stalyart was not sure how he did it, but knew he did it. I know how, though. That boy must have marked the cards with aether. I would have caught him at it easily, but not Denrik. Denrik can barely see into the aether at all, and the effort gives him headaches.

Somewhere out in this world, there is a dark mirror of that boy running free. He is probably as much like Kyrus as Denrik is like me: a magic-less outcast who has had to make do with his wits and daring. What sort of man would that make him, if he truly is Kadrin? Jinzan mused.

There were certain facts of Kyrus's story that were too easily checked for him to have lied about them. Faking a Kadrin accent might be difficult, and faking speaking it entirely would not fool Jinzan in the least. It was galling to think that some little nobody from Acardia had pulled such a ruse on him, but the rest of Kyrus's story was entirely called into question. Was he a highwayman? Was he truly now north of Pevett? Did he truly come by his magic from imitating some itinerant sorcerer who took up with brigands? The last was the most obvious lie in the bunch. If he was to begin questioning Kyrus's story, that was the place to start.

Kadrin was run by sorcerers. The army knew it. The nobles knew it. Even the emperor likely knew it. The Inner Circle wielded more power than the Megrenn High Councilors did, and they were the official seat of power in the kingdom, for Megrenn was a kingdom in name only. The Circle doled out that power generously to the sorcerers of the Empire, giving them free rein and freedom from all but themselves and a scant few others. Those sorcerers that served the noble houses were only slightly less well off, given that the populace was conditioned to treat all sorcerers as a higher class of citizen. The thought of rogue sorcerers making their way by brigandry was ... unlikely, at the least. Nearly any crime could be forgiven, and if the Circle would not have him, a sorcerer could find a patron with ease, if not among the nobles then among the wealthiest of the merchant elite.

So ... what then?

Where would he have learned magic that he would want to keep it secret? Jinzan regretted that Denrik may have shown his hand too soon. Kyrus had not known that he was a Megrenn sorcerer before giving his own story, but that did not excuse the lapse in being so frank with the lad. Kyrus had claimed to harass the Kadrins along the trade-ways, and he had wanted to do him one better. Kyrus had led with a feint, and Denrik had fallen for it.

So the lad was smart. He could accept that and brush aside the sting of being fooled so that he might puzzle through who Kyrus might be in Veydrus. He could not trust him in Tellurak until he knew who he was dealing with. It was about time to start piecing together what he knew and trying to fill in the missing pieces with the best guesses he could make.

Kyrus's counterpart was very likely Kadrin and knew how to use a sword with some skill—that much Kyrus was able to demonstrate, though his counterpart was clearly more fit for such swordplay. He was most likely *not* a robber and had almost certainly not learned magic from some rogue sorcerer. Unless the Empire had changed much since the rebellion, Kadrin had no rogue sorcerers.

Let us begin with where he learned the rudiments of magic. If he had proper training in magic, he would never have been so generally ignorant of spells and the way aether and Sources work. If he was faking being such an ignoramus, he is far, far ahead in this test of wits. I shall consider that eventuality later, perhaps. For now, who would have access to shoddy teaching in spells? A nobleman with a sorcerer in his family's employ, perhaps. A guardsman in the Tower of Contemplation? A possibility. He could be a sibling to a sorcerer, but that would not fit as well as the first two in explaining why he might also be skilled with a blade.

Jinzan blew out a frustrated sigh and ran his fingers through his hair. He needed more information to go on. There were too many unknowns, and he risked deluding himself should he commit too far down an incorrect path. Perhaps Kyrus's twin was nothing worth troubling about. It was possible that he was merely being prudent, especially now that he knew that Denrik's counterpart was Megrenn.

Blast it, if only I had not been so eager to make his alliance and given him a clear answer.

Jinzan was rescued from his self-torment by a Source approaching from behind. Aside from the sorcerers and the assassin, Gkt'Lr, all the goblins Sources looked alike to him. He turned to see who was intruding upon his solitude.

[Cheer up, sorcerer, you are getting your wish,] G'thk greeted him.

The goblin general was in his travel gear, layer upon layer of wolf furs over his uniform. The general clearly intended to ride, as his gait was hindered by the overabundance of warm clothing weighing him down. Jinzan smiled wryly; Megrenn may have been far warmer—lying north of the Kadrin Empire, with the ocean-borne currents bringing warm weather down from tropical regions— but he could brave cold weather that would turn the goblins to worthless, shivering wretches. He could only hope that their skittishness about the cold could be suppressed long enough to conduct a battle in late-autumn weather in the Cloud Wall.

"We are leaving? How soon?" Jinzan got right to the point. He was weary, though truly only mentally, of all the waiting. The sooner they left, the better.

[Mighty Ni'Hash'Tk is planning to catch up with us at the mines. Gather what you need, as we leave immediately,] G'thk said. The general now seemed as eager to go as Jinzan.

"So you deliver messages personally now?" Jinzan joked. G'thk had rarely come to him directly, preferring to send an underling to summon him, or even deliver a message directly.

The general chuckled. [Yes, it seems. The messengers are all afraid of you, sorcerer. They think you are angry and will kill one soon. None wants to be the one to anger you enough that you finally do it.]

"So does this mean we are attacking in two days?" Jinzan asked. He wanted to be sure that there would be no further delays.

[Do not worry, sorcerer. When Ni'Hash'Tk arrives, there will be no question of delaying the attack. This will be glorious. Not only will we win a new lair for Ni'Hash'Tk's whelp, but we will have a great deal of plunder for us as well. We also have word that there are many more of your toys being brought along. The tinkers like them, and the other generals are beginning to request them as well. They have been making them without stop since the first were finished. The ones they bring with them will make our triumph simple.]

"That is … excellent news," Jinzan said.

Well, if by "excellent," you mean "disastrous." I had not anticipated the goblins' zeal for the things. Megrenn had best stay on their good side through this war, else we may find a formidable enemy on our western border.

The general left him to see to his preparations. Jinzan lingered for a moment on the balcony. He looked again to the north and imagined that he could see Raynesdark against the mountain backdrop.

And what might I find when I get there? Will Kyrus turn out to be the son of the lord of the mines? Have I perhaps alerted an Inner Circle guardsman who spies between worlds? Will there be a dozen sorcerers manning the walls when we arrive?

Jinzan left his vantage point and found his way back to the room he had commandeered. Not far from the lord's balcony, the hallways teemed with goblin soldiers. Preparations were already well under way, with much of the equipment the goblins had been storing in the manor house having already been removed. The goblins took their deity's orders to heart and were ill-inclined to displease her.

Fortunately the goblins feared Jinzan enough that none impeded him as he stalked along the stone-walled corridors. The day they had arrived, those same corridors had been adorned with tapestries and paintings but now were bare. The tapestries had been claimed as spoils of war, and the paintings—showing visages of Kadrin noblemen to have inhabited the place—had been relegated to the fireplaces to keep them warm. It felt to Jinzan as if they were beginning the task of rewriting Kadrin history ... and writing the Kadrins right out of it. Illard's Glen may have been a small step along the path Jinzan had chosen to blaze, but Raynesdark would be a much greater achievement. In just a few days' time, he would be walking through the halls of Duke Pellaton's castle in the same manner.

He arrived at his temporary quarters to find them occupied. One of the chambermaids was busily packing his belongings, neatly folding his spare clothes—freshly laundered—and bundling them into his traveling pack. Jinzan glanced around the room, ignoring both her curtsy and greeting of "Milord" as he brushed past her and began to search the room. He scanned though the chest of drawers hastily, finding nothing.

"I have nearly finished packing, milord," the girl claimed, a tremor in her voice.

She was one of the pretty ones he had allowed to share his bed, though he had not bothered putting a name to her. She was clearly ill at ease about something, and he had not recalled her being so timid when last she was in his room.

"Why are you disturbing my belongings?" Jinzan demanded.

"The ... The goblins are preparing to leave. I assumed ... you would be departing with them. I was helping you pack. I ... wanted to repay your ... kindness," she finished quietly, starting to sob.

Jinzan had indeed made a habit of seeing that the manor staff were treated well, even if many of them had been pressed into service from other backgrounds and knew little of their assigned work. The goblins cared little either way, and Jinzan got much more ... cooperation than he would have otherwise as a tyrant. He was suspicious of her motives nonetheless.

"Step aside, girl," he barked at her and then swept her out of his way as he ripped open the pack and began removing its contents.

He found what he was looking for buried near the bottom of the folded clothing: a pair of scroll cases. He popped the end of one and was satisfied that its contents were intact. As he was opening the other, his aether-sense felt the girl moving for the door behind him. He whirled suddenly and caught her by the wrist as she tried to bolt.

"What have we here?" He grabbed her hand, now clenched in a fist, and pried it open. There were slight ink stains on her fingers, no doubt from the documents he had just inspected. "Curious, were we? What were you looking for in my belongings?"

Without warning, a plume of fire in front of his face startled Jinzan. Stumbling backward, singed but not otherwise injured, Jinzan lost his grip on the chambermaid, who made her escape out of the bedroom door. Feeling his face briefly to make sure he still had everything he began the day with, he found only eyebrows to be lacking. Other than that one omission, his face felt as if he had been in the sun too long but not bleeding or weeping as a severe burn might.

Thus satisfied, he took off after the chambermaid. She was half his age and had a head start, but he liked his odds. He had real magic—not like her feeble attempt at firehurling—and an entire city full of goblins on his side.

As he reached the hallway, he shouted, "Stop that girl!" then corrected himself and hoarsely crackled [Stop that girl!] in goblin speech, nearly choking himself in the process. He hated speaking the worthless language even at a conversational volume, but shouting was more than his voice could bear. Still, the nearest goblins began to give chase and spread the alarm. [Alive!] he added, almost not bothering due to the trouble of giving the order loudly enough to hear over the din in the manor.

Jinzan did not even bother to give chase personally. Far from a feeble old man, life extension had been good to him, but he was no athlete. Let less important men—or in this case, goblins—do the work instead. If she had any other tricks, let them find out firsthand instead of him.

A few moments later, she was hauled back before him. A dozen goblins trained spears on her, guarding the two that held ropes tethered to her bound wrists. The front of her chambermaid's dress was torn and bloodied at knee height, and her hands and elbows were raw and bloodied, likely by the goblins dragging her to the ground. Her face was bruised and bloody as well, evidence that the goblins had felt she needed more subduing than just the ropes.

[Good work,] he praised the group in general, seeing no officer among the goblins who had captured the girl.

"Who are you?" Jinzan asked, speaking Kadrin.

He looked the girl over in a different light now, trying to divine what he could without her answer, rather than doing his thinking with his loins. She was fair-skinned, common among Kadrins native to the southern half of the Empire, with dark hair, bordering on black. That she kept it cropped short at jaw length was either a sign of low status or a part of her disguise. Nothing prevented highborn women from keeping their hair short, but fashioning elaborate hairstyles was a common hobby among the idle elite, sorcerer and noble alike. Her disappearing act showed that she had some muscle beneath the deceptive curves of hers, but youth could often provide such, even when less active habits were preferred.

"Celia Mistfield, Seventh Circle," she replied defiantly. "The Circle will ransom my safe return."

"Seventh Circle. That would explain why you could barely even singe me with hurled fire. I suppose, though, your weak Source was the only reason you could even pass among the common folk in the first place. How old are you, girl?"

Celia was silent for a moment, as if considering whether she should answer at all. "Nineteen autumns, if I live to tomorrow," she said, not meeting his gaze.

"Nineteen autumns ... and already such a good spy. What did you hope to find among my things? Were you hoping to discover my plan and warn someone?" Jinzan asked.

"No," she said simply, defiant in her lack of explanation. Her head was lowered, but she was still watching him, glaring death at him through her drooping bangs.

If she had any power behind those eyes, I would likely be in great pain right now, Jinzan mused.

[Drop the ropes. I will handle her,] Jinzan ordered quietly.

The two goblins looked wary of their captive as they turned her loose, but neither questioned the order nor hesitated in carrying it out.

Times like this remind me of why I began dealing with them in the first place. Such efficient little minions. No fuss, just obedience among the rank and file.

Celia was still ringed by spear points and was going nowhere, as the former rope-holders ducked under the circle of sharpened steel to safety. Jinzan used a bit of silent magic and the slackened rope came alive, swirling around her and binding the girl's arms to her sides, then looping around her neck. By the force of the magic pulling on the ropes, he dragged her toward him, motioning to the goblins to allow her to pass. She stumbled as he drew her in, but the force of the ropes kept her from toppling over. If there was one thing that goblins respected, it was a good show of magical force. They saw that the human sorcerer had the situation well in hand now; after the first one of them bowed and took his leave, the rest soon followed suit.

"I see you have thrown your lot in with these goblins, rather than you own kind," Celia jeered at him.

She was obviously frightened and lashing out, but he respected that kind of bravado. He made a point of being brutally honest with himself, though, and knew that the satisfaction he was feeling was just trying to compensate for the fool he had been made by *another* young Kadrin sorcerer, who seemed both cleverer than this one and a thousand times more dangerous.

"My own kind? I assure you my own kind is Megrenn, not goblin ... nor is it Kadrin, I might add. Your Empire has overstayed its welcome on the continent, and we are driving you out of it, slowly but inevitably. We took back our own lands at great cost, and now we have rebuilt and have the power to put an end to your dominion," Jinzan said.

The goblins knew his general plan but were absorbed in their own concerns.

Stalyart knew well enough as well, but only cared for the money he could make. It felt good to lord it over someone of some tiny import among the Kadrins—this less-than-promising sorceress of the Seventh Circle even—and tell them of the vengeance that awaited them.

Still, he felt his point may be lost on her. She was only nineteen, and the rebellion had ended before she was born. She had grown up in a world that had only known a Megrenn free of Kadrin occupation.

Jinzan took a moment to compose himself after his little rant, while Celia remained silent, having no response other than to continue glaring at him.

"Very well, let me assure you that I do not intend to kill you ... *on the condition* that you make no other attempt to escape or cause me or these goblins harm. I care little enough for their infantrymen, but neither will I protect you from them if you anger them enough to warrant them wishing you dead," Jinzan told her.

He stepped back into his room, leaving her in the hall but still within easy earshot, He went about finishing the packing that she had begun, and which he had largely undone. He was untidy about it, though, merely stuffing garments and gear into the pack well enough to get it all in.

"We will be making one more stop. Come along," Jinzan told her as he strode past. He gave a tug on the ropes and dragged her along until she decided to keep up willingly. "You will be accompanying me. I will not have you freezing on the way. We will find you something suitable."

Jinzan brought them to Lord Feldrake's chambers and threw open the doors. G'thk had been using the lord's room as his own but had largely left the lord's clothing unmolested; the wardrobes were too high to be any use to him, and the garments were neither valuable nor offensive to him. Luckily the same apathy extended to Lady Feldrake's wardrobe as well, which Jinzan tore open and began to pillage. He grabbed the first dress that came to hand and brought it over to Celia.

"It seems Lady Feldrake was thicker around the middle and the bust than you, but she was near to your height. Put this on," and with that, ropes uncoiled from around her and dropped to the floor. He pressed the dress into her hands, and she looked at it critically.

"This is much too large for me," she said, holding up the maroon-and-white dress to her middle and wrapping it well over halfway around her.

"I suppose that is what bearing heirs does to a lady's figure," Jinzan called out from the wardrobe, where he was already picking out more suitable travel gear from among Lady Feldrake's belongings. He found petticoats and a long jacket, picked one from an astonishingly large collection of scarves, and found some fur-lined boots, which like as not would be too large for the girl. He tossed each in her general direction as he found them.

He retreated from the wardrobe to find her dutifully struggling into the dress he had handed her. It was wool and much warmer than the damaged chambermaid's outfit she had been wearing, and it seemed she was having trouble lacing up the back. It was a lady's dress and it was expected that a lady would have servants to help with such tasks. Jinzan was impressed by the dexterity she showed in even getting as far as she had, working at the laces behind her back, and he could not help if his gaze lingered down the loose-fitting front of it before taking her by the shoulder and turning her about. He deftly finished up tying the back and pointed to the belt he had left at her feet—the last item he had taken from the Lady Feldrake's collection.

As expected, the boots flopped loosely as she walked; Lady Feldrake must have been a largish woman. Celia took the liberty of obtaining an ermine hat and matching gloves as well, before they departed.

"Are you not going to put something warmer on," Celia asked with unexpected concern in her voice, as they approached the main door of the manor.

"No. It is a simple work of magic to spare myself the worst of the elements, and it reminds the goblins that I am not so weak as they are," Jinan said. "I will see that you get a horse to ride, and you will keep by my side. If the goblins see you alone, outside my sight, they will beat you and send you back to me … and that is if you are lucky. Now come along and you can witness the fall of Raynesdark. Once we are safely within the captured city, we can figure out how to best to see to your situation."

"Are you not worried you waited too long? I would expect that they would have sent reinforcements by now, and be ready for you," Celia said.

Jinzan wondered if she might perhaps be cleverer than she let on as well. Since when did a Seventh Circle know or care anything about military matters? *What is it that they teach Kadrin children these days? Do they all feign incompetence to lull you into underestimating them?*

"The goblins' dragon-goddess is joining the battle. We will meet her at the city in two days' time. I do not care about the reinforcements they might have added—and I doubt they will have any—the dragon will overwhelm them. Kadrin has grown weak. Their armies have shrunk as they trade for their wealth now instead of plundering for it, and the Imperial Circle is a cowardly bunch of old men, with no combat experience worth wooden sword."

"So you have not heard then?" Celia asked, goading him.

"Heard what?" Jinzan could not help but take the bait she had left for him.

"That we have a warlock again." She grinned.

Jinzan studied her face for a moment. The self-satisfaction was evident and seemed genuine. *No, Kadrin is producing too good a crop of liars these days for me to take a prisoner's word for such news. Perhaps she is referring to the demon that the goblins heard reports of. Ni'Hash'Tk will have to deal with that. I have my own plans to attend to.*

"We shall see," was all Jinzan could counter with.

Even he had to admit that he had not made it sound as ominous as he had hoped.

* * * * * * *

[Bring me the assassin,] Ni'Hash'Tk demanded. She loped along, forcing the rest of her army to keep up with her and brooking no rest.

[Your Magnificence, the assassin has already departed some hours ago,] said the priest beside her.

He rode a ground-hawk, a large short-feathered, flightless bird that was strong enough to bear the weight of armed and armored goblin cavalry. They were fierce creatures that were difficult to train, but they were the fastest land creatures that would bear a goblin in combat.

Ni'Hash'Tk's army had shrunk some since she had given the order to quicken their pace. While the troop had been intended for quick travel, there were still not enough mounts to go around. Many of the goblins had managed to crowd atop the chk'p'dn lizards that drew the human rock-launchers, and all the available ground-hawks were being ridden, whereas many had been led on leashes previously, to keep them fresh for battle.

All the goblins who could not find faster transportation than their own feet had fallen behind hours ago. Ni'Hash'Tk assumed that Gkt'Lr was among these.

[Send someone back for him. Bring him a ground-hawk and order him to rejoin us.]

The dragon's angry growl spooked the priest's bird, causing him a moment's panic as he fought to regain control of the skittish animal.

[He did not fall behind, Mighty One,] the priest said, careful not to "correct" her. [He went on ahead of us. If he cares to maintain stealth, we could not catch him even if we sent up skyriders to search for him.]

[Curse that impudent little mouse. He had best make good use of his early arrival. If I find he has not taken enough hearts when we arrive, I will crush him in my jaw and spit him upon the ground,] Ni'Hash'Tk swore.

The eating of a goblin as punishment was at least seen as a noble death—a service to the goddess. Being spat out, though, was a horrible insult, the ultimate rejection by the dragon, beasts known to eat anything they wished, even things most would consider to be inedible.

[As you wish, Your Magnificence,] the priest responded.

Ni'Hash'Tk looked ahead to the east. Through breaks in the trees, she could make out the mountain range the Kadrins called Cloud Wall. The translation of its draconic name was "Godsforge." The volcanoes had been dormant for millennia, but at one time, they belched forth fire and ash and were the home of the fiercest of dragons, before the stone warlords came and took them back for the metals they hid.

Unlike the goblins, who could just see the mountains when the terrain allowed them an unobstructed view, Ni'Hash'Tk's superior eyesight allowed her to make out the city, nestled against the mountainside: the future home of her son, Ruuk'Pt'Kaan.

Chapter 29 - Tour of Duty

Try the road and see the woods,
And feel the wind at sea,
Just pack up all your worldly goods,
And come along with me.

We'll see their sights and eat their food,
And tarry with their lasses,
If their lads break up our mood,
We'll kick their scrawny asses.

Whene'er we stop, which shan't be soon,
With no place left to roam,
We'll pack up 'fore the next day's noon,
And set off back for home!

They sang as they rode, the mood lighter than it had been upon their departure. When traded stories began to wear thin, the mood of the travelers had grown solemn. Brannis had a lot churning in his thoughts, and he had grown prone to long periods of introspection, lost in thought as the others carried on quiet discussions around him, careful not to disturb him. The effects of the tattoo Kyrus had inscribed on his shoulder made Brannis nervous. It had seemed like such a clever idea when he had conceived of it—taking a cultural difference between the worlds and combining two arts into a formidable defense. Kyrus seemed no worse for the ward he bore two days later, but how long would that be the case?

He had made casual inquiries about the use of wards for protecting their persons and the troops, on the pretense of finding innovative ways to combat the goblins' expected attack. None of the four sorcerers had thought it a prudent idea. Iridan worked with wards regularly and thought that it would be unhealthy, though it might work temporarily. Ruuglor thought that simply writing on the skin would not hold up to the rigors of sweat and rubbing cloth, and the rune would be ruined before it provided any real benefit. Brannis could not convey the idea of a tattoo without having to get into more detail than he thought appropriate. He let the matter drop, not satisfied at all with what he had heard.

Brannis knew that it was dangerous to go into battle with troops whose morale was poor, but these were not "troops" in the conventional sense. When conscripts and knights often jested and sang on their way to battle, it felt different. The conscripts, especially if they were completely green, as many were, were easily deluded into the gloried notions of battle that the troubadours peddled. Knights … well, knights were hard to deter. They knew the sins of blood and flesh they were about to face, and faced it anyway; the brotherhood of the knighthood was what they leaned on to get them through.

With Iridan, Ruuglor, Faolen, and Juliana, he was traveling with educated, cultured, and, except for Iridan, untested neophytes. Wars were pages in history books, celebrated with parades. They knew they would see things they had never wished to see, and would fear for their lives, and Brannis could not just sing a trail song to get them to forget that.

It was Juliana, of all people, who had broken the mood by breaking into song. She had an impressive repertoire of trail and tavern songs, many of them bawdy enough to make him blush—though only because the tawdriness of the lyrics was accentuated when a young lady sang them. She did *not*, however, have the voice for them. She could keep time well enough, but the notes held little melody after she was done wringing the tune out of them.

"I apologize for the ones with overly strained meter and poor rhymes," Juliana said. "I learned them from the traders that frequent the city, and translated many of them into Kadrin myself. Much of Kadris is boring, and the songs our bards write are the same. Things are much more entertaining down by the wharfs, where you find all manner of exotic foreigners."

Brannis suspected that young sorceresses of the Sixth Circle needed to be kept busier if she had so much time to spend hanging around dockside barrooms, where she said she learned most of the songs she knew. The songs sounded vaguely familiar, at least as best as Juliana could render them, but Brannis knew the words to only a few.

"I used to wonder what you did with your free time," Brannis joked. "I guess now I know."

"Brannis, that is no way to talk about a lady!" Iridan jumped in, indignantly defending a perceived slight to his betrothed's honor.

"Well … I had meant the translations," Brannis clarified, and Iridan might have begun to blush, if the cold air rushing by them had not already reddened his face.

Onward they flew—for in truth their horses had not touched the ground in hours—and the mountains engulfed them. They made their own passage as best they could, but their luck only held so long before they were forced to ascend. The sights all around them were magnificent as they worked their way up the steep grade of the mountainside. The horses, trained as they were to obey without question, carried along as if they were on level ground and not mounting the vast craggy rocks of the Cloud Wall.

Their ascent brought them up above the snow line, the point where it was winter every season and where the ice no longer melted before it took on snow again. As they crested the peak—a flat-topped caldera of an inactive volcano that was a tower's height deep in snow—they could see much of their day's ride ahead of them. There would be at least three more mountain crossings before they could reach the other side of the range, perhaps four if there was one obscured from view by larger mountains.

Brannis resisted the urge to call a halt, unsure of what sort of footing was presently beneath them. So long as the horses kept in motion, they would continue to remain airborne just above whatever paltry ground lay below them.

"Keep moving. Resist the temptation to stop and gawk!" Brannis urged as he took his own advice and allowed his mount to continue on down the far side of the mountain.

The effect was both thrilling and terrifying. As they had ascended, it was easy to look forward and see the height of the peak shrink as they approached it. Now that he was heading down, Brannis could see the entire descent in its vast panoramic glory, spread out before and below him, with nothing to save him from a fatal plunge but the magic of the horseshoes his mount wore.

With gravity to aid them and no footing to worry about, the horses sped ever faster as they went down. Brannis kept a light hold on the reins, hoping that the horse could react faster to obstacles in their path than he could, since the scenery was hurtling past as an awesome rate. Within moments, his horse had cleared the snow line and, not long afterward, reached the valley between mountains in less than a tenth the time they had taken to ascend.

For three more mountains, they repeated the exercise, speeding down one mountain and carrying that momentum halfway up the next. The whole endeavor was upsetting to both the nerves and the stomach, and all but Juliana managed to lose some portion of their morning meal along the way. The sorceress seemed, however, to enjoy the ride.

* * * * * * *

"Well, at least the goblins will be hampered by the weather," Brannis said, feeling cheerful. "And we seem to have reached the city before them."

Indeed, there was no goblin host camped out in sight of the city, nor any sign of their imminent approach. Brannis's course had brought them out just north of the city. Winter had come early to the western face of the Cloud Wall, and they stood in ankle-deep snow beside their mounts, thankful to be near the end of their journey.

Between them and the city lay Neverthaw Lake, through which the blue-green glacial waters of the Neverthaw River ran. The lake had once been a quarry during the early days of Raynesdark's construction. With wards to keep them intact, the stone structures of the city had little need for additional stone, and the quarry eventually fell to disuse and was allowed to fill with water.

Into the lake crashed Draxel Falls, named after the sorcerer who had diverted the Neverthaw's headwaters to fill the old quarry. It was a majestic sight, especially in winter when the falls partially froze. Though not yet winter, it was late enough into the autumn that Brannis and his companions were able to see the falls in the early phases of its icing over.

The city of Raynesdark sat partway up the mountainside, tucked snugly in against the rock. Naught but stone could be seen of it. The outer walls, the defensive towers, and the tall buildings and castle keep beyond: all were built of the same dark stone once quarried just outside the city. Presumably, in bygone ages, there were wooden structures, but Raynesdark was among the oldest cities in the Empire, and after long enough, folk tired of replacing buildings. Warded stone lasted like nothing else and, with the attentions of a wardkeeper, could be maintained indefinitely.

Brannis knew that while the city was largely hidden by the massive wall as they looked up at it, there was only so much above ground to be seen. Harsh weather had driven many of the inhabitants underground, where whole subterranean districts of the city lay. He had studied maps of the overcity, the undercity, and all of the mines, and the overcity was the smallest part of the whole complex. What was above was mostly commerce and trade, barracks for Duke Pellaton's garrison, and summer abodes for the wealthier of Raynesdark's citizenry. Duke Pellaton's castle was a massive fortified structure that was built into the mountain itself, spanning the overcity and undercity, and offering entrance to the ancient and disused upper mines. The lower mines, the lifeblood of the city, were accessible elsewhere from the undercity.

The road approaching the city paralleled the river, just far enough away that it did not wash out in the spring floods. Upon reaching the base of the mountain, the wide trade-way meandered its way up to the city gates by way of a half dozen switchbacks, keeping the grade low enough for wagon teams to ascend safely. The setup also afforded the city's defenders an excellent vantage overlooking any approaching invaders, who would either have to take the long road or scale numerous smaller cliff faces to climb up directly.

"Though we have made it in time for dinner, I find that I no longer hunger for it," Faolen remarked. He had taken the worst of it throughout the five days' journey, from saddle sores and leg cramps to aching back and nausea over the mountains.

"There now, no need for gloom," Iridan said. "We have arrived, and our journey is finished. We can prevail upon Duke Pellaton for proper accommodations tonight and recover from this ordeal."

"Oh yes," Juliana said. "I feel much better now that we have put ourselves in the path of a goblin army. I cannot be soon enough rid of these *scaaaary* horses and slip into a nice relaxing battle for my life."

"Mind you, only Iridan and I are expected to join the battle," Brannis said. "The three of you are noncombatants once the fighting begins. You will stay with the peasant folk, helping with any evacuation as needed. Beforehand is when I will really need you. There will be much that needs doing, and we do not know how long we have. Hopefully Duke Pellaton will have scouts with a better idea of where the goblin army is. At the most, Illard's Glen is a two-day march from here. It is mostly a matter of when they decide to strike."

"If you do not mind me asking—and mind you, this has played about my mind for days now—but how can you be certain they will strike here and not Korgen?" Ruuglor asked.

"You certainly waited long enough to ask that," Brannis said. "The simple answer: goblins are not stupid. They have a force far too large to have been brought to conquer just Illard's Glen, and Korgen is no more of a threat, nor much more of a prize. The goblins attacked Illard's Glen to field-test their new siege engine before bringing it to bear here at Raynesdark. They would not need a new wall-wrecking weapon if they were to attack Naran Port, which is the only other city in the region that would be a large enough target to justify bringing an army that size."

Brannis tried to sound sure of his answer, but he knew there were several jumps of logic that could easily mislead them if any single one were wrong. Guessing the goblins' motive was the biggest risk in his plan.

"I would hate to hear the complex version," Faolen muttered just loud enough to be sure Brannis heard.

Brannis glared sidelong at the sorcerer but said nothing.

"Well, we are not yet in place to get ourselves attacked," Juliana said cheerfully. "We ought to get moving."

With that, she urged her horse to a gallop and shot off toward Raynesdark like a loosed arrow.

Brannis took a quick glance at the other three sorcerers, shrugged, and took off after her. Iridan, Faolen, and Ruuglor followed in his wake.

* * * * * * * *

There had been no trouble at the city gates. Accompanied by the four sorcerers—one of whom was wearing warlocks' garb—and bearing orders with the imperial seal, Brannis followed the gate guards directly to the castle to meet with Duke Pellaton. The city had been on edge since the arrival of refugees from Illard's Glen, several days earlier, bringing word of the goblin invasion. The walls teemed with soldiers in numbers that could not have been sustainable in peacetime.

As they were escorted through the town to the castle, the streets stood deserted, eerily quiet, and ... curiously warm. Brannis had read that they used the heat from the smelters and forges of the undercity to keep the roads and homes of the city above warm, preventing snowy roads and making the overcity's homes livable in the depths of winter in the heights of the Cloud Wall. Stone ducts ran in a maze between the two layers of the city, mixed in and around the overcity's sewers, venting the immense heats generated below in the belly of the mountain. A low fog hung over much of the city as the moisture left by the snow gently steamed off with nowhere cool to settle.

The castle was no less imposing from up close than it had been from the other side of Neverthaw Lake. Colossal stone blocks formed its walls, each taller than a man and fitted so closely together that no mortar was used in the entirety of the structure. It was impressive to look upon, but less so to Brannis, who had studied the history of the place and knew that the stones had been reshaped by aether to fit so well.

When a stable hand came to take their mounts to the subterranean portion of the city for safekeeping, Brannis looked down at him.

"Shoe them," Brannis said, "and have the old shoes set aside until our departure. The ones they are wearing right now have runes of speed upon them and could cause trouble in the stables if they get loose,"

"Aye, Your Lordship," the lad responded with a nod.

The stable hand then began helping the sorcerers out of their saddles.

Iridan and Faolen had improved a bit over the past few days but were still saddle-weary and aching in the hips, legs, and back. Ruuglor's back was bothering him from all the jostling, especially the last, harrowing run of their ride. Juliana seemed to have fared as well as she had since the first day, stiff from long hours riding but otherwise fine. Brannis had discovered to his pleasant surprise that the runed armor he wore cushioned the worst of the horse's jarring gait, and he could easily have ridden all the rest of the day.

Porters bearing the green-and-gold livery of House Pellaton came and unpacked their belongings from the saddlebags and took their packs. The duke's chamberlain escorted them through the wide, vaulted corridors of the castle to the drawing room where Duke Pellaton awaited them.

"So our warlock suspects the goblins will attack Raynesdark next, and this is what he sends?" Duke Pellaton asked by way of greeting as soon as they entered his presence.

The duke was standing when they arrived, aided by his cane, though it did not detract from his lean stature or erect posture. He wore his own green-and-gold version of a general's uniform, complete with tasseled epaulettes and the sign of House Pellaton—a mountain goat on a heater shield—where an imperial general would bear the emperor's golden hawk. His manicured goatee was shot through with streaks of black where it was not grey, and none would be the wiser if the hair on his head was likewise, for it was waxed bald. The duke's expression was like the rest of him: stern, reserved, and unwelcoming.

"Indeed, Your Grace," Brannis said, skipping the formal introductions. "I suspect you would prefer to get this out of the way directly."

Brannis handed him the orders Rashan had sent with him, as the duke seemed ill inclined toward pleasantries. Two of the three men in the room with him bore striking resemblances to the duke and seemed younger; it took little imagination to see that they were his sons. The third wore a loose black tunic trimmed in the duke's colors, the sign of a house sorcerer. Brannis had only met a few sorcerers who had shunned the Circle to take work in the employ of one of the noble houses. It was more common farther from the heart of the Empire, as the influence of the Circle waned and the nobles had more direct control of their local sorcerers. This specimen seemed to match his master's mood: a dour, scrawny man with a severe, finger-length black beard who was likely much older than the thirty winters he appeared to have seen.

Duke Pellaton took the scroll case from Brannis's hand and, leaning his cane against one of the large maroon-upholstered chairs, removed the document within and began reading. The other eight in the room waited and watched his expression as it ran the gamut from curiosity, to surprise, to puzzlement, then disbelief, anger, and resentment in succession. He handed Rashan's proclamation to the elder of his two sons.

"It seems the warlock has decided to commandeer my own troops. House Pellaton has held Raynesdark against all foes since the earliest days of the Empire, and this is the thanks we receive in return. I find the scant aid he saw fit to send to be more insulting than sending none at all. Now I see that on top of it, he is handing my army to this … boy," Duke Pellaton vented, gesturing to Brannis. Pellaton's face was reddened, and his shoulders heaved slightly as he had run himself short on breath.

"I see that one in the warlock's cloak is Warlock Rashan's son. Caldrax, what do you think of the firehurlers they sent us?" the elder son asked House Pellaton's sorcerer, handing the orders to his brother.

"Let me see," the sorcerer Caldrax said, his eyes losing focus. "I find nothing extraordinary, though the imitation warlock seems to have a respectable Source. Nothing that I would consider to give us any significant tactical advantage, should battle come to our walls."

"The girl is his arranged bride? How sweet … and completely unhelpful," the younger brother added as he reviewed the orders.

Is the whole family soured on the inside? The unadorned stone blocks of the castle seem more friendly than this lot, Brannis thought.

"We are here, and you have all read the orders. I think a tour of the city is in order, and a review of the defenses," Brannis said, trying to remain above the duke's personal dislike of Rashan's plan of how best to defend Raynesdark.

"Hmph. I suppose if we must abide the warlock's decree, we might as well be about it, then," the duke said. "Answer me two things first, however. What did you do to get this assignment?"

"I defeated a goblin army that had destroyed two other scouting expeditions already, and I outwitted Warlock Rashan at chess. He also seems to appreciate the fact that I do not back down from him when I think he is wrong," Brannis replied, trying to word his answers carefully. He could scarcely justify the warlock's confidence in him. Brannis could only hope that two hundred-odd summers' worth of intuition knew what they were doing.

"Hmm, fair enough, then. Second, what would become of me if I ordered you thrown in the dungeons while I conducted the coming battle my way?"

"Since by order of the imperial regent I am in charge here, I would have to do whatever was in my power to maintain my command. I would run you through myself and see if your elder son was more reasonable. And in the event you were successful in removing myself as well as my companions, Rashan would find another noble house to elevate to the duchy of Raynesdark after he killed you and likely your entire family.

"Your Grace, and I say this with due respect to all parties involved, Rashan Solaran is every bit the monster that history reports him as. He finds his position tenuous after discovering treason within the Inner Circle and rectifying it in his own fashion by killing those he deemed to be most responsible. I find him to be utterly loyal · to the Empire and the imperial line. He is also frighteningly powerful, fiendishly intelligent, and surprisingly introspective and thoughtful, but above all, utterly and chillingly ruthless. If he feels you are working against him, he would find himself remiss if he did *not* kill you. The Kadrin Empire did not make enemies of half of Veydrus because of his tolerance and social graces."

Duke Pellaton paused for a moment before responding: "I come from a proud family and find that I enjoy the study of history. I am well familiar with the deeds of Rashan Solaran. There has been some debate ..." The duke looked meaningfully at Caldrax. "... as to whether the reports that Warlock Rashan has returned are indeed true, or whether there is some sort of imposter at work."

"Among the Inner Circle, there is no debate," Ruuglor commented. "There is still a hole in the Sanctum where Gravis Archon was killed."

Brannis noticed Juliana wince at the mention of her grandfather's recent demise. He had been careful not to bring the subject up, but Ruuglor was less concerned about tact. It reminded Brannis as well that his own father was killed in that same purging; he felt oddly detached from it, a fact that he could not muster a sense of shame for.

Duke Pellaton took his leave of them after that, giving them over to the custody of his younger son Mennon, with instructions to show them around the city. Mennon had his father's build but the stooping posture of one who cares little for commanding the respect of others. He seemed morose and aloof, though not as embittered as his father.

As they exited the drawing room, Brannis caught sight of something. As she turned, Juliana's loose over-tunic twirled slightly and there was a glint of something beneath that Brannis was rather convinced was a dagger hilt. He hung back as the group moved into the corridor, and fell into step behind Juliana.

Brannis took her by the arm and slowed their pace. When they had fallen behind a bit, he reached in and pulled the dagger from its hiding place, drawing a small indignant gasp from Juliana—which Brannis cynically suspected was feigned. Fortunately it had not attracted the attention of the rest of the group.

"What is this?" he whispered, holding the dagger out in front of her in accusation. It was carved with runes whose purpose Brannis could at least guess at, if not identify. "Non ... combatant. Understood? No getting involved once the fighting starts."

"Brannis, you brought me here. I am no aspiring warlock. I have no intention of seeking out battle, but if the fighting gets as far as me, I do not intend to go down in flames, hurling fire like some crazed goblin.

"Oh, and I had them there before we even left Kadris, and it took you this long to notice them?" she plucked the dagger deftly from Brannis hand as he was still wondering what "*them*" meant. She twirled the dagger through her fingers before stabbing it deftly back into its sheath. "Did they not teach you juggling at the Academy?"

"We used little cloth balls filled with sand, and you know it," Brannis whispered back, trying to keep their little tiff from alerting the others. It was a rudimentary way that aspiring sorcerers learned to finely control their hand movements, and a great help in developing the dexterity for spellcasting.

"Well, my daggers are runed and deadly, I know how to use them, and I could juggle them better than you could ever juggle those little cloth balls," Juliana countered, and she quickened her pace to rejoin the group.

* * * * * * *

The undercity was oppressive. After days spent in the autumn chill and the icy, biting cold of the mountains, the lower level of Raynesdark felt like summer. Not like the pleasant sunny days of few clouds and balmy nights, but the humid, sticky heat that made breathing seem a chore. Whereas the overcity was deserted, the undercity teemed with activity.

The foundries and forges gave off a reddish-orange light that tinted the entire space. The noise from them pervaded the vast domed space of the undercity, with iron on stone, iron on iron, and the hiss of steam forming an industrial symphony that was discordant to those who had not grown up around it.

"All the heavy labor is ogreish now," Mennon remarked as they watched a gang of ogres trudge by. "We used to still have human labor for work in the diamond mines until a few summers ago, but we have trained them to the point where the ogres can do that as well."

"How do you keep them under control?" Faolen asked.

Brannis knew the answer but left it to Mennon to explain.

"These are all captive-bred," Mennon answered. "Most of ours are sixth generation at least, and we have not had any wild-born in my lifetime. None of them have so much as heard ogreish spoken. We train them from childhood, so they do not know any other way."

Brannis had fought wild ogres, and the difference was stark. These tamed ogres were bigger and better fed—probably stronger as well—but they had a dull look in their eyes. They slaved away in the mines, and that was their entire life. The wild ones had their own culture and worshiped nature gods, painting their faces with colorful mud-like paints before battles to frighten the spirits of their enemies.

Mennon led them to the temporary campground that had been set up for the refugees from Illard's Glen. With no need for protection from the elements, it had sprung up as a sort of open-air barracks, with bedrolls littering the ground and little or no real privacy to be had. Whatever belongings the refugees had managed to bring along with them were lying here and there all about, relying on the openness and a sense of community for security against theft.

Brannis interviewed a number of the refugees, allowing Mennon to take the rest of the group to see the markets and some of the other non-strategic parts of undercity. Brannis was able to tease out the details of the attack from a half dozen different witnesses, the most valuable of whom was a huntsman who had recovered from an apparent case of magical tampering and recalled seeing the goblin encampment before the battle.

The siege weapons they described were most certainly cannons. It seemed that the goblins had been able to cast them out of bronze. There had been no other reports that indicated any earlier tests of the weapons, so it would seem that the goblins had done well enough in their first attempt to pulverize Illard's Glen's walls. The damage had been explained to him and seemed gratuitous; they were likely just working on their aim or performing drills.

Brannis considered the forges and the ready supply of iron, and wondered how long it would take to replicate the goblins' success. The resources were all at hand, he was fairly certain. Kyrus could easily find out the proper way to mix the black powder from the crew of the *Harbinger* or someone in Marker's Point, and he could study the design of the ship's guns. They could make iron versions in Raynesdark, heavier and stronger than the ones the goblins could make from bronze. If they could produce them in time, they could outgun the goblin army. It was a serious problem if the goblins were able to set up their cannons and pound the Raynesdark defenses with impunity from farther away than they could retaliate.

As Brannis considered the cannons that the goblins had, he considered how the goblins had learned of them. That Denrik Zayne was involved seemed nearly certain: he had admitted sharing that marvelous invention of warfare with Veydrus, and the goblins were probably better candidates for producing working black powder than the Megrenn were. The Megrenn were traders, merchants, and philosophers—as well as warriors, Brannis admitted—but not noted alchemists. If Denrik had been in a hurry to get cannons made, it would be easier to trade with the goblins—the plans in exchange for working copies, for instance—than to teach his own people.

If Denrik had to teach the goblins how to make the cannons, could it be possible that he is *the human liaison reportedly traveling with the goblin army?* Brannis's eyes widened. *Yes, that might even be likely. I shall have to try to find out through Kyrus.*

* * * * * * * *

The tour of the undercity had been enlightening, but Brannis hoped that it would have little bearing on the city's defense in the expected battle. If they were driven back to defending the undercity, they might be in serious trouble. The overcity and the walls were what concerned Brannis most.

Mennon took them for a walk on those very walls—fitted stone battlements four times the height of a man, constructed in the same manner as the castle and just as old. Leaning over, Brannis could see runes in a long, unbroken line along the length of the wall.

"Iridan, I want you to get started tomorrow on shoring up these runes," Brannis ordered. "As much power as you can manage, get them near to bursting if you can, and make sure there are no weak spots."

"Thanks, Brannis. I get appointed to the Inner Circle, and not a tenday goes by before you demote me back to wardkeeper," Iridan joked.

Prior to joining Brannis's expedition to Kelvie Forest, wardkeeper had been Iridan's occupation. There were a group of a dozen or so at any given time in the city of Kadrin, keeping up civic wards on wells, sewers, roads, and anything else that required aether to function or last. They would recarve or replace damaged runes and supply aether to depleted ones. Usually new wards were carved by more senior sorcerers for official imperial use, but all the wardkeepers knew the craft well enough, and many did work on the side to earn extra money, earning hefty commissions from paranoid merchants and nobles.

"Faolen, can you create an illusion of a half wall?" Brannis asked.

"To what end?" the sorcerer said.

"I expect this wall to be destroyed in the early goings of the battle. We are going to have to fight within the city itself, and I want to funnel the goblins into a few areas to make them easier to contain. If they approach the wall and find sections that are not completely destroyed, they will avoid them, and it will make them more predictable," Brannis said.

"Why not just make the wall appear whole?" Faolen questioned.

"We want them to believe what they see, or at least not question it overmuch. If they attack the wall and never see any damage, they are going to figure it out and counter it. We need a light touch and some realistically damaged-looking walls to fool them.

"Now, Ruuglor, I want you to rune arrows with magic to carry them farther. On some of them, include runes that will get them through simple shielding constructs," Brannis continued.

"Will that not foul the aim of the archers?" Mennon asked, listening in on a conversation that only tangentially involved him. He held no rank in the Raynesdark army and would be tucked safely underground when the fighting started.

"It may," Brannis said, "but the goblins will set up siege engines out of range of the archers, and it will be our only chance to strike at them. I expect that once arrows start reaching them, the sorcerers will use shielding magics, and then the archers can switch to the arrows with the extra runes. I see no need to rune them all; take the time to make more with the distance runes." Brannis had been giving this thought since he heard about the cannons, and was finally getting the chance to lay his plan out before his politely skeptical sorcerers.

"The arrows ought to reach the goblins without magic," Mennon added, and Brannis wondered if the fellow knew something of use after all. "Our bowmen are quite skilled, and we have them equipped with excellent bows."

"The new weapons of theirs will outdistance the bowmen," Brannis said flatly. He was hoping that he would not have to—

"How can you know that?" Juliana asked.

—explain how he knew that.

"The refugees' estimates of the placement of the weapons when they were fired. It would seem that extended range is a primary advantage of the goblins' latest weapons," Brannis lied.

Well, the statement is probably accurate, but none of the refugees offered anything that specifically useful. I cannot exactly tell them, "I have seen them in action, and trust me: LOOONG range on those things."

"What of Caldrax? Should we assign him some task as well, for the preparations," Iridan asked.

"I am putting you in charge of him. Have him help with the wards on the walls. How long those last may play a key part in the battle," Brannis said.

I can only hope they do not have enough cannonballs to bring down the whole wall. I do not like the thought of laying under siege for long enough for them to finish.

"I did not get the feeling that he was terribly impressed with me. Why would he take orders from me?" Iridan asked.

"You seem to forget, you are Inner Circle now. Even if he is not officially in the Imperial Circle, he would have difficulty justifying any defiance of your orders. If these folk here are not terrified of crossing our new regent, they ought to be," Brannis said.

"It is getting late. We ought to head to the castle for dinner," Mennon suggested.

"Indeed. I shall clarify anything that needs clarifying come morning. We have been long on the road, though walking about all afternoon has felt better than sitting a horse. Lead on, Mennon."

Brannis waited for everyone to start and then began counting down in his head: *Three … two … one …*

"What about me?" Juliana demanded, getting in Brannis's path to block the way to food, wine, and respite until she had been heard.

"Oh, just get to know the locals. I will have you in charge of keeping them safe during the battle," Brannis said in a raised voice. He pulled Juliana close as he started toward the castle after the rest. "I have a different plan for you," he continued in a much lower voice, barely above a whisper. "I want you to weaken the avalanche wards that keep the Neverthaw Glacier from dropping a mountainside of snow over the city. If things go badly, we are going to bury the city under snow and seek the aid of the stone folk. Raynesdark's deepest mines cross their territories, and we do not mine them anymore. They would not fight for our sake, but we could probably buy passage through their caverns for our civilians."

"Would that not destroy the whole city?" Juliana asked, incredulous, slowing them a step farther behind everyone else, lest her voice carry.

"No. The buildings are warded against avalanche as well, though the wards are older. I have been studying magic to make better use of it in warfare, and I was able to recognize the runes as we walked through the city. The avalanche wards on the retaining wall on the cliffs above the city ... I read about in the army's reports on the city's defenses."

"So this was your plan all along? No wonder you played coy," Juliana observed.

"No, it was just my reserve plan in case things go badly. Do you think you can manage it? Use that runed dagger your are so proud of and cross some things out."

"I can."

"Good. Let us catch up before we are missed."

* * * * * * *

House Pellaton's dinners appeared to be rather formal affairs, though thankfully less unwelcoming due to the womenfolk attending. Duke Pellaton may have been the epitome of the denigrating nobleman, but the Duchess Daleighah Pellaton was a charming woman. Of middling summers, with only streaks of white through her light brown hair to betray her age, she looked every bit the young maid her eldest daughter did. Veena Pellaton was the image of her mother, with a tiny upturned nose, high round cheeks, and a curved figure. Mennon attended with his lady wife Aila, a plump cheerful woman who talked almost constantly. The heads of Duke Pellaton's garrison forces attended along with their wives as well, and seemed far more open and personable than their master.

The duke's elder son Harwell did not attend, possibly meaning it as a personal objection to the newcomers' supplanting his father's authority. His lady attended in his place. Gedandra Pellaton was slight of frame and short of womanly charms as well. She slouched like Mennon at the table and had the look of a young lad in the face and the build of one in the body. She was born to the House of Rollack in Naran Port, and the marriage was strictly of convenience. In their brief introduction, Brannis had found her to be quick of wit, which made her instantly more interesting to him than the vapid girl the sorcerer had brought. Caldrax's lady, who was not introduced as his wife, was a pale, curvy creature, with shadowed eyes that rarely lifted to meet the eye of anyone who spoke with her, and who spoke little—which was thankful, as on those occasions that prompted her to speak, she rarely improved upon her standing among those present.

The duke's younger daughters attended as well. Demni and Phaelia were twins, not yet of age to wed as sorcerers would judge it, but the nobles tended to err on the side of marrying their daughters too young. They dressed identically in low-cut, corseted pink dresses, with many-layered petticoats fluffing them out. Brannis was unsure whose idea the dresses were, but he found them to be in poor taste; he had been raised by sorcerers, even if he was not one himself, and found nobles' marriage—and daughter-peddling—practices to be tawdry.

Of course, he was unable to cast blame too far, lest he catch one of his own in the net. While Brannis wore his quicksilver breastplate over mail, and Iridan,

Faolen, and Ruuglor wore their formal Imperial Circle garb—which in Iridan's case was quite impressive—Juliana had taken a different tact. While adhering to the traditional black of the Circle, she wore a strapless gown of scandalously thin material, making the duke's daughters seem prudish by comparison. She cinched it at the waist with a bloodred sash and had a red silk shawl to match, to keep the slight chill of the overcity half of the castle at bay. Brannis wished very much that he had aether-vision at that point, as he was very curious how the dress kept itself in place, and whether there was magic enhancing her figure, or whether he had really just not realized …

Brannis managed to keep his attention focused on the conversation as the meal went on. He was seated at the far end of the long table from the duke, with Juliana just on the far side of Iridan from him. He thought he did well to keep his eyes to his food or to whomever he was speaking, but knew that he was not *entirely* successful. He knew, for instance, that Juliana had left that dagger—or daggers—of hers in her room.

"Sir Brannis." Duke Pellaton stood and raised a goblet of the spiced wine they were drinking. "May the follies of youth plague not your endeavors, and may all of us live to see their fruit."

The others at the table raised their goblets as well, as much out of habit and reflex as out of sympathy for the sentiments offered. Brannis raised his as well but did not drink. Instead he stood and offered a toast of his own.

"And to Duke Pellaton. May he extend the warmth of his hospitality to our goblin foes as well, that they might freeze to death and save us the trouble of killing them."

That drew a chuckle from the table, and a wary look from the duke.

"Your Grace, if the goblins do not attack us, or if your troops turn them aside so easily that no help of ours was needed, I will gladly bear whatever ridicule you wish to heap upon me," Brannis said while still standing—as was Duke Pellaton—at the far end of the table. "And if at that point you wish to voice your displeasure to the regent, Warlock Rashan, I suspect you might find me relieved of my rank, if not my life. And upon my death, if you wish to toast your foresight and laugh over my grave, I will offer no resistance.

"But until such time as we have either defeated the goblins or I am convinced that they have turned their intentions elsewhere, I expect the full cooperation of the forces of Raynesdark and their commanders. That includes yourself, Your Grace. Sometime in the next handful of days, there will be a goblin army at the foot of your mountain, and I have been ordered by the acknowledged ruler of the Empire to defend it. I will do so with or without your help, though I would be obliged for any aid that is available in my charged duty."

"Well spoken, boy, I appreciate blunt words. You will have my cooperation, if not my approval; that you may only have if you are both correct and victorious," Duke Pellaton said.

Brannis did not know if the presence of the duchess softened the duke's mood or tempered his words, but he suspected that the fact Duke Pellaton had no grounds to defy him without risking the ire of Rashan played a part somewhere. Humility was a dish best served to someone else, yet Duke Pellaton had at least lifted a spoonful of it to sniff it experimentally.

The remainder of the meal passed without further incident. Brannis spoke mainly to his own companions and made a bit of light conversation with the commanders of Raynesdark's forces and their wives. The House Pellaton end of the table was quieter and kept their conversation amongst themselves as well.

The day's events had worn Brannis down, and he retired to his borrowed chambers gladly. It felt wonderful to slip into the bath that one of the servants had drawn for him. The runed armor was by far the most comfortable protection he had ever worn, but it was still mail beneath the plates, and hot, sweaty padding below that. Never one for soaking, he washed himself and prepared for a well-earned slumber in a proper bed.

After drying off from the bath, he checked that the books he had brought from the Tower library were still in good order. He had little time to read them while on the road, though he had perused a bit before bed. This night, though, he found that he was more interested in the soft blankets than yellowed old tomes, and put them away once he had seen to their safety.

Sorry, Kyrus. Tomorrow, I promise.

It was chilly in the room, and when the residual warmth from the bath fully left him, it grew unpleasant. The glassed window at the front of the room let in enough light to find the bed with the lanterns out, and lacking magic, he preferred to keep the heavy green curtains wide open. Thankful for the thick carpets on his bare feet, he climbed into the bed.

Brannis closed his eyes and headed off to see what was going on with the crew of the *Harbinger*.

* * * * * * * *

In the darkened hallway of Raynesdark Castle, a figure clung to the shadows. With thick carpets quieting careful feet, the figure felt its way along. It found its objective at the end of the corridor, the last of the rooms in the guests' wing, usually reserved for visiting nobility.

The figure examined the door carefully, running a thin-fingered hand over the wood, searching with a practiced hand. It could find no wire or catch to trigger a trap, nor any ward to interfere with its entry—for it knew the ways of aether and was careful of such things. The same thin hand tried the door and found it opened easily and quietly; it was not even locked. It was almost too easy ...

The slight figure slipped inside and oh-so-quietly closed the door. The floor in the guest room was well covered in rugs as well, and there was no sound as the figure approached the sleeping knight. The chest rose and fell slowly, rhythmically, almost hypnotically. The pale moonlight from the window was even enough to make out the beating of the heart in the knight's neck.

Slowly the figure leaned in closer to the knight, holding its breath lest the knight sense the approach by a disturbance in the air. With dexterity and practiced control, the figure got right down next to the knight's neck ...

... and laid a gentle kiss just above the collarbone. Using the distraction of the kiss and the tickle of hair that fell on Brannis as he stirred in his sleep, Juliana eased herself up onto the bed and beneath the blankets. She had noticed on the journey to Raynesdark just how heavily Brannis slept, and was taking full advantage.

She ran a hand up Brannis's chest and reached her leg across him, slowly drawing herself atop him, straddling his waist. Of course, there were limits to the things even as sound a sleeper as Brannis could slumber through, and some laggardly watchman within his sleeping thoughts saw fit to inform Brannis that "something important is going on."

* * * * * * *

Brannis awoke confused, briefly wondering if he had bedded one of the serving girls from dinner. The smell of honeysuckle brought back a wash of memories and cleared up any doubts as to who his bed-mate was.

She hung her smiling face above his, her unbound hair streaming down around the both of them, creating a curtained area for just herself and Brannis.

"Tonight is ours, Brannis," she whispered and then ran a hand down along his bicep.

"What are you doing here?" Brannis asked softly.

He had not seen that particular smile from her in a long time, and his thoughts began to form small puddles at the bottom of his brain as they melted away. She wore the dress from dinner, but without the sash or shawl to go along with it, or even shoes, as he could feel her cold, bare feet against his legs. Other than her feet, the rest of her felt warm and inviting, the thin fabric of the dress doing nothing to shield him from the warmth of her body.

"We may never get this chance again. Tomorrow we all may die, or be swept up in battle and events carry us away. I do not know. All I need to know is I have you now, for tonight at least," she whispered.

She leaned down and pressed her lips to his. He returned her kiss but hesitated.

Brannis shook his head. "I cannot do this. You are betrothed to my best friend."

"And I still will be, come morning."

"That is not the point," Brannis said.

"But it is," Juliana said. "It is not Iridan that I came to be with tonight. I want you."

"I cannot have you." Brannis barely managed to get the words out. It was the hardest thing he had ever admitted.

She balled up her fist and pounded it on his chest. "Why?" she protested, hitting him again. "Why could you not have been a sorcerer like you were supposed to be? Did your mother bed one of the stable hands? You were supposed to be mine."

She pulled back and seemed about to really slam her fist down, but Brannis caught it this time.

"But I am not. Iridan is going to be yours now. He is a good man ... and a good friend," Brannis replied calmly.

"Brannis, you were more a man at fourteen than I suspect Iridan will ever be."

She seemed about to cry, her breath coming in short gasps in between sniffles. With one wrist in Brannis's grasp, she held down his other arm and leaned in to kiss him again, making one last desperate attempt to overwhelm his reason with her anything-but-reason.

But Brannis ignored her grasp and let go of her other wrist. He took her gently but firmly by the midsection and lifted her up. Held aloft by her center of balance, Juliana could do little to struggle loose as Brannis sat up and plopped her down in a seated position, still kneeling astride him.

Brannis wrapped his arms around Juliana and pulled her close. She curled up in his arms and began to sob. Brannis said nothing, and Juliana was beyond words, just feeling the strength of his arms holding her and letting loose feelings that had been building to a boil for far too long.

When at last she had run dry of tears, Juliana was able to compose herself enough to leave Brannis's bed. She kissed him quickly on the forehead, not trusting herself to try anything more, and quickly disappeared down the corridor to return to her own room.

When she was gone, Brannis got out of bed and found his sword. Drawing Avalanche from its sheath, he walked over to the door and pressed the blade flat against the wood, closest to the handle side and oriented up and down. He released his grip and the sword remained in place, held by rune-forged magic and certain to keep out any further intruders, no matter how welcome their intentions might be.

Having secured the door, Brannis went to stand by the window. The glass let in a chill that felt cleansing, and Brannis thought he could use some about then. He looked at the night view of the abandoned overcity and wondered how soon the attack would come. He watched the view long enough for his passions to cool, and for the warmth of Juliana's body to escape him.

As he climbed back into bed, he noticed that it had managed to acquire a faint whiff of honeysuckle.

I am a fool. Perhaps a good man, perhaps a good friend, but definitely a fool.

Chapter 30 - Sand in the Dragon's Eye

A light steam rose from the murky water that poured from the large circular stone duct that jutted from the rocky base of the mountain, carrying the humans' effluent into the lake. The duct was large enough that a human might pass through, albeit uncomfortably, in order to perform maintenance. There was a grating blocking the opening, made of iron and warded against rusting. The openings in the grating were small enough to keep out goats and bears and other wildlife that might seek respite from the cold of winter within the warm, fetid sewers of Raynesdark. They were even small enough to keep out goblins.

But not all goblins were quite as resourceful as Gkt'Lr. The assassin studied the runes for a moment and measured the gaps in the bars against the width of his shoulders. The wards were not so complex that he could not unravel them and break through the iron of the grating, but it would take time. He reached his pack through the bars and set it quietly on the other side, just above the water level, hoping that it would stay put as he worked to join it. The stone was rough but worn, and the curved slope of the duct threatened to tumble the pack into the murk of the humans' waste. Gkt'Lr was not squeamish about the disgusting mess, but he did not want the stink of it on him for the whole evening; he had work to do and did not want to announce it by his odor.

The goblin assassin reached an arm through the bars and poked his head through as well.

Now for the trick.

He twisted his collarbone at an unseemly angle, farther than nearly any goblin could manage, enough to make an onlooker uncomfortable just watching. There was no pop, no dislocation, as human contortionists might use to fit themselves places that their bodies did not belong, merely a continued stretching as tendons and ligaments relaxed and allowed the lithe body to squeeze through a space no wider than a human forearm.

Once the shoulder was through, the rest came easily. Gkt'Lr reoriented his shoulders to a more anatomically sustainable position—one that let him breathe—and used both arms to push himself the rest of the way through, angling his hips to pass through the square holes.

Scooping up his pack, he set off down the warren of pipes and ducts in search of a way up into the city. The goblin pulled an amulet from beneath his tunic and gave it a bit of aether to start it. The passage was bathed in a purplish light, which he was able to see but which most goblins and all humans would be unable to distinguish from the darkness.

Gkt'Lr was Master of Eternal Night, the second most senior position among the Cult of Knives. The only one above him was the Grandmaster of Darkness. A wizened old goblin named P'ko't, the grandmaster had passed on a great deal of wisdom to his protégées. Gkt'Lr remembered one particularly relevant lesson …

"You cannot just kill a dragon. The dragon is much too strong for you to overcome. Rather, be the sand in the dragon's eye, that it might blink when the blade comes to claim it."

The Cult of Knives was a notoriously impious bunch, left to practice their dark craft more out of practicality than approval. The dragon-god cared little for such backroom blasphemies, though, and appreciated the competence the assassins brought among their followers. So long as the assassins neither openly insulted any dragon nor attempted to put their parables into practice, they were more than tolerated by the dragons.

Ni'Hash'Tk was Gkt'Lr's particular problem, though. She was disappointed in him, possibly bordering on annoyance. That was not a recipe for a long life among her followers. He needed something to prove his worth to her. He could not destroy an army, but he might provide a distraction to the defenders of Raynesdark and wound them as well.

It was time to become the sand in the dragon's eye, and this "dragon" was named Raynesdark.

* * * * * * * *

The sewers had wound a long course, much of it upward, back into the undercity of Raynesdark. Gkt'Lr was more familiar with goblin sewers than human and had to accustom himself to a whole new plethora of foul odors as he made his way through. His hopes of making it through cleanly were dashed at the first drop he had to ascend. With sewage pouring down around him, he had climbed up by rope and hook. It had happened several times after that first one, as the humans had farther to bring their runoff down than across as they drained it out into the lake.

[I wonder if the folk in the downriver cities know they pour their filth into the lake,] the assassin muttered to himself.

He found respite from the foul waters in a back alley of the undercity. The grating that covered the opening to the sewers was not bolted in place, and with the help of a little aether, he was able to dislodge it long enough to make his exit.

He kept to the shadows and away from the noises of the humans' night activities. Few were about, but those that were made enough noise for the vigilant assassin to steer well clear of them. Guards wandered the streets and taverns seemed to still be plying their trade at the late hour of his arrival, but the regular folk seemed to have largely retired for the night.

Gkt'Lr wandered, but not aimlessly. He was reconnoitering the city, looking for three things. The first was the humans' water supply. He could hear the waters flowing and was making his way toward them with all caution.

The architects of Raynesdark had not relied on wells for their water but had instead diverted an underground river through the undercity. Gkt'Lr approached cautiously and examined the canal they had created. The canal flowed in from the north side of the city, and that was the point where Gkt'Lr concerned himself. The canal was cut with dark stone walls, quarried from the same stone as the lake walls outside. He studied the ancient runes inscribed along them—someone around these parts had been intent on placing wards on nearly everything, it seemed—and found ones that kept the stone from wearing away, ones that kept the flow of the water constant and, to the assassins' dismay, ones that kept the water clean and pure.

His pack contained a deadly contaminant that he had intended for the water, but it would have been best used in a well. The free-flowing water would have carried much of the poison—an extract from kokoi grass—out of the city before much had been consumed. Even at that, he would have used it just to try, if not for the wards.

Gkt'Lr had two plans for the water, though, and from the second he would not be dissuaded. There was an archway at the head of the river's entrance to the city, and he walked through it, balancing on the stone blocks that lined the edge. Once safely out of sight of the city, he stripped off his clothes and equipment and laid them on the stones. He slid into the water and washed off the muck of the sewers as best he could.

Once he felt clean enough, he climbed back out and washed his clothing in the waters as well. The wards purified the water so effectively that the filth he left was already dispersing by the time it flowed out into the city.

The foundries were not far from his location, and they were near to where he was headed next anyway. While the city slept, the foundries worked day and night. There was less activity than during daytime hours, but there were still humans about. Gkt'Lr could not exactly run around unnoticed forever, dripping wet from the canal, at least not if he hoped to avoid attracting notice. Gkt'Lr found himself a spot near the fires to dry out, ever alert for iron-workers in the area. He settled in and waited, taking the time to admire the sights of the city—or as much as he could see from his place of hiding.

It was a nice enough place, huge even by goblin standards. The domed ceiling was very practical and avoided the frequent supports that his own people's underground dwellings used. The buildings would have to be refurbished to goblin size, but all the essential elements for goblin habitation were already in place.

Maybe I will purchase land here, once the conquest is complete. Perhaps I can even convince Ni'Hash'Tk to include someplace as a reward for my role in it.

* * * * * * * *

"What this for?" the ogre asked, though his ogreish accent made "what" sound like "whad," as all the hard sounds softened.

The ogre's massive brow knitted in suspicion. He was naked to the waist, wearing just a pair of leather breeches and boots, as were the other male ogres. The females, toward the back of the pen with the children, just wore simple leather skirts and were bare of both chest and foot. A few sat nursing babes, and others kept the naked, unruly children away from their visitor, as much from fear as from politeness.

"Gold ... is ... your," the assassin explained slowly, struggling with the Kadrin words. They had too many vowels.

"Why you givin' us gold?" the ogre persisted, looking down at his knee-high benefactor.

"For help free you," Gkt'Lr said. "Goblins fight humans. Ogres no fight goblins. Goblins give more gold. Goblins set ogres free. No more work mines."

The assassin hoped that got the point across well enough. Speaking Kadrin was tiring, and the ogres only understood properly pronounced Kadrin poorly to begin with.

"So you come fight humans. If we no fight, you give more gold? What we do with gold? We no can go markets," the ogre reasoned out.

Well, he gets half of it at least.

"We make you free. Then you go markets," the assassin clarified.

That gold was a means of trade for goods and services was a bit more than he hoped to have to teach them. At least they knew what markets were, after a fashion.

"What we got do?" the ogre asked, if not fully comprehending the offer, at least understanding that he was being asked to do something. Being given tasks was at least a concept that the ogres were familiar with.

"Humans give weapons. You kill humans, not goblins. Goblins make you free," Gkt'Lr said, thinking that maybe finally they could reach an understanding.

The ogre took the bag of gold coins that the assassin first offered him and looked inside again, getting a feel for the amount of money within, if not a count.

"You give gold. Goblins fight humans in city. You say humans give us weapons?" the ogre paused to ask, and Gkt'Lr nodded an affirmative. "We use weapons and fight humans instead. You give more gold an' make us free, so we go do markets and spend gold. Ya?"

"Yes."

"We make deal."

* * * * * * *

In the darkened hallway of Raynesdark Castle, Gkt'Lr clung to the shadows. With thick carpets quieting careful feet, he felt his way along. He found his objective at the end of the corridor, the last of the rooms in the guests' wing, usually reserved for visiting nobility.

It seemed like the sort of place one would lodge the most important visitors, so it seemed the best place to start. The goblin assassin had made easy work of the passage up from the undercity to the castle, silencing a handful of guards along the way. If he had gotten all of them along the patrol routes, there would be no one left to report the missing guards before daybreak.

The door at the end of the hall was not warded, the assassin concluded after a cursory inspection. There was something with a strong reserve of aether just on the other side of the door though, but it was not any sort of ward. The assassin pushed gently to open the door, but it did not move in the least. He pushed again, harder, and met with the same result.

I could burn through the door, but that would be the end of stealth for the night. I should see what other targets are available.

Gkt'Lr moved on to the next door, across the hallway from the first one. He inspected the wards he found there and saw that it was a simple, temporary construct, likely thrown into place hastily to give the sorcerer within some privacy.

Gkt'Lr was about to begin unraveling it—a skill of which he was especially proud—when he noticed something. The ward he had first found to be so simple was actually a trap, meant to give false security to just such an intruder as himself. He saw that it was linked to other, more subtle wards, scribed within the first so as to pass unnoticed. They would raise an alarm and strike at the one undoing the first ward, with some sort of magic that the assassin could not identify at a glance. It was a masterful work of rune crafting, and Gkt'Lr was thankful to be as much a master at his own craft to have avoided it.

He crossed the hall again to the next door down.

I hope these Kadrins are not all so paranoid, or this night's work could go poorly.

The door was warded again, a bit more thoroughly than the last door appeared at first. Gkt'Lr gave some serious time to going over the runes of the ward in exacting detail, but found that it was merely a plain, unassuming ward to bar the door against entry. He began unraveling it and found that no surprise awaited him upon its final collapse.

The assassin slipped inside and oh-so-quietly closed the door. The floor in the guest room was well covered in rugs as well, and there was no sound as Gkt'Lr approached the sleeping sorcerer. The Kadrin's chest rose and fell slowly, rhythmically, almost hypnotically. The pale moonlight from the window was even enough to make out the beating of the heart in the sorcerer's neck.

Slowly the assassin leaned in closer to the sorcerer, holding his breath lest his victim sense the approach by a disturbance in the air. With dexterity and practiced control, the figure got right down next to the sorcerer's neck …

With expert timing, he simultaneously grabbed the sorcerer's nose and drew his dagger deeply across his victim's throat, at the end of a long breath. The heavy-set sorcerer's involuntary gasp filled his lungs with blood and gave him no breath with which to scream.

It was short work after that to cut the man's heart from his chest, using magics that any Master of Eternal Night would have practiced to the point of doing them blindfolded. He burned the aether out of the sorcerer's Source, more a matter of professional pride than for any real concern about necromancy. There were standards he had to live up to, after all.

After cleaning his dagger on the sorcerer's nightclothes, Gkt'Lr ventured back out into the hall.

The door across from the last one was not warded at all. He checked twice to make sure but could find nothing. The door even opened at his lightest touch and made not a whisper of sound as it swung.

Excellent. This is more like it.

Gkt'Lr was disappointed, however, to find that the room was vacant. He made a circuit of the room to be thorough but could find no occupant.

So much for things going so easily, the goblin thought ruefully.

He closed the door behind him and crossed once again to the other side of the hallway. This door seemed like a trap. The ward upon it was crude and seemed lazily fashioned. It warranted extreme caution after the dangerous trap he had just uncovered within a simple ward, but this was no layered masterwork. It was simply a sloppy ward. Gkt'Lr applied just the slightest pressure with his own aether and it fell to nothingness.

* * * * * * * *

As the door swung inward, a pair of green eyes snapped open, red-rimmed yet fully alert. Using her aether-vision, Juliana noticed her would-be assailant enter the room and close the door. It was a small Source, though far from a weak one. There seemed to be some sort of runed dagger held in one of its hands.

Two can play that game, she thought angrily as she reached silently beneath her pillows to take hold of her daggers. She lay with her back to the door, facing the curtained window. She silently cast a shielding spell and waited for the assassin to draw closer.

The goblin—for it was obvious as to what creature so small would be skulking in the castle with a runed dagger drawn—was taking care not to make the slightest noise. She almost wished she had been snoring so that the goblin would not be so concerned with stealth and just hurry up!

At last, the goblin approached close enough that she felt confident in springing her trap. She whirled in bed and slashed out with one of her daggers. The goblin had been caught by surprise but had reflexively deflected the strike and sprung back.

Juliana then quickly lit the room as bright as daylight and rolled off the bed to confront her attacker. She crouched low to keep the assassin from being able to get beneath her reach, wielding a dagger in each hand.

The assassin tried to strike at her, but she parried with one dagger while striking back with the other. The goblin tried a few more slashes but was finding himself too pressed in return to carry on an offensive.

Gkt'Lr was not above resorting to a bit of firehurling when he was in trouble, and loosed a blast of aether-borne fire toward the Kadrin woman. He would not have thought to call her a sorceress if she was goblin, for minor magical ability was common among them, and she had shown little skill with anything but a blade.

Unfortunately for the assassin, Juliana knew more magic than he had realized—shoddy ward-crafting notwithstanding—and her shield spell deflected the weak flame. Firehurling was useful for many tasks, but breaking through a sorcerer's shielding spell was not among them.

Gkt'Lr had used the diversion of the spell to make his escape, bolting for the door as she instinctively flinched away from the fires. Juliana's reaction did not buy him enough time, though, and he did not make it through the door before she had recovered. Knowing that she would never catch a goblin in a footrace, she flung one of her daggers, catching the goblin assassin low in the back. The assassin sprawled out of sight of the door as he fell.

Juliana quickly pulled on her traveling boots before venturing out into the cold night air in the hallway. She found the assassin struggling to get to his feet, bleeding badly from his lower back. Both the assassin's dagger and her own lay out of reach on the floor, and the assassin turned feebly toward her as she approached him.

"Peace. Me give up," Gkt'Lr begged, holding up an empty hand while the other kept him from collapsing face-first onto the hall carpet.

Juliana walked over next to the goblin, her other dagger still clenched in her hand. "I know better than to trust an assassin," she told him simply.

She proceeded to put her booted foot on the back of the assassin's neck and stepped down. Not heavy for a human, she might as well have been an ox for all the goblin could tell in his weakened state. Her weight flattened him to the ground, and his neck snapped as she shifted her weight onto him.

With reddened eyes and still wearing the dress that Brannis had rejected her in, she was in no mood for mercy.

Chapter 31 - What's in a Name?

"It is called the breech. And that small hole there is called the touch hole. You put the brand to that and light the powder in the vent. That sets off the charge in the chamber, which is the inside part at the bottom of the bore," Crispin explained, pointing as he went along.

"And how do you prepare it for another shot?" Kyrus asked.

He had gone belowdecks to find out more about how cannons worked, since Brannis would be facing them in battle all too soon. If there were weaknesses to be exploited, he wanted to know about them. Crispin had been the gunnery mate aboard the *Harbinger* when it was still an Acardian vessel, and was gunnery mate again aboard the newly rededicated *Fair Trader*, the name Captain Zayne had chosen for his ship.

They had been out of port for a day, and the ship teemed with bodies. They had sailed into Marker's Point with fewer than two dozen men and now departed with over eighty. They might have stayed longer and found even better sailors among the outcasts of Marker's Point, but Captain Zayne had been wary of staying too long after Kyrus's mishap, just in case the authorities were able to make a connection between them and the incident.

"You swab out the bore, wet mind you, and then you load a new charge, wadding, and your shot. Fill the vent with powder again and it is ready to fire," Crispin explained.

He seemed eager to show off his knowledge of the guns, a topic that few aboard were interested in. One was either a gunner or not, and those who were not gunners assumed that it was someone else's job to worry about how they worked.

"Fascinating. And how far can they fire and ..."

* * * * * * *

"So where are we heading now?" Kyrus asked, leaning over the map. It showed the vicinity of Marker's Point and a few days' sailing in any direction.

"We are heading to here."

Stalyart pointed to a small cluster of islands to the southeast, the largest of which was labeled as Denku Appa. They were not as remote as Marker's Point but were still at least a hundred miles off the coast of Feru Maru, the nearest large landmass.

"What is in Denku Appa? It seems a bit out of the way. I mean ... I thought the same of Marker's Point, but this does not seem the sort of place to attract trade the way Marker's Point does."

"You are correct, Mr. Hinterdale. There is not so much there," Stalyart agreed. "But it has two things that very much interest Captain Zayne. He kept a treasure stashed there, one that he had not told me about until just last night. They also have very beautiful women there, and it is warm all year round, so they do not wear much."

Stalyart winked at him. That was all good for Stalyart and Captain Zayne. They could have all the scantily clad island women they wanted for all he cared. He just wanted to find a way to see Abbiley again.

"Well, it looks like we can be there the day after tomorrow," Kyrus concluded, examining the map for a moment and measuring the distance on the map with a compass.

Stalyart had yet to trust him without checking his calculations, but Kyrus had yet to be wrong. The older pirate did his cyphering on a slate with a piece of chalk, accounting for known currents and the prevailing winds. Kyrus managed the same tasks in his head and was quicker about it. It was something Stalyart could not grasp, and it made him assume Kyrus was guessing.

"Mr. Stalyart, can I ask you something?" Kyrus asked, realizing that he had just asked something.

"Of course."

"Who is Captain Zayne in the other world?" Kyrus said. There was no harm in trying, he supposed.

"He is a Megrenn sorcerer. A good one too, by all the pleasant words I hear spoken of him when I travel in Megrenn lands. He was a hero of the war they fought to free themselves from your people. In the city of Zorren, there are five statues in the central square—'The Liberators,' they are called. Captain Zayne is one of those statues."

"Really?" Kyrus was genuinely surprised. "They made a statue of him?"

"Indeed. The Megrenn people suffered much at the hands of the Kadrins. It was a great day when word came that Kadrin had agreed to peace and allowed them to rule themselves once again," Stalyart said.

The first mate seemed to be enamored of the Megrenn, but that seemed appropriate for a merchant such as himself. Megrenn produced little food and was not rich in resources like Kadrin was. They bought and sold, and each time took a little for themselves; it was enough to make a nice living for their people, but it left them vulnerable to blockades and embargoes.

"So who is he? Anyone I would have heard of?" Kryus persisted.

"I think not. Have you heard of Jinzan Fehr?"

"The name does not sound familiar. Is that even a Megrenn name?"

"Hah! Very observant, Mr. Hinterdale. His father was from Gar-Danel. Outside of Kadrin, it is much less uncommon to marry a foreigner. Of Jinzan Fehr's three wives, only one is Megrenn," Stalyart boasted, as if it was his own feat to be proud of.

"Three wives? I did not think the Megrenn kept harems. Is that a holdover from Gar-Danel as well?"

"No. No … they lost many men in the war. Too many. There were widows and daughters and no men to marry them off to. They allowed men to have two wives. For the Liberators, they were allowed as many wives as would have them. If there is one lesson they took from you Kadrin murderers, it is that strong blood keeps a nation strong," Stalyart said.

For the first time, Kyrus heard bitterness in the man's voice. It seemed there was some grudge to be had against Kadrin there too.

"Do you think Megrenn is going to actually manage to conquer Kadrin? Just twenty years ago, they were part of the Empire. I cannot imagine they have changed things there so quickly," Kyrus said.

He did not know why he felt he had to defend the glory of the Empire from a pirate, but he had to get to the core issue at hand as well: what Captain Zayne was up to in Veydrus.

"Hmm. I do not know. I think they will try. I think their cause is right. The one weapon they have that Kadrin never learned is how to make friends. Kadrin has no allies. You stand alone," Stalyart said sadly.

"Mr. Stalyart, what would you say if I told you I would much prefer peace between Kadrin and Megrenn, and that if Captain Zayne starts a war, Megrenn will be wiped out?"

"I would say that in twenty years, Kadrin has grown weaker and Megrenn has grown stronger. With help of knowledge of this world for cannons and black powder, Captain Zayne will make them stronger still. With allies, he will make them strong enough that Kadrin will be forced to surrender."

"No," Kyrus replied. "Kadrin is stronger than you imagine. If you can convince him to make peace, we can save untold lives."

"Why do you care so much? You are a brigand who preys on merchants and who kills when it suits you. Why should you care about Megrenn lives?" Stalyart asked.

Kyrus knew at that point that the canny sailor had not believed his story.

The maps and charts lay forgotten on the table next to them as the ship continued on its course, vaguely in the proper direction. Kyrus had no proper response for Stalyart, at least none that was consistent with the life's story he had given.

"You work with the captain, and you will be fine," Stalyart advised. "There is no need to get involved in the war. Find yourself a nice nobleman to serve, and pass information along to the Megrenn. Captain Zayne will see in return that you are taken care of. The Megrenn are not like you Kadrins. I know, I have traveled in both lands, and I see the differences. You will not be put to slaughter."

Kyrus swallowed hard. "Megrenn will."

"You are young. You do not see the changing of the world. The pendulum swings and then it swings back."

"It just got pulled in back our way," Kyrus said. "I know too much already.

We are ready for war. Please, try to convince the captain."

"Convince him yourself. You have fooled him before; go fool him again if you must. I will not stop you from trying."

* * * * * * * *

"Where did you learn that?" Denrik protested. "I went through the Academy in Kadrin and never have I seen such tactics. I have played many Megrenn sorcerers as well, and I can usually acquit myself well enough, even in losing. I know not a single player who would be your equal."

"There is your problem. You have learned from the wrong world."

Kyrus smiled. He had challenged the captain to a game of chess, and one game had turned into five. Denrik Zayne was a proud man and wanted to at least manage a draw before admitting defeat overall.

"I literally wrote the book on chess, several times," Kyrus said.

"Set up the pieces again. I shall not let you off so easily as that. Try that same trick as last time and I shall have a response for it. And stop making those pointless moves in the middle, taunting me," Denrik said.

The little chess set they had found on the ship consisted of a heavy board with small pegs sticking up at the center of each square, and each piece had a hole in the bottom to fit snugly down onto those pegs. It kept the game from shifting and being ruined by the motion of the ship; the Acardian Navy had too much time on their hands, developing such diversions.

"Those moves you do not understand are the reason I keep beating you. Just because you cannot see what is going on, does not mean that there is nothing happening."

Kyrus worded his statements carefully. He was trying to lead up to the point of his conversation: that he knew what Megrenn was up to, and not just in the general sense, and that they were following a path to ruin.

"So you say."

Another three games passed, and Denrik was finally nearing the point of admitting total defeat. He ran his fingers along his scalp, where a fine stubble was finally starting to resemble hair again, and sighed in frustration. It apparently felt good for him to flex the muscles of his mind, but he wanted to find some result in it.

"I think you must be cheating somehow. I see no other way you could win so many times in a row," Denrik accused after the ninth game.

"You cannot cheat at chess. The pieces are right there in front of both of us the whole time."

"I would not have thought you could cheat at Crackle, either, at least not without my noticing."

Denrik glared at him. Kyrus flushed, unaware that the captain had caught on somehow.

"This is a pirate ship. I assumed everyone else was cheating," Kyrus said.

Denrik chuckled. "So your excuse was that you thought you did not want to be the only one at a disadvantage? Hah! So what were you doing here to win at chess?"

"Outplaying you badly, I am afraid. I have no need to cheat to beat you. I must admit an ulterior motive, though. I wanted to show you that just because you do not always understand what you are seeing, does not mean that it is not a danger."

"What is that supposed to mean?" Denrik asked, his eyes narrowing.

Kyrus sighed within. Denrik was a stubborn man and clearly not prone to enjoying lessons. He would occasionally teach them but preferred to think of himself as having all the answers he needed.

"You are planning a war with Kadrin. You cannot prevail. Lives will be lost on a scale you have not seen in your lifetime, and your cities will burn to the ground," Kyrus said.

"Your loyalty to them is admirable, brigand, but you do not understand the strategic situation as well as I do. Shall I lay it out before you?"

Kyrus saw no need to answer and allowed Denrik to continue.

"Kadrin has been in decline for decades. You overextended your reach under Liead's reign and made enemies of the whole of the continent. Loramar's wars against you sapped your strength and wasted the lives of many of your sorcerers. When Rashan Solaran was destroyed in the Battle of the Dead Earth, it marked the beginning of your fall. The Kadrin Empire curled into a ball and licked its wounds, guarding its sorcerers against harm rather than risking losing their precious bloodlines.

"Even now, with war at hand, they cower in their towers and plot, rather than acting against Megrenn," Denrik said.

"Tides change," Kyrus said, attempting a nautical metaphor. "The rocks are about to be exposed, and if you do not take care, you will run aground."

"Mr. Hinterdale, you should stick to cheating at Crackle. You have no subtlety. What are you on about? What is it that you know that you are trying so desperately *not* to tell me, despite dangling it before me?" Denrik demanded.

"I know what you are planning. I know your goblin allies have taken your cannons to Raynesdark and intend to conquer it. I even suspect you are with them personally," Kyrus guessed. He was fairly certain but had no way of confirming who the human liaison was. If he guessed correctly, he might be able to convince Denrik to avert the disaster he was inviting.

"Still going to insist you are a brigand, Mr. Hinterdale?"

"I have my sources. Rumors travel far and fast, and I believe there is one rumor that you have missed out on, being with the goblins instead of at home in Megrenn," Kyrus said.

He wanted to see if Denrik—or Jinzan, he supposed—had heard about the return of Rashan. He could only surmise that he had not, or his certainty in a Megrenn victory could not be so total.

"Yes, we found out about the demon you keep company with. One of the goblin assassins confronted him and was allowed to escape alive. I am sorry, but if that demon of yours could not kill a simple assassin, the Megrenn army will find nothing to fear, either," Denrik responded, trying to take the wind out of Kyrus's sails.

"So that is it, then? Even with a demon on our side, you still persist in wanting to bring war?" Kyrus asked.

He was not yet ready to reveal that it was Rashan who had returned to them. It was too incredible a story, and even those who had seen him personally had trouble believing it at first.

"Mr. Hinterdale ... Kyrus, you are fighting on the wrong side in this conflict. You will get conscripted—I cannot imagine them tolerating brigandry in wartime—and you will have to fight on the losing side in the coming war. Align yourself with us and you can be a lord of the seas in Tellurak and a nobleman in occupied Kadrin in Veydrus. I could arrange that."

* * * * * * * *

Kyrus had not accepted Denrik's offer, nor had he declined. He was unsure which option would serve him best, though he had no intention of actually joining forces with Jinzan Fehr and his Megrenn compatriots—nor their goblin allies. On the one hand, he might be able to get more information out of Denrik if he agreed to join him. On the other, he might let slip something vital from his own side. It would all come down to his ability to maintain a lie.

That ability had been called into question when he found out that Denrik had caught on to his cheating, though he was unaware what gave him away. Still, it ruled out Crackle as a way of making extra money on board the *Fair Trader*, and was a warning shot across his bow that his lies were not going entirely unnoticed.

Kyrus stared out to sea, watching the endless waters roll. With his aether-vision, he was able to see the sea creatures near the water's surface and paused to watch an enormous school of fish flee from several sharks that had gathered in the area. With practice, it was getting easier to keep his vision split between the aether and the normal world. It was fascinating to him to see the Sources of all those tiny little fish in the water.

As the ship passed over the area where the fray was taking place, Kyrus took pity on the poor little fishes. Locking his attention onto one of the sharks, he felt for its Source—a shabby, weak thing for a creature that large and fierce—and drew at it. The shark had no means of resisting, and its Source gave up its scant aether with little fuss. The shark became a lifeless carcass in the water and continued on for a moment before it floated up to the surface. Kyrus did not even feel the urgency of the aether he had trapped inside him. It was little enough that he could safely hold it without even exerting himself. He killed the other sharks within his reach in a similar manner.

Kyrus had first wondered about whether it was possible for him to kill just by drawing from a Source after he was attacked in Marker's Point. In his panic, he had drawn aether as hard as he could, and though his memories of the event were hazy, he was certain that he remembered the first of his attackers falling limp before the blast that destroyed so much of the area around him.

Marker's Point ... it reminded him of the tattoo on his arm. They were only two days removed from the events of that day, both the tattoo and the attack. The ward carved on his upper arm had saved Kyrus's life that night, there was no doubt. But what had the cost been? Captain Zayne had called him a fool and told him that it would leech from his own Source, but he had yet to feel any such effect.

It is possible that my Source is strong enough that I do not notice the loss of aether I am experiencing? Or perhaps I am just too new at this whole business to be able to tell I am being affected.

* * * * * * *

Kyrus took his meal in the mess with the men that night. He felt more at ease among the rabble of the ship's crew now that he was confident in the workings of his tattoo ward. Let one of them come at him with a blade, and he would not be so helpless as poor Ruuglor, killed in his sleep by a goblin. It was better than dining with the captain and worrying about whether he would accidentally betray the defenders at Raynesdark by something he said. Sooner or later, the goblins would attack, and until then, he would stay clear of the captain as best he could.

Kyrus had learned almost for certain that Denrik's counterpart Jinzan was with the goblin army. He now knew that Jinzan was revered among the Megrenn, so he might make a valuable captive—though that was a new idea and he had no idea how to go about taking captive a sorcerer of the power alluded to by Denrik and Stalyart. He knew that Stalyart had traveled to Kadrin, and that both he and Denrik saw the Kadrin Empire as weakened.

"Hey!" shouted one of the newcomers aboard the *Fair Trader*. "I hear you's a witch."

Kyrus was pressed between two of Denrik's men at the table, Grosh and Jimony, among a throng present in the mess. He could not see who had called out to him.

"I am a wizard, not a witch," Kyrus yelled back to the room in general, keeping his gaze in his tankard. The ale was not half bad, purchased in quantity in Marker's Point by a few discerning men among the crew who liked a change from rum now and again.

"Whassa diff'rence?" he heard another shout back.

"Witches brew potions and cast hexes, and you can never be sure whether they are really using magic at all or just tricking you—and they are female by definition. A wizard such as myself throws fire and commands the winds, and ought not be bothered when he is in his cups," Kyrus retorted.

There was a chuckle among the men at that last part.

"Come on, then. Shows us some magic, then, hey?"

"Ya, put on a show."

"Ha-ha. Dance for us, witch!"

The drunken voices clamored for him to show his power. They had heard rumors about the destruction in Marker's Point, and many were skeptical when they heard that it was the thin, bookish lad that Captain Zayne had aboard.

"Aww, light one of 'em on fire, why don'cha?" Jimony whispered to him. "That'll shut em up right quick."

Kyrus could tell that Jimony was uneasy aboard the *Fair Trader*. He was aware that Captain Zayne had brought some of his fellow prisoners from New Hope colony aboard, and they were every bit as much *not* sailors as he was. Kyrus had shown some empathy with the land-dwellers, and they had begun attaching themselves to him to avoid the wrath of the seafaring cutthroats that were increasing in population on the ship.

"Magic is no toy to be trifled with," Kyrus replied to those who had been egging him on, ignoring Jimony's advice, tempting though it might be. "It is enjoyable, but only for the one using it. If the sight of it amuses you, so be it, but I am not here as your fool. It any of you wish to see me use magic, draw steel with ill intent in my presence."

"Haw, what a load! He ain't no witch."

Kyrus scanned the room, trying to identify the speaker. He did not want to have this conversation every time he decided to take a meal among the crew.

"Whomever just said that, show yourself," Kyrus said, feigning anger and standing suddenly. "Whoever was next to you knows who you are. I shall go to the main deck, and anyone who wishes to have evidence that my magic is real can join me."

With that, Kyrus extracted himself from the crowded bench and made his way through the mess.

I must be crazed. I just threw down a gauntlet before an entire gang of pirates. I could really use someone here who I could trust to talk some sense into me.

Kyrus had expected that a small group might follow him to the deck, but in his wake, nearly every man among them was coming to see. He had underestimated just how little there was of interest aboard a ship, and how much the men craved action.

I wonder what I ought to do to convince them. Jimony would have me kill one just to set an example, but I would rather not become a murderer just to have some peace on this ship.

When they arrived on deck, Kyrus decided on a plan.

"All of you who believe I am a wizard, move to this side of the deck," and Kyrus gestured to the port side of the ship, which was at his left at the moment. "Those who are not sure, step to the other side." The men did not budge at first, but Kyrus snapped at them, "Move!"

Then men lazily arranged themselves to one side of the ship or the other, with many of them seeming undecided. There was much muttering, but after some exhortations, Kyrus was able to get two distinct groups.

First, Kyrus let loose a burst of hurled fire. He made it a quick one, with little risk to the rigging, just a quick jet of flame from his hand. There were gasps among the crew, but he heard skeptics as well.

"Street magician trick."

"I saw a fella in Yulla do that same thing."

"I ain't believin' it still."

Still, a few moved from one side of the ship to the other.

Next, Kyrus lifted one of the belaying pins, using telekinesis. He had been practicing with it silently and was able to manage to move the pin without having to audibly cast the spell. It was the first time he had tried it outside his cabin though, and he was pleased not to have botched it.

"More tricks."

"I was hopin' for somethin' more impressive than that."

Again, though, a handful were swayed.

There still remained more than twenty in the skeptical group, and Kyrus was about to put an end to that.

"Haru bedaessi leoki kwatuan gelora," he chanted, taking no risks this time.

When he swept his arms up, every last one of the group of skeptics lifted into the air.

Telekinesis was a remarkably efficient spell, he found, and despite so many heavy bodies, he barely felt the strain of holding them aloft. Not content to suffer the sworn oaths and pleas for mercy from the now far-less-skeptical group of pirates, he slowly brought them over the railings of the ship. He took care not to let any of them get within arm's reach of the rigging as he guided them out over the open, shark-infested waters with no land in sight in any direction.

"How is this for a trick? Do you like tricks?" Kyrus called out to them. "I told you that none enjoy magic but the one wielding it. Do you believe me now? Would any of you like to see more? I have more."

There were none left among the skeptics when Kyrus returned the airborne men to the deck. He had made enemies that night, he knew, but he would learn to live with that. Let them fear him, despise him even, but he would not be the laughingstock of the ship. He was beginning to suspect that he would not be able to stay long aboard, given the situation with Denrik, and so the prospect of long-term allies was less of a concern for him.

Kyrus stalked past the crew without addressing any of them. He was tired and worried—to some extent about the tattoo and what it might one day do to his Source, but mainly about Brannis. It was time to get to sleep early tonight, to see what was going to befall.

Chapter 32 - Opening Salvo

The sleep that night had been poor for all. The discovery of the assassin had set the castle on alarm, and guards swarmed everywhere. The duke's household was awakened, and Brannis had been forced to cut short his already meager slumber.

"How did he get in?" Brannis asked.

"I smelled a bit of the sewer on him. There, plain as snow, once you get around the smell of blood," the guard captain reported, a lowborn but competent man named Dern. He was dressed in the duke's livery, but it appeared hastily donned. He had his sword belt on but no other arms, and was unarmored. "We lost five o' our own, though we are still checking."

Frantic knocking on the other doors of the hall had roused the rest of Brannis's companions shortly after Juliana dispatched the assassin. Iridan had slept through the incident, confident in his wards. Faolen emerged from his room with one of the duke's daughters, though whether it was Demni or Phaelia, Brannis neither knew nor cared. Faolen had constructed an illusion of an empty bedchamber to guard against scandalizing the castle staff should anyone have come across them. Sending the duke's daughter scampering off to her own chambers in a borrowed cloak had undone his plan, though in the chaos of the assassin's havoc, it passed with little attention paid.

It was hours to dawn, and Brannis was already armored and content to remain so. It took much to rouse him, even after Iridan tore his door off the hinges to check on him, finding that it had been Avalanche that had prevented entrance by less violent means. The sword's power was impressive. A runed weapon would have run out of aether before holding off Iridan's efforts against the door. Being aether-forged, Avalanche was far more stingy with its aether use, able to function for decades or more with no maintenance. Aether-forged weapons were unfortunately uncommon, however, as the process required a rather skilled sorcerer to handcraft the weapon, imbuing it with aether all through the endeavor. Avalanche and Heavens Cry were the only ones Iridan had ever seen.

"Well, anyone who thinks they can get back to sleep, take a few hours, at least until dawn feast," Brannis ordered.

* * * * * * *

Brannis was exploring the lower mines not half an hour later. The others had all gone off to their assigned tasks; none had thought further sleep possible, given the circumstances. While he hoped that the defenses above would hold, the mines were where they would need to hold out if they were overrun. The reported numbers of the goblin army worried him, and the number of the duke's defenders worried him more so.

Duke Pellaton kept two hundred archers, crews for ten siege engines, a pitiful contingent of two-score cavalry, four hundred city guard that would serve as infantry, and a militia of another thousand common folk who could be armed for Raynesdark's defense. That left them outnumbered forty to one, should the reports of the goblin host prove accurate.

"We have near to six hundred ogres working the mines," Mennon suggested as they walked the aether-lit depths of the mines.

The tunnels were huge, cut for ogres to walk three abreast, and they watched ogre workers pass by in both directions, moving ore out and empty carts back in. Brannis was wary of the huge brutes, though they paid him and Mennon every courtesy as they passed. He had fought too many of them to be comfortable in their presence. He expected at any moment for the placid, docile look in their eyes to be replaced by the cunning ferocity he had seen—for one to just snarl and leap at him, take its pick as a war axe and try to cleave him in half.

"Would you trust these brutes with weapons?" Brannis asked, trying to lead the conversation to Mennon ruling the idea out himself.

"I would just let them loose among the goblins with their everyday tools. They would hardly make efficient fighters, nor would they likely follow orders well—not for lack of trying, mind you. They are eager to please but have the intellect of house pets. Train them for winters at simple tasks and they will manage them. Expect them to understand what you are saying conversationally and you will be disappointed."

"I do not like the idea of them loose on a battlefield," Brannis said, stepping around a pile of loose rock that had yet to be removed. "We can set them on the goblins if they make it as far at the undercity, but above ground, I would rather try to hold the overcity with magic and disciplined soldiers."

Mennon nodded.

"Now tell me more about the stone folk," Brannis said.

"We ran into them generation ago, when my great-grandfather was a young man. Our lowest mines ran into their uppermost. There was an accident, and several of our miners were killed when the ground gave out beneath them. The stone folk were at fault and admitted such; they made reparations and we came to an accord on territories."

"Have you kept in contact with them? Do you trade with them at all?"

"We try to keep on good terms with them—last thing we want is a war with the stone folk living right beneath us—but we see them infrequently. They keep to themselves largely. We trade food for ore in the lean times, both ways. They are willing to barter iron ore for deep-lake fish and the large mushrooms they farm. We sell them wheat and mountain goat meat in exchange for gold,"

Mennon said. He was personally responsible for the city's finances, Brannis had discovered, which had explained his detailed knowledge of the city; Mennon had to make sure it was all paid for.

"Do you think they would grant us safe passage if we had to evacuate?" Brannis asked. It was an indelicate question, but it was just him, Mennon, and the ogre workers down this low in the mines.

"Should I be concerned at where your thoughts lead?" Mennon questioned in reply. "I well suspect they would. The price would be rather exorbitant, I expect, but if we come to that point, I expect money will be the least of our concern."

"I plan for the worst. I still expect us to prevail, but my first goal is to ensure the safety of the people of Raynesdark."

"Well, if nothing else, the stone folk might support us to keep Gehlen's Obelisk out of goblin control. The stone folk may not trust us fully, but they know we have kept it safe since the earliest days of the Empire, and they like having it there."

"What is Gehlen's Obelisk?" Brannis asked. It was the first he had heard of it.

"It is an aether-consuming monolith in the upper mines, near the conduit of the volcano. It draws enough of the ambient aether in the area that the volcano cannot erupt. At least, it has not erupted since the obelisk has been there," Mennon said. He was no expert in magical theory, and Brannis knew little more; it was an advanced topic at the Academy, taught to students older than he had been when he had last attended.

"Should I be concerned?"

"I think not. Even if it were destroyed, who knows how long it would be before the volcano became unstable. Besides, if the goblins gain control of it, we will likely be beyond caring at that point. Let the stone folk drive them out of the city and take control of it then. For a high enough price, we might even buy back the city from them," Mennon said.

"Now who is being the pessimist?" Brannis observed.

Mennon smiled for the first time since Brannis had known him.

* * * * * * *

Dawn feast had been light fare. None had wanted a full stomach once the news came from the walls that a thick fog had formed a short ways from the base of the mountain. Brannis confirmed what many had thought: the goblins had arrived.

Brannis was intrigued by their choice of cover. Iridan had used a similar trick in Kelvie Forest, though on a far, far smaller scale. With the Neverthaw right outside the city, conjuring a large fog was all the easier, and would tax the goblin sorcerers rather little.

"Stand ready, but do not cut short any of the preparations," Brannis ordered. "The goblins are unlikely to attack until later in the day. They will have the evening sun at their back, and it is a clear day, so they will want us looking out into the sun during their initial assault."

Brannis stood atop the wall overseeing the removal of all the catapults. He expected the walls to come under heavy bombardment, and the catapults on the wall would not last long against cannons. The officers of Duke Pellaton's garrison had been skeptical, but Brannis knew that he would get better results from arcing shots over the rubble of the wall once the goblin infantry advanced.

Ogres flowed up from the undercity, hauling cart after cart of gravel for the catapults to use as grapeshot. Men shoveled the gravel into open sacks and piled them near the locations Brannis had ordered for the catapults' new positions. Heavy stones would flatten goblins surely enough, but such large expenditures for so few goblins harmed was wasteful. The gravel was often smaller than a cherry, but there were pieces as large as a man's fist mixed in. Any bit of it would be debilitating to a frail little goblin body, and it was far more useful to severely injure a few dozen of them than to kill a handful.

Below, on the outside of the wall, Iridan worked with a handful of Circle sorcerers that were assigned to Raynesdark, none above Sixth Circle. For all its wealth and old-Empire beauty, Raynesdark was a foresaken place in winter and a backwater socially in the Empire. Sorcerers were sent there as needed by the Circle, but it was no prized assignment. Iridan had them gathering what aether they could and shoring up the wards, while he worked recarving them in spots where they were damaged, and making improvements where needed.

Caldrax had been prevailed upon to take over Ruuglor's task of preparing arrows for the archers, allowing them to reach the distant cannons. Brannis was unsure just how useful that would be, now that he knew that the goblins were planning to use the fog as cover for their forces.

They will have to let the fog lift to see what they are shooting at, Brannis thought. *I would gladly trade blind shots with them, if the price is their useless cannons against our useless bows.*

Of Juliana, there was no sign, which was as it should be.

If Duke Pellaton knew what she was doing, I might have a two-front war on my hands. The thought of burying his city beneath the Neverthaw Glacier would probably be enough to have him try to remove me from command.

That is probably why Rashan wanted me to take command. I do not care for the city, but only for the safety of the people and victory over the enemy.

* * * * * * * *

They took their midday meal upon the wall, rather than heading back to the castle for it. The castle's cooks had sent up skewers of goat, soaked in mushroom sauce, and fresh baked bread. The sorcerers working on the wall's wards came up for the meal as well.

"You think they will attack soon?" Iridan asked between bites of goat meat. He had been in his element all morning. Wardkeeping was something he was comfortable with. The business of being trained as a warlock was new to him, and he had hardly even begun before his father had shipped him off to learn under fire.

"They will attack when it suits them. Dusk is my guess. This late in the season, we have a few hours left, no more. In Kelvie, they made us wait overnight, but I think this time the late hours favor them," Brannis answered.

"When the fighting starts, head for the towers if you mean to remain on the walls. The wards there are stronger," Iridan said.

"Where do you intend to be? Did Rashan say where you should position yourself for a battle?" Brannis asked.

He knew that the warlock had taken Iridan aside and tried to convey the basics of his trade. However, where Rashan had generations of experience, Iridan was just trying his hand at the business of war. Kelvie had tested him and nearly broken him.

What could Rashan have taught him in a few days that will make a difference?

"He advised me not to trade spells from the wall, but to keep shield spells on myself at all times, and get close enough to steal aether from the goblins," Iridan said. "I have always known how to use aether bolts silently, so that will be my standby."

"You are going to wade out among the goblins as they charge?" Brannis asked, incredulous. He hoped that Rashan had not inflated Iridan's sense of his own power.

"Ha! Not a chance. I am planning to wait until they approach the wall. I doubt even Rashan is reckless enough to just walk into the middle of an army," he jested.

Brannis noted that he still called the warlock by name and did not refer to him as his father. It was a lot to get used to, and Rashan did not have a very fatherly demeanor.

To be fair, my father never had a fatherly demeanor, either.

"Just keep in mind how dangerous these goblins are," Brannis said. "If you get into trouble, head for the undercity. Do not let them overrun you or separate you from our troops. They will figure out before too long that you are a valuable target."

"Rashan warned me about that as well. His advice was to kill enough of them that they started individually deciding that seeking me out was a bad idea. If enough of them do that, I will be the one chasing them," Iridan said.

"You think that will work?"

"It might have if he let me have his sword. On my own, I doubt I can be that fearsome. Who knows, though, maybe someday ..."

Hours passed after midday, and the sun grew low. Brannis waited. The lower the sun got, the more he caught himself staring out to the west, expecting the first reports of the goblin cannons. He was the only one who would recognize the sound for what it was. For everyone else, it would be terrifying. There was no helping it, though; the cannon was something that had no counterpart in Veydrus. There was magic—terrifying in battle in its own right—and siege weapons, but nothing with the sort of destructive power that could strike from so far away it could not be countered.

All around him, bowmen and officers waited impatiently, conversing in hushed tones and keeping wary eyes on the fog. Fog was not so uncommon around Raynesdark, but even the most skeptical among the soldiers was convinced that the goblins lay beneath that misty blanket, and that the fog was magical. Real fog would have burned off in the late morning.

Kthooom! Kthooom! Kthooom! Kthooom!

There was no warning, no preamble. The air erupted in metal. Low overhead, the whistle of the cannon shot sped by, the shots themselves moving too fast to be seen. There was a crash among the stone buildings of the city where the cannonballs had found a place to cease their flight, though not their intended target. Nearly everyone on the walls moved to the city side to see what had just befallen.

Homes had largely been struck in the first volley, with a smithy taking a shot as well. The sturdy stone construction of Raynesdark's buildings, many of them hundreds of summers old or more, was no match for the goblin version of Acardian cannons.

"Stay low, wait for them to lift the fog. They are firing blindly at us," Brannis yelled out a warning to everyone on the wall.

Following Iridan's advice, he made his way along the wall to one of the large defensive towers that had sported a catapult earlier that day. Without the catapult crews in the way, the tower was an excellent vantage point.

Brrrraaaaaaaaapp. Brrraap. Brrrraaaaap. Brrraaaaaap.

The sound of the horn echoed among the mountains. Brannis eyes widened in comprehension: *They have a spotter!*

"Look to the fields! Find where that horn is sounding from," Brannis shouted.

Men were already rushing to the very edge of the wall to seek out the source of the noise. The fresh fallen snow should have made picking out the goblin spotter easier, but the distance was working against them, and the goblin may have used magic to cover his tracks.

Kthooom! Kthooom! Kthooom! Kthooom!

The volley was less dangerous than the first, smashing into the road leading up to the city. The shots hit various switchbacks, but all were low by roughly the height of the wall. The goblins were adjusting their aim by the spotter's signal.

Brrraap. Brrraap. Brrraaaaaap.

"Iridan, bring one of those can—metal balls up here," Brannis called out, just stopping himself before calling it a cannonball. "And someone fetch Faolen, and quickly."

Brannis had an idea how to play the goblins' blindness against them. If they could fool the spotter, they would not need to find him and kill him.

Kthooom! Kthooom! Kthooom! Kthooom!

Brannis ducked instinctively as the sound of the shots passed close next to him. There was a wet, splattering sound, and one of the archers on the wall nearby was gone. Two other shots had clipped the top of the wall, shattering stone despite the wards.

This is not good. I had hoped that the wards would have done more.

"Brannis, here!" Iridan shouted.

Brannis turned to see an bronze sphere floating his way. Brannis caught the goblins' cannonball as it came close. It was still hot and would have burned his hand if not for the protection his gauntlet offered. It was identical in size to the ones he had seen aboard the *Fair Trader*. He turned it over and around, studying the runes carved into it. He was no expert on runes, but these seemed meant to damage the wards that the walls bore. The cannonball was even in good shape after its impact. It could probably be used again without having to be tended to by a smith.

"Where is Faolen?" Brannis shouted, finding renewed urgency in misleading the goblin spotter.

If we cannot get them to miss the wall, it will not last long.

The accursed horn sounded again: *Brrrraaaaaaaaapp. Brrraap.*

Brannis could only hope that they could get Faolen to the wall before the goblins found their range and brought it down around them.

We need to get the goblins to commit to a charge while the wall is still intact.

Then: *Kthooom! Kthooom! Kthooom! Kthooom!*

The tower where Brannis stood shook under the direct impact of at least two of the shots. The goblins were on target. The tower's wards held, but the wall had not been so lucky. Plumes of stone dust rose skyward as the cannonballs made holes in several places. Some spots just cracked, as the wards spent themselves protecting the walls, but not enough wards were holding.

Dammit, Iridan! Was that all that could be done to shore up those runes?

"Sir Brannis!" Faolen yelled. He was out of breath after being brought back from the safety of the castle and climbing the ladder up to the wall.

"Quickly! Hide that dust cloud. We need to have the goblins think they missed," Brannis ordered.

It may have been too late already, but it was their best chance. If they adjusted their aim again, they might be able to convince them they were hitting wall when all they were destroying was the road below.

"Huaxti janidu deldore wanetexu elu mulaftu sekedori puc'anzu margek lotok junubi," Faolen chanted quickly.

He seemed to paint the air with his fingers, creating an image of clear air in front of the debris made by the cannonballs' impact. It was a much longer incantation than Brannis was used to hearing, but he knew little of illusion and could see how it might need to be a bit more intricate than turning aether into fire or wind.

No way am I going to remember all that; I could barely follow it. That is, if I live to see nightfall at all for Kyrus to make use of the knowledge.

Brannis had to remind himself that there was a horde of goblins who were intent on destroying them, and it was not a foregone conclusion that he would see the next day.

Brannis and the other Kadrin defenders had no perspective that would let them see how the goblins were perceiving Faolen's illusion. The aether construct of a patch of clear air "painted" in the sky was set between the debris cloud and the goblin fog shroud.

They waited.

After a long while, the horn sounded again. The spotter must have been confused.

Brrrraaaaaaaaapp. Brrraap. Brrrraaaaap.

Brannis wished he had been better able to pick out a pattern in the trumpeting. He wanted to know whether he was going to be seeing cannonballs crashing into the rocks below the wall or ducking ones near his head. There was nothing to do but wait. The soldiers along the wall were becoming accustomed to the pattern and hunkered down behind the parapets after the horn's call faded.

Kthooom! Kthooom! Kthooom! Kthooom!

The ground shook but not like it had before. Brannis looked over to see that the shots had missed low. The cannons were striking at the rock just below the base of the wall. A few shots had ricocheted into the wall itself, but the wards had held against the reduced impact.

"Faolen, show them that they hit. Unmask the debris cloud. Make it more visible if you can," Brannis ordered.

"Consider it done," Faolen replied.

They toyed with the goblins for volley after volley. They seemed to be catching on that something was wrong, but the goblin spotter was guessing against them and losing. Faolen adjusted the visible debris and created the appearance of damage where there was none, or revealed earlier damage from the errant shots that occasionally slipped through their web of deceptions and hit the wall anyway.

Brannis wished there was someone that could lend aid to Faolen, but there was no one else who had more than a basic understanding of illusion. It was an ill-reputed discipline, and a highly specialized one; illusion attracted few to its way. Brannis could see the strain it was putting on the slightly built sorcerer's body.

It thus came as no surprise when Faolen collapsed unconscious after one more time having to renew his spell for painting the sky with lies.

"Quickly, get him into town," Brannis said. "Get him water and lay him down. If you can rouse him, help him back to the battle."

This is it. The goblins are going to figure out their range, and we will lose the wall.

Brannis had expected it, but it was no less galling to be driven back. Still, they had not lost the wall yet, and it was possible that they might have run the goblins out of—or at least low on—ammunition or black powder.

Kthooom! Kthooom! Kthooom! Kthooom!
Kthooom! Kthooom! Kthooom! Kthooom!
Kthooom! Kthooom! Kthooom! Kthooom!

There was little they could do but wait it out, and hope the wall still offered some protection when the goblins ran out of shots to fire, or patience, and attacked.

* * * * * * * *

Looking out the flap of the tent, Celia could see little in the heavy, magical fog. There was visibility to a dozen paces or so, but that only showed her the commanders and the Megrenn sorcerer.

He had taken her again that morning, a final human comfort before going into battle beside the goblins. He whispered promises that he would protect her and, for the first time, spoke of not ransoming her back to Kadrin at all. He said he wanted to bring her back to Megrenn with him after conquering Raynesdark and take her for a wife. She would be his fourth wife, he said, and rich as a princess.

"There is no future in Kadrin as a sorceress," he had said.

She was oddly conflicted. Jinzan had been the only one kind to her in the least since the goblin invasion. Her husband had died trying to flee the city— without her—and had been caught by the goblin invaders. He was Lord Feldrake's guard captain and had disgraced himself badly. He had talked bravely, but after a few short months of marriage, she had discovered that he was just a braggart and a bully, and on the day he died, she realized he was a coward who would abandon her to save his own hide. Jinzan was a hero among his people: he had fought for—and won—his people's freedom. He was ruthless, but he was also intelligent and brave in the true sense, backed by actions and not just idle words. Enemy or not, he was more a man than her late husband, and she was now widowed.

Can Megrenn really retake not only their own lands, but steal Kadrin's as well?

An alliance with goblins and the marvelous war machines they had made from Jinzan's plans spoke to a shift in power in favor of the mistreated former vassal. She had been hearing the "cannons," as he called them, for nearly an hour. The noise they made was unlike thunder, which was loud but lasted and faded. These cannons split the air itself with their report. She learned after the first volley to wait for the spotter's horn, then plug her ears.

At least they had left her hands unbound. She did not know whether it was arrogance or oversight. Jinzan had taken no chances with her, certainly. She had slept the night gagged and with her wrists and even fingers tied together. He would treat her as a dangerous enemy, he had told her, until she had chosen her fate. If she agreed to return to Megrenn with him, he promised there would be no more need for such precautions. She believed him too. She had seen his Source and seen his draw. He was far more powerful than Celia, and she knew it.

I wonder how he would treat me if he knew I was Fifth Circle, and not Seventh? Celia mused.

She had lied to keep from being considered even more dangerous than a lesser-ranked sorceress would be. Her Source looked weaker than it truly was, due to her aptitude at life extension. Diverting much of her Source into preserving her youth limited her power, but it was well worth it in her mind. She was seven springtimes older than she claimed but looked young even for the nineteen autumns she pretended to be. For the young sorceresses of Kadrin, it was never too early to begin preserving their looks.

Still, despite summers of habit, she could stop diverting so much of her Source to keeping her youth and instead try to ambush Jinzan. It would cost winters off her life perhaps—life extension was like a dam, and unleashing it would cause much trouble that could not be quickly or completely undone—but she could be a hero to Kadrin.

If we win, she amended to herself.

If things went badly, maybe she would consider his offer.

* * * * * * *

[I grow weary,] Ni'Hash'Tk muttered, heeding the warning G'thk had given her about remaining quiet to retain the element of surprise.

She understood the logic of it and was rather enjoying the sound of K'k'rt's new toys, but it was *cold* outside, and while dragons were warm-blooded and she was in no danger of hypothermia, as were her minions, she longed for the comfort of volcanic caverns.

The city was peopled by humans, with their knights and sorcerers, and according to Gkt'Lr at least, a demon. Aside from the last, the rest barely registered as threats, and she did not fear the demon.

[Patience, Mighty One,] G'thk advised.

His lesser-ranked generals had taken over conducting the battle as soon as she had arrived. G'thk had devoted his energies to trying to placate her and keep her amused while her worshipers dallied about in their conquest of the human city. There was nothing he could do—either by law or through force—to stop her seizing his army from him if she tired of waiting for him to deliver the city.

[We do not wish to waste any of our troops. Let the tinkers' weapons do their work on the K'drn's defenses first.]

[Send for my masseurs. I wish my wings readied for flight,] Ni'Hash'Tk instructed, thinking that once she felt up to it, she would join the battle. It had been some winters since she last flew anything other than lazy loops around her lair to enjoy fine weather or to awe her worshipers on holy days. Her muscles ought to be worked loose before testing them in combat.

G'thk relayed the order and added a few of his own. He could sense her impatience, she could tell; he was an attentive and perceptive minion. While Ni'Hash'Tk was utterly confident in her imperviousness, G'thk was cautious and wished to conduct a proper military operation, with few risks and total victory, or so he claimed. Goblins would need to live in that city when they were done conquering it, and razing it with dragonfire was counterproductive, or so he claimed.

G'thk plugged his ears.

Kthooom! Kthooom! Kthooom! Kthooom!

Ni'Hash'Tk clenched her jaw tight to keep from wincing at the sound, which was beginning to wear on her as much as her general's empty claims. How many more such volleys would she have to put up with before she took matters into her own claws?

* * * * * * * *

"Wolves!" the shout came and then was carried down the wall.

Defenders poked their heads above the ruins of the wall, wherever they could find shelter. Brannis had ordered the evacuation of the wall except for a handful of lookouts, who were posted on the highest remaining points of the wall. Ladders had been moved into place based on where there was still a place worth climbing. All four of the wall's towers had been damaged beyond the point where any sane soldier would man them; thus only a handful remained stationed there, Iridan among them. The would-be warlock was weary of being shot at by unseen engines of war and hungered to show off the real trick his warlock father had taught him during his brief tutelage.

"Man the walls!" Brannis ordered.

Soldiers and militia alike took up spears and climbed the ruins of the wall to gain the hilltop they now formed. Men helped one another up by clasped wrists and knees used as stepladders, any method they could find to get in place to finally face their enemy on the field of battle.

Those at the top saw what appeared to be a stampede of wolves, black furred and near to the height of a horse. These were Ni'Hash'Tk's outriders, though none of the defenders could have known that. For the last two days, the Raynesdark scouts who ventured beyond sight of the city walls were overrun and killed by these same packs of monstrous wolves—and their riders. The wolves carried the goblin equivalent of light cavalry, armed with spears and daggers, and they were having no difficulty traversing the snow-dusted plains that filled the void between the Kadrin defenders and the main goblin host.

The wolves were equipped for battle, with steel helmets that were fanned out at the edges to offer a semicircular screen for the rider to duck behind for cover. Thick leather collars and vests protected their vulnerable necks and underbellies. Goblins left little they dealt with unimproved; their animals were no exception.

The wolves threw up great sprays of powdery snow as they ran, seemingly extending the cloud of fog as they ran. But as the snow fell back upon the earth, it revealed goblins on foot, following in the path trampled by the wolves. The goblins did not hoot and cheer as humans might as they charged into battle. Their tiny voices did not carry far enough or with enough resonance to strike fear into enemies' hearts, and they knew it. Thus onward they came with just the panting of wolves as their herald, still too far away to be heard by their enemies, yet closing rapidly.

Men upon the remains of Raynesdark's battlements shifted nervously and tightened grips on their spears. On the bit of walls and tower that remained, archers arrayed themselves as best they could manage to steady a shot.

"Archers, fire on the wolves as they come into range! Save the enchanted arrows for now!" Brannis shouted.

Bows twanged as the archers took that for liberty to begin firing immediately, and some of the arrows reached their mark.

* * * * * * * *

The view from atop the avalanche wall was breathtaking. Higher than even the top towers of the castle, Juliana could see out over the entire battlefield—though she still could not see what was concealed in the fog.

They must keep their command back there, and obviously there are the cannons, but what else are they hiding? They must have some other trick, or keeping the fog up is just a waste of aether.

The runes were damaged along a long stretch of the avalanche wall. She had struggled with disabling the physical protections of the surface long enough to damage the wards that bore the weight of the Neverthaw Glacier above. She wondered how old the wall was. It was weathered and water stained but in perfectly functional condition. She had never been a strong student of history, but she had gathered that the wall was probably nearly as old as the city itself—thousands of summers. Juliana felt a pang of regret at what she might have just set on a path to destruction. One day, history books might list her as the one who had destroyed Raynesdark's ancient wall, a monument to the early days of the Empire.

But will they see me as a vandal, recklessly toppling a piece of the Empire's heritage, or as the savior who was willing to place the lives of everyone in Raynesdark ahead of the architectural richness of their forebears.

She watched for a moment longer, fascinated by the battle unfolding so far off. The forces arrayed on both sides looked like the tiny ceramic figurines sold in the markets, little clusters of toy people and goblins, too small to be real but so amazingly lifelike in their detail. It was easy to ignore the fact that the figures breathed and bled and screamed, when seen from so far away.

Suddenly the plains erupted in flame. A huge swath of the pack of charging wolves turned into living flame. The charge broke off and diverted around the destruction but kept coming.

Unless that worm Caldrax did that, Iridan must have just cast that firestorm spell. That was no firehurling—not on that scale for sure. Just ... be safe, please, Iridan? You are not your father. Fate willing, you never will be.

* * * * * * * *

[I sensed that!] Ni'Hash'Tk snarled, sending G'thk and the masseurs stumbling away from her reflexive shift to an alert posture.

[Mighty One, I understand your desire for combat. I cannot see any reason you should not join the battle at your leisure. I know you are supremely powerful, but please have care, Holy One. This human feels powerful, and I do not wish to see you injured,] G'thk said, trying to instill some thought of caution in his arrogant goddess.

She knew that she would be fine and wished that her followers would show a bit more confidence in her power. G'thk, she suspected, was more concerned over the damage she might inflict on his new city.

* * * * * * * *

So it seems the demon has joined the battle. If the great beast wishes to confront the thing directly, so be it. It seems strong enough, though I imagine I could hold my own against it, if that is the extent of its power.

Jinzan had spent most of the day pacing. He needed access to the city and did not want to risk open battle if he could at all avoid it. His mission was more important than the overall conquest. The Staff of Gehlen was all that mattered.

Well, maybe not all that matters. The loss of the Raynesdark mines will hurt the Empire, though not fatally. There is the girl, too.

It was a silly, impulsive decision, he knew. Before he had known she was a spy, he had bedded her because she was there and willing, nothing more. But she was a captivating creature now that he knew more of her. Comely enough to be sure, but she was devious and cunning, and did what it took to survive. Oh, he knew that she came to his bed to gain his protection and nothing more; that was simple enough to grasp. But she lied to him at every turn, and did it well. Certainly she was not the same caliber of liar as that snake Kyrus, but Jinzan also had resources that Denrik lacked.

Jinzan has studied her Source thoroughly as she slept. He was no novice and could see subtleties in the swirls and whorls of the aether that most others could not discern. He was able to pick up the signs of extensive life extension taking its toll on the power of her Source. Oh, it was healthy enough, but starved and weakened. If she was nineteen autumns, he was a goblin.

But it was her deceptions and will to survive that he admired in her. She was living the life she was given and making her way. He would take her back to Megrenn as more than a trophy; his interest in her was genuine. She might encounter some small hostility, being Kadrin-born, but Megrenn was nothing if not accepting, and his standing was more than sufficient to validate her among the elite of the kingdom.

Jinzan reached into his pocket, feeling the cold, hard surface of the tiny cannon that was secreted away within. Another pocket held a bag filled with tiny cannonballs, and a pouch contained black powder, wadding, a powder horn, ram, and swab. He had pilfered the materiel from the goblin batteries and used his magic to shrink them down. It was exacting magic, using the aether to crush everything down equally and lightening it proportionally. The little cannon kit moved awkwardly as he fiddled with the pieces; they were intact cannon components, just compressed, and every bit of them was still there. The portion of the spell that made them feel manageably light was not quite as precise, and the pieces did not handle as if they were miniatures made to be the size they were.

Awkward or not, they were the key to his plan. If anything went wrong with the battle, he would not have to rely on the goblins giving him the use of one of the cannons as they fought for their lives.

* * * * * * *

The first of the wolves reached the mountain road up to Raynesdark. Unable to scale the low cliffs that separated the switchbacks, they were forced to weave back and forth as the road wended its way up toward the city gate. Built for defense, Raynesdark had only the one gate.

Arrows fired down from what remained of the wall, expertly picking off the wolves as they ran sidelong to the wall. The armored helmets for the reckless goblin cavalry were designed to protect them as they mounted a frontal charge. The Kadrin arrows were finding flanks left bare to allow for speed.

"Help me with him. Get him down to the ground," one of the lookouts said, holding a slumping Iridan under the arms.

His third firestorm had taken from his own Source for aether and left him spent. He was conscious, but exhausted, and was ready to fall off the wreckage of the tower he had taken up position on if no one else was ready with aid.

Having seen the aid his magic had been, spearmen rushed over to help lower Iridan to ground level, hoping fervently that he would be able to rejoin the battle. The more of the goblins he slew, the fewer that they would have to fend off. Iridan's head lolled to the side as he was handed down into the waiting arms of Duke Pellaton's troops.

Brannis spared a glance after his friend's well-being, but he had to focus on the enemy and the command of his own troops.

Fool. You did it to yourself again. At least this time, you did not burn yourself unconscious.

Brannis gritted his teeth in frustration, wishing his friend had learned better control over his power, or was at least more judicious with it.

"Catapults, all fire!" Brannis shouted back to the siege crews.

The infantry was in range, and he could not let the opportunity pass as he checked on whether Iridan would be in any condition to rejoin the battle.

Crrrk ... Thgggthggthgg.

The catapults loosed sacks full of gravel from the mines, left open such that the gravel lofted free as the sacks arced through the air. The crews were supplied with countless sacks of the stuff, a waste product that was built up and eventually hauled out of the city to be dumped. Brannis had just ordered the process be carried out by catapult and had designated the goblin army as the dumping ground. Much of the gravel was landing on the lower portion of the road as well, possibly impeding the goblin advance.

As Brannis looked to the west, he saw an absolute sea of goblins. More and more emerged from the fog, which had persisted all the way to sunset. The estimates from the survivors of Illard's Glen had been woefully inaccurate. There were likely already sixty thousand goblins upon the plain, and who knew how many more yet to emerge. Yet even with the walls in ruins, the city was defensible, and the humans still held advantages in reach and strength when the battle was joined in hand combat.

"We have waited out their bombardment. We have forced them to face us. Now is our chance to drive them back and throw them off the mountain as they try to take it from us!" Brannis shouted, trying to steel the courage of men who had never seen real combat.

He glanced down the lines, spearmen four deep, archers still picking their shots as the dwindling pack of wolf riders grew closer. None had broken yet and fled in the face of the enemy. None were crying—at least audibly—or talking of retreat, but there were dark looks among those who stood with Brannis; haunted eyes, muttered imprecations, and a few seemed to be catatonic. They might feign bravery well, but Brannis mistrusted them until he saw whether they held against the first charge.

When the wolves were nearly upon them, Brannis took up a position at the fore. Avalanche in hand, he stood out among the grim and dreary mail of soldiers and unarmored winter clothing worn by the militia. The sorcerers had the sense to dress in black for battle, and the knights' bright steel and green-on-black livery shone, but Brannis Solaran looked every bit the commander of an imperial army in his gold-and-quicksilver armor, the polished surfaces reflecting the last moments of sunlight.

The wolves came across the rocky ruin at the approach to the wall, fanning out and making a break for the interior of the city. Wolves as large as mules danced like mountain goats across the uneven terrain, few even missing a step as they leaped and sprang from boulder to flat spot to fallen masonry. The growls and snarls as their prey stood waiting were fearsome, and the wolves fearless, and they plowed heedless into the waiting line of spears, trained to trust in their frilled helms and leather armor to keep death from finding them before they dealt it.

A golden statue amid tin soldiers, Brannis was sought out by several wolf riders eager for the kill of an obviously important commander. The goblin spears deflected harmlessly off his armor as they charged him, not even connecting with enough force to rock him backward, as Rashan's demonstration had. Avalanche swept through the air like one of the goblin-swords the Kelvie expedition had brought, but unlike those wisps of steel, his enchanted blade moved with the force of a mountain behind it. Neither wolf, nor armor, nor goblin rider impeded its path in the slightest. Brannis could only even tell he was finding his target by the sound and the mess. Wolves were cloven in twain, strikes that hit flat-bladed sprayed buckets of blood and gore across the crushed rock hilltop they defended. Men who had previously bunched close to defend their commander now offered him wide space. Brannis retreated only against the onslaught of carrion that was piling in front of him.

All down the wall, the defenders held their ground. The wolf riders were brave and foolhardy, seeking out the well-armored knights in search of trophies rather than probe for weakness among the lines. But their charge had bought time for the infantry behind them. Unlike their mounted comrades, the infantry were climbing the rock faces and heading directly up the side of the mountain toward the fortifications.

Brannis and the rest of the Kadrin defenders had no way to know that the whole of the goblin infantry wore special climbing gear. Crude brass claws, cast by the score in the goblin forges, were strapped to the backs of their hands, and toothy spikes dug down from the tips of their boots, giving them bite into the loose rock of the mountain bottom, and—should they reach that far—the masonry pile higher up. Thus they surprised the defenders with the speed at which they ascended, making time up the mountainside quicker than even the wolves had, running fast but needing to follow the road until nearly at the top. The goblins were light, fragile creatures, but what there was of them was mostly muscle and sinew. They were able to pull their own weight up easily as they climbed, and it fatigued them little. Their short, razor-sharp spears could even be clutched in one hand while the claw strapped to its back held their grip on the rocks.

Brannis saw it and knew there was going to be a slaughter the likes of which he had never witnessed. The goblins knew that many of them, perhaps even most of them, had little chance of surviving the earliest phase of the assault, but they knew that their brethren would follow behind, and trusted that the humans would wear down and eventually succumb. Brannis could only hope that they were wrong, and that, with magic and stamina, they could withstand the onslaught.

*Rrrrrrrr*OOOOOOOOO*AAAAAAAAAAAAAAAAR!*

The battlefield stilled as the goblins paused in their ascent. Goblin and human alike turned to find the source of the great bellow that sundered the air and shook the ground beneath them. Lesser slopes to the north and south of Raynesdark, with no wards to stop them, saw avalanches begin due to the noise. The fog over the goblin campsite dissipated rapidly as a rush of massive wings flapping created a tempest near the Neverthaw River, where it seemed that the command tents were pitched.

"KNEEL DOWN, HUMANS, AND FACE YOUR DOOM. I AM JADEFIRE, GODDESS OF THESE, MY LOYAL FOLLOWERS, AND YOU DIE AT MY COMMAND!" a mammoth dragon bellowed in excellent Kadrin, going so far as to use the name that humans knew her by, or at least once did some centuries past.

With a great beating of wings, the monstrous dragon took to the air. The massive silhouette as she ascended was awe-inspiring, even at the great distance separating the defenders from her. Scale was difficult to judge, but it was so far away ... and still looked so large ...

"Fall back! Take up defenses of the streets. Use the houses. Keep the houses between you and the dragon's fire," Brannis ordered.

His troops needed little prompting to abandon the wall and the scant cover it would offer against an aerial assault. His challenge would be to get them to stop and fight rather than head for the undercity.

Iridan, still weak enough that he needed help being moved, fumbled inside his tunic for the stone Rashan had given him, fighting against the two soldiers who had lifted him up and carried him from where he had taken respite at the base of one of the fallen towers.

* * * * * * * *

Juliana heard the dragon's roar and thought that the wall she had just finished sabotaging was about to give way beneath her. The wall held, but just barely. Its sturdy stone construction was enough, even without the aid of the wards, that it held the advance of the ice against the disruption cause by Jadefire's bellow. She watched as the dragon took wing, and two hints were quite enough for her to decide to take leave of her vantage.

She looked down from the wall to the city streets far below. The wall rose a hundred and more feet above the top of the cliff wall, which itself stood forty feet from the level ground of the overcity. The gate to the undercity was directly beneath her, and there was no provision for getting from where she was to where she was going.

She jumped.

Her unbound hair streaked behind her as she plummeted, a pennant of reddish-gold announcing her own charge toward the ground. The frigid air was both exhilarating and numbingly cold at the same time and she relished it. To all appearances, she slammed into the cobblestone path to the undercity with force enough to splatter her body like the unfortunate wolves that crossed the path of Brannis's sword. Instead she spiked down onto the street on one knee, with a hand out to steady herself. Magic had cushioned her fall, of course, a spell she knew well enough to trust to it mid fall and silently cast.

She considered joining the fighting, but thought better of it. *I am no warlock. I can keep my head on my own shoulders if it comes to a fight, but in a war, I am not prepared to stand out there amid the chaos and trust my magic to keep me alive.*

Instead Juliana contented herself to loiter in the gate area. She was still undercover in case the avalanche wall gave way, but had a view of the streets of Raynesdark and enough of a view to know if the army was being routed or not. She would also be able to hear any further proclamations from the dragon.

* * * * * * * *

"If any portion of the claim is called into question, you have but to request my presence and I will appear with all haste," the knight spoke.

He wore no armor and carried no sword within the emperor's audience chamber. Sir Kaelar Montagu wore his family's coat of arms upon his tabard, green swords crossed facing north and west, upon a white shield, and the fashions of a court dandy about the rest of him. Wide sleeves, green hose, and pointed shoes that turned up slightly at the tip. Rashan was disgusted by him.

Sir Kaelar had just spent half the morning delivering the claim of his lord's cousin, sired by Emperor Dharus's uncle Maolen. They had brought birth records, accounts of interviews with the lord's staff, the travel itinerary of the emperor's uncle on and around the time of the conception, and sketches drawn by some artist that Lord Avewind sponsored that purported to be both hauntingly lifelike and clearly show the resemblance to the boy's supposed sire.

Rashan had stood next to the emperor's throne, a position he had attended on more court audiences than he cared to count. As regent, he felt it unseemly to take his seat upon the vacant throne, particularly as he heard one among the dozens of claims that were beginning to flow in from across the Empire. He was frankly astonished at the lengths the nobles went to document and verify their ruttings, both legitimate and otherwise. Astonished and sickened. They took no pride in their breeding, leaving to chance what sorts of nobles they ended up with as the generations passed, to say nothing of the emperors it engendered, when tragedies such as this occurred.

The knight's claim on his master's behalf was at least well presented, if not wholesome and reassuring. Rashan suspected that there may have been dark dealings in the deaths of those who may have been able to present more legitimate claims. The Inner Circle had likely been taking its time and slowly culling the royal line out of the nobility, but he could prove nothing. His general calling for all claims on the throne was trouble from the start, as he knew it would be. He promised that no claimant should face retribution for bringing their case, however tangential, so long as they made no false representations to him. He also promised protection of all claimants, in the form of a *personal* investigation of any strange deaths.

An army arriving at one's castle gate and demanding to conduct an investigation was wholly anathema to a noble house. It affronted their dignity and took the shine from their reputation, guilty or not, and there was nothing to be done about it save meeting the army in the field. A warlock arriving at one's castle gate and demanding to conduct an investigation was, if possible, less welcome. Whereas armies tended to be subject to misdirection, bribery and a rather unfortunate reputation for rigid thinking, warlocks were notoriously difficult to persuade to any path but the one they had chosen, and saw through ruses too often and too easily.

"Very well, Sir Kaelar, I accept your claim as truth until such time—"

"*DRAGO*—" a voice in Rashan's head screamed, interrupting his thoughts, before being abruptly cut off.

Curse that shoddy stone. I ought to have put more time into its crafting.

"—as I have reason to believe otherwise," Rashan finished his previous sentence after a brief hesitation. "I am afraid I must attend to an urgent military matter. I will hold audience in three days' time." Rashan figured that would be enough time to deal with whatever had befallen at Raynesdark.

It seemed that the goblins had brought along one of their dragon-gods. It was an unusual addition to a goblin assault, and an unfortunate one. Dragons were lazy, indolent creatures, content to remain idle for scores of summers at a time while their minions amassed wealth to give to them in tribute. However, for all their sloth, dragons were the most ferocious creatures imaginable. The goblins would have been wiped from the lands entirely long ago had it not been for the pact they had formed with the dragons, elevating them as deities in exchange for protection. For a dragon to join in attacking Raynesdark, there must have been something that it wanted greatly.

Despite his great age and vast experience, Rashan had never battled a dragon before, nor even strongly considered it. During his time as warlock—the first time, anyway—Kadrin was feared as a conquering, expansionist empire. None but Loramar had dared attack them, including the goblins. However, launching an attack on the goblin lands was nothing to be considered. While a single dragon taking initiative to attack a Kadrin city was troubling, invading them and having *all* the dragons of the pact allied against him was unquestionably stupid, unthinkable even.

He knew he would need to gather aether before he left. The transference spell by itself required massive amounts of aether, and the area around the palace was always a bit dry of aether to begin with.

Not to be helped, with so many sorcerers about.

After that, he would need a reserve in case he ended up in the thick of battle immediately upon arrival. He had no misconceptions about sneaking up on a dragon—or even the goblins, quite frankly—when using a transference spell. They just caused too much disruption in the aether to pass unnoticed by anyone sensitive to it.

It was sorely tempting to draw the aether right out of the Sources of the useless slackwits that had been inflicted upon him. Of all those at court, he could count a handful worth the space they took up: Lord Dergh was a shrewd and keen man, the Duchess Wensaka had sent a reliable knight to court in Sir Darwey, and there were a pair of house sorcerers he would have much liked to recruit back into the Imperial Circle ... perhaps a few others but no more than that few.

It was tempting to rid himself of them and use their aether to go into battle with, but no, he would not. Murder in the name of justice, and you might find yourself ruling a kingdom. Murder in the name of convenience, and you find yourself a pariah, no matter how powerful. He might hold the Empire together for a while through fear, but eventually alliances would form against him and he would not survive the aftermath.

Instead Rashan dashed down the stairs of the dais and quickstepped across the large audience chamber, watching as a path presented itself in the direction he faced, courtiers elbowing and jostling each other to remove themselves from his way. A few tried to ask questions or favors of the regent as he passed, but he studiously ignored them.

I am in charge, at least for now. When I say an audience is at an end, there are no further petitions.

Once free of the press of bodies in the audience chamber and free of the rather ill-defined obligation to maintain decorum, he broke into a run. The dark jest he had played out in his head about the Sources of those courtiers had given him an idea.

* * * * * * *

The lizard was an obstinate beast, unused to the weight of a human on its head. It bore Jinzan's heft but disliked having to. The lizard and rider were both camouflaged with magic, appearing as little more than a distortion of the air to those at a distance, no more substantial than the wavy look the air gets above a fire. The complex system of bladders and tubes that wound around the lizard to keep warm was well-heated by Jinzan's aether, and the creature carried him, but he had to take a harsh hold on its reins to keep its willfulness in check.

He had taken it on a northerly vector, heading away from the main body of the goblin army. The walls were not so damaged to that side of the city, where worked stone met unworked. The cannoneers had wanted to breach the central area of the wall to best make use of the road for the approach, and the far northerly and southerly ends of the wall had taken fewer shots than had the rest. But it was to the north that his destination lay. Between the city wall and the castle, there was an entrance to the old upper mines. There was no map that showed the location of the Staff of Gehlen, but it was known to be in the upper mines.

Chapter 33 - Dragon Goddess

Down the corridors Rashan raced, as fast as his legs would carry him without expending magic to quicken his pace. Palace servants fled at his approach, and a few even threw themselves to the floor to escape his path. For all his lack of stature and smooth, youthful features, he was a terrifying sight when focused. White hair and black cape streamed out behind him, the latter billowing, and his vile sword bounced at his hip, occasionally tapping the floor with its scabbard. It was the eyes, though, that frightened. They were cold, unblinking, staring eyes that saw a destination and brooked nothing pass between him and it. None who saw that gaze wished to have their own visage reflected in it.

He came to the flight of stairs he sought, heading down into the dungeons below the palace. Not slowing his pace, he hopped as he reached the corner and kicked against the wall to make his turn. He touched just one stair and leaped down the rest, then repeated the maneuver as he descended two more flights.

The halls of the lower levels were much as he remembered them from a few days earlier, when he had darkened the mood with flickers reminiscent of torchlight. He turned not to the special wing of the dungeon reserved for sorcerous prisoners but rather toward the cells where plainer men were left to rot.

He slowed his pace to a brisk walk as he entered the cell block. The jailor on duty he dismissed with a wave of his hand and a perfunctory "begone," which was more than enough instruction to set the stout man to flight.

The first door the warlock came to was of solid iron, with a small, barred window at an average man's eye level. The window was too high for Rashan's eyes by more than a head, but he could easily discern the Sources of the men locked up within. They were nothing special, these Sources, save one simple distinguishing fact: they were expendable.

Reaching up, Rashan grabbed the door by the little window that was the only opening in the solid iron plate that constituted its bulk. With a quick tug, he ripped the door from the wall, tearing thick iron bolts from the stonework in the process. He tossed the heavy iron door down the corridor ahead of him, and it rang with a great clatter of iron on stone.

The prisoners within mistook the violent opening of their cell for a jailbreak and clamored to reach the door. The first two to do so dropped dead at Rashan's feet, as the warlock tore the vital aether completely from their Sources. Even down in the depths of the dungeons, men had heard of the warlock's return, and seeing their fellows fall at his whim was enough to turn back the rest and set them begging mercy of the demon.

There was none to be had.

Rashan cleared that cell of living prisoners and two more after it. The screams had set the dungeons into a panicked frenzy. Violent, desperate men lashed out when the door to their cell were ripped open, but they were pathetic wretches—murderers, rapists, and thieves, not a warrior among them, not that it would have mattered. Rashan scythed their aether free of them and built up the power he felt the need to bring with him to the battlefield that Raynesdark had become.

Not bothering even to levitate himself free of the ground, Rashan formed the sphere of aether around him that would swap places with an identically sized spot at his destination. Should the dungeons in the emperor's palace sport a sod-filled hole a demon's-height deep, so be it.

The aether surged into Rashan as he drew in whatever remnants were left about after draining the prisoners, and then suddenly the sphere vanished.

I come for you, dragon.

* * * * * * * *

The defenders scrambled to avoid the path of the dragon's flight as she banked and turned toward the city to come at them from the northwest. The stone-built houses became their battlements in the new fight to hold off the dragon while the goblin infantry poured into the city. The cobblestones thumped beneath thousands of booted feet in what had turned into a large-scale version of the children's game hide-from-his-lordship, with the dragon playing the part of the lord, seeking the humans and scolding them with fire instead of words.

It was the dragon's third pass. The first two had left wide holes in the Kadrin defensive lines and shallow, smoldering channels where the dragonfire had melted the streets and washed the newly molten rock away.

"Engage the goblins!" Brannis ordered. "Keep close to them so the dragon cannot burn us at will without hitting her own forces as well."

Brannis hoped that his knights were relaying his orders as he gave them. He lacked the vantage necessary to see the bulk of his troops, with them running in and between buildings, ducking for cover as the dragon approached. They stopped at any opportunity to hold their ground against the goblins or push them back from a small area.

Will it even matter? Brannis wondered. *If we kill every one of those goblins, we still have no plan to deal with that dragon.*

The dragon was the size of a tavern, or a warship, if you did not count the massive wingspan or the tail. Her maw could swallow men whole, with fangs the size of swords. Brannis had gotten a close view on the last pass, as Jadefire flew past just above the rooftops not ten paces from him.

Brannis had been issuing orders and checking on the goblin advance, and neglected to take account of the dragon's approach. He turned when he heard the great intake of breath that preceded her blasts of dragonfire. She was bearing down right for him, picking out his gaudy armor as a likely enough target for her fiery breath. Brannis was caught in the middle of the road, with no time to make it to cover on either side before Jadefire closed in to incinerate him.

Brannis prepared to die.

* * * * * * * *

The sphere of aether appeared on the plains before Raynesdark, near the city, but still on flat ground among the advancing goblins host, near the rear. Most of the goblins had already reached the mountain and were either on the road or already within the city's walls. A pair of severed spearheads lay just outside the stone circle of the dungeon floor that Rashan had brought with him.

All across the battlefield, aether-sensitive combatants took note of his arrival. Several had noticed the power that was unleashed with Iridan's hellfire spells, but the transference the demon performed had just ripped a chunk of the world loose and transported it across half the Empire. The aether necessary to accomplish that was more than any of them, save the dragon, could have even channeled. The aether shook with the force of his arrival, and the currents of the sea of goblins around him shifted.

Rashan found himself surrounded by infantry, startled to be sure, but accustomed enough to magic that they recovered their wits and brought spears to bear against him. The warlock allowed a spear tip to slide off his shielding spell and reached out absently to grasp its owner by the top of his head and twisted, snapping the neck. He was not so much as looking at the enemies all about him, but searched for the reason he had come so far to join the battle. With his highly developed aether-vision, he was able to locate the vast and powerful Source, even as it was obscured from his view by the buildings of the city as it flew low above them.

Ahh, found you, Rashan thought.

Then something curious happened. There was a twisting in his gut that he had not felt in a long time, since before he had become a demon. It was a feeling that he had thought lost to him, a weakness that he had overcome permanently.

He was afraid.

He had led armies into battle for over a hundred summers in the service of the Kadrin Empire, had thrown down castles and slaughtered kings and armies alike, and hardly remembered the fear that came in deadly conflict. He had faced the horrors of Loramar's dead horde, and vaguely recalled a similar unease to what he now felt. But a century of placid existence among others of his kind, and the occasional killing of those who were unable to threaten him, had softened his heart. Worse, it had taken away something that might possibly have been necessary for true bravery: the knowledge of mortality. A man who accepts death as his inevitable fate will not shy from spending his death well; it was the stuff from which knights and heroes were forged.

But Rashan had unlocked the ultimate secret: eternal life. He was not indestructible, though he was formidable in every way he knew possible. But the thought whispered inside him that rather than risking just the manner and timing of his death, he risked the fact of it entirely; he had hundreds, if not thousands of summers or more of his existence ahead of him, and the possibility of losing that hit him in a manner he had not anticipated.

He saw the great Source and knew the creature it represented. A dragon was the best the gods had created, more formidable, longer lived, and with a stronger Source than any other race they had forged. Like him, they were nearly impervious, save for extraordinary means, and their vast ages ought to have given them a perspective similar to his own. Their supreme arrogance was the thing that goaded them to combat for the satisfaction of greed and pride; they mostly believed there was nothing that could truly oppose them.

Perhaps he could use that, if he could convince the creature he was dangerous enough.

Rashan did not engage the dragon but instead turned his focus fully on the enemy army that surrounded him. Without even paying it attention, he had been killing those who got too close to him.

Lightning stabbed out from his hands, shattering goblin bodies by the score. Superheated chunks of goblin gore splattered the snowy plains and fellow goblins alike. Turning, he unleashed a shock wave of air that sent even more goblins to their deaths, pinwheeling into the air like leaves before a gale, spears and limbs becoming missiles to further maim their comrades as the pieces landed.

An aether bolt took him in the side, hammering against his shielding spell but not getting through.

A strong one, for a goblin, Rashan mused.

He turned and used the hellfire spell he had taught Iridan, noticing a slight resistance from two goblin sorcerers caught in the blast, as their own shielding spells were crushed just before their bodies burned. With the failing light of dusk, the lingering flames of the dead goblins' clothing and spear shafts stood out against the growing blackness. In the city above, hitching posts, rain barrels, and the thick woolen coats of the unarmored militia provided similar light to Raynesdark as night set in.

* * * * * * * *

Ni'Hash'Tk dove low for the shining knight, lining up for a killing blast of dragonfire, speeding low above the rooftops as she approached. Her lungs filled, and she drew aether to give her dragonfire its power. Before she loosed her deadly breath, she noticed just how fine was the armor the human knight before her wore. She saw the sword in his hand, and saw not a deadly weapon but a priceless masterwork of aether-forged steel.

Rather than ruin the spoils of her conquest—and aside from having the city for her son's lair, this knight's armor and Avalanche were the finest prizes she had seen—she belched a halfhearted gout of flame down a side street as she passed, her momentum carrying the flames in a strafing run along several buildings. The stones blackened with the heat, but without concentrated fire, the buildings did not melt or topple as had so many others under the dragon's withering assaults. Dropping even lower, she prepared to scoop up the shining knight in a claw and kill him carefully, lest she damage the armor needlessly.

* * * * * * *

Brannis saw Jadefire's dragonfire spew errantly to the side and watched as the window shutters ignited and awnings transformed into ash. He saw the dragon approaching even lower and realized she was going to attack with claw and fang.

She is going to eat me, he thought suddenly.

He hesitated, trying to decide which way to dive when she made her strike, and realized that the dragon's reach and quickness meant he would likely be doomed either way.

Thinking quickly, he waited to the last moment and held Avalanche out before him, blade up, and dropped to the ground, releasing the blade to hang in the air above him. The dragon's claws moved to close around him but found an immovable impediment instead. The dragon's scream of pain was deafening, heard across the city and down upon the plains. The angle of the blade had not been such that the dragon's toes were severed upon the impact, but the claws that caught upon the blade were bent back unnaturally, breaking bones and wrenching toes from their proper places at the end of the dragon's forelimbs. The sudden jerk was also enough to skew Jadefire in her flight. Already perhaps too low above the rooftops, she pitched forward far enough upon grasping Avalanche that she could not keep her wings from snagging among the buildings.

With a great crash, the dragon hit the cobblestone streets of Raynesdark, her wings wrenched back by stone walls that could not withstand the force of her breath or her bulk, but which held firm—though not unscathed—against the impact of her massive wings.

Brannis was struck a glancing blow as the dragon's broken toes popped free from around his sword. He was spun over thrice and dizzied, but Liead's armor saved him from any real injury.

I wonder how many more such blows this armor can deflect before its wards give way?

He scrambled to his feet and retrieved his sword from its place in the air a few paces away. He gave it a cursory inspection and found it to be intact.

What a blade this is! It suits me so much better than Massacre ever did.

He looked and saw the dragon sprawled upon the street several blocks away. He fortunately found himself unmolested by goblins troops, who had given their goddess a wide berth and who were doubly frightened by the prospect of something having injured her. Great gutters had been carved in the street where her back claws had dragged behind her, and masonry from the buildings that lined the street was all about, the sinewy wings still having bulk enough to damage all that they struck.

The dragon twitched and squirmed, trying to gather herself and get her limbs back under her. She was obviously disoriented, if not fatally wounded, and

Brannis was drawn to pursue. He set off at a bit more than a jog but a bit less than a run, cautiously making his way down the rubble-littered street. He saw the sign of a bootblack lying face up in the road, and a set of draperies that had been pulled down along with the window they had fallen with. There were bits of a shattered cart and the wares that had been left in it. He had to avoid the remains of a stone balcony that had been dislodged from its vantage and now barred half the road.

And now I go to chase down what creature did all this, and by accident? I must be crazed!

Unbeknownst to him, Brannis's pursuit of the fallen dragon coincided with the arrival of the warlock, Rashan, upon the battlefield. Being blind and insensitive to the aether, he had no way of perceiving the massive disruption in the flow of the aether all around the city that heralded Rashan's appearance on the plains below, but many others had been keenly aware. Jadefire snapped her head up, twisting her long neck in the direction of the disturbance.

* * * * * * * *

Ni'Hash'Tk had assumed until then that the demon had been hiding among the troops somewhere, biding its time. It had just been a matter of waiting until it showed itself and then destroying it.

This was a bit different, though. The transference spell shook and warped the aether like few others, and she knew the power it took to perform one. Had she been the size of a goblin, or even a human, she could have managed one herself, but Ni'Hash'Tk's vast bulk required too large a chunk of the world be moved for even her mighty Source to bear.

Whatever it was that had just appeared—and she reasoned that it was most likely the demon her assassin seemed so frightened of—it was strong. She feared no creature of muscle and bone, save perhaps another dragon, for none were her equal. Magic … now that was a different matter. She had just had an object lesson in the pitfalls of the hidden powers of magic—*Blast that dratted human knight and his trick sword!*—and had paid a price for it. She watched in the aether as the newcomer drew great surges of the stuff, and kept watching as the tiny, sturdy little Sources of her followers turned from vibrant and healthy to tiny little decaying candles, wafting out their last bits of living aether.

Too many. Too quickly.

The Kadrin demon was laying waste to the goblin ground forces. Her right foreleg was a wreck of broken bones, and her wings ached badly. She worked the wings and felt confident they would hold her in flight, though maybe not for a prolonged engagement in the air.

She noticed movement in her peripheral vision and drew a quick breath. A burst of flame sent the seeking human knight diving headlong behind one of the buildings.

Sneak up on me? Not likely, she thought spitefully.

She could not spare the time or effort to chase after a single knight. She contented herself to claim his magics for herself later.

Something must be done about that demon, she told herself but did not relish the thought of fighting in her current condition.

"Greetings, Mighty One," a voice called in her head, and she found that perhaps she had an alternative to pitting her dragonfire against that demon's spells.

* * * * * * * *

Jinzan, too, had felt the rush of power in the aether, and had quickened the pace of his mount.

Stealth be gutted, I must get away before I am caught up in that.

He could feel a gentle pull in the whole of the aether as more and more of it was drawn over to where the massive surge had originated.

I think we just found the real demon, unless there were two to begin with.

Jinzan kept an eye to the south, where the carnage was beginning. He could pick out no Source at the center of the growing maelstrom of fire, lightning, and telekinetic energy that was engulfing the goblins forces. No Source ... the hallmark of a demon.

That other one, I would have fought should I have found it blocking my path. Should that one come between me and the mines, all is lost.

Jinzan had never seen anything like the display to his south. It was a garish display of power, obscene in its excess.

War was a time for judicious use of aether, if a sorcerer were to enter the battle at all. There was only so much aether to be had before the field was run dry and there was no more aether left to power spells. Once that happened, the sorcerer was left defenseless, save for whatever skill at arms he might possess—dreadfully little in his own case—and what aether slowly spilled anew from the combatants over time. Jinzan knew from Denrik's life what the feel of a sword in his hand was like. But he recalled also seeing Kyrus wield one, knowing only its use in another world. Jinzan would be no better off for Denrik's knowledge, and despite a bit of life extension, he was not so young a man as to make up for such deficiencies with youthful vigor and strength.

On a whim, he decided to take a better look to see what had befallen.

"Makto enfusi delgaja," he spoke, loosening his hold on the reins to touch thumb to thumb and forefinger to forefinger of each hand and drawing them wide to expand the circle they formed. A shimmering disc formed in the air and followed along with the bouncing gait of his mount as they ambled along the plains, rapidly approaching the base of the mountain.

Through the disc, everything seemed larger, clearer, and closer. It mimicked the effects of a spyglass from Tellurak and did its job far better. Jinzan adjusted the view and panned around, following the carnage back to its source. Goblins kept trying to attack, to their credit, but the view was kept clear as wave upon wave of them were thrown back like the little cloth-knot dolls the poor children of Megrenn played with.

There within the wide ring of dead bodies was a human, slight of build, with long, pure-white hair flowing over the black, red, and gold garb of a warlock. He was only head and shoulders taller than the goblins he fought, once Jinzan saw one get close enough before dying to make the comparison. Jinzan himself was tall enough that most of the goblins only came to his waist, and he was not accorded as a tall man. At the demon's hip was a sword that dragged nearly to the ground, though he eschewed its use in favor of spells and his bare hands. Twice Jinzan saw lone goblins approach close enough to land blows, which the demon turned aside with disdain before disposing of his attackers.

This is not *good. The Kadrins have themselves a true warlock it seems, and a demonic one as well. Where could he have come from?*

For all the demon's ferocity, he seemed passive on the offensive. He had not advanced and, in lulls in the fighting, stood with a distant look on his face. Jinzan was not certain what that portended, but he took the chance to bring his view even closer, focusing on just the demon and ignoring the area around him.

It cannot be! Jinzan protested in his own thoughts.

He was as good a student of history as the Academy had seen in quite a long time, centuries perhaps, and he had an obsessive interest in the conquest of his own homeland. He had read *The Diplomacy of Fire and Steel* a dozen times from cover to cover, bringing his blood to a boil anew with each reading. He had seen sketches of Rashan Solaran in its pages and had even once viewed the bust of him in the Sanctuary of the Tower of Contemplation.

It is him!

Jinzan's stomach knotted. He was not a man prone to idle fears and had steeled himself against many a foe, taking his magic into battle time and again, despite the risks and despite not having the skill of a warlock. But here ... here was a warlock so notorious that his whole civilization despised the memory of him; the name was a curse for them.

If that is not Rashan Solaran, he has had a descendant with all the power the histories attribute to him. Either thought was discomforting and reinforced his desire to reach the Staff of Gehlen so that he might possibly stand against such a monster.

As he watched in his aetherial spyglass, the distant look left the demon's face. It turned to look *right at him,* and the eyes narrowed, as if in annoyance. The visage appeared for a moment to be indecisive and then it disappeared from view.

Jinzan panicked. He released the spell of far-sight and scanned the battlefield south of him. He caught sight of a blur of motion—the demon, headed up the mountain pass to the city. In a series of great leaps and strides that would shame a stripe-cat or a mountain goat, he disappeared from view into the city in mere moments.

Jinzan had reached the base of the mountain himself by then, his mount making easy work of the slopes with its long claws digging in to grab footholds. He urged it on, conveying his need for haste to the beast, which was not quite so dumb as it first appeared. The lizard picked up its pace, and they ascended the uncut rocky slope with nearly the speed they had kept on level ground.

Jinzan clutched at the miniaturized cannon kit in his pockets and held the pieces secure as he bumped along atop the lizard's head. He could only hope that whatever had distracted the demon had done a good enough job that he could reach the upper mines unhindered.

* * * * * * * *

"Greetings, Mighty One," Rashan spoke once he contacted the great dragon's mind. *"Whose army do I have the privilege of destroying?"*

The goblins continued to throw themselves at him heedlessly. For creatures possessed of the cunning he had long attributed to goblins, it seemed a senseless waste. He paid them scant attention as he began his negotiation with their god.

After a brief wait, he got a reply: *"What are you doing in my head? I am Jadefire, demon, no mind for your petty magics to trifle with,"* the dragon replied telepathically.

"'Jadefire'? Come now, what sort of name is that? You have a proper one, as do I. My name is Rashan Solaran, Warlock of the Kadrin Empire. I have conquered kingdoms and slaughtered armies. Grant me the honor of the name your mother gave you upon your hatching," Rashan replied.

Draconic was the language of the dragons, but not everyone knew that it was the same as the runic language used for spellcasting. Rashan understood it fully as well as Kadrin. He would deign to address the dragon in its own tongue once he knew its given name.

"Hmph. Very well. I am Nihaxtukali—Ni'Hash'Tk in goblin-speech—Queen of the goblins of Feduwliax—F'd'lsh in their own tongue," Ni'Hash'Tk replied. *"The goblins of the cities of Ni'Stb, Dl'Rzl, and Tnk'Ch'Nck worship me as their goddess. Enough with pleasantries. Why do you parley?"*

"As you wish, Nihaxtukali. I believe that we have three options left to us to choose from. First, we could tear each other's followers to pieces as we are doing now and then contest between the two of us at the end, leaving the winner as the sole survivor of a massacre. Second, we could seek each other out and battle singly, the winner free to wipe out the other's forces unopposed," Rashan's mind spoke now in draconic, fluent enough that Ni'Hash'Tk was pleased to hear it spoken. The goblin tongue was so much pidgin draconic. It grew wearisome at times, and proper draconic was rare to be heard. *"I despise both options as wasteful."*

"Hah, you value your minions too closely," Ni'Hash'Tk replied. *"My goblins live to serve my whim, and when many die, I simply permit more of them to breed. Worry over your pitiful humans if you must, but I shed no tear for goblins that die obeying my command."*

"You misunderstand me. I care as little for my followers as you do yours," Rashan lied. He was willing to put lives to use and was willing to risk them, but wantonness was never a trait of his. The dragon's point about the goblins' breeding habits was well taken, though; the Kadrins would suffer far more from such a loss. *"In both my first two options, one of us dies. I am twelve-score summers old and have no end to the days before me. I suspect you are far older, with ages yet unborn before you. What a shame that after tonight one of us would see no more days.*

"Thus is my third option. Let us remove ourselves from this battle and contest it among our minions only. We take up a vantage above the city and watch, each monitoring the other that

we do not interfere. The loser might return to their home afterward, no matter which side wins," Rashan said.

He wondered if he had done enough to the goblin army to show the dragon that there was no way she could rely on her minions in the battle against him. He needed her to be sure that not only was he disdainful of the goblins' ability to harm him, he was personally dangerous enough that she should worry for her own fate if facing him alone.

"Is that cowardice I hear for your mind's voice, demon?" Ni'Hash'Tk laughed at Rashan mentally. *"If you offer such a deal, it means you must fear me. You reveal your weakness."*

"Cowardice? Have you heard of Loramar? I faced him and destroyed his army of the dead. I swear to you, I would not allow you to survive a battle against me. Even in death, I would wound you mortally. No, I merely wish to take no chances, for however sure I am of your death, should it come down to combat between us, I am not so certain of my own survival. Instead let us choose to live long after this day."

"Loramar? I have not heard the name. Still, I can see merit in your plan. You are not so weak as your minions," the dragon said. *"I will cease my attacks upon your minions, and you shall do likewise. We will watch each other and view the battle together. I will see the routing of your forces."*

"Nor are you as weak as your minions, Nihaxtukali," Rashan replied. *"Meet me atop the glacier above the city. It is the only flat spot large enough for both of us at once, with a view of all the fighting."*

"Agreed."

Rashan broke off the contact at that point and reoriented himself to the swirling chaos around him. Hardly noticing, he had killed scores more goblins, fools who had no notion that he was beyond their ability to harm. What he did notice was that he was being watched.

Off to the north, a human sorcerer hid himself against the backdrop of the mountains and snow, using aether to camouflage himself. It worked well enough against most foes but shone a light upon him in Rashan's ever-present vision in the aether. He looked right at the sorcerer, Megrenn by the slightly darker skin and hair than was typical among Kadrins, and narrowed his gaze. Had he not just agreed with the dragon to cease assaulting her allies, he would have been tempted to slay the Megrenn sorcerer out of hand. Unfortunately he preferred to honor his agreement and keep dragonfire off his list of worries … at least for the time being.

"Iridan," Rashan called out to his son, using the same spell he had used to contact the dragon's mind. *"There is a human sorcerer—Megrenn, it seems— camouflaging himself and riding a lizard. He appears headed to the northern part of the city in some haste. His likely target is the upper mines. Intercept him."*

"All right," a weary Iridan replied.

Rashan sped off toward the city and beyond, rushing to reach the top before the dragon got there and had a chance to grow impatient at his absence. He could already see the beast ponderously taking to the air, clearly not in the best of health.

Ahh, someone had drawn dragon blood today. Was that you, Iridan?

* * * * * * * *

Celia watched the battle from the entrance to her tent. First the fog then the onset of darkness obscured her view, but she much preferred the poor view to one any closer. The tent was icy cold from having the flap open at length, as Celia could not help but stare out into the torch-lit gloom and watch her fate playing out. The heavy coat she wore kept her warm, but not entirely on its own. She had been leaking tiny bits of aether into it since mid afternoon, warming the thick wool against the bone-gnawing cold. It was risky—it was all too easy to set fire to a garment—but she felt it worth the gamble, lest she suffer frostbite watching the two armies clash.

Dark as it was, she could still see the fires burning where the warlock had made his stand. She had known at once who it had to be when someone seemed to shatter the very aether around them, someone who had a draw such as she had never witnessed before. It was impressive that she could even notice the draw of a particular combatant from so far away, her tent being well back where the cannons had been before the goblins advanced them. It had left no doubt in her mind that the rumors of the return of Rashan Solaran were true. It also made her decision about the Megrenn sorcerer, Jinzan, much simpler.

As had all good little boys and girls at the Academy, Celia had studied the Empire's history. There were dates and places and emperors' names to remember, but nearly every student paid rapt attention when the subject turned to war. Bloody and gory and speaking of the glory of the mighty Kadrin Empire, the children could not get enough of the stories of the ancient warlocks of old. There were no defeats mentioned in the Kadrin histories; the details of those were for more advanced study by the Circle and the knights. Celia had been devastated to learn that Sir Lornhelm—whose daring rescue of Empress Euphelia some twelve hundred summers ago had set a younger Celia's heart quickening—had been killed ignobly a few months later in a duel behind a tavern. Warlock Rashan had been different. When the legends of his exploits were peeled back by more mature versions of his life's story, there were no secret shames to hide. The perspective given in the children's histories remained largely intact and was merely expanded on to show his personal flaws: megalomania, ruthlessness, and a vicious and capricious temper. He was, simply, what anyone would infer a man to be who had whispered in the ears of emperors and convinced them to make war on anything their armies could reach.

If this was the Rashan of history that she witnessed before her, Celia felt that history had treated him ill. His magic was inspiring, casual in its destruction of literally thousands of goblins, as best she could estimate. Of the warlock himself, she could see no sign. There was a wall of Sources between her and the spot where he battled, and if his Source was as powerful as she expected it must be, she could still not make it out so far away.

With a warlock on the field and among the goblin army, she knew that even a dragon would not swing the balance in the goblins' favor. Jinzan's offer would be rendered worthless before daybreak. She needed to plan an escape.

Chapter 34 - Rashan's Bargain

Juliana had watched from the gate down to the undercity for some time. Twice she had retreated back down the tunnel to avoid the dragon's passes as it raked the ground with dragonfire. None of the strikes had been particularly close by, but Juliana knew little of the dragon's abilities and limitations, and took precautions as she passed.

She had heard the crash of the great beast as it was brought to the ground amid a residential district on the wealthier side of town nearer the cliff wall. She heard the shriek of pain and surprise, the crush of stone, and various other debris being flung about. Juliana rushed back to the gate entrance and saw wings flexing and flapping, as if to test them after the dragon's fall. She heard the smaller gout of flame sent down the street and saw the light from it, though she could not see the flame itself. Highlighted against the small fires burning in the city, she saw the dragon crane her head and look westward.

Juliana hunkered down in the entryway, trying to avoid attracting the dragon's notice. Something was going on. The dragon had ceased her attack and was just looking out to the plains. With the dragon so near and the great bellows of dragonfire being spewed forth, Juliana was too close to massive shifts in the aether to have noticed Rashan's arrival. She watched the dragon in rapt fascination. With a closer view and the dragon still, she could see what a beautiful creature it was: sleek, graceful, and majestic.

Her musings were broken when the creature turned suddenly in her direction. Juliana ducked and pressed herself against the stones of the arched gateway, but the dragon paid her no heed. Jadefire extended her wings and, with a great heave, thrust herself aloft, wings raising a cloud of dust and debris as she cleared the site of her tumble and gained altitude. Juliana got an excellent view of the dragon's underbelly—a slightly lighter shade of the deep green scales about the rest of her—as the beast passed above her toward the top of the glacier. She heard a great crunch of snow and ice as the dragon settled above her location.

I hope the wall can hold her weight along with that of ice and snow, Juliana thought.

* * * * * * * *

Iridan ached. He could move—that much of him worked at least—but that was the most he could credit himself with. He remembered the layout of the city well enough that he would be able to find his way to the mine entrance easily enough. That was not the problem he faced.

Actually it was two and perhaps even three problems rolled up into one giant problem that he was preparing to deal with. He had exhausted himself, body and Source, in the battles for the wall. He was only now feeling up to drawing aether again, should he have to, and it seemed that he would have to. He could walk and possibly even jog a bit, but his aching muscles probably did not have a run in them. If it was to be a race to the mine entrance, he did not like his chances.

Once he got there, he was to stop the human traitor who had taken up with the goblins. It seemed safe to assume that the goblins had not taken on the least sorcerer they could find among the Megrenn, so he was expecting to face a true foe when he got there.

Iridan was slouching in a chair in the sitting room closest to the castle's door, where the soldiers assigned to oversee the retreat of the downed sorcerers had been bringing them. The sitting room was littered with spent sorcerers. Two of the lesser Circle sorcerers were laid out on blankets, unconscious, possibly dead. Caldrax was about, but he was up and alert, seemingly having withdrawn himself from the battle before his last energies were spent. If any of the goblin forces breached the castle entrance, it was comforting to Iridan that someone at least was fit to put up a resistance. Faolen was laid out on a chaise, unmoving. He rose to take water when the servants brought it, so Iridan knew that he was at least still living.

As for Iridan, he was neither in the best nor worst shape of the lot of them, but he was the one who had received orders directly from the Warlock of the Empire himself—and he was the one training to follow in the way of the warlocks. Iridan forced himself to his feet and stretched his back, working out the stiffened muscles that had settled into unhelpful places as he recuperated.

"Caldrax, watch over them," Iridan ordered, making clear his intent to depart. "I have a task from the warlock. There is a sorcerer trying to reach the upper mines. I must go to stop him."

"You seem in no condition," Caldrax said. "Do not waste yourself in combat in your current state." The older sorcerer looked haggard when Iridan turned to look at him, and scared.

I suppose he would rather I was here to defend this part of the castle instead of just him alone, Iridan thought.

Instead Iridan chose not to answer at all but made for the castle's front entrance. The guards obliged when he ordered the portcullis opened for him, despite the fighting that grew nearer by the moment. The Kadrin troops were fighting a slow withdrawal action, never holding ground at too great a cost, but making the goblins pay for their advance every pace of the way.

Iridan's back groaned in protest as he ducked under the portcullis; the guards had lifted it just enough for him to pass beneath. The streets were deserted in the immediate area of the castle but did not seem as if they would remain so for long. The fighting was close by and growing closer. The chittering cries of the goblins and the screams and yells of the Kadrins mixed together with the sounds of steel striking steel and occasionally stone. There was light of a sort, but it was haphazard and not nearly adequate. The fires of collateral damage were too far and too little, and the starry sky grew dimmer as the smoke from those fires wafted upward and became thicker. Iridan switched over to aether-vision.

Rashan had warned that the sorcerer was camouflaging himself, so even in good lighting, it seemed a better bet to watch in the aether than in the light. His aether-vision was keen enough that he could make out the streets and buildings by the disruptions in the aether's flow, so he worried but little about stumbling blindly. As a bonus, it allowed him to keep an eye toward the advancing goblins infantry as well and keep well clear of them.

The entrance to the mines was not far. The castle was built largely into the north mountainous wall of the city, just a short way from the defensive walls. The entrance to the mines lay between the two, the primary concern of the original lords of Raynesdark—who were no dukes in those early days—and the primary reason for the construction of the walls in the first place. The gold of the upper mines was the life's blood of Raynesdark in those bygone days.

Iridan saw the mine entrance as he hurried—not quite jogging but rushing his steps at least. The mine seemed undisturbed, with no excess traces of aether to suggest that someone powerful of Source had passed there. The entrance was of stone "timbers," with runes all about them like much of the old, preserved architecture of the city. There was a pair of rusted iron rails running out from it, which had been less well preserved. There was no debris or refuse kept in the mine entrance, and it seemed well preserved, though Iridan knew not why.

If no one has passed through yet, I am in time to stop him, Iridan reasoned.

He found a small civic garden a few dozen paces away and crouched behind a hardy evergreen shrub. The shrub's own Source was unimpressive, but it was the strongest of the meager plants that the Raynesdark folk grew, and large enough to hide him from light as well as obscure his Source some. He began to hold back his aether to husband it for the expected battle, as well as to disguise its power.

He had not long to wait, as he saw a pair of Sources coming from the direction of the wall. One was a lizard of some sort, being used as a mount. The other was his prey.

With neither parley nor warning, Iridan struck from ambush, loosing a bolt of aether with most of what he had held. The blast was considerable and silently cast, one of the spells Iridan had first learned to cast in such a manner. He took the head clean off the lizard that the sorcerer rode, and the sorcerer himself was thrown to the earth some paces distant. The invader's shielding spell had shattered but had saved his life. Iridan had eschewed such defenses himself lest they be seen by an alert foe before he struck.

With surprise lost, Iridan quickly saw to his own defensive shields, quickly armoring himself silently in aether. The Megrenn sorcerer was no fool, though, taking the initiative and attacking immediately, before even seeing to the replacement of his own shields.

"Kolo ketenxu mafira."

Still lying on his side from where Iridan's spell had hurled him, the Megrenn sorcerer made a claw-like gesture down. Iridan was unfamiliar with the spell but learned the gist of it quickly enough when the ground turned liquidy beneath his feet. With no magic ready to support him, Iridan sunk quickly into the soupy soil.

A second gesture, the complement to the first, solidified the ground again with Iridan stuck chest deep, his arms trapped below the surface before he was able to raise them.

Iridan drew as hard as he could, his Source aching with the effort. The Megrenn sorcerer was already launching into a new spell, and Iridan needed to do something or he was going to be a stationary target for it.

"*Hakvea golotanu dexjahi ecalamu,*" the Megrenn intoned, drawing himself to his feet.

Iridan knew the spell and diverted all the aether he had just drawn into reinforcing his shield construct. He hoped it would be enough.

His adversary formed a sphere with his two hands, and within grew a distortion in the air. Once it grew to the size of a wheel of cheese, it shot forth, crossing the distance to Iridan in the beat of a swallow's wing.

* * * * * * * *

Jinzan watched in satisfaction as the apprentice in warlock's garb was torn asunder, the top half of his body gone to gore and splintered bone where it had once protruded above the soil.

Satisfied that he had no further opposition, Jinzan rechecked the contents of his pockets and headed into the mines. There was no light within, so he quickly made one for himself, not trusting to his aether-vision. He had no map of the mines, so he needed to be alert for any signs of his direction. The goblin advance was proceeding well, but since the arrival of the demon—*Is it truly Rashan Solaran, or just a descendant?*—he would bet no amount on their chances, let alone the success of his whole mission.

* * * * * * * *

"Your little ones are doing poorly, demon," Nihaxtukali commented, gazing down at the city far below.

She and Rashan stood upon the crest of the Neverthaw Glacier, the only flat spot around that offered the vantage of the whole battle that they were looking for. Despite her protestations against the cold earlier, the dragon was thankful to be able to bury her maimed forelimb in the ice to sooth the shooting pains it gave her. The icy cold on the rest of her seemed a small price now for such relief.

"Perhaps," Rashan answered, speaking draconic. "But we will not settle this until one side surrenders or is wiped out. I have trust in my followers."

He was not three paces from the dragon, each on guard against treachery by the other. Despite his fears of the mighty beast, his mind tangled and untangled plots of how he might slay it, bargain or no.

The dragon knew that Rashan's magic was formidable, possibly able to cut through her nigh-impervious scales or even affect her monolithic Source itself. She also knew that the demon was quick afoot and might well dodge claw or tail or even dragonfire as he worked his magic against her.

For his part, Rashan knew that the claws and teeth of the great dragon were little concern to him. His physical body was a tool of his Source, not the reverse, and despite horrifying wounds, he would be able to fight on. The dragonfire was his real fear. While fire was a power that had many counters in the ways of magic, dragonfire was mostly aether, borne on flame. It could cut through wards and stone alike, and burn things that no other fire would harm. Caught in a full blast of it, he was almost sure to perish; even his shields could not withstand more than a short or incidental burst of the stuff.

What Nihaxtukali did not know, however, was the true nature of Heavens Cry. His boast about Loramar was the first gambit he had made in his thoughts of bringing the dragon down. When she claimed never to have heard of the necromancer—whose few score winters of prominence could easily have escaped the notice of the ages-old dragon—he knew that she must have been ignorant of Heavens Cry as well, for their tales were interwoven too closely. Sadly it would not be so easy to kill a dragon with the blade. Its poisons would not do much to dragon scales, certainly not quickly enough to make use of in combat. Getting Nihaxtukali to inhale the vapors might work, but that was an uncertain ploy. He needed something better before he would strike. He might only get one chance.

* * * * * * *

With the dragon's withdrawal, the goblins pressed the attack, no longer fearing the collateral carnage their deity was wont to inflict. Brannis had seen Jadefire fly up to the glacier and had noticed Rashan follow shortly thereafter.

When did he arrive? And what is he scheming at? Brannis wondered when no sign of fighting broke out between the bloodthirsty demon and the green-scaled force of nature. *I do not know how he got the dragon to stop attacking, but I like our chances better against the army of goblins than against that beast.*

"Fall back! Reform ranks!" Brannis shouted.

With the dragon out of the calculation, the battle could be fought on Kadrin terms, no longer dodging around buildings to keep out of the path of the dragonfire that had claimed all too many of Duke Pellaton's men already.

"Sir Garen, take command of the north half and have them fall back to the castle. I shall hold the main gate to the undercity."

The fighting was chaotic. The goblins were still equipped with climbing claws from their initial ascent of the mountainside. Now that the battle was being fought in the streets, the goblin soldiers were taking advantage of the urban terrain and scaling the walls of buildings to gain advantage on the Kadrins, who were staying at ground level.

A spear clanged against the side of Brannis's helmet. The wards on the armor prevented him from even feeling the blow.

How many times over would I have died today had I been armored as my knights? The soldiers wear just mail, and the militia just what they have for sturdy clothes.

Brannis saw the goblin whose spear had sought him, on the third-story balcony of a nearby house. Brannis dug Avalanche into the ground and gave a flick of his wrist. The irresistible blade uprooted paving stones and flung them skyward in a spray in the direction of the spear-thrower, who ducked back inside the building. Brannis paid it no mind and turned his attentions back to the organization of his forces.

The Kadrins were reforming, but slowly. The goblins outnumbered them badly and were taking their toll on the scattered human fighters, sealing off many pockets of defenders and hedging them in, cutting them down. There were enough, though, that two fronts could both make a disciplined retreats back to the castle and undercity gates, respectively.

Brannis stood at the fore of the retreat, keeping a wide swath around him clear of invaders. The goblins were no fools and made every effort to avoid the gold-armored purveyor of death, covered in much blood of their kind. Spear-and-shield was a slow fighting style, easy to defend with and wearying to push back. Numbers. It was all down to numbers, as the Kadrin soldiers could only hold out so long against exhaustion and the cold.

Cold was one ally, however, that Brannis could not afford to underestimate. The goblins were a thin, wiry people, with little insulating their bodies. They wore heavy—for them, at least—clothing, but they just did not generate the kind of body heat to keep apace with the Raynesdark nightfall. They fought like crazed animals knowing this; it kept their bodies warm, and it drove the humans farther and farther toward the warm security of the sheltering undercity. Once the goblins took the fighting underground, the cold would no longer hamper the scrawny invaders.

Yet minute by minute, the goblins advanced, despite Brannis's best efforts to hold them back. Brannis moved up and down the line of spearmen, forcing the goblins back anywhere he found a spot weakening against the onslaught. He had lost all track of time once the sun had set. Fires burned here and there still from the dragon's attacks, but the battle was being fought largely by moonlight. The endless horde of goblins seemed to pour out of the dark nothingness beyond his vision. A score would die at his feet, and from down side streets and around corners came more. Brannis knew rationally that there was an end to them somewhere, but he doubted whether they would see it.

Kthooom!

Brannis and two men behind him were thrown clear of the front lines by cannon fire. The artillery had arrived.

* * * * * * * *

Iridan vomited all down his chin and chest. With his arms trapped at his sides beneath the dirt and held upright, he could hardly manage otherwise. He saw nothing of his torso and just a gruesome half-man left buried in the soil just beneath his head. He ached throughout, especially the parts that were not there anymore.

"It is not real. Pull yourself together," Faolen spoke quietly, yet harshly. The illusionist wiped away the tableau of gore and blood he had painted over the stricken Iridan. "It fooled that Megrenn at least. Now let us get you out of there." Faolen looked pale and moved stiffly, but seemed alert and in command of his power.

Iridan tried to turn to see his fellow sorcerer but could not turn anything below his neck. Faolen saw his struggle and moved to Iridan's front. He looked down at the trapped apprentice warlock and smiled reassuringly. He poked Iridan in the chest, clothed again in a black tunic, trimmed in red and gold, and entirely *there*.

"I promise. You are not dead."

Iridan shook his head to clear it. The world sounded a little fuzzy and muted. Faolen sounded a long way off.

"Ears," he mumbled.

Faolen took Iridan's head in his hands and turned his ear toward the half moon for better light.

"There is some blood. You shall likely feel worse for this, but you have lived through it," Faolen assured him. Iridan only believed the part about feeling worse. "I do not have much for spells to undo this sort of thing. If you have any strength left to lend aid, start moving earth."

Through a series of small telekinesis, the two began to un-plant Iridan from the soil.

* * * * * * *

Juliana cried out in shock. She had heard the cannon fire and saw Brannis disappear from view—she had been watching him the whole time—but did not see where he ended up. The fight was drawing closer to the gate, and she resisted the urge to rush out to his aid to see if he had survived. She suspected he had, wearing that fabulously enchanted armor Warlock Rashan had outfitted him with, but there were limits to all magic, and she hoped that Liead's armor had not found its own.

Kthooom!

Juliana saw that the goblins had discovered grapeshot, when crushed paving stone clattered against her shielding spell. The spell held, but the soldiers nearby had not been so well protected by their armor. Juliana saw that the men who had hung by the gate along with her were largely gone, bleeding their last upon the stone roadway that led down into the bowels of the city.

Time to end this vigil and shut the gate.

"Get inside!" Juliana shouted. "I am dropping the portcullis!"

A short way from the gateway, there was a heavy wooden door, from whence the guards controlled the workings of the portcullis. She rushed inside and saw there was no one within.

Must have been among those killed while watching the battle, she assumed.

There was a crank like a ship's wheel, with handholds all around, and beside it a lever. If she were to pull the lever, it would release the catch that kept back the weight of the portcullis. The whole thing would crash down, and any who were caught on the wrong side would be trapped at the mercy of the goblin army.

Back to the doorway, she poked her head out and watched as the Kadrins withdrew to the safety of the undercity side of the gate. They did not flee, but gave ground and kept back the goblins from following them in, at least as well as they could. When she saw that the line held right at the entrance, she went in and gave the lever a great heave. It took all her weight on it to move the handle, but it was enough, and outside she could hear the great iron grate crash down into place, separating the two armies. She collapsed against the doorway in relief, watching to see the Kadrin defenders and goblin invaders jabbing through the bars at each other with their spears.

Suddenly the goblins pulled back and scattered. The Kadrin defenders did not react in time, but Juliana dove back within the gate control room.

Kthooom! Kthooom! Kthooom! Kthooom!

Metal shrieked and groaned, screams of iron and men mingled, and a light rain of rock fell from the ceiling of the passageway. Juliana peered outside and saw that there was a hole in the portcullis large enough for the goblins to run through three abreast. She quickly pulled the door closed behind her and barred it before they got around to doing so.

There was a second door within the control room, on the far side from the one she had entered from. She opened in and rushed through. She caught herself immediately, though, grabbing the doorjamb before she slammed into the next wall, not a full running pace away. The door had led her to nothing more than a garderobe, put in place for the soldiers stationed at the gate.

Juliana could hear the goblins pouring through the ruins of the gate, driving the surviving human defenders before them. She ran back across to the outside door—still barred and as yet disregarded by the goblins—and pulled out one of her daggers. Frantically she carved the runes of a protective ward on the wood of the door.

* * * * * * * *

"Hmm, it seems your army is retreating underground, demon," Nihaxtukali observed, chuckling—a deep bass that was felt through the warlock's whole body.

Why, yes, I had noticed, you great reptilian town crier.

The dragon's eyes were far better than his own, but Rashan wagered that his aether-vision was stronger. He used it nearly constantly and saw what befell in the gateway and just before it, where the dragon's eyesight was blocked by rock and snow. Nihaxtukali most certainly could see the aether too, but through so much dead earth, he doubted she could watch what he saw.

"Those toys your tinkers made have done admirably," Rashan commented sweetly, trying to keep the contempt out of his voice.

He had not found a weakness to exploit, and the battle was going toward the sewers, both literally and figuratively. His eyes played along the scales and curves of the dragon's form, watching the interplay of muscle and sinew from her fidgeting and deducing the anatomy beneath.

"Why do you keep looking at me, demon?" Nihaxtukali demanded, suddenly suspicious.

She brought her head down level with Rashan. The great dragon's nostrils were at his head height, her fangs longer than his body. It was beginning to occur to her that the demon was *much* too small to be a threat physically. If she could just wait until she could draw up all the aether in the immediate area—starving him of magic—she could have her chance to destroy him.

"I have never seen a dragon before, let alone so close up. Pardon me if I cannot help myself marveling at your beauty. Would that the ancient gods had taken so much care in crafting humans," Rashan said.

It was commonly held that dragons were vain creatures, and his musings on their beauty had enough truth to it that he hoped it assuaged Nihaxtukali's suspicions. He had not worked magic since they had taken up their vantage on the glacier. His Source, ever industrious, had been supplying more than his body required for that whole time. His normal habit of siphoning that excess off into multitudes of tiny magics had been put on hold, and his reserve of aether was growing. Soon he would either have to find his spot for an ambush, or find a way to begin venting off that extra aether without Nihaxtukali noticing.

* * * * * * *

Brannis spat blood, nauseated. It was not his own. Whomever had fallen atop him had only done so from the collarbone up. It took him a moment to gather himself once he realized he had been blown clear of the immediate fighting. Fallen among the corpses, he had been ignored by the goblin forces. It would seem that they trained their soldiers well enough that they did not stop mid battle to plunder.

Brannis wished he was sensitive enough to tell if the warded armor was depleted. He could barely believe the blow he had just survived, both the initial impact and slamming into the western cliff wall of the city afterward. He was still mashed against the rock, blood dripping all over him. Gagging at the mess and smell, he turned onto his hands and knees.

Where is it? Brannis wondered, not seeing his sword about. He looked to see if it had driven itself clear into the rock, but found no hole to mark its entrance. *It must have been knocked loose when I was hit. When ... I ... dropped it.*

Realization dawned, and Brannis remembered the nature of Avalanche. He looked up and found the sword hanging in the air a few paces back the way he had flown.

Looking back that way, he saw that the portcullis had been blasted though, and goblins poured through into the undercity. Of the defenders at the gate, he saw none. There were cannons being wheeled through as well, interrupting the flow of troops as their heavy carriages were maneuvered through the ragged opening.

I have got to put a stop to this, Brannis thought. *There is no one around. I have to find a way to bring the avalanche wall down.*

Brannis looked to the sword, hung from nothing, waiting to be reclaimed.

Time for you to earn that name of yours, he silently told it.

The sword accepted the news stoically. Avalanche was not too far from the corner of a house, so Brannis used the building as cover and then sneaked up and made a short leap for the sword, pulling it out of the air. Goblins took notice, but those who first took notice were quickly dispatched with a swipe of the blade. After that, Brannis ran off, ducking behind the houses and occasional shop that formed the neighborhood around the gate. Goblins continued streaming down the main trade road, making their way straight from the main city gate (recently destroyed) to the undercity gate (even more recently destroyed).

Brannis made his way to a more remote section of the western cliffs and searched for a handhold. Climbing had never been a hobby of his, even as a boy, but this was a circumstance that demanded risks be taken. Keeping Avalanche drawn and ready, he found twofold purpose for it in his climb. He was able to use its irresistible blade to carve spots for hands and feet to grip, and more importantly, he was able to let go the hilt and use it as a brace, trusting that the armor that could hold back a cannonball could protect him from the blade of Avalanche as he leaned on it.

He made slow progress up the side of the cliff. Goblins below noticed before long and threw spears and tiny daggers at him, but all bounced off Brannis's armor to no effect.

Were those hitting wards, or was that the metal turning those blades?

For Brannis's plan, it would be very useful if the wards had not exhausted themselves.

At length, Brannis made it to the base of the avalanche wall and carefully walked along the narrow flat area before it to the gate to the undercity. Goblins took note of him, but he was beyond the reach of their thrown weapons, and out in the cold, by himself, when there was a war and warm air to be found in the city below, Brannis seemed to be better left to the attention of "someone else." Brannis managed to keep free of interference as he steeled himself to do the craziest thing he had ever considered.

Taking Avalanche in both hands, he leaped and swung the blade flat-first through the wall in a great diagonal slash. He felt the barest of resistance as rock shattered at his sword's passing. Without waiting to see the results of his handiwork, he hopped backward, off the cliff, leaving the sword out in front of him to drag through the rocky cliff face all the way down.

Above him, Brannis heard the groan and crack as rock, snow, and ice shifted and began to fall. Downward he plummeted, rolling and turning to try to fall with the sword *aside* him rather than risk falling with it atop him, or him atop it. The resistance of blade in stone was minimal but slowed him from being fully in free fall. The remains of the portcullis bent and then shattered as the sword caught it. After that, it was the duration of a blink before Brannis slammed into the road on his side, crushing goblins beneath him.

Brannis was stunned by the fall, his left arm exploding in pain where it was caught beneath him.

So much for the wards, Brannis mused.

Then the Neverthaw Glacier fell atop knight and goblin alike, dropping a hundred feet of snow and ice across the entrance to the undercity.

* * * * * * *

Rashan had tensed as he watched Brannis inch along the avalanche wall, rune-forged blade in hand.

Clever boy. Do it! It is the chance I need.

When Brannis's blade breached the wall, the city's protection against the Neverthaw Glacier gave way. The glacier shifted and began to fall, the support it had relied on for countless generations suddenly no longer sufficient to hold back its awesome weight.

The dragon panicked. She and Rashan had been watching her forces overrun the undercity gate below and bringing siege to the castle on the north side of the city. All was going in the goblins' favor, then without warning, the ground began to give way beneath them. The dragon's instincts caused her to stiffen her forelimbs against the falling motion, even as she unfurled her wings to slow her fall and take flight.

But in that short moment, she seemed to forget the demon she had been holding vigil over. Rashan did not hesitate. He had spent his time with the dragon mapping out her muscles and scales, finding where best to strike if the chance was presented. He could tell by the expansion of Nihaxtukali's chest as she breathed where her lungs ended. His aether-vision saw the shielding construct built around her and where he could penetrate it. She was an impressive beast, but a middling sorceress, and he had his pick of spots where his own magic could whelm hers.

Rashan aimed his strike just behind her left forelimb as she extended it to halt her slide. On a human, it would have been a strike aimed roughly at the chink most armor had beneath the arm. Dragon scales were not so clumsily assembled, but they faced the unnatural strength of a demon. Drawing Heavens Cry and lunging with a two-handed grip in one blinding action, he sent an aether blast to his target ahead of the blade. The magical attack weakened the dragon's shielding construct just enough that Rashan's strike was able to drive the point home.

The rune-forged sword punctured dragon scale, and Rashan's blade plunged to the hilt. Unleashing the terrible magic of his creation, he pumped all his stored aether through the blade. The sword was lodged in Nihaxtukali's left lung, and the plume of toxic fumes not only filled the dragon's lung but melted through it, eating away the heart and other lung as well.

Nihaxtukali screamed … or tried to at least. The great bellows that had earlier announced the doom of the Kadrin forces now choked off in strangled agony, accompanied by a billowing cloud of the noxious vapor that had been forced into her. The dragon's pain was short lived, though, as it was already a corpse by the time it pitched face-first into the snow, ensuring that the avalanche would take the whole glacier with it. With the dragon's added bulk, there was no stopping that.

Rashan rode the dragon's corpse, hanging onto the blade until they had nearly reached the ground. Before the impact, the warlock leaped free of the monstrous, dead sledge. It was a gleeful, liberated demon, drunk with bloodlust, that fell amid the teeming masses of goblins. It was a stake thrust into history with Rashan Solaran's name upon it. Dragon-slayers were the stuff of storybooks, not histories, for dragons resisted slaying like no other creatures. The mantle of "Dragon-slayer" would fit nicely among his boasted titles, Rashan thought.

Out on the streets of Raynesdark, and afterward on the plains below, goblins died. And died. And died …

* * * * * * * *

Juliana heard the immense thunder of the crash, and felt the ground shake as if the whole of the mountain would come down atop her. She heard the frightened goblins running down the passageway and then the relative silence that followed. She put away one of her daggers and risked unbarring the door.

Outside, the corridor was clear. Magic lit it—left by some goblin sorcerer most likely—and she saw bodies all about, mostly human, some goblin. At the gate entrance, she saw the whole of it blocked by fallen ice and snow, some of it forming a slope back into the corridor. Here and there, a limb or a spear or bit of shining metal shone through the debris. She caught a flash of gold …

Brannis!

Juliana rushed over, heedless that any goblins backtracking to the entrance would have her trapped. She put away her other dagger and rushed over to begin digging in the snow with her hands.

"Brannis? Brannis! Can you hear me?" Juliana asked.

"Yph," came a muffled response from beneath the snow. A minute's effort had revealed Brannis's face. Once she knew better where he was, Juliana drew aether and warmed the snow around him. She pulled off one of the vicious gauntlets of his armor and took him by the hand with both of hers. She heaved and pulled as she melted the snow that pressed down on him, slowly dragging him free enough that he could help the rest of the way.

"Thank you," Brannis said, collapsing on his back to catch his breath.

Juliana plunked herself down beside him, sitting in the melted runoff and not caring. Brannis unclasped the demon helm and pulled it off, and his hot, sweaty head steamed in the icy air.

"You stopped them," she said.

"Good. Any idea how many got through?"

"Too many. They are overrunning the undercity by now. Not many of your troops were left to hold them off," Juliana said.

Brannis looked at her and saw the concern in her eyes. She knew that he was not going to give up, take his rest, and leave the defense of the undercity to those with more left to give.

Brannis sat up and cupped her cheek in his ungloved hand. He leaned over and kissed her. The snow had cleaned much of the gore from him, albeit haphazardly. He looked nothing like the heroes drawn in the fairy stories that Juliana had grown up worshiping. He was bruised and bloody, with matted hair and dripping sweat, but he was everything she ever really wanted in a hero.

"I have to go help them. I cannot just rest here, much as I might need it. If I think too much, I might not be able to move at all."

Brannis grinned ruefully. He took up his helm and put his gauntlet back on. Avalanche was lost somewhere amid the snow, and he had no time to look for it. He took up a discarded spear from the floor and headed down toward the undercity.

"Stay here, or at least stay back. I have to go."

It was all she heard, all she ever heard from Brannis anymore. The rest did not matter. She would follow. She would never stop following him unless that phrase changed to: "I want to go."

* * * * * * * *

The undercity was in chaos. Goblins were everywhere. The Kadrin defenders were few, and civilians were all over. Some reinforcements were arriving from the castle, but the castle defenders had been hard pressed as well. Brannis looked about and saw that there was no organization to the defense. If there were commanders about, they had been overwhelmed by the maelstrom of flesh and steel.

Mennon's plan was the only solution Brannis could think of. The ogre pens were along the south wall of the undercity and well away from where the civilians and their defenders were making their stand, at the mine entrances. It was hard to tell from the overlook at the lower interior gate to the undercity, but it seemed like pockets of Kadrins might even have been surrendering.

Brannis ran.

Brannis *tried* to run but managed a hustle. His back hurt, and his left arm was likely broken. The enchantment on the armor had saved his life, but it was done saving him until a sorcerer saw to it.

I guess I should be glad the quicksilver stays solid when it runs out of aether, Brannis mused, mid hustle.

When he got to the ogre cages, he found them in a highly agitated mood. They strode over to the barred door that marked the entrance to their little community.

"Who is your leader?" Brannis demanded.

From what he knew of ogres, they dealt in strength, using simple, straightforward chains of command that were often topped by the strongest warrior. He hoped these were at least sensible enough to follow someone who spoke good Kadrin.

"That be me," one near the door answered.

The ogre towered over Brannis the way he did over Iridan. Brannis's bloody face came to the ogre's sternum, so he had to look up to see the furrowed brow and suspicious glare the ogre met him with.

"What is your name?" Brannis asked.

He refused to treat them with the dishonor the nobles of Raynesdark did. He wanted them to fight for him, not as slaves but as warriors. He hoped that the instinct for it still lurked behind the docile front they had showed so far. The cunning he saw in their leader's gaze gave him some hope.

"Me Glumg. Who you?" the ogre responded.

"I am Sir Brannis Solaran. I lead the Kadrin army. I am the big boss. I am boss of all bosses. I want you to fight for me." Brannis gestured to all of the ogres in the pen. There were hundreds of them, and most would be battle ready without training if the opponents were just measly little goblins. "All of you."

"Huh? You have us fight goblins? They everywhere! See 'em?" Glumg pointed out into the city.

"So what? You are ogres. You are a lot bigger. Step on them. Kick them. Hit them with tools. Killing goblins is easy. There are a lot of them to kill," Brannis said. "And it is fun. You will like killing goblins. They make a crunch noise when you step on them." Brannis mimicked a crunching noise as best he could. It was a skill all little boys learned at an early age, and he got the point across. Glumg grinned.

"But goblin give us gold. Say you give us weapons to fight goblins, we fight humans instead," Glumg said.

Brannis was impressed at the point he was managing to convey.

The goblins paid the ogres off? So it would seem.

"I make you a better offer. You fight for *me*, you get freedom. You fight for me, kill goblins, I make you free. No more cages. You get paid for working. Same as humans. You work, you get gold, you buy things you like. You come and go when it is not work time. Free," Brannis promised.

Duke Pellaton hates me anyway. If he still has a city left in the morning, he will be needing more than just slaves to populate it.

"Hmm. Deal," Glumg decided after a moment's pondering with his chin cupped in one massive hand.

"Deal," Brannis removed his gauntlets and extended a hand through the bars. Glumg had seen the human custom of clasping hands and tried it for the first time. Brannis hand was engulfed in a stone-like grip of Glumg, and they made their deal in the custom of free men.

"Juliana, burn through the hinges," Brannis said over his shoulder.

He had not watched her sneak up behind him, but he had caught Glumg's gaze flicking over to her on occasion, and he had assumed she would follow him anyway.

"*Kohtho ilextiumane veeru,*" Brannis heard from just behind him

He smiled with amusement that he had outguessed her for once. The hinges glowed red and soft. Putting his gauntlets back on, he reached out with his good hand, grabbed the door not far from the hinge, and heaved. The weakened metal gave way, and he stumbled back with the door in his grasp. Not trying to balance the heavy and awkward piece of iron, he turned and let it fall away. He hoped the display was impressive enough for his new allies to respect his strength.

Kthooom!

Brannis turned at the sound.

That did not sound right. The cannons were buried under the falling glacier, and if they had others out there, the snow and rock would have muffled the sound almost completely. Where was that sound coming from?

"Hey, everybody. We goin' do kill goblins. All goblins. Big boss say it gonna be fun," Glumg shouted back, beckoning his fellows with a great sweeping gesture, and the leader of the captive ogres strode past Brannis out into the undercity.

* * * * * * * *

Brannis jogged through the city, Juliana in tow, looking for someone knowledgeable to ask. He had a suspicion about where the sound of cannon fire could be coming from. He had not seen Jinzan on the battlefield, and he had begun to suspect the sorcerer wished to use those cannons to destroy Gehlen's Obelisk and sabotage the city. The plan seemed overly complex, especially if, as Mennon claimed, stopping the obelisk's function would have no immediate effect on the city. He needed to find out where the echoes were emanating from, though. That would tell him what he needed to know.

The front lines of the running battle were impossible to define. The goblins were cut off from their senior commanders, and their organized charges and flanking maneuvers from the battle for the overcity were gone, replaced by small roving bands of twenty to fifty goblins that were operating under lesser-ranked commanders. Brannis and Juliana avoided one such band and sent another scattering. They recognized Brannis and wanted no part of him, disengaging as quickly as they found and attacked them.

At length, Brannis found Mennon, protected by a regiment of his father's personal guards, near the undercity entrance to the castle. Brannis gave him credit for getting within sight of the battle, even if his men's posture was strictly defensive.

"Where is that noise coming from?" Brannis asked. Twice more they had heard the cannon fire, and with no clearer understanding of whence the noise came. "Could we be hearing it from the upper mines?"

"Quite possibly. There is a cross-link between the upper and lower mines from one of the earlier horizontal shafts. The way between is boarded up, but sound certainly travels down from the upper mines when we have men working up there," Mennon replied.

"I thought you said the upper mines were abandoned," Brannis said.

"As mines, yes, but we use the old mine shafts for storage now. There is far more space than we would ever need there, and the castle is not so large that the extra storage is wasted," Mennon said.

"What is the quickest way there?" Brannis asked.

"Through the castle, there is an entrance from the kitchens, cut through into the old mines to use for dry goods and wines," Mennon replied.

"Lead the way! All of you," Brannis said, gesturing to the duke's guards, "are coming with me. There is a sorcerer in those mines, and we have to stop him."

* * * * * * *

Jinzan swept away chunks of stone from the base of the obelisk with a bristle broom he had found within the warren of tunnels that constituted the upper mines. The Kadrins had apparently been using the abandoned shafts as a dumping ground for all manner of excess supplies: barrels, nails, iron ingots, old books, horse tack, cured meats, and anything else they did not wish to store elsewhere.

It had taken him far too long to find his way through it, much of the wasted time coming when he had to climb over clutter and push things out of his way. He was thankful that the cannon had been miniaturized, or he would have been delayed far longer maneuvering it through the mess in the mines.

The cannon and its accessories were back to their normal size now. Jinzan had managed the enlargement as deftly as he had shrunken them in the first place, and he could detect no flaws in the aspect of them. The cannon now was set facing the obelisk from a dozen paces away at the entrance to the obelisk chamber. The "chamber" was a dead end in the mines, a widened area with one entrance, and a rather suspect exit—it had an exposed view of the conduit of the volcano. If it were to ever erupt, the lava would rise through that very same vertical shaft.

The obelisk was a genius work of ward crafting. Half again the height of a man and shoulder width on each side, every bit of it was covered in a single intricate ward with numerous functions all mingled into its web of runes. It drew aether in from all about it—Jinzan could approach no closer than a pace without feeling deathly ill, and even three paces away was uncomfortable—and it undid all magics that approached too close to it. It was formed of a light grey stone that was unfamiliar to Jinzan and was not native to the Cloud Wall.

His first few shots had been promising, but the broken pieces the cannonballs blasted free had slid slowly back toward the rest of the ward and reformed themselves. Jinzan had tried to keep ahead of it, hoping to shatter the ward through force faster than it could repair itself, but alone he could not clean, load, and fire the cannon fast enough, even using telekinesis to do all the hard work. He had gone back into the mines to find the broom at that point.

Now, after each blast, he approached as near as he could and reached out with the broom to brush away the loose pieces. If he moved them beyond five paces or so from the obelisk, they no longer tried to rejoin the rest.

It is only a matter of time now. Jinzan grinned.

Kthooom!

Jinzan fired again, and the cannonball cracked a large chunk free from one corner. The heavy iron sphere ricocheted off and through the archway that led off into the nothingness of the volcano's conduit. Runes were carved all along the archway, even along the floor from one side to the other, forming a ward that prevented the toxic fumes of the deep earth from wafting up into the inhabited portion of the mines. The obelisk seemed not to hinder those wards, despite their proximity. Jinzan suspected they might be somehow linked.

The fallen chunk of rock was too heavy to yield to the broom's bristles, so Jinzan picked up one of the cannonballs in his hand. Using telekinesis yet again, he "threw" the ball at the loose piece of the obelisk, releasing the magic before the ward stole the aether from him. *Crack!* The rock split, but both of the two largest chunks—along with the cannonball—went down the shaft as well, into the vast depths whence came a faint red glow.

Back to his work, Jinzan loaded the cannon again, impatience making him forget to clean the gun before firing it again.

Kthooom!

Another huge chunk fell loose and did not seem to move thereafter. Jinzan's eyes lit. He saw it then, a glint of white wood, the core of the obelisk: the Staff of Gehlen. Jinzan realized that he had finally done enough to the ward that it no longer drew against him. He inched carefully closer and discovered to his glee that there was no further effect on him.

Jinzan drew up a reserve of aether and prepared to free the staff from its stony prison the way he knew best: with magic.

It is mine!

* * * * * * *

Kthooom!

Brannis, Juliana, and twelve of the duke's guards hustled down the passages of the mine, pausing to recheck their bearings each time they heard the cannon fire. They were growing close.

When they had arrived at the kitchen entrance to the mines, Brannis had picked out the dozen men he had taken, and Juliana had taken advantage of the pause to re-infuse his armor with aether, hopefully enough to protect him in the event that they managed to find the Megrenn sorcerer and engage him in combat.

There ought to be a crew of four or five goblins working that cannon. This should be more than enough men to deal with them.

Brannis had also traded his spear for a sword from one of the guards he left to defend Mennon—there were only so many men that could travel swiftly together through the mines, and twelve was already stretching it.

"This way!" Brannis whispered urgently after the most recent report.

The group took a left at the next intersection they came to, based on Brannis's hearing of the noise.

Kthooom!

There had been little pause that time between blasts.

Not good. They are rushing. Either they know they are being pursued, or they are eager about something. Neither option bodes well for us.

Despite their attempts at swift stealth, a group of fourteen, mostly in armor, could not avoid detection for long. The last blast had been close, and Brannis increased his pace, wincing at each step as his injured arm was jolted. The time for quiet was over, though, and the chase was on.

BOOM!

There was a great explosion, followed by a clatter of rock. It sounded distinctly different from the sharp report of the cannons. It sounded like destructive magic. It had come from just ahead and around the corner.

Brannis led the way and stopped short when from a dozen paces away he saw the Megrenn sorcerer standing before an archway that was lit from the far side with a red glow. The sorcerer was a ghost from another world. It was Denrik Zayne, younger looking perhaps, and sporting longer hair, but definitely the pirate he had come to know. In his hands, he was holding a long white staff, topped with a pair of stylized wooden wings, cut at sharp angles.

"Kyrus!" Jinzan gasped, eyes wide in shock. The staff leveled toward him. "Stay back!"

"Hello, Captain Zayne," Brannis replied evenly, smirking. "You are caught. There is no escape now. Drop the staff and surrender, and I shall guarantee your safety."

"Kyrus, you were not lying after all. You *are* just a brigand. No, I think I shall not surrender. With the Staff of Gehlen, I can fight my way out now," Jinzan said.

The sorcerer seemed much the same man Kyrus knew from Tellurak, perhaps a bit less reserved, but the voice, the manner, everything seemed to Brannis that this was Denrik dressed for a masquerade.

"Not with a demon warlock outside. He would never let you escape, and I do not think it would be wise to draw against him," Brannis said.

His companions seemed ill-inclined to move past him toward the Megrenn sorcerer their grand marshal parleyed with.

"The only deal I will make is this. I will spare your life here, and you will spare me *there*. Understood? I know my predicament all too well now," Jinzan bargained. "We can discuss this later. But for now …

"Fetru oglo daxgak sevdu wenlu," Jinzan began, leveling the staff at Brannis and his companions.

Brannis reacted instinctively. He did not recognize the spell, but he understood Jinzan's intent all too clearly. He dove and drove Juliana to the ground an instant before the air erupted in lightning. He heard the sizzle of flesh and felt a tingle along his back where the armor was probably saving him from a similar fate. He checked to see that Juliana was untouched by the lightning and then turned to see what Jinzan was doing as the duke's guards fell dead all about him.

Brannis saw nothing but an opaque sphere around where Captain Zayne's counterpart had just been. He heard indistinguishable mutterings from within, and for the first time in his life, Brannis *felt* the flow of the aether, this time as it was drawn inward toward that same sphere. Juliana stirred beneath him in obvious distress. Brannis worried that whatever was happening was about to kill her as well.

Then it ended. Jinzan was gone, as was a curved scoop of stone from the mine floor. In its place was gently turned soil and a few flowers.

Chapter 35 - That Awkward Morning After

I am still here, Kyrus mused, blinking up at the wooden beams of the ceiling above him.

He lay on his back in his bunk aboard the *Free Trader,* feeling the roll of the ship beneath him. He ached everywhere, and his left arm felt the break that Brannis's had in it, though he could tell that his own was intact. He looked over to the door and, in his aether-vision, found it to be intact with its wards undisturbed.

Kyrus sat up and looked around in the aether to see what befell aboard the ship. He saw sailors bustling all about, no different than any other day he had seen since taking to the seas himself. If there was unease about the ship's wizard, they were betraying no sign of it. The deck was being cleaned, there were men in the rigging, and the galley was manned with cook and hungry sailor alike.

Kyrus could not see the whole of the ship from his quarters, so he could not check on the whereabouts of Captain Zayne, and he was fairly certain he did not want to go looking for him, either.

What would I even say?

There were twelve men in his immediate company who had died at Captain Zayne's hands, and Juliana had narrowly avoided being another of his victims.

"I will spare your life here, and you will spare me there," Jinzan had said.

Was it even binding? Brannis had agreed to nothing, and Kyrus certainly had not been there. Where was the line between Kyrus and Brannis, between Captain Zayne and Jinzan?

Kyrus had much to think about before he opened that warded door and left the cozy safety of his cabin. If Captain Zayne bore him ill will from their encounter in Veydrus, Kyrus knew he had best leave prepared to do battle.

No, that is ludicrous. I must remember that here, I am the sorcerer. Jinzan may know a thousand tricks of aether for all I care, and Captain Zayne can manage none of that. He would be a fool to try anything to harm me.

Kyrus examined the ward tattooed into the flesh of his shoulder. It glowed reassuringly in his aether-vision, its protections solid and unyielding. Of the warnings of dire peril that Captain Zayne had predicted, Kyrus still noticed nothing. If aether were being drawn into the ward directly from his Source, he was none the worse for it.

Maybe my Source is just a bit stronger than Jinzan's, and better able to shrug off the additional burden. Captain Zayne has always seemed impressed with my Source and how powerful it supposedly is.

Kyrus had tried looking in the mirror, but mirrors only reflected the light, not aether. It was awkward trying to view his own Source, some quirk of how Source and aether-vision interacted that prevented him getting a good look at his own. The best he could do was infer. There seemed in general to be more aether about his person than he saw near others, and when it came time to draw it, it came readily and speedily to his call. All other aspects of his Source, any that needed direct observation, were obscured to him. Was he so different from Jinzan, who rivaled the Inner Circle members in power?

Brannis had heard tell of Iridan's battle with Captain Zayne's alter ego, having both reports and firsthand accounts of how the battle went on all fronts before taking his slumber. Though tired and worn down, Iridan had drawn against Jinzan and lost, saved only by the quick-thinking illusionist, Faolen.

Would that it had been Rashan who crossed Jinzan's path, and not just Iridan. I could suffer Captain Zayne's presence in good conscience if I did not have to worry that he worked against my homeland and friends in another world.

In theory, Kyrus knew that dispatching the captain of the *Free Trader* would have been a simple matter. Neither pistol, not blade, nor the presence of four-score loyal sailors could stop Kyrus—and the loyalty of so new a crew was a paltry thing when asked to stand in the way of a sorcerer with murderous intent. But that was the rub: murder. Kyrus had been wronged in no way by Denrik Zayne—indeed, he had been helped at many turns by the captain and his associates. Brannis had even been explicitly spared by Jinzan, who by all rights ought to have obliterated them all before using a transference spell to flee the mines.

Kyrus's stomach growled, reminding him that no matter the moral dilemma, he could not remain in his cabin indefinitely. Outside on deck, the men sang a song that reminded him of the ones Juliana had them singing on the way to Raynesdark. Kyrus would much rather have been there in the wreckage of Raynesdark than isolated and alone on a Megrenn sorcerer's ship.

* * * * * * * *

"Ha-ha, so I was right to think he was lying to us." Stalyart grinned. The first mate sat straddling one of the chairs in the captain's cabin, his crossed arms resting on the back of it. "So everything else went according to your plan?"

"Largely, yes. I did not stay to witness the battle's end, but there was a dragon and a warlock back from the dead there, and I did not wish to risk the staff's safety around either of them. Once I got it, I got myself out by magic and back to Megrenn lands. I sleep right now in my very own bed for the first time in months. In the morning, it will be a hero's reception for me again," Denrik said, letting out a satisfied sigh. Denrik Zayne was a hard, solitary man, but Jinzan at least had known love in his life.

"So what is our little sorcerer like in the other world, hmm? I admit, I had guessed him to be a useless noble son, seventh in line to some worthless scrap of

Kadrin with a fencing tutor who had taught him to use a blade. Bookish, timid, much like our Kyrus, that was my guess. Oh, but how wrong, hey?" Stalyart joked. He had little stake in the war between Kadrin and Megrenn, certainly nothing beyond just the financial gain to be had in supplying foreign-bred mounts and iron ore for their military efforts.

"He tried to bargain with me, offered to take me alive and guaranteed my safety if I gave myself up. Typical Kadrin ploy. I bet they would have had my throat before dawn. No, I read my history. No fop shall be made of me in the stories written about the fall of Kadrin. I bartered my life here for his twin's life there. I slew the rest of his companions, save for one slip of a sorceress that he shielded with his body. I took a moment's panic, thinking I had killed him accidentally, but his armor was warded strongly and turned aside my attack. I know not what Kyrus would have done if I had slain his twin, and once I realized he would sacrifice himself to save the girl, I spared her as well. That boy has violence within him, even if it is not at the surface. I still worry that he might not hold to his end."

"What would we do if he did not?" Stalyart asked, shrugging. "You saw the smoke from the fires in Marker's Point. Eleven men, he said. Would it make a difference if it had been a hundred? We have no sorcerer here to balance against him. My advice to you is better now than before: befriend him. You know his secret now. Let the tide wash the footprints from the sand. Make new ones. Are you Jinzan? Is he the Kadrin knight you saw? Let him search the ship all he likes; the Staff of Gehlen is not here. He can choose a life of drinking and whoring and plundering, or he can slink off to the hills of some desolate backwater to make his home away from those who would shun him as a witch."

"And what if he decides he can make himself a king?" Denrik countered. "Surely people will fear and shun him, but let him slay an army and they will kneel to him. I doubted the boy had it in him, but I bet you that knight does. That means Kyrus is capable as well, there is no mistaking. The lessons of the one world carry into the other. *You* explained that one to me. The 'Rule of the Twinborn,' you called it."

"Then do not let him think of the possibility. Make a grand gesture of your acceptance of him. Make him truly your friend. Then maybe he does not think of running and conquering. Oh, and I understand too, if he decides he is a lion among kittens, we are dead men the day he chooses to leave us. We would be just an angry tantrum as he carves an empire of his own—men who knew too much."

"I will have to think on it," Denrik muttered, half to himself. Stalyart took that as a sign he ought to be going and stood up. "One last thing, Stalyart. Has Kyrus left his cabin yet today?"

"I shall check, but I had not seen him yet this morn," Stalyart replied.

What can *I do?* Denrik wondered as soon as the door shut behind his friend and first mate.

The door provided no answer as he stared at it. He was suddenly wary of that door. Somewhere on the other side was a man who might well feel wronged by him, or at least stood as a mortal enemy—kingdom to empire—not far away.

Will today be my end, not at the gibbet, but at the hands of an angry Kadrin sorcerer? Will he weigh the life I spared in the mines of Raynesdark against my own life here? If it were me, I would honor the bargain, even though I had not agreed to it. A man's life is not his own to barter at times like that. I had his life in my hands and gave it back to him. Does a Kadrin even have enough honor to understand that debt?

Denrik felt the comforting shape of the pistol in his belt and ran a hand along it.

Fool or not, that ward makes this pistol a condemned man's last resort. Source like his, he is unlikely to let that ward of his falter, especially after what has transpired.

No amount of staring at the cabin door was going to change his fate, but Denrik tried nonetheless.

* * * * * * * *

Kyrus ate his morning meal in the mess, keeping to himself. After the previous night's display—which Kyrus had nearly forgotten about after the war he had witnessed in his dreams—few were eager to share his company. Even Jimony, who had tried to warm to Kyrus in order to be shielded beneath his aura of power and influence with the captain, took his own meal at another table. Kyrus poked his spoon a bit at a lackluster fish strew—how anyone could undersalt saltwater fish was beyond him—but ate little.

He caught a glimpse of Stalyart, but there was no sign that the captain was about.

Is he afraid of me? Kyrus wondered.

The ship's first mate had made no eye contact with Kyrus, and that was unusual for the outgoing and boisterous southlander.

There was shouting up on deck, but Kyrus could not make out what was going on. He could see Sources congregating outside the captain's quarters. Curiosity started picking off the others in the mess as they went to see what was going on above. Kyrus sat at the table, mindlessly staring into his stew until he was the last remaining.

"Everyone on deck. Captain's orders," came a shout from above.

Kyrus could only imagine that his presence had been missed. If it was to be a call for his head or a duel between him and the captain, so be it. Kyrus steeled himself and pushed away his bowl.

As he started for the stairs, he checked his ward for what must have been the twentieth time since he awoke. It was still fine, and he added a bit of aether to it to be safe. Thinking on it, he also drew a bit of aether to hold onto. Kyrus was getting used to retaining aether for emergencies, out of habit, and was to the point where it barely burned to hold it anymore. Even without any proper spells for battle, simple firehurling would be enough to defend him against any of the ship's inhabitants.

"All right, men," Kyrus heard as he reached the top of the stairs. Captain

Zayne was holding court from the aft castle, addressing his men like a king from a palace balcony. "Gather 'round. This is a joyous time. Look at you all," Denrik shouted, grinning. "A proper pirate crew if I ever saw one. It had been too long since I had seen the likes of you. We will make our mark upon the world. Men will fear us. The sound of the name *Fair Trader* will be spoken in reverent whispers among the seafaring merchants much as *Honest Merchant* once was.

"But today, tonight, we will make for a gentler port. Tonight we will feast in Denku Appa."

A cheer rose up from a scattering of the men, those worldly enough to have known or heard of the tiny island. Kyrus had seen it on the ship's maps but knew little of it. It was but one strange name among many, a lone island far from most others, though close enough to Marker's Point that they were reaching it in just two days at sea.

"So I gather that some of you have heard of Denku Appa, but not all," Captain Zayne continued once the cheer died down.

Men were continuing to press closer about the deck below where he held court, while Kyrus kept to the back of the assembly. There was an energy about the captain that Kyrus had not seen before. He had realized the charisma of the captain not long after their proper introduction, but he seemed to have enthralled his men, though Kyrus saw no hint of tampering with them in the aether.

"For those who have not, it is a paradise. The natives who live there are friendly, and their hospitality is unmatched. We will drink and feast and take the company of their women, and all for the price of a little steel, which they cannot make themselves."

"Tell more about them women," someone shouted.

There were murmurs and shouts of agreement. And so the captain did, as Kyrus watched. He felt detached, wondering how the men of the crew could be so gullible.

You would really sell your lives to this man for the chance at primitive women and shoddily distilled liquor?

It was a magic that Kyrus did not know but which he envied. It was the power to plant seeds in men's minds and make them grow into ideas that they think are their own. It was like planting a garden of dreams.

Ask a man what he wants in life, and there are many who would answer: riches, drink, and the company of many beautiful women. Not every man dreams so simply or so crudely, but Denrik Zayne need only choose his crew from among those who do.

And where do I fit in among these? Can I even truly dream, or is it not a "dream" in quite that sense? If it is just to unlock the key to the heart's desires, all I want is to find a way to be with Abbiley again. The rest ... It would work itself out, and I could be content however it befell.

By the time the captain had finished, the crew was clamoring to get to Denku Appa and sate their gluttony and lusts among the welcoming savages who lived there. Kyrus wondered what it would actually be like once they got there. Could enough rum allow a man to imagine a primitive paradise where there is only squalor? Could dreams make a spit-charred grouper taste of lemon-brushed salmon, or an awkward and nervous native girl seem an exotic temptress? Captain Zayne was promising a Garden of Ma'Lai, and there was no way he would be able to deliver all he boasted of. Like the merchants Kyrus had met in Acardia, there was an art to such selling that he just could not fully wrap his mind about.

As the speech finished, Captain Zayne ordered the men back about their work, and they complied eagerly, excited by the prospect of exotic island delights by nightfall, if they kept their course and speed. They pushed and jostled as too many men moved about the deck to get to where they were headed. None touched Kyrus. There was an area about him that might well have been forged of steel, a pillar into which no man could enter. It was magic that managed it but not of the aetherial sort; Kyrus had them scared of him. Glances did not long linger on him—lest a sailor make accidental eye contact—save for one. Denrik Zayne locked gazes with Kyrus and gave him an even look, not betraying any intent but interest.

As the last of the men were clearing the area of the aft castle, the captain yelled down, just loudly enough for Kyrus to hear clearly: "Mr. Hinterdale, a word in my cabin, if you will."

It was an order but a politely delivered one. Kyrus did not see Stalyart lingering about, so he wondered if it was to be a private conversation, with no ally ready at hand. Kyrus kept his walk slow as he crossed to the door of the captain's cabin, hanging back long enough for Captain Zayne to make the walk down from the castle and meet him at his own door without having to wait.

"Come in. Come in." Denrik gestured as he entered his own quarters.

Kyrus followed and closed the door behind him. He knew his ward was still ready in case of treachery, but the captain's jovial mood did not suddenly shift once they were alone, as he had feared it would.

"Ah, Kyrus, that was marvelous," the captain beamed.

"Which do you mean?" Kyrus asked.

He was unused to the captain being jolly, but it was all he could think to describe the mood he saw. There was wine set out at the captain's private table, and two stout goblets made of silver, inlaid with rubies. Captain Zayne slumped into one of the chairs and threw his feet up onto the table. He took one of the goblets and drank deeply, then gestured for Kyrus to join him.

"I mean everything," Denrik stated. "What has gone awry for me these past weeks? A month ago, I was sitting in a prison cell on Rellis Island in Tellurak and treating with goblins in Veydrus, trying to get them to go to war with my enemies. Today I have my own ship, practically smelling of fresh paint and filled with new cannons, and I have secured the Staff of Gehlen and begun the downfall of the Kadrin Empire."

"Seems a bit premature to gloat, do you not think?" Kyrus asked. "You may have your staff, but at what cost? Any allies you might have had among the goblins are dead. Rashan Solaran has returned and taken over his duties as Warlock of the Empire and has already slain a dragon and routed an army." Kyrus saw Denrik's brow furrow at the mention of a dead dragon, momentarily cracking the façade of joviality he presented. "Staff or no staff, you fled rather than face him. If you thought you could stand against him, you ought to have done it right there, before he knew you possessed it; now that chance is gone. Life here is good, I shall not deny, but you have more troubles than you think in Veydrus."

"Before you decide that I have troubles in this world after all, let me assure you of one thing: this world is not Veydrus. The dead feel no pain; I will shed no tears for my slain allies. They served their purpose, and in truth, their company had worn on me awfully. I suspected the battle was lost when I puzzled out that it was truly your dead warlock reborn. I bear no ill will toward you for whatever role you play in the Kadrin army or the defeat of my clever little associates, though I do begrudge you the Kadrin habits that seep over into you from the other world. I may have called you a brigand, but that was Jinzan speaking, and to whomever your twin may be, not to you. If you do not mind me asking, what is your name in the other world? Who are you? Mind you, every word I have spoken about my life in Veydrus has borne true, while you have confronted me with lie upon lie. Have it out: who was the man I spared in Raynesdark's mines?" Denrik said, and the word "Raynesdark" sounded so odd to Kyrus with its Kadrin sound to it, spoken in Acardian.

"The truth?" Kyrus supposed it was past hiding at this point. "I am Sir Brannis Solaran, Grand Marshal of the Imperial Army."

Denrik shook his head and gave a small smile. "Fine, if you do not wish to tell me, then—"

"No, that is the truth of it. That armor that saved my life from whatever spell you intended for everyone else? That was from the personal collection of the emperor, once worn in battle by Liead the Only, not runed but aether-forged. I was the one who matched wits with your goblin allies, the one who escaped Kelvie Forest to warn of your approach and to put a ready army at the walls of Raynesdark when you arrived, cannons in tow."

"Hmm, perhaps this time it is the truth after all. Well, then, let us toast to a friendship in this world while we begin our rivalry in the other. I say this: let this ship be as an embassy of the Kadrin Empire. We can treat here with no hint of our activity showing among our own allies and keep each other apprised of diplomatic messages.

"House Solaran, you say," Denrik mused. "It seems they have gone downwind in their pursuit of sorcerous perfection. I think they made you too good, and when your Source broke in half from the strain, the whale's share ended up here, rather than in Kadrin. You tell me that Rashan Solaran is returned among you, but I think I would more greatly fear Kyrus Solaran, properly trained among those of the Imperial Circle. You may lack for guile and ruthlessness compared with him, but they would have put that into you at the

Academy had you shown this sort of promise."

"In fact, I did attend the Academy. They expected much of me, given my birthright, and for some time suffered my slow development in magic, before casting me out. I joined with the knighthood instead, and my family ties came to my advantage only once I met Rashan," Kyrus said. "It was he who elevated me to grand marshal."

"Tell me, what is the monster like? How was it he has kept himself alive so long? He must be near to two hundred fifty by now," Denrik asked, leaning toward Kyrus a bit.

"He is a philosopher and a keen observer, thoughtful and kind. His knowledge and wisdom span centuries, and he teaches and guides. The next moment, he is bloody to the elbows with a score of corpses in his wake over some slight or misstep, with a look in his eyes akin to madness, even joy. The moment after, he will calmly resume his pleasant demeanor, as if no one had noticed what he had done. It preys on his thoughts, I think, the rage that lurks inside him, and I think that is why he was away so long—to find some other way of being.

"As to his longevity, he had found the secret of the demons, of a perfect Source that loses no aether. He is a demon now himself, and a monster in both the classical and literal senses," Kyrus said.

It felt odd speaking of Rashan while in Tellurak, since the warlock was so alien to it, a creature of naught but magic in a world that did not even admit the existence of it.

"Tell me this, Kyrus, why do you follow him, if you see this so clearly? You seem to understand the evils you consort with—the monster who enslaved my homeland six generations ago—yet you serve him." Denrik seemed perplexed.

"If you wish him slain, do it yourself with that staff you are so proud of plundering. He killed a dragon and I cannot count the thousands of goblins. When I fell exhausted into my bed last night, Rashan Solaran was still chasing down anything that survived in the plains below the city. I am loyal to Kadrin, and for now at least, he is our best weapon against you. I could not stand against him if I wished to, and at present, I do not wish to," Kyrus said.

"Well, I shall let it go at that for now. I shall make it my goal to sell you the merits of a free Megrenn ruling over Kadrin. You may be too highborn to see it, but your people suffer for the rule of the powerful houses—noble and sorcerous alike—and I intend to see them free to live as Megrenn do, as equals to be judged on their own merits. I will win you over. I will find what it is you love in life, and you shall have it. You are made of different stuff that those men out there." Denrik gestured broadly beyond the walls of his cabin. "But I will find your heart's song and a bard to play it for you." Denrik smiled at Kyrus.

I bet you cannot find me another Abbiley, nor take her aboard the Fair Trader. *You will find no hold over me.*

* * * * * * *

423

The boats held ten men each, and Kyrus had been summoned to the first one with Captain Zayne. They were to head ashore first to meet with the chieftain of the people on the island. The boat swayed a bit as each man climbed aboard, down the rope ladder over the *Fair Trader*'s side. Three nights they had been promised, to take in the pleasures of the island's hospitality. The Denku—for Denku Appa literally meant "Denku Place" in their own tongue—would be expecting them, having seen the ship from their little fishing boats.

The water was placid and calm, with just the slightest of rolls to give any hint of being at sea at all. The ship anchored a ways from shore, as the island was surrounded by reefs and shallow waters all about. The long boats would be the only way to go ashore.

Kyrus went with more than a bit of trepidation. He meant to keep his magics to himself; if a cosmopolitan people like the Acardians could be driven to stake-burning frenzy at the prospect of magic, how much worse would savages react to having a witch in their midst? Kyrus might survive, but what might he wreak in the meantime? Would he kill half his own crew this time? Perhaps the boats ...

Four poor men had the unlucky draw to get duty on the oars, and slowly they began making their way to shore. The night air was warm, and the clouds sparse in the starry sky. The moon and starlight sparkled against the tepid waters of the southern Katamic. The sound of the oars rhythmically breaching the water brought to mind memories of illicit visits to Dragon's Eye Island back in Kadrin, when a younger Kyrus—err, Brannis—was wooing a younger Juliana Archon. Kyrus smiled, but amid the eager smiles of the lusty sailors about him, its nostalgia felt tainted amid less pure intentions.

As they neared the shore, smaller boats came out to meet them and guide them in to shore. These boats were little more than a pair of hollowed tree trunks, lashed together with wooden poles that held them separated by two paces or so. In each boat, one of the hollowed trunks carried a small mast and little triangular sail little taller than a man's height. The Denku sailors wore little but loincloths and an occasional ornament—a necklace of sharks' teeth, a leather bracelet—and they carried small lanterns hung from poles, which they dangled a bit in front of the long boat to light its way. It was an unnecessary gesture on the brightly lit night, but it was just that: a gesture. The native Denku seemed eager to appear welcoming to their visitors.

Fires appeared on the shore, lighting areas of broad, white sand and casting the small figures gathered around them into sharp contrast. There were scores of the Denku out to greet them once they reached shore. Kyrus saw no sign of weapons among them, which he found curious.

Even Marker's Point had guns trained on us and boarded the ship before we were allowed in, and one ship is no real threat to them. Four-score pirates could slaughter these people, yet they guide us to them with unarmed fishermen?

The fires on the beach multiplied as the island's residents continued their preparations. Kyrus tried to guess how many there were among them but gave up as there were too many obscured in the darkness where the fires did not reach. But the numerous fires were enough that he could begin to make out the plant life that lived not far from the beach. There were brilliant greens of leaf and bush, tall trees that had no leaves at all until very near the top, and little specks of color that must have been flowers, all oranges and reds and yellows.

Off to the port side of the boat they passed a sea-worn rock, jutting from the water. Their guides had veered them around it. Kyrus paid a bit more attention to the surrounding waters after that and noticed many more rocks not far above the surface.

It would be suicide to pilot these waters blindly without guides. Well, aside from the water being warm and us being so close to shore, Kyrus corrected himself.

Aside from the late hour and not wishing to sleep wet, it was tempting to swim the waters. Kyrus dragged a hand in the water, feeling the warmth and wondering what creatures might lurk beneath the surface.

Drat!

Kyrus had once again forgotten and let his vision slip back solely into the light. It was a hard habit to get into—easier aboard ship where his paranoia lent him focus—and the beauty of the night landscape had lulled him into a reverie of light without aether. He willed his vision into the mixed view he wanted to maintain, and looked down again.

Below the boats, the waters teemed with life. Schools of fish abounded, hundreds of schools, and thousands, perhaps millions of fish! There was a wall of life not far beneath them; it ran in a circle about the island, as far as he could see into the aether. It could only have been the reef. He did not know the draft of the *Free Trader*, but it could not possibly have made it over the reef without running aground.

Kyrus's musings were again interrupted when the drums began, followed by chanting in a language he did not understand. There was a five-beat pattern with syncopation—*dum dum da-dum dum*—and accompaniment by a clacking of wood on wood. The words did not change much. If it was a song, it seemed only to have perhaps two verses, but it sounded festive, and there were at least a hundred among the chanters, if not more.

"They know how to welcome visitors here," Denrik spoke quietly to Kyrus.

Kyrus had forgotten about his reservations about Captain Zayne, caught up in the wonder and mystery of this little island and its inhabitants.

Could it be that this place is all that he promised? Kyrus wondered.

* * * * * * * *

The party that first greeted them as they pulled the boat ashore was led by a trio of older men. Two had the look of the island's natives, lean with bronzed skin; smooth, soft features and round faces, and dark black hair, which they wore close-cropped. They wore nothing but loincloths and trinkets, and their bodies bore numerous tattoos—plainer in style and cruder in form than the ones he had seen in Marker's Point, but he had seen their like among the crew. The third was a grey-bearded northerner, Acardian by the look of him, dressed like the Denku:

loincloth, tattoos and all.

One of the Denku spoke at length in his own language, and the Acardian translated: "Welcome back, sir. Kappi wishes to welcome the Zayne ship and its crew. His fishermen did not recognize your ship, but he is pleasantly surprised to find it is you."

The one who must have been Kappi spoke again. "He says the feast will begin shortly, once the hunters return. You and your men will share drinks and songs. They may lie with any women who will have them but warns that they must behave themselves," the Acardian translated.

"It will not be like last time," Denrik assured him. "Rathbone was hung years ago and is no longer among my crew. Tell Kappi that it is a pleasure as always, and we have much to trade and much to discuss." To the rest of his men, he ordered, "And you lot, bring the chest ashore and have it here."

Kyrus had not seen the small chest loaded aboard the longboat. It had been covered with a canvas tarp to protect against the sea spray and had not attracted his notice.

On the other hand, the natives most certainly had caught Kyrus's notice. The garb of the men that met them was typical of the Denku, man and woman alike. Not a one of them wore the clothes he would consider adequate to be modestly asleep in his own bed. The women were of all ages, but the old crones and mothers did not catch his eye; it was the younger maids. Whether primitive or not, there was something to a diet of fish and hunted game, combined with an active life, that seemed quite agreeable to the figure. Kyrus had been to the museums of Scar Harbor and Golis, and had seen the works of Dard the Lesser and Hallay Fellbird—and the Denku women looked much like those statues in form, if not about the face. He had never seen so much of his beloved Abbiley as he now saw of these strange women.

After the official greeting, the Denku pressed forward to greet the newcomers themselves. There were smiles and indecipherable greetings in the Denku tongue. Two comely young women took Kyrus in arm and escorted him toward the fires. Tattooing seemed to be mostly for the menfolk, but the women had decoration of their own. The younger ones especially seemed to like to dye their hair fanciful colors. The one who had hold of his right arm had brightly colored green hair, which might have been shoulder length had it not been teased out in every direction. She wore a double-stranded necklace of seashells about her neck and a needle through the top of one ear. The one on his left arm was scarlet haired— the red of ripe apples, not the more natural strawberry blonde of Juliana's—and wore hers in four braids, two pulled forward over each shoulder. This one wore no necklace, but the clatter of beads as she walked made him guess that perhaps her loincloth was naught but stranded beads—Kyrus pointedly did not look.

Kyrus was finding it hard to look anywhere at all on the island without embarrassment. He was a head taller than either of his escorts, so even looking down at their faces—which smiled up guilelessly each time they noticed his attention—was an invitation to blush as he saw too much else. The two who had claimed him took him off to a long bench at the sand's edge, made from a felled tree and carved flat and made smooth on the top surface. They waded through a throng of cheerful Denku on the way there, smiling at him, touching him, offering greetings or blessings. It was hard to tell which, since Kyrus could barely distinguish words among their speech, let alone put meaning to them.

Once they were seated, the girls began fussing over him. He was touched and felt, and they talked past him to each other considerably. They pressed close against him on either side and managed to arrange it such that each of his arms encircled one of them. Kyrus hardly knew how to resist—and was beginning to wonder why it was occurring to him to try—as he could hardly touch anyplace on them in any modesty to push them away. Drinks were brought around in bowls not much smaller than dinner plates. The two girls, whose hands were free when they chose them to be, held the bowl to Kyrus's lips so that he did not need to release them from his embrace to drink. The liquid was slightly thick, not quite a syrup, and sweet, with just a hint of alcohol to it. It was delicious, some sort of fermented melon if he had to guess, and the three of them shared it.

Kyrus saw others from the crew come to join the revelry, but he paid them little mind. His attention was being drawn to the area immediately beneath each of his arms by the attentions of the two young lasses who seemed intent on keeping it all for themselves. When the feasting started, they took spits of the meat of some furry animal the hunters had killed—halfway between a bear and a badger—and fish, as well as fruits from the island. As with the drink, they held the spit up for him as well, feeding him like a Takalish prince.

As the night wore on, the music played and drunken men and women danced about the fires. Drinks were replaced when they were emptied, and spits of meat came regularly. At some point, Kyrus had his tunic confiscated—he was a bit fuzzy on the "how," but figured out the "who" easily enough—and the two girls curled more closely against him, their warmth contrasting with the pleasantly cool night breeze on his back. The girl to his left had marveled at his tattoo, tracing it with her fingers and kissing it. It seemed like they thought it was a symbol of status, or perhaps his prowess as a warrior.

Well, perhaps it is, at that.

Kyrus felt guilty somewhere in his heart. He longed for home, but the night was surreal and dreamlike, in a way his dreams never were. It seemed magical, but not in the way that he was growing to understand magic. Kyrus allowed the revelry to sweep him up and away, like a leaf borne on the wind. He was not Brannis, nor were these girls betrothed of anyone he had ever met.

Chapter 36 - A Feast for Heroes

The repairs and cleanup began at dawn. The townsfolk were out in numbers, clearing the bodies from the streets and carting off debris from the wreckage of buildings or the wall. The combatants of the night before were allowed to sleep to noontime, but all other able-bodied folk were at work by the duke's orders. Brannis had ignored his privilege of a late slumber and was seeing to the organization of the repair and recovery efforts.

He had slept fitfully, with his broken arm set by aether construct to prevent it from breaking any worse, but Caldrax's handiwork had done nothing for the pain of the break, or any of the other lesser hurts Brannis had suffered when his armor's aether had failed.

Brannis was not sure what to do about Jinzan. Only Juliana had heard what befell in the chamber of the Obelisk of Gehlen and still lived. She had heard Brannis call to him by name, and not the name he was known by in Veydrus. She had also heard Jinzan call him by Kyrus's name. Then again, she had hit the floor solidly when he tackled her. Perhaps she would not even remember such a mincing detail as two unfamiliar names traded just before a blow to the head.

Should I bother trying to explain it away, just in case? Maybe if I do not bring it up, she will let it pass, or forget about it in the face of all else that has befallen.

"Marshal Brannis, a word," came a shout from down the hall, bearing the duke's voice.

Brannis had been giving orders to a few others of the knights who could not bear the extra sleep, sending them to begin accounting for the dead. With the destruction wrought of dragonfire and cannon alike, a count of skulls would be the best way to determine how many had been lost—by both sides. While he was less concerned with the families of the goblins, he wanted to know what strength they had faced, and how many fewer were the goblin numbers than they had been the previous day.

"Marshal Brannis," the voice came again as Duke Pellaton made his way through the throng in the overcity entrance chamber of the castle. "Finally! I have been looking all over for you. What have you done to my city? I heard that you were the one who sabotaged the avalanche wall and brought the Neverthaw Glacier down across the entrance to the undercity and buried half the overcity in snow and ice! What were you thinking?"

"Go out, do what you can," Brannis ordered the knights who had surrounded him, then turned his attention to the duke. "What would you have had me do, fight them in the undercity, outnumbered twenty to one? The whole population was down there; I could not just let an army make their way down unhindered. As it was, too many got through, and we had to let the ogres loose among the goblins to stop them."

"That is another thing. My steward tells me that the ogres are demanding payment. They said the 'big boss' said so," Duke Pellaton said, his face reddening.

"It has already been taken care of. I had Mennon give them a few hundred lions and they seemed happy enough with that," Brannis said.

"That is not the point. They do not get paid. They are mining animals, nothing more. My family has kept and bred them for winters," Duke Pellaton growled, pointing his cane menacingly at Brannis.

"They showed last night that they were more than that. They fought to defend their homes and their keepers. So pay them a pittance and make them buy the bread and meat they eat. Give them the same illusion of freedom as the peasants, and you shall find them just as loyal and useful.

"I might add that it is the same illusion of freedom that you enjoy, Duke. You have your lands and your wealth, but there is an angry demon outside dissecting the corpse of a dragon he slew inside the walls of your city. Any freedom you think you have is at the pleasure of Warlock Rashan. He treats you better than you treat the ogres, but he could easily show you how tenuous that freedom really is, show you firsthand how simple it is to take away," Brannis said.

"Why do you care for the ogres? They are just dumb brutes." Duke Pellaton's eye narrowed accusingly. "You got some *thing* for ogres, do you?"

"I spent two summers fighting them in the borderlands. They are fierce warriors. You tamed them and made them dumb. I am not claiming them to be scholars, but they are cunning enough fighters and have their own ways, their own language. Your ogres are useless, or at least were until last night, when they showed they can be trusted."

Brannis snatched the cane from the old duke with his good hand and thrust it back at him, jamming it flatly against his chest. The old duke stumbled backward against a chair and bobbled the cane, which clattered against the floor.

"If you do not like the manner in which I kept your people alive, or the manner in which I treat your slaves, take it up with the warlock," Brannis barked, drawing stares from all about, as those who had been attending to other business stopped to watch the confrontation.

"This is my city, you insolent pup! I shall have you—"

Suddenly Brannis had closed the gap and stood face-to-face with the duke, towering over the older man from a handspan away.

"You shall have me ... what?" Brannis asked through gritted teeth. After all that had transpired the previous night, he was ill-inclined to suffer threats from the worthless Duke Pellaton and his feigned outrage. "You forget yourself, Duke. I was sent here to save your city, and I have. I was not sent here to save your old walls, or keep your ogres docile. There is a dead dragon outside, and you somehow survived the night. Warlock Rashan put me in command here, and I have not yet relinquished it, nor yet been relieved of it. If you insist on interfering with my efforts to put Raynesdark back in order, you can spend the night in one of your own dungeons. Any appeal will not take long, since the Imperial Regent is just outside. Fair warning, he is not so forgiving of fools."

Brannis was glad that Avalanche was still buried somewhere under a mountain of ice. Had the clean-up crews retrieved it for him already, Duke Pellaton's elder son might have been made duke.

* * * * * * *

Iridan listened as best he could, but his attention wandered at times. The dragon was fascinating, but he'd had a hard night and had not slept. Rashan poked and carved at the corpse, studying the creature's anatomy, marveling at the strength in the scales and the beauty of the dragon as a whole. Rashan had walked all about the dragon's body and climbed around on it, Iridan following dutifully in his wake as the warlock explained his findings and his methodology to his protégé. Iridan had not looked in a mirror since the battle and would hardly have recognized the reflection if he had. His face was ashen, with dark shadows around reddened, heavy-lidded eyes. A fresh bruise swelled the left side of his face at the cheekbone, and blood crusted at the corner of his mouth and left eye from the force of Jinzan's spell, even though Iridan's shield had saved his life from the blast.

"Look at this. I can bend it just a bit but cannot break it or keep it from springing back to shape, and I am truly trying," Rashan said, flexing one of the dragon's scales between his hands.

The scale in question was the size of a supper plate, one of the larger scales on the dragon's body—they ranged down to tiny scales the size of a thumbnail. The warlock handed the scale to Iridan to see for himself, and Iridan gamely tried to bend it, finding it as inflexible as steel, though it felt like glass or polished stone in his hands.

"Yes. Sturdy," Iridan muttered sleepily, handing it back.

Warlock Rashan had pried it loose from the dragon's back with some difficulty, an indication of how well it was attached, to have put the demon to some trouble over it. Iridan was just noticing that it was late morning, as the sun was coming up over the mountaintops. Raynesdark saw little of the sun even in the warm months, but as the Solstice holiday approached, it was lucky to have a few hours of light a day, between the shortened days and the sheltering mountains to the east.

Townsfolk had begun gathering at the base of the fallen glacier, tradesmen by the look of them. They were dressed for warmth in the frigid morning air, but Iridan identified them by their tools. There were blacksmiths with tongs and hammers, standing out from their peers by their bulk as well. He saw butchers, with meat hooks and cleavers, a couple even carrying saws along with their more commonly seen tools. The duke's apothecary was there with his apprentices, pulling a hand cart filled with empty vials, flasks, and jars. Drovers came in numbers, with oxcarts, mostly empty, some filled with crates and sacks. Other tradesmen Iridan could not name, but he knew that they had some part in Rashan's current undertaking: disassembling the dragon.

It was to be gruesome work, but Rashan had emphasized just how rare a thing a dragon kill was, and how valuable every piece of it. The scales and bones were stronger than steel and took runes as readily as a mop took water. The leather was strong and supple even before any curing, and was impervious to fire. Less was known of the uses of the dragon's fluids, but Rashan wanted none wasted that could otherwise be preserved, that they might find what uses they held.

The ground at the edge of the glacier was wet, and further away steamed lightly. The fires of the forges below still heated the overcity and the snow was melting, albeit at a rate which would not clear the hilltop-sized mount of snow before springtime. The more adventurous of the tradesmen did not just stand in the great puddle waiting for instruction but came up onto the snow and approached the dragon.

"Welcome, people of Raynesdark," Rashan addressed them, tearing his attention away from the fascinating specimen upon which he stood.

The warlock placed one foot upon the dragon's head, posing as a prize hunter might atop a kill—and no monohorn or gelnon looked so impressive beneath a hunter's boot as the dragon who called herself Jadefire looked beneath Rashan's.

"Last night was a night of war and suffering and loss, but today is a day for celebrating those who yet live, and the mighty deeds they have wrought. This dragon brought forth her goblin minions against us, and the Kadrin people have made her pay for her folly. Her minions are slaughtered in the fields before the city, at the wall, and in the streets of Raynesdark. Beneath the Neverthaw lie countless others. Yet more lie dead in the streets of the undercity, given no quarter or mercy by Raynesdark's miners," Rashan said, rather diplomatically referring to the ogres, declining to call them either slaves or citizens. Brannis's actions the previous night had cast their status into question.

"As for you, good folks, you will be helping us take our trophy. For while goblins sell their lives cheaply in battle, dragons are more cautious creatures, and more dangerous. To my knowledge, there have been no slayings of dragons in at least six hundred summers. You look upon a spectacle none of your ancestors has seen in thirty generations, if they were even so lucky. We will harvest and put to use every part of this dragon save for one. The skull will remain just where it is now, allowing for the melting of a few feet of snow beneath it. The area around will be cleared and a monument erected, celebrating the defeat of Nihaxtukali." The draconic word sounded odd with Rashan's traditional pronunciation, amid all the Kadrin words about it. "Do not fear, I will show the stonemasons how to spell it," the warlock joked, smiling. There were a few chuckles among the tradesmen, mostly out of politeness.

The tradesmen had been informed of who Rashan Solaran was, and in a few cases had it explained to them what a warlock was, as there had not been one within the lifetime of anyone in the city. They were a bit uneasy around him in person as he directed them about the butchering and harvesting of the dragon. There was a way he walked, moved, and spoke, that unnerved folks. His movements were swift and sure, his head snapped around quickly when he changed focus, his eyes seemed to meet the gaze of each man and woman in the crowd as he spoke to the assembly, all from a single glance. Sorcerers were not so unusual a sight among the folk of Raynesdark, but they were not used to the pent up energy they saw in the warlock. Their own sorcerers were aloof, bookish sorts, prone to long periods indoors and little real work. Rashan directed the tradesmen the way a harbormaster oversees a port—at the center of all, checking on all he saw and demanding reports of all he did not.

Iridan had no tasks assigned him. He was present to watch and learn but seemed near the point of falling asleep on his feet. When he quietly slipped away, Rashan made sure to overlook his absence. While Iridan's contributions to the battle has been less than he had hoped, he had shown promise.

But Iridan had been the one assigned to stop the Megrenn sorcerer, and that failing was likely to prove quite costly someday. The Staff of Gehlen was an object whose powers few were familiar with. Rashan was quite familiar with them. He wanted no part of facing one who wielded it.

Rashan busied himself demonstrating to the fifth group of would-be dragon-skinners the technique he had found that removed the scales from the hide most quickly. All men who used blades were carrying whetstones and cloths as well. The blades dulled quickly against the resilient dragon hide. The warlock had considered runing a few blades to speed the work but decided that his time was better spent in organization.

Flay my flesh, this is vanity! I have but three I somewhat trust among the Inner Circle, and two only because they are kin. I have no spies of my own and rely on Caladris for information across the Empire. Most of the Circle thinks I have usurped the imperial throne, and much of the populace thinks I killed the emperor myself. Yet here I am, carving trophies from my greatest kill.

As the snow continued to melt, the dragon sank slowly toward the city streets, sometimes shifting ominously as the melt was uneven. Bodies were exposed as the glacier receded against the combined heat of the undercity's furnaces and forges, and the heat generated by the bodies and efforts of the workers around the dragon. Workers were diverted from dragon duty to the clearing of the goblin corpses. It was a duty for those who were found slacking, displeased the warlock in some way, or otherwise fell to those of least social standing.

The goblins bodies were frozen from a night packed in ice, and their frail bodies came apart all too easily with the effort it took to disengage them from the snow. Exposed again to air after a partial night's decay prior to freezing, their odor was fetid and nauseating. Men wore dampened cloths over their faces to move them, despite the frigid air, preferring the cold to the retch-inducing smell.

"Fool!" Rashan barked, directing his ire at one of the drovers, who had just thrown a claw the size of a greatsword into his cart. "Those are not unbreakable. They are sturdy but worth more than you will earn in a lifetime. Treat them with more care."

Who is the fool? I essentially just told them all that a little petty thievery will make them rich enough to retire. Now I am going to have to watch them all the more carefully. There is no count of scales, nor of the claws, and I do not yet know all the internal bits we are to excavate. Something is bound to go missing and never be missed.

Annoyed at his revelation, Rashan drove the tradesmen all the harder, reminding them not only of the value of those scraps of dragon they were hauling but also the blood of friends and kinsmen that had been paid for it.

Let guilt keep them honest, the warlock figured.

Even in his most optimistic mood, it was unlikely to work, but it was better than leaving them to plot their little larcenies from the comfort of a clear conscience.

* * * * * * * *

Brannis slumped against the wall of his bedchamber, wincing as the impact jarred his broken arm. He breathed deeply to calm his nerves, slowly regaining his composure after his confrontation with Duke Pellaton.

Have I gone completely mad? I just threatened one of the highest nobles in the western Empire. If I had been carrying a blade, I would have killed him.

Brannis's thoughts turned to the fables that he remembered from Kyrus's youth. *The Test of Kings* sprang painfully to mind. It was a long tale, told through a succession of unlikely men elevated to the crown by unlikely circumstance. Each had gone in as a good man, with the best of intentions, but in turn, each was corrupted by the power of a crown on his head. Brannis was no king, but he felt as though he had just failed *The Test of Kings,* as had so many in the eponymous tale. He could not recall quite how it ended, but it was something to do with a king finally realizing that the only real power he had derived from the love of his people and their loyalty.

Brannis had never been the most honorable of knights. He considered himself more of a pragmatist in battle, willing to sully himself with deceits and ruses rather than restricting himself to fighting his enemy on even terms. While his dealings within the Empire were honest, and he treated his subordinates and peers alike with respect, he was far from the ideal of the old guard among the knighthood. The old guard would have been proud of him, though, standing his ground to challenge an insult from one who was not his liege. Placing honor above self-preservation was something that Brannis had not learned at a young enough age for it to have ever made sense to him. His family and his early schooling taught him that self-preservation was the ideal.

Do not touch that—it is hot and will burn you. Do not eat that—it will make you sick. Do not provoke that man—he will plot against you and you will die under suspicious circumstances that will never be investigated with any rigor.

Knights did not think like that, or at least were not taught to.

Do not break your word—no man will ever accept it again. Do not visit treachery upon your foe—one day you may be in their power, and they will remember. Do not let stand an untrue word against you—your honor can never be fully cleaned once sullied. Do not take that woman to your bed—she is the betrothed of your best friend, who could magic you into ash if he was angry enough.

Brannis sighed. At least one lesson of the knights had overridden his more cosmopolitan upbringing among the sorcerers. Juliana would have gone through with it and trusted to discretion as her shield.

He knew that he could not be long from the activities going on below in the lower levels of the castle, out in the city, and down in the undercity. He was the focus of the recovery and repair efforts; the soldiers would look to him once they were recalled to duty from their well-earned respite, and the citizens already were busily obeying Brannis's orders, knowing him to not only be the Grand Marshal of the Empire, but a key to the costly victory the night before. His presence would be missed, folk would be seeking him out and asking for him. He could not be found cowering in his room from his own temper.

To put at ease any wondering as to why he had run off, Brannis hastily grabbed his cloak from the wardrobe where the servants had left it and threw it about his shoulders. It was a poor excuse, but it would do. He would have to make a point of heading outside at some point soon though, so it would appear as if he had just wanted something warmer to go out in. He knew what Rashan was doing out in the city, carving up the dragon into its component parts, and he had little stomach for it. The dragon *was* fascinating, but Brannis had seen it from close up already, at great speed and hurling toward him intent on his death. He would be just as happy to not see it again, no matter the number of pieces.

* * * * * * *

Pompous ass. He should be grateful he has a city left at all after that dragon attacked.

Juliana had watched the encounter between Brannis and Duke Pellaton, as had many of those in the castle that morning. For a moment, she actually believed that Brannis was going to run him through—and she would not have blamed him—but he had left his sword somewhere under the collapsed glacier. The duke was myopic, seeing only the damage done to his city—no, not to the city, but to his treasury. She had paid attention, and heard every word, and not once had the duke mentioned the loss of life, either those suffered or those lives saved by Brannis's actions and orders. She had seen the glacier wall collapse, had seen the host of goblins that had been assembled to enter through the gate the avalanche blocked, and had seen the cannons they'd brought with them.

Cut off from the battle outside, she had heard secondhand what Rashan had done. After taking the dragon by surprise when the ice gave way beneath its feet, the warlock had fallen upon the goblins like the demons of the fairy stories, untouchable by the weapons brought to bear against him and slaying all that he encountered. Actually Rashan had gone far out of his way, hunting long into the predawn hours to chase down survivors who had fled the battle. As best everyone could tell, there were no survivors down on the plains, save one lone human sorceress, whom the goblins had kept captive at the behest of their human ally.

Juliana had not seen the woman herself, who had named herself a Fifth Circle when the demon confronted her, but Juliana was no fool. A sorceress of the Fifth Circle could have escaped capture if she had really wanted to, and by all accounts, the goblins had taken no real precaution to hold her against her will. The girl was a harlot or a turncoat, in Juliana's opinion. The sorcerer they had encountered in the upper mines no doubt held some sway over her, but she doubted that it was by magic. That Megrenn was strong—Inner Circle strong—but that was no excuse for failing to slay a man whose bed she no doubt shared. A threat to the Empire was worth taking a risk for; it was worth murdering for, even if it meant her own death if caught or unsuccessful.

Juliana had never met this woman but hated her already.

After the duke had finished his argument with Brannis, they each had left in opposite directions: Brannis to the upper floors, and Duke Pellaton to the feast hall. Overcoming her natural inclination to trail after Brannis, Juliana decided to lurk after the duke instead. The old man fumed and was carrying his cane in his hand like a sword, limping along down the main corridor of the castle with servants and workers alike scattering at his approach. Someone was bound to feel that seething wrath, and she was interested to find out who.

He was an old man and slow even with the aid of his cane, so she had no trouble keeping pace with him even as the ranks of those busy about their duties closed in behind him and business resumed its course in his wake. Sorceresses were not far below angry noblemen on the list of people who are not harassed by crowds, and Juliana found that her black Circle garb was heraldry enough to announce her status. The duke showed no sign that he knew he was being followed. There were people all about, too many to keep track of with the extra people all about.

She followed through the corridors until the duke reached the great hall, which was apparently his destination. Preparations were under way for a huge feast—by order of the warlock. She had heard about it shortly before turning in for the night, but it seemed that the duke had not been quite so well informed.

"What is all this?" Duke Pellaton bellowed to the room at large, not seeing anyone who appeared to be in charge of the efforts.

Juliana had not entered the great hall with him but rather kept to the corridor outside, so she could not hear what must have been an unsatisfactory response.

"I do not care what that usurper said! Get this all out of here at once. This is still *my* city. I have walls, homes, and shops to be rebuilding! I cannot afford feasting at a time like this. If I find so much as one bottle of wine or brandy missing from my personal stores, I shall have your hide."

The room had grown silent in light of the duke's tirade, but not quite enough for her to make out the response. The pause was long, though, before the duke spoke again.

"You ought to think who shall still be here next week. I assure you it will not be that ... that creature ... outside. Now clear the hall! All of you!" the duke shouted.

Juliana's jaw clenched—she despised petty tyrants. Greater tyrants were new to her, and she had yet to settle an opinion on her future oathfather, but the men who enjoyed belittling those weaker than themselves when insecure about their own authority were a particular peeve of hers. She knew that the warlock was going to be angry that his orders were countermanded, and whom Rashan held accountable might go a long way in helping her form opinions of those greater tyrants.

And if she did not see justice done, there was a certain dagger she had picked from the corpse of her would-be assassin. Duke Pellaton may have been a horrid ruler and awful father, but those were forgivable. The danger he posed to Brannis, should he carry through with any of his blustering threats, was not.

* * * * * * * *

The room had been cleaned, and the bedclothes changed, but Celia knew of the murder that had taken place in the room they had given her. One of the Circle sorcerers from Kadris had been lodging here and had been slain by a goblin assassin. The floor still smelled of lye where the servants had no doubt scrubbed away blood. It seemed that it was the only room left that had been deemed suitable for a sorceress to stay in, but Celia would have preferred a room whose dark history was more a subject of ancient history than yesterday's gossip.

"I have been invited to the feasting tonight, and I have naught but borrowed clothes to wear. Ill-fitting ones, I might add," Celia informed the ladies' maid that had been assigned to attend her during her stay.

The girl's name was Chartra—she refused to call her "Miss Chartra," as the Duchess Pellaton had—and she seemed to be as young as Celia looked, perhaps eighteen summers, give or take a summer here or there.

"I know this is scant notice," Celia said, "but what can you do?"

"Well, milady, I can take that dress in if you like. I am a fair seamstress, and it should not take long," Chartra said.

Celia looked down at the dress she wore, stolen from the wardrobe of the rather plump Lady Feldrake, and shook her head.

"No, I think not," Celia replied. "Even if I cared for it in the least, it is dirty and battle worn, and I slept in it besides. Are there dresses to be purchased anywhere in the city? I have no coin, but the warlock assured me that all costs I incurred would be covered by the imperial treasury. He said I was to be well attired for the revelry, so let coin be no object."

"Well, milady, I think I can find you something nice that is close enough to be fitted. I shall do the fitting myself, or we can have the dressmaker do it in her shop," Chartra said.

"Well, in the shop is out of the question. As soon as you depart for the dressmaker, I would like you to have someone sent up to draw a bath. I have needed one for some time," Celia told the girl, though she was not about to go into detail as to why. "Get me at least three dresses to choose from. Oh, and find some jewelry to match each. Remember, cost be forgotten."

"Of course, milady." Chartra smiled.

Celia knew that the girl would enjoy spending the Empire's coin at the dressmaker. She hoped the girl had a sense of style to go along with her enthusiasm.

Warlock Rashan had made it quite clear she was to look her best. She had gotten no impression of lechery from the ancient demon, but she suspected that there was some deeper reason to his insistence. Regardless, she had seen *real* power out on the plains below Raynesdark, personified in the diminutive warlock who had collected her from the ruins of the goblin encampment. She was not inclined to cross him at any cost.

After the battle, he had brought her to the castle and ordered that a room be made ready for her, and told her she was invited to the victory feast: *"You will be honored along with those who fought. Your account of your time with the goblins does you credit,"* he had told her. *"You should find better garb, though, to grace the feast hall properly with your beauty. Erase all sign of hardship and show how the victorious celebrate. Whatever costs are incurred, I shall see to them."*

Am I to be the example held up before all or am I to be part of the decorations? Little matter, I suppose. I am neither prisoner nor dead. I shall play the role I am given.

Celia soaked for what felt like hours, once her bath had been drawn. She had not asked for the water to be hot, preferring to heat it herself with her aether, adjusting it to match her ideal temperature exactly. She cleaned herself thoroughly, then sank back to relax in the warm water. She was nearly asleep in the tub when Chartra returned with a porter in tow, carrying an array of dresses and accessories.

"Milady will find something to her tastes, I am sure," she assured Celia, directing the porter to lay the clothing upon the bed before shooing him from the room. "Let us get you out of there and dried off, and we can pick out your favorite.

Chartra helped Celia out of the bath and brought her a towel to dry herself. A fancier sorceress might have just let the water wick from her body by magic, but Celia was not skilled enough for such a trick; she had to rely on the fabric to do the hard part.

Sufficiently but incompletely dry, Celia pulled the first of the dresses on. It was red and frilly, with slightly puffed shoulders, and laced up the back, leaving much of her back exposed. Bits were trimmed in gold here and there, and translucent fabric layered over other areas.

"Quite fetching," Chartra remarked, pulling the fabric taut against Celia's middle.

The dress would need to be taken in, and Chartra apparently wanted to show how it might look if properly fitted. Celia twisted a bit to her left and right and regarded herself in the full-length mirror on the wall.

"No, I think not. Pretty, but not quite right for me," Celia judged. Her skin tone was middling, neither light enough nor dark enough to throw the red into contrast, and she wanted something striking.

The second they tried was a rather severe black gown, and Celia dismissed it without even trying it on.

Too much like Circle robes. I want to look my best, not look important.

The third dress was blue, with accents of a more greenish hue of blue, and thin white lace trim. It had stays built into the front and sides to slim the figure, and it felt like it was cutting her in half as Chartra laced up the back—which was more warmly covered than that of the red dress. It was low cut, and both lifted and enhanced her curves. Celia tugged a bit at the front, seeing her figure cast in the mirror as she had not shown it off since she had been married. The blue also matched well with the color of her eyes.

"This ... will do. Just ... loosen ..." Celia said with the dress squeezing her lungs. Chartra eased off the laces. "Much better. Take it out a bit so it can be laced properly and this will do nicely. Unless you found some rather tall shoes as well, it shall need hemming."

Celia kicked her bare feet under the folds of the dress as it spilled onto the floor about her.

"Afraid not, milady. Slippers seemed best without you there to fit them. They might not be perfect, but they will form a bit to the foot. I shall take the hem up for you."

"Good. Now show me what you brought for jewelry."

Celia had been told to look her best. She was just following orders. Yes, just following orders ...

* * * * * * * *

Voices were raised, and so were mugs and tankards. The duke's feast hall was packed with soldiers and militia alike, not to mention enough of their womenfolk to make the atmosphere festive. Music from the fiddle, flute, and drum trio in the middle of the room played a lively, bouncing melody, and people danced to it. The duke's wine cellar was emptied to the bottle at Rashan's order. The duke had been chased off to his own private quarters—whence he could no doubt hear the revelry still—and the only stay upon the excesses of drink was the hope that the stores would last them the night. To ensure the wine and spirits lasted, there was ale in plenty to make up for any shortcomings.

The young and not-so-old crowded the hall and spilled out into the adjoining rooms and corridors, making their merriment as they drank it. The grey-beards hung about the fringes, enjoying their drink with less reckless abandon, talking amongst themselves and watching the younglings make fools of themselves.

Young though he was, Brannis took his place among the grey-beards, remembering his position as Grand Marshal of the Empire and keenly aware of the public threat he had made to the ruler of the city just a few hours earlier. His was not a position to be taken lightly, and he was intent on seeing that he did not. He stood near one of the long tables set against the walls of the room with refreshments, a tankard of good dark ale in his hand, which he nursed carefully.

At Brannis's elbow was the demon warlock, taking swigs from an unstoppered decanter of horse whiskey—so called because a glass of it cost about the same as a good horse. The demon neither needed drink nor particularly enjoyed its taste, but it was Duke Pellaton's, and it was being drunk spitefully, as retribution for overstepping his bounds in trying to cancel the feast. Rashan had plans for the feast larger than the coin-clutching concerns of a miserly nobleman.

"You know," Rashan murmured to Brannis, "you could sweep up any lass out there and have a dance with her. There are plenty to be had, and no man would gainsay you."

"Hmph," Brannis harrumphed. "Tell that to the husband or sweetheart of the one I pick. There may be maids out there, but my guess is most are spoken for. You know, history has given you too much credit as a tactician. That was a clumsy attempt and you should know better."

Brannis cast a wry smile at the warlock, who was clearly still intent on steering him away from Juliana. *If only he knew how much I was already on his side. It is her you need to work on.*

"That has not deterred Faolen, it would seem," Rashan remarked.

Indeed the illusion specialist was decked out like a palace courtier, outshining most of the ladies present in his finery. While those who attended the feast had worn their holiday best, they were largely common folk with little money for exotic fashions. Faolen was arrayed in red and gold silk, with green hose beneath. He was taking ladies from their menfolk at every turn, allaying anger only by his lack of persistence with any one of them.

Warlock and Grand Marshal watched in silence for a time, seeing couples twirl and bounce and hop to the rhythm of the musicians' song. Brannis was surprised when he noted Juliana and Iridan dancing—albeit awkwardly—in the middle of the hall. Juliana was much taller than her betrothed, and though Brannis was no expert on dancing, she appeared to be leading. Iridan was no clumsier than half the men dancing but seemed more conscious of his shortcoming than the more inebriated celebrants. Juliana was gamely trying to adjust to his frequent missteps and corrections, where he would stop for a moment and try to join back in on-beat with the music.

Well, it is a start at least. She is trying. Brannis hoped that his rebuke of her two nights prior had gotten the message through to her.

As he watched the hand-fast couple, Rashan broke in upon his musings: "Ahh, Sir Brannis," the warlock caught his attention and tugged, addressing him formally against his usual custom.

Brannis turned and saw a young woman approaching the warlock. His breath caught in his lungs momentarily as he briefly had a vision of Abbiley; the girl bore some resemblance, but he quickly put to rest any serious thought that the object of Kyrus's affection was in both worlds as well. It would have been too great a coincidence.

"Allow me to introduce Celia Mistfield, Fifth Circle."

"Sorceress Celia." Brannis inclined his head politely toward the sorceress.

She was stunning in a dress the colors of the South Katamic—blues and blue-greens, with white lace for foam or sea spray—to match her striking blue eyes, which were alive and alert, unlike many of the court ladies, whose eyes seemed bored and unfocused much of the time. She wore teardrop sapphire earrings and a necklace of pearls and sapphires intermixed. She *was* about Abbiley's height, and far more womanly endowed than was Juliana. She looked right into his eyes as he greeted her, with no hint of shyness about her.

"Grand Marshal Brannis. I have heard so much about you since arriving last night," Celia responded.

"All exaggerations, I assure you," Brannis could not stop himself. He just could not help his self-deprecation in front of ladies. He was being led down a steep slope, he now realized.

"Not exaggerated in the least, I assure you," Rashan interjected. "Sir Brannis, Sorceress Celia has had an arduous journey to Raynesdark and is a stranger to everyone present. As I am now responsible for all the Imperial Circle, I would consider it as a personal favor if you could look after her for the evening among all these unfamiliar faces."

Brannis had of course heard the report of a human sorceress held captive by the goblins from the sacking of Illard's Glen. While he had been gladdened to hear the report of a survivor of the night's slaughter among the goblins, he had more pressing concerns than delving into the details of the girl's ordeal. He thought he remembered her being described as a widow, however.

"Of course, my lady," Brannis extended an arm to her, setting aside his tankard on a nearby table with the other.

Well played, Warlock. Save your prize lamb from the wolf by feeding it another. There was no possible way to refuse the warlock's request with any dignity, and the sorceress was intriguing in her own right. *Maybe I can just move on and put my troubles with Juliana in my past for good. The only other path opposes Rashan, and I can only push him so far.*

Brannis escorted Celia out amid the dancers, and they joined in with the merriment. Brannis danced poorly, but so did Celia, and neither of them saw fit to mention it. Brannis's arm ached and occasionally reminded him of his injury even more forcefully when he twirled Celia beneath his hand, but he was sporting about staying out among the dancers and showing the sorceress a good time. After the first couple dances passed, he even managed to forget that he had been manipulated into taking her, and genuinely enjoyed her company.

"What was ... that?" Celia asked, breathing hard from the quick pace of their dancing.

"What ... was what?" Brannis asked back, seeking clarification of one of the vaguest possible questions—which Brannis knew from long experience at verbal jousting were the ones most dangerous to answer blindly.

"There, you ... just did it ... again. You wince at each pass of this dance," Celia said sternly. She seemed to have caught on.

"Broken ... in the battle last night," Brannis admitted, puffing out his answer between breaths.

"Well ..." Celia redirected their course along the dance floor, off to one side of the room. "No more ... for now." She paused at the edge of the dance to gather up her breath, and allowed Brannis to do likewise. She clung to him still but carefully chose the unbroken arm for her own arm to encircle. "You ought to have said something."

"It was fine. I enjoyed myself completely. The bone is set with aether; I was doing no harm to it." Brannis smiled down at Celia. She was so approachable in her manner, he found it easy to talk to her.

"Care to buy a lady a tankard of wine?" Celia jested.

Brannis, too, had noted the distinct lack of couth in the manner Duke Pellaton's wines were being consumed. Generations-old vintages were being swilled from the bottle and poured into mugs not entirely drained empty of ale.

* * * * * * * *

As Brannis took Celia in arm over to the makeshift wine steward—a stable hand who had no taste for the stuff and was thus deemed fit for duty dispensing it—a malicious glare followed them. With Iridan held tight to her bosom, Juliana could stare clear over his head and saw all of Brannis's exchange with the harlot sorceress Rashan had retrieved from the goblins. Juliana had dressed in her Circle garb so as to avoid the attention of so many drunken, wandering hands amid the festival. The harlot had taken the opposite tack, outshining every lady present such that she could secure the grand marshal's attention fully.

"Ow," Iridan yelped, as Juliana crushed his hand as her grip tightened in anger.

"Sorry," she apologized, hastily relaxing her grip and returning as much of her attention as she could manage back to her future husband.

* * * * * * * *

"May I have your attention," Rashan boomed, his voice carrying clearly throughout much of the castle.

He was standing atop a table, giving everyone present a clear view of him. He was bedecked in his formal warlock's garb, as he had arrived the night before, and was at once both a magnificent and terrifying sight. Those few who saw him on the field of battle had reported his savagery and his power, and those tales had spread throughout the city. As conversations and dancing stopped, the musicians ceased playing.

"Thank you. Thank all of you. This is a day that Raynesdark—and all of Kadrin—will long remember. But first, I must insist that many of those present must leave. While our friends and kin have livened our merrymaking, tonight is a feast for heroes. It is for those who stood upon the city walls when the enemy bombarded us. It is for those who carried the battle to the undercity and protected the citizens. It is for those whose spells defended us and caused havoc among the goblin host. It is for all those who encountered the enemy and acted against them to bring us victory. For those others gathered here within the sound of my voice, I bid you good evening and ask that you do honor to those to whom you owe your lives."

The hall began to clear somewhat, as wives and maidens exited, along with a few of the men who had not been part of the militia, including the old man who played drums for the dancing.

Celia thought it was her time to depart as well but felt a gentle force keeping her from leaving. She made eye contact with the warlock and knew that he meant for her to remain.

"Spies are valuable as well. Never doubt that," she heard in her head.

"Now that we have cleared the regular folk, gather 'round, all you heroes of Raynesdark," Rashan's voice resonated.

Men who had not fit into the feast hall before entered now, and the room filled back to near its previous capacity, though now the surrounding castle was largely vacant.

"Tonight we dine as few have ever done. Tonight we feast on dragon flesh!" Rashan proclaimed.

At that, the side door to the feast hall opened, and porters carried in large covered platters. The crowd stared at the platters as they were brought through, and each was set out on one of the tables around the room's perimeter. At a gesture from the warlock, the covers to all were removed simultaneously as men jostled to see what was on them.

There was a heap of strip meat on each, a hand's length long and two fingers wide, sliced thinly.

"Eat up, and you will one day have a tale fit for your grandchildren, and your ancestors will brag of possessing the blood of dragons in their veins."

"Hey, this is raw!" came an indignant complaint from one of the first soldiers to try the dragon meat. There were voices of assent in the evaluation of the fare.

"Cooking is the application of fire to food. Dragons are utterly immune to fire, as is their flesh," Rashan explained, taking a strip for himself and tearing off a bite in front of everyone. "This is not a delicacy to savor but a trophy well earned. Take in the meat of dragons and take for yourself some small measure of their power. Eat your fill, for there is more than all Raynesdark could eat in a month."

Brannis took his first strip of the raw dragon flesh and bit into it. The cooks had made some attempts at it. There was a smoky flavor to it, and the meat had been salted and spiced, but it still had the strong taste of blood that no amount of non-cooking could fully disguise. It did not taste *bad* exactly, but he worried what the raw meat would do to his digestion later. He expected there to be many a sick soldier in the morning, and many partially eaten scraps of dragon meat found kicked beneath tables or hidden under the edges of platters.

Celia, for her part, nibbled dutifully on the over-spiced raw meat. She found it barbaric—and she had lived among goblins for over week—and wished she had something to wipe her hands on after handling the gummy meat. If Celia had any thoughts of ending her night with lovemaking, they had been run off the road by the macabre feast. She had just heard the very dragon she ate talking the day before.

Juliana, on the other hand, was well and drunk. She had given herself over to the debauchery presented to her and—for the time being at least—was intent on making do with what she was given. She finished her first strip of the dragon meat, hardly tasting it over the ale she washed it down with, and ate a second and even third piece of it. Far from Celia's revulsion, Juliana thought the salted meat went well with her thirst. She was contemplating a fourth when a thought occurred to her, and she put the dragon meat back onto the platter she had found it on.

Brusquely giving Iridan a look up and down, she threaded her arm through his and hauled him away from the feast hall. Iridan had been gamely attempting to choke down a third piece of his own to keep up with his betrothed and was startled by his sudden movement—without his having intended to move at all. He was somewhat less drunk than Juliana but was still not piecing together the whole of what was going on.

Juliana was just sober enough to know that she was drunk, and she was planning to make the most of it. She would need to bed Iridan one day, sooner or later, and she was mad at Brannis right then.

Chapter 37 - The Last to Find Out

Kyrus awoke to the sound of the waves washing up on the beach and the smell of the sea. However, the subtle rush of the waves was complemented by distant voices, the bustle of activity, and the sweet fragrance of tropical flowers added to the briny, nautical fragrance of the Katamic. He was content for a while just to relax and listen, and feel the occasional breeze across his skin. He had opened his eyes enough to realize he was in a small building—a hut or tent of some sort—and it was at least partly open to the outside. He was alone but had not been when he had fallen asleep. He did not know the hour but assumed that his companions had awakened rather earlier and with less of a hangover than he had.

Why do I keep doing this to myself?

Kyrus was growing weary of awakening with a skull-cracking headache every fourth night or so. He pushed himself up to his hands and knees and crawled to the doorway, finding that the floor of the hut was covered by a woven blanket of some sort. Peeking out through the leather flap that served as a door, Kyrus saw the sea and the white sands of the beach but little else. He poked his head completely out, keeping the door flap tight to his neck to hide his nakedness. He looked about and saw a few of the Denku going about their daily chores. Men and women—as immodest at work as they had been at revelry—were making and repairing fishing nets, seeing to the boats, and hauling in fish from the morning's catch. Of his two companions from the night before, he saw no sign.

Less awkward this way, I suppose. I shall have time to dress before they see I have awakened.

Kyrus did not know if anything was expected of him after having the pleasure of their company—or at least he thought he had. The previous night's events were not entirely clear to him. The bright sunshine of the late-morning sky was hurting his aching head and making it even more difficult to recall what had befallen. He had been drinking and laughing and had been fed spits of what tasted like pork. The two young women who had claimed him had been very affectionate, they had left the feast and then ... *blank* ... waking up just shortly ago. Kyrus frowned. The last time he had blacked out after drinking, he had worked magic and thought it a dream.

Kyrus heard a shout, unintelligible in the Denku tongue, but it seemed clear that someone had spotted him, as one of the men down by the beach pointed to another then up toward Kyrus's hut. It sounded friendly and good-natured—at

444

least as far as unintelligible shouting goes—but it also meant he would likely be receiving visitors shortly. He pulled his head back inside and quickly pulled on pants and tunic, eschewing shoes as less than ideal in sand. Luckily his clothes had been neatly piled in a corner—certainly not his own doing—and nothing appeared to be missing.

"Hey there," Kyrus heard from outside.

It was an unfamiliar voice, but it seemed as though one of the Denku spoke at least a bit of Acardian. Kyrus quickly checked that his clothes were properly adjusted and stepped outside the hut.

Several of the Denku were heading over to see him, heading down the shoreline from the north. They seemed largely older men, middling years at least, accompanied by one younger man. It was hard to hide age among the islanders, as wrinkled flesh and sagging muscle could not be hidden behind clothing when you wore almost none.

"Good morning, Spirit Man Kyrus," the younger one addressed him.

The accent he had was easy on the ears, with all the harsh sounds of the Acardian tongue softened and smoothed out, particularly the hard "T" and "K" sounds. Kyrus wondered what Captain Zayne had told them to have them calling him a "spirit man," though. It boded ill to Kyrus's thinking.

"Good morning," Kyrus replied politely.

He glanced around to see that others from among the Denku were drifting in from their various activities to see what was going on. Of the other members of the *Fair Trader*'s crew, he could see none.

"I see you are well this morning," the younger one said. "My name is Gahalu. A few of us speak your tongue. I learned from sailing with the foreign ships for three years. The elders do not speak your tongue, but I will translate for you."

Kyrus was impressed if Gahalu's command of Acardian was gained from just three years at sea among native speakers. Aside from the accent, you would hardly have been able to tell he had not grown up in Golis.

"Thank you for your kind welcome last night," Kyrus said, addressing the rest of the small group.

He waited a moment as Gahalu relayed his words in the Denku language. The elders heads bobbed in approval as his thanks were translated. One of the elders spoke for a bit, and Kyrus waited his turn for Gahalu's explanation.

"Toktu says, if he knew a spirit man was coming, he would have had a bigger feast, but he is happy you enjoyed it anyway."

Toktu was the oldest-looking of the elders. His face had wrinkles like the lines on a map of the sea currents, with hollowed cheeks and bushy grey eyebrows. His head was shaved bare like his face, and his bones showed prominently in his limbs and chest, but he stood tall and proud—though the tall part only got him as high as Kyrus's shoulder. He wore the same loincloths as the rest of the Denku, but also bore ornaments of seashell and shark teeth, and a gold chain with a ruby stone that must have come from the traders that sometimes stopped at Denku Appa.

"I do not need anything fancy," Kyrus said. "The feast was remarkable. Speaking of which, who are the two women who ... um ... kept me company at the feast last night?" Kyrus tried to put that as diplomatically as possible. He was not sure what the accepted custom was in such circumstances and hoped he had done nothing to give offense.

Gahalu relayed his sentiments but did not wait for a reply before answering Kyrus's question: "That was Tippu and Kahli. Tippu was the one with green hair, and Kahli was the one with the red hair." Gahalu smiled. "They are very lucky to have laid claim on a spirit man. There are many jealous women this morning."

Kyrus found himself blushing.

"Um ... laid claim?" Kyrus asked shyly, leaning a bit toward Gahalu and keeping his voice low.

"Well, yes. They got you first. They did not know you were a spirit man, though, so they are either very smart or just very lucky. They did not wake you up for morning-meal, but we will get you something to eat. You slept a long time, so you must be hungry by now," Gahalu said.

"Well, I suppose I am, at that. Where are the others from my ship?" Kyrus asked.

He had looked about but had not seen any of them yet. He assumed they had either slept even later than he had or there was somewhere else they had been housed.

"Oh, your ship left just before dawn," Gahalu said matter-of-factly.

Kyrus felt his blood chill.

They ... left me. No. He *left me here.* Kyrus realized he had been played for a fool.

"Captain Zayne left a message for you." Gahalu turned and spoke briefly to one of the other elders beside Toktu, who handed him a scroll case. Gahalu in turn handed it to Kyrus. "Here. I can speak Acardian fine, but none of us can read it."

* * * * * * * *

Kyrus stared at the parchment, not absorbing the meaning of the words. It was all plainly written in Acardian in Denrik Zayne's crisp, efficient penmanship—the quality of the writing was a feature of the letter that Kyrus had grasped far better than the concepts they were trying to convey. Kyrus sat in the sand, his back pressed against the scaly trunk of one of the tall trees that had its branches all up near the top.

He tried for the fourth time to get through the letter without his brain shutting off on him like a lantern going out in a storm.

Kyrus Hinterdale (or whomever you may really be),

Welcome to your new life on the island of Denku Appa. After the events of the past few days, I finally decided that I just could not risk keeping you aboard the Fair Trader. Your powers are impressive, frightening even, and therein lies the rub. You are frankly too powerful and possessing of too little control to be trusted aboard my ship. And if the Marker's Point incident was not enough to convince me of your incompetence, finding you in the mines of Raynesdark was enough to have me questioning your trustworthiness. I have worked with men with dark pasts and men who do not speak of their earlier days at all, but never have I worked with one who had such personal reasons to mistrust and hate me. Life on a ship, pirate or otherwise, requires a certain understanding, a commonality of purpose, such that even the vilest of miscreants can grasp that by working together, we profit more than by subterfuge amongst ourselves. While I may have rotten maggots infesting my ship, they will eventually be found out and disposed of. With you, a more subtle approach was required. Be flattered, for there are few men who have crossed me and lived to see their twilight years, but you have earned well such distinction. By whatever means, you have rendered yourself too dangerous and too difficult to kill safely, and thus I found it easier to maroon you instead.

As to your current circumstances, I hope that in time you will come to bear me no ill will over them. I imagine that you could eventually find your way to just about anywhere, either through magic or just waiting until another ship anchors at Denku Appa, but my hope is that before then, you will decide that you do not want to leave. There are fewer places more beautiful than that island, and I have seen much of Tellurak. They also have a great deal of respect for magic, and their spirit men are revered. Make yourself a home among them and you will live out your days in a paradise as a respected adviser, and likely have your pick of women.

If you choose to hunt me down instead, I have no doubt you will one day find and destroy me. You have the resourcefulness and magical power to do so. But give the Denku a chance and I think you will find life there preferable to a life of vengeance-seeking.

And if we are to ever face one another on the field of battle as knight and sorcerer, I will bear you no special malice.

Captain Denrik Zayne
Grand Sorcerer Jinzan Fehr

Kyrus still could barely grasp the concept that he was suddenly stranded on a tiny island in a remote part of the Katamic.

"Did he tell you anything when he left this?" Kyrus asked Gahalu later, once he had a chance to gather his composure. Kyrus had been so clearly disturbed by the contents of the letter that the Denku had left him in peace while he pored over it time and again.

"He just said to give it to you when you awoke. We figured that he meant it by way of good-bye. He seemed a little afraid of you, Spirit Man. He is not a goodly man. We Denku are not stupid: we know he is a pirate, but with us he trades fairly and brings word from the outside world, so we tolerate him. But a spirit man is one he can have no hold over. A spirit man has a heart too strong to be controlled by threats or force. I am sorry if his message to you causes you troubled thoughts," Gahalu said.

The Denku interpreter was perhaps half a dozen years older than Kyrus, but he had the manner of an old man about him, wise and understanding of the ways of the world.

"You could not have known. We had a disagreement, and I had thought that we had resolved it. Obviously he was able to deceive me. But how did they all manage to sneak off in the night and leave just me? Surely others must have drunk as much as I did, and we were expecting to stay three nights, not one," Kyrus said. Just what lengths had Captain Zayne gone to rid himself of his sorcerer?

"Actually … no. Captain Zayne had us mix the others' drinks with unfermented mango juice. Only your own was kept strong. The rest of his men grew drunk, but only you and one other passed out," Gahalu said.

"So you mean there is another from the *Fair Trader* here on Denku Appa?" Kyrus asked eagerly, hoping that some familiar face might be stranded with him—and also hoping it was one of the crewmen he got on well with.

"No, Spirit Man. The other one who drank too much was carried to the boat. You were the only one he had wanted to stay here."

Gahalu sounded sad. Kyrus was not sure just how complicit the Denku had been in getting him stuck on the island, but Gahalu at least seemed contrite.

"So what now?" Kyrus asked simply, at a loss.

He had never felt so lost, even when he had thrown in with Captain Zayne and his crew. At least then, he had some inkling that he would eventually find his way back to Acardia, perhaps parting ways at a major port and taking a different ship. Now he found himself off the trade-ways, on a little island that had little to draw ships to its shores.

"First, I think you still need to eat this morning. No feast is big enough to keep your belly full forever. Then after that, I can show you your new home. It is nice here. I have traveled, and I have still not seen any place I would rather live. One thing I think you should prepare yourself for: our people have much respect for spirit men. The outside world is not so respectful, but here you will be treated well by everyone, even the elders."

* * * * * * *

Kyrus's meal had been strange, but not entirely bad. He liked the reef fish they had cooked for him, but the meat from the melons with the rock-hard shells would take some accustoming to appreciate. A small crowd had gathered to watch him eat, and Kyrus found the attention a bit unsettling as they watched for his reactions to the foods he was trying for the first time—though the fish tasted much like he had eaten back home.

After the meal, Gahalu took Kyrus on a bit of a tour of at least the region of the island where his village was. It seemed that there were several villages spread throughout the island, which must have been larger than Kyrus initially realized. Tiny dots on a map still covered vast reaches when traveled by foot, he had to remind himself. The interior of the island was still relatively untamed, with dangerous creatures bearing names Gahalu could not translate in Acardian, as the Acardians had no name for them.

"So these other villages, do you trade with them, or war with them?" Kyrus asked.

Acardian history showed that any contact between two peoples invariably resulted in one or the other. Leaving another people entirely alone could not persist, even among those who styled themselves xenophobes—those usually went to war with the "dangerous" outsiders at some point.

"We used to war with them, long ago. Now we just trade. All the villages are near the coast, and we each fish near our own shores. The ocean is huge, and the reefs are ripe with fish. We do not fight over who fishes where," Gahalu said. "Some men like to travel the island as traders, but most things that one village can make, the others can make too, so there are not too many traders. Many have friends in other villages, though, so travel is common. When word reaches the others that there is a spirit man here, *many* will come to see."

"So what is it that I am supposed to do? I do not know how to be a spirit man."

Kyrus was growing worried that he might not be able to live up to the expectations that these people obviously had of him.

"You are a spirit man. It is not up to us to tell you what to do. You have powers we do not understand, though Captain Zayne told us some of what you can do. We hope to have the aid of your wisdom, the help of your powers. You will have every comfort the island can offer in return, as well as the love and respect of its people. No worry, you will do fine," Gahalu told him.

Kyrus was not yet certain, though. Even as a sorcerer, he had much to learn … and he was still prone to rather dangerous mistakes.

"So what did Captain Zayne tell you?"

"He showed us the marks you bear and the protection they give you. Pardon us, but we poked you with spear points to see that it worked; Captain Zayne assured us you would be unharmed, and you were. He also said you can make fire from air and move even heavy things without touching them. Is that not true?" Gahalu asked.

"I suppose all that is true, though I dislike hearing that I was jabbed with spears in my sleep, though I suppose that the ward protected me well enough that it did not so much as wake me. Please do not try that again, though," Kyrus warned. "So what do I do all day as a spirit man? I do not expect that you will need me to make fire for you; I can see that you do that fine without me. And I do not see many heavy things to move, certainly not enough to fill my days."

"You are still young to Denku Appa. For now, just learn of the island and our people. I am sure that in time you will find what you wish to do, and if need arises, we will ask you for your help."

The tour of the island lasted hours. Gahalu showed Kyrus the freshwater streams that they drank from and the crude roads that cut through the island to reach the other villages. He showed Kyrus groves of cultivated trees that grew the fruits the Denku liked best. All the while, a cluster of Denku with no better tasks to occupy themselves with had followed them around, listening without understanding as Kyrus and Gahalu spoke in Acardian—though Gahalu occasionally answered questions from the gawkers in their native tongue. They pressed close around him, and Kyrus noticed that many were young women with their hair dyed various colors, from reds to violets to yellow-whites. He noticed that unlike the night before, none actually came close enough to touch him, keeping an arm's reach back from him. It was not much space, but it did not feel so confining without them pressed physically against him.

At length, the heat of the island convinced Kyrus to remove at least his shirt, and the gawkers found interest anew in examining his pale body. Of special note was the tattoo on his arm, which amusingly shifted the crowd almost entirely to his left side. There was much pointing and discussion among the Denku, who used tattoos of their own. Kyrus figured there was significance to the designs they wore, but had not discovered the meanings of each. After trying to continue the tour despite the distraction, Gahalu eventually relented to the questioning of the other Denku.

"Spirit Man, they are asking what the marks on your shoulder mean. Could you tell them so they will let me continue in peace?" Gahalu asked.

"It is a protective ward," Kyrus said. "Watch. Here, have that man there give me his knife."

Kyrus gestured to one of the Denku fishermen who carried a steel knife on a leather cord slung over one shoulder. It was undoubtedly a valuable tool, since Kyrus saw no evidence of smelting or metalworking among the Denku, unless one or more of the other villages was more advanced. He suspected instead that it had been traded from the rare visitors the island had received. Despite the knife's value, it was handed over immediately after Gahalu translated the request, with no question asked.

Kyrus took the knife and pressed it hard against the bare skin of his forearm, then drew it quickly across his flesh. He startled the Denku, who seemed worried that he had just injured himself badly. Though Kyrus knew it not, the Denku held that steel was the sharpest thing possible, and it seemed incredible to them that the knife had not cut Kyrus's arm to the bone, the way he slashed himself with it. Instead they gaped in awe at their new spirit man, as his skin was unmarred by the blade.

At that point, the tour ended. Gradually the crowd drew Kyrus back to the main village, pressing him for further displays of his powers. Gahalu translated the requests spottily, as dozens of people were clamoring to make their requests of their newest resident. Kyrus made lights of various colors appear for their amusement. He created bursts of flame is midair, and jets of it shooting from his hands to catch the tips of sticks they held out for him, or roasting bits of meat held on spear tips. He spent a long while lifting different Denku high in the air, much to their delight. It was a frightening experience but also an exhilarating one, and it seemed nearly all wanted to take a turn once they found out it was within his power. At one point, he tried to walk through a tree, which was met with mixed results. He was able to turn himself insubstantial again, much like he

450

had during his Acardian jailbreak; however, he did no better at keeping his clothing in the process. He did not have to understand a word of Denku to grasp the thrust of the ribald jokes and leering looks cast his way as he scurried to retrieve his pants.

* * * * * * * *

By nightfall, Kyrus was exhausted. He had never used his draw so extensively, but more than anything, he was footsore and mentally drained from being what amounted to a stage performer for nearly the whole afternoon. His Source, by comparison, felt limber and ready to continue.

At least part of me is not worn out. Nothing they asked of me was particularly taxing.

There was to be another feast but a different sort from that of the previous night. When the *Fair Trader* had arrived, none of the Denku had known that they were welcoming a new spirit man, and had certainly not expected one who would be staying with them. So while the feast of the night before had been lively and festive, it had been planned with little notice. A day of preparation had allowed the residents of the village to hunt for choice game and practice their festival entertainments.

The feast was held in the center of the village itself, with the central bonfire as its focal point. Kyrus was given a seat of honor, the front row around the fire, where he would have an unfettered view of the night's entertainment. He was also joined again by Tippu and Kahli, who took up their same positions as they had at the previous night's revels. Kyrus had asked Gahalu about them and discovered that he had been claimed by them in what amounted to a semi-official reservation. Kyrus was free to spurn them any time he wished, but unless he did so, no others would approach him.

Kyrus had asked Gahalu about why there were two of them, and whether that was common among the Denku. As Gahalu had explained it: "When twenty children are born, there are ten boys, ten girls. One boy and one girl die young, due to illness or weakness. One boy dies in his test of manhood. Two boys die of wounds taken while hunting. So we are left with nine girls and six boys. Each girl cannot have one boy all her own, so some choose to share. They do not share spear-makers and fishermen. They choose hunters and chieftains—and spirit men."

Kyrus looked and saw only a few at the festival who were likewise attended. Kyrus was unsure what to do about Tippu and Kahli, but he expected that it would be … rude … to spurn them after apparently sharing his bed with them the night before. Yes … rude.

The feast was three whole boars—or what looked close enough to be called such in Acardian at least—spitted over small fires about the villages. Around the main fire, men and women danced and sang, wearing masks and paint, seeming to act out historical scenes.

This must be something akin to opera, Kyrus mused.

He tried to follow the action, but between not understanding Denku and his other distractions, he settled for just enjoying the spectacle of it.

The drink he was served was so weak he wondered if there was any alcohol in it at all this time. It was cloyingly sweet and fruity, and he needed the saltiness of the boar meat to cut the edge off its flavor. He found himself intoxicated again, but by the atmosphere of the festival and not the liquor.

At the end of the night, his two escorts led him out of the village toward a hilltop where Gahalu had explained there was a hut for him. The tour had been cut short before he had seen it, but it had been the home of their last spirit man, kept empty since his death many years ago, but cleaned and prepared for him to have as his own.

When they arrived, Kyrus was quite surprised to find that it was not of the same wood and grass construction as the rest of the Denku homes. It was made of square-cut stone blocks, fitted as would a mason from anywhere in the more civilized world Kyrus knew, with proper windows and all. The roof was of clay tiles, and they looked to be in excellent repair.

On the inside, there was a small fireplace complete with a hook to hang a cooking pot, and the cooking pot was there as well, all cast iron in defiance of the Denku's poverty of metal. A wooden writing desk and chair graced one wall, and a low bed occupied the other. The bedding was unusual, made of the woven grass mats that the Denku used for sleeping, but the headboard and footboard were of a style he would not have been shocked to see in Acardia.

Tippu and Kahli waited respectfully as Kyrus examined his new abode. They seemed to think of the bed as a place that the sleeping mats were stored and quickly took a few of the thick-piled mats and covered the floor with them. Kyrus sighed as he watched them but lacked the language skill to properly explain the situation to them. Besides, there was barely room for two in the bed, and he was not going to upset them by sending them away so late at night.

Instead Kyrus met them halfway. He lay down upon the mats and waited for the two Denku women to join him. When Tippu moved to divest him of his pants, he took hold of her wrist and shook his head slowly. Instead he motioned to the mat next to him. Disappointed but understanding his meaning, both Tippu and Kahli curled up next to him to sleep. Both of them were a little tipsy from the same drink Kyrus had imbibed, and fell asleep after not very long at all. Kyrus breathed a sigh of relief. He was still plenty sober enough to keep his wits about him. As easy as it would have been to give in to every temptation—and he could not deny the temptation—the two sweet young girls sleeping peacefully next to him were not who he wanted.

The mystery of the previous occupant of the un-Denku-like home could wait for another time. As for Kyrus, his thoughts were elsewhere. He turned his head slightly to the side and looked at Kahli sleeping there. The red of her hair was all wrong, but it brought his thoughts in the wrong direction. Turning to Tippu, he imagined away the green hair and tried to picture Abbiley's dark hair in its place.

I wonder if Abbiley would enjoy life in a place like this.

It was Kyrus's last thought before sleep took him.

Chapter 38 - Solstice Feast

The halls of Solaran Estate felt different as Brannis walked along its corridors. He had not long been Grand Marshal of the Imperial Army when last he had been in his family's ancestral home. Now the servants who hurried about seemed more deferential; his relatives seemed to noticed his presence and grant him acknowledgment when he passed them in the halls. He had not realized just how diminished he had been in their eyes until he had finally earned a position worthy of their respect.

The torrent of activity was due to preparations for the Solstice celebration. Elsewhere in the Empire, Solstice had been observed days ago, but Brannis had just arrived back from Raynesdark the night before, having stayed long enough to ensure the orderly progress of the city's repairs. Initially he had not intended to stay long after the victory over the goblin forces, but Duke Pellaton's assassination had thrust him into the forefront of the recovery planning.

Two nights after the Heroes' Feast, as it was being called, the duke had been found dead in his quarters with a goblin dagger in his chest. A search had been launched to find and capture—or kill—the second goblin assassin to have infiltrated the castle, but the skill of the second assassin was greater than that of the first. Either that or the second assassin had just chosen his victim more carefully and not tried to kill everyone in the guest wing, as had seemed to be the plan of the one Juliana had caught and killed.

After the duke's death, his elder son Harwell had inherited the title of Duke of Raynesdark. With the assassin undiscovered, he was a wreck of nerves and little use to his people. Brannis had taken over the day-to-day operations of the city with Mennon's help, and arranged for the repairs to be made to the walls and other damaged parts of the city. The tradesmen of Raynesdark numbered few stonemasons among their brethren, given that the city was thousands of summers old and was maintained by wards, not manual labor. Little had needed to be repaired or built within the lifetime of anyone in the Empire, so the skill was limited to those who had immigrated from less ancient and warded parts of the Empire, and those who had learned to practice new trades while in the city.

So Brannis had arranged for Mennon to contact the stone folk. Living for centuries as neighbors since their mutual excavations had run together, neither the folk of Raynesdark nor the stone folk had seemed interested in engaging in close contact, other than occasional trade in dire times. Brannis considered the times sufficiently dire to engage with the folk again.

The stone folk proved to be tough negotiators but straightforward in their manner. They were wide, stocky people, hairless and covered in thick, hard skin that lent them the name Kadrins called them. They spoke their own tongue, but it was based on the rune language, and in written form Brannis could communicate enough to arrange with them what he needed. The stone folk were all stonemasons in the manner that all humans are cooks. Not all were expert in the working of stone, but all could manage to some degree, and they had among their numbers those whose work was artistry itself.

The cost of all the repairs the city needed was to be a majority share of the materials that had been gathered from Jadefire's corpse. Brannis found it appropriate that the beast whose predations cost the city so much would be the source of their payment for rebuilding, with plenty still to spare for the Empire's own use.

Rashan had claimed choice bits of the creature for his own personal use, namely fangs and claws, along with a selection of choice scales from among the smallish ones near the joints. The rest he had allowed Brannis to allocate as he saw fit, and Brannis had traded much of it away. The stone folk had no interest in the flesh but coveted the bones and scales for their armor. Brannis knew not of the conflicts among the races that dwelt deep beneath the ground, but the stone folk were reputed to be fabulous armorers and weapon-smiths, scoffing at Brannis's warnings about the difficulty of working the dragon-bits and their resistance to fire.

As for that dragon flesh, men who had eaten it had largely grown sick. Raw meat sits well in few human stomachs, but those who braved the delicacy and kept it down saw certain benefits. In the several days Brannis had kept in the city, he had seen many a soldier impressing folk by holding his hand over a flame with no ill effect. After such displays, a small group devoted themselves to consuming as much of the dragon meat as they could stomach, for as long as it lasted.

Brannis knew not what to make of that particular group of culinary adventurers, but he wished them all the best and left them to their curious choice of foods. Brannis had felt no different for his meal of dragon and wanted no part in more of it.

* * * * * * * *

"There you are. I looked over half the estate to find you," Brannis commented, spying Iridan on one of the balconies overlooking the lake.

The young warlock in training was staring out at the water. He did not turn to look at Brannis when he heard him call out.

"I was not hiding, if that is what you are driving at," Iridan replied. "I just came out here for the quiet. I always took Solstice as a quiet holiday, with no feasting. What is going on inside there is madness."

"It does not sound like you are finding peace out here, either. I can go," Brannis said and then turned to leave Iridan to his solitude.

"How do you deal with her?" Iridan asked, finally turning toward Brannis.

Aha, the real reason he is out here alone, thought Brannis.

"Everything I say to her comes out wrong, and it never passes without comment. It does not matter if there are others about, she takes every chance to diminish my dignity."

"Well, first off, do not blame yourself for whatever you say. She is good at twisting words and ascribing double meanings where none were meant. She knows what you mean as well as you do, so do not let her fool you into thinking you have offended her. There is *very* little that I have found that truly offends her, and if she persists in harassing you, I just might let you in on what a few of those are. It would be cruel, but on occasion, she has to be reminded that she often is as well. I honestly think that at times she forgets that," Brannis said.

It felt odd putting Juliana's person into so few words. She was complicated, and even Brannis only understood her partially. She often cried at night, or at least did when she was younger, and would angrily deny having done so if it was ever mentioned. Brannis thought he knew her as well as anyone, but it still did not explain the half of her. She was outwardly aggressive and confident, but he had glimpsed beyond the façade a few times. Iridan would too, in time, he was sure.

"She has taken me to her bed twice now," Iridan confided, his tone and sudden lack of eye contact making his embarrassment obvious. "And when she lies atop me, I cannot help to think back to when she would beat me up as a boy. She looks the same now as then, at least in the face. I know it is foolish, but ..."

"It *is* foolish. That was almost fifteen winters ago. You are a grown man now, and she is a grown woman. She could not beat you now if she tried." Brannis tried to sound convincing, even if he would not have laid good odds to anyone betting against Iridan in such a fight. "Besides, Rashan sees a warlock when he looks at you. Maybe you should start seeing one as well, and not remembering a time when you were the weaker one."

"Well, maybe, but—"

"She is your problem now. Learn how to deal with her," Brannis advised. "I cannot be there to protect you from her anymore."

Brannis continued on his departure, leaving Iridan to ponder what to do about his future wife.

* * * * * * *

Brannis could not bear any longer to talk with Iridan about Juliana.

She is your problem now. She has been my problem for a long time, so it is about time someone else had to deal with her.

Brannis could not help Iridan in good faith, since he still held on to the remote hope that Juliana would still be his. He just did not know how. Somehow he thought that if he suggested they both abandon their lives in the Empire and run off together, she would agree.

I am Grand Marshal of the Imperial Army. I am favored by the warlock. Would I really give that all away just to be with her?

Brannis found himself greedy: he wanted to have her and all the benefits of his rank and station as well. The decision might not have been as simple as that, either. The warlock was unlikely to be kind in the face of not only his desertion but also his interference in his son's betrothal.

The trip back from Raynesdark had been filled with temptation as well. He well understood that Celia had been sent to him to divert him from his interest in Juliana, but he had found himself drawn to her regardless. There was a familiarity about her that Kyrus had felt with Abbiley. She was unpretentious, witty, and easy to talk to. She even looked enough like Abbiley that he found himself lusting after her, perhaps on Kyrus's behalf.

He had objected when Rashan had suggested inviting her to the Solstice celebration with the Solaran household. Brannis had won a tilt against the warlock when he said he thought it ought to just be family present, which would mean that Juliana would not be invited, either. It would give him time with his family and relieve him from the headache of having the two most life-complicating women he knew present at once. Even in the brief time they had both been around, Brannis could not help but notice the enmity between the two—or rather, the enmity that Juliana bore Celia.

* * * * * * * *

By early afternoon, the festivities began outdoors at Solaran Estate. Two games of yalter had begun on the grounds, one for the children and one for the adults. Since Solstice was an event for the household, and not just the family, both games were being played family versus the help. While the kitchen staff was occupied with preparing the evening feast, there were stable hands, porters, gardeners, stewards, and advisers, as well as their own families, all eligible to play.

Upon the great stone terrace of the manor house sat many of the elder members of the household and the women who felt the game too rough for their sensibilities. They drank warmed cider and watched those at play, commenting amongst themselves upon the game or holding discussions unrelated. The common folk kept their own gathering, just outside the roped-off fields of play, and were much more exuberant in their attention to the games. Many looked forward to the yalter games at Solstice, and the delay for Brannis's return only increased their hunger for the event.

Brannis had always enjoyed the game. His family was generally outmatched by their servants in the adult games, and he had been playing amongst the elders since he was fourteen, trying to even the match in the Solarans' favor. The older a sorcerer grew, the greater the temptation to leave physical tasks to others or just use magic to complete them. With the strict ban on magic in the friendly games of yalter, this left the laborers of the estate in greater position. A sorcerer in his fortieth summer might still retain much of the vigor of youth, but not so much as a lad of twenty who wrangled horses all day, or a courier whose days were naught but rushing about carrying missives.

Brannis arrived late to the game and found his family already hard pressed.

He considered seating himself among the elders and relaxing to watch the game, thinking that finally yalter might be beneath his station. When the players caught sight of him, though, he was quickly disabused of that notion.

"Brannis, there you are. Get over here, now," his sister Aloisha shouted from the playing field. "This is getting embarrassing."

Aloisha was eight summers his senior and recently appointed to the Inner Circle, and yet she was out on the yalter field, running and sweating among the commoners and his other relatives. Brannis was thankfully unarmored, safe as he was in his family's own home, but he carried Avalanche at his hip out of long habit of having a blade wherever he went. He unbuckled his sword belt and left it on the terrace, then ran off to join the game.

* * * * * * *

"I forget at times how young he is," Rashan commented quietly to Axterion, who sat beside him watching the children's game.

He had been pleased to learn that the old man was still alive, though he had been in his forties when Rashan had left the Empire. He had thought at the time he killed Gravis Archon that the last living person who remembered him from his early days had died.

"Hmph. You look younger still. Looks lie. You are no more an unblooded lad than you look, and Brannis is no more a boy than he looks. Thinks too much to be a knight, if you ask me. Broods. Not so much as that boy of yours, though. No, that one thinks the world watches him, and is shamed by it."

Axterion was in a lucid mood and liked having someone older than him around. Though by rights he could have reclaimed the head position in the household, Rashan had left the honor to Axterion, deferring to him in matters of family. It seemed only fitting, since Axterion knew them all from babes, and Rashan had only recently met most of them.

"He will grow out of that. He has been looked down on for too long. I shall just have to show him the sort of power he really possesses," Rashan said.

The warlock took a sip of the cider and remembered days that had passed centuries ago. Tradition meant more to those who had more remote times to remember. Rashan had sat upon the same terrace during the reign of Escelon the Fourth, and had drunk cider that tasted much the same as that which he held in his hand.

"You do not even see him out playing at yalter. Boy his age ought to enjoy his vigor while he has it. Too young to be getting caught up in this warlock business," Axterion said. He was good at complaining; one of the few benefits he saw of his extreme old age was that he could complain about nearly anything with authority.

"I was warlock much younger than him," Rashan observed, grinning at his great nephew Axterion.

"Bah, and look what that got you! Off to war before you knew a woman. Caught up in bloodthirst and plots of war. Made enemies of well near everyone but the emperors and a few apprentices. You even left a grand mess to clean up when you ran off after the Dead Earth," Axterion ranted, growing crotchety and loud as he went.

"That is not how—"

"I was not done! You got too much power and responsibility at a young age, and got arrogant for it. It turned you into a liar, a warmonger, and a bully. You thought you were the best at everything, and you were not."

"Wait a moment—"

"No, I think I will not wait. You turned the Kadrin Empire into a pariah among all the nations of Koriah. Folk would not trade with us, and our folk would turn up dead when they traveled widely. Spent a good many winters trying to prevent them allying together to come crush us after you disappeared. You may have been a good general, but you were a lousy diplomat, a bad father, and a worse author," Axterion harrumphed.

The old man was breathing heavily after his tirade, and many of the family were surreptitiously listening in to hear the warlock torn down a bit by someone who had little to fear from retribution.

"Are you quite finished?" Rashan asked.

"I think so, yes. Been meaning to yell at you since I heard you were back. First good chance I got. Colossally large mess of yours I had to clear up," Axterion replied civilly. The fire had gone out of him after he had given his grievances a proper airing.

"I understand the rest, but what was that about being a bad author?" Rashan suspected he had just discovered a key piece of a puzzle he had been curious about since he had found that his room at the palace had been violated.

The old man paused for a moment before answering, as a cheer went up from the yalter field. Someone had just scored for the servants. It seemed that Brannis's presence was not enough on its own to swing the balance to the family's favor.

"That book of prophecy you wrote. Pure drivel. Glad you only gave it the one go and stuck with—"

"It was *you* that broke into my room!" Rashan said. He did not sound quite angry but had rather just found the answer to a question that had dogged him since learning of the book's disappearance.

"Well … yes. You were thought dead. I was your replacement as High Sorcerer, and I felt it my duty to get into your quarters and see if anything was amiss," Axterion stated. "You always had an overblown opinion of your rune-carving skills. Those wards were good, but I was better."

"How did you break through? I found nothing amiss after a century away when I checked on them."

Rashan was more curious than angry. The old man was entitled to his bragging if he had truly been the one to break into his quarters. Gravis Archon had seemed to think it an impossible task.

"I set up wards all around it, on floors above and below even, diverting aether away from the area. Your ward relied on having a draw of its own. I denied it aether until it weakened, and broke it," Axterion said. "Then after making a search of the room, I took your book of prophecy and sealed it back up. That ward you saw was my copy of yours."

A row erupted on the children's field, as one of the Solaran children was caught using magic on the field of play. Axterion did not have to look to know that it was Danilaesis that was at fault. The boy was too full of his own skills to abide by the simplest of rules. Being among the youngest of the players allowed onto the field, he was too immature to cope with being physically outmatched. He was too short to pass the yalt over his opponents' heads, and his hands were too small to catch it well. He had settled for spending his time chasing after it and had now started sneaking spells in to disrupt the servants' children. He was being escorted from the field by his father Caladris, who was overseeing the children's game.

"Of all the treasures in that room, all you took was that worthless book?" Rashan was incredulous. "After all that work, you found nothing else to your liking?"

"I had no designs of becoming the next warlock. I had no need of your finery or that sword of yours that Brannis now carries." The old sorcerer nodded in the direction of where Brannis had left Avalanche to go play yalter. "I wanted something distinctive, such that anyone who challenged me could see that I had really been inside. But alas, not one but you ever seemed interested."

"So where is it? What have you done with it? That sort of thing is dangerous in the wrong hands," Rashan said, but Axterion waved away his concerns.

"I taught out of it at the Academy for a time, but I have kept it in the family library ever since."

"You *taught* from it? You old fool, what kind of troubles have you caused with that nonsense?" Rashan seemed genuinely annoyed with the old man.

"Pshaw. I taught from it, surely. I did not represent what you had written as true prophecy, though. I do not believe there is aether strong enough to pierce the mists of time, but I see the benefits of crafting prophecy to manipulate events. Many prophecies have altered the course of events, but for the knowing of them, not because some pompous fool actually saw it coming. Knowledge of the future, even false knowledge—no, *especially* false knowledge—is powerful stuff," the wily old sorcerer said. "Your book was a good example of bland, generic prophecy, written with no talent for it. I used it as an example of prophecy written to sow discord rather than actually predict anything."

"The others say that your wits are failing you in your dotage, Axterion. I begin to suspect you have them all fooled," Rashan said, and Axterion just smiled. "So you have not tried to act on any of the prophecies written within? There is one in particular I would worry to have in general knowledge."

"The one about the Empire being consumed in fire in … oh, about seventy winters from now?" Axterion asked.

Rashan had written that one after a particularly bad day, promising volcanoes and wildfires consuming the Empire in a great blaze from which none would escape.

"No, not that one. There was another, about a monster in the form of a sorcerer ..." Rashan did not wish to relate the rest of it with others possibly around to hear.

"Oh, that one. Boring. Never had much use for it. Worried folk might think you predicted your own impersonator, demon?" Axterion hinted. "I would give you more credit than you deserve if you had actually managed that trick. If a demon in your form was undone and discovered by this 'prophecy' of yours, it would be the first use for it I have ever found. You are too much of Rashan Solaran to be an imposter."

Another cheer went up from the yalter field, as the Solarans had scored. With the early twilight approaching, the game would be ending soon, and the Solarans had barely scored all match. Iridan had decided to join in for a while but had wearied of it quickly and excused himself with a vaguely explained injury.

"I should like the book back, in any event," Rashan told the old sorcerer.

Axterion shrugged by way of reply. "Very well. It is yours after all, I suppose. I shall fetch it this evening."

"Good. The less people see of prophecy the better I shall like it."

Rashan did not state it, but there were other things within those pages that he did not want seen or spoken about. They had been the idle ramblings of his poorest moods, but many of the "prophecies" had laid bare secret fears and fearful secrets. Of all in the Empire, he most feared Brannis reading what lay within its pages. The boy was too clever by far. Prophecy or no, there was knowledge to be gleaned from those pages, more than Rashan had even realized at the time he wrote them. He would feel safer once he had it safely back in his possession.

* * * * * * * *

The feast had been festive enough, but Brannis's thoughts were elsewhere. As he retired to his rooms, he did not intend to sleep. He had been to the libraries of the Tower of Contemplation on his way back home and had selected a number of volumes to take back with him for study.

War with Megrenn was a foregone conclusion. Despite the devastation visited upon the goblin army, the Megrenn had lost nothing in the assault and had gained for themselves the Staff of Gehlen. It was an object so old that none Brannis had spoken to had any idea of its powers, save for how it had been used in Raynesdark to keep the volcano dormant. While the winter cold bought Kadrin time, Megrenn would be certain to begin a campaign against them when the weather warmed. With much of their cavalry comprising exotic beasts purchased from across the northern seas, they fought best in hotter climates. It was not an ideal composition for an army, but Megrenn was playing to their strength as great traders and buying what they could not scavenge from their resource-poor lands. With less magical strength than Kadrin, at least for a period stretching from mid springtime to early autumn, they would have the advantage in strength of arms.

But Brannis would have time to devise strategies against the Megrenn before the season turned. Winter had not even begun in earnest to sink its icy talons into Kadris, and the whole of winter would pass before any serious threat from Megrenn could be mounted. Kyrus, on the other hand, could use his help much more immediately. While his twin was stranded on a remote island, he seemed to be in little actual danger. Still, Brannis felt he owed much to his counterpart, both for the help he had been against Jinzan Fehr and for the richness he added to the sleeping portion of his life. In a strange and mildly uncomfortable way, he yearned for Abbiley as well and wanted to see Kyrus returned to her.

And so, for Kyrus, he read.

Aetherial Navigation was a treatise on the use of the aether as a means of finding one's way over long distances. *The Greatest of Ptakk's Works* explained how to form permanent structures out of materials at hand, with particular emphasis on how to build them to last. *Spirit Magic* was of questionable use, but it explored the view of aether as a spiritual medium and many of the beliefs that sprung from that view. The one that Brannis felt held the most promise was *To Anywhere*, a volume that held the transference spell that Rashan had used to cross half of Koriah to reach Raynesdark. With any luck, Kyrus would be able to use it one day to return home. The spell was much more complex than any Kyrus had learned previously, and there were many warnings of the dire consequences of mistakes in its use, but it seemed the best option.

Brannis settled in to his bed with the stack of borrowed books at his bedside table.

No fear, Kyrus. I will find a way to rescue you, or at least to find you a way to rescue yourself.

Chapter 39 - Letter Home

Dearest Abbiley,

I barely know where to begin my tale. The events of the last few months deny description, though I must try. Understand that half of what you have heard about me is indeed true, while the other half are exaggerations and falsehoods, borne of fear and misunderstanding.

I have discovered that magic does exist in our world, not relegated to the bedtime tales we heard as children. I have been blessed with a glimpse into another world, one of magic and wonder, where fantastical things are possible. I have learned from what I have seen there and have put it to practice. I made a record of my studies, after the manner of Sir Waldon, Lord Candelwright, or Professor Hawkweave, seeking to use the methods of science to find reason where there is naught but mysticism. I admit that my scholarly endeavors were led astray by something rather embarrassing: I had fun with it.

I can only imagine the joy you feel seeing your paintings leap into life upon the canvas as your brush transforms bits of sticky multicolored pastes into visions of reality or fancy as you choose them. I have not the eye to be an artist. Neither do I have the voice to sing or ear to compose. I have not the heart nor arm to be a warrior, and I lack the slick tongue to enter politics. I lack all the faculties that allow a man to change the world, save for a new one that I have discovered.

I find before me the choice of how to use the gift I have discovered. What was not so long ago a barely understood trick of trial and error, I now find under some nascent degree of real control. Had I learned such mastery before my unfortunate encounter with the fearful custodians of law in Scar Harbor, I might have held them at bay long enough to make them see reason. Alas, the hordes of fear and superstition fell upon me and sought to claim my life for their peace of mind. At the time you last saw me, I was frightened and uncertain, wondering if some aspect of my newly found ability might secure my freedom.

The events after that night bear much explanation, for as fanciful as my tale so far has been, it grows stranger still. The notorious pirate, Denrik Zayne, had escaped from his exile and was lurking about in Scar Harbor when he heard of my plight. Not one for pity, he believed in magic and knew some paltry amount of it himself. Seeing in me a potential ally, scorned alike by the authorities of Acardia, he effected my escape from the prison, and took me on as a part of his crew when he stole the Harbinger from its berth.

I admit my mistake now, seeing it with the benefit of hindsight. Though I knew not how to harness my power, I could have stayed and defended myself until such time as I could make men see reason, that I was not a threat, and that my magics were harmless—nay, beneficial even— to the community at large. Instead I took the coward's path and allowed whatever rumors might flourish after my escape to run unchecked, no doubt growing to monstrous proportions.

As my short time among the pirates passed, it became clear that I would never fit in with them and that I was not the sort of man they wished to keep among them. As what they claimed was a small kindness, they have stranded me upon a remote isle, inhabited by an inoffensive native people who have, I must say, treated me well enough.

I am in good health and sound of mind. It is only my heart that aches. For whatever kindness is visited upon me by my gracious hosts, they cannot provide the only desire I find myself lacking: the pleasure of your company. There has not been a day to pass that I have not wished to be with you, either to be back home with you in Acardia to escape the distasteful sights I have seen among the squalor of a pirate's life, or to have you with me to see the wonders of the world beyond the horizon from all you have known.

Ships are a rarity here, with merchants having little reasons to travel here, to this place called Denku Appa. I find myself discontent with waiting upon the next lucky vessel to come my way to take me from here and back to the civilized lands where I might book passage home. Instead I look to my own studies, for in magic, should not all be possible? If by chance some errant vessel may pass, I shall leap upon it, with a farewell to my hosts upon my lips and a song in my heart, but I will not sit idly by and count upon such fortune.

One way, though I know not how as yet, I will make my way back to see you again. You may have my solemn word upon it.

With All My Heart,
Kyrus Hinterdale

When all the words had arranged themselves, Kyrus ceased his spell and let the rest of the ink from Denrik Zayne's message pour into the inkwell. Once the ink on the letter dried, Kyrus carefully folded and rolled up the only paper upon the island of Denku Appa, then bound it around the leg of the parrot he had enspelled. The colorful bird watched him curiously as he worked but offered no comment, nor objected to bearing the message it was being given.

"Find your way, little friend," Kyrus told the parrot, lifting it to the air to help it take flight.

The bird headed off to the north and west, a long journey ahead of it, and with just a few mental images from Kyrus to guide its way.

"Find your way to Abbiley, so that I might one day follow."

About The Author

Born in New Hampshire in 1977, J.S. Morin found himself captivated by the wonders of fantasy novels at a young age. He was introduced to the genre via the works of R.A. Salvatore, Ed Greenwood, and Margaret Weiss and Tracy Hickman. He loved exploring other people's worlds, from Shadowdale to Hyrule. He also quickly found Dungeons and Dragons to be a creative outlet for stories, characters, and new worlds of his own creation.

His other passion was for building and designing things, and when it came time to choose a career, he went down that road. A Mechanical Engineer by day, he spends his evenings with his wife in their New Hampshire home, enjoying the simplicity of life in a quiet state.

By night he dreams elaborate dreams of visiting fanciful worlds, performing acts of heroism, and solving intriguing puzzles, which inspire him to craft stories that he hopes will help shape the lives of the next generation of fantasy readers. He hopes to avoid finishing growing up.